THE ESSENTIAL CLIVE BARKER

THE ESSENTIAL
CLIVE BARKER

SELECTED FICTION

WITH FOREWORD BY
ARMISTEAD MAUPIN

HarperCollins*Publishers*

Library of Congress Cataloging-in-Publication Data
Barker, Clive, 1952–
   [Selections. 1999]
   The essential Clive Barker: selected fiction/Clive Barker. — 1st ed.
      p.   cm.
   ISBN 0-06-019529-0
   1. Fantasy literature, English. 2. Horror tales, english. I. Title.
   PR052.A6475A6   1999
823'.914—dc21   99–32574

00 01 02 03 04 ❖/RRD 10 9 8 7 6 5 4 3

For Jane Johnson

I am a man, and men are animals who tell stories. This is a gift from God, who spoke our species into being, but left the end of our story untold. That mystery is troubling to us. How could it be otherwise? Without the final part, we think, how are we to make sense of all that went before; which is to say, our lives?

So we make stories of our own, in fevered and envious imitation of our Maker, hoping that we'll tell, by chance, what God left untold. And finishing our tale, come to understand why we were born.

—*from Sacrament*

CONTENTS

ACKNOWLEDGMENTS

J ane Johnson, to whom this book is dedicated, has been my editor and my friend for many years now. A gifted novelist herself, she is intimately familiar with the agonies of the writing process, her advice always a powerful and rare mingling of high ideals and practicality. More than that, she's a *celebrant*, and her companionship on these journeys has made them both more ambitious and more pleasurable.

I'd also like to thank my publisher, Eddie Bell. In 1986 he brought me to HarperCollins with *Weaveworld* and since then has unfailingly supported every sea change that my fictions have undergone. He has a brilliant, but incredibly old-fashioned theory about publishing: he trusts his authors. Such trust is a rare gift for a writer to receive, and I love him for it.

Finally, a word of thanks to my team here in Los Angeles. To David Dodds, Robb Humphreys, and Joseph Daley, who have juggled a dozen different projects for me while this book was being brought into being.

ARMISTEAD MAUPIN

A quick confession: I discovered Clive Barker's work through a comic book, a graphic rendition of his brilliant story "In the Hills, the Cities" that had the good sense to leave much of his language intact. The story was nothing less than a waking nightmare—perfectly suited for illustration—but what lingered with me was the absolute authority of Barker's voice. He wrote with the easy confidence of a tribal storyteller, an elder who had seen every-thing and committed most of it to scripture. And every novel of his I've read since has been embued with the same quality, the same stately Biblical cer-titude. Somehow, through an alchemy other writers can only envy, even Barker's most bizarre tales have the ring of history to them, a core of ancient truth that allows us—no, compels us—to follow him anywhere.

And anywhere, for him, means everywhere. Nothing is off limits to this free-range fabulist. He can fold a dusty Persian carpet into the contours of the world itself and wring delight from every lustrous thread. He can build a battling giant out of thousands of contorted human bodies and enlist our aid in its construction. He can make us believe we're fondling the genitals of an alien—and thoroughly enjoying it to boot. And though he's also mas-tered the visual arts on both canvas and celluloid, he accomplishes these wonders with words alone, manipulating our dreads and desires until we believe the unbelievable, think the unthinkable. Or, as one of his charac-ters puts it so well in *Imajica*, until we "stop looking and *see*."

This happens, in part, because we are led into these incredible realms by such credible guides. Barker's people are as real as anyone in Updike or Welty, flawed and idiosyncratic, anything but the stick figures that too often inhabit the work of best-selling fantasists. And most of his characters live in low-tech landscapes we can readily recognize. They endure the hardships of inner-city housing projects, or cruise the bars in San Francisco's Castro District, or rage against the tedium of a heartland post office. They are prigs and libertines, monsters and angels, the casually evil and the profoundly ordinary. They long for love and strive for fulfillment and seek meaning from the random struggles of existence. Barker will never be confined to a "genre"—that most condescending of literary labels—having grasped something basic about his art: when the horrific and the humane coexist believably in a work of fiction, the reader's experience of each is heightened.

Then there's the sex. Barker writes about human desire in the most visceral—and fearless—way imaginable, stimulating all our senses at once. And while he's one of the few globally popular artists to be off-handedly frank about his homosexuality, his celebration of the body and its pleasures is thoroughly ecumenical. I can think of no other writer who writes so generously about everyone's passion, whether hetero-, homo- or omni-, rough sex or gentle; all are acceptable in Barker's dominion. And why not? he seems to be saying. In a world so chock-a-block with shape-shifters and mystifs, creatures who can morph into anything at the blink of an eye, why deny us lowly mortals a few interesting options of our own?

As a writer, I'm always intrigued by Barker's reverence for the power of myth-making, a theme that pervades much of his work. He sees storytelling as a tool for spiritual growth, a means of making sense of things, not just for the reader but for the writer himself. Listen to his narrator in *Galilee*:

> Now I had the answer to the question: what lay at the center of all the threads of my story? It was myself. It wasn't an abstracted recaunter of these lives and loves. I was—I *am*—the story itself; its source, its voice, its music. Perhaps to you that doesn't seem like much of a revelation. But for me, it changes everything. It makes me see, with brutal clarity, the person I once was. It makes me understand for the first time who I am now. And it makes me shake with anticipation of what I must become. . . . In other words, there must inevitably be unholy business here, just as there will be sacred, but I cannot guarantee to tell you—or even sometimes to know—which is which. . . . All I want now is the time to enchant you . . .

And who could decline such an offer? The symphonic grace of Barker's prose, his loping, muscular imagination, his sharp eye on the human dilemma—all serve a seamless, remarkable whole. Add to that his uncanny gift for scaring the daylights out of you and there's more than enough reason to be grateful he's on the planet.

Assuming, of course, he is.

PRIVATE LEGENDS

AN INTRODUCTION

private 1 *archaic*: one not in public life or office 2: a secret message
3: privates pl. genitalia.
legend 1: the story of the life of a saint 2: a story coming down from
the past 3: an explanatory list of the symbols appearing on a map or
chart.

I

There are three stories at the heart of this introduction. One concerns
a Bird Man, one a Magician, and one, the Sea. They are all true;
accounts of events that happened in my life which I've attempted to tell as
plainly as possible. On the face of it their presence here might seem a little
odd. This is, after all, the introduction to a book of imaginings; selections
from volumes that take reality as a starting point for journeys into other
states of soul and bone. But these journeys, however remote their destina-
tions, are always rooted in some personal experience. Their truth is the
truth of things seen, things felt. I wanted that fact to be somehow reflected
in these pages; to mingle some observations on the kind of work I make —
and the means by which I make it — with examples of events which have
moved and marked me.

This exchange between the world and the work is a two-way street. I hope
to make stories powerful enough to reflect back upon reality, and perhaps, in
some subtle way, transform it. I want to charge up the minds of my readers
with a taste of *otherness*, and deliver them back into the world ready to make
a new sense of it. Arguably, all art intends this. But the fantastique, as I will
dub the fruit of the imagination, performs this duty in a fashion quite unlike

that of novels or films or paintings that are created to be mirrors of life. The fantastique is not content, let's say, to show us a horse. Or a man standing beside a horse. Instead it says: let's marry the horse and the man, to see what comes of it. The resulting creature, a centaur, is of course familiar to us from classical mythology; though in fact a primal confluence of beast and man appears in the earliest known examples of art, cave paintings. It's a game, this marrying of disparate pieces, which seems fundamental to us. Children play it with instinctive ease. Left to their own devices they will match and marry forms without a thought to propriety. They let the world melt in their own minds, and pluck whatever pleases them out of the resulting stew. Many of these liaisons are often simply a diverting nonsense; which is a perfectly acceptable end in itself. But sometimes, as for instance in the case of the centaur, these forms carry a potency all their own. When we look at the man who is also a horse a plethora of fascinating questions arise. We may be inspired to think in a new way about our sexuality, or our bestiality, or our history as a species that has tamed and domesticated other species. We may find ourselves strangely aroused by the image: by its nakedness, its power, its enviable lack of inhibitions. The image of the horse-man has become a vessel for a cluster of thoughts that might otherwise slip away, lost in the crush and din of the solid world.

The history of the fantastique presents us with an extraordinary array of such vessels, including, but by no means limited to: stories of the womb; stories of the state or states which precede the womb; ruminations on the origin of the soul; ruminations on the destination of the soul; nonsense rhymes, nursery tales; lullabies and prayers; heroic tales of a Golden Age; fairy tales of a Magic Age; tales of lost time, tales of lost sanity; tales of lost love, returned from the grave; tales of any manner of creature returned from the grave; histories of supernatural species or tribes of supernatural species including angels, demons, vampires, werewolves; accounts of the efficacy of occult forces; accounts of pacts made with Infernal Powers, and their consequences; all unholiness; all holiness; all tales of spiritual endeavor; topographies of invented islands; descriptions of invented voyages; scenes set in floating cities and lost continents; books set in Heaven; books set in Hell; books set in the mind of God, especially those which purport to explain the will of God; anything with scenes of talking animals, anything with scenes of articulate stones, or wells or roses; *grimoires*, operas, drag shows; stories of removal to other worlds or dimensions by means which do not yet exist; stories set in those worlds or dimensions; stories in which paranoid delusions are substantiated; hallucinations and deliriums, opiated dreamscapes; reports of the monstrous, the grotesque, and the freakish; uncollected gospels; visions of the end of the world; visions of what will come after the end of the world; erotic fantasias upon the rituals of love; stories in which one or other lover is miraculously transformed (into a cloud, a bull, a rain of gold); stories in which the object of desire survives impossible vicissitudes in order to entertain the author; stories in which the genitalia speak; stories of obscene excess; stories of eternal love; stories of eternal virgins; stories of the impregnation of such virgins by the Holy Spirit; and so, as in some inevitable circle, back to stories of the womb.

II

There have been countless, mostly misbegotten, attempts to divide the various modes of the fantastique: the sorry consequences of these divisions are visible at your local bookstore. You'll find one species of imagining dubbed science fiction, another shelved under horror; yet another under fantasy. Some—magic realism, for instance—are simply collected on the literature shelves. Away with that nonsense, here and now. A lot of good reading time can be wasted arguing whether Nathaniel Hawthorne belongs with Italo Calvino, or Kurt Vonnegut with the Brothers Grimm.

One particularly fruitless definition of the fantastic, offered by literary critic Tzvetan Todorov, cites it at a place in a story in which two possibilities (one defying the laws of reality, the other caused by a dislocation of the senses) exist side by side. The moment the narrative chooses one road or the other, Todorov argues, the fantastic mode passes away. In my experience these attempts to organize and compartmentalize the labors of the imagination are strictly for the entertainment of theorists. Let me give you a case in point.

Sitting in various stacks around my desk as I write are the four books I presently have in progress. One is this, *The Essential Clive Barker*, another is an untitled collection of short fiction, the third a book of erotic prose and paintings, called *The Scarlet Gospels*, and the fourth a book I've been working on for three years called *The Book of Hours*. None of them is remotely like another. There is work here which will be published as children's fiction, and work which plays into the heart of my sexual obsessions; there's a story in the collection set in a future which I hope is wholly unlike any created, and another set in a canyon inspired by the landscape outside the window. Some days, when an idea strikes me, I will hop from one text to another; and every day, without fail, I will put my pen down at the end of the afternoon and go to paint the pictures for *The Book of Hours* in my studio next door, never feeling as though I have to actively remove myself from one world and beg entrance to another. Why? Because my mind is not divided like a bookshop. It doesn't have a compartment into which my erotic feelings are put, and another where my prophetic aspirations go, and another where I put my hunger to make an archipelago for children: it's all one place. Of course I'm not going to write in the erotic mode for an audience of children, nor drop a scene about enchanted hats into a story about Hell, but that doesn't mean there isn't a connection between these subjects. Where, for instance, is the bridge that leads from the dream-sea Quiddity, and the islands of the Ephemeris that are set in that sea, to the five Dominions of the Imajica? Or from the Weaveworld, with its Fugue and Gyre, to Hood's Holiday House? From the ruins of Warsaw in 1944 to the *Rub al Khali*, the Empty Quarter of the Sahara?

To help answer those questions, I've put excerpts of the stories side by side, so that the connections become more apparent. To take an example: in chapter 11, Making and Unmaking, there are pieces of wild fantasy (a chapter titled "The Miracle of the Loom," from *Weaveworld*, and a portion of the climax of *The Thief of Always*) alongside a key passage from *Galilee* in which the narrator, Maddox Barbarossa, ruminates on the scale of his ambition for the story he is about to tell. And then, from *Sacrament*, two much darker passages, which concern themselves with a boy coming to understand his power in the world. It matters not at all how these various books might be described generically: the thematic material is more important than the way a bookseller may decide (or be obliged) to position the book. What does the terminology matter? The urgency of the story is what drove me to write these passages in the first place. The rest is just packaging. It's irrelevant the moment a reader invests his or her time and imagination in the work.

Of course there's an exploratory element to such organization. Arguably some of the selections might well belong in more than one chapter. There's nothing definitive in any of this. But that may be part of the essence of such pathfinding. As Gentle, the protagonist in *Imajica*, muses toward the end of that novel: "maps weren't cursed by the notion of a definitive original . . . [they] were always works in progress."

III

So, it's a work in progress. And I don't expect anybody to pick this book up, begin on page one, and dutifully read on to the end. Very few people, I think, will do that. I put up my signposts, in the full knowledge that they will largely go ignored. I think one of the pleasures of a collection like this is that it encourages a nomadic spirit. You wander here and there, guided only by some vague instinct.

I feel the same way as a writer. I do my best to lay out the trip I want to take when I begin to write a book, but I seldom stay very close to it. The fantastique lends itself to digression; it feeds upon its own spiraling inventions. The first appearances of such storytelling—in folklore and myth and in fairy tale (later, in urban legend)—are celebrations of their own fecundity. Heaven and Hell are populated by such stories, seas and species and stars spun into being. Here let me be quite clear: the primary impulse behind such creations is not escapism. That implies a kind of cowardice in the face of the world, which is not what inspires such visions. Quite the reverse. It is a hunger to see more clearly that fuels the true fantasist. A desire to express the world's transforming heart.

Sometimes, of course, events uncover their mythic selves without any help from a writer. Such events often become part of our personal landscape; pivotal moments around which our lives seem to organize themselves.

My first confrontation, in the flesh, with an image that had this kind of mythic resonance occurred when I was very young. In May 1956, as a four year old, I was taken to an air show at Speke Airport, on the outskirts of Liverpool. It was a big event. The city was still getting out of its postwar doldrums, and entertainment was hard to come by. I have a very clear memory of what happened that day, a memory sharpened by the process of describing it in the drafts of this piece, and by several conversations with my father, who also plays a significant part in these events. I remember the heat of an intemperate English August, and a tiny car filled with people: my parents; my aunt and uncle; my cousin, still a babe in arms; and myself. The air was stagnant, the sky blindingly bright. The family, lacking the wherewithal to get everyone inside the airfield so as to watch the fly-bys from the tarmac like the paying crowd, stood near the car, parked at the edge of a cornfield close to the perimeter fence. I was bored, I think; the periods of waiting between the passing of the planes seemed interminable. My shirt stuck to the back of my neck; there were late summer wasps buzzing around, coming after our sandwiches.

The high point of the afternoon's entertainment was to be a flight by a much-celebrated Bird Man. His name was Leo Valentin, and his performance, which had been seen throughout Europe (the man was French) was this: he jumped from a circling plane and glided on homemade balsa wood wings until he reached a certain altitude, at which point he pulled his rip cord and parachuted to earth.

My family waited through the heat of the afternoon for this last part of the show to begin, my father doing his best to interpret the words of the announcer on the airfield loudspeaker. Was that the Frenchman's plane: that tiny dark dot up there in the wide, empty sky? (This was the fifties; the sky was emptier then.) Yes, that was the plane, because look, there was Leo Valentin tumbling out, an even tinier dot. My uncle helped me follow him, explaining what I was seeing; but it didn't interest me very much. I was too hot and tired; too distracted by the wasps. And the spectacle, such as it was, seemed so remote, so undramatic. It required an adult's comprehension of the risks this man was taking to make the diminishing shape of the plane and Valentin's tumbling form seem significant.

I think my aunt began to panic first, her voice shrill. My uncle attempted to calm her, but her distress simply grew, as she watched the Bird Man descend.

Vaguely I began to understand what was happening. Something was wrong with the trick we were here to see. The man up there in the sky wasn't flying the way he was supposed to: *he was falling*.

Was there any concern being expressed by the voice on the airfield loudspeaker? Perhaps; I don't remember. But I do remember the mounting panic of the adults, a panic not simply fueled by the fact that Valentin was dropping out of the sky, but by their growing comprehension that he was going to hit the ground very close to us.

I think my mother must have taken me back to the car at this point. Certainly my next memory is of the hot confines of a vehicle, and my mother instructing me not to look. This was a sight I must not see. You can imagine what a goad to my curiosity that was. Something was about to happen so terrible I was forbidden sight of it.

"Don't look," my mother said, over and over. "Don't look. Don't look. Don't look." My aunt was also in the car (perhaps she'd preceded us there) and my baby cousin was bawling in her arms.

In the confusion I defied my mother's repeated edict, and looked out toward the cornfield. My father and my uncle were standing at the edge of the field, their hands cupped over their brows to shield their eyes from the blazing sun, watching Leo Valentin plummet to his death.

(The image of a man falling out of the sky, his body and his ambitions dashed against the earth, is one that trails mythologies, of course. But it would be many years before I learned the story of Icarus, or read *Paradise Lost*. All I knew at that moment was the panic, and my hunger to see what the men out there were seeing; the thing I was forbidden.)

I was denied it, however. Probably my mother averted my eyes at the last minute, though it's unlikely I would have seen much. A blurred form dropping out of the blue, with the silk plume of a parachute following behind. It would have meant nothing.

My father, on the other hand, saw it all, and was one of the first to reach Valentin's body. I asked him about it, much, much later. He is a plain-spoken, pragmatic man, not given to waxing poetic, but when he answered my questions his vocabulary grew dreamy and evocative. The Bird Man's body, he said, had made a shape from the flattened grain, and he lay with his wings spread wide, so that it looked as though an enormous bird had fallen to earth. Of course they knew he was dead, but they turned him over anyway, I suppose to be absolutely sure. His face, my father told me, was not bloody, though a newspaper piece I later found about the accident speaks of "severe head injuries." His eyes were closed.

Perhaps, for completeness' sake, I should tell you how the tragedy came about. That flight, on May 21, 1956, was to have been Leo Valentin's last; he'd been experimenting with the technology of unaided human flight since 1950, when he'd made his first jump at Villacoublay, and was now, at thirty-seven, ready to pursue a safer avenue of work. He was a superstitious man. He had asked for Room 123 at the hotel where he'd stayed (that was the number he called out before jumping); he would let no hands touch his wings but his own. Nobody is entirely certain what went wrong, but the favored theory is that his wings clipped the plane as he jumped. He started to spin, and the damage to his wings prevented his controlling the descent. He attempted to open his parachute but it caught in the fractured wings, and candled.

So that was Valentin's story. Now let me return to the way it affected me. Though I saw nothing, and left the event undiscussed for thirty years or more, what happened that day marked me deeply. The sight of a winged man (sometimes flying, sometimes falling) comes up over and over again in the work I make. In the opening chapters of *Weaveworld* a character called Cal Mooney "falls" into a world in a carpet: "*The tumult of the birds grew louder, crowing their delight at his descent. He, the usurper of their element; he, who had snatched a glimpse of the miracle, would now be dashed to death upon it.*"

In the play *Crazyface*, the fool-hero Tyl Eulenspiegel escapes at the end, rising from the dirt and grief of his life on the wings of a failed Bird Man. There is a shot in *Nightbreed*, a movie I directed, in which the hero, Aaron Boone, is gunned down in a field of rushes. The sequence ends with a crane shot, rising from his face, to show him splayed on the ground, his arms spread wide. I had no idea what I was doing when I created that shot. If I had, I would probably not have been moved to do it.

My paintings and drawings also contain more than their share of winged figures. One of those images, created for a limited edition of *Weaveworld*, later became the symbol of my film company. Even the Bird Man's name appears in a story of mine ("The Last Illusion") and as a character in the film adaptation, *Lord of Illusions*. None of this, as I say, was conscious. But nor, I believe, was any of it accidental. On that afternoon in 1956 the death of Leo Valentin entered the life of a four-year-old Clive Barker. The fact that I had no way to interpret the event doesn't mean it went away. Indeed its power to impose itself upon my imagination may have been made all the stronger because I lacked those skills. It became, as it were a private legend, an image drawn on the rock of my skull, from which all manner of other tales and pictures would in time be derived.

There are no other events in my early life that carry quite the primal power of Leo Valentin's fall, but every childhood, however unremarkable, has its share of strangenesses and wonders, which the mind files away and puts to later purpose. Though in 1956 I was many years from realizing I wanted to write for a living, I certainly knew from an early age that I was a natural inventor of imagined things. I knew how to tell stories; how to create pictures in other people's heads. I also knew that there was power in those inventions; that I, as their creator, felt special, even unique.

Jorge Luis Borges, a writer for whose works and wisdom I have the greatest admiration, says at the end of his poem, *The Maker*, that: "*A man sets himself the task of portraying the world. Over the years he fills a given surface with images of provinces and kingdoms, mountains, bays, ships, islands, fish, rooms, instruments, heavenly bodies, horses, and people.*

Shortly before he dies, he discovers that this patient labyrinth of lines is a drawing of his own face."

I wonder if the reverse is not also in some way true. That the artist is constantly working on an elaborate and fantasticated self-portrait, but at the end has drawn, unbeknown, a picture of the world.

Before I move on from the story of Leo Valentin, let me describe the other image that remains with me from that day: the one I did see. I'm looking out of the car window, and there, at the edge of the cornfield, stand my father and uncle, watching the last moments of the Bird Man's fall. No doubt they were as panicked as everyone else, but that's not how I remember them. What I picture in my mind's eye are two stoic witnesses to this terrible scene. This was maleness, this witnessing; or so in that moment I came to believe. And if my early work is marked by a certain hunger to see what should not be seen, to show what should not be shown, the beginning of that appetite may be here, at the edge of the cornfield with the men watching the sky, and me, struggling in my mother's arms because I was forbidden the sight.

IV

The notion of the forbidden—of a subject so unspeakable that it cannot be visited without terrible consequences—lies at the root of the subgenre of fantastic art which has drawn most public attention in the last few years: horror fiction. Given that a significant number of the books I've written, and most of the film projects I've worked on, have been dubbed works of horror, it may be time to talk about it a little.

In the grand scheme of the fantastique, horror fiction—which I will define as narratives that seek chiefly or solely to scare or horrify—is a relatively small subgenre. It's also a modern phenomenon. That's not to say that the horrific has not always been a part of the storyteller's repertoire; only that the singularity of focus is recent; say, since the middle of the eighteenth century, when Gothic fiction began to depict lives entirely consumed by darkness and terror. Before that, the horrific was always part of a larger story-scheme. In a number of my early short stories I attempted this single-minded approach; making tales that only went after shock and horror. Their titles announce their intent: "The Midnight Meat Train," "Rawhead Rex," "Pig Blood Blues." But after writing a few of them, I quickly tired of the trick, and I started to expand my palette, while attempting to keep an element of hardcore horror in play. It's harder to do than it looks: distressing images and ideas are so potent that they often outweigh all other elements. It's difficult for character-based work, or felicities of philosophy, to make any impression on a reader when bodies are being disemboweled and heads are flying. But there were occasions, I think, when I struck a reasonable balance. "In the Hills, the Cities," for instance, achieves a potent surreality amid the bloodshed. A couple of stories, "Son of Celluloid" and "Dread," operate as *metafictions*, debating their use of the grotesque and the horrific even as they dramatize them. With three books of short stories under my belt I turned my hand to a novel: *The Damnation Game*. It is a Faust story (after Marlowe rather than Goethe), and though it's much shorter than my later novels it still spins an elaborate narrative, which allowed me to expand the place of metaphysics in my storytelling. This is the first time a religious tone appears in the fiction, I think; and I took courage from the readers' response to these deeper chords. When I returned to short stories for the next three books the narratives are much more explicitly metaphysical. Again, the titles tell all: "Down Satan!," "The Madonna," "The Life of Death." And again, there are attempts to create metafictions, the most lucid of which, I believe, is "The Forbidden." The film *Candyman* was derived from this story, and drew some serious critical attention. For anyone who might have missed the subtext, I drove it home by making the heroine a semiotician: an intellectual in pursuit of what she believes to be a monstrous myth, who finds halfway through the narrative that the myth is alive and well, and that she's become its quarry.

In a sense this story dramatizes a vital dynamic in these early books. They gain much of their energy from the tension between my intellectual and stylistic ambitions and the often disgusting ferocity of their images. I had learned some of the key creative lessons from the cinema. From Georges Franju's poetic and horrible *Les Yeux Sans Visage* (*Eyes Without a Face*); from Cronenberg's brutal, eloquent films, and of course from *The Exorcist*, which still stands as a benchmark of resonant cruelty. My own attempt to create something memorable for the screen, *Hellraiser*, was made soon after the delivery of these short stories, and in a way completed the first arc of my career. I was effectively finished with writing horror fiction. The next book I wrote was *Weaveworld*: a new world, a new direction.

That's not to say that my reputation as a purveyor of Grand Guignol hasn't followed me. I have, to be honest, an ambiguous response to that reputation. It has been all too often an easy peg for lazy journalists to hang a headline on; and for a certain order of reviewers, more interested in turning a phrase than exercising their intellects, it has been a stick to beat me with. But then if it hadn't been that it would have been something else; we all make rods for our own backs. I still enjoy crafting horror movies. It's a genre, which, for all its inanities, can still stir people up, which is always pleasing. It's such a primal form—it deals in the meat and bone of our existence—yet the moral issues it raises can be surprisingly complex: that's an attractive package.

As to writing horror, I think I'm done, barring a few pieces I still have in the works, designed to finish mythologies that still need closure. Of course I'll still go after a *frisson* if I see that the narrative offers me one; I just can't imagine devoting an entire novel to the business of scaring the reader. Sometimes, in fact, there's more potency in a darkness that creeps out of nowhere, its presence unsuspected, than in a fiction that announces from the first word that it intends to scare. There are passages in *Sacrament*, for instance, which are as disturbing as anything in "The Midnight Meat Train," but they arise organically from a story that has a lot of other things on its mind. In that sense this perhaps more closely approximates the way images of horror occur in real life. More often than not they come out of nowhere. But perhaps that also can be said of other areas of our experience. Out of nowhere, something strange.

V

Something strange.

One of my teachers at university, a notable literary scholar, railed against my appetite for invented worlds. Why, she demanded, did I waste my time reading about Middle-earth and Wonderland, when the real world was so rich and diverse? True artists weren't interested in inventing places, she said. It was a narcissistic game; writers who played it were arrested in adolescence. The woman intimidated me; I kept my enthusiasms to myself thereafter. Now, of course, I'd remind her that Shakespeare, surely the greatest model for storytellers in the Western tradition, was no stranger to invented worlds. Prospero's island, the woods of *A Midsummer Night's Dream*, even the history plays, with their ghosts and omens, are fearless marriages of the real and the fantastical. What I believe she was objecting to, in hindsight, was a perceived hollowness in the conventions of the fantastic; and had she made that argument I would have been obliged to see its merit. Emptied of meaning or belief, the forms of the fantastic often become mere filigree, no question. Books become catalogues of nonsense names and empty cliché: elaborate conceits, lacking the power to move us. But at its best, I would have countered, the fantastic is as rich and truthful and humane as any piece of realism.

I'm not sure I would have convinced her. There was something in her nature that made her unsympathetic to imaginative labors. When we were studying Ibsen, I voiced my admiration for *Peer Gynt*. She was scornful, directing my attention back to Ibsen's naturalistic plays. They had all kinds of merits, she insisted, that *Peer Gynt* lacked; it was a thin work by contrast. Her admiration (indeed her understanding) of Ibsen's work was directly connected with his powers as a social observer. It was as though she could not quantify the excellence of a scene involving the Kingdom of Trolls, for instance, because she had no personal experience by which to measure it. Put plainly like this, the notion sounds absurd, but there's some truth in it, I think. In short, the very qualities that define the fantastique were at the heart of her problem with it.

Of course, *Peer Gynt* isn't simply fantastical; it's profligate in its imaginings. And such profligacy is one of those defining qualities. There are exceptions to the rule (Beckett's plays, for instance) but, broadly speaking, the imagination, once unleashed, is defiantly excessive. The journeys the protagonists of fantastic fiction take are seldom less than staggering, the countries or planets or dimensions they discover either surpassingly beautiful or hellish, the characters and creatures they meet there prodigious in form and feeling. As befits a literature with its roots in myth, the wars and romances which the narratives describe are likely to be vast in their consequences.

Perhaps it's not surprising that the critics panic. Schooled to analyze the spartan aesthestics of modernity, the sheer spectacle of the fantastique looks, to their eye, deeply suspect. They're like architecture critics who've spent their formative years in minimalist houses and are suddenly removed into a Gothic cathedral. They don't have the vocabulary to describe or critique the complexity, the confidence, the sheer exuberance of what's in front of them. It intimidates them. In what is finally a supreme act of self-defense, they put on shrugs and walk away, saying that there's nothing here that deserves their scrutiny.

Readers have no such difficulties. They don't need screeds of criticism to help them understand what the books are attempting to do: they trust their sense of direction in these invented places. Nor do they flinch when the author explores his appetite for transgression. Though readers of contemporary fantasy are often characterized as conservative, even reactionary —half in love with places where life is simpler, and sex is invisible—they are, in my experience, quite the reverse. Over the last fifteen years I've played both pornographer and pulpit-pounder in the books I've written, without meeting significant objection.

I've created a character (Pie 'oh' pah in *Imajica*) whose gender is dependent on the erotic desires of those it's coupling with; I've made gay heroes and lesbian heroines; I've described confrontations with both the God of the Israelites and with pagan Goddesses; I've explored Gnosticism, Hermeticism, numerous forms of Sex Magic and Earth Magic; I've celebrated the perversities of the Devil and pictured Christ as a sun-addled egotist. I've made paintings and photographs depicting every kind of physical and spiritual conjunction and found audiences eager to see what I've made.

One of the things that surprises observers about the crowds who come to my book signings and lectures is how eclectic they are. The appetite for imaginative material is not circumscribed; it reaches out into every part of our society. I can still be astonished myself by the passion which these readers express for some of the darker, more byzantine elements of my work. The book to which many readers feel most fiercely loyal is *Imajica*. It's without question the most difficult thing I've written, both thematically and structurally. It is also the most ambitious, using the tropes of classical fantasy—the quest, the doppelgangers, the separated lovers, the villain with access to dark forces—as the bones of a far stranger body. Just as the alchemical writers used their pseudoscience as a way to encode a theory of spirit—the burning away of ego in search of a purer being—so in *Imajica* I attempted to encode a whole belief system into a single ambitious narrative. Have readers broken that code? Yes; in their tens of thousands. The most moving letters that I receive are related to this book, and to the breaking of that code. From a priest in Russia, who had been restored in his faith by reading the book, from a man with AIDS who relates that the book did more good than months of counseling, from a prisoner in England who paralleled the book with another spiritual quest, *Pilgrim's Progress*, which is one of the two books *Imajica*'s protagonist, Gentle, purchases on his journey. (The other is *Fanny Hill*.)

Returning to my forbidding lecturer, with her contempt for *Peer Gynt*, I wonder why the code of that play was so impenetrable to her. She was a very bright woman, the author of several influential texts; she understood perfectly well the idea of metaphor. She had undoubtedly read books by fellow academics analyzing Ibsen's intentions in *Peer Gynt*. But the moment any artist removed his or herself from a context which she identified as real something disconnected in her. The work no longer made sense.

This is, I suspect a peculiarly modern problem. Our century has been a time of investigation: everything has been made visible, made quantifiable. Mystery retreats; or, when it survives, it does so in the most broken-backed fashion: as a preoccupation with aliens or, worse, with the necessity to prove their existence.

The fantastic has nothing to do with proof; nothing to do with what might once have been true, or might yet come to pass. Hence my contempt for Todorov; for that mealymouthed negotiation with what *might* be possible. Why concern oneself with the plausible? What use is it in the grip of a dream? Would it help us comprehend the wisdom of *The Tempest* if we could be persuaded that there was once an entity called Ariel? Not at all. Only the frailest of cultures, afraid of its own shadow-self, will judge the excellence of its dreamscapes by a standard of verifiable truth.

VI

A second story, then. My tale of the Magician.

In the autumn of 1960, I was sick, quite seriously so, with the flu. I think we must just have gotten a television; a small black and white set. Enraptured by the thing, and too light-headed to do anything else with myself anyway, I sat and watched it through the gloomy afternoon. At some point an elderly man was interviewed; his words were translated from the French as he spoke. He was a strange character to my unsophisticated eye, but he fascinated me, with his fluttering hands, his old maid's mouth, the sorrowful wrinkle in his eyes. At the end of the interview came an excerpt from a film that he'd made. It was called, though the title meant nothing to me at the time, *The Testament of Orpheus*, and in it this same old man appeared, dressed much as he'd been dressed in his interview. He was wandering in a rather fake-looking landscape of ruins, where he encountered a menacing woman dressed in a cloak and elaborate helmet, armed with a spear. Flanking her were men wearing horse-masks. There was some exchange between the two, then the old man turned his back and walked away. Suddenly, the woman threw the spear, and it sank into the man's back, appearing through the middle of his chest. He fell to the ground, transfixed. One of the man-horses went to him, and pulled the spear out. This I remember very vividly: the spear sliding out of the dead man's body.

That was it. I'd never seen anything like it in my life. Visits to the cinema were extremely rare events for the family, and when we did see movies they were the usual juvenile fare. This was like a thunderbolt; I couldn't get it out of my head. I grasped nothing of what was meant by what I'd seen, or so it seemed at the time. But it had transfixed me nevertheless, as the spear had transfixed the old man.

It would be several years before I discovered who the man being interviewed was. It was, of course, Jean Cocteau. *The Testament of Orpheus* was his last film; he was to die a year later. The film was by no means the best he made; it's mawkish in places, and Cocteau is not a great screen presence by any means. But it is a testament, and it serves that purpose well. There are references throughout to his work as an artist or, as he would have preferred it, "a poet." He did not mean to limit himself with this definition. A poet might work in any medium and still express his poetic visions. Cocteau did just that. He made a number of films (two of them, *Orphée* and *La Belle et la Bête*, masterpieces of fantastic cinema), he painted frescoes, designed tapestries and ballets, illustrated books (on two occasions with groundbreaking homoerotic frankness), wrote books, and yes, poetry.

I don't recall asking my parents any questions about the man I'd seen that afternoon on the little television screen. Perhaps I knew they wouldn't be familiar with him; or that I wasn't ready to understand him yet. But the image of the ruins and the horse-headed men, and the terrible tenderness with which the spear was drawn out of the dead man's body, remained with me. It was only a matter of time before I went back into the world Cocteau had made. When I did so I was probably fifteen. I saw some of his drawings in a book: the grace and beauty of the men he rendered in such confident lines spoke loudly to me. I found a biography: saw *La Belle et la Bête* at a local film society screening; stumbled through some of his poetry; and, by degrees, began to interpret his very particular code. I don't have the space here to detail what I learned: but it had in some measure to do with being homosexual, in some measure to do with his faith in mythic models, and a great deal to do with his fearless belief that he was a king in his own country, and could legislate freely there. As it happened, I was learning much the same lesson from another poet, William Blake. "Make your own laws," Blake says, "or be a slave to another man's." (Blake was, of course, a polymath like Cocteau: poet, mystic, painter, engraver.) The lesson seems clear enough: make what your heart instructs, and don't let anyone persuade you to compromise with your own truth.

In practical terms, of course, this can be difficult. Both of these men were obliged to be workers for hire at periods in their lives; sometimes your stomach instructs more loudly than your heart. But when we look back over their lives (I hesitate to say careers; these men lived their careers), we see that they were wholly committed to being conduits for a vision which was in one sense theirs, of their essence, and in another wholly remote, unconcerned with the particularities of their lives, their unhappiness, their frustration, their addictions (in Cocteau's case), their grinding poverty (in Blake's). Though their circumstances were very different—Cocteau worked and played among some of the greatest artists of the century, Blake was barely noticed by the potentates and tastemakers of his age—they had this in common: they saw the world with a gaze that was peculiarly their own; and they scarcely deviated from the business of communicating what they saw to others.

My early encounter with Cocteau changed me. Seeing him living and dying I had, without being able to articulate what had happened, understood something; and all understanding brings change. I understood that the books I'd read and the paintings I'd seen were all *pieces* of their maker. That was what the image of the old man walking in the ruins showed me: an artist present in his own creation. Blake is even more audacious: he populates the city of London, familiar places like Camden Town and Mary-le-Bone, with the warring tribes of his homemade pantheon. Together these two artists provided me with an almost complete education in the methodologies of the fantastique. One draws the reader/spectator into his own kingdom; the other expels his creations into the known world, transforming it in the process. One centers his world around Christian iconography, though with a very personal slant; the other is inspired by pagan images and ideas. None of these dichotomies is strict, I should add. Cocteau, the classicist, painted frescoes for chapels, and Blake's Christian convictions contain a healthy portion of pantheism. They both brim over, defying any simple description of their ambitions or achievements. That's perhaps why, having been familiar with the work of both men for three decades or more, I am nowhere near exhausting them. They continue to teach, and I am still their apprentice.

Cocteau, my first magician, died on October 11, 1963. He had already planned the circumstances of his burial. He lies in a chapel he had decorated, sacred to the order of Saint-Blaise-des-Simples, the members of which had been known for their use of healing herbs. Shaping his world to the end, he inscribed his epitaph with his own hand: "*Je reste avec vous*" (I remain with you).

There is a herb garden around the chapel. Among the medicinal plants that grows there is the opium poppy.

VII

I originally had more than three stories to tell as part of this piece. Indeed one version was simply a patchwork of stories sewn together. The truth is, any intellectual grasp I have upon my fiction, and the context of my fiction, is framed inside a telling. I have no means at my disposal but to say: this happened, then this, then this.

Let me tell something about telling, then.

People are curious, I think, about how a writer makes a world. The process is assumed to be very different from the writing of a so-called realistic novel. In my experience, that's true. When I write about places I know — the Hebridean island of Tiree, for instance, in *Sacrament*, or Liverpool in *Weaveworld*, or London or New York — I write quickly, reporting to the page scenes which play out in my mind's eye. I'm almost a journalist. When the narrative is removed to new worlds, however, the rhythm of working changes completely. Very seldom does the scene I'm attempting to create spring immediately into my head. It's misty at first; I have a feeling about it, little more. The first exploratory paragraphs are likely to be about that feeling; they seldom make it to a final draft.

Before I describe the process any further perhaps I should retreat to an even earlier point: to the urge which makes me want to remove myself to these imagined spaces. This is best described as a phase of yearning: a powerful need to be in some other place. There's a melancholy aspect to this state; indeed the melancholy may be an essential part of the process. We feel this yearning when we wake from a particularly pleasing dream: a sense of separation from something wonderful. The Freudian will claim that it's the comfort of our mother's arms we yearn for, but I believe that's simplistic. I don't think it's Mama we're thinking of when we stare at the open sea, or at a road cresting a hill, leading away into some undiscovered place. But having stated with such certainty what it's not, I can't really supply any alternative explanation. I suppose if I knew the root of the yearning that gets me to work, its power over me would be diminished.

(Perhaps the medium best suited to an expression of this yearning, by the way, is music. I hear that longing in countless pieces: in Barber's Adagio, in the "In Paradisum" from the *Fauré Requiem*, in the "Liebestod" from *Tristan and Isolde*; in Max Steiner's film scores, in folk songs like "Blow the Wind Southerly" and "Shenandoah." It expresses both a dissatisfaction with things as they are and a suspicion that there are places, just out of sight, where life is better, richer, more meaningful. Across the Jordan or the wide Missouri some world waits to be restored to us.)

Returning now to the nuts and bolts of the process, I find that the restoration I'm describing occurs for me in increments. Having begun by setting down the feelings this as yet unspecified world arouses, I work, sentence by sentence, to make it come clear to me. Sometimes it simply refuses. Or rather, I've misread the signs, and am searching in the wrong place. There are countless abandoned explorations in my bottom drawer: the remains of searches for places that simply weren't there to be discovered. It's no use trying to fake it. If I can't see this place in my head what hope do I have of evoking it for my readers? I suppose you could cobble together a collection of secondhand thoughts, but there's no joy in that. If the place refuses to become real to you, you give up on the pursuit and look elsewhere. One of the tools I have on hand as I work on specifying the landscape is a lexicon of names and invented words, which I usually assemble when I start work on a book, and supplement as I go on. They may not stay in place as the drafts proceed, but they help to make the characters and places a reality. I always know when I've alighted upon the right name: Pie 'oh' pah and John Furie Zacharias; the twin cities of Yzorrdorex and Patashoqua; Mamoulian, the Last European and his companion Anthony Breer, the Razor-Eater; the names sound right to me.

As the work progresses all the senses come into play. I come to know the texture of a certain skin, the timbre of a certain voice. I've heard writers speak of the magical moment when a character "talks back" to them; when someone they have created attempts to wrest from the creator control of his or her destiny. It's an illusion, of course: they're all you, in the end; different parts of your being in conversation with one another. But the illusion can be potent, for all that. My equivalent of this feeling is less about voice than about something I suppose I must call *presence*. A character becomes so real that I can walk all the way around them, as it were; I can imagine how they'll respond to any stimulus I might toss at them: waltz music or the prospect of a bagel with lox.

Once the work is up and under way, once the world is breathing, you have to surrender to it: to its rhythms, to its intentions, to its ugliness, sometimes; to its beauty, others. Sometimes this surrender, which is the second state of creation, feels perilous. You float in a murky place for long periods, waiting for the sense of things to show itself. Doubt devours you. This time, you think, there's nothing there to bear you up. You're just going to sink, while these illusions you created watch you go down.

And then, miraculously, something begins to happen. The story begins to move before you, like a pageant. Still surrendering, you describe it. If you're lucky, there are days when this other world is so familiar to you that you can operate in that journalistic fashion I described before and simply report what you see. Some days too when you have to wait, not pushing too hard, not demanding that the sense of all this show itself before it wants to; listening, deeply; watching, deeply.

And when you're very lucky, a third state comes your way: what I'll call the ecstatic. It doesn't happen very often, at least to me, and when it does it never lasts very long, but when it's gone you know it. What is this state? Damned if I know. I do know that it invariably comes when you least expect it. Suddenly you're expressing feelings you didn't know you had, you're seeing patterns you didn't know were there to be found, and better still, you find you have the words to express those feelings, those patterns. When it's over, you come down from the experience feeling tender and vulnerable. But what has happened on the page is somehow new to you, as though another mind has created it. More than once I've been tempted to reject or even destroy work I made in this state, motivated by an unhealthy desire to recall the text within the boundaries of what's recognizably mine.

Somebody asked me at a lecture a few weeks ago whether I took drugs when I wrote. It's not the first time the question has been asked of me; and it's not surprising, perhaps, given what is on the page. I told the questioner that while I thoroughly enjoy certain altered states, I've never done good work when out of my head. Later, I realized that wasn't entirely true. I found titles to several of the stories in *The Books of Blood* one evening, high on hashish-laced brownies, and I've jotted down paranoid fantasies on cocaine, which I later used in stories. But that's about it. The paintings I've made high I always destroyed. They seemed thinly felt. And though I've made a few grandiose schemes for films and books in such states, they've never seemed as interesting—or indeed, as ambitious—as those I made on a Monday morning, clearheaded. That's not to say the method is unworkable. I'm happy to believe that Coleridge wrote "Kubla Khan" while in a laudanum fugue; and that great works of nineteenth-century poetry and painting were made under the influence of absinthe. Keith

Haring made wonderful, lucid images while high as a kite; Faulkner wrote beautifully when drunk. There are no rules here, except the rules of the dominant culture, which I—old Romantic that I am—firmly believe artists have no place obeying. It's just that I'm not wired to work while I'm high. Maybe I fear the consequences. I see quite enough visions as it is. Too many, some days. Some days I feel abused by their brightness, their elaboration. Perhaps I'm afraid that they have more than enough heat to cook me alive as it is; drugs would only stoke the fire.

Even as I write that, I see my own ambiguities clearly. How much, on the one hand, I want to be consumed, I want the fire to burn me up; and how much on the other I retreat from the prospect. And then, perhaps both appetites need to be in play, in balance even, for the work to be made. The surrendering self has to be matched by the aggressor; the man who wants to be lost in his worlds forever, erased by them, has to be met halfway by his other self, the one who is making this work out of a neurotic need for self-description.

VIII

I observed at the beginning of this introduction that it would contain its share of contradictory statements; so here's one. Having stated clearly that the fantastic is not motivated by an appetite to escape, I think that it was some part of what drew me to these forms at the start. I was born in 1952, in Liverpool: an unpromising place for a child. There were great areas of rubble-strewn bombed-out sites, wounds of the Second World War, all about the city; there was a sense (not consciously grasped by a child, but informing my experience in many subtle ways) that the best years were over and a slow decline from greatness begun. I remember in the autumn, thick, choking fogs the color of phlegm still seizing the city, stinking of the coal-fire smoke that created them. And, in the summer, the grass in the parks burned brown.

But also I remember the little library in Allerton Road; and the adventure of going there. The smell of old books; the covetousness that seized me when I found something new; the sense, when I got home and sat down to read, of a new world opening up. There is an intimacy in reading, of course, that is the essence of experience. The reader is being personally addressed by the author, mind to mind. That intimacy was a major part of what drew me to books. They made me feel connected to something beyond the limits of my life, the city, my schooling. My perception of language changed as I devoured the volumes I borrowed. Words were no longer to be taken for granted. Chosen and arranged with care, they were like spells. They could make things appear to me; pictures and feelings. I began to remember some of these enchantments by heart, as defenses against the dull world: sentences from a favorite novel, or more often, poems. I favored tight rhyme schemes over free verse. Not only were they easier to remember, their incantatory power was stronger. "In Midnights of November" by A. E. Housman, for instance; Stevenson's "Requiem," John Masefield's "Sea-Fever": "I must go down to the sea again, to the lonely sea and the sky, And all I ask is a tall ship and a star to steer her by."

As my tastes widened, and my grasp of how poetry worked deepened, my choice of pieces to be committed to memory became more ambitious. Chunks of Shakespeare, W. B. Yeats, and Robert Frost; even bits of Eliot. Often I had at best a partial understanding of the meaning, but the music in these pieces was enough. I felt protected by what I had remembered; I repeated them quietly to myself when the world got too much for me.

The incantations were transforming me, by degrees. I became more certain of myself; and more certain that I would be capable of making changes in the world, when my time came.

That, in a sense, is the greatest source of optimism we can have as children: to believe that we will be able to change things, when our turn comes.

IX

A final story.
In order to make the selection for this book, I took copies of all my plays, novels, and short stories away with me to my home in Hawaii; to the Garden Island of Kaua'i. I hadn't intended to do much more than glance through them, but my sleep patterns were oddly disturbed when I got to the island, so I found myself waking a little before dawn, lighting a fire, making some tea, and working for a few hours before the household rose. After some initial trepidation about returning to old prose, I found myself enjoying the process, digging through the novels to find nuggets that I deemed "essential." As I did so, I made notes for this introduction, some of which, in hindsight, almost read like tiny stories themselves: "I'm like a man who's hired to break into his own house, who finds—much to his astonishment—that he's asleep in his own bed."

Some were simply lists of things that enchanted me, work that carried the unmistakable stamp of profound imagining: Max Ernst's forests; also *Of This Men Shall Know Nothing*; opening of Korda's *Thief of Baghdad*, Carlo Crivelli's *Annunciation*, Britten's *A Ceremony of Carols*, Tarkovsky's *Andrei Rublev*, de Sade's *120 Days of Sodom*, Poe's *Masque of the Red Death*, David Lindsay's *Voyage to Arcturus* . . .

I made several such lists; attempts, I suppose, to see myself more clearly by naming the things that had given me inspiration.

So, that was my work, between five and eight-thirty every morning. The only sounds were those of the sea (the house is twenty yards from the water), and sometimes the January rains lashing against the roof of our house. These were wonderful, even magical, times.

A little after dawn one day, I had a visitor. A woman I didn't know, who came knocking on the door, visibly distressed. She was sorry to be bothering me so early, she said, but did I have a large container of some kind: maybe a laundry bin or its like? I asked her what she needed it for, and she told me that her husband had found a baby dolphin stranded in the shallows a little way along the shore. It was hurt, and needed to be taken out of the water before any further harm came to it. I could find nothing to the purpose, but went with the woman down the beach. Her husband had gone back to their house to see if he could get the police to come out and help or at least to get some advice; the animal was floating in the surf, buffeted by wave after wave. He was tiny—no more than two, perhaps two-and-a-half, feet long—and he was audibly distressed. When I waded in and attempted to comfort him, the sounds he made were uncannily like the cries of a baby. I examined him as best I could, as the waves came in against us. The night had been exceptionally stormy, and the infant dolphin had plainly been thrown up against the rocks in the bay repeatedly. He had open gashes on his head and snout. I have seldom felt so ignorant and powerless. What were we to do? Bring the creature up out of the water where he wouldn't be knocked about by the waves, or leave him in his native element? The woman and I debated for a minute or two, then compromised. I lifted the animal out on to the sand to see just how bad his wounds were, and then, having made a perfunctory examination, carried him back into the shallows. He had no energy left, he simply lay in my arms, buoyed by the water but protected from the worst assaults of the waves. We talked to him, we stroked him, and by degrees his mewling cries ceased. I kept looking at his bright black eyes, wondering what he saw when he looked at me; wondering what he imagined me to be. We stayed there together for half an hour or so; me cradling him in the water, the woman standing in the shallows close by. At last he died. It was my companion who realized it, not me. "I think we lost him," she said quietly. I lifted the dolphin out of the water. I said I could feel his heart beating. She gently pointed out that it was my own pulse I was feeling, not his. She was right. Fatigue—and, who knows, perhaps despair?—had claimed him.

We laid him on the sand, and sat with him silently for a few minutes. Then I picked him up and carried him back to the woman's house. Later, she came to report that a man from the Marine Research Unit on the island, who had been alerted by her husband, had come out to collect the body. He'd ascertained several things. First, that the animal was not diseased (apparently diseased animals often deliberately beach themselves); second, that the dolphin was barely twenty-four-hours old, and had not even fed in his short life, which suggested that his mother had been taken by a shark, or that they had somehow become separated, and the infant had been carried to the shore, where he had been powerless to resist being thrown against the rocks. The man was happy that we'd reported the situation, because the animal was not, as we'd thought, a spinner dolphin (a species which is much in evidence around the islands, often close to shore) but a striped dolphin; altogether rarer, and much less studied. He was surprised, he said, that the animal had been washed up: they were thought to live in much deeper waters.

That, in a sense, is the end of the story. I suppose it's more anecdote than story. But it belongs here, I think. For the next few days, as I went on reading and reflecting, my thoughts returned over and over to the time I had been with the infant. The memory of holding his silky, wounded body in my arms moved me deeply: he was utterly strange to me, and I to him, no doubt. I tried to imagine what the creature must have been feeling—though of course it was an exercise in futility to try to do so. Still I kept coming back to the brightness of his eyes, to the pitifulness of his mewling. What a world to have been delivered into! One moment you're safe in your mother's womb, the next you're expelled from her, then separated from her, and driven up onto a shore, where two creatures tend you, whisper to you in a language you cannot understand, and hold you until you die. Was I being too much the sentimentalist, to think that our words and touches had comforted the creature at the last? Were we in truth so alien to him that what we intended as solace was just another terror? I want to believe that there are signs that all living things understand; at least all mammals. That he knew there was gentleness in our touch and concern in our voices; and that that went some little way to easing his death.

The sea plays a significant role in the books I've written. Quiddity, the dream-sea which lies at the heart of *The Great and Secret Show* and *Everville*, is presented as a source of all mythologies, and finally perhaps, the source of consciousness itself. In *Imajica* the rise of the Goddesses at the end of the novel is signaled by an invasion of water, which playfully but irrevocably undoes the labors of God and His Kings. In *Galilee*, of course, the eponymous hero is a lonely seafarer, who chooses not to set foot on solid ground except when his responsibilities require it. He always comes to the same place when he makes landfall. The same island, the same beach. It is, of course, the beach I have been describing. Though I moved its location a mile or two to preserve the anonymity of the little bay where we spend a few weeks each year, it is the very place where I knelt in the surf with the dolphin.

X

We all live in separate worlds.

The man watching the fire may be standing just a few yards from the man consumed by it, but his experience of the world is utterly different. At various points in our lives we all feel like the one who's watching the flames; at other times, we feel like the one burning. Then we find ourselves looking out through the waves of heat and wondering how it's possible for anyone to laugh, or look at the sky, or simply breathe.

The challenge is this: how do we remember, when we're out in the cool air, and our breath is easy, what it feels like in the fire? How do we extend our intellects, our emotions, our sympathies from one place into another; in fact, into many others? This is the defining business of the imagination: how to be *other than ourselves*, and in that experience look back at what we are, and know ourselves better. It is Terence, the great Roman dramatist, who offers the nicest summary of this adventure. "*Humani nil a me alienum puto*," he says: Nothing human is alien to me. The traditions of storytelling and picturemaking which I've been celebrating here press beyond Terence's profound humanism. They invite us not only to understand what it feels like to be another human being, but what it feels like to be another species entirely. To play in the Bestiary, openhearted. The realist objects that there is no merit in this: what does it matter, he protests, that a story takes us into the condition of invented beasts? The answer is this: that we are all invented beasts, all pieces of fiction, suspended in the solution of mind, and to keep a certain sense of that fact as we go about the hard business of daily life is to be more alive, more protean, more open to the possibility of flow. Sometimes we hope to flow into the pain of someone we know, and diminish it. Sometimes into the refreshing strangeness of a bird, or a dog. And finally, perhaps, we may flow out from our own narrowness completely, and be returned to the sea.

Clive Barker
LOS ANGELES
MARCH 1999

ONE

DOORWAYS

We pass through doorways all the time; they're so familiar to us we fail to appreciate their mythic resonance. In the language of the fantastic, doorways present the reader with passage into other worlds, other times, other states of being. The most widely known example is probably in the film of *The Wizard of Oz*, when Dorothy tentatively opens the door of her house and discovers that she has been living in a black and white world, and that the experience that awaits her on the other side is rainbow-colored. What more perfect analogy for the power of the imagination?

In the chapter that follows there are very few literal *doorways*; but all the selections describe moments when a character discovers that the rules of the world are changing in front of his or her eyes. Nothing will ever be the same again.

Cal Mooney topples from the wall of a yard and falls into an enchanted carpet. Private detective Harry D'Amour stumbles into a place of passage between this world and Quiddity, the dream-sea. A boy called Will Rabjohns discovers that killing a living thing is also a doorway; a place in the world where everything changes. This, of course, is the reverse of the scene from *Oz*. Some color goes *out* of the world when Will is taught to kill.

Most of the journeys these characters are about to take are outlandish. But the experience isn't completely remote from us, is it? We've all crossed a threshold or turned a corner and come upon some revelation that has changed our lives. A face to fall in love with; a library filled with undiscovered books; a doctor, making a small, sad smile as he rises to beckon us in . . .

1

From *Weaveworld*

The birds did not stop their spiraling over the city as Cal approached.
For every one that flew off, another three or four joined the throng.

The phenomenon had not gone unnoticed. People stood on the pavement and on doorsteps, hands shading their eyes from the glare of the sky, and stared heavenward. Opinions were everywhere ventured as to the reason for this congregation. Cal didn't stop to offer his, but threaded his way through the maze of streets, on occasion having to double back and find a new route, but by degrees getting closer to the hub.

And now, as he approached, it became apparent that his first theory had been incorrect. The birds were not feeding. There was no swooping nor squabbling over a six-legged crumb, nor any sign in the lower air of the insect life that might have attracted these numbers. The birds were simply circling. Some of the smaller species, sparrows and finches, had tired of flying and now lined rooftops and fences, leaving their larger brethren—carrion-crows, magpies, gulls—to occupy the heights. There was no scarcity of pigeons here either; the wild variety banking and wheeling in flocks of fifty or more, their shadows rippling across the rooftops. There were some domesticated birds too, doubtless escapees like 33. Canaries and budgerigars: birds called from their millet and their bells by whatever force had summoned the others. For these birds being here was effectively suicide. Though their fellows were at present too excited by this ritual to take note of the pets in their midst, they would not be so indifferent when the circling spell no longer bound them. They would be cruel and quick. They'd fall on the canaries and the budgerigars and peck out their eyes, killing them for the crime of being tamed.

But for now, the parliament was at peace. It mounted the air, higher, ever higher, busying the sky.

The pursuit of this spectacle had led Cal to a part of the city he'd seldom explored. Here the plain square houses of the council estates gave way to a forlorn and eerie no-man's-land, where streets of once-fine, three-story terraced houses still stood, inexplicably preserved from the bulldozer, surrounded by areas leveled in expectation of a boomtime that had never come; islands in a dust sea.

It was one of these streets—*Rue Street* the sign read—that seemed the point over which the flocks were focused. There were more sizable assemblies of exhausted birds here than in any of the adjacent streets; they twittered and preened themselves on the eaves and chimney tops and television aerials.

Cal scanned sky and roof alike, making his way along Rue Street as he did so. And there—a thousand-to-one chance—he caught sight of his bird. A solitary pigeon, dividing a cloud of sparrows. Years of watching the sky, waiting for pigeons to return from races, had given him an eagle eye; he could recognize a particular bird by a dozen idiosyncrasies in its flight pattern. He had found 33; no doubt of it. But even as he watched, the bird disappeared behind the roofs of Rue Street.

He gave chase afresh, finding a narrow alley which cut between the terraced houses halfway along the road, and let on to the larger alley that ran behind the row. It had not been well kept. Piles of household refuse had been dumped along its length; orphan dustbins overturned, their contents scattered.

But twenty yards from where he stood there was work going on. Two removal men were maneuvering an armchair out of the yard behind one of the houses, while a third stared up at the birds. Several hundred were assembled on the yard walls and windowsills and railings. Cal wandered along the alley, scrutinizing this assembly for pigeons. He found a dozen or more among the multitude, but not the one he sought.

"What d'you make of it?"

He had come within ten yards of the removal men, and one of them, the idler, was addressing the question to him.

"I don't know," he answered honestly.

"Maybe they're goin' to migrate," said the younger of the two armchair carriers, letting drop his half of the burden and staring up at the sky.

"Don't be an idiot, Shane," said the other man, a West Indian. His name—Gideon—was emblazoned on the back of his overalls. "Why'd they migrate in the middle of the fuckin' summer?"

"Too hot," was the idler's reply. "That's what it is. Too fuckin' hot. It's cookin' their brains up there."

Gideon had now put down his half of the armchair and was leaning against the backyard wall, applying a flame to the half-spent cigarette he'd fished from his top pocket.

"Wouldn't be bad, would it?" he mused. "Being a bird. Gettin' yer end away all spring, then fuckin' off to the South of France as soon as yer get a chill on yer bollocks."

"They don't live long," said Cal.

"Do they not?" said Gideon, drawing on his cigarette. He shrugged. "Short and sweet," he said. "That'd suit me."

Shane plucked at the half-dozen blond hairs of his would-be mustache. "Yer know somethin' about birds, do yer?" he said to Cal.

"Only pigeons."

"Race 'em, do you?"

"Once in a while—"

"Me brother-in-law keeps whippets," said the third man, the idler. He looked at Cal as though this coincidence verged on the miraculous, and would now fuel hours of debate. But all Cal could think of to say was:

"Dogs."

"That's right," said the other man, delighted that they were of one accord on the issue. "He's got five. Only one died."

"Pity," said Cal.

"Not really. It was fuckin' blind in one eye and couldn't see in the other."

The man guffawed at this observation, which promptly brought the exchange to a dead halt. Cal turned his attention back to the birds, and he grinned to see—there on the upper window-ledge of the house—*his* bird.

"I see him," he said.

Gideon followed his gaze. "What's that then?"

"My pigeon. He escaped." Cal pointed. "There. In the middle of the sill. See him?"

All three now looked.

"Worth something is he?" said the idler.

"Trust you, Bazo," Shane commented.

"Just asking," Bazo replied.

"He's won prizes," said Cal, with some pride. He was keeping his eyes glued to 33, but the pigeon showed no sign of wanting to fly; just preened his wing feathers, and once in a while turned a beady eye up to the sky.

"Stay there . . . ," Cal told the bird under his breath, "don't move." Then, to Gideon: "Is it all right if I go in? Try and catch him?"

"Help yourself. The auld girl who had the house's been carted off to hospital. We're taking the furniture to pay her bills."

Cal ducked through into the yard, negotiating the bric-a-brac the trio had dumped there, and went into the house.

It was a shambles inside. If the occupant had ever owned anything of substance it had long since been removed. The few pictures still hanging were worthless; the furniture was old, but not old enough to have come back into fashion; the rugs, cushions, and curtains so aged they were fit only for the incinerator. The walls and ceilings were stained by many years' accrual of smoke, its source the candles that sat on every shelf and sill, stalactites of yellowed wax depending from them.

He made his way through the warren of poky, dark rooms, and into the hallway. The scene was just as dispiriting here. The brown linoleum rucked up and torn, and everywhere the pervasive smell of must and dust and creeping rot. *She was well out of this squalid place*, Cal thought, *wherever she was; better off in hospital, where at least the sheets were dry.*

He began to climb the stairs. It was a curious sensation, ascending into the murk of the upper story, becoming blinder stair by stair, with the sound of birds scurrying across the slates above his skull, and beyond that the muted cries of gull and crow. Though it was no doubt self-deception, he seemed to hear their voices *circling*, as though this very place were the center of their attentions. An image appeared in his head, of a photograph from *National Geographic*. A study of stars, taken with a slow-release camera, the pinpoint lights describing circles as they moved, or appeared to move, across the sky, with the Pole Star, the Nail of Heaven, steady in their midst.

The wheeling sound, and the picture it evoked, began to dizzy him. He suddenly felt weak, even afraid.

This was no time for such frailties, he chided himself. He had to claim the bird before it flew off again. He picked up his pace. At the top of the stairs he maneuvered past several items of bedroom furniture, and opened one of the several doors that he was presented with. The room he had chosen was adjacent to the one whose sill 33 occupied. Sun streamed through the curtainless window; the stale heat brought fresh sweat to his brow. The room had been emptied of furniture, the only souvenir of occupancy a cal-endar for the year 1961. On it, a photograph of a lion beneath a tree, its shaggy, monolithic head laid on vast paws, its gaze contemplative.

Cal went out on to the landing again, selected another door, and was this time delivered into the right room. There, beyond the grimy glass, was the pigeon.

Now it was all a question of tactics. He had to be careful not to startle the bird. He approached the window cautiously. On the sun-drenched sill 33 cocked its head, and blinked its eye, but made no move. Cal held his breath, and put his hands on the frame to haul the window up, but there was no budging it. A quick perusal showed why. The frame had been sealed up years ago, a dozen or more nails driven deep into the wood. A primitive form of crime prevention, but no doubt reassuring to an old woman living alone.

From the yard below, he heard Gideon's voice. Peering down, he could just see the trio dragging a large rolled-up carpet out of the house, Gideon giving orders in a ceaseless stream.

"To my left, Bazo. *Left!* Don't you know which is your left?"

"I'm going left."

"Not *your* left, yer idiot. *My* left."

The bird on the sill was undisturbed by this commotion. It seemed quite happy on its perch.

Cal headed back downstairs, deciding as he went that the only option remaining was to climb up onto the yard wall and see if he couldn't coax the bird down from there. He cursed himself for not having brought a pocketful of grain. Coos and sweet words would just have to do.

By the time he stepped out into the heat of the yard once more, the removal men had successfully manhandled the carpet out of the house, and were taking a rest after their exertions.

"No luck?" said Shane, seeing Cal emerge.

"The window won't budge. I'll have to try from down here."

He caught a deprecating look from Bazo. "You'll never reach the bug-ger from here," the man said, scratching the expanse of beer-gut that gleamed between T-shirt and belt.

"I'll try from the wall," said Cal.

"Watch yerself—" Gideon said.

"Thanks."

"—you could break yer back—"

Using pits in the crumbling mortar for footholds, Cal hauled himself up on to the eight-foot wall that divided this yard from its neighbor.

The sun was hot on his neck and the top of his head, and something of the giddiness he'd experienced climbing the stairs returned. He straddled the wall as though it were a horse, until he got used to the height. Though the perch was the width of a brick, and offered ample enough walking space, heights and he had never been happy companions.

"Looks like it's been a nice piece of handiwork," said Gideon, in the yard below. Cal glanced down to see that the West Indian was now on his haunches beside the carpet, which he'd rolled out far enough to expose an elaborately woven border.

Bazo wandered over to where Gideon crouched, and scrutinized the property. He was balding, Cal could see, his hair scrupulously pasted down with oil to conceal the spot.

"Pity it's not in better nick," said Shane.

"Hold yer horses," said Bazo. "Let's have a better look."

Cal returned his attention to the problem of standing upright. At least the carpet would divert his audience for a few moments; long enough, he prayed, for him to get to his feet. There was no breath of wind here to alleviate the fury of the sun; he could feel sweat trickle down his torso and glue his underwear to his buttocks. Gingerly, he started to stand, bringing one leg up into a kneeling position—both hands clinging to the brick like grim death.

From below, there were murmurs of approval as more of the carpet was exposed to light.

"Look at the work in that," said Gideon.

"Are you thinkin' what I'm thinkin'?" said Bazo, his voice lowered.

"I don't know 'til you tell me," came Gideon's reply.

"What say we take it down to Gilchrist's. We might get a price for this."

"The Chief'll know it's gone," Shane protested.

"Keep it down," said Bazo, quietly reminding his companions of Cal's presence. In fact Cal was far too concerned with his inept tightrope act to bother himself with their petty theft. He had finally got the soles of both feet up on to the top of the wall, and was about to try standing up.

In the yard, the conversation went on.

"Take the far end, Shane, let's have a look at the whole thing . . ."

"D' you think it's Persian?"

"Haven't a fuckin' clue."

Very slowly, Cal stood upright, his arms extended at ninety degrees from his body. Feeling as stable as he was ever going to feel, he chanced a quick look up at the windowsill. The bird was still there.

From below he heard the sound of the carpet being unrolled further, the men's grunts punctuated with words of admiration.

Ignoring their presence as best he could, he took his first faltering step along the wall.

"Hey there . . . ," he murmured to the escapee, "remember me?"

33 took no notice. Cal advanced a second trembling step, and a third, his confidence growing. He was getting the trick of this balancing business now.

"Come on down," he coaxed, a prosaic Romeo.

The bird finally seemed to recognize his owner's voice, and cocked his head in Cal's direction.

"Here, boy. . . ," Cal said, tentatively raising his hand toward the window as he risked another step.

At that instant either his foot slipped or the brick gave way beneath his heel. He heard himself loose a yell of alarm, which panicked the birds lining the sill. They were up and off, their wing beats ironic applause, as he flailed on the wall. His panicked gaze went first to his feet, then to the yard below.

No, not the yard; that had disappeared. It was the carpet he saw. It had been entirely unrolled, and it filled the yard from wall to wall.

What happened next occupied mere seconds, but either his mind was lightning fast, or the moments played truant, for it seemed he had all the time he needed—

Time to appreciate the startling intricacy of the design laid out beneath him; an awesome proliferation of exquisitely executed detail. Age had bled brightness from the colors of the weave, mellowing vermilion to rose, and cobalt to a chalky blue, and here and there the carpet had become threadbare, but from where Cal teetered the effect was still overwhelming.

Every inch of the carpet was worked with motifs. Even the border brimmed with designs, all subtly different from their neighbors. The effect was not over-busy; every detail was clear to Cal's feasting eyes. In one place a dozen motifs congregated as if banded together; in another, they stood apart like rival siblings. Some kept their station along the border; others spilled into the main field, as if eager to join the teeming throng there.

In the field itself ribbons of color described arabesques across a background of sultry browns and greens, forms that were pure abstraction—

bright jottings from some wild man's diary—jostling with stylized flora and fauna. But this complexity paled beside the center piece of the carpet: a huge medallion, its colors as various as a summer garden, into which a hundred subtle geometries had been cunningly woven, so that the eye could read each pattern as flower or theorem, order or turmoil, and find each choice echoed somewhere in the grand design.

He saw all of this in one prodigious glance. In his second the vision laid before him began to change.

From the corner of his eye he registered that the rest of the world—the yard, and the men who'd occupied it, the houses, the wall he'd been toppling from—all were winking out of existence. Suddenly he was hanging in the air, the carpet vaster by the moment beneath him, its glorious configurations filling his head.

The design was shifting, he saw. The knots were restless, trembling to slip themselves, and the colors seemed to be merging into each other, new forms springing from this marriage of dyes.

Implausible as it seemed, the carpet was coming to life.

A landscape—or rather a confusion of landscapes thrown together in fabulous disarray—was emerging from the warp and the weft. Was that not a mountain he could see below him, pressing its head up through a cloud of color? And was that not a river? And could he not hear its roar as it fell in white water torrents into a shadowed gorge?

There was a *world* below him.

And he was suddenly a bird, a wingless bird hovering for a breathless instant on a balmy, sweet-scented wind, sole witness to the miracle sleeping below.

There was more to claim his eye with every thump of his heart.

A lake, with myriad islands dotting its placid waters like breaching whales. A dappled quilt of fields, their grasses and grains swept by the same tides of air that kept him aloft. Velvet woodland creeping up the sleek flank of a hill, on whose pinnacle a watchtower perched, sun and cloud-shadow drifting across its white walls.

There were other signs of habitation too, though nothing of the people themselves. A cluster of dwellings hugging a river bend; several houses beetling along the edge of a cliff, tempting gravity. And a town too, laid out in a city-planner's nightmare, half its streets hopelessly serpentine, the other half cul-de-sacs.

The same casual indifference to organization was evident everywhere, he saw. Zones temperate and intemperate, fruitful and barren were thrown together in defiance of all laws geological or climatic, as if by a God whose taste was for contradiction.

How fine it would be to walk there, he thought, with so much variety pressed into so little space, not knowing whether turning the next corner would bring ice or fire. Such complexity was beyond the wit of a cartographer. To be there, in that world, would be to live a perpetual adventure.

And at the center of this burgeoning province, perhaps the most awesome sight of all. A mass of slate-colored cloud, the innards of which were in perpetual, spiraling motion. The sight reminded him of the birds wheeling above the house in Rue Street—an echo of this greater wheel.

At the thought of them, and the place he'd left behind, he heard their voices—and in that moment the wind that had swept up from the world below, keeping him aloft, faltered.

He felt the horror in his stomach first, and then his bowels: he was going to fall.

The tumult of the birds grew louder, crowing their delight at his descent. He, the usurper of their element; he, who had snatched a glimpse of a miracle, would now be dashed to death upon it.

He started to yell, but the speed of his fall stole the cry from his tongue. The air roared in his ears and tore at his hair. He tried to spread his arms to slow his descent but the attempt instead threw him head over heels, and over again, until he no longer knew earth from sky. There was some mercy in this, he dimly thought. At least he'd be blind to death's proximity. Just tumbling and tumbling until—

The world went out.

He fell through a darkness unrelieved by stars, the birds still loud in his ears, and hit the ground, hard.

It hurt, and went on hurting, which struck him as odd. Oblivion, he'd always assumed, would be a painless condition. And soundless too. But there were voices.

"Say something . . . ," one of them demanded, "if it's only good-bye."

There was laughter now.

He opened his eyes a hair's breadth. The sun was blindingly bright, until Gideon's bulk eclipsed it.

"Have you broken anything?" the man wanted to know.

Cal opened his eyes a fraction wider.

"Say something, man."

He raised his head a few inches, and looked about him. He was lying in the yard, on the carpet.

"What happened?"

"You fell off the wall," said Shane.

"Must have missed your footing," Gideon suggested.

"Fell," Cal said, pulling himself up into a sitting position. He felt nauseous.

"Don't think you've done much damage," said Gideon. "A few scrapes, that's all."

Cal looked down at himself, verifying the man's remark. He'd taken skin off his right arm from wrist to elbow, and there was tenderness down his body where he'd hit the ground, but there were no sharp pains. The only real harm was to his dignity, and that was seldom fatal.

He got to his feet, wincing, eyes to the ground. The weave was playing dumb. There was no telltale tremor in the rows of knots, no sign that hidden heights and depths were about to make themselves known. Nor was there any sign from the others that they'd seen anything miraculous. To all intents and purposes the carpet beneath his feet was simply that: a carpet.

He hobbled toward the yard gate, offering a muttered thanks to Gideon. As he stepped out into the alley, Bazo said:

"Yer bird flew off."

Cal gave a small shrug and went on his way.

What had he just experienced? A hallucination, brought on by too much sun or too little breakfast? If so, it had been startlingly real. He looked up at the birds, still circling overhead. *They* sensed something untoward here too; that was why they'd gathered. Either that, or they and he were sharing the same delusion.

All, in sum, that he could be certain of was his bruising. That, and the fact that though he was standing no more than two miles from his father's house, in the city in which he'd spent his entire life, he felt as homesick as a lost child.

From *Sacrament*

The worst of the storm had cleared to the southwest by the time Will and Jacob came within sight of the summit. Through the thinning snow, Will saw that up ahead there was a stand of trees. Leafless, of course (what the season had not taken the night's wind had surely stripped), but growing so close together, and sufficiently large in number that each had protected the other in their tender years, until they had matured into a dense little wood.

Now, with the gale somewhat diminished, Will asked a question out loud:

"Is that where we're going?"

"It is," said Jacob, not looking down at him.

"Why?"

"Because we have work to do."

"What?" Will asked. The clouds were coming unknitted over the heights, and even as he put this question a patch of dark and star-pricked sky appeared beyond the trees. It was as though a door were opening on the far side of the wood, the sight so perfect Will almost believed it had been stage-managed by Jacob. But perhaps it was more likely—and more marvelous, in its way—that they had arrived at this moment by chance, he and Jacob being blessed travelers.

"There's a bird in those trees, you see," Jacob went on. "Actually there's a pair of birds. And I need you to kill them for me." He said this without any particular emphasis, as though the matter was relatively inconsequential. "I have a knife I'd like you to use for the job." Now he looked Will's way, intently. "Being a city boy you're probably not as experienced with birds as you are with moths and such."

"No, I'm not . . . ," Will admitted, hoping he didn't sound doubtful or questioning. "But I'm sure it's easy."

"You eat bird meat, presumably," Jacob said.

Of course he did. He enjoyed fried chicken, and turkey at Christmas. He'd even had a piece of the pigeon pie Adele had made once she'd explained that the pigeon wasn't the filthy kind he knew from Manchester. "I love it," he said, the notion of this deed easier when he thought of a barbecued chicken leg. "How will I know which birds you want me to . . ."

"You can say it."

". . . kill?"

"I'll point them out, don't worry. It's as you say: *easy.*" He had said that, hadn't he? Now he had to make good on the boast. "Be careful with this," Jacob said, passing the knife to him. "It's uncommonly sharp."

He received the weapon gingerly. Was there some charge passed through its blade into his marrow? He thought so. It was subtle, to be sure, but when his hand tightened around the hilt he felt as though he knew the knife like a friend; as though he and it had some long-standing knowledge of one another.

"Good," Jacob said, seeing Will fearlessly clasping the weapon. "You look as if you mean business."

Will grinned. He did; no doubt of it. Whatever business this knife was capable of, he meant.

They were at the fringes of the wood now, and with the clouds parted, the starlight polished every snow-laden twig and branch until it glittered. There remained in Will a remote tic of apprehension regarding the deed ahead—or rather, his competency in the doing of it; he entertained no doubts about the killing itself—but he showed no sign of this to Jacob. He strode between the trees a pace ahead of his companion, and was all at once enveloped in a silence so profound it made him hold his breath for fear of breaking it.

A little way behind him, Jacob said: "Take it slowly. Enjoy the moment."

Will's knife-hand had a strange agitation in it, however. It didn't want any delay. It wanted to be at work, *now*.

"Where are they?" Will whispered.

Jacob put his hand on the back of Will's neck. "Just look," he murmured, and though nothing actually changed in the scene before them, at Jacob's words Will saw it with a sudden simplicity, his gaze blazing through the lattice of branches and mesh of brambles, through the glamour of sparkling frost and starlit air, to the heart of this place. Or rather to what seemed to him at that moment its heart: two birds, huddled in a niche at the juncture of branch and trunk. Their eyes were wide and bright (he could see them blinking, even though they were ten yards from him) and their heads were cocked.

"They see me," Will breathed.

"See them back."

"I do."

"Fix them with your eyes."

"I am."

"Then finish it. *Go on*."

Jacob pushed him lightly, and lightly Will went, like a phantom in fact, over the decorated ground. His eyes were fixed on the birds every step of the way. They were plain creatures. Two bundles of ragged brown feathers, with a sliver of sheeny blue in their wings. No more remarkable than the moths he'd killed in the Courthouse, he thought. He didn't hurry toward them. He took his time, despite the impatience in his hand, feeling as though he were gliding down a tunnel toward his target, which was the only thing in focus before him. If they fled now, they still could not escape him; of that he was certain. They were in the tunnel with him, trapped by his hunter's will. They might flutter, they might peck, but he would have their lives whatever they did.

He was perhaps three strides from the tree—raising his arm to slit their throats—when one of the pair took sudden flight. His knife-hand astonished him. Up it sped, a blur in front of his face, and before his eyes could even find the bird the knife had already transfixed it. Though strictly speaking it had not been his doing, he felt proud of the deed.

Look at me! he thought, knowing Jacob was watching him. *Wasn't that quick? Wasn't that beautiful?*

The second bird was rising now, while the first flapped like a toy on a stick. He hadn't time to free the blade. He just let his left hand do as the right had done, and up it went like five-fingered lightning to strike the bird from the air. Down the creature tumbled, landing belly up at Will's feet. His blow had broken its neck. It feebly flapped its wings a moment, shitting itself. Then it died.

Will looked at its mate. In the time it had taken to kill the second bird, the first had also perished. Its blood, running down the blade, was hot on his hand.

Easy, he thought, just as he'd said it would be. A moment ago they'd been blinking their eyes and cocking their heads, hearts beating. Now they were dead, both of them; spilled and broken. Easy.

"What you've just done is *irreversible,*" said Jacob, laying his hands upon Will's shoulders from behind. "Think of that." His touch was no longer light. "This is not a world of resurrections. They've gone. Forever."

"I know."

"No you don't," Jacob said. There was as much weight in his words as in his palms. "Not yet, you don't. You see them dead before you, but knowing what that means takes a little time." He lifted his left hand from Will's shoulder, and reached around his body. "May I have my knife back? If you're sure you've finished with it, that is."

Will slid the bird off the blade, bloodying the fingers of his other hand in the doing, and tossed the corpse down beside its mate. Then he wiped the knife clean on the arm of his jacket—an impressively casual gesture, he thought—and passed it back into Jacob's care, as cautiously as he'd been lent it.

"Suppose I were to tell you," Jacob said softly, almost mournfully, "that these two things at your feet—which you so efficiently dispatched—were the last of their kind?"

"The last birds?"

"No," Jacob said, indulgently. "Nothing so ambitious. Just the last of *these* birds."

"Are they?"

"*Suppose they were*," Jacob replied. "How would you feel?"

"I don't know," Will said, quite honestly. "I mean, they're just birds."

"Oh now," Jacob chided, "*think again.*"

Will obeyed. And as had happened several times in Steep's presence, his mind grew strange to itself, filling with thoughts it had never dared before. He looked down at his guilty hands, and the blood seemed to throb on them, as though the memory of the bird's pulse was still in it. And while he looked he turned over what Jacob had just said.

Suppose they were the last, the very last, and the deed he'd just done irreversible. No resurrections here. Not tonight; not ever. *Suppose they were the last*, blue and brown. The last that would ever hop that way, sing that way, court and mate and make more birds who hopped and sang and courted that way.

"Oh . . . ," he murmured, beginning to understand. "I . . . changed the world a little bit, didn't I?" He turned and looked up at Jacob. "That's it, isn't it? That's what I did! I changed the world."

"Maybe . . . ," Jacob said. There was a tiny smile of satisfaction on his face, that his pupil was so swift. "If these were the last, perhaps it was more than a little."

"Are they?" Will said. "The last, I mean?"

"Would you like them to be?" Will wanted it too much for words. All he could do was nod. "Another night, perhaps," Jacob said. "But not tonight. I'm sorry to disappoint you, but these"— he looked down at the bodies in the grass—"are as common as moths." Will felt as though he'd just been given a present, and found it was just an empty box. "I know how it is, Will. What you're feeling now. Your hands tell you you've done something wonderful, but you look around and nothing much seems to have changed. Am I right?"

"Yes," he said. He suddenly wanted to wipe the worthless blood off his hands. They'd been so quick and so clever; they deserved better. The blood of something rare; something whose passing would be of consequence. He bent down and, plucking up a fistful of sharp grass, began to scrub his palms clean.

"So what do we do now?" he said as he worked. "I don't want to stay here any longer. I want to . . ."

He didn't finish his chatter, however, for at that moment a ripple passed through the air surrounding them, as though the earth itself had expelled a tiny breath. He ceased his scrubbing and slowly rose to his feet, letting the grass drop.

"What was that?" he whispered.

"You did it, not I," Jacob replied. There was a tone in his voice Will had not heard before, and it wasn't comforting.

"What did I do?" Will said, looking all around for some explanation. But there was nothing that hadn't been there all along. Just the trees, and the snow and the stars.

"I don't want this," Jacob was murmuring. "Do you hear me? I don't want this." All the weight had vanished from his voice; so had the certainty.

Will looked around at him. Saw his stricken face. "Don't want *what?*" Will asked him.

Jacob turned his fretful gaze in Will's direction. "You've more power in you than you realize, boy," he said. "A lot more."

"But I didn't *do* anything," Will protested.

"You're a conduit."

"I'm a *what?*"

"Damn it, why didn't I see? Why didn't I *see?*" He backed away from Will, as the air shook again, more violently than before. "*Oh Christ in Heaven. I don't want this.*"

His anguish made Will panic. This wasn't what he wanted to hear from his idol. He'd done all he'd been asked to do. He'd killed the birds, cleaned and returned the knife; even put a brave face on his disappointment. So why was his deliverer retreating from him as though Will were a rabid dog?

"*Please . . . ,*" he said to Steep, "I didn't mean it, whatever it was I did, I'm sorry . . ."

But Jacob just continued to retreat. "It's not you. It's *us.* I don't want your eyes going where I've been. Not there, at least. Not to him. Not to *Thomas—*"

He was starting to babble again, and Will, certain his savior was about to run, and equally certain that once he was gone it would be over between them, reached and grabbed hold of the man's sleeve. Jacob cried out, and tried to shake himself free, but in doing so Will's hand, seeking better purchase, caught hold of his fingers. Their touching had made Will strong before; he'd climbed the hill light-footed because Jacob's flesh had been laid on his. But the business of the knife had wrought some change in him. He was no longer a passive recipient of strength. His bloodied fingers had been granted talents of their own, and he could not control them. He heard Jacob cry out a second time. Or was it his own voice? No, it was *both*. Two sobs, rising as though from a single throat.

Jacob had been right to be afraid. The same rippling breath that had distracted Will from cleaning his hands was here again, increased a hundredfold, and this time it inhaled the very world in which they stood. Earth and sky shuddered and were in an instant reconfigured, leaving them each in their terror: Will sobbing that he did not know what was happening; Jacob, that he did.

From *The Thief of Always*

Harvey said nothing about his peculiar visitor to either his mom or his dad, in case they put locks on the windows to stop Rictus returning to the house. But the trouble with keeping the visit a secret was that after a few days Harvey began to wonder if he'd imagined the whole thing. Perhaps he'd fallen asleep at the window, he thought, and Rictus had simply been a dream.

He kept hoping nevertheless. "Watch for me," Rictus had said, and Harvey did just that. He watched from the window of his room. He watched from his desk at school. He even watched with one eye when he was lying on his pillow at night. But Rictus didn't show.

And then, about a week after that first visit, just as Harvey's hope was waning, his watchfulness was rewarded. On his way to school one foggy morning he heard a voice above his head, and looked up to see Rictus floating down from the clouds, his coat swelled up around him so that he looked fatter than a prize pig.

"Howya doin'?" he said, as he descended.

"I was starting to think I'd invented you," Harvey replied. "You know, like a dream."

"I get that a lot," Rictus said, his smile wider than ever. "Particularly from the ladies. You're a dream come true, they say." He winked. "And who am I to argue? You like my shoes?"

Harvey looked down at Rictus's bright blue shoes. They were quite a sight, and he said so.

"I got given 'em by my boss," Rictus said. "He's very happy you're going to come visit. So, are you ready?"

"Well . . ."

"It's no use wasting time," Rictus said. "There may not be room for you tomorrow."

"Can I just ask *one* question?"

"I thought we agreed—"

"I know. But just one."

"All right. One."

"Is this place far from here?"

"Nah. It's just across town."

"So I'd only be missing a couple of hours of school?"

"That's two questions," Rictus said.

"No, I'm just thinking out loud."

Rictus grunted. "Look," he said, "I'm not here to do a great song and dance persuading you. I got a friend called Jive does that. I'm just a smiler. I smile, and I say: Come with me to the Holiday House, and if folks don't want to come—" He shrugged. "Hey, it's their hard luck."

With that, he turned his back on Harvey.

"Wait!" Harvey protested. "I want to come. But just for a little while."

"You can stay as long as you like," Rictus said. "Or as little. All I want to do is take that glum expression off your face and put one of *these* up there." His grin grew even larger. "Is there any crime in that?"

"No," said Harvey. "That's no crime. I'm glad you found me. I really am."

So what if he missed *all* of the morning at school, he thought, it'd be no great loss. Maybe an hour or two of the afternoon as well. As long as he was back home by three. Or four. Certainly before dark.

"I'm ready to go," he said to Rictus. "Lead the way."

Millsap, the town in which Harvey had lived all his life, wasn't very big, and he thought he'd seen just about all of it over the years. But the streets he knew were soon behind them, and though Rictus was setting a fair speed Harvey made sure he kept a mental list of landmarks along the way, in case he had to find his way home on his own. A butcher's shop with two pigs' heads hanging from hooks; a church with a yard full of old tombs beside it; the statue of some dead general, covered from hat to stirrups in pigeon dung: all these sights and more he noted and filed away.

And while they walked, Rictus kept up a stream of idle chatter.

"I hate the fog! Just hate it!" he said. "And there'll be rain by noon. We'll be out of it, of course . . ." He went on from talk of rain to the state of the streets. "Look at this trash, all over the sidewalk! It's shameful! And the mud! It's making a fine old mess of my shoes!"

He had plenty more to say, but none of it was very enlightening, so after a while Harvey gave up listening. How far *was* this Holiday House, he began to wonder. The fog was chilling him, and his legs were aching. If they didn't get there soon, he was going to turn back.

"I know what you're thinking," said Rictus.

"I bet you don't."

"You're thinking this is all a trick. You're thinking Rictus is leading you on a mystery tour and there's nothing at the end of it. Isn't that true?"

"Maybe a little."

"Well, my boy, I've got news for you. Look up ahead."

He pointed, and there—not very far from where they stood—was a high wall, which was so long that it disappeared into the fog to right and left.

"What do you see?" Rictus asked him.

"A wall," Harvey replied, though the more he stared at it the less certain of this he was. The stones, which had seemed solid enough at first sight, now looked to be shifting and wavering, as though they'd been chiseled from the fog itself, and piled up here to keep out prying eyes.

"It *looks* like a wall," Harvey said, "but it's *not* a wall."

"You're very observant," Rictus replied admiringly. "Most people just see a dead end, so they turn around and take another street."

"But not us."

"No, not us. We're going to keep on walking. You know why?"

"Because the Holiday House is on the other side?"

"What a *mir-ac-u-lous* kid you are!" Rictus replied. "That's exactly right. Are you hungry, by the way?"

"Starving."

"Well, there's a woman waiting for you in the House called Mrs. Griffin, and let me tell you, she is the greatest cook in all of Americaland. I swear, on my tailor's grave. Anything you can dream of eating, she can cook. All you have to do is ask. Her deviled eggs—" He smacked his lips. "Perfection."

"I don't see a gate," Harvey said.

"That's because there isn't one."

"So how do we get in?"

"Just keep walking!"

Half out of hunger, half out of curiosity, Harvey did as Rictus had instructed, and as he came within three steps of the wall a gust of balmy, flower-scented wind slipped between the shimmering stones and kissed his cheek. Its warmth was welcome after his long, cold trek, and he picked up his pace, reaching out to touch the wall as he approached it. The misty stones seemed to reach for him in their turn, wrapping their soft, gray arms around his shoulders, and ushering him through the wall.

He looked back, but the street he'd stepped out of, with its gray sidewalks and gray clouds, had already disappeared. Beneath his feet the grass was high and full of flowers. Above his head, the sky was midsummer blue. And ahead of him, set at the summit of a great slope, was a house that had surely been first imagined in a dream.

He didn't wait to see if Rictus was coming after him, nor to wonder how the gray beast February had been slain and this warm day risen in its place. He simply let out a laugh that Rictus would have been proud of, and hurried up the slope and into the shadow of the dream house.

From *Paradise Street*

EXTERIOR. THE WALL. NIGHT. A SOFT WIND IS BLOWING UP FROM THE RIVER. BELLS TINKLE; SNATCHES OF SONG CAN BE HEARD FROM SOMEWHERE FAR OFF.

ENTER JUDE. A GROAN.

JUDE: Who's there?

MULROONEY: *(Off)* Help me.

JUDE CAUTIOUSLY INVESTIGATES BEHIND THE WALL.

JUDE: Oh my God.

MULROONEY: *(Off)* Ah. Careful.

JUDE: I'm sorry.

> JUDE AND MULROONEY EMERGE FROM BEHIND THE WALL. MUL-
> ROONEY HAS A BLOODY NOSE, HIS CLOTHES TORN.

MULROONEY: *(Looking at the blood on his hands)* Where am I bleeding
from?

JUDE: *(Gives him a handkerchief)* Your nose. Here. Where does it hurt?

MULROONEY: Where doesn't it?

JUDE: What did you do? Fall off the wall?

MULROONEY: Damn fool question. What do I want climbing on a wall?
Where are my papers?

> HE GOES ROUND THE WALL AGAIN.

MULROONEY: They're gone.

JUDE: The wind must have caught them.

MULROONEY: Impatient to be off and away from me.

JUDE: Were they important?

MULROONEY: Only my life's work.

JUDE: It's a hospital for you—

MULROONEY: It is not.

JUDE: You may have broken bones.

MULROONEY: I can roll with a blow. I'm not moving from here. What
time is it?

JUDE: I don't know, my watch has stopped. About four in the morning.

MULROONEY: What's a woman like you doing out here?

JUDE: It's so hot.

MULROONEY: It is hot.

JUDE: I had the window open. I heard voices, and music. I looked out, and
you know what? Somebody was performing a play in the middle of
the street. I went down to find out what they were doing, and they'd
gone. Have you noticed the smell?

MULROONEY: My nose is in no fit state to smell.

JUDE: There's a scent, scents, in the air, like flowers; no, not like flowers;
like the day before flowers. Some March morning, waking up.
There's a green smell in the air.

MULROONEY: Four o'clock, you say? Oh fuck.

JUDE: What's wrong?

MULROONEY: All my life, I've been waiting for one particular train: collecting the timetables, the ticket stubs, the signs of it. And when it
comes, where am I? Dead to the world. The visit's over. It must be. I

have to join the queue of people who just missed the miracles. The man who had diarrhea, and missed the Last Supper. The fellow who was blowing his nose when Lazarus took his first breath. Oh God—I think I've wet my pants.

JUDE: You can't stay here.

MULROONEY: I'll walk down to the river.

JUDE: What for?

MULROONEY: To throw myself in.

JUDE: Mulrooney.

MULROONEY: What do I care if the land sinks, if the whole world's only fit for fishes? (*Yelling, to the sleeping city*) Drown, you blind ignorant bastards! Starved of fancy, aren't you? Gray with truth. Wandering the world up and down. Well, I tried to tell them. Did my best. They took no notice. There's visions over Dogger Bank, Viking, Forties, lights on the Irish Sea, and all the promise of Jerusalem rolling away to meet the Pole, and do they care?

JUDE: They dream.

MULROONEY: (*Reluctantly conceding the point*) Sure, they do that.

JUDE: Isn't that something?

MULROONEY: I don't distrust the internal vision. I don't say what the mind sees is less than what the eye sees. I say there's a threshold, where one becomes the other. Where the fruit of the mind becomes edible, where the waters of the imagination become available to wash in. The rest is politics, the rest is sociology, the rest is commerce with dissolution and I want none of it.

APPLAUSE FROM BEHIND THE WALL.

MULROONEY: Listen to yourself, Mulrooney.

THE WALL OPENS. A GLORIOUS LIGHT SPILLS OUT ONTO THE FILTHY STREET. MULROONEY HASN'T NOTICED YET. JUDE HAS. SHE'S IN AWE.

MULROONEY: Piss soaking in your socks and you're talking like a madman. How long does it take to drown?

IN THE ROSY HEART OF THE LIGHT STANDS GLORIANA HERSELF, ELIZABETH I, WITH HER MANDRILL, BENNY, ON A SILVER CHAIN. BEHIND HER STAND ROBERT DEVEREUX, EARL OF ESSEX, AND LUCY LOVELACE, HER LADY-IN-WAITING.

ELIZABETH: We applaud your sentiments.

MULROONEY: They're not sentiments; they're accusations.

JUDE: Mulrooney. I don't think you missed the miracle after all.

MULROONEY: What? *(Turns)*

ESSEX: Bow your head, you heathen. You stand before Her Majesty Queen Elizabeth of England, Scotland, and Ireland.

LUCY: *(To Jude)* Curtsy.

JUDE: *(Curtsies)* What am I doing?

MULROONEY: Do you know you're the spitting image of somebody?

ELIZABETH: We are Gloriana.

MULROONEY: Been to a party have you? Fancy dress, is it? *(To Jude)* Or are these maybe the actors you saw in the street? The monkey's very fine, by the way.

ELIZABETH: *(To Essex)* It's a pretty irony when the entertainment presumes the patron to be on show.

MULROONEY: I'm no entertainment.

ELIZABETH: It was certainly a well-written speech you just delivered.

MULROONEY: I'm suicidal is what I am. It's the right of every man within an ace of dying to say his piece.

ELIZABETH: Your name's Mulrooney?

MULROONEY: Yes.

ESSEX: Acknowledge Her Majesty.

ELIZABETH: Hush, Robin—

ESSEX: Ma'am, he has not so much as bowed his head.

MULROONEY: Breed pimps with a bit of bite these days, don't they?

ELIZABETH: *(To Jude)* You?

JUDE: What?

ELIZABETH: Who are you?

JUDE: Jude Colquhoun.

ELIZABETH: Scottish name.

JUDE: Is this a joke?

ELIZABETH: Of course, you don't expect us.

MULROONEY: The woman's drunk.

ESSEX: *(Unsheathing his sword)* What?

ELIZABETH: Robin—

MULROONEY: Oh Lord, where's Jonson? He swore he'd keep you off my back.

JUDE: Who are you?

ELIZABETH: We are Elizabeth. Queen of—

MULROONEY: Drunk. Every one of them.

JUDE: She's been dead four hundred years.

ELIZABETH: We were dead before we were born, yet we were born.

ESSEX: This is Her Infinite Majesty.

ELIZABETH: Absolute Majesty.

ESSEX: In flesh and blood.

JUDE: And you?

ESSEX: I am Robert Devereux, Earl of Essex. You may touch me if you doubt it—

JUDE: No thank you. Why have you no shoes on?

ELIZABETH: It is our punishment. We are displeased with him in the matter of Ireland.

MULROONEY: Ireland is it?

ELIZABETH: He has mislaid several thousand good Englishmen in that country.

ESSEX: No man could have done better, ma'am.

ELIZABETH: That's not our opinion. Our opinion is that you were both arbitrary and vicious. Until he solves the Irish question he will go barefoot.

MULROONEY: Then his cobbler will get no more business from him.

ESSEX: I bristle, ma'am. Allow me to cut this Irish clod in two.

MULROONEY: *(Re Essex's sword)* Have you got a license for that, by the way?

ESSEX: Every Irishman is half phlegm and half mud.

MULROONEY: And what are you, her bum-boy?

ESSEX: No more!

    ESSEX STEPS FORWARD AND SWIFTLY BRINGS MULROONEY TO THE FLOOR, HIS SWORD-POINT TO MULROONEY'S NECK.

ESSEX: This is where you belong.

MULROONEY: You bloody coward! I'm unarmed!

JUDE: Leave him alone!

ESSEX: May I dispatch him?

ELIZABETH: You may not.

ESSEX: Ma'am, he as good as called me a catamite.

ELIZABETH: If you harm him, Robin, we'll have you beheaded again. And this time we won't be so quick to resurrect you.

JUDE: This isn't funny anymore. Stop it.

ELIZABETH: You still think this is a pretense?

JUDE: Of course.

ELIZABETH: Touch us, Jude. Come on. Close to us. Touch our skin. Are we warm?

JUDE: That doesn't prove anything.

ELIZABETH: *Touch us.*

> JUDE IS INTIMIDATED. BUT SHE TOUCHES ELIZABETH.

JUDE: Lord, you smell. Powder and sweat a year old.

ELIZABETH: We don't like to bathe. It is our opinion it takes the youthful vigor out of us.

JUDE: Mulrooney.

MULROONEY: Yes?

JUDE: Suppose it is her. Just . . . suppose.

MULROONEY: Then you're welcome to her.

JUDE: Suppose this is your miracle. Not out of the sky, but out of the past. Why are you here?

ELIZABETH: We've come to look at England. And if it suits us, to unmake it. We do not like what we see. Not remotely. This was a glorious country in our age. It could have been Paradise on earth.

JUDE: And how do you intend to change it?

ELIZABETH: With daughters. A country's like a body. A system of physical states, a geography of entrails, limbs, and bones. A head: us. A trunk: the people. A hand to fight: the army. A hand to trade with: the merchants. A leg to hop to heaven on: the Church. Another to skip to hell on: government. Now, look at this England. It is a body at war with itself. It bites its own tongue, so its voice is half sores, it tears out its hair, it weeps, it bleeds, it bleeds and weeps again. Now ask yourself, what sex is this body, England? Male. The army, male. The Church, male. Philosophy, commerce, government, male, male, all male. So, I say, if the male body cannot live without mutilating itself, setting its parts in war against each other, dividing head from heart from lung from stomach, then let us unsex it. Tear off its manhood and fling it into France, dig a hole where our men built towers; no longer aspire to being steel, but make a glory of love's body, where we shall be pocketed in peace, where the rule of Venus is law, and every breath is pleasure.

MULROONEY: I thought she was the Virgin Queen.

> ESSEX UNSHEATHES HIS SWORD.

ESSEX: One more word—

ELIZABETH: You apologize for that.

MULROONEY: If you're Elizabeth the First, I'm Mickey Mouse.

ELIZABETH: That's your fucking problem. Now apologize. Or your neck
will wonder where your head went.

JUDE: A very male display, ma'am, if I may say so.

ELIZABETH: What?

JUDE: You were saying something about being pocketed in peace.

ELIZABETH: We must have them in their place, or they'll tread on us. (*To
Mulrooney*) Apologize!

JUDE: (*To Mulrooney*) She means it.

MULROONEY: I won't do it.

JUDE: I'm squeamish. Do it. For me.

MULROONEY: (*Reluctantly*) Oh Christ. All right. Yes.

ELIZABETH: Yes what?

MULROONEY: I apologize.

ELIZABETH: Very nice. That was much to our pleasure. You may kiss us,
and leave.

JUDE: (*Reluctantly*) Go on.

    MULROONEY KISSES HER HAND. ELIZABETH DOESN'T LET GO OF IT.

MULROONEY: Can I have my hand back?

ELIZABETH: What age are you?

MULROONEY: Forty-one.

ELIZABETH: I'm sick of boys, Jack Mulrooney. My appetite is for wisdom
without platitudes, and a bed without lust. Your hand is shaking.
"Cras amet qui numquam amavit quique amavit cras amet."

MULROONEY: My Latin's shite. What did she say?

ESSEX: Tomorrow . . . er . . .

ELIZABETH: "Tomorrow may he love who has never loved before, and may
he who has loved love too."

    SHE LETS MULROONEY GO. HE LOOKS AT HER AS SHE BACKS AWAY.

ELIZABETH: Go to bed. Dream of us.

MULROONEY: Not if I can help it.

    MULROONEY EXITS.

ELIZABETH: (*To Jude*) Your business is the pox?

JUDE: Yes.

ELIZABETH: Tomorrow, we will debate syphilis.

JUDE: We will?

ELIZABETH: We will. We've learned much already, being here. This age
is America's, as the age before was ours, as the age before that was

Bethlehem's. We shan't be great as we were; but greatness is defined by men, who mean a metaphor for how full they find their codpieces. I say, we shall not be great, but deep, as our cunts, and moist and mighty. You will attend on us tomorrow. 'Til then, goodnight.

EXIT ELIZABETH, HAVING PETTED HER APE, AND PASSED IT TO ESSEX.

JUDE: What am I smiling for?

From *The Great and Secret Show*

At first, it was drudgery. Pure hell, day after day, going through the sacks.

The piles didn't seem to diminish. Indeed they were several times fed by a leering Homer, who led a trail of peons in with further satchels to swell the number.

First Jaffe sorted the interesting envelopes (bulky; rattling; perfumed) from dull; then the private correspondence from official, and the scrawl from the Palmer method. Those decisions made, he began opening the envelopes, in the first week with his fingers, till his fingers became callused, thereafter with a short-bladed knife he bought especially for the purpose, digging out the contents like a pearl-fisher in search of a pearl, most of the time finding nothing, sometimes, as Homer had promised, finding money or a check, which he dutifully declared to his boss.

"You're good at this," Homer said after the second week. "You're really good. Maybe I should put you on this full time."

Randolph wanted to say fuck you, but he'd said that too many times to bosses who'd fired him the minute after, and he couldn't afford to lose this job: not with the rent to pay and heating his one-room apartment costing a damn fortune while the snow continued to fall. Besides, something was happening to him while he passed the solitary hours in the Dead Letter Room, something it took him to the end of the third week to begin to enjoy, and the end of the fifth to comprehend.

He was sitting at the crossroads of America.

Homer had been right. Omaha, Nebraska, wasn't the geographical center of the USA, but as far as the Post Office was concerned, it may as well have been.

The lines of communication crossed, and recrossed, and finally dropped their orphans here, because nobody in any other state wanted them. These letters had been sent from coast to coast looking for someone to open them, and had found no takers. Finally they'd ended with him: with *Randolph Ernest Jaffe*, a balding nobody with ambitions never spoken and rage not expressed, whose little knife slit them, and little eyes scanned them, and who—sitting at his crossroads—began to see the private face of the nation.

There were love letters, hate letters, ransom notes, pleadings, sheets on which men had drawn round their hard-ons, Valentines of pubic hair, blackmail by wives, journalists, hustlers, lawyers, and senators, junk mail and suicide notes, lost novels, chain letters, résumés, undelivered gifts, rejected gifts, letters sent out into the wilderness like bottles from an island, in the hope of finding help, poems, threats, and recipes. So much. But these were the least of it. Though sometimes the love letters got him sweaty, and the ransom notes made him wonder if, having gone unanswered, their senders had murdered their hostages; the stories of love and death they told touched him only fleetingly. Far more persuasive, far more moving, was another story, which could not be articulated so easily.

Sitting at the crossroads he began to understand that America had a secret life; one which he'd never even glimpsed before. Love and death he knew about. Love and death were the great clichés; the twin obsessions of songs and soap operas. But there was another life, which every fortieth letter, or fiftieth, or hundredth, hinted at, and every thousandth stated with a lunatic plainness. When they said it plain, it was not the whole truth, but it was a beginning, and each of the writers had their own mad way of stating something close to unstatable.

What it came down to was this: the world was not as it seemed. Not *remotely* as it seemed. Forces conspired (governmental, religious, medical) to conceal and silence those who had more than a passing grasp of that fact, but they couldn't gag or incarcerate every one of them. There were men and women who slipped the nets, however widely flung; who found backroads to travel where their pursuers got lost, and safe houses along the way where they'd be fed and watered by like visionaries, ready to misdirect the dogs when they came sniffing. These people didn't trust Ma Bell, so they didn't use telephones. They didn't dare assemble in groups of more than two for fear of attracting attention to themselves. But they *wrote*. Sometimes it was as if they *had* to, as if the secrets they kept sealed up were too hot, and burned their way out. Sometimes it was because they knew the hunters were on their heels and they'd have no other chance to describe the world to itself before they were caught, drugged, and locked up. Sometimes there was even a subversive glee in the scrawlings, sent out with deliberately indistinct addresses in the hope that the letter would blow the mind of some innocent who'd received it by chance. *Some of the missives were stream-of-consciousness rantings, others precise, even clinical, descriptions of how to turn the world inside out by sex-magic or mushroom-eating. Some used the nonsense imagery of* National Enquirer *stories to veil another message. They spoke of UFO sightings and zombie cults; news from Venusian evangelists and psychics who tuned into the dead on the TV.* But after a few weeks of studying these letters (and *study* it was; he was like a man locked in the ultimate library) Jaffe began to see beyond the nonsenses to the hidden story. He broke the code; or enough of it to be tantalized. Instead of being irritated each day when Homer opened the door and had another half-dozen satchels of letters brought in, he welcomed the addition. The more letters, the more clues; the more clues the more hope he had of a solution to the mystery. It was, he became more certain as the weeks turned into months and the winter mellowed, not several mysteries but *one.* The writers whose letters were about the Veil, and how to draw it aside, were finding their own way forward toward revelation; each had his own particular method and metaphor; but somewhere in the cacophony a single hymn was striving to be sung.

It was not about love. At least not as the sentimentalists knew it. Nor about death, as a literalist would have understood the term. *It was—in no particular order—something to do with fishes, and the sea (sometimes the Sea of Seas); and three ways to swim there; and dreams (a lot about dreams); and an island which Plato had called Atlantis, but had known all along was some other place. It was about the end of the World, which was in turn about its beginning. And it was about Art.*

Or rather, the Art.

That, of all the codes, was the one he beat his head hardest against, and broke only his brow. *The Art was talked about in many ways. As the Final Great Work. As the Forbidden Fruit. As da Vinci's Despair or the Finger in the Pie or the Butt-Digger's Glee.* There were many ways to describe it, but only one Art. And (here was a mystery) no *Artist.*

"So, are you happy here?" Homer said to him one May day.

Jaffe looked up from his work. There were letters strewn all around him. His skin, which had never been too healthy, was as pale and etched upon as the pages in his hand.

"Sure," he said to Homer, scarcely bothering to focus on the man. "Have you got some more for me?"

Homer didn't answer at first. Then he said: "What are you hiding, Jaffe?"

"Hiding? I'm not hiding anything."

"You're stashing stuff away you should be sharing with the rest of us."

"No I'm not," Jaffe said. He'd been meticulous in obeying Homer's first edict, that anything found among the dead letters be shared. The money, the skin magazines, the cheap jewelry he'd come across once in a while; it all went to Homer, to be divided up. "You get everything," he said. "I swear."

Homer looked at him with plain disbelief. "You spend every fucking hour of the day down here," he said. "You don't talk with the other guys. You don't drink with 'em. Don't you like the smell of us, Randolph? Is that it?" He didn't wait for an answer. "Or are you just a *thief?*"

"I'm no thief," Jaffe said. "You can look for yourself." He stood up, raising his hands, a letter in each. "Search me."

"I don't want to fucking touch you," came Homer's response. "What do you think I am, a fucking fag?" He kept staring at Jaffe. After a pause he said: "I'm going to have somebody else come down here and take over. You've done five months. It's long enough. I'm going to move you."

"I don't want—"

"What?"

"I mean . . . what I mean to say is, I'm quite happy down here. Really. It's work I like doing."

"Yeah," said Homer, clearly still suspicious. "Well starting Monday you're out."

"Why?"

"Because I say so! If you don't like it find yourself another job."

"I'm doing good work, aren't I?" Jaffe said.

Homer was already turning his back.

"It smells in here," he said as he exited. "Smells real bad."

There was a word Randolph had learned from his reading which he'd never known before: synchronicity. He'd had to go buy a dictionary to look it up, and found it meant that sometimes events coincided. The way the letter writers used the word it usually meant that there was something significant, mysterious, maybe even miraculous in the way one circumstance collided with another, as though a pattern existed that was just out of human sight.

Such a collision occurred the day Homer dropped his bombshell, an intersecting of events that would change everything. No more than an hour after Homer had left, Jaffe took his short-bladed knife, which was getting blunt, to an envelope that felt heavier than most. He slit it open, and out fell a small medallion. It hit the concrete floor: a sweet ringing sound. He picked it up, with fingers that had been trembling since Homer's exit. There was no chain attached to the medallion, nor did it have a loop for that purpose. Indeed it wasn't attractive enough to be hung around a woman's neck as a piece of jewelry, and though it was in the form of a cross, closer inspection proved it not to be of Christian design. Its four arms were of equal length, the full span no more than an inch and a half. At the intersection was a human figure, neither male nor female, arms outstretched as in a crucifixion, but not nailed. Spreading out along the four routes were abstract designs, each of which ended in a circle. The face was very simply rendered. It bore, he thought, the subtlest of *smiles*.

He was no expert on metallurgy, but it was apparent the thing was not gold or silver. Even if the dirt had been cleaned from it he doubted it would ever gleam. But there was something deeply attractive about it nevertheless. Looking at it he had the sense he'd sometimes had waking in the morning from an intense dream but unable to remember the details. This was a significant object, but he didn't know why. Were the sigils spreading from the figure vaguely familiar from one of the letters he'd read, perhaps? He'd scanned thousands upon thousands in the last twenty weeks, and many of them had carried little sketches, obscene sometimes, often indecipherable. Those he'd judged the most interesting he'd smuggled out of the Post Office, to study at night. They were bundled up beneath the bed in his room. Perhaps he'd break the dream-code on the medallion by careful examination of those.

He decided to take lunch that day with the rest of the workers, figuring it'd be best to do as little as possible to irritate Homer any further. It was a mistake. In the company of the good ol' boys talking about news he'd not listened to in months, and the quality of last night's steak, and the fuck they'd had, or failed to have, after the steak, and what the summer was going to bring, he felt himself a total stranger. They knew it too. They talked with their backs half-turned to him, dropping their voices at times to whisper about his weird look, his wild eyes. The more they shunned him the more he felt happy to be shunned, because they *knew*, even fuckwits like these *knew*, he was different from them. Maybe they were even a little afraid.

He couldn't bring himself to go back to the Dead Letter Room at one-thirty. The medallion, its mysterious signs, was burning a hole in his pocket. He had to go back to his lodgings and start the search through his private library of letters *now*. Without even wasting breath telling Homer, he did just that.

It was a brilliant, sunny day. He drew the curtains against the invasion of light, turned on the lamp with the yellow shade, and there, in a jaundiced fever, began his study, taping the letters with any trace of illustration to the bare walls and, when the walls were full spreading them on the table, bed, chair, and floor. Then he went from sheet to sheet, sign to sign, looking for anything that even faintly resembled the medallion in his hand. And as he went, the same thought kept creeping back into his head: that he knew there was an Art, but no Artist, a practice but no practitioner, and that maybe *he* was that man.

The thought didn't have to creep for long. Within an hour of perusing the letters it had pride of place in his skull. The medallion hadn't fallen into his hands by accident. It had come to him as a reward for his patient study, and as a way to draw together the threads of his investigation and finally begin to make some sense of it. Most of the symbols and sketches on the pages were irrelevant, but there were many, too many to be a coincidence, that echoed images on the cross. No more than two ever appeared on the same sheet, and most of these were crude renderings, because none of the writers had the complete solution in their hands the way he did, but they'd all comprehended some part of the jigsaw, and their observations about the part they had, whether haiku, dirty talk, or alchemical formulas, gave him a better grasp of the system behind the symbols.

A term that had cropped up regularly in the most perceptive of the letters was the *Shoal*. He'd passed over it several times in his reading, and never thought much about it. There was a good deal of evolutionary talk in the letters, and he'd assumed the term to be a part of that. Now he understood his error. The Shoal was a cult, or a church of some kind, and its symbol was the object he held in the palm of his hand. What it and the Art had to do with each other was by no means clear, but his long-held suspicion that this was *one* mystery, *one* journey, was here confirmed, and he knew that with the medallion as a map he'd find his way from Shoal to Art eventually.

In the meantime there was a more urgent concern. When he thought back to the tribe of coworkers, with Homer at its head, he shuddered to think that any of them might ever share the secret he'd uncovered. Not that they had any chance of making any real progress decoding it: they were too witless. But Homer was suspicious enough to at least sniff along the trail a little way, and the idea of anybody—but especially the boorish Homer—tainting this sacred ground was unbearable. There was only one way to prevent such a disaster. He had to act quickly to destroy any evidence that might put Homer on the right track. The medallion he'd keep, of course: he'd been entrusted with it by higher powers, whose faces he'd one day get to see. He'd also keep the twenty or thirty letters that had proffered the best information on the Shoal; the rest (three hundred or so) had to be burned. As to the collection in the Dead Letter Room, they had to go into the furnace too. All of them. It would take time, but it had to be done, and the sooner the better. He made a selection of the letters in his room, parceled up those he didn't need to keep, and headed off to the Sorting Office.

It was late afternoon now, and he traveled against the flow of human traffic, entering the office by the back door to avoid Homer, though he knew the man's routine well enough to suspect he'd punched out at five-thirty to the second, and was already guzzling beer somewhere. The furnace was a sweaty rattling antique, tended by another sweaty rattling antique, called Miller, with whom Jaffe had never exchanged a single word, Miller being stone deaf. It took some time for Jaffe to explain that he was going to be feeding the furnace for an hour or two, beginning with the parcel he'd brought from home, which he immediately tossed into the flames. Then he went up to the Dead Letter Room.

Homer had not gone guzzling beer. He was waiting, sitting in Jaffe's chair under a bare bulb, going through the piles around him.

"So what's the scam?" he said as soon as Jaffe stepped through the door.

It was useless trying to pretend innocence, Jaffe knew. His months of study had carved knowledge into his face. He couldn't pass for a naïf any longer. Nor—now that it came to it—did he want to.

"No *scam*," he said to Homer, making his contempt for the man's puerile suspicions plain. "I'm not taking anything you'd want. Or could use."

"I'll be the judge of that, asshole," Homer said, throwing the letters he was examining down among the rest of the litter. "I want to know what you've been up to down here. 'Sides jerking off."

Jaffe closed the door. He'd never realized it before, but the reverberations of the furnace carried through the walls into the room. Everything here trembled minutely. The sacks, the envelopes, the words on the pages tucked inside. And the chair on which Homer was sitting. And the knife, the short-bladed knife, lying on the floor beside the chair on which Homer was sitting. The whole place was moving, ever so slightly, like there was a rumble in the ground. Like the world was about to be flipped.

Maybe it was. Why not? No use pretending the *status* was still *quo*. He was a man on his way to some throne or other. He didn't know which and he didn't know where, but he needed to silence any pretender quickly. Nobody was going to find him. Nobody was going to blame him, or judge him, or put him on Death Row. He was his own law now.

"I should explain . . . ," he said to Homer, finding a tone that was almost flippant, "what the *scam* really is."

"Yeah," Homer said, his lip curling. "Why don't you do that?"

"Well it's real simple . . ."

He started to walk toward Homer, and the chair, and the knife beside the chair. The speed of his approach made Homer nervous, but he kept his seat.

"I've found a secret," Jaffe went on.

"Huh?"

"You want to know what it is?"

Now Homer stood up, his gaze trembling the way everything else was. Everything except Jaffe. All the tremors had gone out of his hands, his guts, and his head. He was steady in an unsteady world.

"I don't know what the fuck you're doing," Homer said. "But I don't like it."

"I don't blame you," Jaffe said. He didn't have his eyes on the knife. He didn't need to. He could sense it. "But it's your job to know, isn't it?" Jaffe went on, "what's been going on down here."

Homer took several steps away from the chair. The loutish gait he liked to affect had gone. He was stumbling, as though the floor was tilting.

"I've been sitting at the center of the world," Jaffe said. "This little room . . . this is where it's all happening."

"Is that right?"

"Damn right."

Homer made a nervous little grin. He threw a glance toward the door.

"You want to go?" Jaffe said.

"Yeah." He looked at his watch, not seeing it. "Got to run. Only came down here—"

"You're afraid of me," Jaffe said. "And you should be. I'm not the man I was."

"Is that right?"

"You said that already."

Again, Homer looked toward the door. It was five paces away; four if he ran. He'd covered half the distance when Jaffe picked up the knife. He had the door handle clasped when he heard the man approaching behind him.

He glanced round, and the knife came straight at his eye. It wasn't an accidental stab. It was synchronicity. His eye glinted, the knife glinted. Glints collided, and the next moment he was screaming as he fell back against the door, Randolph following him to claim the letter opener from the man's head.

The roar of the furnace got louder. With his back to the sacks Jaffe could feel the envelopes nestling against each other, the words being shaken on the pages, till they became a glorious poetry. Blood, it said; like a sea; his thoughts like clots in that sea, dark, congealed, hotter than hot.

He reached for the handle of the knife, and clenched it. Never before in his life had he shed blood; not even squashed a bug, at least intentionally. But now his fist on the hot wet handle seemed wonderful. A prophecy; a proof.

Grinning, he pulled the knife out of Homer's socket, and before his victim could slide down the door stuck it into Homer's throat to the hilt. This time he didn't let it lie. He pulled it out as soon as he'd stopped Homer's screams, and he stabbed the middle of the man's chest. There was bone there, and he had to drive hard, but he was suddenly very strong. Homer gagged, and blood came out of his mouth, and from the wound in his throat. Jaffe pulled the knife out. He didn't stab again. Instead he wiped the blade on his handkerchief and turned from the body to think about his next move. If he tried to lug the sacks of mail to the furnace he risked being discovered, and sublime as he felt, high on the boor-slob's demise, he was still aware that there was danger in being found out. It would be better to bring the furnace *here*. After all, fire was a moveable feast. All it required was a light, and Homer had those. He turned back to the slumped corpse and searched in the pockets for a box of matches. Finding one, he pulled it out, and went over to the satchels.

Sadness surprised him as he prepared to put a flame to the dead letters. He'd spent so many weeks here, lost in a kind of delirium, drunk with mysteries. This was good-bye to all that. After this—Homer dead, the letters burned—he was a fugitive, a man without a history, beckoned by an Art he knew nothing about, but which he wished more than anything to practice.

He began to screw up a few of the pages, to provide some initial fodder for the flame. Once begun, he didn't doubt that the fire would sustain itself: there was nothing in the room—paper, fabric, flesh—that wasn't combustible. With three heaps of paper made, he struck a match. The flame was bright, and looking at it he realized how much he hated brightness. The dark was so much more interesting; full of secrets, full of threats. He put the flame to the piles of paper and watched while the fires gained strength. Then he retreated to the door.

Homer was slumped against it, of course, bleeding from three places, and his bulk wasn't that easy to move, but Jaffe put his back into the task, his shadow thrown up against the wall by the burgeoning bonfire behind him. Even in the half minute it took him to move the corpse aside the heat grew exponentially, so that by the time he glanced back at the room it was ablaze from side to side, the heat stirring up its own wind, which in turn fanned the flames.

It was only when he was clearing out his room of any sign of himself— eradicating every trace of Randolph Ernest Jaffe—that he regretted doing what he'd done. Not the burning—that had been altogether wise—but leaving Homer's body in the room to be consumed along with the dead letters. He should have taken a more elaborate revenge, he realized. He should have hacked the body into pieces, packaged it up, tongue, eyes, testicles, guts, skin, skull, divided piece from piece—and sent the pieces out into the system with scrawled addresses that made no real sense, so that chance (or synchronicity) would be allowed to elect the doorstep on which Homer's flesh would land. The mailman mailed. He promised himself not to miss such ironic possibilities in the future.

The task of clearing his room didn't take long. He had very few belongings, and most of what he had meant little to him. When it came down to basics, he barely existed. He was the sum of a few dollars, a few photographs, a few clothes. Nothing that couldn't be put in a small suitcase and still leave room alongside them for a set of encyclopedias.

By midnight, with that same small suitcase in hand, he was on his way out of Omaha, and ready for a journey that might lead in any direction. Gateway to the East, Gateway to the West. He didn't care which way he went, as long as the route led to the Art.

From *Everville*

The interior smelled of stale incense and week-old sushi—the odors, in short, of bad magic. It made Harry's heart hammer to smell those smells. How many times do I have to do this? he found himself wondering as he advanced into the murk. How many times into the maw, into the sickened body? How many times before I've done my penance?

Ted laid his hand on Harry's shoulder.

"There," he murmured, and directed Harry's gaze off to the right. Some ten yards from where they stood was a further flight of stairs, and from the bottom a wash of silvery light.

Ted's hand remained on Harry's shoulder as they crossed to the top of the flight and began the descent. It grew colder with every step, and the smell became steadily stronger: signs that what they sought lay somewhere at the bottom. And, if any further evidence was required, Harry's tattoos supplied it. The new one itched more furiously than ever, while the old ones (at his ankles, at his navel, in the small of his back, and down his sternum) tingled.

Three steps from the bottom, Harry turned to Ted, and in the lowest of voices murmured, "I meant it: about not being responsible for you."

Ted nodded and took his hand off Harry's shoulder. There was nothing more to be said; no further excuse to delay the descent. Harry reached into his jacket and lightly patted the gun in its holster. Then he was down the last three steps and, turning a corner was delivered into a sizable brick chamber, the far wall of which was fifty feet or more from where he stood, the vaulted ceiling twenty feet above his head. In the midst of this was what at first glance resembled a column of translucent drapes, about half as wide as the chamber itself, which was the source of the silvery light that had drawn them down the stairs. Second glance, however, showed him that it was not fabric, but some kind of ether. It resembled the melting folds of a Borealis, draped over or spun from a cat's cradle of filaments that crisscrossed the chamber like the vast web of an ambitious spider.

And amid the folds, figures: the celebrants he'd seen coming here through the afternoon. They no longer wore their coats and hats, but wandered in the midst of the light nearly naked.

And *such* nakedness! Though many of them were partially concealed by the drooping light, Harry had no doubt that all he'd heard about the Zyem

Carasophia was true. These were exiles; no doubt of it. Some were plainly descended from a marriage of bird and man, their eyes set in the sides of their narrow heads, their mouths beakish, their backs feathered. Others gave credence to a rumor Harry'd heard that a few of Quiddity's infants were simply *dreamed* into being, creatures of pure imagination. How else to explain the pair whose heads were yellowish blurs, woven with what looked like bright blue fireflies, or the creature who had shrugged off the skin of her head in tiny ribbons, which attended her raw face in a fluttering dance.

Of the unholy paraphernalia Harry had expected to see, there was no sign. No sputtering candles of human fat, no ritual blades, no gutted children. The celebrants simply moved in the cradle of light as if drifting in some collective dream. Had it not been for the smell of incense and sushi he would have doubted there was even error here.

"What's going on?" Ted murmured in Harry's ear.

Harry shook his head. He had no clue. But he knew how to find out. He shrugged off his jacket and proceeded to unbutton his shirt.

"What are you doing?"

"I'm going to join them," he replied.

"They'll be on to you in a minute."

"I don't think so," Harry said, heeling off his shoes as he pulled his shirt out of his trousers. He watched the wanderers as he did so, looking for any trace of belligerence among them. But there was none. It was as if they were moving in a semimesmerized state, all aggression dulled.

There was every possibility they wouldn't even notice if he went among them clothed, he suspected. But some instinct told him he would be safer in this throng if he were as vulnerable as they.

"Stay here," he said to Ted.

"You're out of your mind, you know that?" Ted replied.

"I'll be fine," Harry said, glancing down at his near-naked body and patted his belly. "Maybe I need to lose a pound or two . . ." Then he turned from Ted and walked toward the cradle.

He hadn't realized until now that either the light or the filaments was making a low, fluctuating whine, which grew louder as he approached. It throbbed in his skull, like the beginning of a headache, but uncomfortable as it was it could not persuade him to turn round. His skin was gooseflesh now, from head to foot, the tattoos tingling furiously.

He raised his left arm in front of him and pulled the dressing off his fresh ink. The tattoo looked livid in the silvery light, as though it had been pricked into his flesh moments before: a ruby parabola that suddenly seemed an utter redundancy. *Norma had been right*, he thought. *What defense was a mere mark in a world so full of power?*

He cast the dressing aside and continued to advance toward the cradle, expecting one of the celebrants to look his way at any moment. But none did. He stepped into the midst of the drapes without so much as a glance being cast in his direction and, weaving among the wanderers, made his way toward the center of the Borealis. He raised his arms as he did so, and his fingers brushed one of the filaments, sending a small charge of energy, too minor to be distressing, down to his shoulders and across his chest. The Borealis shook, and for a moment he feared that it intended to expel him, for the shimmering folds closed around him from all sides. Their touch was far from unpleasant, however, and whatever test they had put him to he apparently passed, for a moment later they retreated from him again, and returned to their gentle motion.

Harry glanced back, out into the chamber, in search of Ted, but everything beyond the light—the walls, the stairs, the roof—had become a blur. He didn't waste time looking, but turned his attention back to whatever mystery lay waiting in the center of the cradle.

The ache in his head grew more painful as he approached, but he bore it happily enough. There was something ahead of him, he saw: a sliver of darkness at the core of this cradle of light. It was taller than he was, this sliver, and it almost seemed to exercise some authority over him, because now that he had it in view he could not turn his eyes from it.

And with the sight, another sound, audible beneath the whine, like the repeated roll of muffled drums.

Mystified and mesmerized though he was, the identity of the sound was not lost on him. It was the sea he was hearing.

His heartbeat grew urgent. Tremors ran through his body. The sea! My God, the sea! He breathed its name like a blessing.

"Quiddity—"

The word was heard. He felt a breath upon his back and somebody said, "Hold back."

He glanced round, to find that one of the exiles, its face an eruption of color, was close to him.

"We must wait before the *neirica*," the creature said. "The blessing will come."

The blessing? Harry thought. Who were they expecting down here, the Pope?

"Will it be soon?" Harry said, certain that at any moment the creature would see him for the simple *Homo sapiens* he was.

"Very soon," came the reply, "he knows how impatient we are." The creature's gaze went past Harry to the darkness. "He knows how we ache to return. But we must do it with the blessing, yes?"

"Yes," said Harry. "Of course. Yes."

"Wait . . . ," the creature said, turning its head toward the outside world, "is that not him?"

There was a sudden flurry of activity in the vicinity as the creatures—including Harry's informant—moved off toward the edge of the Borealis. Harry was torn between the desire to see whoever this was, coming to bless them, and the urge to see Quiddity's shore. He chose the latter. Turning on his heel he took two quick strides toward the sliver of darkness, his momentum speeded by the force it exercised. He felt the ground grow uncertain beneath him, felt a gust of rainy wind against his face, fresh and cold. The darkness opened before him, as though the gust had blown open a door, and for an instant his sight seemed to race ahead of him, his lumpen flesh stumbling after, out, out across a benighted shore.

Above him the sky was spired with clouds, and creatures trailing dusty light swooped and soared in lieu of stars. On the stones below, crabs made war or love, claws locked as they clattered toward the surf. And in that surf, shoals leaped the waves as though aspiring to sky or stones, or both.

All this he saw in a single hungry glance.

Then he heard a cry behind him, and with the greatest reluctance looked back over his shoulder toward the chamber. There was some consternation there, he saw. The cradle was shaking, the veils that circled the crack, like bandages wrapped around a wound, torn here and there. He tried to focus his eyes to better see the cause, but they were slow to shake off the wonders they'd just witnessed, and while they did so screams erupted to right and left of him. Their din was sufficient to slap him from his reverie. Suddenly fearful for his life he took off from his place beside the sliver, though its claim on him was powerful, and it took all his strength to do so.

As he ran he caught sight of the creature who had so recently addressed him, stumbling through the veils with a wound in its chest the size of a fist. As it fell to its knees its glistening eyes fixed on Harry for a moment, and it opened its bony mouth as to beg some explanation. Blood came instead, black as squid's ink, and the creature toppled forward, dead before it hit the ground. Harry searched for its killer among the shaking veils, but all he found were victims: creatures reeling and falling, their wounds atrocious. A lopped head rolled at his feet; a creature with half its body blown away took hold of him in its agony, and expired sobbing in his arms.

As to the cradle, which had so suddenly become a grave, it shook from one end to the other, the veils shaken down by the violence in their midst, and bringing the filaments with them. They spat and spasmed on the ground, the light they'd lent the veils dying now, and steadily delivering the chamber into darkness.

Shielding his head against the falling cradle, Harry gained the outer limit of the circle, and now—finally—had sight of the creature that had visited these horrors on the scene.

It was a man. No more, no less. He had the beard of a patriarch, and the robes of a prophet. Blue robes once, but now so stained with blood he looked like a butcher. As to his weapon, it was a short staff, from which spurts of pallid fire broke, going from it almost languidly. Harry saw one go, snaking through the air to catch a victim who had so far avoided harm. It struck the creature (one of the blur-and-firefly couple) above her buttocks and ran up her back, gouging out the flesh to either side of her spine. Despite the appalling scale of her wounding, she was not felled, but swung round to face her wounder.

"Why?" she sobbed, extending her flabby arms in his direction. "Why?"

He made no answer. Simply raised his staff a second time, and let another burst of energy go from it, striking his victim in the mouth. Her pleas ceased on the instant, and the fire climbed up over her skull, turning it to ruin in a heartbeat. Even then she didn't fall. Her body shook as it stood, her bowels and bladder voiding. Wearing a look close to amusement, the prophet stepped over the bloody litter that lay between them and with one backhanded swipe struck the seared face with the staff, the blow so hard her head was separated from her neck.

Harry let out an involuntary cry, more of rage than of horror. The killer, who was already striding past the beheaded woman toward the crack, stopped in mid-step, and stared through the blood-flecked air. Harry froze. The prophet stared on, a look of puzzlement on his face.

He doesn't see me, Harry thought.

That was perhaps overly optimistic. The man continued to look, as though he glimpsed some trace of a presence in the deepening darkness, but could not quite decide whether his eyes were deceiving him. He wasn't about to take any chances. Even as he stared on in puzzlement he raised his staff.

Harry didn't wait for the fire to come. He made a dash for the stairs, hoping to God that Ted had escaped ahead of him. The killing fire sighed past him, close enough for Harry to feel its sickly heat, then burst against the opposite wall, its energies tracing the cracks as it dispersed. Harry looked back toward the prophet, who had already forgotten about the phantom and had turned toward the dark crack that let on to Quiddity.

Harry's gaze went to the sliver. In the diminishing light of the chamber the shore and sea were more visible than they had been, and for a moment it was all he could do not to turn back; to race the prophet to the threshold and be out under that steepled sky.

Then, from the murk off to his left, a pained and weary voice.

"I'm sorry, Harry . . . please . . . I'm sorry—"

With a sickening lurch in his stomach Harry turned and sought out the source of the voice. Ted lay seven or eight yards from the bottom of the stairs, his arms open wide, his chest the same. Such a wound, wet and deep, it was a wonder he had life enough to breathe, much less to speak. Harry went down at his side.

"Grab my hand, will you?" Ted said.

"I've got it," Harry said.

"I can't feel anything."

"Maybe that's for the best," Harry said. "I'm going to have to pick you up."

"He came out of nowhere—"

"Don't worry about it."

"I was keepin' out of the way, like you said, but then he just came out of nowhere."

"Hush, will you?" Harry slid his arms under Ted's body. "Okay, now, are you ready for this?"

Ted only moaned. Harry drew a deep breath, stood up, and without pausing began to carry the wounded man toward the stairs. It was harder to see the flight by the moment, as the last of the light in the filaments died away. But he stumbled on toward it, while little spasms passed through Ted's body.

"Hold on," Harry said. "Hold on."

They had reached the bottom of the flight now, and Harry began to climb. He glanced back toward the center of the chamber just once, and saw that the prophet was standing at the threshold between Cosm and Metacosm. No doubt he would step through it presently. No doubt that was what he had come here to do. Why had it been necessary to slaughter so many souls in the process was a mystery Harry did not expect to solve any time soon.

From *Imajica*

"Tnere are some things you should understand before we leave." Pie said, tying their wrists together, left to right, with a belt. "This is no easy journey, Gentle. This Dominion, the Fifth, is unreconciled, which means that getting to the Fourth involves risk. It's not like crossing a bridge. Passing over requires considerable power. And if anything goes wrong, the consequences will be dire."

"Tell me the worst."

"In between the Reconciled Dominions and the Fifth is a state called the In Ovo. It's an ether, in which things that have ventured from their worlds are imprisoned. Some of them are innocent. They're there by accident. Some were dispatched there as a judgment. They're lethal. I'm hoping we'll pass through the In Ovo before any of them even notice we're there. But if we were to become separated—"

"I get the picture. You'd better tighten that knot. It could still work loose."

Pie bent to the task, with Gentle fumbling to help in the darkness.

"Let's assume we get through the In Ovo," Gentle said. "What's on the other side?"

"The Fourth Dominion," Pie replied. "If I'm accurate in my bearings, we'll arrive near the city of Patashoqua."

"And if not?"

"Who knows? The sea. A swamp."

"Shit."

"Don't worry. I've got a good sense of direction. And there's plenty of power between us. I couldn't do this on my own. But together . . ."

"Is this the only way to cross over?"

"Not at all. There are a number of passing places here in the Fifth: stone circles, hidden away. But most of them were created to carry travelers to some particular location. We want to go as free agents. Unseen, unsuspected."

"So why have you chosen Patashoqua?"

"It has . . . sentimental associations," Pie replied. "You'll see for yourself, very soon." The mystif paused. "You *do* still want to go?"

"Of course."

"This is as tight as I can get the knot without stopping our blood."

"Then why are we delaying?"

Pie's fingers touched Gentle's face. "Close your eyes."

Gentle did so. Pie's fingers sought out Gentle's free hand and raised it between them.

"You have to help me," the mystif said.

"Tell me what to do."

"Make a fist. Lightly. Leave enough room for a breath to pass through. Good. Good. All magic proceeds from breath. Remember that."

He did, from somewhere.

"Now," Pie went on. "Put your hand to your face, with your thumb against your chin. There are very few incantations in our workings. No pretty words. Just pneuma like this, and the will behind them."

"I've got the will, if that's what you're asking," Gentle said.

"Then one solid breath is all we need. Exhale until it hurts. I'll do the rest."

"Can I take another breath afterward?"

"Not in this Dominion."

With that reply the enormity of what they were undertaking struck Gentle. They were leaving Earth. Stepping off the edge of the only reality he'd ever known into another state entirely. He grinned in the darkness, the hand bound to Pie's taking hold of his deliverer's fingers.

"Shall we?" he said.

In the murk ahead of him Pie's teeth gleamed in a matching smile.

"Why not?"

Gentle drew breath.

Somewhere in the house, he heard a door slamming and footsteps on the stairs leading up to the studio. But it was too late for interruptions. He exhaled through his hand, one solid breath which Pie 'oh' pah seemed to snatch from the air between them. Something ignited in the fist the mystif made, bright enough to burn between its clenched fingers . . .

At the door, Jude saw Gentle's painting almost made flesh: two figures, almost nose to nose, with their faces illuminated by some unnatural source, swelling like a slow explosion between them. She had time to recognize them both—to see the smiles on their faces as they met each other's gaze—then, to her horror, they seemed to turn inside out. She glimpsed wet red surfaces, which folded upon themselves not once but three times in quick succession, each fold diminishing their bodies, until they were slivers of stuff, still folding, and folding, and finally gone.

She sank back against the doorjamb, shock making her nerves cavort. The dog she'd found waiting at the top of the stairs went fearlessly to the place where they'd stood. There was no further magic there, to snatch him after them. The place was dead. They'd gone, the bastards, wherever such avenues led.

The realization drew a yell of rage from her, sufficient to send the dog scurrying for cover. She dearly hoped Gentle heard her, wherever he was. Hadn't she come here to share her revelations with him, so that they could investigate the great unknown together? And all the time he was preparing for his departure without her. Without her!

"How dare you?" she yelled at the empty space.

The dog whined in fear, and the sight of its terror mellowed her. She went down on her haunches.

"I'm sorry," she said to it. "Come here. I'm not cross with you. It's that little fucker Gentle."

The dog was reluctant at first but came to her after a time, its tail wagging intermittently as it grew more confident of her sanity. She rubbed its head, the contact soothing. All was not lost. What Gentle could do, she could do. He didn't have the copyright on adventuring. She'd find a way to go where he'd gone, if she had to eat the blue eye grain by grain to do so.

Church bells began to ring as she sat chewing this over, announcing in their ragged peals the arrival of midnight. Their clamor was accompanied by car horns in the street outside and cheers from a party in an adjacent house.

"Whoopee," she said quietly, on her face the distracted look that had obsessed so many of the opposite sex over the years. She'd forgotten most of them. The ones who'd fought over her, the ones who'd lost their wives in their pursuit of her, even those who'd sold their sanity to find her equal: all were forgotten. History had never much engaged her. It was the future that glittered in her mind's eye, now more than ever.

The past had been written by men. But the future—pregnant with possibilities—the future was a woman.

TWO

JOURNEYS

In *Everville* the travelers go by covered wagon. In *Imajica* Jude is carried by a stone, skipping from one vision to another. In *Sacrament,* Will enters the House of the World on foot. And in *Galilee*—a book of the sea, of course—it is Galilee's boat, *The Samarkand,* that carries him away. These are all journeys of the spirit. The means of transport is, finally, neither here nor there.

Perhaps the clearest statement of this occurs in one of the passages from *Imajica* I selected for this section. In it, a character called Gentle comes to the deathbed of his friend Taylor. They talk about the past for a little while, but move on to discuss love and death. There are mysteries in both their lives that are presently beyond their comprehension. But the journeys they are discussing in this scene will help them solve those mysteries. And, though Clem dies, his part in assisting Gentle in his search is far from over. As is so often the case in works of the fantastique, death is an enlightenment; the revelation of a landscape that is just out of human sight, waiting to be traveled.

From *Weaveworld*

Before the explorers, the *Rub al Khali* had been a blank space on the map of the world. After them, it remained so.

Its very name, given to it by the Bedu, the desert nomads who'd lived for unnumbered centuries in the deserts of the Arab peninsula, meant: the Empty Quarter. That they, familiar with wildernesses that would drive most men insane, should designate this place *empty* was the most profound testament to its nullity imaginable.

But among those Europeans for whom names were not proof enough, and who had, from the beginning of the nineteenth century, gone looking for places to test their mettle, the *Rub al Khali* rapidly acquired legendary status. It was perhaps the single greatest challenge the earth could offer to adventurers, its barrenness unrivaled by any wasteland, equatorial or arctic.

Nothing lived there, nor could. It was simply a vast nowhere, 250,000 square miles of desolation, its dunes rising in places to the height of small mountains, and elsewhere giving way to tracts of heat-shattered stone large enough to lose a people in. It was trackless, waterless, and changeless. Most who dared its wastes were swallowed by it, its dust increased by the sum of their powdered bones.

But for that breed of man—as much ascetic as explorer—who was half in love with losing himself to such an end—the number of expeditions that had retreated in the face of the Quarter's maddening absence, or disappeared into it, was simply a spur.

Some challenged the wasteland in the name of cartology, determined to map the place for those who might come after them, only to discover that there was nothing *to* map but the chastening of their spirit. Others went looking for lost tombs and cities, where fabled wealth awaited that man strong enough to reach into Hell and snatch it out. Still others, a patient, secretive few, went in the name of Academe, seeking verification of theories geological or historical. Still others looked for the Ark there; or Eden.

All had this in common: that if they returned from the Empty Quarter—even though their journey might have taken them only a day's ride into that place—they came back changed men. Nobody could set his eyes on such a void and return to hearth and home without having lost a part of himself to the wilderness forever. Many, having endured the void once, went back, and back again, as if daring the desert to claim them; not content until it did. And those unhappy few who died at home, died with their eyes not on the loving faces at their bedside, nor on the cherry tree in blossom outside the window, but on that waste that called them as only the Abyss can call, promising the soul the balm of nothingness.

From *Galilee*

S o Galilee sailed away; I cannot tell you where. If this were a different kind of book I might well invent the details of his route, culled from books and maps. But in doing so I would be trading on your ignorance; assuming you wouldn't notice if I failed to get the details right.

It's better I admit the truth: Galilee sailed away, and I don't know where he went. When I close my eyes, and wait for an image of him to come I usually find him sitting on the rolling deck of *The Samarkand* looking less than happy with his lot. But though I've searched the horizon for some clue as to his whereabouts I see only the wastes of the ocean. To an eye more canny than mine perhaps there are clues even here, but I'm no sailor. To me, one seascape looks much like the next.

I will confess that I tried to apply what I thought would be simple logic to the question. I took down from the shelves several maps I'd been given over the years (the older ones may even have belonged to Galilee himself; long before he left to wander the world, he loved to trace imaginary journeys) and having spread them out on the floor of my study I walked among them with a book on celestial navigation in one hand and a volume on tides and currents in the other, trying to plot the likeliest course for *The Samarkand* to have taken. But the challenge defeated me. I set his course north past the island (that much I remember seeing, through Rachel's eyes); I began to calculate the prevailing winds at that time, and set *The Samarkand* before them, but I became hopelessly distracted by the very charts that were supposed to be anchoring my imagination. They were, as I said, old charts; made at a time when knowledge was not so vigorously (some would say calamitously) divided from the pleasures of fancy. The makers of these maps had seen nothing wrong with adding a few decorative touches here and there: filigreed beasts that rose out of the painted ocean to foam at passing ships; flights of windy angels poised at every quarter, with streaming hair and trumpeter's cheeks; even a great squid on one of the maps with eyes like twin furnaces and tentacles (so the note informed me) the length of six clippers.

In the midst of such wonders, my pathetic attempts at rational projections went south. I left off my calculations and sat in the midst of the maps like a man trading in such things, waiting for a buyer.

Galilee had been in love before, of course, and survived to tell the tale. But he'd only once before been in love with a Geary, and that made all the difference in the world. Loving a woman who belonged in the family of your enemy wasn't wise; there were plenty of tragedies that testified to that. And in his experience love always ended up a bitter business. Sweet for a time yes, but never for long enough to justify the consequences: the weeks of self-recrimination, the months of lost sleep, the years of loneliness. Every time a romance ended, he'd tell himself that he'd never fall again. He'd stay out at sea, where he was safe from his own appetites.

What did he want from love anyway? A mate or a hiding place? Both perhaps. And yet hadn't he raged again and again against the witless contentment of his animal self, smug in its nest, in its ease, in the comfort of its own dirt? He hated that part of himself: the part that wanted to be wrapped in the arms of some beloved; that asked to be hushed and sung to and forgiven. What stupidity! But even as he railed against it, fled it, out to sea, he shuddered at the thought of what lay ahead, now that love was gone again. Not just the loneliness and the sleepless nights, but the horror of being out in the fierce, hard light that burned over him, set there by his own divinity.

As he guided *The Samarkand* out into the ocean currents, he wondered how many more times he'd be able to sail away before the toll of partings became intolerable. Perhaps this was the last. That wouldn't be such a terrible oath to take: to swear that after Rachel there'd be no more seductions, no more breaking of hearts. It would be his mark of respect to her, though she'd never know he'd made it: to say that after her there would only be the sea.

That said, he couldn't readily put the woman from his mind. He sat out on deck through the night, while *The Samarkand* was carried further and further from land, thinking about what had passed between them. How she'd looked, lying in the carved bed that first night; how she'd talked to him as he told the story of Jerusha and the riverman, asking questions, prodding him to make the story better, finer, deeper. How she'd imitated the child bride while she lay there, pulling the sheet off her body to show herself to him; and how exquisite that sight had been. How they'd touched; how he thought of her all the time they were parted, wondering whether to risk bringing her on board the boat. He'd never let a woman set foot on *The Samarkand* before, holding to ancient superstition on the matter. But her presence made such fears seem nonsensical. What boat would not be blessed to have such a creature tread its boards?

Nor did he now regret the decision. Sitting under the stars he seemed to see her, turning to smile at him. There she was, with her arms open to welcome him in. There she was, saying she loved him. Whatever wonders he saw after this—and he'd seen wonders: the sea turned silver with squid, storms of gold and vermilion—there would be no vision out of sea or sky that would command his devotion as she had.

If only she hadn't been a Geary.

So, Galilee sailed away, and—as I said—I don't know where he wandered. I do know where he ended up, however. After three weeks *The Samarkand* put into the little harbor at Puerto Bueno. There had been storms all along that coast earlier in the month, and the town had taken a severe battering. Several houses close to the quay, repeatedly assaulted by waves breaking over the harbor wall, had been damaged; and one had collapsed entirely, killing the widow who'd lived there. But Galilee's house at the top of the hill was virtually unharmed, and it was here he returned, climbing the steep streets of the town without speaking to anyone he encountered, though he knew them all, and they all knew him.

The roof of the Higgins house had leaked during the storms, and the place smelled damp. There was mildew everywhere; and much of the furniture in the upper rooms had begun to rot. He didn't care. There was nothing here that mattered to him. Any vague dreams he might have once entertained of bringing a companion here, and living a kind of ordinary life, now seemed foolish; laughable. What a perfect waste of time, to indulge dreams of domesticity.

By chance the weather brightened the day after he appeared—which fact did nothing to harm his reputation as a man of power among the townspeople—but the scene from the windows of his house—the clouds steadily sculpted to nothingness by the wind, the sea glittering in the sun—gave him no pleasure. He'd seen it all before. This, and every other glory. There was nothing new to watch for; no surprises left in earth or heaven. He could close his eyes forever, and pass away without regret, knowing he'd seen the best of things.

Oh, and the worst. He'd seen the worst, over and over again.

He wandered from one stagnant room to the next, and up the stairs and down; and everywhere he went, he saw visions of things he wished he'd never witnessed. Some of them had seemed like brave sights at the time. In his youth, bloody business had excited him; why did its echoes now come to bruise him the way they did?

Why when he lay down on the mildewed bed did he remember a whorehouse in Chicago, where he'd chased down two men and slaughtered them like the cattle they made such profit from? Why, after all these years, did he remember how one of them had made a little speech as he lay dying, and thanked his murderer for the ease of it all?

Why when he sat down to empty his bowels did his mind conjure up a yellow dog, which had shit itself in terror, seeing its master with his throat cut on the stairs, and Galilee sitting at the bottom of the flight, drinking the dead man's champagne?

And why, when he tried to sleep—not in the bed but on the threadbare sofa in the living room—did he remember a rainy February night and a man who had no better reason to die than that he'd crossed the will of one mightier, and he, Galilee, no better reason to commit murder than that he served that same will? Oh that was a terrible memory. In some ways— though it was not the bloodiest of his recollections—it was the most distressing because it had been such an intimate encounter. He remembered it so clearly: the car rocking as gusts of wind came off the ocean; the rain rattling on the car roof; the stale heat of the interior, and the still staler heat that came off the man who died in his arms.

Poor George; poor, innocent George. He'd looked up at Galilee with such confusion on his face; his lips trying to form some last coherent question. He'd been too far gone to shape the words; but Galilee had supplied the answer anyway.

"I was sent by your father," he'd said.

The confounded look had slipped away and George's face had become oddly placid, hearing that he was dying at the behest of his father; as though this were some last, wretched service he could render the old man, after which he was finally free of Cadmus's jurisdiction.

Any ambition Galilee might have entertained of fathering a child had gone at that moment: to be the father's agent in the murder of a son had killed all appetite in him. Not simply the appetite for parenthood—though that had been the saddest casualty of the night at Smith Point Beach—the very desire to live had lost its piquancy at that moment. Destroying a man because he stood between your family and its ascendance was one thing (all kings did it, sooner or later); but to order the death of your own child because he disappointed you: that was another order of deed entirely, and to have been obliged to perform it had broken Galilee's heart.

And still, after all this time, he couldn't get the scene out of his head. The hours of the whorehouse in Chicago, and his memories of the yellow dog shitting on the stairs, were bad enough; but they were nothing by comparison with the memory of the look on George Geary's face that rainy night.

And so it went on for a week and a half: memories by day and dreams by night, and nothing to do but endure them. He ventured out of the house at evening, and went down to check that all was well with *The Samarkand*, but even that journey became harder as time passed; he was so exhausted.

This could not go on. The time had come to make a decision. There was no great heroism in suffering, unless perhaps it was for a cause. But he had no causes, nor ever had; not to live for, not to die for. All he had was himself.

No, that wasn't true. If he'd just had himself he wouldn't have been haunted this way.

She'd done this to him. The Geary woman; the wretched, gentle Geary woman, whom he'd wanted so badly to put out of his heart, but could not. It was she who'd reminded him of his capacity for feeling, and in so doing had opened him up as surely as if she'd wielded a knife, letting these unwelcome things have access to his heart. It was she who'd reminded him of his humanity, and of all that he'd done in defiance of his better self. She who'd stirred the voice of the man on the whorehouse floor, and roused the yellow dog, and put the sight of George Geary before him.

His Rachel. His beautiful Rachel, whom he tried not to conjure but who was there all the time, holding his hand, touching his arm, telling him she loved him.

Damn her to hell for tormenting him this way! Nothing was worth this pain, this constant gnawing pain. He no longer felt safe in his own skin. She'd invaded him, somehow; possessed him. Sleeplessness made him irrational. He began to hear her voice, as though she were in the next room, and calling to him. Twice he came into the dining room and found the table set for two.

There was no happy end to this, he knew. There would be no escaping her, however patiently he waited. She had too strong a hold on his soul for him to hope for deliverance.

It was as though he were suddenly old—as though the decades in which time had left him untouched had suddenly caught up with him—and all he could look forward to now was certain decline; an inevitable descent into obsessive lunacy. He would become the madman on the hill, locked away in a world of rotted visions; seeing her, hearing her, and tormented day and night by the shameful memories that came with love: the knowledge of his cruelties, his innumerable cruelties.

Better to die soon, he thought. Kinder to himself, though he probably didn't deserve the kindness.

On the sixth evening, climbing the hill to the house, he conceived his plan. He'd known several suicides in his life, and none of them had made a good job of it. They'd left other people with a mess to clear up, for one thing, which was not his style at all. He wanted to go, as far as it were possible, invisibly.

That night, he made fires in all the hearths in the house, and burned everything that might be used to construe some story about him. The few books he'd gathered over the years, an assortment of bric-a-brac from the shelves and windowsills, some carvings he'd made in an idle hour (nothing fancy, but who knew what people would read into what they found here?). There wasn't a lot to burn, but it took time nevertheless, what with his state of mind so dreamy and his limbs aching from want of rest.

When he had finished, he opened all the doors and windows, every one, and just before dawn headed down the hill to the harbor. His neighbors would get the message, seeing the house left open. After a couple of days some brave soul would venture inside, and once word spread that he'd made a permanent departure the place would be stripped of anything useful. At least so he hoped. Better somebody was using the chairs and tables and clocks and lamps than that they all rot away.

The wind was strong. Once The Samarkand was clear of the harbor, its sails filled; and long before the people of Puerto Bueno were up and brewing their morning coffee or pouring their breakfast whiskies their sometime neighbor was gone.

His plan was very simple. He would sail The Samarkand a good distance from land, and then—once he was certain neither wind nor current would bear him back the way he'd come—he'd surrender his captaincy over both vessels, his body and his boat, and let nature take its course. He would not trim his sails if a storm arose. He would not steer the boat from reef or rocks. He would simply let the sea have him, whenever and however she chose to take him. If she chose to overturn The Samarkand and drown him, so be it. If she chose to dash the boat to pieces, and him along with it, then that was fine too. Or if she chose to match his passivity with her own, and let him linger becalmed until he perished on deck, and was withered by the sun, then that lay in her power too, and he wouldn't lift a hand to contradict her will.

He had only one fear: that if hunger and thirst made him delirious he might lose the certainty that moved him now, and in a moment of weakness attempt to take control of the vessel again, so he scoured the boat for anything that might be put to practical use, and threw it all overboard. His mariner's charts, his life jackets, his compass, his flares, his inflatable life raft: all of it went. He left only a few luxuries to sweeten these last days, reasoning that suicide didn't have to be an uncivilized business. He kept his cigars, his brandy, a book or two. Thus supplied, he gave himself over to fate and the tides.

From *Imajica*

Though Jude had been invited to a number of New Year's Eve parties, she'd made no firm commitment to attend any of them, for which fact, after the sorrows the day had brought, she was thankful. She'd offered to stay with Clem once Taylor's body had been taken from the house, but he'd quietly declined, saying that he needed the time alone. He was comforted to know she'd be at the other end of the telephone if he needed her, however, and said he'd call if he got too maudlin.

One of the parties she'd been invited to was at the house opposite her flat, and on the evidence of past years it would raise quite a din. She'd several times been one of the celebrants there herself, but it was no great hardship to be alone tonight. She was in no mood to trust the future, if what the New Year brought was more of what the old had offered.

She closed the curtains in the hope that her presence would go undetected, lit some candles, put on a flute concerto, and started to prepare something light for supper. As she washed her hands, she found that her fingers and palms had taken on a light dusting of color from the stone. She'd caught herself toying with it several times during the afternoon, and pocketed it, only to find minutes later that it was once again in her hands. Why the color it had left behind had escaped her until now, she didn't know. She rubbed her hands briskly beneath the tap to wash the dust off, but when she came to dry them found the color was actually brighter. She went into the bathroom to study the phenomenon under a more intense light. It wasn't, as she'd first thought, dust. The pigment seemed to be in her skin, like a henna stain. Nor was it confined to her palms. It had spread to her wrists, where she was sure her flesh hadn't come in contact with the stone. She took off her blouse and to her shock discovered there were irregular patches of color at her elbows as well. She started talking to herself, which she always did when she was confounded by something.

"What the hell is this? I'm turning blue? This is ridiculous."

Ridiculous, maybe, but none too funny. There was a crawl of panic in her stomach. Had she caught some disease from the stone? Was that why Estabrook had wrapped it up so carefully and hidden it away?

She turned on the shower and stripped. There were no further stains on her body that she could find, which was some small comfort. With the water seething hot she stepped into the bath, working up a lather and rubbing at the color. The combination of heat and the panic in her belly was dizzying her, and halfway through scrubbing at her skin she feared she was going to faint and had to step out of the bath again, reaching to open the bathroom door and let in some cooler air. Her slick hand slid on the doorknob, however, and cursing she reeled around for a towel to wipe the soap off. As she did so she caught sight of herself in the mirror. Her neck was blue. The skin around her eyes was blue. Her brow was blue, all the way up into her hairline. She backed away from this grotesquerie, flattening herself against the steam-wetted tiles.

"This isn't real," she said aloud.

She reached for the handle a second time and wrenched at it with sufficient force to open the door. The cold brought gooseflesh from head to foot, but she was glad of the chill. Perhaps it would slap this self-deceit out of her. Shuddering with cold she fled the reflection, heading back into the candlelit haven of the living room. There in the middle of the coffee table lay the piece of blue stone, its eye looking back at her. She didn't even remember taking it out of her pocket, much less setting it on the table in this studied fashion, surrounded by candles. Its presence made her hang back at the door. She was suddenly superstitious of it, as though its gaze had a basilisk's power and could turn her to similar stuff. If that was its business she was too late to undo it. Every time she'd turned the stone over she'd met its glance. Made bold by fatalism, she went to the table and picked the stone up, not giving it time to obsess her again but flinging it against the wall with all the power she possessed.

As it flew from her hand it granted her the luxury of knowing her error. It had taken possession of the room in her absence, had become more real than the hand that had thrown it or the wall it was about to strike. Time was its plaything, and place its toy, and in seeking its destruction she would unknit both.

It was too late to undo the error now. The stone struck the wall with a loud hard sound, and in that moment she was thrown out of herself, as surely as if somebody had reached into her head, plucked out her consciousness, and pitched it through the window. Her body remained in the room she'd left, irrelevant to the journey she was about to undertake. All she had of its senses was sight. That was enough. She floated out over the bleak street, shining wet in the lamplight, toward the step of the house opposite hers. A quartet of partygoers—three young men with a tipsy girl in their midst—was waiting there, one of the youths rapping impatiently on the door. While they waited, the burliest of the trio pressed kisses on the girl, kneading her breasts covertly as he did so. Jude caught glimpses of the discomfort that surfaced between the girl's giggles: saw her hands make vain little fists when her suitor pushed his tongue against her lips, then saw her open her mouth to him, more in resignation than lust. As the door opened and the four stumbled into the din of celebration, she moved away, rising over the rooftops as she flew and dropping down again to catch glimpses of other dramas unfolding in the houses she passed.

They were all, like the stone that had sent her on this mission, fragments: slivers of dramas she could only guess at. A woman in an upper room, staring down at a dress laid on a stripped bed; another at a window, tears falling from beneath her closed lids as she swayed to music Jude couldn't hear; yet another rising from a table of glittering guests, sickened by something. None of them women she knew, but all quite familiar. Even in her short remembered life she'd felt like all of them at some time or other: forsaken, powerless, yearning. She began to see the scheme here. She was going from glimpse to glimpse as if to moments of her life, meeting her reflection in women of every class and kind.

In a dark street behind King's Cross she saw a woman servicing a man in the front seat of his car, bending to take his hard pink prick between lips the color of menstrual blood. She'd done that too, or its like, because she'd wanted to be loved. And the woman driving past, seeing the whores on parade and righteously sickened by them: that was her. And the beauty taunting her lover out in the rain, and the virago applauding drunkenly above: she'd been in those lives just as surely, or they in hers.

Her journey was nearing its end. She'd reached a bridge from which there would perhaps have been a panoramic view of the city, but that the rain in this region was heavier than it had been in Notting Hill, and the distance was shrouded. Her mind didn't linger but moved on through the downpour—unchilled, unwetted—toward a lightless tower that lay all but concealed behind a row of trees. Her speed had dropped, and she wove between the foliage like a drunken bird, dropping down to the ground and sinking through it into a sodden and utter darkness.

There was a momentary terror that she was going to be buried alive in this place; then the darkness gave way to light, and she was dropping through the roof of some kind of cellar, its walls lined not with wine racks but with shelves. Lights hung along the passageways, but the air here was still dense, not with dust but with something she only understood vaguely.

There was sanctity here, and there was power. She had felt nothing like it in her life: not in St. Peter's, or Chartres, or the Duomo. It made her want to be flesh again, instead of a roving mind. To walk here. To touch the books, the bricks; to smell the air. Dusty it would be, but *such* dust: every mote wise as a planet from floating in this holy space.

The motion of a shadow caught her eye, and she moved toward it along the passageway, wondering as she went what volumes these were, stacked on every side. The shadow up ahead, which she'd taken to be that of one person, was two, erotically entangled. The woman had her back to the books, her arms grasping the shelf above her head. Her mate, his trousers around his ankles, was pressed against her, making short gasps to accompany the jabbing of his hips. Both had their eyes closed; the sight of each other was no great aphrodisiac. Was this coupling what she'd come here to see? God knows, there was nothing in their labors to either arouse or educate her. Surely the blue eye hadn't driven her across the city gathering tales of womanhood just to witness this joyless intercourse. There had to be something here she wasn't comprehending. Something hidden in their exchange, perhaps? But no. It was only gasps. In the books that rocked on the shelves behind them? Perhaps.

She drifted closer to scrutinize the titles, but her gaze ran beyond spines to the wall against which they stood. The bricks were the same plain stuff as all along the passages. The mortar between had a stain in it she recognized, however: an unmistakable blue. Excited now, she drove her mind on, past the lovers and the books and through the brick. It was dark on the other side, darker even than the ground she'd dropped through to enter this secret place. Nor was it simply a darkness made of light's absence, but of despair and sorrow. Her instinct was to retreat from it, but there was another presence here that made her linger: a form, barely distinguishable from the darkness, lying on the ground in this squalid cell. It was bound— almost cocooned—its face completely covered. The binding was as fine as thread, and had been wound around the body with obsessive care, but there was enough of its shape visible for her to be certain that this, like the ensnared spirits at every station along her route, was also a woman.

Her binders had been meticulous. They'd left not so much as a hair or toenail visible. Jude hovered over the body, studying it. They were almost complementary, like corpse and essence, eternally divided: except that she had flesh to return to. At least she hoped she did: hoped that now she'd completed this bizarre pilgrimage, and had seen the relic in the wall, she'd be allowed to return to her tainted skin. But something still held her here. Not the darkness, not the walls, but some sense of unfinished business. Was a sign of veneration required of her? If so, what? She lacked the knees for genuflection, and the lips for hosannas: she couldn't stoop; she couldn't touch the relic. What was there left to do? Unless—God help her—she had to *enter* the thing.

She knew the instant she'd formed the thought that this was precisely why she'd been brought here. She'd left her living flesh to enter this prisoner of brick, cord, and decay, a thrice-bounded carcass from which she might never emerge again. The thought revolted her, but had she come this far only to turn back because this last rite distressed her too much? Even assuming she could defy the forces that had brought her here, and return to the house of her body against their will, wouldn't she wonder forever what adventure she'd turned her back on? She was no coward; she would enter the relic and take the consequences.

No sooner thought than done. Her mind sank toward the binding and slipped between the threads into the body's maze. She had expected darkness, but there was light here, the forms of the body's innards delineated by the milk-blue she'd come to know as the color of this mystery. There was no foulness, no corruption. It was less a charnel house than a cathedral, the source, she now suspected, of the sacredness that permeated this underground. But, like a cathedral, its substance was quite dead. No blood ran in these veins, no heart pumped, no lungs drew breath. She spread her intention through the stilled anatomy, to feel its length and breadth. The dead woman had been large in life, her hips substantial, her breasts heavy. But the binding bit into her ripeness everywhere, perverting the swell and sweep of her. What terrible last moments she must have known, lying blind in this filth, hearing the wall of her mausoleum being built brick by brick. What kind of crime hung on her, Jude wondered, that she'd been condemned to such a death? And who were her executioners, the builders of that wall? Had they sung as they worked, their voices growing dimmer as the brick blotted them out? Or had they been silent, half ashamed of their cruelty?

There was so much she wished she knew, and none of it answerable. She'd finished her journey as she'd begun it, in fear and confusion. It was time to be gone from the relic, and home. She willed herself to rise out of the dead blue flesh. To her horror, nothing happened. She was bound here, a prisoner within a prisoner. God help her, what had she done? Instructing herself not to panic, she concentrated her mind on the problem, picturing the cell beyond the binding, and the wall she'd passed so effortlessly through, and the lovers, and the passageway that led out to the open sky. But imagining was not enough. She had let her curiosity overtake her, spreading her spirit through the corpse, and now it had claimed that spirit for itself.

A rage began in her, and she let it come. It was as recognizable a part of her as the nose on her face, and she needed all that she was, every particular, to empower her. If she'd had her own body around her it would have been flushing as her heartbeat caught the rhythm of her fury. She even seemed to hear it—the first sound she'd been aware of since leaving the house—the pump at its hectic work. It was not imagined. She felt it in the body around her, a tremor passing through the long-stilled system as her rage ignited it afresh. In the throne room of its head a sleeping mind woke and knew it was invaded.

For Jude there was an exquisite moment of shared consciousness, when a mind new to her—yet sweetly familiar—grazed her own. Then she was expelled by its wakefulness. She heard it scream in horror behind her, a sound of mind rather than throat, which went with her as she sped from the cell, out through the wall, past the lovers shaken from their intercourse by falls of dust, out and up, into the rain, and into a night not blue but bitterest black. The din of the woman's terror accompanied her all the way back to the house, where, to her infinite relief, she found her own body still standing in the candlelit room. She slid into it with ease, and stood in the middle of the room for a minute or two, sobbing, until she began to shudder with cold. She found her dressing gown and, as she put it on, realized that her wrists and elbows were no longer stained. She went into the bathroom and consulted the mirror. Her face was similarly cleansed.

Still shivering, she returned to the living room to look for the blue stone. There was a substantial hole in the wall where its impact had gouged out the plaster. The stone itself was unharmed, lying on the rug in front of the hearth. She didn't pick it up. She'd had enough of its delirium for one night. Avoiding its baleful glance as best she could, she threw a cushion over it. Tomorrow she'd plan some way of ridding herself of the thing. Tonight she needed to tell somebody what she'd experienced, before she began to doubt it. Someone a little crazy, who'd not dismiss her account out of hand; someone already half believing. Gentle, of course.

From *Imajica*

Bedrooms were only ever this hot for sickness or love. Gentle thought as Clem ushered him in: for the sweating out of obsession or contagion. It didn't always work, of course, in either case, but at least in love failure had its satisfactions. He'd eaten very little since he'd departed the scene in Streatham, and the stale heat made him feel lightheaded. He had to scan the room twice before his eyes settled on the bed in which Taylor lay, so nearly enveloped was it by the soulless attendants of modern death: an oxygen tank with its tubes and mask; a table loaded with dressings and towels; another, with a vomit bowl, bedpan, and towels; and beside them a third, carrying medication and ointments. In the midst of this panoply was the magnet that had drawn them here, who now seemed very like their prisoner. Taylor was propped up on plastic-covered pillows, with his eyes closed. He looked like an ancient. His hair was thin, his frame thinner still, the inner life of his body—bone, nerve, and vein— painfully visible through skin the color of his sheet. It was all Gentle could do not to turn and flee before the man's eyes flickered open. Death was here again, so soon. A different heat this time, and a different scene, but he was assailed by the same mixture of fear and ineptitude he'd felt in Streatham.

He hung back at the door, leaving Clem to approach the bed first and softly wake the sleeper.

Taylor stirred, an irritated look on his face until his gaze found Gentle. Then the anger at being called back into pain went from his brow, and he said. "You found him."

"It was Judy, not me," Clem said.

"Oh. Judy. She's a wonder," Taylor murmured.

He tried to reposition himself on the pillow, but the effort was beyond him. His breathing became instantly arduous, and he flinched at some discomfort the motion brought.

"Do you want a painkiller?" Clem asked him.

"No, thanks," he said. "I want to be clearheaded, so Gentle and I can talk." He looked across at his visitor, who was still lingering at the door. "Will you talk to me for a while, John?" he said. "Just the two of us?"

"Of course," Gentle said.

Clem moved from beside the bed and beckoned Gentle across. There was a chair, but Taylor patted the bed, and it was there Gentle sat, hearing the crackle of the plastic undersheet as he did so.

"Call if you need anything," Clem said, the remark directed not at Taylor but at Gentle. Then he left them alone.

"Could you pour me a glass of water?" Taylor asked.

Gentle did so, realizing as he passed it to Taylor that his friend lacked the strength to hold it for himself. He put it to Taylor's lips. There was a salve on them, which moistened them lightly, but they were still split, and puffy with sores. After a few sips Taylor murmured something.

"Enough?" Gentle said.

"Yes, thanks." Taylor replied. Gentle set the glass down. "I've had just about enough of everything. It's time it was all over."

"You'll get strong again."

"I didn't want to see you so we could sit and lie to each other." Taylor said. "I wanted you here so I could tell you how much I've been thinking about you. Night and day. Gentle."

"I'm sure I don't deserve that."

"My subconscious thinks you do," Taylor replied. "And, while we're being honest, the rest of me too. You don't look as if you're getting enough sleep, Gentle."

"I've been working, that's all."

"Painting?"

"Some of the time. Looking for inspiration, you know."

"I've got a confession to make," Taylor said. "But first, you've got to promise you won't be angry with me."

"What have you done?"

"I told Judy about the night we got together," Taylor said. He stared at Gentle as if expecting there to be some eruption. When there was none, he went on, "I know it was no big deal to you," he said. "But it's been on my mind a lot. You don't mind, do you?"

Gentle shrugged. "I'm sure it didn't come as any big surprise to her."

Taylor turned his hand palm up on the sheet, and Gentle took it. There was no power in Taylor's fingers, but he closed them round Gentle's hand with what little strength he had. His grip was cold.

"You're shaking," Taylor said.

"I haven't eaten in a while," Gentle said.

"You should keep your strength up. You're a busy man."

"Sometimes I need to float a little bit," Gentle replied.

Taylor smiled, and there in his wasted features was a phantom glimpse of the beauty he'd had.

"Oh, yes," he said. "I float all the time. I've been all over the room. I've even been outside the window, looking in at myself. That's the way it'll be when I go, Gentle. I'll float off, only that one time I won't come back. I know Clem's going to miss me—we've had half a lifetime together—but you and Judy will be kind to him, won't you? Make him understand how things are, if you can. Tell him how I floated off. He doesn't want to hear me talk that way. but you understand."

"I'm not sure I do."

"You're an artist," he said.

"I'm a faker."

"Not in my dreams, you're not. In my dreams you want to heal me, and you know what I say? I tell you I don't want to get well. I say I want to be out in the light."

"That sounds like a good place to be," Gentle said. "Maybe I'll join you."

"Are things so bad? Tell me. I want to hear."

"My whole life's fucked, Tay."

"You shouldn't be so hard on yourself. You're a good man."

"You said we wouldn't tell lies."

"That's no lie. You are. You just need someone to remind you once in a while. Everybody does. Otherwise we slip back into the mud, you know?"

Gentle took tighter hold of Taylor's hand. There was so much in him he had neither the form nor the comprehension to express. Here was Taylor pouring out his heart about love and dreams and how it was going to be when he died, and what did he, Gentle, have by way of contribution? At best, confusion and forgetfulness. Which of them was the sicker, then? he found himself thinking. Taylor, who was frail but able to speak his heart? Or himself, whole but silent? Determined he wouldn't part from this man without attempting to share something of what had happened to him, he fumbled for some words of explanation.

"I think I found somebody," he said. "Somebody to help me . . . remember myself."

"That's good."

"I'm not sure," he said, his voice gossamer. "I've seen some things in the last few weeks. Tay . . . things I didn't want to believe until I had no choice. Sometimes I think I'm going crazy."

"Tell me."

"There was someone in New York who tried to kill Jude."

"I know. She told me about it. What about him?" His eyes widened. "Is this the somebody?" he said.

"It's not a him."

"I thought Judy said it was a man."

"It's not a man," Gentle said. "It's not a woman, either. It's not even human, Tay."

"What is it then?"

"Wonderful," he said quietly.

He hadn't dared use a word like that, even to himself. But anything less was a lie, and lies weren't welcome here.

"I told you I was going crazy. But I swear if you had seen the way it changed . . . it was like nothing on earth."

"And where is it now?"

"I think it's dead," Gentle replied. "I waited too long to find it. I tried to forget I'd ever set eyes on it. I was afraid of what it was stirring up in me. And then when that didn't work I tried to paint it out of my system. But it wouldn't go. *Of course*, it wouldn't go. It was *part* of me by that time. And then when I finally went to find it . . . it was too late."

"Are you sure?" Taylor said. Knots of discomfort had appeared on his face as Gentle talked, and were tightening.

"Are you all right?"

"Yes, yes," he said. "I want to hear the rest."

"There's nothing else to hear. Maybe Pie's out there somewhere, but I don't know where."

"Is that why you want to float? Are you hoping—" He stopped, his breathing suddenly turning into gasps. "You know, maybe you *should* fetch Clem," he said.

"Of course."

Gentle went to the door, but before he reached it Taylor said, "You've got to understand, Gentle. Whatever the mystery is, you'll have to see it for us both."

With his hand on the door, and ample reason to beat a hasty retreat, Gentle knew he could still choose silence over a reply, could take his leave of the ancient without accepting the quest. But, if he answered, and took it, he was bound.

"I'm going to understand," he said, meeting Taylor's despairing gaze. "We both are. I swear."

Taylor managed to smile in response, but it was fleeting. Gentle opened the door and headed out onto the landing. Clem was waiting.

"He needs you," Gentle said.

Clem stepped inside and closed the bedroom door. Feeling suddenly exiled, Gentle headed downstairs. Jude was sitting at the kitchen table, playing with a piece of rock.

"How is he?" she wanted to know.

"Not good," Gentle said. "Clem's gone in to look after him."

"Do you want some tea?"

"No, thanks. What I really need's some fresh air. I think I'll take a walk around the block."

There was a fine drizzle falling when he stepped outside, which was welcome after the suffocating heat of the sickroom. He knew the neighborhood scarcely at all, so he decided to stay close to the house, but his distraction soon got the better of that plan and he wandered aimlessly, lost in thought and the maze of streets. There was a freshness in the wind that made him sigh for escape. This was no place to solve mysteries. After the turn of the year everybody would be stepping up to a new round of resolutions and ambitions, plotting their futures like well-oiled farces. He wanted none of it.

As he began the trek back to the house he remembered that Jude had asked him to pick up milk and cigarettes on his journey, and that he was returning empty-handed. He turned and went in search of both, which took him longer than he expected. When he finally rounded the corner, goods in hand, there was an ambulance outside the house. The front door was open. Jude stood on the step, watching the drizzle. She had tears on her face.

"He's dead," she said.

He stood rooted to the spot a yard from her. "When?" he said, as if it mattered.

"Just after you left."

He didn't want to weep, not with her watching. There was too much else he didn't want to stumble over in her presence. Stony, he said, "Where's Clem?"

"With him upstairs. Don't go up. There's already too many people." She spied the cigarettes in his hand and reached for them. As her hand grazed his, their grief ran between them. Despite his intent, tears sprang to his eyes, and he went into her embrace, both of them sobbing freely, like enemies joined by a common loss or lovers about to be parted. Or else souls who could not remember whether they were lovers or enemies and were weeping at their own confusion.

From *Imajica*

There was a balmy rain falling as they left London the next day, but by the time they'd reached the estate the sun was breaking through, and the parkland gleamed around them as they entered. They didn't make any detours to the house but headed straight to the copse that concealed the Retreat. There was a breeze in the branches, and they flickered with light leaves. The smell of life was everywhere, stirring her blood for the journey ahead.

Oscar had advised her to dress with an eye to practicality and warmth. The city, he said, was subject to rapid and radical shifts in temperature, depending on the direction of the wind. If it came off the desert, the heat in the streets could bake the flesh like unleavened bread. And if it swung and came off the ocean, it brought marrow-chilling fogs and sudden frosts. None of this daunted her, of course. She was ready for this adventure as for no other in her life.

"I know I've gone on endlessly about how dangerous the city's become," Oscar said as they ducked beneath the low-slung branches, "and you're tired of hearing about it, but this isn't a civilized city, Judith. About the only man I trust there is Peccable. If for any reason we were to be separated—or if anything were to happen to me—you can rely upon him for help."

"I understand."

Oscar stopped to admire the pretty scene ahead, dappled sunlight falling on the pale walls and dome of the Retreat. "You know, I used only to come here at night," he said. "I thought that was the sacred time, when magic had the strongest hold. But it's not true. Midnight Mass and moonlight is fine, but miracles are here at noon as well; just as strong, just as strange."

He looked up at the canopy of trees.

"Sometimes you have to go away from the world to see the world," he said. "I went to Yzordderrex a few years back and stayed—oh, I don't know, two months, maybe two and a half, and when I came back to the Fifth I saw it like a child. I swear, like a child. This trip won't just show you other Dominions. If we get back safe and sound—"

"We will."

"Such faith. If we do, this world will be different, too. Everything changes after this, because you'll be changed."

"So be it," she said.

She took hold of his hand, and they started toward the Retreat. Something made her uneasy, however. Not his words—his talk of change had only excited her—but the hush between them, perhaps, which was suddenly deep.

"Is there something wrong?" he said, feeling her grip tighten.

"The silence . . ."

"There's always an odd atmosphere here. I've felt it before. A lot of fine souls died here, of course."

"At the Reconciliation?"

"You know about that, do you?"

"From Clara. It was two hundred years ago this midsummer, she said. Perhaps the spirits are coming back to see if someone's going to try again."

He stopped, tugging on her arm. "Don't talk about it, even in jest. Please. There'll be no Reconciliation, this summer or any other. The Maestros are dead. The whole thing's—"

"All right," she said. "Calm down. I won't mention it again."

"After this summer it'll be academic anyway," he said, with a feigned lightness, "at least for another couple of centuries. I'll be dead and buried long before this hoopla starts again. I've got my plot, you know? I chose it with Peccable. It's on the edge of the desert, with a fine view of Yzordderrex."

His nervous babble concealed the quiet until they reached the door; then he let it drop. She was glad he was silent. The place deserved reverence. Standing at the step, it wasn't difficult to believe phantoms gathered here, the dead of centuries past mingling with those she'd last seen living on this very spot: Charlie for one, of course, coaxing her inside, telling her with a smile that the place was nothing special, just stone; and the voiders too, one burned, one skinned, both haunting the threshold.

"Unless you see any just impediment," Oscar said, "I think we should do this."

He led her inside, to the middle of the mosaic.

"When the time comes," he said. "We have to hold on to each other. Even if you think there's nothing to hold on to, there is; it's just changed for a time. I don't want to lose you between here and there. The In Ovo's no place to go wandering."

"You won't lose me," she said.

He went down on his haunches and dug into the mosaic, pulling from the pattern a dozen or so pieces of pyramidal stone the size of two fists, which had been so designed as to be virtually invisible when set in their places.

"I don't fully understand the mechanisms that carry us over," he said as he worked. "I'm not sure anybody does completely. But according to Peccable there's a sort of common language into which anybody can be translated. And all the processes of magic involve this translation."

He was laying the stones around the edge of the circle as he spoke, the arrangement seemingly arbitrary.

"Once matter and spirit are in the same language, one can influence the other in any number of ways. Flesh and bone can be transformed, transcended—"

"Or transported?"

"Exactly."

Jude remembered how the removal of a traveler from this world into another looked from the outside: the flesh folding upon itself, the body distorted out of all recognition.

"Does it hurt?" she said.

"At the beginning, but not badly."

"When will it begin?" she said.

He stood up. "It already has," he said.

She felt it, as he spoke: a pressure in her bowels and bladder, a tightness in her chest that made her catch her breath.

"Breathe slowly," he said, putting his palm against her breastbone. "Don't fight it. Just let it happen. There's no harm going to come to you."

She looked down at his hand, then beyond it to the circle that enclosed them, and out through the door of the Retreat to the sunlit grass that lay just a few paces from where she stood. Close as it was, she couldn't return there. The train she'd boarded was gathering speed around her. It was too late for doubts or second thoughts. She was trapped.

"It's all right," she heard Oscar say, but it didn't feel that way at all.

There was a pain in her belly so sharp it felt as though she'd been poisoned, and an ache in her head, and an itch too deep in her skin to be scratched. She looked at Oscar. Was he enduring the same discomforts? If so he was bearing them with remarkable fortitude, smiling at her like an anesthetist.

"It'll be over soon," he was saying. "Just hold on . . . it'll be over soon."

He drew her closer to him, and as he did so she felt a tingling pass through her cells, as though a rainstorm was breaking inside her, sluicing the pain away.

"Better?" he said, the word more shape than sound.

"Yes." she told him and, smiling, put her lips to his, closing her eyes with pleasure as their tongues touched.

The darkness behind her lids was suddenly brightened by gleaming lines, falling like meteors across her mind's eye. She lifted her lids again, but the spectacle came out of her skull, daubing Oscar's face with streaks of brightness. A dozen vivid hues picked out the furrows and creases of his skin; another dozen, the geology of bone beneath; and another, the lineaments of nerves and veins and vessels, to the tiniest detail. Then, as though the mind interpreting them had done with its literal translation and could now rise to poetry, the layered maps of his flesh simplified. Redundancies and repetitions were discarded, the forms that emerged so simple and so absolute that the matter they represented seemed wan by comparison, and receded before them. Seeing this show, she remembered the glyph she'd imagined when she and Oscar had first made love: the spiral and curve of her pleasure laid on the velvet behind her eyes. Here was the same process again, only the mind imagining them was the circle's mind, empowered by the stones and by the travelers' demand for passage.

A motion at the door distracted her gaze momentarily. The air around them was close to dropping its sham of sights altogether, and the scene beyond the circle was blurred. But there was enough color in the suit of the man at the threshold for her to know him even though she couldn't make out his face. Who else but Dowd wore that absurd shade of apricot? She said his name, and though she heard no sound from her throat, Oscar understood her alarm and turned toward the door.

Dowd was approaching the circle at speed, his intention perfectly clear: to hitch a ride to the Second Dominion. She'd seen the gruesome consequences of such interference before, on this very spot, and she braced herself against Oscar for the coming shock. Instead of trusting to the circle to dispatch the hanger-on, however, Oscar turned from her and went to strike Dowd. The circle's flux multiplied his violence tenfold, and the glyph of his body became an illegible scrawl, the colors dirtied in an instant. The pain she'd thought washed away swept back over her. Blood ran from her nose and into her open mouth. Her skin itched so violently she'd have brought blood to that too had the pain in her joints not kept her from moving.

She could make no sense of the scribble in front of her until her glance caught sight of Oscar's face, smeared and raw, screaming back at her as he toppled from the circle. She reached to haul him back, despite the searing pain her motion brought, and took hold of an arm, determined that wherever they were delivered, to Yzordderrex or death, they'd go there together. He returned her grasp, seizing her outstretched arms and dragging himself back onto the Express. As his face emerged from the blur beyond the smile she realized her error. It was Dowd she'd hauled aboard.

She let go of her hold, in revulsion more than rage. His face was horribly contorted, blood streaming from eyes, ears, and nose. But the mind of passage was already working on this fresh text, preparing to translate and transport it. She had no way of braking the process, and to leave the circle now would be certain suicide. Beyond it, the scene was blurred and darkening, but she caught sight of Oscar, rising from the ground, and thanked whatever deities protected these circles that he was at least alive. He was moving toward the circle again, she saw, as though to dare its flux a second time, but it seemed he judged the train to be moving too swiftly now, because he retreated, arms up over his face. Seconds later the whole scene disappeared, the sunlight at the threshold burning on for a heartbeat longer than the rest, then that too folding away into obscurity.

The only sight left to her now was the matrix of lines which were the translator's rendering of her fellow traveler, and though she despised him beyond words she kept her eyes fixed upon them, having no other point of reference. All bodily sensation had disappeared. She didn't know if she was floating, falling, or even breathing, though she suspected she was doing none of these things. She had become a sign, transmitted between Dominions, encoded in the mind of passage. The sight before her—Dowd's shimmering glyph—was not secured by sight but by thought, which was the only currency valid on this trip. And now, as if her powers to purchase were increasing with familiarity, the absence around her began to gain detail. The In Ovo, Oscar had called this place. Its darkness swelled in a million places, their skins stretching until they gleamed and split, glutinous forms breaking out and in their turn swelling and splitting, like fruit whose seeds were sown inside each other and nourished to corruption by their predecessors' decay. Repulsive as this was, there was worse to come, as new entities appeared, these no more than scraps from a cannibal's table, sucked bloodless and gnawed: idiot doodles of life that didn't bear translation into any material form. Primitive though they were, they sensed the presence of finished life forms in their midst and rose toward the travelers like the damned to passing angels. But they swarmed too late. The visitors moved on and away, the darknesses sealing up their tenants and receding.

Jude could see Dowd's body in the midst of his glyph, still insubstantial but brightening by the moment. With the sight, the agonies of ferriage returned, though not as sharply as those that had pained her at the outset of the journey. She was glad to have them if they proved her nerves were hers again; surely it meant the journey was almost over. The horrors of the In Ovo had almost disappeared entirely when she felt the faint heat on her face. But the scent this heat raised to her nostrils brought more certain proof that the city was near: a mingling of the sweets and sours she'd first smelled on the wind that had issued from the Retreat months before.

She saw a smile come over Dowd's face, cracking the blood already dried on it: a smile which became a laugh in a beat or two, ringing off the walls of the merchant Peccable's cellar as it grew solid around them. She didn't want to share his pleasure, after all the harms he'd devised, but she couldn't help herself. Relief that the journey hadn't killed her, and sheer exhilaration that after all this time she was here, brought laughter onto her face and, with every breath between, the air of the Second Dominion into her lungs.

From *Everville*

B ut the heat went out of the world even before August was over, and by the end of the third week, with the Blue Mountains not yet visible even to the keenest eye, and food so severely rationed that some were too weak to walk, the word had spread around the campfires that according to friendly natives, storms of unseasonal severity were already descending from the heights. Sheldon Sturgis, who had led the train thus far with a loose hand (some said that was his style; others that he was simply weak and prone to drink), now began to hasten along those who were slowing progress. But with a growing number of frail and sickened pioneers, mistakes and accidents proliferated, adding to the delays that were an inevitable part of such journeys: wheels lost, animals injured, trails blocked.

Death became a fellow traveler sometime in early September, that was Maeve's belief. She did not see him at first, but she was certain of his presence.

He was in the land around them, killing living things with his touch or his breath. Trees that should have been fruitful in this season had already given up their leaves and were going naked. Animals large and small could be seen dead or dying beside the trail. Only carcass-flies were getting fat this September; but then Death was a friend to flies, wasn't he?

At night, waiting for sleep to come, she could hear people praying in the wagons nearby, begging God to keep Death at bay.

It did no good. He came anyway. To Marsha Winthrop's baby son, William, who had been born in Missouri just two weeks before the trek began. To Jack Pottruck's father, a beast of a man like his son, who suddenly weakened and perished in the middle of the night (not quietly, like the Winthrop child, but with terrible cries and imprecations). To the sisters Brenda and Meriel Schonberg, spinsters both, whose passing was only discovered when the train stopped at dusk and their wagon went unhalted, the women being dead at the reins.

Maeve could not help wonder why Death had chosen these particular souls. She could understand why he had taken her mother: she had been very beautiful and gracious and loving. He had wanted to make the world the poorer by removing her, and himself the richer. But what did he want with a baby and an old man and two withered sisters?

She didn't bother her father with such questions; he was fretful and beset enough. Though their wagon showed no sign of failing, and their horse was as healthy as any in the train, it was clear from the look in his sunken eyes that he too knew Death was an unwelcome outrider these days. She began to watch for the horseman more clearly, hoping to reassure her father by identifying the enemy; to say, I know the color of his horse and of his hat, and if he comes near us I'll know him and frighten him off with a prayer or a song. More than once she thought she caught sight of him, weaving between the wagons up ahead, dark in the dust. But she was never certain of any sighting, so she kept her silence rather than give her father an unverified report.

And the days passed, and the cold deepened, and when finally the Blue Mountains came into view, their slopes were white down below the tree line, and the clouds behind them black and bruised by their burden of ice.

And Abilene Welsh and Billy Baxter, whose antics in the summer had been the subject of much gossip (and clucking from Martha Winthrop), were found frozen in each other's arms one morning, touched by death as they enjoyed each other's company away from the warmth of the fires.

Even as they were being buried, and Doc Hodder was speaking of how they would be eternally united in the Kingdom of the Lord, and those sins they might have committed in the name of love forgiven, Maeve looked up at the gray heavens and saw the first flakes of snow spiraling down. And that was the beginning of the end.

She gave up looking for Death the Outrider after that. If he had ever accompanied the wagons on horseback, as she'd suspected, he had now put off that shape. He had become simpler. He was ice.

It killed many of the travelers quickly, and those it did not kill it tormented with intimations of the state ahead. It slowed the brain and the blood; it made the fingers fumble and the feet numb; it stiffened the sinews; it lined the lungs with a dusting of frost.

Sometimes, even now, with so many people dead and the rest dying, Maeve would hear her father say: "It wasn't supposed to be this way," as though some promise had been made to him that was presently being broken. She did not doubt the identity of the promise-maker. Mr. Buddenbaum. It was he who had filled her father's heart with ambition, who had given him gifts and told him to go West and build. It was he who had first whispered the word *Everville*. Perhaps, she began to think, Whitney had been right. Perhaps the Devil *had* come to tempt her father in the form of Mr. Buddenbaum, and filled his trusting heart with dreams for the pleasure of watching that heart broken. The problem vexed her night and day—never more so than when her father, in the midst of the storm—leaned over to her and said: "We must be strong, sweet. We mustn't die, or Everville dies with us!"

Hunger and exhaustion had her teetering on delirium now—sometimes she would imagine herself on the ship coming from Liverpool, clinging to the icy deck with her fingertips; sometimes she was back in Ireland, eating grass and roots to keep her belly from aching—but in times of lucidity she wondered if perhaps this was some kind of test; Buddenbaum's way of seeing whether the man to whom he'd given the dream of Everville was strong enough to survive. The notion seemed so plausible she could not keep it to herself.

"Papa?" she said, grabbing hold of his coat.

Her father looked round at her, his face barely visible beneath his hood. She could only see one of his eyes, but it looked at her as lovingly as ever.

"What, child?" he said.

"I think maybe—maybe it *was* meant to be this way."

"What are you saying?"

"Maybe Mr. Buddenbaum's watching us, to see if we deserve to build his city. Maybe just when we think we can't go on any longer he'll appear, and tell us it was a test, and show us the way to the valley."

"This isn't a test, child. It's just what happens in the world. Dreams die. The cold comes out of nowhere and kills them." He put his arm around his daughter, and hugged her to him, though there was precious little strength left in him.

"I'm not afraid, Papa," she said.

"Are you not?"

"No I'm not. We've come a long way together."

"That we have."

"Remember how it was back at home? How we thought we'd die of starvation? But we didn't. Then on the ship. Waves washing people overboard to right and left of us, and we thought we'd drown for certain. But the waves passed us by. Didn't they?"

His cracked, white lips managed a tiny smile. "Yes, child, they did."

"Mr. Buddenbaum knew what we'd come through," Maeve said. "He knew there were angels watching over us. And Mama too—"

She felt her father shudder at her side. "I dreamed of her last night—" he said.

"Was she beautiful?"

"Always. We were floating, side by side, in this calm, calm sea. And I swear, if I'd not known you were here, child, waiting for me—"

He didn't finish the thought. A sound like a single blast of a trumpet came out of the blind whiteness ahead; a note of triumph that instantly raised a chorus of shouts from the wagons in front and behind.

"Did ya hear that?"

"There's somebody up here with us!"

Another blast now, and another, and another, each rising from the echo of the last till the whole white world was filled with brazen harmonies.

The Sturgises' wagon, which was ahead of the O'Connells', had come to a halt, and Sheldon was calling back down the line, summoning a party of men to his side.

"Stratton! Whitney! O'Connell! Get your guns!"

"Guns?" said Maeve. "Papa, why does he want guns?"

"Just climb up into the wagon, child," Harmon said, "and stay there till I come back."

The din of trumpets had died away for a moment, but now it came again, more magnificent than ever. As she climbed up onto the wagon, Maeve's skinny frame ran with little tremors at the sound, as though the music was shaking her muscles and marrow. She started to weep, seeing her father disappear, rifle in hand. Not because she feared for him but because she wanted to go out into the snow herself and see what manner of trumpet made the sound that moved in her so strangely, and what manner of man played upon it. Perhaps they were not men at all, her spinning head decided. Perhaps the angels she'd been gabbing about minutes before had come to earth, and these blasts were their proclamations.

She started out into the snow, suddenly and uncontrollably certain that this was true. Their heavenly guardians had come to save them, and Mama too, more than likely. If she looked hard she would see them soon, gold and blue and purple. She stood up on the seat, clinging to the canvas, to get a better view, scanning the blank snow in every direction. Her study was rewarded. Just as the trumpets began their third hallelujah, the snow parted for a few moments. She saw the mountains rising to left and right like the teeth of a trap, and ahead of her a single titanic peak, its lower slopes forested. The perimeter of the trees lay no more than a hundred yards from the wagon, and the music she heard was coming from that direction, she was certain of it. Of her father, and of the men accompanying him, there was no sign, but they had surely disappeared among the trees. It would be quite safe to follow them, and wonderful to be there at her father's side when he was reunited with Mama. Wouldn't that be a blissful time, kissing her mother in a circle of angels, while Whitney and all the men who had scorned her father looked on agog?

The opening in the veil of snow was closing again, but before it did so she jumped down from the wagon and started off in the direction of the trees. Within moments, snow had obliterated the wagons behind her, just as it had covered the forest ahead, and she was following her nose through a blank world, stumbling with every other step. The drifts lay perilously deep in places, and several times she dropped into drifts so deep she was almost buried alive. But just as her frozen limbs threatened to give up on her, the trumpets came again, and the music put life back into her sinews and filled her head with bliss. There was a piece of paradise up ahead. Angels and Mama and her loving father, with whom she would build a city that would be the wonder of the world.

She would not die, of that she was certain. Not today, not for many years to come. She had great work to do, and the angels would not see her perish in the snow, knowing how far she had traveled to perform that labor.

And now she saw the trees, pines higher than any house, like a wall of sentinels in front of her. Calling for her father she ran toward them, careless of the cold and the bruises and her spinning head. The trumpets were close, and there were bursts of color in the corner of her eye, as though some of the angelic throng, who had not yet picked their instruments, were clustered about her, the tips of their beating wings all that she was allowed to glimpse.

Borne by invisible hands, she was ushered beneath the canopy of trees and there, where the snow could not come, and the ground was soft with pine needles, she sank down onto her knees and drew a dozen heaving breaths while the sound of trumpets touched her in every part.

From *Sacrament*

The braids of light in which the Nilotic had been wed to itself were dispersing now, and as they did so the creature turned and looked at Will. Simeon had not done too badly with the portrait he'd painted, Will thought. He'd caught the grace of the creature well enough. What he'd failed to capture was the alien cadences of its proportions; its subtle otherness, which made Will a little fearful it would do him harm.

But when it spoke, his fears fled.

"*We have come such a distance together,*" it said, its voice mellifluous. "*What will you do now?*"

"I want to go a little further," Will replied, glancing back over his shoulder.

"*I'm sure you do,*" the Nilotic said. "*But believe me when I tell you it wouldn't be wise. Every step we take we go deeper into the living heart of the world. It will take you from yourself, and at last, you will be lost.*"

"I don't care."

"*But those who love you will care. They'll mourn you, more than you know. I would not wish to be responsible for another moment's suffering.*"

"I just want to see a little more," Will said.

"*How much is a little?*"

"I'll let you be the judge of that," Will said. "I'll walk with you for a while, and we'll turn back when you tell me it's time."

"*I won't be coming back,*" the Nilotic said. "*I intend to unmake the House, and must unmake it from its heart.*"

"Then where will you go?"

"*Away. From men and women.*"

"Is there anywhere like that left?"

"*You'd be surprised,*" the Nilotic said, and so saying, moved past Will and proceeded on into the mystery.

It had not explicitly forbidden Will to follow it, which was all the invitation he needed. He went in cautious pursuit of it, like a spawning fish climbing waters that would have dashed him to death without the Nilotic ahead of him to breast the flow. Even so, he quickly understood the truth in its warnings. The deeper they ventured the more it seemed he was treading not among the echoes of the world, but the world itself, his soul a thread of bliss passing into its mysteries.

He lay with a pack of panting dogs on a hill overlooking plains where antelope grazed. He marched with ants, and labored in the rigors of the nest, filing eggs. He danced the mating dance of the bowerbird, and slept on a warm rock with his lizard kin. He was a cloud. He was the shadow of a cloud. He was the moon that cast the shadow of a cloud. He was a blind fish; he was a shoal; he was a whale; he was the sea. He was the lord of all he surveyed. He was a worm in the dung of a kite. He did not grieve, knowing his life was a day long, or an hour. He did not wonder who made him. He did not wish to be other. He did not pray. He did not hope. He only was; and was; and was; and that was the joy of it.

Somewhere along the way, perhaps among the clouds, perhaps among the fish, he lost sight of his guide. The creature that had been, in its human incarnations, both his maker and his tormentor, slipped away and was gone out of his life forever. He was vaguely aware of its departure, and knew its going to be a signal that he should stop and turn round. It had trusted him with his destiny; it was his responsibility not to abuse the gift. Not for his sake, but for those who would mourn him if he was lost to them.

He shaped all these thoughts quite clearly. But he was too besotted to act upon them. How could he turn his back on these glories, with so much more to see?

On he went then, where only souls who had learned the homeward paths by heart dared to go.

THREE

VISIONS AND DREAMS

I often use dreams in stories as stepping-stones. They're a way to unknit the character's certainty in the here and now and begin the process of transferring him to a new place. Or perhaps reminding him of something very old.

In the passage I've selected from *Weaveworld*, for instance, Cal Mooney has forgotten his visit into a miraculous country, but is reminded of it when he eats a dried-up Giddy Fruit, picked from an orchard in that country. The fruit induces a waking vision, and he sets off in pursuit of what he's witnessed. An even more expansive vision seizes Maddox Barbarossa in the passage from *Galilee*. Trapped in the Sky Room of his mother's house, he is granted a glimpse of her legendary origins. It transforms him. Though he enters a room a cripple, the vision heals him; and incites him to begin work on the story that is the matter of the book.

There is another order of experience among these pieces, however: one which hovers on the borderline between the real and the imagined. In a sequence from *Imajica*, the aggressively heterosexual John Furie Zacharias, known as Gentle, is visited by a creature called Pie 'oh' pah. Pie is a mystif, a species able to project the mirror image of their partners' profoundest erotic desires. Gentle makes love to what he imagines is his ex-lover, Judith. Then he discovers the truth; or perhaps another version of it.

Here the dream state bleeds into reality, and it's no longer possible readily to say what is true and what's not.

In some ways the material in this chapter suggests that that issue can never be truly resolved, nor perhaps needs to be. We're like Peer Gynt, in Ibsen's play, going through life peeling away its layers like the skin of some infinite onion, one vision supplanted by another, and each—for a little while, at least—looking like reality.

From *Weaveworld*

The Mersey was high tonight, and fast; its waters a filthy brown, its spume gray. Cal leaned on the promenade railing and stared across the churning river to the deserted shipyards on the far bank. Once this waterway had been busy with ships, arriving weighed down with their cargo and riding high as they headed for faraway. Now, it was empty. The docks silted up, the wharves and warehouses idle. Spook City; fit only for ghosts.

He felt like one himself. An insubstantial wanderer. And cold too, the way the dead must be cold. He put his hands in his jacket pocket to warm them, and his fingers found there half a dozen soft objects, which he took out and examined by the light of a nearby lamp.

They looked like withered plums, except that the skin was much tougher, like old shoe leather. Clearly they were fruit, but no variety he could name. Where and how had he come by them? He sniffed at one. It smelled slightly fermented, like a heady wine. And appetizing; tempting even. Its scent reminded him that he'd not eaten since lunchtime.

He put the fruit to his lips, his teeth breaking through the corrugated skin with ease. The scent had not deceived; the meat inside did indeed have an alcoholic flavor, the juice burning his throat like cognac. He chewed, and had the fruit to his lips for a second bite before he'd swallowed the first, finishing it off, seeds and all, with a fierce appetite.

Immediately, he began to devour another of them. He was suddenly ravenous. He lingered beneath the wind-buffeted lamp, the pool of light he stood in dancing, and fed his face as though he'd not eaten in a week.

He was biting into the penultimate fruit when it dawned on him that the rocking of the lamp above couldn't entirely account for the motion of the light around him. He looked down at the fruit in his hand, but he couldn't quite focus on it. God alive! Had he poisoned himself? The remaining fruit dropped from his hand and he was about to put his fingers down his throat to make himself vomit up the rest when the most extraordinary sensation overtook him.

He rose up; or at least some part of him did.

His feet were still on the concrete, he could feel it solid beneath his soles, but he was still floating up, the lamp shining *beneath* him now, the promenade stretching out to right and left of him, the river surging against the banks, wild and dark.

The rational fool in him said: *you're intoxicated; the fruits have made you drunk.*

But he felt neither sick nor out of control; his sight (sights) were clear. He could still see from the eyes in his head, but also from a vantage point high above him. Nor was that all he could see. Part of him was with the litter too, gusting along the promenade; another part was out in the Mersey, gazing back toward the bank.

This proliferation of viewpoints didn't confuse him: the sights mingled and married in his head, a pattern of risings and fallings; of looking out and back and far and near.

He was not *one* but *many.*

He Cal; he his father's son; he his mother's son; he a child buried in a man, and a man dreaming of being a bird.

A *bird!*

And all at once it *all* came back to him; all the wonders he'd forgotten surged back with exquisite particularity. A thousand moments and glimpses and words.

A bird, a chase, a house, a yard, a carpet, a flight (and he the bird; *yes! yes!*); then enemies and friends; Shadwell, Immacolata; the monsters; and Suzanna, his beautiful Suzanna, her place suddenly clear in the story his mind was telling itself.

He remembered it all. The carpet unweaving, the house coming apart; then into the Fugue, and the glories that the night there had brought.

It took all his newfound senses to hold the memories, but he was not overwhelmed. It seemed he dreamed them all at once; held them in a moment that was sweet beyond words: a reunion of self and secret self which was an heroic remembering.

And after the recognition, tears, as for the first time he touched the buried grief he felt at losing the man who'd taught him the poem he'd recited in Lo's orchard: his father, who'd lived and died and never once known what Cal knew now.

Momentarily, sorrow and salt drew him back into himself, and he was single-sighted once more, standing under the uncertain light, bereft—

Then his soul soared again, higher now, and higher, and this time it reached escape velocity.

Suddenly he was up, *up* above England.

Below him moonlight fell on bright continents of cloud, whose vast shadows moved over hillside and suburb like silent ushers of sleep. He went too, carried on the same winds. Over tracts of land which pylons strode in humming lines; and city streets the hour had emptied of all but felons and wild dogs.

And this flight, gazing down like a lazy hawk, stars at his back, the isle beneath him, this flight was companion to that other he'd taken, over the carpet, over the Fugue.

No sooner had his mind turned to the Weaveworld than he seemed to sniff it—seemed to know where it lay beneath him. His eye was not sharp enough to pick out its place, but he knew he could find it, if he could only keep this new sense intact when he finally returned to the body beneath him.

The carpet was north-northeast of the city, that he *was* certain of; many miles away and still moving. Was it in Suzanna's hands? Was she fleeing to some remote place where she prayed their enemies wouldn't come? No, the news was worse than that, he sensed. The Weaveworld and the woman who carried it were in terrible jeopardy, somewhere below him—

At that thought his body grew possessive of him once more. He felt it around him—its heat, its weight—and he exalted in its solidity. Flying thoughts were all very well, but what were they worth without muscle and bone to act upon them?

A moment later he was standing beneath the light once more, and the river was still churning and the clouds he'd just seen from above moved in mute flotillas before a wind that smelled of the sea. The salt he tasted was not sea salt; it was the tears he'd shed for the death of his father, and for his forgetting, and for his mother too perhaps—for it seemed all loss was one loss, all forgetting one forgetting.

But he'd brought new wisdom from the high places. He knew now that things forgotten might be recalled; things lost, found again.

That was all that mattered in the world: to search and find.

He looked north-northeast. Though the many sights he'd had were once more narrowed to one, he knew he could still find the carpet.

He saw it with his heart. And seeing it, started in pursuit.

From *Galilee*

Nothing happened. I lay there, my breaths quick and shallow, my stomach ready to revolt, my body sticky with sweat, and the room just waited. The unfixable forms all around me—which had by now entirely blotted out every detail of windows and walls, even carpeted the floor—were almost still, their evolutionary endeavors at an end, at least for the moment.

Had the fact that I'd been injured shocked the presence, or presences, here into reticence, I wondered? Perhaps they felt they'd overstepped the bounds of enthusiasm, and now wanted nothing more than for me to crawl away and tend my wounds? Were they waiting for me to call down to Luman, perhaps? I thought about doing so, but decided against it. This was not a room in which to speak a simple word unless it was strictly necessary. I would be better lying still and quiet, I decided, and let my panicked body calm itself. Then, once I had governed myself, I would try to crawl back to the door. Sooner or later, Luman would come up and fetch me; I felt certain of that. Even if I had to wait all night.

Meanwhile I closed my eyes so as to put the images around me out of the way. Though the pain in my side was by now only a dull throb, my head and eyes were throbbing too; indeed it was not hard to imagine my body had become one fat heart, lying discarded on the floor, pumping its last.

I'm not afraid, I'd boasted, moments before the bolt had struck me. But now? Oh, I was very much afraid now. Afraid that I would die here, before I'd worked my way through the catalogue of unfinished business that sat at the back of my skull, awaiting my attention and of course never getting it, while all the time growing and growing. Well, it was most likely too late; there would not be time for me to flagellate myself for every dishonorable deed in that list, nor any chance to make good the harms I'd done. Minor harms, to be sure, in the scheme of things; but large enough to regret.

And then, on the back of my neck, a touch; or what I believed to be a touch.

"Luman?" I murmured, and opened my eyes.

It wasn't Luman; it wasn't even a human touch, or anything resembling a human touch. It was some presence in the shadows; or the shadows themselves. They had swarmed upon me while my eyes were closed, and were now pressing close, their intimacy in no way threatening, but curiously *tender*. It was as though these roiling, senseless forms were concerned for my well-being, the way they brushed my nape, my brow, my lips. I stayed absolutely still, holding my breath, half expecting their mood to change and their consolations to turn into something crueler. But no; they simply waited, close upon me.

Relieved, I drew breath. And in the instant of drawing, knew I had again unwittingly done something of consequence.

On the intake I felt the marked air about my head rush toward my open lips, and down my throat. I had no choice but to let it in. By the time I knew what was happening it was too late to resist. I was a vessel being filled. I could feel the marks on my tongue, against my tonsils, in my windpipe—

Nor did I want to choke them off, once I felt them inside me. At their entrance the pain in my side seemed instantly to recede, as did the throbbing in my head and eyes. The fear of a lonely demise here went out of my head and I was removed—in one breath—from despair to pleasurable ease.

What a maze of manipulations this chamber contained! First banality, then a blow, then this opiated bliss. I would be foolish, I knew, to believe that it did not have more tricks in its repertoire. But while it was content to give me some relief from my pains I was happy to take what was offered. Greedy for it, indeed. I gulped at the air, drawing in great draughts of it. And with every breath I felt further removed from my pain. Nor was it just the hurt in my flank and the throb in my head that was becoming remote; there was a much older ache—a dull, wretched pain that haunted the dead terrain of my lower limbs—that was now, for the first time in almost two human spans, relieved. It wasn't, I think, that the pain was taken away; only that I no longer knew it as pain. Need I say I gladly banished it from my mind, sobbing gratitude to be relieved of an agony that had attended me so closely I'd forgotten how profound a hurt it was?

And with its passing my eyes—which were more acute than I could ever remember their being, even in my youth—found a new sight to astonish them. The air that I was expelling from my lungs had a bright solidity of its own; it came from me filled with flecks of delicate brilliance, as though a fire was stoked in me, and I was breathing out shards of flame. Was this some representation of my pain, I wondered? The room's—or my own delirium's—way of demonstrating the expulsion? That theory floated for ten seconds, then it was gone. The motes were about to show me their true nature, and it had nothing to do with pain.

They were still flowing from my mouth with every breath, but I wasn't watching those I'd just exhaled. It was those that had flown from me first which drew my startled sight. They were seeding their luminescence in the shadows—disappeared into the cloudy bed around me. I watched with what I'd like to think was almost scientific detachment. There was a certain logic to all that happened to me here; or so I now supposed. The shadows were only half the equation: they were a site of possibilities, no more than that; the fertile mud of this chamber, waiting for some galvanizing spark to bring forth—to bring forth *what*?

That was the question. What did the marriage of fire and shadow want to show me?

I didn't have to wait more than twenty seconds to discover the answer. No sooner had the first of the motes embedded themselves than the shadows surrendered their uncertainty, and blossomed.

The limits of the dome room had been banished. When the visions came—*and oh, how they came!*—they were vast.

First, out of the shadows, a landscape. The most primal of landscapes, in fact: rock and fire, and a flowing mass of magma. It was like the beginning of the world; red and black. It took me only a moment to make sense of this scene. The next, I was besieged with images, the scene before me transforming with every beat of my heart. Something flowered from the fire, gold and green, rising into a smoky sky. As it rose the blossoms it bore became fruit, and fell back onto the laval ground. I didn't have time to watch them be consumed. A motion in the smoke off to my right drew my gaze. An animal of some kind—with pale, scarred flanks—galloped through my field of vision. I felt the violence of its hooves in my bowels. And before it had passed from sight came another, and another, then a herd of these beasts—not horses, but something close to them. Had I made these creatures? I wondered. Had I exhaled them with my pain; and the fire too, and the rock and tree that rose from the rock? Was all this my invention, or perhaps some remote memory, which the enchantments of the room had somehow made visible?

Even as I shaped that thought the pale herd changed direction and came pounding at me. I instinctively covered my head, to keep my brains from being beaten out. But for all the fury of their hooves, the passage of the herd did me no more harm than a light breeze; they passed over me, and away.

I looked up. In the few seconds I'd had my eyes averted the ground had given prodigious birth. There were now sights to be seen on every side. Close by me, sliding through the very air from which it was being carved, a snake came, bright as a flower. Before it was even finished with its own creation another creature snatched it up, and my eyes rose to find before me a form that was vaguely human, but winged and sleek. The snake was gone in an instant, swallowed down the throat of this thing, which then settled its fiery eyes on me as though wondering if I too were edible. Plainly I looked like poor fare. Pumping its massive wings the creature rose like a curtain to reveal another drama, stranger still, behind it.

The tree I'd seen born had spread its seeds in every direction. In a few seconds a forest had sprung up, its churning canopy as dark as a thunderhead. And flitting between the trees were all manner of creatures, rising to nest, falling to rot. Close by me, an antelope stood in the dapple, shitting itself in terror. I looked for the cause. There; a few yards from the creature, something moved between the trees. I glimpsed only the glint off its eye, or tooth, until it suddenly broke cover, and came at its prey in one vast bound. A tiger, the size of four or five men. The antelope made to dart away, but its hunter was too fast. The tiger's claws sank into the antelope's silken flank and finished its leap with its prey beneath it. The death wasn't quick or pretty. The antelope thrashed wildly, though its body was torn wide open, and the tiger was tearing out its stringy throat. I didn't look away. I watched until the antelope was steaming meat, and the tiger sank down to dine. Only then did my eyes wander in search of new distractions.

There was something bright between the trees, I saw; brighter by the moment. Like a fire in its appetite, it climbed through the canopy as it approached, its advance above outpacing its steadier progress below. There was chaos in the thicket, as every species—hunter and hunted alike—fled before the blaze. But above me there was no escape. The fire came too fast, consuming birds in their flight, the chicks in their nests, monkeys and squirrels on the bough. Countless corpses fell around me, blackened and smoking. White hot ash came with them, powdering the ground.

I wasn't in fear for my life. By now I knew enough about this place to be confident of my immunity. But the scene appalled me nevertheless. What was I witnessing? Some primal cataclysm that had scoured this world? Undone it from sky to ground? If so, what was its source? This was no natural disaster, I was certain of that. The blaze above me had made itself into a kind of roof, creating in the moment of destruction a fretted vault, in which the dying were immortalized in fire. Tears started into my eyes, the sight moved me so. I reached to brush them out, so as not to miss whatever new glories or horrors were imminent, and as I did so I heard in my heart the first human utterance—other than my own noise—to come my way since I'd entered this chamber.

It was not a word; or if it was it was no word I knew. But it had meaning; at least that was my belief. To my ear it sounded like an open-throated shout raised by some newborn soul in the midst of the blaze; a yell of celebration and defiance. *Here I am!* it seemed to say. *Now we begin!*

I raised myself up on my hands to see if I could find the shouter (whether it was man or woman I couldn't yet decide) but the rain of ash and detritus was like a veil before me: I could see almost nothing through it.

My arms could not support me for more than a few moments. But as I sank back down to the ground, frustrated, the fire overhead—having perhaps exhausted its fuel—went out. The ash ceased falling. And there, standing no more than twenty yards from where I lay, the blaze surrounding her like a vast, fiery flower, was Cesaria. There was nothing about her attitude or her expression that suggested the fire threatened her. Far from it. She seemed rather to be luxuriating in its touch; her hands moving over her body as the conflagration bathed it, as though to be certain its balm penetrated every pore. Her hair, which was even blacker than her skin, flickered and twitched; her breasts seeped milk, her eyes ran silvery tears, her sex, which now and then she fingered, issued streams of blood.

I wanted to look away, but I couldn't. She was too exquisite, too ripe. It seemed to me that all I had seen before me in the last little while—the laval ground, the tree and its fruit, the pale herd, the hunted antelope and the tiger that took it; even the strange, winged creature that had briefly appeared in my vision—all of these were *in* and *of* the woman before me. She was their maker and their slaughterer; the sea into which they flowed and the rock from which they'd sprung.

I'd seen enough, I decided. I'd drunk down all I could bear to drink, and still keep my sanity. It was time I turned my back on these visions, and retreated to the safety of the mundane. I needed time to assimilate what I'd seen—and the thoughts that the sights had engendered.

But retreat was no easy business. Ungluing my eyes from the sight of my father's wife was hard enough; but when I did so, and looked back toward the door, I could not find it. The illusion surrounded me on every side; there was no hint of the real remaining. For the first time since the visions had begun I remembered Luman's talk of madness, and I was seized with panic. Had I carelessly let my hold on sanity slip, without even noticing that I'd done so? Was I now adrift in this illusion with no solid ground left for my senses?

I remembered with a shudder the crib in which Luman had been bound; and the look of unappeasable rage in his eyes. Was that all that lay before me now? A life without certainty, without solidity; this forest a prison I'd breathed into being, and that other world, where I'd been real and in my wounded fashion content, now a dream of freedom to which I could not return?

I closed my eyes to shut out the illusion. Like a child in terror, I prayed.

"*Oh Lord God in Heaven, look down on your servant at this moment; I beg of you . . . I need you with me.*

"*Help me. Please. Take these things out of my head. I don't want them, Lord. I don't want them.*"

Even as I whispered my prayer I felt a rush of energies against me. The blaze between the trees, which had come to a halt a little distance from me, was on the move again. I hastened my prayer, certain that if the fire was coming for me, then so was Cesaria.

"*Save me, Lord—*"

She was coming to silence me. That was my sudden conviction. She was a part of my insanity and she was coming to hush the words I'd uttered to defend myself against it.

"*Lord, please hear me—*"

The energies intensified, as though they intended to snatch the words away from my lips.

"*Quickly, Lord, quickly! Show me the way out of here! Please! God in Heaven, help me!*"

"Hush . . . ," I heard Cesaria say. She was right behind me. It seemed to me I could feel the small hairs at the nape of my neck fizzle and fry. I opened my eyes and looked over my shoulder. There she was, still cocooned in fire, her dark flesh shining. My mouth was suddenly parched; I could barely speak.

"I want . . . ,"

"I know," she said softly. "I know. I know. Poor child. Poor lost child. You want your mind back."

"Yes . . . ," I said. I was close to sobbing.

"But here it is," she said. "All around you. The trees. The fire. Me. All of it's *yours*."

"No," I protested. "I've never been in this place before."

"But it's been in you. This is where your father came looking for me, an age ago. He dreamed it into you when you were born."

"Dreamed it into me . . . ," I said.

"Every sight, every feeling. All he was and all he knew and all he knew was to come . . . it's in your blood and in your bowels."

"Then why am I so afraid of it?"

"Because you've held on to a simpler self for so long, you think you're the sum of what you can hold in your hands. But there are other hands holding you, child. Filled with you, these hands. Brimming with you . . . "

Did I dare believe any of this?

Cesaria replied as though she'd heard the doubt spoken aloud.

"I can't reassure you," she said. "Either you trust that these visions are a greater wisdom than you've ever known, or you try to rid yourself of them, and fall again."

"Fall where?"

"Why back into your own hands, of course," she said. Was she amused by me? By my tears and my trembling? I believe she was. But then I couldn't blame her; there was a part of me that also thought I was ridiculous, praying to a God I'd never seen, in order to escape the sight of glories a man of faith would have wept to witness. But I was afraid. Over and over I came back to that: *I was afraid.*

"Ask your question," Cesaria said. "You have a question. Ask it."

"It sounds so childish."

"Then have your answer and move on. But first you have to ask it."

"Am I . . . safe?"

"Safe?"

"Yes. Safe."

"In your flesh? No. I can't guarantee your safety in the flesh. But in your immortal form? Nothing and nobody can unbeget you. If you fall through your own fingers, there're other hands to hold you. I've told you that already."

"And . . . I think I believe you," I said.

"So then," Cesaria said, "you have no reason not to let the memories come."

She reached out toward me. Her hand was covered with countless snakes: as fine as hairs but brilliantly colored, yellow and red and blue, weaving their way between her fingers like living jewelry.

"Touch me," she said.

I looked up at her face, which wore an expression of sweet calm, and then back at the hand she wanted me to take.

"Don't be afraid," she said to me. "They don't bite."

I reached up and took her hand. She was right, the snakes didn't bite. But they *swarmed*; over her fingers and onto mine, squirming across the back of my hand and up onto my arm. I was so distracted by the sight of them that I didn't realize that she was pulling me up off the ground until I was almost standing up. I say *standing* though I can't imagine how that's possible; my legs were, until that moment, incapable of supporting me. Even so I found myself on my feet, gripping her hand, my face inches from her own.

I don't believe I had ever stood so close to my father's wife before. Even when I was a child, brought from England and accepted as her stepson, she always kept a certain distance from me. But now I stood (or seemed to stand) with my face inches from her own, feeling the snakes still writhing up my arm, but no longer caring to look down at them: not when I had the sight of her face before me. She was flawless. Her skin, for all its darkness, was possessed of an uncanny luminescence, her gaze, like her mouth, both lush and forbidding. Strands of her hair were lifted by gusts off the blaze around us (to the heat of which I seemed invulnerable) and brushed against my cheek. Their touch, though it was light, was nevertheless profoundly sensual. Feeling it, and seeing her exquisite features, I could not help but imagine what it would be like to be received into her arms. To kiss her, to lie with her, to put a child into her. It was little wonder my father had obsessed on her to his dying day, though all manner of argument and disappointment had soured the love between them.

"So now . . . ," she said.

"Yes?" I swear I would have done anything for her at that moment. I was like a lover standing before his beloved; I could deny her nothing.

"Take it back . . . ," she said.

I didn't comprehend what she was telling me. "Take what back?" I said.

"The breath. The pain. Me. Take it all back. It belongs to you Maddox. *Take it back.*"

I understood. It was time to repossess all that I'd attempted to put away from myself: the visions that were a part of my blood, though I'd hidden them from myself; the pain that was also, for better or worse, mine. And of course the very air from my lungs, whose expulsion had begun this journey.

"*Take it back.*"

I wanted to beg a few moments' grace, to talk with her, perhaps; at least to gaze at her, before my body was returned into its agony. But she was already easing her fingers from my grip.

"*Take it back,*" she said a third time, and to be certain I obeyed her edict she put her face close to mine and drew a breath of her own, a breath so swift and strong it emptied my mouth, throat, and lungs in an instant.

My head reeled; white blotches burned at the corners of my vision, threatening to occlude the sight before me. But my body acted with a vigor of its own, and without instruction from my will, did as Cesaria had demanded: it took the breath back.

The effect was immediate, and to my enchanted eyes distressing. The fabled face in front of me dissolved as though it had been conjured out of mist and my needy lungs had unmade it. I looked up—hoping to snatch a glimpse of the ancient sky before it too dissolved, but I was too late.

What had seemed unquestionably real moments before came to nothing in a heartbeat. No; not to nothing. It unknitted into marks such as had haunted the air when I'd first entered the room. Some of them still carried traces of color. There were smudges of blue and white above, and around me, where the thicket had not been consumed by fire, a hundred kinds of green; and ahead of me glints of gold from the flame and scarlet-flecked darkness where my father's wife had stood. But even these remains evaporated in the next heartbeat, and I was back in the arena of gray on gray which I had mistaken for a maze of stained walls.

From *Everville*

In sleep, Tesla found herself walking on an unearthly shore. Snow had lately fallen there, but she felt none of its chill. Light-footed, she wandered down to the sea. It was thick and dark, its turbulent waters scummy, and here and there she saw bodies in the surf, turning their stricken faces her way as if to warn her against entering.

She had no choice. The sea wanted her, and would not be denied. Nor, in truth, did she want to resist it. The shore was drear and desolate. The sea, for all its freight of corpses, was a place of mystery.

It was only once she was wading into the surf, the waves breaking against her breasts and her belly, that her dreaming mind put words to what place this was. Or rather, one word.

Quiddity.

The dream-sea leaped up against her face when she spoke its name, and its undertow pulled at her legs. She didn't attempt to fight it, but let it lift her off her feet and carry her away like an eager lover. The waves, which were substantial enough at the shore, soon grew titanic. When they raised her up on their shoulders she could see a wall of darkness at the horizon, the likes of which she remembered from her last moments in Kissoon's Loop. The lad, of course. Mountains and fleas; fleas and mountains. When they dropped her into their troughs, and she plunged below the surface, she glimpsed another spectacle entirely: vast shoals of fish, moving like thunderheads below her. And weaving between the shoals, luminous forms that were, she guessed, human spirits like herself. She seemed to see vestigial faces in their light; hints of the infants, lovers, and dying souls who were dreaming themselves here.

She had no doubt as to which of the three she was. Too old to be a baby, too crazy to be a lover, there was only one reason why her soul was journeying here tonight. Miss Perfection had been right. Death was imminent. This was the last time she would sleep before her span as Tesla Bombeck was over.

Even if she'd been distressed at this, she had no time to feel it. The adventure at hand demanded too much of her attention. Rising and falling, on shoulder and in trough, she was carried on toward a place where the waters, for some reason she could not comprehend, grew so utterly calm they made an almost perfect mirror for the busy sky.

She thought at first she was alone in these doldrums, and was about to test her powers of self-propulsion in order escape them, when she realized that a light was flickering beneath her. She looked down into the water, and saw that some species of fish with luminous flesh had congregated in the deep, and was now steadily rising toward the surface. When she raised her head from the water again she found that she was not alone. A long-haired, bearded man was casually crouching on the water as though it were as solid as a rock, idly creating ripples in the glassy surface. He had been there all along, she assumed, and she'd missed him. But now, as if roused from some reverie by her gaze, he looked up.

His face was scrawny—his bones sharp, his black eyes sharper—but the smile he offered was so sweetly tentative, as though he was a little embarrassed to have been caught unawares, that she was instantly charmed. He rose, the water dancing around his feet, and ambled over to her. His water-soaked robes were in tatters, and she could see that his torso was covered with small, pale scars, as though he'd been wrestling in broken glass.

She sympathized with his condition. She too was scarred, inside and out; she too had been stripped of all she'd worn in the world: her profession, her self-esteem, her certainty.

"Do we know each other?" he said to her as he approached. His voice lacked music, but she liked the sound of it nevertheless.

"No," she said, suddenly tongue-tied. "I don't believe so."

"Somebody spoke of you to me, I'm certain. Was it Fletcher perhaps?"

"You know Fletcher?"

"Then it was," the man said, smiling again. "You're the one who martyred him."

"I hadn't thought of it that way—but yes, I guess that was me."

"You see?" he said. He went down on his haunches beside her, while the water buoyed her up. "You wanted connections, and they're there to be found. But you have to look in the terrible places, Tesla. The places where death comes to take love away, where we lose each other and lose ourselves; that's where the connections begin. It takes a brave soul to look there and not despair."

"I've tried to be brave," she said.

"I know," he said softly. "I know."

"But I wasn't brave enough, is that what you're saying? The thing is, I didn't ask to be part of this. I wasn't ready for it. I was just going to write movies, you know, and get rich and smug. I guess that sounds pathetic to you."

"Why?"

"Well, I don't suppose you get to see a lot of movies."

"You'd be surprised," the man said with a little smile. "Anyway, it's the stories that matter, however they're told."

She thought of the child at the crossroads—

We saw your face, and we said: She knows about the story tree.

"What's the big deal about stories?" she said.

"You love them," he said, his gaze leaving her face and slipping down to the water. The glowing forms she'd seen rising from below were within a few fathoms of the surface now. The water was beginning to simmer with their presence. "You do, don't you?" he said.

"I suppose I do," she said.

"That's what the connections are, Tesla."

"Stories?"

"Stories. And every life, however short, however meaningless it seems, is a leaf—"

"A leaf."

"Yes, a leaf." He looked up at her again, and waited, unspeaking, until she grasped the sense of what he was saying.

"On the story tree," she said. He smiled. "Lives are leaves on the story tree."

"Simple, isn't it?" he said. The bubbles were breaking all around them now, and the surface was no longer glacial enough to bear him up. He started to sink into the water; slowly, slowly. "I'm afraid I have to go," he said. "The 'shu have come for me. Why do you look so unhappy?"

"Because it's too late," she said. "Why did I have to wait until now to know what I was supposed to do?"

"You didn't need to know. You were doing it."

"No I wasn't," she said, distressed now. "I never got to tell a story I gave a damn about."

"Oh but you did," he said. He was almost gone from sight now.

"What story was that?" she begged him, determined to get an answer before he disappeared. "What?"

"Your own," he told her, slipping from sight. "*Your own.*"

Then he was gone.

She stared down into the bubbling water, and saw that the creatures he'd called the 'shu—which resembled cuttlefish as far as she could see, and were congregated below her in their many millions—were describing a vast spiral around the sinking man, as though drawing him down into their midst.

From *Paradise Street*

CAROLINE STEPS FORWARD: THE ROOM DISAPPEARS BEHIND HER. SHE SPEAKS TO THE AUDIENCE.

CAROLINE: I had this dream. I was in my mother's kitchen. I was only small. She was cutting open a fish. I'd seen her do it a hundred times. Our family was very fond of fish. She took a sharp knife and slit it open. And my father, who was leaning on the sink with a glass of dark beer, beer froth on his mustache, my father laughed. My mother reached into the guts of the fish she'd cut open and pulled out another fish. But this one—dreams are strange, aren't they?— this one was bigger, much bigger than the first, wet and shining and alive. It smelled fresh: of the sea, of the deep sea, of the dark sea. My father throws his glass of beer into the sink, and before we can help him, the living fish has leaped out of my mother's hand and eaten him up, in our kitchen. I woke up right then. I swear I was smiling. CAROLINE EXITS.

From *The History of the Devil*

THE DEVIL HOLDS UP A FILTHY, PATCHED-UP BOOK.

CATHARINE LAMB: What is that?

THE DEVIL: The diary of Jesus Christ.

POPPER: Diary?

THE DEVIL: In his own hand: given to me at Golgotha, by his far from virginal mother. There is in it a passage relating to me—

POPPER: Prosecution? What are your views on this?

CATHARINE LAMB: It could be a forgery.

THE DEVIL: M'lord, it would not be wise for a creature in my condition, knowing I'm overlooked by Heaven, to present to the Court a forgery. If this book is not the true word of God's son, may I be struck down now. (He waits, watching the sky) See?

POPPER: Well?

CATHARINE LAMB: By all means, let's have the evidence. It was the episode in the desert I was interested in.

THE DEVIL: (Smiling) It's here. It's all here.

POPPER: Milo. Do you want to read it to the Court?

MILO MILO: (Taking the book) Where from?

THE DEVIL: Below the wine stain.

MILO MILO: (Reads) It was hot. My hair went yellow. I met a lion. I met another lion. I saw two baboons having a fuck. When I was in the desert four weeks, I was hungry. I was being chased. I ran away, but they chased me. I was thirsty. I met a man—

THE SCENE CHANGES. THE COURT DISAPPEARS. WE'RE IN A BLAZING DESERT. ENTER THE DEVIL, CLOSELY PURSUED BY JESUS CHRIST, WHO CARRIES TWO SHARPENED STICKS.

CHRIST: Don't move.

THE DEVIL: *(Raising his arms in surrender)* I'm past moving. Impale me.

CHRIST: No tricks.

THE DEVIL: Me, tricks?

CHRIST: And if you see the little blue wheels, tell me. Empty your pockets.

THE DEVIL: Nothing.

CHRIST: You must have some food.

THE DEVIL: You're right, I must have some food.

CHRIST: I'll take pork.

THE DEVIL: I'll take it first.

CHRIST: What sort of world is this?

THE DEVIL: An empty one, inside and out. What's your name?

CHRIST: Jesus Christ. The Nazarene.

THE DEVIL: I heard of you, down south.

CHRIST: I'm famous; that's why the blue wheels are after me.

THE DEVIL: My friend, you are suffering from hallucinations.

CHRIST: You think I don't know that? Before you fade away, scratch my back.

THE DEVIL: Anything for a fellow Messiah. *(He obliges)*

CHRIST: Higher: left: left: there. You say you're a Messiah, too?

THE DEVIL: Yes.

CHRIST: That's why I'm here: to purify myself. If I could only stop itching.

THE DEVIL: Ticks.

CHRIST: Nits, ticks, fleas. But you have to go among the multitudes.

THE DEVIL: Do you want to put those sticks down?

CHRIST: Any good at hunting? I've seen lizards. Do you think lizard's kosher?

THE DEVIL: Everything's kosher in desperation. Moses ate his mother. Mama from heaven.

CHRIST: *(Outraged)* I wouldn't eat my mother.

THE DEVIL: *(Pained by his lack of humor)* No, I didn't mean—

CHRIST: That's not very kind.

THE DEVIL: No, it isn't.

CHRIST: I think I ought to tell you, you may as well as go home. I'm the
    Messiah.

THE DEVIL: I think not.

CHRIST: They love me.

THE DEVIL: Cautionary tales. Coins, rainbows: it's not sufficient to win the
    world, Jesus.

CHRIST: *(Like a child)* Well, we'll fight it out, then.

THE DEVIL: No.

CHRIST: Come on: fight me.

THE DEVIL: I don't want to fight.

CHRIST: Fight! Fight!

> THE DEVIL DOESN'T MOVE, SO CHRIST ATTACKS HIM. THE DEVIL
> QUICKLY WRESTLES HIM TO THE FLOOR.

CHRIST: I won't give up. I won't, you hear me? I won't!

THE DEVIL: What would it take to dissuade you?

CHRIST: I'm the Messiah.

THE DEVIL: I could give you a great deal.

CHRIST: Like what?

THE DEVIL: I've got contacts. Solomon's wife is in the family. People in
    power all across the known world. I could give you cities.

CHRIST: Rome?

THE DEVIL: It might be arranged. But you'd have to give up your preten-
    sions to Messiahdom.

CHRIST: I couldn't do that.

THE DEVIL: What a pity. *(He takes out rope)*

CHRIST: What's that for? *(Realizes)* You can't kill me.

THE DEVIL: Who's to see?

CHRIST: My father. Didn't I tell you? My father in Heaven. I'm the Son of
    God.

THE DEVIL: What?

CHRIST: So I wouldn't try to hurt me: unless—you wanted to do it in pub-
    lic.

THE DEVIL: Strangle you?

CHRIST: No, no. But the time's coming when I have to make an exit.

THE DEVIL: Why?

CHRIST: I'm running out of stories. And I'm tired. So I'll have to die. You
    could arrange it.

THE DEVIL: No.

CHRIST: A terrible death.

THE DEVIL: I'm not an executioner.

CHRIST: The worst death imaginable.

THE DEVIL: Torn apart by dogs.

CHRIST: Too messy: I don't want to be resurrected in pieces. I must be
marked but . . . intact.

THE DEVIL: Run over by a horse?

CHRIST: It could be comic. No, I want something spectacular. On a hill. A
good view. A sunset. Clouds.

THE DEVIL: Crucifixion.

CHRIST: Everyone gets that. They do it to sodomites these days. Half of
Israel should be up there. Isn't there something they do in the East
with hooks through the skin? Swing you round a pole on hooks?
Takes days. And so unusual.

THE DEVIL: I don't know of it.

CHRIST: Damn.

THE DEVIL: You'll have to compromise.

CHRIST: What? Crucifixion?

THE DEVIL: Unless we think of something better.

CHRIST: *(Grabs the Devil)* Will you promise me? Promise you'll arrange it.

THE DEVIL: Yes, I promise.

CHRIST: *(With relish)* I want to be publicly flogged. I must be bloodied,
humiliated, reduced to a wounded, whimpering animal. Something
on the head—

THE DEVIL: Roses—

CHRIST: Or some such. I'll be naked, hung up there like a slab of meat,
then the clouds'll boil, lions roar, perhaps an earthquake, and I'll die.
And they'll all know what they did, killing me—you promise you'll
do it?

THE DEVIL: I told you, yes. Sure as God made little apples.

CHRIST: Good man. Now get thee behind me.

THE DEVIL: Why?

CHRIST: You're in my way.

> EXIT JESUS, AT A RUN, LEAVING THE DEVIL BEMUSED AND
> EXHAUSTED. THE COURT REAPPEARS.

THE DEVIL: *(To the audience)* I kept my word. There was a demon called
Carreau posing as a Roman governor. He had the man crucified. I
was there. He saw me in the crowd: instructed his mother to give me

the diary. Even thanked me. He was quite changed: sick looking, thinking better of it. But he got his roses.

POPPER: This makes him sound like an imbecile.

THE DEVIL: Oh no, I was the dupe. Here was me, thinking I was getting rid of a competitor, and in fact I was stage managing his apotheosis. I tell you, when I saw them fall down on their knees at Golgotha, I wept. I was tricked, tricked!—and you called me the Father of Lies. You put me on trial while he goes free. He gets a cult to himself, but my synagogue is blasphemy. When I think . . .

A DIN OF SUPPORT HAS RISEN FROM THE DEMONS IN THE EARTH.

POPPER: Order in the Court! Please! Please! *(To the Devil)* Will you hush your faction?

THE DEVIL: *(He puts his fingers to his lips. The din quietens.)* The earth was given to me: remember that. I was to be Prince of the World. But now, it was Christian. Though I was an exile, they found me everywhere. Here's the Devil, they said, possessing pigs and small boys. Ha! Here's the Devil, they said, in everything diseased and putrescent. The world rose against me. Everywhere: slandered, my works twisted, my ambitions destroyed and my face dragged in fear and loathing.

SAM KYLE: Could we have a recess?

POPPER: No!

THE DEVIL: That's right: no sympathy for the Devil.

POPPER: Sit down!

THE DEVIL: Do you know how difficult it is not to believe what people say about you? Not to become your own publicity? Be thankful, Felix Popper, I'm not the Devil you think I am, because if I were, if I once believed the image of myself, I'd devour you.

POPPER: Order! Order!

THE DEVIL: Judgment! Judgment!

POPPER: Sit down!

FROM THE EARTH, THE DEMONS CHANT: "JUDGMENT! JUDGMENT!"

POPPER: Order! Order! Silence your faction or I'll throw them out of Court!

THE DEVIL: They've been thrown out of finer places.

From *Sacrament*

I t was very simple. Sherwood, poor Sherwood, was dead, sprawled there on the floor, and his murderer was standing here right in front of Will, and there was a knife in Will's hand, trembling to be put to its purpose. It didn't care that Steep had once been its owner; it only wanted to be used. *Now; quickly!* Never mind that the flesh it would be butchering belonged to the man who'd treated it like a holy relic. All that mattered was to glint and glitter in the deed; to rise and fall and rise again red.

"Have you come to give that back to me?" Steep said.

Will could barely fumble a reply, his mind was so filled with the knife's advertisements for its skills. How it would lop off Steep's ears and nose; reduce his beauty to a wound. He sees you still? Scoop out his eyes! His screams distress you? Cut out his tongue!

They were terrible thoughts; sickening thoughts. Will didn't want them. But they kept coming.

Steep on his back now, naked. And the knife opening his chest—one, two—exposing his beating heart. You want his nipples for souvenirs? Here! Something more intimate perhaps? Meat for the fox—

And before Will knew what he was doing, his hand was up, the knife exalting. It would have opened Steep's face to the bone a moment later had Steep not reached up and caught the blade in his fist. Oh it stung him; even him. His perfect lips curled in pain, and a hiss came between his perfect teeth; a soft hiss that died into a sigh, as he expelled every vestige of air.

Will attempted to pull the knife out of his grip. Surely it would slice the sheath of Steep's palm, and free itself; its edges were too keen to be contained. But it didn't move. He tugged again, harder. Still it didn't move. And again he pulled; but still Steep held it fast.

Will's eyes flickered from the knife to his enemy's face. Steep had not drawn breath since he'd exhaled his sigh; he was staring at Will, his mouth open a little way, as though he were about to speak.

Then, of course, he inhaled. It was no common breath; no simple summoning of air. It was Steep's reprise of what had happened on the hill, thirty years before, except that this time he was the one commanding the moment, unknitting the world around them. It flickered out on the instant, the floor seeming to fall away beneath their feet, so that Will and Steep seemed to hang above a velvet immensity, connected only by the blade.

"I want you to share this with me," Steep said softly, as though he had found a fine wine and was inviting Will to drink from the same cup. The darkness was solidifying beneath their feet: a roiling dust, ebbing, and flowing. But all around them otherwise, darkness. And above, darkness. No clouds; nor stars, nor moon.

"Where are we?" Will breathed, looking back at Steep. Jacob's face was not as solid as it had been. The once smooth skin of his brow and cheek had become grainy, and the murk behind him seemed to be leaking through his eye. "Can you hear me?" Will wanted to know. But the face before him continued to lose coherence. And now, though Will knew this was just a vision, panic began to grow in him. Suppose Steep deserted him here, in this emptiness?

"Stay . . . ," he found himself saying, like a child afraid to be left alone in the dark. "Please stay . . ."

"What are you frightened of?" Steep said. The darkness had almost claimed his face entirely. "You can tell me."

"I don't want to get lost," Will replied.

"There's no help for that," Steep said. "Not unless we know our way to God. And that's hard in this confusion. This *sickening* confusion." Though his image had almost disappeared completely now, his voice remained, soft and solicitous. "Listen to that din . . ."

"Don't go."

"*Listen,*" Steep told him.

Will could hear the noise Steep was referring to. It wasn't a single sound, it was a thousand, a thousand thousand, coming at him from every direction at once. It wasn't strident, nor was it sweet or musical. It was simply insistent. And its source? That was coming, too, from all directions. Tidal multitudes of pale, indistinguishable forms, crawling toward him. No, not crawling: *being born.* Creatures spreading their limbs and purging themselves of infants that, even in the moment of their birth, were ungluing their legs to be fertilized; and before their partners had rolled off them were spreading their limbs to expel another generation. And on; and on; in sickening multitudes, their mingled mewlings and sighings and sobs the din that Steep had said drowned out God.

It wasn't hard for Will to fathom what he was witnessing. This was what Steep saw when he looked at living things. Not their beauty, not their particularity, just their smothering, deafening fecundity. Flesh begetting flesh, din begetting din. It wasn't hard to fathom, because he'd thought it himself, in his darkest times. Seen the human tide advancing on species he'd loved—beasts too wild or too wise to compromise with the invader—and wished for a plague to wither every human womb. Heard the din and longed for a gentle death to silence every throat. Sometimes not even gentle. He understood. Oh Lord, he understood.

"Are you still there?" he said to Steep.

"Still here . . . ," the man replied.

"Make it go away."

"That's what I've been trying to do all these years," Steep replied.

The rising tide of life was almost upon them, forms being born and being born, spilling around Will's feet.

"Enough," Will said.

"You understand my point of view?"

"Yes . . ."

"Louder."

"*Yes!* I understand. Perfectly."

The admission was enough to banish the horror. The tide retreated, and a moment later was gone entirely, leaving Will hanging in the darkness again.

"Isn't this a finer place?" Steep said. "In a hush like this we might have a hope of knowing who we are. There's no error here. No imperfection. Nothing to distract us from God."

"This is the way you want the world?" Will murmured. "Empty?"

"Not empty. Cleansed."

"Ready to begin again?"

"Oh no."

"But it will. Steep. You might drive things into hiding for a while, but there'll always be some mudflat you missed, some rock you didn't lift. And life *will* come back. Maybe not human life. Maybe something better. But *life*, Jacob. You can't kill the world."

"I'll reduce it to a petal," Jacob replied, lightly. Will could hear the smile in the man's voice as he spoke. "And God'll be there. Plain. I'll see Him, plain. And I'll understand why I was made." His face was starting to congeal again. There was the wide, pale brow, sheltering that deep, troubled gaze; the fine nose, the finer mouth.

"Suppose you're wrong," Will said. "Suppose God wanted the world to be filled? Ten thousand kinds of buttercup? A million kinds of beetle? No two of anything alike. Just suppose. Suppose you're the enemy of God, Jacob. Suppose . . . you're the Devil and you don't know it?"

"I'd know. Though I can't see Him yet. God moves in me."

"Well," said Will, "He moves in me too." And the words, though he'd never thought he'd hear them from his own tongue, were true. God *was* in him now. Always had been. Steep had the rage of some Judgmental Father in his eye, but the divinity Will had in him was no less a Lord, though He talked through the mouth of a fox and loved life more than Will had supposed life could be loved. A Lord who'd come before him in innumerable shapes over the years. Some pitiful, to be sure, some triumphant. A blind polar bear on a rubbish heap; two children in painted masks; Patrick sleeping. Patrick smiling, Patrick speaking love. Camellias on a windowsill and the skies of Africa. His Lord was there, everywhere, inviting him to see the soul of things.

Sensing the certainty moving in Will, Steep countered in the only way he knew how.

"I put the hunger for death in you," he said. "That makes you mine. We might both regret it, but it's the truth."

How could Will deny it, while that knife was still in his hand? Taking his gaze from Steep's face, he sought the weapon out, following the form of the man's shoulder, along his arm to the fist that was still gripping the blade, and down, down to his own hand, which still grasped the hilt.

Then, seeing it, he let it go. It was so simple to do. The sum of the blade's harms would not be swelled by his wielding of it; not by a single wound.

The consequence of his letting go was instantaneous. The darkness was instantly extinguished, and the solid world sprang up around him: the hallway, the body, the staircase that led up to the open roof, through which straight beams of sun were coming.

And in front of him, Steep; staring at him with a curious look on his face. Then he shuddered, and his fingers opened just enough to allow the blade to slide from his grip. It had opened his palm, deeply, and the wound was seeping. It wasn't blood that came, however. It was the same stuff that had seeped from Rosa's body; finer threads from a smaller wound, but the same bright liquor. Fragments of it curled lazily around his fingers, and without thinking what he was doing, Will reached out to touch it. The threads sensed him, and came to meet his hand. He heard Steep tell him no, but it was too late. Contact had been made. Once again, he felt the matter pass into him and through him. This time, however, he was prepared to watch for its revelation, and he wasn't disappointed. The face before him unveiled itself, its flesh confessing the mystery that lay beneath. He knew it already. The same strange beauty he'd seen lurking in Rosa was here in Steep too: the form of the Nilotic, like something carved from the eternal.

"What did Rukenau do to you two?" Will said softly.

The flesh inside Steep's flesh stared out at him like a prisoner, despairing of release. "Tell me," Will pressed. Still it said nothing. Yet it wanted to speak; Will could see the desire to do so in its eyes; how it wanted to tell its story. He leaned a little closer to it. "Try," he said.

It inclined its head toward him, until their mouths were only three or four inches apart. No sound escaped it; nor could, Will suspected. The prisoner had been mute too long to find its voice again so quickly. But while they were so close, gaze meeting gaze, he could not waste its proximity. He leaned another inch toward it, and the Nilotic, knowing what was coming, smiled. Then Will kissed it, lightly, reverently, on the lips.

The creature returned his kiss, pressing its cool mouth against his.

The next moment, as had happened with Rosa, the thread of light burned itself out in him, and was gone. The veil fell instantly, obscuring what lay beneath, and the face Will was kissing was Steep's face.

Jacob pushed him away with a shout of disgust, as though he'd momentarily shared Will's trance and only now realized what the power inside him had sanctioned. Then he fell back against the wall, tightly clenching his wounded hand closed to be certain no more of this traitorous fluid escaped, and with the back of his other hand, wiped his lips clean. He scoured every trace of gentility from his face as he did so. All perplexity, all doubt, were gone. Fixing Will with a rabid gaze, he reached down and picked up the knife that lay between them. There was no room for further exchange, Will knew. Steep wasn't going to be talking about God or forgiveness any longer. All he wanted to do was kill the man who'd just kissed him.

Even though he knew there was no hope of peace now, Will took his time as he retreated to the door, studying Steep. When next they met, it would be death for one of them; this would most likely be his last opportunity to look at the man whose brotherhood he had so passionately wanted to share. A kiss such as they'd exchanged was nothing to a man who was certain of himself. But Steep was not certain; never had been. Like so many of the men Will had watched and wanted in his life, he lived in fear of his manhood being seen for what it was, a murderous figment; a trick of spit and swagger that concealed a far stranger spirit.

He could watch no longer; another five seconds and the knife would be at his throat. He turned, and took himself off across the threshold, down the path, and out into the street. Steep didn't follow. He would brood a while, Will guessed, putting his thoughts in murderous order before he began his final pursuit.

And pursue he would. Will had kissed the spirit in him, and that was a crime the figment would never forgive. It would come, knife in hand. Nothing was more certain.

From *Imajica*

W hen he got back to the hotel, Gentle's first instinct was to call Jude. She'd made her feelings toward him abundantly clear, of course, and common sense decreed that he leave this little drama to fizzle out, but he'd glimpsed too many enigmas tonight to be able to shrug off his unease and walk away. Though the streets of this city were solid, their buildings numbered and named, though the avenues were bright enough even at night to banish ambiguity, he still felt as though he was on the margin of some unknown land, in danger of crossing into it without realizing he was even doing so. And if *he* went, might Jude not also follow? Determined though she was to divide her life from his, the obscure suspicion remained in him that their fates were interwoven.

He had no logical explanation for this. The feeling was a mystery, and mysteries weren't his specialty. They were the stuff of after-dinner conversation, when—mellowed by brandy and candlelight—people confessed to fascinations they wouldn't have broached an hour earlier. Under such influence he'd heard rationalists confess their devotion to tabloid astrologies; heard atheists lay claim to heavenly visitations; heard tales of psychic siblings and prophetic deathbed pronouncements. They'd all been amusing enough, in their way. But this was something different. This was happening to him, and it made him afraid.

He finally gave in to his unease. He located Marlin's number and called the apartment. The lover boy picked up. He sounded agitated and became more so when Gentle identified himself.

"I don't know what your goddamn game is," he said.

"It's no game," Gentle told him.

"You just keep away from this apartment—"

"I've no intention—"

"Because if I see your face. I swear—"

"Can I speak to Jude?"

"Judith's not—"

"I'm on the other line," Jude said.

"Judith, put down the phone! You don't want to be talking with this scum."

"Calm down, Marlin."

"You heard her, Mervin. Calm down."

Marlin slammed down the receiver.

"Suspicious, is he?" Gentle said.

"He thinks this is all your doing."

"So you told him about Estabrook?"

"No, not yet."

"You're just going to blame the hired hand, is that it?"

"Look, I'm sorry about some of the things I said. I wasn't thinking straight. If it hadn't been for you maybe I'd be dead by now."

"No maybe about it," Gentle said. "Our friend Pie meant business."

"He meant *something*," she replied. "But I'm not sure it was murder."

"He was trying to smother you, Jude."

"Was he? Or was he just trying to hush me? He had such a strange look—"

"I think we should talk about this face to face," Gentle said. "Why don't you slip away from lover boy for a late-night drink? I can pick you up right outside your building. You'll be quite safe."

"I don't think that's such a good idea. I've got packing to do. I've decided to go back to London tomorrow."

"Was that planned?"

"No, I'd just feel more secure if I was at home."

"Is Mervin going with you?"

"It's Marlin. And no, he isn't."

"More fool him."

"Look, I'd better go. Thanks for thinking of me."

"It's no hardship," he said. "And if you get lonely between now and tomorrow morning—"

"I won't."

"You never know. I'm at the Omni. Room one-oh-three. There's a double bed."

"You'll have plenty of room, then."

"I'll be thinking of you," he said. He paused, then added. "I'm glad I saw you."

"I'm glad you're glad."

"Does that mean you're not?"

"It means I've got packing to do. Good night. Gentle."

"Good night."

"Have fun."

He did what little packing of his own he had to do, then ordered up a small supper: a club sandwich, ice cream, bourbon, and coffee. The warmth of the room after the icy street and its exertions made him feel sluggish. He undressed and ate his supper naked in front of the television, picking the crumbs from his pubic hair like lice. By the time he got to the ice cream he was too weary to eat, so he downed the bourbon—which instantly took its toll—and retired to bed, leaving the television on in the next room, its sound turned down to a soporific burble.

His body and his mind went about their different businesses. The former, freed from conscious instruction, breathed, rolled, sweated, and digested. The latter went dreaming. First, of Manhattan served on a plate, sculpted in perfect detail. Then of a waiter, speaking in a whisper, asking if sir wanted *night*; and of night coming in the form of a blueberry syrup, poured from high above the plate and falling in viscous folds upon the streets and towers. Then, Gentle walking in those streets, between those towers, hand in hand with a shadow, the company of which he was happy to keep, and which turned when they reached an intersection and laid its feather finger upon the middle of his brow, as though Ash Wednesday were dawning.

He liked the touch and opened his mouth to lightly lick the ball of the shadow's hand. It stroked the place again. He shuddered with pleasure, wishing he could see into the darkness of this other and know its face. In straining to see, he opened his eyes, body and mind converging once again. He was back in his hotel room, the only light the flicker of the television, reflected in the gloss of a half-open door. Though he was awake the sensation continued, and to it was added sound: a milky sigh that excited him. There was a woman in the room.

"Jude?" he said.

She pressed her cool palm against his open mouth, hushing his inquiry even as she answered it. He couldn't distinguish her from the darkness, but any lingering doubt that she might belong to the dream from which he'd risen was dispatched as her hand went from his mouth to his bare chest. He reached up in the darkness to take hold of her face and bring it down to his mouth, glad that the murk concealed the satisfaction he wore. She'd come to him. After all the signals of rejection she'd sent out at the apartment—despite Marlin, despite the dangerous streets, despite the hour, despite their bitter history—she'd come, bearing the gift of her body to his bed.

Though he couldn't see her, the darkness was a black canvas, and he painted her there to perfection, her beauty gazing down on him. His hands found her flawless cheeks. They were cooler than her hands, which were on his belly now, pressing harder as she hoisted herself over him. There was everywhere in their exchange an exquisite synchronicity. He thought of her tongue and tasted it: he imagined her breasts, and she took his hands to them: he wished she would speak, and she spoke (oh, how she spoke), words he hadn't dared admit he'd wanted to hear.

"I had to do this . . ." she said.

"I know. I know."

"Forgive me."

"What's to forgive?"

"I can't be without you, Gentle. We belong to each other, like man and wife."

With her here, so close after such an absence, the idea of marriage didn't seem so preposterous. Why not claim her now and forever?

"You want to marry me?" he murmured.

"Ask me again another night," she replied.

"I'm asking you now."

She put her hand back upon that anointing place in the middle of his brow. "Hush," she said. "What you want now you might not want tomorrow . . ."

He opened his mouth to disagree, but the thought lost its way between his brain and his tongue, distracted by the small circular motions she was making on his forehead. A calm emanated from the place, moving down through his torso and out to his fingertips. With it, the pain of his bruising faded. He raised his hands above his head, stretching to let bliss run through him freely. Released from aches he'd become accustomed to, his body felt new minted: gleaming invisibly.

"I want to be inside you," he said.

"How far?"

"All the way."

He tried to divide the darkness and catch some glimpse of her response, but his sight was a poor explorer and returned from the unknown without news. Only a flicker from the television, reflected in the gloss of his eye and thrown up against the blank darkness, lent him the illusion of a luster passing through her body, opaline. He started to sit up, seeking her face, but she was already moving down the bed, and moments later he felt her lips on his stomach, and then upon the head of his cock, which she took into her mouth by degrees, her tongue playing on it as she went, until he thought he would lose control. He warned her with a murmur, was released, and, a breath later, swallowed again.

The absence of sight lent potency to her touch. He felt every motion of tongue and tooth in play upon him, his prick, particularized by her appetite, becoming vast in his mind's eye until it was his body's size: a veiny torso and a blind head lying on the bed of his belly wet from end to end, straining and shuddering, while she, the darkness, swallowed him utterly. He was only sensation now, and she its supplier, his body enslaved by bliss, unable to remember its making or conceive of its undoing. God, but she knew how he liked to be pleasured, taking care not to stale his nerves with repetition, but cajoling his juice into cells already brimming, until he was ready to come in blood and be murdered by her work, willingly.

Another skitter of light behind his eye broke the hold of sensation, and he was once again entire—his prick its modest length—and she not darkness but a body through which waves of iridescence seemed to pass. Only *seemed*, he knew. This was his sight-starved eyes' invention. Yet it came again, a sinuous light, sleeking her, then going out. Invention or not it made him want her more completely, and he put his arms beneath her shoulders, lifting her up and off him. She rolled over to his side, and he reached across to undress her. Now that she was lying against white sheets her form was visible, albeit vaguely. She moved beneath his hand, raising her body to his touch.

"Inside you . . . ," he said, rummaging through the damp folds of her clothes.

Her presence beside him had stilled; her breathing lost its irregularity. He bared her breasts, put his tongue to them as his hands went down to the belt of her skirt, to find that she'd changed for the trip and was wearing jeans. Her hands were on the belt, almost as if to deny him. But he wouldn't be delayed or denied. He pulled the jeans down around her hips, feeling skin so smooth beneath his hands it was almost fluid; her whole body a slow curve, like a wave about to break over him.

For the first time since she'd appeared she said his name, tentatively, as though in this darkness she'd suddenly doubted he was real.

"I'm here," he replied. "Always."

"This is what you want?" she said.

"Of course it is. Of course," he replied, and put his hand on her sex.

This time the iridescence, when it came, was almost bright, and fixed in his head the image of her crotch, his fingers sliding over and between her labia. As the light went, leaving its afterglow on his blind eyes, he was vaguely distracted by a ringing sound, far off at first but closer with every repetition. The telephone, damn it! He did his best to ignore it, failed, and reached out to the bedside table where it sat, throwing the receiver off its cradle and returning to her in one graceless motion. The body beneath him was once again perfectly still. He climbed on top of her and slid inside. It was like being sheathed in silk. She put her hands up around his neck, her fingers strong, and raised her head a little way off the bed to meet his kisses. Though their mouths were clamped together he could hear her saying his name— "Gentle? Gentle?"—with that same questioning tone she'd had before. He didn't let memory divert him from his present pleasure, but found his rhythm: long, slow strokes. He remembered her as a woman who liked him to take his time. At the height of their affair they'd made love from dusk to dawn on several occasions, toying and teasing, stopping to bathe so they'd have the bliss of working up a second sweat. But this was an encounter that had none of the froth of those liaisons. Her fingers were digging hard at his back, pulling him onto her with each thrust. And still he heard her voice, dimmed by the veils of his self-consumption: "Gentle? Are you there?"

"I'm here," he murmured.

A fresh tide of light was rising through them both, the erotic becoming a visionary toil as he watched it sweep over their skin, its brightness intensifying with every thrust.

Again she asked him, "Are you there?"

How could she doubt it? He was never more present than in this act, never more comprehending of himself than when buried in the other sex.

"I'm here," he said.

Yet she asked again, and this time, though his mind was stewed in bliss, the tiny voice of reason murmured that it wasn't his lady who was asking the question at all, but the woman on the telephone. He'd thrown the receiver off the hook, but she was haranguing the empty line, demanding he reply. Now he listened. There was no mistaking the voice. It was Jude. And if Jude was on the line, who the fuck was he fucking?

Whoever it was, she knew the deception was over. She dug deeper into the flesh of his lower back and buttocks, raising her hips to press him deeper into her still, her sex tightening around his cock as though to prevent him from leaving her unspent. But he was sufficiently master of himself to resist and pulled out of her, his heart thumping like some crazy locked up in the cell of his chest.

"*Who the hell are you?*" he yelled.

Her hands were still upon him. Their heat and their demand, which had so aroused him moments before, unnerved him now. He threw her off and started to reach toward the lamp on the bedside table. She took hold of his erection as he did so and slid her palm along the shaft. Her touch was so persuasive he almost succumbed to the idea of entering her again, taking her anonymity as carte blanche and indulging in the darkness every last desire he could dredge up. She was putting her mouth where her hand had been, sucking him into her. He regained in two heartbeats the hardness he'd lost.

Then the whine of the empty line reached his ears. Jude had given up trying to make contact. Perhaps she'd heard his panting and the promises he'd been making in the dark. The thought brought new rage. He took hold of the woman's head and pulled her from his lap. What could have possessed him to want somebody he couldn't even see? And what kind of whore offered herself that way? Diseased? Deformed? Psychotic? He had to see. However repulsive, he had to see!

He reached for the lamp a second time, feeling the bed shake as the harridan prepared to make her escape. Fumbling for the switch, he brought the lamp off its perch. It didn't smash, but its beams were cast up at the ceiling, throwing a gauzy light down on the room below. Suddenly fearful she'd attack him, he turned without picking the lamp up, only to find that the woman had already claimed her clothes from the snarl of sheets and was retreating to the bedroom door. His eyes had been feeding on darkness and projections for too long, and now, presented with solid reality, they were befuddled. Half concealed by shadow the woman was a mire of shifting forms—face blurred, body smeared, pulses of iridescence, slow now, passing from toes to head. The only fixable element in this flux was her eyes, which stared back at him mercilessly. He wiped his hand from brow to chin in the hope of sloughing the illusion off, and in these seconds she opened the door to make her escape. He leaped from the bed, still determined to get past his confusions to the grim truth he'd coupled with, but she was already halfway through the door, and the only way he could stop her was to seize hold of her arm.

Whatever power had deranged his senses, its bluff was called when he made contact with her. The roiling forms of her face resolved themselves like pieces of a multifaceted jigsaw, turning and turning as they found their place, concealing countless other configurations—rare, wretched, bestial, dazzling—behind the shell of a congruous reality. He knew the features, now that they'd come to rest. Here were the ringlets, framing a face of exquisite symmetry. Here were the scars that healed with such unnatural speed. Here were the lips that hours before had described their owner as nothing and nobody. It was a lie! This nothing had two functions at least: assassin and whore. This nobody had a name.

"Pie 'oh' pah!"

Gentle let go of the man's arm as though it were venomous. The form before him didn't redissolve, however, for which fact Gentle was only half glad. That hallucinatory chaos had been distressing, but the solid thing it had concealed appalled him more. Whatever sexual imaginings he'd shaped in the darkness—Judith's face, Judith's breasts, belly, sex—all of them had been an illusion. The creature he'd coupled with, almost shot his load into, didn't even share her sex.

He was neither a hypocrite nor a puritan. He loved sex too much to condemn any expression of lust, and though he'd discouraged the homosexual courtships he'd attracted, it was out of indifference, not revulsion. So the shock he felt now was fueled more by the power of the deceit worked upon him than by the sex of the deceiver.

"What have you done to me?" was all he could say. "What have you done?"

Pie 'oh' pah stood his ground, knowing perhaps that his nakedness was his best defense.

"I wanted to heal you," he said. Though it trembled, there was music in his voice.

"You put some drug in me."

"No!" Pie said.

"Don't give me *no!* I thought you were Judith! You let me think you were Judith!" He looked down at his hands, then up at the hard, lean body in front of him. "I felt *her,* not you."

Again, the same complaint. "What have you done to me?"

"I gave you what you wanted," Pie said.

Gentle had no retort to this. In its way, it was the truth. Scowling, he sniffed his palms, thinking there might be traces of some drug in his sweat. But there was only the stench of sex on him, of the heat of the bed behind him.

"You'll sleep it off," Pie said.

"Get the fuck out of here," Gentle replied. "And if you go anywhere near Jude again, I swear . . . I *swear* . . . I'll take you apart."

"You're obsessed with her, aren't you?"

"None of your fucking business."

"It'll do you harm."

"Shut up."

"It will, I'm telling you."

"I told you," Gentle yelled, *"shut the fuck up!"*

"She doesn't belong to you," came the reply.

The words ignited new fury in Gentle. He reached for Pie and took him by the throat. The bundle of clothes dropped from the assassin's arm, leaving him naked. But he put up no defense; he simply raised his hands and laid them lightly on Gentle's shoulders. The gesture only infuriated Gentle further. He let out a stream of invective, but the placid face before him took both spittle and spleen without flinching. Gentle shook him, digging his thumbs into the man's throat to stop his windpipe. Still he neither resisted nor succumbed, but stood in front of his attacker like a saint awaiting martyrdom.

Finally, breathless with rage and exertion, Gentle let go his hold and threw Pie back, stepping away from the creature with a glimmer of superstition in his eyes. Why hadn't the fellow fought back or fallen? Anything but this sickening passivity.

"Get out," Gentle told him.

Pie still stood his ground, watching him with forgiving eyes.

"Will you get out?" Gentle said again, more softly, and this time the martyr replied.

"If you wish."

"I wish."

He watched Pie 'oh' pah stoop to pick up the scattered clothes. Tomorrow, this would all come clear in his head, he thought. He'd have shat this delirium out of his system, and these events—Jude, the chase, his near rape at the hands of the assassin—would be a tale to tell Klein and Clem and Taylor when he got back to London. They'd be entertained. Aware now that he was more naked than the other man, he turned to the bed and dragged a sheet off it to cover himself with.

There was a strange moment then, when he knew the bastard was still in the room, still watching him, and all he could do was wait for him to leave. Strange because it reminded him of other bedroom partings: sheets tangled, sweat cooling, confusion and self-reproach keeping glances at bay. He waited, and waited, and finally heard the door close. Even then he didn't turn, but listened to the room to be certain there was only one breath in it: his own. When he finally looked back and saw that Pie 'oh' pah had gone, he pulled the sheet up around himself like a toga, concealing himself from the absence in the room, which stared back at him too much like a reflection for his peace of mind. Then he locked the suite door and stumbled back to bed, listening to his drugged head whine like the empty telephone line.

FOUR

LIVES

Every story concerns itself with lives, of course: so why try to gather pieces together under this heading? Because there is a certain magic in the ways that words can summarize the arc of life, lingering for a sentence or two to offer some piece of a character's history, then moving on, skipping years perhaps, until another significant event is alighted upon. This is very much the case in the story of Zelim, excerpted here from *Galilee*. In one sense, the tale is a self-contained element in the novel. Though Zelim appears as a ghost in latter portions of the book it isn't strictly necessary to tell his life-story. But *Galilee* has a strange, digressionary structure, and Zelim's story a peculiar poignancy which reflects on the lives of characters he never even meets.

There is a far less wholesome life documented in "The Last European," from *The Damnation Game*. Anthony Breer, the Razor-Eater, is discovered in what he intends to be his last minutes on earth. His attempt at suicide is halted by the intervention of one Mamoulian, the self-styled Last European. In the few pages of this excerpt we get a snapshot, as it were, of a life lived in the shadow of its own corruption.

Also collected here is a short story called "The Departed," which is one of the very few short stories I have written on commission. I was invited to create the story for the op-ed page of the *New York Times*, on Halloween. It's a ghost story, of sorts. In their wisdom, the editors retitled the story "Hermione and the Moon," apparently finding my original title, restored here, too "dark." The story is in fact quite optimistic, in a bittersweet way, and at its heart is a philosophical nugget which I was delighted to be able to slip into the minds of *Times* readers while they drank their morning coffee.

119

From *Galilee*

Let me tell you what happened to Zelim after he left Atva.

Determined to prove—if only to himself—that the forest from which the family had emerged was not a place to be afraid of, he made his departure through the trees. It was damp and cold, and more than once he contemplated retreating to the brightness of the shore, but after a time such thoughts, along with his fear, dissipated. There was nothing here that was going to do harm to his soul. When shit fell on or about him, as now and then it did, the shitter wasn't some child-devouring beast as he'd been brought up to believe it'd be, just a bird. When something moved in the thicket, and he caught the gleam of an eye, it was not the gaze of a nomadic djinn that fell on him, but that of a boar or a wild dog.

His caution evaporated along with his fear, and much to his surprise his spirits grew lighter. He began to sing to himself as he went. Not the songs the fishermen sang when they were out together, which were invariably mournful or obscene, but the two or three little songs he remembered from his childhood. Simple ditties which brought back happy memories.

For food, he ate berries, washed down with water from the streams that wound between the trees. Twice he came upon nests in the undergrowth and was able to dine on raw eggs. Only at night, when he was obliged to rest (once the sun went down he had no way of knowing the direction in which he was traveling), did he become at all anxious. He had no means to light a fire, so he was obliged to sit in the darkened thicket until dawn, praying a bear or a pack of wolves didn't come sniffing for a meal.

It took him four days and nights to get to the other side of the forest. By the time he emerged from the trees he'd become so used to the gloom that the bright sun made his head ache. He laid down in the grass at the fringe of the trees, and dozed there in the warmth, thinking he'd set off again when the sun was a little less bright. In fact, he slept until twilight, when he was awoken by the sound of voices rising and falling in prayer. He sat up. A little distance from where he'd laid his head there was a ridge of rocks, like the spine of some dead giant, and on the narrow trail that wound between these boulders was a small group of holy men, singing their prayers as they walked. Some were carrying lamps, by which light he saw their faces: ragged beards, deeply furrowed brows, sunbaked pates; these were men who'd suffered for their faith, he thought.

He got up and limped in their direction, calling to them as he approached so that they wouldn't be startled by his sudden appearance. Seeing him, the men came to a halt; a few suspicious glances were exchanged.

"I'm lost and hungry," Zelim said to them. "I wonder if you have some bread, or if you can at least tell me where I can find a bed for the night."

The leader, who was a burly man, passed his lamp to his companion, and beckoned Zelim.

"What are you doing out here?" the monk asked.

"I came through the forest," Zelim explained.

"Don't you know this is a bad road?" the monk said. His breath was the foulest thing Zelim had ever smelled. "There are robbers on this road," the monk went on. "Many people have been beaten and murdered here." Suddenly, the monk reached out and caught hold of Zelim's arm, pulling him close. At the same time he pulled out a large knife, and put it to Zelim's throat. "*Call them!*" the monk said.

Zelim didn't understand what he was talking about. "Call who?"

"The rest of your gang! You tell them I'll slit your throat if they make a move on us."

"No, you've got me wrong. I'm not a bandit."

"Shut up!" the monk said, pressing his blade into Zelim's flesh so deeply that blood began to run. "*Call to them!*"

"I'm on my own," Zelim protested. "I swear! I swear on my mother's eyes, I'm not a bandit."

"Slit his throat, Nazar," said one of the monks.

"Please, don't do that," Zelim begged. "I'm an innocent man."

"There are no innocent men left," Nazar, the man who held him, said. "These are the last days of the world, and everyone left alive is corrupt."

Zelim assumed this was high-flown philosophy, such as only a monk might understand. "If you say so," he replied. "What do I know? But I tell you I'm not a bandit. I'm a fisherman."

"You're a very long way from the sea," said the ratty little monk to whom Nazar had passed his lamp. He leaned in to peer at Zelim, raising the light a little as he did so. "Why'd you leave the fish behind?"

"Nobody liked me," Zelim replied. It seemed best to be honest.

"And why was that?"

Zelim shrugged. Not too honest, he thought. "They just didn't," he said.

The man studied Zelim a little longer, then he said to the leader: "You know, Nazar, I think he's telling the truth." Zelim felt the blade at his neck dig a little less deeply into his flesh. "We thought you were one of the bandits' boys," the monk explained to him, "left in our path to distract us."

Once again. Zelim felt he was not entirely understanding what he was being told. "So . . . while you're talking to me, the bandits come?"

"Not *talking*," Nazar said. His knife slid down from Zelim's neck to the middle of his chest; there it cut at Zelim's already ragged shirt. The monk's other hand slid through the shirt, while the knife continued on its southward journey, until it was pressed against the front of Zelim's breeches.

"He's a little old for me, Nazar," the monk's companion commented, and turning his back on Zelim sat down among the rocks.

"Am I on my own then?" Nazar wanted to know.

By way of answering him, three of the men closed on Zelim like hungry dogs. He was wrested to the ground, where his clothes were pulled seam from seam, and the monks proceeded to molest him, ignoring his shouts of protest, or his pleas to be left alone. They made him lick their feet and their fundaments, and suck their beards and nipples and purple-headed cocks. They held him down while one by one they took him, not caring that he bled and bled.

While this was going on the other monks, who'd retired to the rocks, read, or drank wine or lay on their backs watching the stars. One was even praying. All this Zelim could see because he deliberately looked away from his violators, determined not to let them see the terror in his eyes, and equally determined not to weep. So instead he watched the others, and waited for the men who were violating him to be finished.

He fully expected to be murdered when they were done with him, but this, at least, he was spared. Instead the monks had the night with him, on and off, using him every way their desires could devise, and then, just before dawn, they left him there among the rocks, and went on their way.

The sun came up, but Zelim closed his eyes against it. He didn't want to look at the light ever again. He was too ashamed. But by midday the heat made him get to his knees and drag himself into the comparative cool of the rocks. There, to his surprise, he found that one of the holy men—perhaps the one who had been praying—had left a skin of wine, some bread, and a piece of dried fruit. It was no accident, he knew. The man had left it for Zelim.

Now, and only now, did the fisherman allow the tears to come, moved not so much by his own agonies, but by the fact that there had been one who'd cared enough for him to do him this kindness.

He drank and ate. Maybe it was the potency of the wine, but he felt remarkably renewed, and covering his nakedness as best he could, he got up from his niche among the rocks and set off down the trail. His body still ached, but the bleeding had stopped, and rather than lie down when night fell he walked under the stars. Somewhere along the way a bony-flanked she-dog came creeping after him, looking perhaps for the comfort of human company. He didn't shoo her away; he too wanted company. After a time the animal became brave enough to walk at Zelim's heel, and finding that her new master didn't kick her, was soon trotting along as though they'd been together since birth.

The hungry bitch's arrival in his life marked a distinct upturn in Zelim's fortunes. A few hours later he came into a village many times larger than Atva, where he found a large crowd in the midst of what he took to be some kind of celebration. The streets were thronged with people shouting and stamping, and generally having a fine time.

"Is it a holy day?" Zelim asked a youth who was sitting on a doorstep, drinking.

The fellow laughed. "No," he said, "it's not a holy day."

"Well then why's everybody so happy?"

"We're going to have some hangings," the youth replied, with a lazy grin.

"Oh . . . I . . . see."

"You want to come and watch?"

"Not particularly."

"We might get ourselves something to eat," the youth said. "And you look as though you need it." He glanced Zelim up and down. "In fact you look like you need a lot of things. Some breeches, for one thing. What happened to you?"

"I don't want to talk about it."

"That bad, huh? Well then you should come to the hangings. My father already went, because he said it's good to see people who are more unfortunate than you. It's good for the soul, he said. Makes you thankful."

Zelim saw the wisdom in this, so he and his dog accompanied the boy through the village to the market square. It took them longer to dig through the crowd than his guide had anticipated, however, and by the time they got there all but one of the men who were being hanged were already dangling from the makeshift gallows. He knew all the prisoners instantly: the ragged beards, the sunburned pates. These were his violators. All of them had plainly suffered horribly before the noose had taken their lives. Three of them were missing their hands; one of them had been blinded; others, to judge by the blood that glued their clothes to their groins, had lost their manhood to the knife.

One of this unmanned number was Nazar, the leader of the gang, who was the last of the gang left alive. He could not stand, so two of the villagers were holding him up while a third slipped the noose over his head. His rotted teeth had been smashed out, and his whole body covered with cuts and bruises. The crowd was wildly happy at the sight of the man's agonies. With every twitch and gasp they applauded and yelled his crimes at him. "Murderer!" they yelled. "Thief!" they yelled. "Sodomite!" they yelled.

"He's all that and more, my father says," the youth told Zelim." 'He's so evil, my father says, that when he dies we might see the Devil come up onto the gallows and catch his soul as it comes out of his mouth!"

Zelim shuddered, sickened at the thought. If the boy's father was right, and the sodomite robber-monk had been the spawn of Satan, then perhaps that unholiness had been passed into his own body, along with the man's spittle and seed. Oh, the horror of that thought; that he was somehow the wife of this terrible man and would be dragged down into the same infernal place when his time came.

The noose was now about Nazar's neck, and the rope pulled tight enough that he was pulled up like a puppet. The men who'd been supporting him stood away, so that they could help haul on the rope. But in the moments before the rope tightened about his windpipe, Nazar started to speak. No; not speak; *shout*, using every last particle of strength in his battered body.

"*God shits on you all!*" he yelled. The crowd hurled at him. Some threw stones. If he felt them breaking his bones, he didn't respond. He just kept shouting. *"He put a thousand innocent souls into our hands! He didn't care what we did to them! So you can do whatever you want to me—"*

The rope was tightening around his throat as the men hauled on the other end. Nazar was pulled up onto tiptoe. And still he shouted, blood and spittle coming with the words.

"There is no hell! There is no paradise! There is no—"

He got no further; the noose closed off his windpipe and he was hauled into the air. But Zelim knew what word had been left unsaid. *God.* The monk had been about to cry: *there is no God.*

The crowd was in ecstasies all around him; cheering and jeering and spitting at the hanged man as he jerked around on the end of the rope. His agonies didn't last long. His tortured body gave out after a very short time, much to the crowd's disapproval, and he hung from the rope as though the grace of life had never touched him. The boy at Zelim's side was plainly disappointed.

"I didn't see Satan, did you?"

Zelim shook his head, but in his heart he thought: maybe I did. Maybe the Devil's just a man like me. Maybe he's many men; all men, maybe.

His gaze went along the row of hanged men, looking for the one who had prayed while he'd been raped; the one Zelim suspected had left him the wine, bread, and fruit. Perhaps he'd also persuaded his companions to spare their victim; Zelim would never know. But here was the strange thing. In death, the men all looked the same to him. What had made each man particular seemed to have drained away, leaving their faces deserted, like houses whose owners had departed, taking every sign of particularity with them. He couldn't tell which of them had prayed on the rock, or which had been particularly vicious in their dealings with him. Which had bitten him like an animal; which had pissed in his face to wake him when he'd almost fainted away; which had called him by the name of a woman as they'd plowed him. In the end, they were virtually indistinguishable as they swung there.

"Now they'll be cut up and their heads put on spikes," the youth was explaining, "as a warning to bandits."

"And holy men," Zelim said.

"They weren't holy men," the youth replied.

His remark was overheard by a woman close by. "Oh yes they were," she said. "The leader, Nazar, had been a monk in Samarkand. He studied some books he should never have studied, and that was why he became what he became."

"What kind of books?" Zelim asked her.

She gave him a fearful look. "It's better we don't know," she said.

"Well, I'm going to find my father," the youth said to Zelim. "I hope things go well with you. God be merciful."

"And to you," Zelim said.

Zelim had seen enough; more than enough, in truth. The crowd was working itself up into a fresh fever as the bodies were being taken down in preparation for their beheading; children were being lifted up onto their parents' shoulders so they could see the deed done. Zelim found the whole spectacle disgusting. Turning away from the scene, he bent down, picked up his flea-bitten dog, and started to make his way to the edge of the assembly.

As he went he heard somebody say: "Are you sickened at the sight of blood?"

He glanced over his shoulder. It was the woman who'd spoken of the unholy books in Samarkand.

"No, I'm not sickened," Zelim said sourly, thinking the woman was impugning his manhood. "I'm just bored. They're dead. They can't suffer anymore."

"You're right," the woman said with a shrug. She was dressed, Zelim saw, in widow's clothes, even though she was still young; no more than a year or two older than he. "It's only us who suffer," the woman went on. "Only us who are left alive."

He understood absolutely the truth in what she was saying, in a way that he could not have understood before his terrible adventure on the road. That much at least the monks had given him: a comprehension of somebody else's despair.

"I used to think there were reasons . . . ," he said softly.

The crowd was roaring. He glanced back over his shoulder. A head was being held high, blood running from it, glittering in the bright sun.

"What did you say?" the woman asked him, moving closer to hear him better over the noise.

"It doesn't matter," he said.

"Please tell me," she replied, "I'd like to know."

He shrugged. He wanted to weep, but what man wept openly in a place like this?

"Why don't you come with me?" the woman said. "All my neighbors are here, watching this *stupidity*. If you come back with me, there'll be nobody to see us. Nobody to gossip about us."

Zelim contemplated the offer for a moment or two. "I have to bring my dog," he said.

He stayed for six years. Of course after a week or so the neighbors began to gossip behind their hands, but this wasn't like Atva; people weren't forever meddling in your business. Zelim lived quite happily with the widow Passak, whom he came to love. She was a practical woman, but with the front door and the shutters closed she was also very passionate. This was especially true, for some reason, when the winds came in off the desert; burning hot winds that carried a blistering freight of sand. When those winds blew the widow would be shameless—there was nothing she wouldn't do for their mutual pleasure, and he loved her all the more for it.

But the memories of Atva, and of the glorious family that had come down to the shore that distant day, never left him. Nor did the hours of his violation, or the strange thoughts that had visited him as Nazar and his gang hung from the gallows. All of these experiences remained in his heart, like a stew that had been left to simmer, and simmer, and as the years passed was becoming steadily more tasty and more nourishing.

Then, after six years, and many happy days and nights with Passak, he realized the time had come for him to sit down and eat that stew.

It happened during one of these storms that came off the desert. He and Passak had made love not once but three times. Instead of falling asleep afterward, however, as Passak had done, Zelim now felt a strange irritation behind his eyes, as though the wind had somehow whistled its way into his skull and was stirring the meal one last time before serving it.

In the corner of the room the dog—who was by now old and blind—whined uneasily.

"Hush, girl," he told her. He didn't want Passak woken; not until he had made sense of the feelings that were haunting him.

He put his head in his hands. What was to become of him? He had lived a fuller life than he'd ever have lived if he'd stayed in Atva, but none of it made any sense. At least in Atva there had been a simple rhythm to things. A boy was born, he grew strong enough to become a fisherman, he became a fisherman, and then weakened again, until he was as frail as a baby, and then he perished, comforted by the fact that even as he passed from the world new fishermen were being born. But Zelim's life had no such certainties in it. He'd stumbled from one confusion to another, finding agony where he had expected to find consolation, and pleasure where he'd expected to find sorrow. He'd seen the Devil in human form, and the faces of divine spirits made in similar shape. Life was not remotely as he'd expected it to be.

And then he thought: I have to tell what I know. That's why I'm here; I have to tell people all that I've seen and felt, so that my pain is never repeated. So that those who come after me are like my children, because I helped shape them, and made them strong.

He got up, went to his sweet Passak where she lay, and knelt down beside the narrow bed. He kissed her cheek. She was already awake, however, and had been awake for a while.

"If you leave, I'll be so sad," she said. Then, after a pause: "But I knew you'd go one day. I'm surprised you've stayed so long."

"How did you know—?"

"You were talking aloud, didn't you realize? You do it all the time." A single tear ran from the corner of her eye, but there was no sorrow in her voice. "You are a wonderful man, Zelim. I don't think you know how truly wonderful you are. And you've seen things . . . maybe they were in your head, maybe they were real, I don't know . . . that you have to tell people about." Now it was he who wept, hearing her speak this way, without a trace of reprimand. "I have had such years with you, my love. Such joy as I never thought I'd have. And it'd be greedy of me to ask you for more, when I've had so much already." She raised her head a little way, and kissed him. "I will love you better if you go quickly," she said.

He started to sob. All the fine thoughts he'd had a few minutes before seemed hollow now. How could he think of leaving her?

"I can't go," he said. "I don't know what put the thought in my head."

"Yes, you will," she replied. "If you don't go now, you'll go sooner or later. So go."

He wiped his tears away. "No," he said. "I'm not going anywhere."

So he stayed. The storms still came, month on month, and he and the widow still coupled fiercely in the little house, while the fire muttered in the hearth and the wind chattered on the roof. But now his happiness was spoiled; and so was hers. He resented her for keeping him under her roof, even though she'd been willing to let him go. And she in her turn grew less loving of him, because he'd not had the courage to go, and by staying he was killing the sweetest thing she'd ever known, which was the love between them.

At last, the sadness of all this killed her. Strange to say, but this brave woman, who had survived the grief of being widowed, could not survive the death of her love for a man who stayed at her side. He buried her, and a week later, went on his way.

He never again settled down. He'd known all he needed to know of domestic life; from now on he would be a nomad. But the stew that had bubbled in him for so long was still good. Perhaps all the more pungent for those last sad months with Passak. Now, when he finally began his life's work, and started to teach by telling of his experiences, there was the poignancy of their soured love to add to the account: this woman, to whom he had once promised his undying devotion—saying what he felt for her was imperishable—soon came to seem as remote a memory as his youth in Atva. Love—at least the kind of love that men and women share—was not made of eternal stuff. Nor was its opposite. Just as the scars that Nazar and his men had left faded with the years, so had the hatred Zelim had felt for them.

Which is not to say he was a man without feeling; far from it. In the thirty-one years left to him he would become known as a prophet, as a storyteller, and as a man of rare passion. But that passion did not resemble the kind that most of us feel. He became, despite his humble origins, a creature of subtle and elevated emotion. The parables he told would not have shamed Christ in their simplicity, but unlike the plain and good lessons taught by Jesus, Zelim imparted through his words a far more ambiguous vision; one in which God and the Devil were constantly engaged in a game of masks.

Three times in his life Zelim joined a caravan on the Silk Road and made his way to Samarkand. The first time was just a couple of years after the death of Passak, and he traveled on foot, having no money to purchase an animal strong enough to survive the trek. It was a journey that tested to its limits his hunger to see the place: by the time the fabled towers came in sight he was so exhausted—his feet bloody, his body trembling, his eyes red-raw from days of walking in clouds of somebody else's dust—that he simply fell down in the sweet grass beside the river and slept for the rest of the day there outside the walls, oblivious.

He awoke at twilight, washed the sand from his eyes, and looked up. The sky was opulent with color; tiny knitted rows of high cloud, all amber toward the west, blue purple on their eastern flank, and birds in wheeling flocks, circling the glowing minarets as they returned to their roosts. He got to his feet and entered the city as the night fires around the walls were being stoked, their fuel such fragrant woods that the very air smelled holy.

Inside, all the suffering he'd endured to get here was forgotten. Samarkand was all that his father had said it would be, and more. Though Zelim was little more than a beggar here, he soon realized that there was a market for his storytelling. And that he had much to tell. People liked to hear him talk about the baptism at Atva; and the forest; and Nazar and his fate. Whether they believed these were accounts of true events or not didn't matter: they gave him money and food and friendship (and in the case of several well-bred ladies, nights of love) to hear him tell his tales. He began to extend his repertoire: extemporize, enrich, invent. He created new stories about the family on the shore, and because it seemed people liked to have a touch of philosophy woven into their entertainments, introduced his themes of destiny into the stories, ideas that he'd nurtured in his years with Passak.

By the time he left Samarkand after that first visit, which lasted a year and a half, he had a certain reputation, not simply as a fine storyteller, but as a man of some wisdom. And now, as he traveled, he had a new subject: Samarkand.

There, he would say, the highest aspirations of the human soul, and the lowest appetites of the flesh, are so closely laid, that it's hard sometimes to tell one from the other. It was a point of view people were hungry to hear, because it was so often true of their own lives, but so seldom admitted to. Zelim's reputation grew.

The next time he went to Samarkand he traveled on the back of a camel, and had a fifteen-year-old boy to prepare his food and see to his comfort, a lad who'd been apprenticed to him because he too wanted to be a storyteller. When they got to the city, it was inevitably something of a disappointment to Zelim. He felt like a man who'd returned to the bed of a great love only to find his memories sweeter than the reality. But this experience was also the stuff of parable; and he'd only been in the city a week before his disappointment was part of a tale he told.

And there were compensations: reunions with friends he'd made the first time he'd been here; invitations into the palatial homes of men who would have scorned him as an uneducated fisherman a few years before, but now declared themselves honored when he stepped across their thresholds. And the profoundest compensation, his discovery that here in the city there existed a tiny group of young scholars who studied his life and his parables as though he were a man of some significance. Who could fail to be flattered by that? He spent many days and nights talking with them, and answering their questions as honestly as he was able.

One question in particular loitered in his brain when he left the city. "Do you think you'll ever see again the people you met on the shore?" a young scholar had asked him.

"I don't suppose so," he'd said to the youth. "I was nothing to them."

"But to the child, perhaps . . . ," the scholar had replied.

"To the child?" said Zelim. "I doubt he even knew I existed. He was more interested in his mother's milk than he was in me."

The scholar persisted, however. "You teach in your stories," he said, "how things always come round. You talk in one of them about the Wheel of the Stars. Perhaps it will be the same with these people. They'll be like the stars. Falling out of sight—"

"And rising again," Zelim said.

The scholar offered a luminous smile to hear his thoughts completed by his master. "Yes. Rising again."

"Perhaps," Zelim had said. "But I won't live in expectation of it."

Nor did he. But, that said, the young scholar's observation had lingered with him, and had in its turn seeded another parable: a morose tale about a man who lives in anticipation of a meeting with someone who turns out to be his assassin.

And so the years went on, and Zelim's fame steadily grew. He traveled immense distances—to Europe, to India, to the borders of China, telling his stories, and discovering that the strange poetry of what he invented gave pleasure to every variety of heart.

It was another eighteen years before he came again to Samarkand; this—though he didn't know it—for the last time.

By now Zelim was getting on in years and though his many journeys had made him wiry and resilient, he was feeling his age that autumn. His joints ached; his morning motions were either water or stone; he slept poorly. And when he did sleep, he dreamed of Atva; or rather of its shore, and of the holy family. His life of wisdom and pain had been caused by that encounter. If he'd not gone down to the water that day then perhaps he'd still be there among the fishermen, living a life of utter spiritual impoverishment; never having known enough to make his soul quake, nor enough to make it soar.

So there he was, that October, in Samarkand, feeling old and sleeping badly. There was little rest for him, however. By now the number of his devotees had swelled, and one of them (the youth who'd asked the question about things coming round) had founded a school. They were all young men who'd found a revolutionary zeal buried in Zelim's parables, which in turn nourished their hunger to see humanity unchained. Daily, he would meet with them. Sometimes he would let them question him, about his life, about his opinions. On other days—when he was weary of being interrogated—he would tell a story.

This particular day, however, the lesson had become a little of both. One of the students had said: "Master, many of us have had terrible arguments with our fathers, who don't wish us to study your works."

"Is that so?" old Zelim replied, raising an eyebrow. "I can't understand why." There was a little laughter among the students. "What's your question?"

"I only wondered if you'd tell us something of your own father."

"My father . . . ," Zelim said softly.

"Just a little."

The prophet smiled. "Don't look so nervous," he said to the questioner. "Why do you look so nervous?"

The youth blushed. I was afraid perhaps you'd be angry with me for asking something about your family."

"In the first place," Zelim replied gently, "I'm far too old to get angry. It's a waste of energy and I don't have much of that left. In the second place, my father sits before you, just as all your fathers sit here in front of me." His gaze roved the thirty or so students who sat cross-legged before him. "And a very fine bunch of men they are too." His gaze returned to the youth who'd asked the question. "What does your father do?"

"He's a wool merchant."

"So he's out in the city somewhere right now, selling wool, but his nature's not satisfied with the selling of wool. He needs something else in his life, so he sends you along to talk philosophy."

"Oh no . . . you don't understand . . . he didn't send me."

"He may not think he sent you. You may not think you were sent. But you were born your father's son and whatever you do, you do it for him." The youth frowned, plainly troubled at the thought of doing anything for his father. "You're like the fingers of his hand, digging in the dirt while he counts his bales of wool. He doesn't even notice that the hand's digging. He doesn't see it drop seeds into the hole. He's amazed when he finds a tree's grown up beside him, filled with sweet fruit and singing birds. But it was his hand did it."

The youth looked down at the ground. "What do you mean by this?" he said.

"That we do not belong to ourselves. That though we cannot know the full purpose of our creation, we should look to those who came before us to understand it better. Not just our fathers and our mothers, but *all* who went before. They are the pathway back to God, who may not know, even as He counts stars, that we're quietly digging a hole, planting a seed . . . "

Now the youth looked up again, smiling, entertained by the notion of God the Father looking the other way while His human hands grew a garden at His feet.

"Does that answer the question?" Zelim said.

"I was still wondering . . . ," the student said.

"Yes?"

"Your own father—?"

"He was a fisherman from a little village called Atva, which is on the shores of the Caspian Sea." As Zelim spoke, he felt a little breath of wind against his face, delightfully cool. He paused to appreciate it. Closed his eyes for a moment. When he opened them again; he knew something had changed in the room; he just didn't know what.

"Where was I?" he said.

"Atva," somebody at the back of the room said.

"Ah, yes, Atva. My father lived there all his life, but he dreamed of being somewhere quite different. He dreamed of Samarkand. He told his children he'd been here, in his youth. And he wove such stories of this city; such stories . . . "

Again, Zelim halted. The cool breeze had brushed against his brow a second time, and something about the way it touched him seemed like a sign. As though the breeze was saying *look, look* . . .

But at what? He gazed out of the window, thinking perhaps there was something out there he needed to see. The sky was darkening toward night. A chestnut tree, still covetous of its leaves despite the season, was in perfect silhouette. High up in its branches the evening star glimmered. But he'd seen all of this before: a sky, a tree, a star.

He returned his gaze to the room, still puzzled.

"What kind of stories?" somebody was asking him.

"Stories . . . ?"

"You said your father told stories of Samarkand."

"Oh yes. So he did. Wonderful stories. He wasn't a very good sailor, my father. In fact he drowned on a perfectly calm day. But he could have told tales of Samarkand for a year and never told the same one twice."

"But you say he never came here?" the master of the school asked Zelim.

"Never," Zelim said, smiling. "Which was why he was able to tell such fine stories about it."

This amused everyone mightily. But Zelim scarcely heard the laughter. Again, that tantalizing breeze had brushed his face; and this time, when he raised his eyes, he saw somebody moving through the shadows at the far end of the room. It was not one of the students. They were all dressed in pale yellow robes. This figure was dressed in ragged black breeches and a dirty shirt. He was also black, his skin possessing a curious radiance, which made Zelim remember a long-ago day.

"Atva . . . ?" he murmured.

Only the students closest to Zelim heard him speak, and even they, when debating the subject later, did not agree on the utterance. Some thought he'd said *Allah*, others that he'd spoken some magical word, that was intended to keep the stranger at the back of the room at bay. The reason that the word was so hotly debated was simple: it was Zelim's last, at least in the living world.

He had no sooner spoken than his head drooped, and the glass of tea which he had been sipping fell from his hand. The murmurings around the room ceased on the instant; students rose on all sides, some of them already starting to weep, or pray. The great teacher was dead, his wisdom passed into history. There would be more stories, no more prophecies. Only centuries of turning over the tales he'd already told, and watching to see if the prophecies came true.

Outside the schoolroom, under that covetous chestnut tree, two men talked in whispers. Nobody saw them there; nobody heard their happy exchange. Nor will I invent those words; better I leave that conversation to you: how the spirit of Zelim and Atva, later called Galilee, talked. I will say only this: that when the conversation was over, Zelim accompanied Galilee out of Samarkand; a ghost and a god, wandering off through the smoky twilight, like two inseparable friends.

Need I say that Zelim's part in this story is far from finished? He was called away that day into the arms of the Barbarossa family, whose service he has not since left.

In this book, as in life, nothing really passes away. Things change, yes; of course they change; they must. But everything is preserved in the eternal moment—Zelim the fisherman, Zelim the prophet, Zelim the ghost; he's been recorded in all his forms, these pages a poor but passionate echo of the great record that is holiness itself.

From *The Damnation Game*
THE LAST EUROPEAN

Anthony Breer, the Razor-Eater, returned to his tiny flat in the late afternoon, made himself instant coffee in his favorite cup, then sat at the table in the failing light and started to tie himself a noose. He'd known from early morning that today was the day. No need to go down to the library; if, in time, they noticed his absence and wrote to him demanding to know where he was, he wouldn't be answering. Besides, the sky had looked as grubby as his sheets at dawn, and being a rational man he'd thought: why bother to wash the sheets when the world's so dirty, and I'm so dirty, and there's no chance of ever getting any of it clean? The best thing is to put an end to this squalid existence once and for all.

He'd seen hanged people aplenty. Only photographs of course, in a book he'd stolen from work about war crimes, marked "*Not for the open shelves. To be issued only on request.*" The warning had really got his imagination working: here was a book people weren't really meant to see. He'd slipped it in his bag unopened, knowing from the very title—*Soviet Documents on Nazi Atrocities*—that this was a volume almost as sweet in the anticipation as in the reading. But in that he'd been wrong. Mouth-watering as that day had been, knowing that his bag contained this taboo treasure, that delight was nothing compared to the revelations of the book itself.

There were pictures of the burnt-out ruins of Chekhov's cottage in Istra, and others of the desecration of the Tchaikovsky residence. But mostly—and more importantly—there were photographs of the dead. Some of them heaped in piles, others lying in bloody snow, frozen solid. Children with their skulls broken open, people lying in trenches, shot in the face, others with swastikas carved into their chests and buttocks. But to the Razor-Eater's greedy eyes, the best photographs were of people being hanged. There was one Breer looked at very often. It pictured a handsome young man being strung up from a makeshift gallows. The photographer had caught him in his last moments, staring directly at the camera, a wan and beatific smile on his face.

That was the look Breer wanted them to find on *his* face when they broke down the door of this very room and found him suspended up here, pirouetting in the breeze from the hallway. He thought about how they would stare at him, coo at him, shake their heads in wonder at his pale white feet and his courage in doing this tremendous thing. And while he thought, he knotted and unknotted the noose, determined to make as professional a job of it as he possibly could.

His only anxiety was the confession. Despite his working with books day in, day out, words weren't his strongest point: they slipped away from him, like beauty from his fat hands. But he wanted to say something about the children, just so they'd know, the people who found him and photographed him, that this wasn't a nobody they were staring at, but a man who'd done the worst things in the world for the best possible reasons. That was vital: that they knew who he was, because maybe in time they'd make sense of him in a way that he'd never been able to.

They had methods of interrogation, he knew, even with dead people. They'd lay him in an ice-room and examine him minutely, and when they'd studied him from the outside they'd start looking at his inside, and oh!, what things they'd find. They'd saw off the top of his skull and take out his brain; examine it for tumors, slice it thinly like expensive ham, probe at it in a hundred ways to find out the why and how of him. But that wouldn't work, would it? He, of all people, should know that. You cut up a thing that's alive and beautiful to find out *how* it's alive and *why* it's beautiful and before you know it, it's neither of those things, and you're standing there with blood on your face and tears in your sight and only the terrible ache of guilt to show for it. No, they'd get nothing from his brain, they'd have to look further than that. They'd have to unzip him from neck to pubis, snip his ribs and fold them back. Only then could they unravel his guts, and rummage in his stomach, and juggle his liver and lights. There, oh yes, there, they'd find plenty to feast their eyes on.

Maybe that was the best confession then, he mused as he retied the noose one final time. No use to try and find the right words, because what were words anyway? Trash, useless for the hot heart of things. No, they'd find all they needed to know if they just looked inside him. Find the story of the lost children, find the glory of his martyrdom. And they'd know, once and for all, that he was of the Tribe of the Razor-Eaters.

He finished the noose, made himself a second cup of coffee, and started work on getting the rope secure. First he removed the lamp that hung from the middle of the ceiling, then he tied the noose up there in its place. It was strong. He swung from it for a few moments to make certain of it, and though the beams grunted a little, and there was a patter of plaster on his head, it bore his weight.

By now it was early evening, and he was tired, the fatigue making him more clumsy than usual. He shunted around the room tidying it up, his pig-fat body wracked with sighs as he bundled up the stained sheets and tucked them out of sight, rinsed his coffee-cup, and carefully poured away the milk so that it wouldn't curdle before they came. He turned on the radio as he worked; it would help to cover the sound of the chair being kicked over when the time came: there were others in the house and he didn't want any last-minute reprieve. The usual banalities filled the room from the radio station: songs of love and loss and love found again. Vicious and painful lies, all of them.

There was little strength left in the day once he'd finished preparing the room. He heard feet in the hallway and doors being opened elsewhere in the house as the occupants of the other rooms came home from work. They, like him, lived alone. He knew none of them by name; none of them, seeing him taken out escorted by police, would know his.

He undressed completely and washed himself at the sink, his testicles small as walnuts, tight to his body, his belly flab—the fat of his breasts and upper arms—quivering as the cold convulsed him. Once satisfied with his cleanliness, he sat on the mattress edge and cut his toenails. Then he dressed in freshly laundered clothes: the blue shirt, the gray trousers. He wore no shoes or socks. Of the physique that shamed him, his feet were his only pride.

It was almost dark by the time he finished, and the night was black and rainy. Time to go, he thought.

He positioned the chair carefully, stepped up onto it, and reached for the rope. The noose was, if anything, an inch or two too high, and he had to go on tiptoe to fit it snugly round his neck, but he fitted it securely with a little maneuvering. Once he had the knot pulled tight against his skin he said his prayers and kicked the chair over.

Panic began immediately, and his hands, which he'd always trusted, betrayed him at this vital juncture, springing up from his sides and tearing at the rope as it tightened. The initial drop had not broken his neck, but his spine felt like a vast centipede sewn into his back, writhing now every way it could, causing his legs to spasm. The pain was the least of it: the real anguish came from being out of control, smelling his bowels giving out into his clean trousers without his say-so, his penis stiffening without a lustful thought in his popping head, his heels digging the air looking for purchase, fingers still scrabbling at the rope. All suddenly not his own, all too hot for their own preservation to hold still and die.

But their efforts were in vain. He'd planned this too carefully for it to go awry. The rope was tightening still, the cavortings of the centipede weakening. Life, this unwelcome visitor, would leave very soon. There was a lot of noise in his head, almost as though he was underground, and hearing all the sounds of the earth. Rushing noises, the roar of great hidden weirs, the bubbling of molten stone. Breer, the great Razor-Eater, knew the earth very well. He'd buried dead beauties in it all too often, and filled his mouth with soil as penitence for the intrusion, chewing on it as he covered their pastel bodies over. Now the earth noises had blotted out everything— his gasps, the music from the radio, and the traffic outside the window. Sight was going too; lace darkness crept over the room, its patterns pulsing. He knew he was turning—there was the bed, now the wardrobe, now the sink—but the forms he fitfully saw were decaying.

His body had given up the good fight. His tongue flapped perhaps, or maybe he imagined the motion, just as surely as he imagined the sound of somebody calling his name.

Quite abruptly, sight went out completely, and death was on him. No flood of regrets attended the ending, no lightning regurgitation of a life-history encrusted with guilt. Just a dark, and a deeper dark, and now a dark so deep night was luminous by comparison with it. And it was over, easily.

No; not over.

Not quite over. A cluster of unwelcome sensations swarmed over him, intruding on the privacy of his death. A breeze warmed his face, assaulting his nerve ends. An ungracious breath choked him, pressing into his flaccid lungs without the least invitation.

He fought the resurrection, but his savior was insistent. The room began to reassemble itself around him. First light, then form. Now color, albeit drained and grimy. The noises—fiery rivers and liquid stone alike—were gone. He was hearing himself cough, and smelling his own vomit. Despair mocked him. Could he not even kill himself successfully?

Somebody said his name. He shook his head, but the voice came again, and this time his upturned eyes found a face.

And *oh* it was not over: far from it. He had not been delivered into Heaven or Hell. Neither would dare boast the face he was now staring up into.

"I thought I'd lost you, Anthony," said the Last European.

He had righted the chair Breer had stood on for his suicide attempt, and was sitting on it, looking as unsullied as ever. Breer tried to say something, but his tongue felt too fat for his mouth, and when he felt it his fingers came back bloody.

"You bit your tongue in your enthusiasm," said the European. "You won't be able to eat or speak too well for a while. But it'll heal, Anthony. Everything heals given time."

Breer had no energy to get up off the floor; all he could do was lie there, the noose still tight around his neck, staring up at the severed rope depending from the light fixture. The European had obviously just cut him down and let him fall. His body had begun to shake; his teeth were chattering like a mad monkey's.

"You're in shock," said the European. "You lie there . . . I'll make some tea, shall I? Sweet tea is just the thing."

It took some effort, but Breer managed to haul himself off the floor and on to the bed. His trousers were soiled, front and back: he felt disgusting. But the European didn't mind. He forgave all, Breer knew that. No other man Breer had ever met was quite so capable of forgiveness; it humbled him to be in the company and the care of such easy humanity. Here was a man who knew the secret heart of his corruption, and never once spoke a word of censure.

Propped up on the bed, feeling the signs of life reappearing in his wracked body, Breer watched the European making the tea. They were very different people. Breer had always felt awed by this man. Yet hadn't the European told him once: "*I am the last of my tribe, Anthony, just as you are the last of yours. We are in so many ways the same.*" Breer hadn't understood the significance of the remark when he'd first heard it, but he'd come to understand in time. "*I am the last true European; you are the last of the Razor-Eaters. We should try to help each other.*" And the European had gone on to do just that, keeping Breer from capture on two or three occasions, celebrating his trespasses, teaching him that to be a Razor-Eater was a worthy estate. In return for this education he'd asked scarcely anything: a few minor services, no more. But Breer wasn't so trusting that he didn't suspect a time would come when the Last European—please call me Mr. Mamoulian, he used to say, but Breer had never really got his tongue round that comical name—when this strange companion would ask for help in his turn. It wouldn't be an odd-job or two he'd ask either; it would be something terrible. Breer knew that, and feared it.

In dying he had hoped to escape the debt ever being called in. The longer he'd been away from Mr. Mamoulian—and it was six years since they'd last met—the more the memory of the man had come to frighten Breer. The European's image had not faded with time: quite the contrary. His eyes, his hands, the caress of his voice had stayed crystal-clear when yesterday's events had become a blur. It was as if Mamoulian had never *quite* gone, as though he'd left a sliver of himself in Breer's head to polish up his picture when time dirtied it; to keep a watch on his servant's every deed.

No surprise then, that the man had come in when he had, interrupting the death scene before it could be played out. No surprise either that he was talking to Breer now as though they'd never been parted, as though he was the loving husband to Breer's devoted wife, and the years had never intervened. Breer watched Mamoulian move from sink to table as he prepared the tea, locating the pot, setting out the cups, performing each domestic act with hypnotic economy. The debt would have to be paid, he knew that now. There would be no darkness until it *was* paid. At the thought, Breer began to sob quietly.

"Don't cry," said Mamoulian, not turning from the sink.

"I wanted to die," Breer murmured. The words came out as though through a mouthful of pebbles.

"You can't perish yet, Anthony. You owe me a little time. Surely you must see that?"

"I wanted to die," was all Breer could repeat in response. He was trying not to hate the European, because the man would know. He'd feel it for certain, and maybe lose his temper. But it was so difficult: resentment bubbled up through the sobbing.

"Has life been treating you badly?" the European asked.

Breer sniffed. He didn't want a father-confessor, he wanted the dark. Couldn't Mamoulian understand that he was past explanations, past healing? He was shit on the shoe of a Mongol, the most worthless, irredeemable thing in creation. The image of himself as a Razor-Eater, as the last representative of a once-terrible tribe, had kept his self-esteem intact for a few perilous years, but the fantasy had long since lost its power to sanctify his vileness. There was no possibility of working the same trick twice. And it *was* a trick, just a trick, Breer knew that, and hated Mamoulian all the more for his manipulations. I want to be dead, was all he could think.

Did he say the words out loud? He hadn't heard himself speak, but Mamoulian answered him as though he had.

"Of course you do. I understand, I really do. You think it's all an illusion: tribes, and dreams of salvation. But take it from me, it isn't. There's purpose in the world yet. For both of us."

Breer drew the back of his hand across his swollen eyes, and tried to control his sobs. His teeth no longer chattered; that was something.

"Have the years been so cruel?" the European inquired.

"Yes," Breer said sullenly.

The other nodded, looking across at the Razor-Eater with compassion in his eyes; or at least an adequate impersonation of same.

"At least they didn't lock you away," he said. "You've been careful."

"You taught me how," Breer conceded.

"I showed you only what you already knew, but were too confused by other people to see. If you've forgotten, I can show you again."

Breer looked down at the cup of sweet, milkless tea the European had set on the bedside table.

"Or do you no longer trust me?"

"Things have changed," Breer mumbled with his thick mouth.

Now it was Mamoulian's turn to sigh. He sat on the chair again, and sipped at his own tea before replying.

"Yes, I'm afraid you're right. There's less and less place for us here. But does that mean we should throw up our hands and die?"

Looking at the sober, aristocratic face, at the haunted hollows of his eyes, Breer began to remember why he'd trusted this man. The fear he'd felt was dwindling, the anger too. There was a calm in the air, and it was seeping into Breer's system.

"Drink your tea, Anthony."

"Thank you."

"Then I think you should change your trousers."

Breer blushed, he couldn't help himself.

"Your body responded quite naturally, there's nothing to be ashamed of. Semen and shit make the world go round."

The European laughed, softly, into his tea cup, and Breer, not feeling the joke to be at his expense, joined in.

"I never forgot you," Mamoulian said. "I told you I'd come back for you and I meant what I said."

Breer nursed his cup in hands that still trembled, and met Mamoulian's gaze. The look was as unfathomable as he'd remembered, but he felt warm toward the man. As the European said, he hadn't forgotten, he hadn't gone away never to return. Maybe he had his own reasons for being here now, maybe he'd come to squeeze payment out of a long-standing debtor, but that was better, wasn't it, than being forgotten entirely?

"Why come back now?" he asked, putting down his cup.

"I have business," Mamoulian replied.

"And you need my help?"

"That's right."

Breer nodded. The tears had stopped entirely. The tea had done him good: he felt strong enough to ask an insolent question or two.

"What about me?" came the reply.

The European frowned at the inquiry. The lamp beside the bed flickered, as though the bulb was at crisis-point, and about to go out.

"What *about* you?" he asked

Breer was aware that he was on tricky ground, but he was determined not to be weak. If Mamoulian wanted help, then he should be prepared to deliver something in exchange.

"What's in it for me?" he asked.

"You can be with me again," the European said.

Breer grunted. The offer was less than tempting.

"Is that not enough?" Mamoulian wanted to know. The lamplight was more fitful by the moment, and Breer had suddenly lost his taste for impertinence.

"*Answer me, Anthony,*" the European insisted. "If you've got an objection, voice it."

The flickering was worsening, and Breer knew he'd made an error, pressing Mamoulian for a covenant. Why hadn't he remembered that the European loathed bargains and bargainers alike? Instinctively he fingered the noose-groove around his neck. It was deep, and permanent.

"I'm sorry . . . ," he said, rather lamely.

Just before the lamp bulb gave out completely, he saw Mamoulian shake his head. A tiny shake, like a tick. Then the room was drowned in darkness.

"Are you with me, Anthony?" the Last European murmured.

The voice, normally so even, was twisted out of true.

"Yes . . . ," Breer replied. His lazy eyes weren't becoming accustomed to the dark with their usual speed. He squinted, trying to sort out the European's form in the surrounding gloom. He needn't have troubled himself. Scant seconds later something across the room from him seemed to ignite, and suddenly, awesomely, the European was providing his own illumination.

Now, with this lurid lantern show to set his sanity reeling, tea and apologies were forgotten. The dark, life itself, were forgotten; and there was only time, in a room turned inside out with terrors and petals, to stare and stare and maybe, if one had a sense of the ridiculous, to say a little prayer.

From *Sacrament*

There was a meager lamp burning beside Hugo's bed, its sallow light throwing a monumental shadow of the man upon the wall. He was semirecumbent amid a Himalayan mass of pillows, his eyes closed.

He'd grown a beard, and nurtured it to a formidable size. A solid ten inches long, trimmed and waxed in emulation of the beards of great dead men: Kant, Nietzsche, Tolstoy. The minds by which Hugo had always judged contemporary thought and art, and found it wanting. The beard was more gray than black, with streams of white running in it from the corners of his mouth, as though he'd dribbled cream into it. His hair, by contrast, had been clipped short and lay flat to his scalp, delineating the Roman dome of his skull. Will watched him for fifteen or twenty seconds, thinking how magisterial he looked. Then Hugo's lips parted, and very quietly he said:

"So you came back."

Now his eyes opened and found Will. Though there was a pair of spectacles at the bedside table, he stared at his visitor as though he had Will in perfect focus, his stare as unrelenting as ever; and as judgmental.

"Hello, Pa," Will said.

"Into the light," Hugo said, beckoning for Will to approach the bed. "Let me see you." Will duly stepped into the throw of the lamp to be scrutinized. "The years are showing on you," he said. "It's the sun. If you have to tramp the world at least wear a hat."

"I'll remember."

"Where were you lurking this time?"

"I wasn't lurking, Pa. I was—"

"I thought you'd deserted me. Where's Adele? Is she here?" He reached out to pluck his glasses off the nightstand. In his haste he instead knocked them to the ground. "Damn things!"

"They're not broken," Will said, picking them up.

Hugo put them on, one-handed. Will knew better than to help. "Where is she?"

"Waiting outside. She wanted us to have a little quality time together."

Now, paradoxically, he didn't look at Will, but studied the folds in the bedcover, and his hands, his manner perfectly detached. "Quality time?" he said. "Is that an Americanism?"

"Probably."

"What does it *mean* exactly?"

"Oh . . ." Will sighed. "Are we reduced to that already?"

"No, I'm just interested," Hugo said. "Quality time." He pursed his lips.

"It's a stupid turn of phrase," Will conceded. "I don't know why I used it."

Stymied, Hugo looked at the ceiling. Then: "Maybe you could just ask Adele to come in. I need a few toiletry items brought—"

"Who did it?"

"Just some toothpaste and some—"

"*Pa.* Who did it?"

The man paused, his mouth working as though he were chewing a piece of gristle. "Why do you assume I know?" he said.

"Why do you have to be so argumentative? This isn't a seminar. I'm not your student. I'm your son."

"Why did you take so long to come back?" Hugo said, his eyes returning to Will. "You knew where to find me."

"Would I have been welcome?"

Hugo's stare didn't waver. "Not by me, particularly," he said with great precision. "But your mother was very hurt by your silence."

"Does Eleanor know that you're in here?"

"I certainly haven't told her. And I doubt Adele has. They hated one another."

"Shouldn't she be told?"

"Why?"

"Because she'll be concerned."

"Then why tell her?" Hugo said neatly. "I don't want her here. There's no love lost between us. She's got her life. I've got mine. The only thing we have in common is you."

"You make that sound like an accusation."

"No. You simply *hear* it that way. Some children are palliatives in a troubled marriage. You weren't. I don't blame you for that."

"So can we get back to the subject?"

"Which was?"

"Who did this?"

Hugo returned his gaze to the ceiling. "I read a piece you wrote in *The Times*, about eighteen months ago—"

"What the hell has—"

"Something about elephants. You did write it?"

"It had my name on it."

"I thought perhaps you'd had some amanuensis write it for you. I daresay you thought you were waxing poetic, but Christ, how could you put your name to that kind of indulgence?"

"I was describing what I felt."

"There you are then," Hugo said, his tone one of weary resignation. "If you feel it then it must be true."

"How I disappoint you," Will said.

"No. No. I never hoped, so how could I be disappointed?" There was such a profundity of bitterness in this, it took Will's breath away. "None of it means a damn thing, anyway. It's all shit in the end."

"Is it?"

"Christ, yes." He looked at Will with feigned surprise. "Isn't that what you've been shrieking about all these years?"

"I don't shriek."

"Put it this way. It's a little shrill for most people's ears. Maybe that's why it's not having any effect. Maybe that's why your beloved Mother Earth—"

"Fuck Mother Earth—"

"No, you first, I insist."

Will raised his hands in surrender. "Okay, you win," he said. "I don't have the appetite for this. So . . . "

"Oh, come now."

"I'll fetch Adele," he said, turning from the bed.

"*Wait*—"

"What for? I didn't come here to be sniped at. If you don't want a peaceful conversation, then we won't have *any* conversation." He was almost at the door.

"I said *wait*," Hugo demanded.

Will halted, but didn't turn.

"It was him," Hugo said, very softly. Now Will glanced over his shoulder. His father had taken off his spectacles and was staring into middle distance.

"Who?"

"Don't be so dense," Hugo said, his voice a monotone. "You *know* who."

Will heard his heart quicken. "Steep?" he said. Hugo didn't reply. Will turned back to face the bed. "Steep did this to you?"

Silence. And then, very quietly, almost reverentially, "This is your revenge. So enjoy it."

"Why?"

"Because you won't get another like it."

"No, *why* did he do this to you?"

"Oh. To get to you. For some reason that's important to him. He did state his devotion. Make what you will of that."

"Why didn't you tell the police?" Again, Hugo kept his counsel, until Will came back to the bedside. "You should have told them."

"*What* would I tell them? I don't want any part of this . . . connection . . . between you and these creatures."

"There's nothing sexual, if that's what you think."

"Oh, I don't give a damn about your bedroom habits. *Humani nil a me alienum puto.* Terence—"

"I know the quote, Dad," Will said wearily. "*Nothing human is alien to me.* But that doesn't apply here, does it?"

Hugo narrowed his puffy eyes. "This is the moment you've been waiting for, isn't it?" he said, his lip curling. "You feel quite the master of ceremonies. You came in here, pretending you wanted to make peace but what you *really* want is revenge."

Will opened his mouth to deny the charge, then thought better of it, and instead told the truth: "Maybe a little."

"So. You have your moment," Hugo said, staring up at the ceiling. "You're right. Terence does not apply. These . . . creatures . . . are not human. There. I've said it. I've thought a lot about what that means, while I've been lying here."

"And?"

"It doesn't mean very much in the end."

"I think you're wrong."

"Well, you would, wouldn't you?"

"There's something extraordinary in all of this. Waiting at the end."

"Speaking as a man who *is* waiting at the end I see nothing here but the same tiresome cruelties and the same stale old pain. Whatever they are, they're not angels. They're not going to show you anything miraculous. They're going to break your bones the way they broke mine."

"Maybe they don't *know* what they really are," Will replied, realizing as he spoke that this was indeed at the heart of what he believed. "Oh, Jesus," he murmured almost to himself. "Yes . . . They don't know what they are any more than we do."

"Is this some kind of revelation?" Hugo said in his driest tone. Will didn't dignify his cynicism with a reply. "*Well?*" he insisted. "Is it? Because if you know something about them I don't, I want to hear it."

"Why should you care, if none of it means anything anyway?"

"Because I have a better chance of surviving another meeting with them if I know what I'm dealing with."

"You won't see them again," Will said.

"You sound very certain of that."

"You said Steep wants me," Will replied. "I'll make it simple for him. I'll go to him."

A look of unfeigned alarm crossed Hugo's face. "He'll kill you."

"It's not that simple for him."

"You don't know what he's like—"

"Yes I do. Believe me. *I do*. We've spent the last thirty years together." He touched his temple. "He's been in my head and I've been in his. Like a couple of Russian dolls."

Hugo looked at him with fresh dismay. "How did I get you?" he said, looking at Will as though he were something venomous.

"I assumed it was fucking, Dad."

"God knows, God *knows* I tried to put you on the right track. But I never stood a chance, I see that now. You were queer and crazy and sick to your sorry little heart from the beginning."

"I was queer in the womb," Will said calmly.

"Don't sound so damn proud of it!"

"Oh, that's the worst, isn't it?" Will countered. "I'm queer and I like it. I'm crazy and it suits me. And I'm sick to my sorry little heart because I'm dying into something new. You don't get that yet, and you probably never will. But that's what's happening."

Hugo stared at him, his mouth so tightly closed it seemed he would never utter another word; certainly not to Will. Nor did he need to, at least for now, because at that moment there was a light tapping at the door. "Can I interrupt?" Adele said, putting her head around the door.

"Come on in," Will said. Then, glaring back at Hugo, "The reunion's pretty much over."

Adele came directly to the bed and kissed Hugo on the cheek. He received the kiss without comment or reciprocation, which didn't seem to bother Adele. How many kisses had she bestowed this way, Will wondered; Hugo taking them as his right? "I brought you your toothpaste," she said, digging in her handbag and depositing the tube on the bedside table. Will saw the glint of fury in his father's eye, to have been seen addle-headed, asking for something he'd already requested. Adele was happily unaware of this. She fairly bubbled in Hugo's presence, Will saw, sweetly content to be coddling him—straightening his sheets, plumping up his pillow— though he gave her no thanks for her efforts.

"I'm going to leave you two to talk," Will said. "I need a cigarette. I'll see you out by the car, Adele."

"Fine," she said, all her focus upon the object of her affections. "I won't be long."

"Good-bye, Dad," Will said. He didn't expect a reply, and he didn't get one. Hugo was staring up at the ceiling again, with the glassy-eyed gaze of a man who has more important things on his mind than a child he would rather had never been born.

"The Departed"

I t was not only painters who were connoisseurs of light, Hermione had come to learn in the three days since her death; so too were those obliged to shun it. She was a member of that fretful clan now—a phantom in the world of flesh—and if she hoped to linger here for long she would have to avoid the sun's gift as scrupulously as a celibate avoided sin, and for much the same reason. It tainted, corrupted and finally drove the soul into the embrace of extinction.

She wasn't so unhappy to be dead; life had been no bowl of cherries. She had failed at love, failed at marriage, failed at friendship, failed at motherhood. That last stung the sharpest. If she could have plunged back into life to change one thing she would have left the broken romances in pieces and gone to her six-year-old son Finn to say: trust your dreams, and take the world lightly, for it means nothing, even in the losing.

She had shared these ruminations with one person only. His name was Rice; an ethereal nomad like herself who had died wasted and crazed from the plague but was now in death returned to corpulence and wit. Together they had spent that third day behind the blinds of his shunned apartment, listening to the babble of the street and exchanging tidbits. Toward evening, conversation turned to the subject of light.

"I don't see why the sun hurts us and the moon doesn't," Hermione reasoned. "The moon's reflected sunlight, isn't it?"

"Don't be so logical," Rice replied, "or so damn *serious*."

"And the stars are little suns. Why doesn't starlight hurt us?"

"I never liked looking at the stars," Rice replied. "They always made me feel lonely. Especially toward the end. I'd look up and see all that empty immensity and—" He caught himself in midsentence. "Damn you, woman, listen to me! We're going to have to get out of here and *party*."

She drifted to the window.

"Down there?" she said.

"Down there."

"Will they see us?"

"Not if we go naked."

She glanced round at him. He was starting to unbutton his shirt.

"I can see you perfectly well," she told him.

"But you're dead, darling. The living have a lot more trouble." He tugged off his shirt and joined her at the window. "Shall we dare the dusk?" he asked her, and without waiting for a reply, raised the blind. There was just enough power in the light to give them both a pleasant buzz.

"I could get addicted to this," Hermione said, taking off her dress and letting the remnants of the day graze her breasts and belly.

"Now you're talking," said Rice. "Shall we take the air?"

All Hallows' Eve was a day away, a night away, and every store along Main Street carried some sign of the season. A flight of paper witches here; a cardboard skeleton there.

"Contemptible," Rice remarked as they passed a nest of rubber bats. "We should protest."

"It's just a little fun," Hermione said.

"It's our holiday, darling. The Feast of the Dead. I feel like . . . like Jesus at a Sunday sermon. How dare they *simplify* me this way?" He slammed his phantom fists against the glass. It shook, and the remote din of his blow reached the ears of a passing family, all of whom looked toward the rattling window, saw nothing, and—trusting their eyes—moved on down the street.

Hermione gazed after them.

"I want to go and see Finn," she said.

"Not wise," Rice replied.

"Screw wise," she said. "I want to see him."

Rice already knew better than to attempt persuasion, so up the hill they went, toward her sister Elaine's house, where she assumed the boy had lodged since her passing.

"There's something you should know . . ." Rice said as they climbed. "About being dead."

"Go on."

"It's difficult to explain. But it's no accident we feel safe under the moon. We're *like* the moon. Reflecting the light of something living; something that loves us. Does that make any sense?"

"Not much."

"Then it's probably the truth."

She stopped her ascent and turned to him. "Is this meant as a *warning* of some kind?" she asked.

"Would it matter if it were?"

"Not much."

He grinned. "I was the same. A warning was always an invitation."

"End of discussion?"

"End of discussion."

There were lamps burning in every room of Elaine's house, as if to keep the night and all it concealed at bay.

How sad, Hermione thought, to live in fear of shadows. But then didn't the day now hold as many terrors for her as night did for Elaine? Finally, it seemed, after thirty-one years of troubled sisterhood, the mirrors they had always held up to each other—fogged until this moment—were clear. Regret touched her, that she had not better known this lonely woman whom she had so resented for her lack of empathy.

"Stay here," she told Rice. "I want to see them on my own."

Rice shook his head. "I'm not missing this," he replied, and followed her up the path, then across the lawn toward the dining room window.

From inside came not two voices but three: a woman, a boy, and a man whose timbre was so recognizable it stopped Hermione in her invisible tracks.

"Thomas," she said.

"Your ex?" Rice murmured.

She nodded. "I hadn't expected—"

"You'd have preferred him not to come and mourn you?"

"That doesn't sound like mourning to me," she replied.

Nor did it. The closer to the window they trod, the more merriment they heard. Thomas was cracking jokes, and Finn and Elaine were lapping up his performance.

"He's such a *clown!*" Hermione said. "Just listen to him."

They had reached the sill now, and peered in. It was worse than she'd expected. Thom had Finn on his knee, his arms wrapped around the child. He was whispering something in the boy's ear, and as he did so a grin appeared on Finn's face.

Hermione could not remember ever being seized by such contrary feelings. She was glad not to find her sweet Finn weeping—tears did not belong on that guileless face. But did he have to be quite so content; quite so forgetful of her passing? And as to Thom the clown, how could he so quickly have found his way back into his son's affections, having been an absentee father for five years? What bribes had he used to win back Finn's favor, master of empty promises that he was?

"Can we go trick-or-treating tomorrow night?" the boy was asking.

"Sure we can, partner," Thomas replied. "We'll get you a mask and a cape and—"

"You too," Finn replied. "You have to come too."

"Anything you want—"

"Son of a bitch," Hermione said.

"From now on—"

"He never even *wrote* to the boy while I was alive."

"Anything you want."

"Maybe he's feeling guilty," Rice suggested.

"Guilty?" she hissed, clawing at the glass, longing to have her fingers at Thomas's lying throat. "He doesn't know the meaning of the word."

Her voice had risen in pitch and volume, and Elaine—who had always been so insensitive to nuance—seemed to hear its echo. She rose from the table, turning her troubled gaze toward the window.

"Come away," Rice said, taking hold of Hermione's arm. "Or this is going to end badly."

"I don't care," she said.

Her sister was crossing to the window now, and Thomas was sliding Finn off his knee, rising as he did so, a question on his lips.

"There's somebody . . . watching us," Elaine murmured. There was fear in her voice.

Thomas came to her side; slipped his arm around her waist.

Hermione expelled what she thought was a shuddering sigh, but at the sound of it the window shattered, a hail of glass driving man, woman, and child back from the sill.

"*Away!*" Rice demanded, and this time she conceded; went with him, across the lawn, out into the street, through the benighted town and finally home to the cold apartment where she could weep out the rage and frustration she felt.

———

Her tears had not dried by dawn; nor even by noon. She wept for too many reasons, and for noting at all. For Finn, for Thomas, for the fear in her sister's eyes; and for the terrible absence of sense in everything. At last, however, her unhappiness found a salve.

"I want to touch him one last time," she told Rice.

"Finn?"

"Of course Finn."

"You'll scare the bejeezus out of him."

"He'll never know it's me."

She had a plan. If she was invisible when naked, then she would clothe every part of herself, and put on a mask, and find him in the streets, playing trick-or-treat. She would smooth his fine hair with her palm, or lay her fingers on his lips, then be gone, forever, out of the twin states of living death and Idaho.

"I'm warning you," she told Rice, "you shouldn't come."

"Thanks for the invitation," he replied a little ruefully. "I accept."

His clothes had been boxed and awaited removal. They untaped the boxes, and dressed in motley. The cardboard they tore up and shaped into crude masks—horns for her, elfin ears for him. By the time they were ready for the streets All Hallows' Eve had settled on the town.

It was Hermione who led the way back toward Elaine's house, but she set a leisurely pace. Inevitable meetings did not have to be hurried to; and she was quite certain she would encounter Finn if she simply let instinct lead her.

There were children at every corner, dressed for the business of the night. Ghouls, zombies, and fiends every one; freed to be cruel by mask and darkness, as she was freed to be loving. One last time, and then away.

"Here he comes," she heard Rice say, but she'd already recognized Finn's jaunty step.

"You distract Thom," she told Rice.

"My pleasure," came the reply, and the revenant was away from her side in an instant.

Thom saw him coming, and sensed something awry. He reached to snatch hold of Finn, but Rice pitched himself against the solid body, his ether forceful enough to throw Thom to the ground. He let out a ripe curse, and rising the next instant, snatched hold of his assailant. He might have landed a blow, but that he caught sight of Hermione as she closed on Finn, and instead turned and snatched at her mask.

It came away in his hands, and the sight of her face drew from him a shout of horror. He retreated a step; then another.

"Jesus . . . Jesus . . . ," he said.

She advanced upon him, Rice's warning ringing in her head.

"What do you see?" she demanded.

By way of reply he heaved up his dinner in the gutter.

"He sees decay," Rice said. "He sees rot."

"*Mom?*"

She heard Finn's voice behind her; felt his little hand tug at her sleeve. "Mom, is that you?"

Now it was she who let out a cry of distress; she who trembled.

"Mom?" he said again.

She wanted so much to turn; to touch his hair, his cheek; to kiss him good-bye. But Thom had seen rot in her. Perhaps the child would see the same, or worse.

"Turn round," he begged.

"I . . . can't . . . Finn."

"*Please.*"

And before she could stop herself, she was turning, her hands dropping from her face.

The boy squinted. Then he smiled.

"You're so *bright*," he said.

"I am?"

She seemed to see her radiance in his eyes; touching his cheeks, his lips, his brow as lovingly as any hand. So this was what it felt like to be a moon, she thought; to reflect a living light. It was a fine condition.

"Finn . . . ?"

Thom was summoning the boy to his side.

"He's frightened of you," Finn explained.

"I know. I'd better go."

The boy nodded gravely.

"Will you explain to him?" she asked Finn. "Tell him what you saw?"

Again, the boy nodded. "I won't forget," he said.

That was all she needed; more than all. She left him with his father, and Rice led her away, through darkened alleyways and empty parking lots to the edge of town. They discarded their costumes as they went. By the time they reached the freeway, they were once more naked and invisible.

"Maybe we'll wander a while," Rice suggested. "Go down South."

"Sure," she replied. "Why not?"

"Key West for Christmas. New Orleans for Mardi Gras. And maybe next year we'll come back here. See how things are going."

She shook her head. "Finn belongs to Thom now," she said. "He belongs to life."

"And who do we belong to?" Rice asked, a little sadly.

She looked up. "You know damn well," she said, and pointed to the moon.

FIVE

OLD HUMANITY

The title of this chapter comes from *The Damnation Game*, which is a Faust novel without the Devil. Under its general heading I've collected only three pieces. But all seem to me to belong in this book of essentials. From *Weaveworld*, a chapter in which a member of the Seerkind—an ancient, magical race—witnesses the madness that can seize our species. From *The Damnation Game*, another witnessing: this time by a girl called Carys, who sees into the mind of the book's villain, Mamoulian, and comprehends something of his origins.

The story at the center of the chapter is "The Forbidden," which is probably familiar to more people from its cinematic incarnation than it is from its life as a short story. The film is called *Candyman*, and it's a very effective piece of horror filmmaking, dutifully terrifying its audiences with a mingling of shocks and suspense. But something of the subtextual life of the tale gets sacrificed in the transfer to film. The sense that the Candyman is summoned by words, by the *telling of tales*, is inevitably diluted when the medium changes. "The Forbidden" carries a metafictional punch that *Candyman* can't, simply because it's written down.

That said, there is something wonderfully satisfying about finding out, as I did recently, that my invented urban legend has now attained the condition of "urban truth." I have it on good authority that in Cabrini Green, the housing project in Chicago where the movie is set, the kids tell tales of the horror of the Candyman. They haven't encountered him personally, of course. But they all know someone who did.

From *Weaveworld*

"So much *desire*," Apolline commented to Suzanna, as they walked the streets of Liverpool.

They'd found nothing at Gilchrist's Warehouse but suspicious stares, and had made a quick exit before inquiries were made. Once out, Apolline had demanded to take a tour of the city, and had followed her nose to the busiest thoroughfare she could find, its pavements crammed with shoppers, children, and *deadbeats*.

"Desire?" said Suzanna. It wasn't a motive that sprang instantly to mind on this dirty street.

"Everywhere," said Apolline. "Don't you see?"

She pointed across at a billboard advertising bed linen, which depicted two lovers languishing in a postcoital fatigue; beside it a car advertisement boasted the Perfect Body, and made its point as much in flesh as steel. "And there," said Apolline, directing Suzanna to a window display of deodorants, in which the serpent tempted a fetchingly naked Adam and Eve with the promise of confidence in crowds.

"The place is a whorehouse," said Apolline, clearly approving.

Only now did Suzanna realize that they'd lost Jerichau. He'd been loitering a few paces behind, his anxious eyes surveying the parade of human beings. Now he'd gone.

They retraced their steps through the throng of pedestrians and found him standing in front of a video rental shop, entranced by bank upon bank of monitors.

"Are they prisoners?" he said, as he stared at the talking heads.

"No," said Suzanna. "It's a show. Like a theater." She plucked at his oversized jacket. "Come on," she said.

He looked around at her. His eyes were brimming. The thought that he had been moved to tears by the sight of a dozen television screens made her fear for his tender heart.

"It's all right," she said, coaxing him away from the window. "They're quite happy."

She put her arm through his. A flicker of pleasure crossed his face, and together they moved through the crowd. Feeling his body trembling against hers it was not difficult to share the trauma he was experiencing. She'd taken the harlot century she'd been born into for granted, knowing no other, but now—seeing it with *his* eyes, hearing it with *his* ears—she understood it afresh; saw just how desperate it was to please, yet how dispossessed of pleasure; how crude, even as it claimed sophistication; and, despite its zeal to spellbind, how utterly unenchanting.

For Apolline, however, the experience was proving a joy. She strode through the crowd, trailing her long black skirts like a widow on a post-funereal spree.

"I think we should get off the main street," said Suzanna when they'd caught up with her. "Jerichau doesn't like the crowd."

"Well he'd best get used to it," said Apolline, shooting a glance at Jerichau. "This is going to be *our* world soon enough."

So saying, she turned and started away from Suzanna again.

"Wait a minute!"

Suzanna went in pursuit, before they lost each other in the throng.

"Wait!" she said, taking hold of Apolline's arm. "We can't wander around forever. We have to meet with the others."

"Let me enjoy myself awhile," said Apolline. "I've been asleep too long. I need some entertainment."

"Later maybe," said Suzanna. "When we've found the carpet."

"Fuck the carpet," was Apolline's prompt reply.

They were blocking the flow of pedestrians as they debated, receiving sour looks and curses for their troubles. One pubescent boy spat at Apolline, who promptly spat back with impressive accuracy. The boy retreated, with a shocked look on his bespittled face.

"I like these people," she commented. "They don't pretend to courtesy."

"We've lost Jerichau again," Suzanna said. "Damn him, he's like a child."

"I see him."

Apolline pointed down the street, to where Jerichau was standing, striving to keep his head above the crowd as though he feared drowning in this sea of humanity.

Suzanna started back toward him, but she was pressing against the tide, and it was tough going. But Jerichau didn't move. He had his fretful gaze fixed on the empty air above the heads of the crowd. They jostled and elbowed him but he went on staring.

"We almost lost you," Suzanna said when she finally reached his side.

His reply was a simple:

"Look."

Though she was several inches shorter than he, she followed the direction of his stare as best she could.

"I don't see anything."

"What's he troubling about now?" Apolline, who'd now joined them, demanded to know.

"They're all so sad," Jerichau said.

Suzanna looked at the faces passing by. Irritable they were; and sluggish some of them, and bitter; but few struck her as sad.

"Do you see?" said Jerichau, before she had a chance to contradict him: "The lights."

"No she doesn't see them," said Apolline firmly. "She's still a Cuckoo, remember? Even if she has got the menstruum. Now come on."

Jerichau's gaze now fell on Suzanna, and he was closer to tears than ever. "You *must* see," he said. "I want you to see."

"Don't do this," said Apolline. "It's not wise."

"They have colors," Jerichau was saying.

"Remember the Principles," Apolline protested.

"Colors?" said Suzanna.

"Like smoke, all around their heads."

Jerichau took hold of her arm.

"Will you listen?" Apolline said. "Capra's Third Principle states—"

Suzanna wasn't attending. She was staring at the crowd, her hand now grasping Jerichau's hand.

It was no longer simply his senses she shared, but his mounting panic, trapped among this hot-breathed herd. An empathic wave of claustrophobia rose in her; she closed her lids and told herself to be calm.

In the darkness she heard Apolline again, talking of some Principle. Then she opened her eyes.

What she saw almost made her cry out. The sky seemed to have changed color, as though the gutters had caught fire, and the smoke was choking the street. No one seemed to have noticed, however.

She turned to Jerichau, seeking some explanation, and this time she let out a yell. He had gained a halo of fireworks, from which a column of light and vermilion smoke was rising.

"Oh Christ," she said. "What's happening?"

Apolline had taken hold of her shoulder, and was pulling on her.

"Come away!" she shouted. "It'll spread. *After three, the multitude.*"

"Huh?"

"The Principle!"

But her warning went uncomprehended. Suzanna—her shock becoming exhilaration—was scanning the crowd. Everywhere she saw what Jerichau had described. Waves of color, plumes of it, rising from the flesh of Humankind. Almost all were subdued; some plain gray, others like plaited ribbons of grimy pastel; but once or twice in the throng she saw a pure pigment; brilliant orange around the head of a child carried high on her father's back; a peacock display from a girl laughing with her lover.

Again, Apolline tugged at her, and this time Suzanna acquiesced, but before they'd got more than a yard a cry rose from the crowd behind them—then another, and another—and suddenly to right and left people were putting their hands to their faces and covering their eyes. A man fell to his knees at Suzanna's side, spouting the Lord's prayer—somebody else had begun vomiting, others had seized hold of their nearest neighbor for support, only to find their private horror was a universal condition.

"Damn you," said Apolline. "Now look what you've done."

Suzanna could see the colors of the haloes changing, as panic convulsed those who wore them. The vanquished grays were shot through with violent greens and purples. The mingled din of shrieks and prayers assaulted her ears.

"Why?" said Suzanna.

"Capra's Principle!" Apolline yelled back at her. "*After three, the multitude.*"

Now Suzanna grasped the point. What two could keep to themselves became public knowledge if shared by three. As soon as she'd embraced Apolline and Jerichau's vision—one they'd known from birth—the fire had spread, a mystic contagion that had reduced the street to bedlam in seconds.

The fear bred violence almost instantly, as the crowd looked for scapegoats on which to blame these visions. Shoppers forsook their purchases and leaped upon each other's throats; secretaries broke their nails on the cheeks of accountants; grown men wept as they tried to shake sense from their wives and children.

What might have been a race of mystics was suddenly a pack of wild dogs, the colors they swam in degenerating into the gray and umber of a sick man's shit.

But there was more to come. No sooner had the fighting begun than a well-dressed woman, her makeup smeared in the struggle, pointed an accusing finger at Jerichau.

"Him!" she shrieked. "It was him!"

Then she flung herself at the guilty party, ready to take out his eyes. Jerichau stumbled back into the traffic as she came after him.

"Make it stop!" she yelled. "Make it stop!"

At her cacophony, several members of the crowd forgot their private wars and set their sights on this new target.

To Suzanna's left somebody said: "Kill him." An instant later, the first missile flew. It hit Jerichau's shoulder. A second followed. The traffic had come to a halt, as the drivers, slowed by curiosity, came under the influence of the vision. Jerichau was trapped against the cars, as the crowd turned on him. Suddenly, Suzanna knew, the issue was life and death. Confused and frightened, this mob was perfectly prepared, *eager* even, to tear Jerichau and anyone who went to his rescue limb from limb.

Another stone struck Jerichau, bringing blood to his cheek. Suzanna advanced toward him, calling for him to *move*, but he was watching the advancing crowd as if mesmerized by this display of human rage. She pushed on, climbing over a car bonnet and squeezing between bumpers to get to where he stood. But the leaders of the mob—the smeared woman and two or three others—were almost upon him.

"Leave him be!" she yelled. Nobody paid the least attention. There was something almost ritualistic about the way victim and executioners were playing this out, as though their cells knew it of old, and had no power to rewrite the story.

It was the police sirens that broke the spell. The first time Suzanna had heard that gut-churning wail and been thankful for it.

The effect was both immediate and comprehensive. Members of the crowd began to moan as though in sympathy with the sirens, those still in combat forsaking their enemies' throats, the rest staring down at their trampled belongings and bloodied fists in disbelief. One or two fainted on the spot. Several others began weeping again, this time more in confusion than fear. Many, deciding discretion bettered arrest, took to their heels. Shocked back into their Cuckoo blindness they fled in all directions, shaking their heads to dislodge the last vestiges of their vision.

Apolline had appeared at Jerichau's side, having maneuvered her way round the back of the mob during the previous few minutes.

She bullied him from his trance of sacrifice, shaking him and shouting. Then she hauled him away. Her rescue attempt came not a moment too soon, for though most of the lynching party had dispersed, a dozen or so weren't ready to give up their sport. They wanted blood, and would have it before the law arrived.

Suzanna looked around for some escape route. A small street off the main road offered some hope. She summoned Apolline with a shout. The arrival of the patrol cars proved a useful distraction: there was a further scattering of the mob.

But the hard core of dedicated lynchers came in pursuit. As Apolline and Jerichau reached the street corner the first of the mob, the woman with the smeared face, snatched at Apolline's dress. Apolline let go of Jerichau and turned on her attacker, delivering a punch to the woman's jaw that threw her to the ground.

A couple of the officers had caught sight of the chase and were now chasing in their turn, but before they could step in to prevent violence, Jerichau stumbled. In that second the mob was on him.

Suzanna turned back to lend him a hand. As she did so a car raced toward her, skirting the curb. The next second it was at her side, the door flung open, and Cal was yelling:

"Get in! Get in!"

"Wait!" she called to him, and looked back to see Jerichau being flung against a brick wall, cornered by the hounds. Apolline, who'd laid another of the mob out for good measure, was now making for the open car door. But Suzanna couldn't leave Jerichau.

She ran back toward the knot of bodies that now eclipsed him, blotting out the sound of Cal's voice calling her to get away while she could. By the time she reached Jerichau he'd given up all hope of resistance. He was just sliding down the wall, sheltering his bloodied head from a hail of spittle and blows. She shouted for the assault to stop but anonymous hands dragged her from his side.

Again she heard Cal shout, but she couldn't have gone to him now if she'd wanted to.

"*Drive!*" she yelled, praying to God he heard her and got going. Then she flung herself at the most vicious of Jerichau's tormentors. But there were simply too many hands holding her back, some covertly molesting her in the confusion of the moment. She struggled and shouted, but it was hopeless. In desperation she reached for Jerichau, and hung on to him for dear life, covering her head with her other arm as the bruising hail intensified.

Quite suddenly, the beating and the cursing and the kicks all ceased, as two officers broke into the ring of lynchers. Two or three of the mob had already taken the opportunity to slip away before they could be detained, but most of them showed not the least sign of guilt. Quite the reverse; they wiped the spit from their lips and began to justify their brutality in shrill voices.

"They started it, officer," said one of the number, a balding individual who, before the blood had stained his knuckles and shirt, might have been a bank cashier.

"Is that right?" said the officer, taking a look at the black derelict and his sullen mistress. "Get the fuck up, you two," he said. "You've got some questions to answer."

From *The Damnation Game*
THE FORBIDDEN

Like a flawless tragedy, the elegance of which structure is lost upon those suffering in it, the perfect geometry of the Spector Street Estate was visible only from the air. Walking in its drear canyons, passing through its grimy corridors from one gray concrete rectangle to the next, there was little to seduce the eye or stimulate the imagination. What few saplings had been planted in the quadrangles had long since been mutilated or uprooted; the grass, though tall, resolutely refused a healthy green.

No doubt the estate and its two companion developments had once been an architect's dream. No doubt the city planners had wept with pleasure at a design that housed three and thirty-six persons per hectare, and still boasted space for a children's playground. Doubtless fortunes and reputations had been built upon Spector Street, and at its opening fine words had been spoken of its being a yardstick by which all future developments would be measured. But the planners—tears wept, words spoken—had left the estate to its own devices; the architects occupied restored Georgian houses at the other end of the city, and probably never set foot here.

They would not have been shamed by the deterioration of the estate even if they had. Their brainchild (they would doubtless argue) was as brilliant as ever: its geometries as precise, its ratios as calculated; it was *people* who had spoiled Spector Street. Nor would they have been wrong in such an accusation. Helen had seldom seen an inner-city environment so comprehensively vandalized. Lamps had been shattered and backyard fences overthrown; cars whose wheels and engines had been removed and chassis burned blocked garage facilities. In one courtyard three or four ground-floor maisonettes had been entirely gutted by fire, their windows and doors boarded up with planks and corrugated metal shutters.

More startling still were the graffiti. That was what she had come here to see, encouraged by Archie's talk of the place, and she was not disappointed. It was difficult to believe, staring at the multiple layers of designs, names, obscenities, and dogmas that were scrawled and sprayed on every available brick, that Spector Street was barely three and a half years old. The walls, so recently virgin, were now so profoundly defaced that the Council Cleaning Department could never hope to return them to their former condition. A layer of whitewash to cancel this visual cacophony would only offer the scribes a fresh and yet more tempting surface on which to make their mark.

Helen was in seventh heaven. Every corner she turned offered some fresh material for her thesis: "Graffiti: The Semiotics of Urban Despair." It was a subject that married her two favorite disciplines—sociology and aesthetics—and as she wandered around the estate she began to wonder if there wasn't a book, in addition to her thesis, in the subject. She walked from courtyard to courtyard, copying down a large number of the more interesting scrawlings and noting their location. Then she went back to the car for her camera and tripod and returned to the most fertile of the areas, to make a thorough visual record of the walls.

It was a chilly business. She was not an expert photographer, and the late October sky was in full flight, shifting the light on the bricks from one moment to the next. As she adjusted and readjusted the exposure to compensate for the light changes, her fingers steadily became clumsier, her temper correspondingly thinner. But she struggled on, the idle curiosity of passersby notwithstanding. There were so many designs to document. She reminded herself that her present discomfort would be amply repaid when she showed the slides to Trevor, whose doubt of the project's validity had been perfectly apparent from the beginning.

"The writing on the wall?" he'd said, half smiling in that irritating fashion of his. "It's been done a hundred times."

This was true, of course; and yet not. There certainly were learned works on graffiti, chock full of sociological jargon: *cultural disenfranchisement*; *urban alienation*. But she flattered herself that *she* might find something among this litter of scrawlings that previous analysts had not: some unifying convention perhaps, that she could use as the lynchpin of her thesis. Only a vigorous cataloguing and cross-referencing of the phrases and images before her would reveal such a correspondence; hence the importance of this photographic study. So many hands had worked here; so many minds left their mark, however casually: if she could find some pattern, some predominant motive, or *motif*, the thesis would be guaranteed some serious attention, and so, in turn, would she.

"What are you doing?" a voice from behind her asked.

She turned from her calculations to see a young woman with a stroller on the pavement behind her. She looked weary, Helen thought, and pinched by the cold. The child in the stroller was mewling, his grimy fingers clutching an orange lollipop and the wrapping from a chocolate bar. The bulk of the chocolate, and the remains of previous jujubes, were displayed down the front of his coat.

Helen offered a thin smile to the woman; she looked in need of it.

"I'm photographing the walls," she said in answer to the initial inquiry, though surely this was perfectly apparent.

The woman—she could barely be twenty, Helen judged—said, "You mean the filth?"

"The writing and the pictures," Helen said. Then: "Yes. The filth."

"You from the council?"

"No, the university."

"It's bloody disgusting," the woman said. "The way they do that. It's not just kids, either."

"No?"

"Grown men. Grown men, too. They don't give a damn. Do it in broad daylight. You see 'em . . . broad daylight." She glanced down at the child, who was sharpening his lollipop on the ground. "Kerry!" she snapped, but the boy took no notice. "Are they going to wipe it off?" she asked Helen.

"I don't know," Helen said, and reiterated: "I'm from the university."

"Oh," the woman replied, as if this were new information, "so you're nothing to do with the council?"

"No."

"Some of it's obscene, isn't it. Really dirty. Makes me embarrassed to see some of the things they draw."

Helen nodded, casting an eye at the boy in the stroller. Kerry had decided to put his lollipop in his ear for safekeeping.

"Don't do that!" his mother told him, and leaned over to slap the child's hand. The blow, which was negligible, started the child bawling. Helen took the opportunity to return to her camera. But the woman still desired to talk. "It's not just on the outside, either," she commented.

"I beg your pardon?" Helen said.

"They break into the flats when they get vacant. The council tried to board them up, but it does no good. They break in anyway. Use them as toilets, and write more filth on the walls. They light fires, too. Then nobody can move back in."

The description piqued Helen's curiosity. Would the graffiti on the *inside* walls be substantially different from the public displays? It was certainly worth an investigation.

"Are there any places you know of around here like that?"

"Empty flats, you mean?"

"With graffiti."

"Just by us, there's one or two," the woman volunteered. "I'm in Butts's Court."

"Maybe you could show me?" Helen asked.

The woman shrugged.

"By the way, my name's Helen Buchanan."

"Anne-Marie," the mother replied.

"I'd be very grateful if you could point me to one of those empty flats."

Anne-Marie was baffled by Helen's enthusiasm and made no attempt to disguise it, but she shrugged again and said, "There's nothing much to see. Only more of the same stuff."

Helen gathered up her equipment and they walked side by side through the intersecting corridors between one square and the next. Though the estate was low-rise, each court only five stories high, the effect of each quadrangle was horribly claustrophobic. The walkways and staircases were a thief's dream, rife with blind corners and ill-lit tunnels. The rubbish-dumping facilities—chutes from the upper floors down which bags of refuse could be pitched—had long since been sealed up, thanks to their efficiency as firetraps. Now plastic bags of refuse were piled high in the corridors, many torn open by roaming dogs, their contents strewn across the ground. The smell, even in the cold weather, was unpleasant. In high summer it must have been overpowering.

"I'm over the other side," Anne-Marie said, pointing across the quadrangle. "The one with the yellow door." She then pointed along the opposite side of the court. "Five or six maisonettes from the far end," she said. "There's two of them been emptied out. Few weeks now. One of the family's moved into Ruskin Court; the other did a bunk in the middle of the night."

With that, she turned her back on Helen and wheeled Kerry, who had taken to trailing spittle from the side of his stroller, around the side of the square.

"Thank you," Helen called after her. Anne-Marie glanced over her shoulder briefly but did not reply. Appetite whetted, Helen made her way along the row of ground-floor maisonettes, many of which, though inhabited, showed little sign of being so. Their curtains were closely drawn; there were no milk bottles on the doorsteps, or children's toys left where they had been played with. Nothing, in fact, of *life* here. There *were* more graffiti however, sprayed, shockingly, on the doors of occupied houses. She granted the scrawlings only a casual perusal, in part because she feared that one of the doors might open as she examined a choice obscenity sprayed upon it, but more because she was eager to see what revelations the empty flats ahead might offer.

The malign scent of urine, both fresh and stale, welcomed her at the threshold of number 14, and beneath that the smell of burned paint and plastic. She hesitated for fully ten seconds, wondering if stepping into the maisonette was a wise move. The territory of the estate behind her was indisputably foreign, sealed off in its own misery, but the rooms in front of her were more intimidating still: a dark maze which her eyes could barely penetrate. But when her courage faltered she thought of Trevor, and how badly she wanted to silence his condescension. So thinking, she advanced into the place, deliberately kicking a piece of charred timber aside as she did so, in the hope that she would alert any tenant into showing himself.

There was no sound of occupancy, however. Gaining confidence, she began to explore the front room of the maisonette, which had been—to judge by the remains of a disemboweled sofa in one corner and the sodden carpet underfoot—a living room. The pale green walls were, as Anne-Marie had promised, extensively defaced, both by minor scribblers—content to work in pen, or even more crudely in soft charcoal—and by those with aspirations to public works, who had sprayed the walls in half a dozen colors.

Some of the comments were of interest, though many she had already seen on the walls outside. Familiar names and couplings repeated themselves. Though she had never set eyes on these individuals she knew how badly Fabian J. (A OK!) wanted to deflower Michelle; and that Michelle, in her turn, had the hots for somebody called Mr. Sheen. Here, as elsewhere, a man called White Rat boasted of his endowment, and the return of the Syllabub Brothers was promised in red paint. One or two of the pictures accompanying, or at least adjacent to, these phrases were of particular interest. An almost emblematic simplicity informed them. Beside the word *Christos* was a stick man with his hair radiating from his head like spines, and other heads impaled on each spine. Close by was an image of intercourse so brutally reduced that at first Helen took it to illustrate a knife plunging into a sightless eye. But fascinating as the images were, the room was too gloomy for her film and she had neglected to bring a flash. If she wanted a reliable record of these discoveries she would have to come again and for now be content with a simple exploration of the premises.

The maisonette wasn't that large, but the windows had been boarded up throughout, and as she moved farther from the front door the dubious light petered out altogether. The smell of urine, which had been strong at the door, intensified too, until by the time she reached the back of the living room and stepped along a short corridor into another room beyond, it was as cloying as incense. This room, being farthest from the front door, was also the darkest, and she had to wait a few moments in the cluttered gloom to allow her eyes to become useful. This, she guessed, had been the bedroom. What little furniture the residents had left behind them had been smashed to smithereens. Only the mattress had been left relatively untouched, dumped in the corner of the room among a wretched litter of blankets, newspapers, and pieces of crockery.

Outside, the sun found its way between the clouds, and two or three shafts of sunlight slipped between the boards nailed across the bedroom

window and pierced the room like annunciations, scoring the opposite
wall with bright lines. Here, the graffitists had been busy once more: the
usual clamor of love letters and threats. She scanned the wall quickly, and
as she did so her eye was led by the beams of light across the room to the
wall that contained the door she had stepped through.

Here, the artists had also been at work, but had produced an image the
like of which she had not seen anywhere else. Using the door, which was
centrally placed in the wall, like a mouth, the artists had sprayed a single
vast head onto the stripped plaster. The painting was more adroit than
most she had seen, rife with detail that lent the image an unsettling verac-
ity. The cheekbones jutting through skin the color of buttermilk; the teeth,
sharpened to irregular points, all converging on the door. The eyes were,
owing to the room's low ceiling, set mere inches above the upper lip, but
this physical adjustment only lent force to the image, giving the impression that the head was thrown back. Knotted strands of hair snaked from
the scalp across the ceiling.

Was it a portrait? There was something naggingly *specific* in the details of
the brows and the lines around the wide mouth; in the careful picturing of
those vicious teeth. A nightmare certainly: a facsimile, perhaps, of something
from a heroin fugue. Whatever its origins, it was potent. Even the illusion of
door-as-mouth worked. The short passageway between living room and bedroom offered a passable throat, with a tattered lamp in lieu of tonsils. Beyond
the gullet, the day burned white in the nightmare's belly. The whole effect
brought to mind a ghost-train painting. The same heroic deformity, the same
unashamed intention to scare. And it worked; she stood in the bedroom
almost stupefied by the picture, its red-rimmed eyes fixing her mercilessly.
Tomorrow, she determined, she would come here again, this time with high-
speed film and a flash to illuminate the masterwork.

As she prepared to leave the sun went in, and the bands of light faded.
She glanced over her shoulder at the boarded windows, and saw for the
first time that one four-word slogan had been sprayed on the wall beneath
them.

"Sweets to the sweet," it read. She was familiar with the quote, but not
with its source. Was it a profession of love? If so, it was an odd location for
such an avowal. Despite the mattress in the corner, and the relative privacy of this room, she could not imagine the intended reader of such
words ever stepping in here to receive her bouquet. No adolescent lovers,
however heated, would lie down here to play at mothers and fathers; not

under the gaze of the terror on the wall. She crossed to examine the writing. The paint looked to be the same shade of pink as had been used to color the gums of the screaming man; perhaps the same hand?

Behind her, a noise. She turned so quickly she almost tripped over the blanket-strewn mattress.

"Who—?"

At the other end of the gullet, in the living room, was a scabby-kneed boy of six or seven. He stared at Helen, eyes glittering in the half-light, as if waiting for a cue.

"Yes?" she said.

"Anne-Marie says do you want a cup of tea?" he declared without pause or intonation.

Her conversation with the woman seemed hours past. She was grateful for the invitation however. The damp in the maisonette had chilled her.

"Yes," she said to the boy. "Yes, please."

The child didn't move but simply stared at her.

"Are you going to lead the way?" she asked him.

"If you want," he replied, unable to raise a trace of enthusiasm.

"I'd like that."

"You taking photographs?" he asked.

"Yes. Yes, I am. But not in here."

"Why not?"

"It's too dark," she told him.

"Don't it work in the dark?" he wanted to know.

"No."

The boy nodded at this, as if the information somehow fitted well into his scheme of things, and about-turned without another word, clearly expecting Helen to follow.

If she had been taciturn in the street, Anne-Marie was anything but in the privacy of her own kitchen. Gone was the guarded curiosity, to be replaced by a stream of lively chatter and a constant scurrying between half a dozen minor domestic tasks, like a juggler keeping several plates spinning simultaneously. Helen watched this balancing act with some admiration; her own domestic skills were negligible. At last, the meandering conversation turned back to the subject that had brought Helen here.

"Them photographs," Anne-Marie said, "why'd you want to take them?"

"I'm writing about graffiti. The photos will illustrate my thesis."

"It's not very pretty."

"No, you're right, it isn't. But I find it interesting."

Anne-Marie shook her head. "I hate the whole estate," she said. "It's not safe here. People getting robbed on their own doorsteps. Kids setting fire to the rubbish day in, day out. Last summer we had the fire brigade here two, three times a day, till they sealed them chutes off. Now people just dump the bags in the passageways, and that attracts rats."

"Do you live here alone?"

"Yes," she said, "since Davey walked out."

"That your husband?"

"He was Kerry's father, but we weren't never married. We lived together two years, you know. We had some good times. Then he just upped and went off one day when I was at me Mam's with Kerry." She peered into her tea cup. "I'm better off without him," she said. "But you get scared sometimes. Want some more tea?"

"I don't think I've got time."

"Just a cup," Anne-Marie said, already up and unplugging the electric kettle to take it to the sink for a refill. As she was about to turn on the tap she saw something on the draining board and drove her thumb down, grinding it out. "Got you, you bugger," she said, then turned to Helen. "We got these bloody ants."

"Ants?"

"Whole estate's infected. From Egypt, they are: pharaoh ants, they're called. Little brown sods. They breed in the central heating ducts, you see; that way they get into all the flats. Place is plagued with them."

This unlikely exoticism (ants from Egypt?) struck Helen as comical, but she said nothing. Anne-Marie was staring out of the kitchen window and into the backyard.

"You should tell them," she said, though Helen wasn't certain whom she was being instructed to tell. "Tell them that ordinary people can't even walk the streets any longer—"

"Is it really so bad?" Helen said, frankly tiring of this catalogue of misfortunes.

Anne-Marie turned from the sink and looked at her hard.

"We've had murders here," she said.

"Really?"

"We had one in the summer. An old man he was, from Ruskin. That's just next door. I didn't know him, but he was a friend of the sister of the woman next door. I forget his name."

"And he was murdered?"

"Cut to ribbons in his own front room. They didn't find him for almost a week."

"What about his neighbors? Didn't they notice his absence?"

Anne-Marie shrugged, as if the most important pieces of information—the murder and the man's isolation—had been divulged and any further inquiries into the problem were irrelevant. But Helen pressed the point.

"Seems strange to me," she said.

Anne-Marie plugged in the filled kettle. "Well, it happened," she replied, unmoved.

"I'm not saying it didn't, I just—"

"His eyes had been taken out," she said, before Helen could voice any further doubts.

Helen winced. "No," she said under her breath.

"That's the truth," Anne-Marie said. "And that wasn't all that'd been done to him." She paused for effect, then went on: "You wonder what kind of person's capable of doing things like that, don't you? You wonder." Helen nodded. She was thinking precisely the same thing.

"Did they ever find the man responsible?"

Anne-Marie snorted her disparagement: "Police don't give a damn what happens here. They keep off the estate as much as possible. When they do patrol all they do is pick up kids for getting drunk and that. They're afraid, you see. That's why they keep clear."

"Of this killer?"

"Maybe," Anne-Marie replied. Then: "He had a hook."

"A hook?"

"The man what done it. He had a hook, like Jack the Ripper."

Helen was no expert on murder, but she felt certain that the Ripper hadn't boasted a hook. It seemed churlish to question the truth of Anne-Marie's story, however; though she silently wondered how much of this—the eyes taken out, the body rotting in the flat, the hook—was elaboration. The most scrupulous of reporters was surely tempted to embellish a story once in a while.

Anne-Marie had poured herself another cup of tea and was about to do the same for her guest.

"No thank you," Helen said. "I really should go."

"You married?" Anne-Marie asked, out of the blue.

"Yes. To a lecturer from the university."

"What's his name?"

"Trevor."

Anne-Marie put two heaped spoonfuls of sugar into her cup of tea. "Will you be coming back?" she asked.

"Yes, I hope to. Later in the week. I want to take some photographs of the pictures in the maisonette across the court."

"Well, call in."

"I shall. And thank you for your help."

"That's all right," Anne-Marie replied. "You've got to tell somebody, haven't you?"

"The man apparently had a hook instead of a hand."

Trevor looked up from his plate of tagliatelle con prosciutto. "Beg your pardon?"

Helen had been at pains to keep her recounting of this story as uncolored by her own response as she could. She was interested to know what Trevor would make of it, and she knew that if she once signaled her own stance he would instinctively take an opposing view out of plain bloody-mindedness.

"He had a hook," she repeated, without inflection.

Trevor put down his fork and plucked at his nose, sniffing. "I didn't read anything about this," he said.

"You don't read the local papers," Helen returned. "Neither of us do. Maybe it never made any of the nationals."

"'Geriatric Murdered by Hook-Handed Maniac'?" Trevor said, savoring the hyperbole. "I would have thought it very newsworthy. When was all of this supposed to have happened?"

"Sometime last summer. Maybe we were in Ireland."

"Maybe," said Trevor, taking up his fork again. Bending to his food, the polished lens of his spectacles reflected only the plate of pasta and chopped ham in front of him, not his eyes.

"Why do you say *maybe*?" Helen prodded.

"It doesn't sound quite right," he said. "In fact it sounds bloody preposterous."

"You don't believe it?" Helen said.

Trevor looked up from his food, tongue rescuing a speck of tagliatelle from the corner of his mouth. His face had relaxed into that noncommittal expression of his—the same face he wore, no doubt, when listening to his students. "Do *you* believe it?" he asked Helen. It was a favorite time-gaining device of his, another seminar trick, to question the questioner.

"I'm not certain," Helen replied, too concerned with finding some solid ground in this sea of doubts to waste energy scoring points.

"All right, forget the tale," Trevor said, deserting his food for another glass of red wine. "What about the teller? Did you trust her?"

Helen pictured Anne-Marie's earnest expression as she told the story of the old man's murder. "Yes," she said. "Yes, I think I would have known if she'd been lying to me."

"So why's it so important, anyhow? I mean, whether she's lying or not, what the fuck does it matter?"

It was a reasonable question, if irritatingly put. Why *did* it matter? Was it that she wanted to have her worst feelings about Spector Street proved false? That such an estate be filthy, be hopeless, be a dump where the undesirable and the disadvantaged were tucked out of public view—all that was a liberal commonplace, and she accepted it as an unpalatable social reality. But the story of the old man's murder and mutilation was something other. An image of violent death that, once with her, refused to part from her company.

She realized, to her chagrin, that this confusion was plain on her face, and that Trevor, watching her across the table, was not a little entertained by it.

"If it bothers you so much," he said, "why don't you go back there and ask around, instead of playing believe-it-or-not over dinner?"

She couldn't help but rise to his remark. "I thought you liked guessing games," she said.

He threw her a sullen look. "Wrong again," he said.

The suggestion that she investigate was not a bad one, though doubtless he had ulterior motives for offering it. She viewed Trevor less charitably day by day. What she had once thought in him a fierce commitment to debate she now recognized as mere power play. He argued, not for the thrill of dialectic, but because he was pathologically competitive. She had seen him, time and again, take up attitudes she knew he did not espouse, simply to spill blood. Nor, more's the pity, was he alone in this sport. Academe was one of the last strongholds of the professional time-waster. On occasion their circle seemed entirely dominated by educated fools, lost in a wasteland of stale rhetoric and hollow commitment.

From one wasteland to another. She returned to Spector Street the following day, armed with a flashgun in addition to her tripod and high-sensitivity film. The wind was up today, and it was arctic, more furious still for being trapped in the maze of passageways and courts. She made her way to number 14 and spent the next hour in its befouled confines, meticulously photographing both the bedroom and living-room walls. She had half expected the impact of the head in the bedroom to be dulled by reacquaintance. It was not. Though she struggled to capture its scale and detail as best she could, she knew the photographs would be at best a dim echo of its perpetual howl.

Much of its power lay in its context, of course. That such an image might be stumbled upon in surroundings so drab, so conspicuously lacking in mystery, was akin to finding an icon on a rubbish heap: a gleaming symbol of transcendence from a world of toil and decay into some darker but more tremendous realm. She was painfully aware that the intensity of her response probably defied her articulation. Her vocabulary was analytic, replete with buzzwords and academic terminology, but woefully impoverished when it came to evocation. The photographs, pale as they would be, would, she hoped, at least hint at the potency of this picture, even if they couldn't conjure up the way it froze the bowels.

When she emerged from the maisonette the wind was as uncharitable as ever, but the boy waiting outside—the same child as had attended upon her yesterday—was dressed as if for spring weather. He grimaced in his effort to keep the shudders at bay.

"Hello," Helen said.

"I waited," the child announced.

"Waited?"

"Anne-Marie said you'd come back."

"I wasn't planning to come until later in the week," Helen said. "You might have waited a long time."

The boy's grimace relaxed a notch. "It's all right," he said. "I've got nothing to do."

"What about school?"

"Don't like it," the boy replied, as if not obliged to be educated if it wasn't to his taste.

"I see," said Helen, and began to walk down the side of the quadrangle. The boy followed. On the patch of grass at the center of the quadrangle several chairs and two or three dead saplings had been piled.

"What's this?" she said, half to herself.

"Bonfire Night," the boy informed her. "Next week."

"Of course."

"You going to see Anne-Marie?" he asked.

"Yes."

"She's not in."

"Oh. Are you sure?"

"Yeah."

"Well, perhaps *you* can help me . . ." She stopped and turned to face the child; smooth bags of fatigue hung beneath his eyes. "I heard about an old man who was murdered near here," she said to him. "In the summer. Do you know anything about that?"

"No."

"Nothing at all? You don't remember anybody getting killed?"

"No," the boy said again, with impressive finality. "I don't remember."

"Well, thank you anyway."

This time, when she retraced her steps back to the car, the boy didn't follow. But as she turned the corner out of the quadrangle she glanced back to see him standing on the spot where she'd left him, staring after her as if she were a madwoman.

By the time she had reached the car and packed the photographic equipment into the trunk there were specks of rain in the wind, and she was sorely tempted to forget she'd ever heard Anne-Marie's story and make her way home, where the coffee would be warm even if the welcome wasn't. But she needed an answer to the question Trevor had put the previous night. Do *you* believe it? he'd asked when she'd told him the story. She hadn't known how to answer then, and she still didn't. Perhaps (why did she sense this?) the terminology of verifiable truth was redundant here; perhaps the final answer to his question was not an answer at all, only another question. If so, so. She had to find out.

Ruskin Court was as forlorn as its fellows, if not more so. It didn't even boast a bonfire. On the third-floor balcony a woman was taking washing in before the rain broke; on the grass in the center of the quadrangle two dogs were absentmindedly rutting, the fuckee staring up at the blank sky. As she walked along the empty pavement she set her face determinedly; a purposeful look, Bernadette had once said, deterred attack. When she caught sight of two women talking at the far end of the court she crossed over to them hurriedly, grateful for their presence.

"Excuse me?"

The women, both middle-aged, ceased their animated exchange and looked her over.

"I wonder if you can help me?"

She could feel their appraisal, and their distrust; they went undisguised. One of the pair, her face florid, said plainly, "What do you want?"

Helen suddenly felt bereft of the least power to charm. What was she to say to these two that wouldn't make her motives appear ghoulish? "I was told . . . ," she began, and then stumbled, aware that she would get no assistance from either woman. "I was told there'd been a murder near here. Is that right?"

The florid woman raised eyebrows so plucked they were barely visible. "Murder?" she said.

"Are you from the press?" the other woman inquired. The years had soured her features beyond sweetening. Her small mouth was deeply lined; her hair, which had been dyed brunette, showed a half-inch of gray at the roots.

"No, I'm not from the press," Helen said. "I'm a friend of Anne-Marie's, in Butts's Court." This claim of *friend* stretched the truth, but it seemed to mellow the women somewhat.

"Visiting, are you?" the florid woman asked.

"In a manner of speaking—"

"You missed the warm spell—"

"Anne-Marie was telling me about somebody who'd been murdered here, during the summer. I was curious about it."

"Is that right?"

"Do you know anything about it?"

"Lots of things go on around here," said the second woman. "You don't know the half of it."

"So it's true," Helen said.

"They had to close the toilets," the first woman put in.

"That's right. They did," the other said.

"The toilets?" Helen said. What had this to do with the old man's death?

"It was terrible," the first said. "Was it your Frank, Josie, who told you about it?"

"No, not Frank," Josie replied. "Frank was still at sea. It was Mrs. Tyzack."

The witness established, Josie relinquished the story to her companion, and turned her gaze back upon Helen. The suspicion had not yet died from her eyes.

"This was only the month before last," Josie said. "Just about the end of August. It was August, wasn't it?" She looked to the other woman for verification. "You've got the head for dates, Maureen."

Maureen looked uncomfortable. "I forget," she said, clearly unwilling to offer testimony.

"I'd like to know," Helen said. Josie, despite her companion's reluctance, was eager to oblige.

"There's some lavatories," she said, "outside the shops—you know, public lavatories. I'm not quite sure how it all happened exactly, but there used to be a boy . . . well, he wasn't a boy really. I mean he was a man of twenty or more, but he was"—she fished for the words—"mentally subnormal, I suppose you'd say. His mother used to have to take him around like he was a four year old. Anyhow, she let him go into the lavatories while she went to that little supermarket, what's it called?" She turned to Maureen for prompting, but the other woman just looked back, her disapproval plain. Josie was ungovernable, however. "Broad daylight, this was," she said to Helen. "Middle of the day. Anyhow, the boy went to the toilet, and the mother was in the shop. And after a while, you know how you do, she's busy shopping, she forgets about him, and then she thinks he's been gone a long time . . ."

At this juncture Maureen couldn't prevent herself from butting in: the accuracy of the story apparently took precedence over her wariness.

"She got into an argument," she corrected Josie, "with the manager. About some bad bacon she'd had from him. That was why she was such a time."

"I see," said Helen.

"Anyway," said Josie, picking up the tale, "she finished her shopping and when she came out he still wasn't there—"

"So she asked someone from the supermarket—" Maureen began, but Josie wasn't about to have her narrative snatched away at this vital juncture.

"She asked one of the men from the supermarket," she repeated over Maureen's interjection, "to go down into the lavatory and find him."

"It was terrible," said Maureen, clearly picturing the atrocity in her mind's eye.

"He was lying on the floor, in a pool of blood."

"Murdered?"

Josie shook her head. "He'd have been better off dead. He'd been attacked with a razor"—she let this piece of information sink in before delivering the coup de grâce—"and they'd cut off his private parts. Just cut them off and flushed them down a toilet. No reason on earth to do it."

"Oh my God."

"Better off dead," Josie repeated. "I mean, they can't mend something like that, can they?"

The appalling tale was rendered worse still by the sangfroid of the teller, and by the casual repetition of "Better off dead."

"The boy," Helen said. "Was he able to describe his attackers?"

"No," said Josie, "he's practically an imbecile. He can't string more than two words together."

"And nobody saw anyone go into the lavatory? Or leaving it?"

"People come and go all the time," Maureen said. This, though it sounded like an adequate explanation, had not been Helen's experience. There was not a great bustle in the quadrangle and passageways; far from it. Perhaps the shopping mall was busier, she reasoned, and might offer adequate cover for such a crime.

"So they haven't found the culprit," she said.

"No," Josie replied, her eyes losing their fervor. The crime and its immediate consequences were the nub of this story; she had little or no interest in either the culprit or his capture.

"We're not safe in our own bed," Maureen observed. "You ask anyone."

"Anne-Marie said the same," Helen replied. "That's how she came to tell me about the old man. Said he was murdered during the summer, here in Ruskin Court."

"I do remember something," Josie said. "There *was* some talk I heard. An old man, and his dog. He was battered to death, and the dog ended up . . . I don't know. It certainly wasn't here. It must have been one of the other estates."

"Are you sure?"

The woman looked offended by this slur on her memory. "Oh yes," she said, "I mean if it had been here, we'd have known the story, wouldn't we?"

Helen thanked the pair for their help and decided to take a stroll around the quadrangle anyway, just to see how many more maisonettes were unoccupied.

As in Butts's Court, many of the curtains were drawn and all the doors locked. But then if Spector Street *was* under siege from a maniac capable of the murder and mutilation such as she'd heard described, she was not surprised that the residents took to their homes and stayed there. There was nothing much to see around the court. All the unoccupied maisonettes and flats had been recently sealed, to judge by a litter of nails left on a doorstep by the council workmen. One sight *did* catch her attention however. Scrawled on the paving stones she was walking over—and all but erased by rain and the passage of feet—the same phrase she'd seen in the bedroom of number 14: "Sweets to the sweet." The words were so benign; why did she seem to sense menace in them? Was it in their excess, perhaps, in the sheer overabundance of sugar upon sugar, honey upon honey?

She walked on, though the rain persisted, away from the quadrangles and into a concrete no-man's-land through which she had not previously passed. This was—or had been—the site of the estate's amenities. Here was the children's playground, its metal-framed rides overturned, its sand-pit fouled by dogs, its paddling pool empty. And here too were the shops. Several had been boarded up; those that hadn't were dingy and unattractive, their windows protected by heavy wire-mesh.

She walked along the row, and rounded a corner, and there in front of her was a squat brick building. The public lavatory, she guessed, though the signs designating it as such had gone. The iron gates were closed and padlocked. Standing in front of the charmless building, the wind gusting around her legs, she couldn't help but think of what had happened here. Of the man-child, bleeding on the floor, helpless to cry out. It made her queasy even to contemplate it. She turned her thoughts instead to the felon. What would he look like, she wondered, a man capable of such a depravity? She tried to make an image of him, but no detail she could conjure up carried sufficient force. But then monsters were seldom very terrible once hauled into the plain light of day. As long as this man was known only by his deeds he held untold power over the imagination; but the human truth beneath the terrors would, she knew, be bitterly disappointing. No monster he, just a whey-faced apology for a man more needful of pity than awe.

The next gust of wind brought the rain on more heavily. It was time, she decided, to be done with adventures for the day. Turning her back on the public lavatories, she hurried back through the quadrangles to the refuge of the car, the icy rain needling her face to numbness.

_____

The dinner guests looked gratifyingly appalled at the story, and Trevor, to judge by the expression on his face, was furious. It was done now, however; there was no taking it back. Nor could she deny the satisfaction she took in having silenced the interdepartmental babble about the table. It was Bernadette, Trevor's assistant in the history department, who broke the agonizing hush.

"When was this?"

"During the summer," Helen told her.

"I don't recall reading about it," said Archie, much the better for two hours of drinking; it mellowed a tongue that was otherwise fulsome in its self-coruscation.

"Perhaps the police are suppressing it," Daniel commented.

"Conspiracy?" said Trevor, plainly cynical.

"It's happening all the time," Daniel shot back.

"Why should they suppress something like this?" Helen said. "It doesn't make sense."

"Since when has police procedure made sense?" Daniel replied.

Bernadette cut in before Helen could answer. "We don't even bother to read about these things any longer," she said.

"Speak for yourself," somebody piped up, but she ignored whoever it was and went on:

"We're punch-drunk with violence. We don't see it any longer, even when it's in front of our noses."

"On the screen every night," Archie put in. "Death and disaster in full color."

"There's nothing very modern about that," Trevor said. "An Elizabethan would have seen death all the time. Public executions were a very popular form of entertainment."

The table broke up into a cacophony of opinions. After two hours of polite gossip the dinner party had suddenly caught fire. Listening to the debate rage, Helen was sorry she hadn't had time to have the photographs processed and printed; the graffiti would have added further fuel to this exhilarating row. It was Purcell, as usual, who was the last to weigh in with his point of view; and—again, as usual—it was devastating.

"Of course, Helen, my sweet," he began, that affected weariness in his voice edged with the anticipation of controversy, "your witnesses could all be lying, couldn't they?"

The talking around the table dwindled, and all heads turned in Purcell's direction. Perversely, he ignored the attention he'd garnered and turned to whisper in the ear of the boy he'd brought—a new passion who would, as in the past, be discarded in a matter of weeks for another pretty urchin.

"Lying?" Helen said. She could already feel herself bristling at the observation, and Purcell had spoken only a dozen words.

"Why not?" the other replied, lifting his glass of wine to his lips. "Perhaps they're all weaving some elaborate fiction or other. The story of the spastic's mutilation in the public toilet. The murder of the old man. Even that hook. All quite familiar elements. You must be aware that there's something *traditional* about these atrocity stories. One used to exchange them all the time; there was a certain frisson in them. Something competitive maybe, in attempting to find a new detail to add to the collective fiction; a fresh twist that would render the tale that little bit more appalling when you passed it on."

"It may be familiar to you—" Helen said defensively. Purcell was always so *poised*; it irritated her. Even if there were validity in his argument, which she doubted, she was damned if she'd concede it. "I've never heard this kind of story before."

"Haven't you?" said Purcell, as though she were admitting to illiteracy. "What about the lovers and the escaped lunatic, have you heard that one?"

"I've heard that," Daniel said.

"The lover is disemboweled—usually by a hook-handed man—and the body left on the top of the car, while the fiancé cowers inside. It's a cautionary tale, warning of the evils of rampant heterosexuality." The joke won a round of laughter from everyone but Helen. "These stories are very common."

"So you're saying that they're telling me lies," she protested.

"Not lies, exactly—"

"You said *lies*."

"I was being provocative," Purcell returned, his placatory tone more enraging than ever. "I don't mean to imply there's any serious mischief in it. But you must concede that so far you haven't met a single *witness*. All these events have happened at some unspecified date to some unspecified person. They are reported at several removes. They occurred at best to the brothers of friends of distant relations. Please consider the possibility that perhaps these events do not exist in the real world at all, but are merely titillation for bored housewives."

Helen didn't make an argument in return, for the simple reason that she lacked one. Purcell's point about the conspicuous absence of witnesses was perfectly sound; she herself had wondered about it. It was strange, too, the way the women in Ruskin Court had speedily consigned the old man's murder to another estate, as though these atrocities always occurred just out of sight—around the next corner, down the next passageway—but never *here*.

"So why?" said Bernadette.

"Why what?" Archie puzzled.

"The stories. Why tell these horrible stories if they're not true?"

"Yes," said Helen, throwing the controversy back into Purcell's ample lap. "*Why?*"

Purcell preened himself, aware that his entry into the debate had changed the basic assumption at a stroke. "I don't know," he said, happy to be done with the game now that he'd shown his arm. "You really mustn't take me too seriously, Helen. *I* try not to." The boy at Purcell's side tittered.

"Maybe it's simply taboo material," Archie said.

"Suppressed—" Daniel prompted.

"Not the way you mean it," Archie retorted. "The whole world isn't politics, Daniel."

"Such naïveté."

"What's so taboo about death?" Trevor said. "Bernadette already pointed out: it's in front of us all the time. Television, newspapers."

"Maybe that's not close enough," Bernadette suggested.

"Does anyone mind if I smoke?" Purcell broke in. "Dessert seems to have been indefinitely postponed."

Helen ignored the remark and asked Bernadette what she meant by "not close enough."

Bernadette shrugged. "I don't know precisely," she confessed, "maybe just that death has to be *near*; we have to *know* it's just around the corner. The television's not intimate enough."

Helen frowned. The observation made some sense to her, but in the clutter of the moment she couldn't root out its significance.

"Do you think they're stories too?" she asked.

"Andrew has a point—" Bernadette replied.

"Most kind," said Purcell. "Has somebody got a match? The boy's pawned my lighter."

"About the absence of witnesses."

"All that proves is that I haven't met anybody who's actually *seen* anything," Helen encountered, "not that witnesses don't exist."

"All right," said Purcell. "Find me one. If you can prove to me that your atrocity monger actually lives and breathes, I'll stand everyone dinner at Apollinaire's. How's that? Am I generous to a fault, or do I just know when I can't lose?" He laughed, knocking on the table with his knuckles by way of applause.

"Sounds good to me," said Trevor. "What do you say, Helen?"

She didn't go back to Spector Street until the following Monday, but all weekend she was there in thought: standing outside the locked toilet, with the wind bringing rain; or in the bedroom, the portrait looming. Thoughts of the estate claimed all her concern. When, late on Saturday afternoon, Trevor found some petty reason for an argument, she let the insults pass, watching him perform the familiar ritual of self-martyrdom without being touched by it in the least. Her indifference only enraged him further. He stormed out in high dudgeon, to visit whichever of his women was in favor this month. She was glad to see the back of him. When he failed to return that night she didn't even think of weeping about it. He was foolish and vacuous. She despaired of ever seeing a haunted look in his dull eyes; and what worth was a man who could not be haunted?

He did not return Sunday night either, and it crossed her mind the following morning, as she parked the car in the heart of the estate, that nobody even knew she had come, and that she might lose herself for days here and nobody would be any the wiser. Like the old man Anne-Marie had told her about: lying forgotten in his favorite armchair with his eyes hooked out, while the flies feasted and the butter went rancid on the table.

It was almost Bonfire Night, and over the weekend the small heap of combustibles in Butts's Court had grown to a substantial size. The construction looked unsound, but that didn't prevent a number of boys from clambering over and into it. Much of its bulk was made up of furniture, filched, no doubt, from boarded-up properties. She doubted if it could burn for any time: if it did, it would be chokingly smoky. Four times, on her way across to Anne-Marie's house, she was waylaid by children begging for money to buy fireworks.

"Penny for the guy," they'd say, though none had a guy to display. She had emptied her pockets of change by the time she reached the front door.

Anne-Marie was in today, though there was no welcoming smile. She simply stared at her visitor as if mesmerized.

"I hope you don't mind me calling . . ."

Anne-Marie made no reply.

"I just wanted a word."

"I'm busy," the woman finally announced. There was no invitation inside, no offer of tea.

"Oh. Well . . . it won't take more than a moment."

The back door was open and a draft blew through the house. Papers were flying about in the backyard. Helen could see them lifting into the air like vast white moths.

"What do you want?" Anne-Marie asked.

"Just to ask you about the old man."

The woman frowned minutely. She looked as if she might be sick. Helen thought her face had the color and texture of stale dough. Her hair was lank and greasy.

"What old man?"

"Last time I was here, you told me about an old man who'd been murdered, do you remember?"

"No."

"You said he lived in the next court."

"I don't remember," Anne-Marie said.

"But you *distinctly* told me—"

Something fell to the floor in the kitchen and smashed. Anne-Marie flinched but did not move from the doorstep, her arm barring Helen's way into the house. The hallway was littered with the child's toys, gnawed and battered.

"Are you all right?"

Anne-Marie nodded. "I've got work to do," she said.

"And you don't remember telling me about the old man?"

"You must have misunderstood," Anne-Marie replied, and then, her voice hushed: "You shouldn't have come. Everybody *knows*."

"Knows what?"

The girl had begun to tremble. "You don't understand, do you? You think people aren't watching?"

"What does it matter? All I asked was—"

"I don't know *anything*," Anne-Marie reiterated. "Whatever I said to you, I lied about it."

"Well, thank you anyway," Helen said, too perplexed by the confusion of signals from Anne-Marie to press the point any further. Almost as soon as she had turned from the door she heard the lock snap closed behind her.

That conversation was only one of several disappointments that morning brought. Helen went back to the row of shops and visited the supermarket that Josie had spoken of. There she inquired about the lavatories and their recent history. The supermarket had changed hands only in the last month, and the new owner, a taciturn Pakistani, insisted that he knew nothing of when or why the lavatories had been closed. She was aware, as she made her inquiries, of being scrutinized by the other customers in the store; she felt like a pariah. That feeling deepened when, after leaving the supermarket, she saw Josie emerging from the launderette and called after her, only to have the woman pick up her pace and duck away into the maze of corridors. Helen followed but rapidly lost both her quarry and her way.

Frustrated to the verge of tears, she stood among the overturned rubbish bags and felt a surge of contempt for her foolishness. She didn't belong here, did she? How many times had she criticized others for their presumption in claiming to understand societies they had merely viewed from afar? And here was she, committing the same crime, coming here with her camera and her questions, using the lives (and deaths) of these people as fodder for party conversation. She didn't blame Anne-Marie for turning her back; had she deserved better?

Tired and chilled, she decided it was time to concede Purcell's point. It *was* all fiction she had been told. They had played with her—sensing her desire to be fed some horrors—and she, the perfect fool, had fallen for every ridiculous word. It was time to pack up her credulity and go home.

One call demanded to be made before she returned to the car however: she wanted to look a final time at the painted head. Not as an anthropologist among an alien tribe, but as a confessed ghost-train rider: for the thrill of it. Arriving at number 14, however, she faced the last and most crushing disappointment. The maisonette had been sealed up by conscientious council workmen. The door was locked; the front window boarded over.

She was determined not to be so easily defeated however. She made her way around the back of Butts's Court and located the yard of number 14 by simple mathematics. The gate was wedged closed from the inside, but she pushed hard against it, and with the effort, it opened. A heap of rub-bish—rotted carpets, a box of rain-sodden magazines, a denuded Christ-mas tree—had blocked it.

She crossed the yard to the boarded-up windows and peered through the slats of wood. It wasn't bright outside, but it was darker still within; it was difficult to catch more than the vaguest hint of the painting on the bedroom wall. She pressed her face close to the wood, eager for a final glimpse.

A shadow moved across the room, momentarily blocking her view. She stepped back from the window, startled, not certain of what she'd seen. Perhaps merely her own shadow, cast through the window? But then *she* hadn't moved; it had.

She approached the window again, more cautiously. The air vibrated; she could hear a muted whine from somewhere, though she couldn't be certain whether it came from inside or out. Again, she put her face to the rough boards, and suddenly, something leaped at the window. This time she let out a cry. There was a scrabbling sound from within as nails raked the wood.

A dog! And a big one to have jumped so high.

"Stupid," she told herself aloud. A sudden sweat bathed her.

The scrabbling had stopped almost as soon as it had started, but she couldn't bring herself to go back to the window. Clearly the workmen who had sealed up the maisonette had failed to check it properly and incarcerated the animal by mistake. It was ravenous, to judge by the slavering she'd heard; she was grateful she hadn't attempted to break in. The dog—hungry, maybe half-mad in the stinking darkness—could have taken out her throat.

She stared at the boarded-up window. The slits between the boards were barely a half-inch wide, but she sensed that the animal was up on its hind legs on the other side, watching her through the gap. She could hear its panting now that her own breath was regularizing; she could hear its claws raking the sill.

"Bloody thing . . . ," she said. "Damn well stay in there."

She backed off toward the gate. Hosts of wood lice and spiders, dis-turbed from their nests by the moving of the carpets behind the gate, were scurrying underfoot, looking for a fresh darkness to call home.

She closed the gate behind her and was making her way around the front of the block when she heard the sirens; two ugly spirals of sound that made the hair on the back of her neck tingle. They were approaching. She picked up her speed, and came around into Butts's Court in time to see several policemen crossing the grass behind the bonfire and an ambulance mounting the pavement and driving around to the other side of the quadrangle. People had emerged from their flats and were standing on their balconies, staring down. Others were walking around the court, nakedly curious, to join a gathering congregation. Helen's stomach seemed to drop to her bowels when she realized *where* the hub of interest lay: at Anne-Marie's doorstep. The police were clearing a path through the throng for the ambulance men. A second police car had followed the route of the ambulance onto the pavement; two plainclothes officers were getting out.

She walked to the periphery of the crowd. What little talk there was among the onlookers was conducted in low voices; one or two of the older women were crying. Though she peered over the heads of the spectators she could see nothing. Turning to a bearded man, whose child was perched on his shoulders, she asked what was going on. He didn't know. Somebody dead, he'd heard, but he wasn't certain.

"Anne-Marie?" she asked.

A woman in front of her turned and said: "You know her?" almost awed, as if speaking of a loved one.

"A little," Helen replied hesitantly. "Can you tell me what's happened?"

The woman involuntarily put her hand to her mouth, as if to stop the words before they came. But here they were nevertheless: "The child—" she said.

"Kerry?"

"Somebody got into the house around the back. Slit his throat."

Helen felt the sweat come again. In her mind's eye the newspapers rose and fell in Anne-Marie's yard.

"No," she said.

"Just like that."

She looked at the tragedienne who was trying to sell her this obscenity, and said "No" again. It defied belief; yet her denials could not silence the horrid comprehension she felt.

She turned her back on the woman and jostled her way out of the crowd. There would be nothing to see, she knew, and even if there had been she had no desire to look. These people—still emerging from their homes as the story spread—were exhibiting an appetite she was disgusted by. She was not one of them; would never *be* one of them. She wanted to slap every eager face into sense; wanted to say: "It's pain and grief you're going to spy on. Why? Why?" But she had no courage left. Revulsion had drained her of all but the energy to wander away, leaving the crowd to its sport.

Trevor had come home. He did not attempt an explanation of his absence but waited for her to cross-examine him. When she failed to do so he sank into an easy bonhomie that was worse than his expectant silence. She was dimly aware that her lack of interest was probably more unsettling for him than the histrionics he had been anticipating. She couldn't have cared less.

She tuned the radio to the local station and listened for news. It came surely enough, confirming what the woman in the crowd had told her. Kerry Latimer was dead. Person or persons unknown had gained access to the house via the backyard and murdered the child while he played on the kitchen floor. A police spokesman mouthed the usual platitudes, describing Kerry's death as an "unspeakable crime," and the miscreant as "a dangerous and deeply disturbed individual." For once, the rhetoric seemed justified, and the man's voice shook discernibly when he spoke of the scene that had confronted the officers in the kitchen of Anne-Marie's house.

"Why the radio?" Trevor casually inquired, when Helen had listened for news through three consecutive bulletins. She saw no point in withholding her experience at Spector Street from him; he would find out sooner or later. Coolly, she gave him a bald outline of what had happened at Butts's Court.

"This Anne-Marie is the woman you first met when you went to the estate. Am I right?"

She nodded, hoping he wouldn't ask her too many questions. Tears were close, and she had no intention of breaking down in front of him.

"So you were right," he said.

"Right?"

"About the place having a maniac."

"No," she said. "No."

"But the kid—"

She got up and stood at the window, looking down two stories into the darkened street below. Why did she feel the need to reject the conspiracy theory so urgently? Why was she now praying that Purcell had been right, and that all she'd been told had been lies? She went back to the way Anne-Marie had been when she'd visited her that morning: pale, jittery; *expectant.* She had been like a woman anticipating some arrival, hadn't she, eager to shoo unwanted visitors away so that she could turn back to the business of waiting? But waiting for what, or *whom?* Was it possible that Anne-Marie actually knew the murderer? Had perhaps invited him into the house?

"I hope they find the bastard," she said, still watching the street.

"They will," Trevor replied. "A baby murderer, for Christ's sake. They'll make it a high priority."

A man appeared at the corner of the street, turned, and whistled. A large Alsatian came to heel, and the two set off down toward the cathedral.

"The dog," Helen murmured.

"What?"

She had forgotten the dog in all that had followed. Now the shock she'd felt as it had leaped at the window shook her again.

"What dog?" Trevor pressed her.

"I went back to the flat today—where I took the pictures of the graffiti. There was a dog in there. Locked in."

"So?"

"It'll starve. Nobody knows it's there."

"How do you know it wasn't locked in to kennel it?"

"It was making such a noise," she said.

"Dogs bark," Trevor replied. "That's all they're good for."

"No," she said very quietly, remembering the noises through the boarded window. "It didn't bark."

"Forget the dog," Trevor said. "And the child. There's nothing you can do about it. You were just passing through."

His words only echoed her own thoughts of earlier in the day, but somehow, for reasons that she could find no words to convey, that conviction had decayed in the last hours. She was not just passing through. Nobody ever just *passed through;* experience always left its mark. Sometimes it merely scratched; on occasion it took off limbs. She did not know the extent of her present wounding, but she knew it was more profound than she yet understood, and it made her afraid.

"We're out of booze," she said, emptying the last dribble of whiskey into her tumbler.

Trevor seemed pleased to have a reason to be accommodating. "I'll go out, shall I?" he said. "Get a bottle or two?"

"Sure," she replied. "If you like."

He was gone only half an hour; she would have liked him to be longer. She didn't want to talk, only to sit and think through the unease in her belly. Though Trevor had dismissed her concern for the dog—and perhaps justifiably so—she couldn't help but go back to the locked maisonette in her mind's eye: to picture again the raging face on the bedroom wall, and hear the animal's muffled growl as it pawed the boards over the window. Whatever Trevor had said, she didn't believe the place was being used as a makeshift kennel. No, the dog was *imprisoned* in there, no doubt of it, running round and round, driven, in its desperation, to eat its own feces, growing more insane with every hour that passed. She became afraid that somebody—kids maybe, looking for more tinder for their bonfire—would break into the place, ignorant of what it contained. It wasn't that she feared for the intruders' safety, but that the dog, once liberated, would come for her. It would know where she was (so her drunken head construed) and come sniffing her out.

Trevor returned with the whiskey, and they drank together until the early hours, when her stomach revolted. She took refuge in the toilet—Trevor outside asking her if she needed anything, her telling him weakly to leave her alone. When, an hour later, she emerged, he had gone to bed. She did not join him but lay down on the sofa and dozed through until dawn.

The murder was news. The next morning it made all the tabloids as a front-page splash, and a found prominent position in the heavyweights too. There were photographs of the stricken mother being led from the house, and others, blurred but potent, taken over the backyard wall and through the open kitchen door. Was that blood on the floor, or shadow?

Helen did not bother to read the articles—her aching head rebelled at the thought—but Trevor, who had brought the newspapers in, was eager to talk. She couldn't work out if this was further peacemaking on his part or a genuine interest in the issue.

"The woman's in custody," he said, poring over the *Daily Telegraph*. It was a paper he was politically averse to, but its coverage of violent crime was notoriously detailed.

The observation demanded Helen's attention, unwilling or not. "Custody?" she said. "Anne-Marie?"

"Yes."

"Let me see."

He relinquished the paper, and she glanced over the page.

"Third column," Trevor prompted.

She found the place, and there it was in black and white. Anne-Marie had been taken into custody for questioning to justify the time lapse between the estimated hour of the child's death, and the time that it had been reported. Helen read the relevant sentences over again, to be certain that she'd understood properly. Yes, she had. The police pathologist estimated Kerry to have died between six and six-thirty that morning; the murder had not been reported until twelve.

She read the report over a third and fourth time, but repetition did not change the horrid facts. The child had been murdered before dawn. When she had gone to the house that morning Kerry had already been dead four hours. The body had been in the kitchen, a few yards down the hallway from where she had stood, and Anne-Marie had said *nothing*. That air of expectancy she had had about her—what had it signified? That she awaited some cue to lift the receiver and call the police?

"My Christ . . . ," Helen said, and let the paper drop.

"What?"

"I have to go to the police."

"Why?"

"To tell them I went to the house," she replied. Trevor looked mystified. "The baby was dead, Trevor. When I saw Anne-Marie yesterday morning, Kerry was already dead."

She rang the number given in the paper for any persons offering information, and half an hour later a police car came to pick her up. There was much that startled her in the two hours of interrogation that followed, not least the fact that nobody had reported her presence on the estate to the police, though she had surely been noticed.

"They don't want to know," the detective told her. "You'd think a place like that would be swarming with witnesses. If it is, they're not coming forward. A crime like this—"

"Is it the first?" she said.

He looked at her across a chaotic desk. "First?"

"I was told some stories about the estate. Murders. This summer."

The detective shook his head. "Not to my knowledge. There's been a spate of muggings; one woman was put in hospital for a week or so. But no; no murders."

She liked the detective. His eyes flattered her with their lingering, and his face with its frankness. Past caring whether she sounded foolish or not, she said: "Why do they tell lies like that? About people having their eyes cut out. Terrible things."

The detective scratched his long nose. "We get it too," he said. "People come in here, they confess to all kinds of crap. Talk all night, some of them, about things they've done, or *think* they've done. Give you it all in the minutest detail. And when you make a few calls, it's all invented. Out of their minds."

"Maybe if they didn't tell you the stories . . . they'd actually go out and do it."

The detective nodded. "Yes," he said. "God help us. You might be right at that."

And the stories *she'd* been told, were they confessions of uncommitted crimes, accounts of the worst imaginable, imagined to keep fiction from becoming fact? The thought chased its own tail: these terrible stories still needed a *first cause*, a wellspring from which they leaped. As she walked home through the busy streets she wondered how many of her fellow citizens knew such stories. Were these inventions common currency, as Purcell had claimed? Was there a place, however small, reserved in every heart for the monstrous?

"Purcell rang," Trevor told her when she got home. "To invite us out to dinner."

The invitation wasn't welcome, and she made a face.

"Apollinaire's, remember?" he reminded her. "He said he'd take us all to dinner if you proved him wrong."

The thought of getting a dinner out of the death of Anne-Marie's infant was grotesque, and she said so.

"He'll be offended if you turn him down."

"I don't give a damn. I don't want dinner with Purcell."

"Please," he said softly. "He can get difficult, and I want to keep him smiling just at the moment."

She glanced across at him. The look he'd put on made him resemble a drenched spaniel. Manipulative bastard, she thought; but said, "All right, I'll go. But don't expect any dancing on the tables."

"We'll leave that to Archie," he said. "I told Purcell we were free tomorrow night. Is that all right with you?"

"Whenever."

"He's booking a table for eight o'clock."

The evening papers had relegated the Tragedy of Baby Kerry to a few column inches on an inside page. In lieu of much fresh news they simply described the house-to-house inquiries that were now going on at Spector Street. Some of the later editions mentioned that Anne-Marie had been released from custody after an extended period of questioning and was now residing with friends. They also mentioned, in passing, that the funeral was to be the following day.

Helen had not entertained any thoughts of going back to Spector Street for the funeral when she went to bed that night, but sleep seemed to change her mind, and she woke with the decision made for her.

Death had brought the estate to life. Walking through to Ruskin Court from the street, she had never seen such numbers out and about. Many were already lining the curb to watch the funeral cortege pass, and looked to have claimed their niche early, despite the wind and the ever-present threat of rain. Some were wearing items of black clothing—a coat, a scarf—but the overall impression, despite the lowered voices and the studied frowns, was one of celebration. Children running around, untouched by reverence; occasional laughter escaping from between gossiping adults—Helen could feel an air of anticipation that made her spirits, despite the occasion, almost buoyant.

Nor was it simply the presence of so many people that reassured her; she was, she conceded to herself, happy to be back here in Spector Street. The quadrangles, with their stunted saplings and their gray grass, were more real to her than the carpeted corridors she was used to walking; the anonymous faces on the balconies and streets meant more than her colleagues at the university. In a word, she felt *home*.

Finally, the cars appeared, moving at a snail's pace through the narrow streets. As the hearse came into view—its tiny white casket decked with flowers—a number of women in the crowd gave quiet voice to their grief.

One onlooker fainted; a knot of anxious people gathered around her. Even the children were stilled now.

Helen watched, dry-eyed. Tears did not come very easily to her, especially in company. As the second car, containing Anne-Marie and two other women, drew level with her, Helen saw that the bereaved mother was also eschewing any public display of grief. She seemed, indeed, to be almost elevated by the proceedings, sitting upright in the back of the car, her pallid features the source of much admiration. It was a sour thought, but Helen felt as though she was seeing Anne-Marie's finest hour; the one day in an otherwise anonymous life in which she was the center of attention. Slowly, the cortege passed by and disappeared from view.

The crowd around Helen was already dispersing. She detached herself from the few mourners who still lingered at the curb and wandered through from the street into Butts's Court. It was her intention to go back to the locked maisonette, to see if the dog was still there. If it was, she would put her mind at rest by finding one of the estate caretakers and informing him of the fact.

The quadrangle was, unlike the other courts, practically empty. Perhaps the residents, being neighbors of Anne-Marie's, had gone on to the crematorium for the service. Whatever the reason, the place was eerily deserted. Only children remained, playing around the pyramid bonfire, their voices echoing across the empty expanse of the square.

She reached the maisonette and was surprised to find the door open again, as it had been the first time she'd come here. The sight of the interior made her lightheaded. How often in the past several days had she imagined standing here, gazing into that darkness. There was no sound from inside. The dog had surely run off—either that, or died. There could be no harm, could there, in stepping into the place one final time, just to look at the face on the wall, and its attendant slogan?

"Sweets to the sweet." She had never looked up the origins of that phrase. No matter, she thought. Whatever it had stood for once, it was transformed here, as everything was; herself included. She stood in the front room for a few moments, to allow herself time to savor the confrontation ahead. Far away behind her the children were screeching like mad birds.

She stepped over a clutter of furniture and toward the short corridor that joined living room to bedroom, still delaying the moment. Her heart was quick in her: a smile played on her lips.

And there! At last! The portrait loomed, compelling as ever. She stepped back in the murky room to admire it more fully and her heel caught on the mattress that still lay in the corner. She glanced down. The squalid bedding had been turned over, to present its untorn face. Some blankets and a rag-wrapped pillow had been tossed over it. Something glistened among the folds of the uppermost blanket. She bent down to look more closely and found there a handful of sweets—chocolates and caramels—wrapped in bright paper. And littered among them, neither so attractive nor so sweet, a dozen razor-blades. There was blood on several. She stood up again and backed away from the mattress, and as she did so a buzzing sound reached her ears from the next room. She turned, and the light in the bedroom diminished as a figure stepped into the gullet between her and the outside world. Silhouetted against the light, she could scarcely see the man in the doorway, but she smelled him. He smelled like cotton candy, and the buzzing was with him or in him.

"I just came to look," she said, ". . . at the picture."

The buzzing went on—the sound of a sleepy afternoon, far from here. The man in the doorway did not move.

"Well," she said, "I've seen what I wanted to see." She hoped against hope that her words would prompt him to stand aside and let her pass, but he didn't move, and she couldn't find the courage to challenge him by stepping toward the door.

"I have to go," she said, knowing that despite her best efforts fear seeped between every syllable. "I'm expected . . . "

That was not entirely untrue. Tonight they were all invited to Apolli-naire's for dinner. But that wasn't until eight, which was four hours away. She would not be missed for a long while yet.

"If you'll excuse me," she said.

The buzzing had quieted a little, and in the hush the man in the door-way spoke. His unaccented voice was almost as sweet as his scent.

"No need to leave yet," he breathed.

"I'm due . . . due . . ."

Though she couldn't see his eyes, she felt them on her, and they made her feel drowsy, like that summer that sang in her head.

"I came for you," he said.

She repeated the four words in her head. *I came for you.* If they were meant as a threat, they certainly weren't spoken as one.

"I don't . . . know you," she said.

"No," the man murmured. "But you doubted me."

"Doubted?"

"You weren't content with the stories, with what they wrote on the walls. So I was obliged to come."

The drowsiness slowed her mind to a crawl, but she grasped the essentials of what the man was saying. That he was legend, and she, in disbelieving him, had obliged him to show his hand. She looked, now, down at those hands. One of them was missing. In its place, a hook.

"There will be some blame," he told her. "They will say your doubts shed innocent blood. But I say what's blood for, if not for shedding? And in time the scrutiny will pass. The police will leave, the cameras will be pointed at some fresh horror, and they will be left alone, to tell stories of the Candyman again."

"Candyman?" she said. Her tongue could barely shape that blameless word.

"I came for you," he murmured so softly that seduction might have been in the air. And so saying, he moved through the passageway and into the light.

She knew him, without doubt. She had known him all along, in that place kept for terrors. It was the man on the wall. His portrait painter had not been a fantasist: the picture that howled over her was matched in each extraordinary particular by the man she now set eyes upon. He was bright to the point of gaudiness: his flesh a waxy yellow, his thin lips pale blue, his wild eyes glittering as if their irises were set with rubies. His jacket was a patchwork, his trousers the same. He looked, she thought, almost ridiculous, with his blood-stained motley, and the hint of rouge on his jaundiced cheeks. But people were facile. They needed these shows and shams to keep their interest. Miracles; murders; demons driven out and stones rolled from tombs. The cheap glamour did not taint the sense beneath. It was only, in the natural history of the mind, the bright feathers that drew the species to mate with its secret self.

And she was almost enchanted. By his voice, by his colors, by the buzz from his body. She fought to resist the rapture, though. There was a *monster* here, beneath this fetching display; its nest of razors was at her feet, still drenched in blood. Would it hesitate to slit her own throat if it once laid hands on her?

As the Candyman reached for her she dropped down and snatched the blanket up, flinging it at him. A rain of razors and candy fell around his shoulders. The blanket followed, blinding him. But before she could snatch the moment to slip past him, the pillow that had lain on the blanket rolled in front of her.

It was not a pillow at all. Whatever the forlorn white casket she had seen in the hearse had contained, it was not the body of Baby Kerry. That was *here*, at her feet, its blood-drained face turned up to her. He was naked. His body showed everywhere signs of the fiend's attentions.

In the two heartbeats she took to register this last horror, the Candyman threw off the blanket. In his struggle to escape from its folds, his jacket had come unbuttoned, and she saw—though her senses protested—that the contents of his torso had rotted away, and the hollow was now occupied by a nest of bees. They swarmed in the vault of his chest, and encrusted in a seething mass the remnants of flesh that hung there. He smiled at her plain repugnance.

"Sweets to the sweet," he murmured, and stretched his hooked hand toward her face. She could no longer see light from the outside world or hear the children playing in Butts's Court. There was no escape into a saner world than this. The Candyman filled her sight; her drained limbs had no strength to hold him at bay.

"Don't kill me," she breathed.

"Do you believe in me?" he said.

She nodded minutely. "How can I not?" she said.

"Then why do you want to live?"

She didn't understand, and was afraid her ignorance would prove fatal, so she said nothing.

"If you would learn," the fiend said, "just a *little* from me . . . you would not beg to live." His voice had dropped to a whisper. "I am rumor," he sang in her ear. "It's a blessed condition, believe me. To live in people's dreams; to be whispered at street corners, but not have to *be*. Do you understand?"

Her weary body understood. Her nerves, tired of jangling, understood. The sweetness he offered was life without living: was to be dead, but remembered everywhere; immortal in gossip and graffiti.

"Be my victim," he said.

"No . . . ," she murmured.

"I won't force it upon you," he replied, the perfect gentleman. "I won't oblige you to die. But think; *think*. If I kill you here—if I unhook you"— he traced the path of the promised wound with his hook; it ran from groin to neck—"think how they would mark this place with their talk . . . point it out as they passed by and say, 'She died there, the woman with the green eyes.' Your death would be a parable to frighten children with. Lovers would use it as an excuse to cling closer together."

She had been right: this was a seduction.

"Was fame ever so easy?" he asked.

She shook her head. "I'd prefer to be forgotten," she replied, "than be remembered like that."

He made a tiny shrug. "What do the good know?" he said. "Except what the bad teach them by their excesses?" He raised his hooked hand. "I said I would not oblige you to die and I'm true to my word. Allow me, though, a kiss at least . . ."

He moved toward her. She murmured some nonsensical threat, which he ignored. The buzzing in his body had risen in volume. The thought of touching his body, of the proximity of the insects, was horrid. She forced her lead-heavy arms up to keep him at bay.

His lurid face eclipsed the portrait on the wall. She couldn't bring herself to touch him, and instead stepped back. The sound of the bees rose; some, in their excitement, had crawled up his throat and were flying from his mouth. They climbed about his lips; in his hair.

She begged him over and over to leave her alone, but he would not be placated. At last she had nowhere left to retreat to; the wall was at her back. Steeling herself against the stings, she put her hands on his crawling chest and pushed. As she did so his hand shot out and around the back of her neck, the hook nicking the flushed skin of her throat. She felt blood come; felt certain he would open her jugular in one terrible slash. But he had given his word, and he was true to it.

Aroused by this sudden activity, the bees were everywhere. She felt them moving on her, searching for morsels of wax in her ears, and sugar at her lips. She made no attempt to swat them away. The hook was at her neck. If she so much as moved it would wound her. She was trapped, as in her childhood nightmares, with every chance of escape stymied. When sleep had brought her to such hopelessness—the demons on every side, waiting to tear her limb from limb—one trick remained. To let go; to give up all ambition to life, and leave her body to the dark. Now, as the Candyman's face pressed to hers, and the sound of bees blotted out even her own breath, she played that hidden hand. And, as surely as in dreams, the room and the fiend were painted out and gone.

She woke from brightness into dark. There were several panicked moments when she couldn't think of where she was, then several more when she remembered. But there was no pain about her body. She put her hand to her neck; it was, barring the nick of the hook, untouched. She was lying on the mattress, she realized. Had she been assaulted as she lay in a faint? Gingerly, she investigated her body. She was not bleeding; her clothes were not disturbed. The Candyman had, it seemed, simply claimed his kiss.

She sat up. There was precious little light through the boarded window—and none from the front door. Perhaps it was closed, she reasoned. But no; even now she heard somebody whispering on the threshold. A woman's voice.

She didn't move. They were crazy, these people. They had known all along what her presence in Butts's Court had summoned, and they had *protected* him—this honeyed psychopath; given him a bed and an offering of bonbons, hidden him away from prying eyes, and kept their silence when he brought blood to their doorsteps. Even Anne-Marie, dry-eyed in the hallway of her house, knowing that her child was dead a few yards away.

The child! That was the evidence she needed. Somehow they had conspired to get the body from the casket (what had they substituted; a dead dog?) and brought it here to the Candyman's tabernacle as a toy, or a lover. She would take Baby Kerry with her—to the police—and tell the whole story. Whatever they believed of it, and that would probably be very little, the fact of the child's body was incontestable. That way at least some of the crazies would suffer for their conspiracy. Suffer for *her* suffering.

The whispering at the door had stopped. Now somebody was moving toward the bedroom. Whoever it was hadn't brought a light. Helen made herself small, hoping she might escape detection.

A figure appeared in the doorway. The gloom was too impenetrable for her to make out more than a slim figure, who bent down and picked up a bundle on the floor. A fall of blond hair identified the newcomer as Anne-Marie: the bundle she was picking up was undoubtedly Kerry's corpse. Without looking in Helen's direction, the mother about-faced and made her way out of the bedroom.

Helen listened as the footsteps receded across the living room. Swiftly, she got to her feet and crossed to the passageway. From there she could vaguely see Anne-Marie's outline in the doorway of the maisonette. No lights burned in the quadrangle beyond. The woman disappeared, and Helen followed as speedily as she could, eyes fixed on the door ahead. She stumbled once, and once again, but reached the door in time to see Anne-Marie's vague form in the night ahead.

She stepped out of the maisonette and into the open air. It was chilly; there were no stars. All the lights on the balconies and corridors were out, nor did any burn in the flats; not even the glow of a television. Butts's Court was deserted.

She hesitated before going in pursuit of the girl. Why didn't she slip away now, cowardice coaxed her, and find her way back to the car? But if she did that the conspirators would have time to conceal the child's body. When she got back here with the police there would be sealed lips and shrugs and she would be told she had imagined the corpse and the Candy-man. All the terrors she had tasted would recede into rumor again. Into words on a wall. And every day she lived from now on she would loathe herself for not going in pursuit of sanity.

She followed. Anne-Marie was not making her way around the quad-rangle but moving toward the center of the lawn in the middle of the court. To the bonfire! Yes; to the bonfire! It loomed in front of Helen now, blacker than the night sky. She could just make out Anne-Marie's figure, moving to the edge of the piled timbers and furniture, and ducking to climb into its heart. This was how they planned to remove the evidence. To bury the child was not certain enough; but to cremate it, and pulverize the bones—who would ever know?

She stood a dozen yards from the pyramid and watched as Anne-Marie climbed out again and moved away, folding her figure into the darkness.

Quickly, Helen moved through the long grass and located the narrow space in among the piled timbers into which Anne-Marie had put the body. She thought she could see the pale form; it had been laid in a hol-low. She couldn't reach it, however. Thanking God that she was as slim as the mother, she squeezed through the narrow aperture. Her dress snagged on a nail as she did so. She turned round to disengage it, fingers trembling. When she turned back she had lost sight of the corpse.

She fumbled blindly ahead of her, her hands finding wood and rags and what felt like the back of an old armchair, but not the cold skin of the child. She had hardened herself against contact with the body; she had endured worse in the last hours than picking up a dead baby. Determined not to be defeated, she advanced a little farther, her shins scraped and her fingers spiked with splinters. Flashes of light were appearing at the corners of her aching eyes; her blood whined in her ears. But there, *there!*—the body was no more than a yard and a half ahead of her. She ducked down to reach beneath a beam of wood, but her fingers missed the forlorn bundle by inches. She stretched farther, the whine in her head increasing, but still she could not reach the child. All she could do was bend double and squeeze into the hidey-hole the children had left in the center of the bonfire.

It was difficult to get through. The space was so small she could barely crawl on hands and knees, but she made it. The child lay face-down. She fought back the remnants of squeamishness and went to pick it up. As she did so, something landed on her arm. The shock startled her. She almost cried out, but swallowed the urge, and brushed the irritation away. It buzzed as it rose from her skin. The whine she had heard in her ears was not her blood but the hive.

"I knew you'd come," the voice behind her said, and a wide hand covered her face. She fell backward and the Candyman embraced her.

"We have to go," he said in her ear, as flickering light spilled between the stacked timbers. "Be on our way, you and I."

She fought to be free of him, to cry out for them not to light the bonfire, but he held her lovingly close. The light grew: warmth came with it; and through the kindling and the first flames she could see figures approaching the pyre out of the darkness of Butts's Court. They had been there all along: waiting, the lights turned out in their homes, and broken all along the corridors. Their final conspiracy.

The bonfire caught with a will, but by some trick of its construction the flames did not invade her hiding place quickly; nor did the smoke creep through the furniture to choke her. She was able to watch how the children's faces gleamed; how the parents called them back from going too close, and how they disobeyed; how the old women, their blood thin, warmed their hands and smiled into the flames. Presently the roar and the crackle became deafening, and the Candyman let her scream herself hoarse in the certain knowledge that nobody could hear her, and even if they had, would not have moved to claim her from the fire.

The bees vacated the fiend's belly as the air became hotter, and mazed the air with their panicked flight. Some, attempting escape, caught fire, and fell like tiny meteors to the ground. The body of Baby Kerry, which lay close to the creeping flames, began to cook. Its downy hair smoked; its back blistered.

Soon the heat crept down Helen's throat and scorched her pleas away. She sank back, exhausted, into the Candyman's arms, resigned to his triumph. In moments they would be on their way, as he had promised, and there was no help for it.

Perhaps they would remember her, as he had said they might, finding her cracked skull in tomorrow's ashes. Perhaps she might become, in time, a story with which to frighten children. She had lied, saying she preferred death to such questionable fame. She did not. As to her seducer, he laughed as the conflagration sniffed them out. There was no permanence for him in this night's death. His deeds were on a hundred walls and ten thousand lips, and should he be doubted again his congregation could summon him with sweetness. He had reason to laugh. So, as the flames crept upon them, did she, as through the fire she caught sight of a familiar face moving between the onlookers. It was Trevor. He had forsaken his meal at Apollinaire's and come looking for her.

She watched him questioning this fire watcher and that, but they shook their heads, all the while staring at the pyre with smiles buried in their eyes. Poor dupe, she thought, following his antics. She willed him to look past the flames in the hope that he might see her burning. Not so that he could save her from death—she was long past hope of that—but because she pitied him in his bewilderment and wanted to give him, though he would not have thanked her for it, something to be haunted by. That, and a story to tell.

From *The Damnation Game*

It wasn't difficult to find the European; her mind went to him with almost distressing readiness, as if into the arms of a long-lost compatriot. She could distinctly feel the pull of him, though not, she thought, a conscious magnetism. When her thoughts arrived at Caliban Street and entered the room at the top of the stairs, her suspicions about his passivity were verified. He was lying on the bare boards of the room in a posture of utter exhaustion. Perhaps, she thought, I *can* do this after all. Like a teasing mistress, she crept to his side, and slipped into him.

She murmured.

Marty flinched. There were movements in her throat, which was so thin he felt he could almost see the words shaping in it. Speak to me, he willed her. Say it's all right. Her body had become rigid. He touched her.

Her muscle was stone, as though she'd exchanged glances with the Basilisk.

"Carys?"

She murmured again, her throat palpitating, but no words came; there was barely breath.

"Can you hear me?"

If she could, she made no sign of it. Seconds passed into minutes and still she was a wall, his questions fracturing against her and falling into silence.

And then she said: "I'm here." Her voice was insubstantial, like a foreign station found on a radio; words from some unfixable place.

"With him?" he asked.

"Yes."

No prevarication now, he charged himself. She'd gone to the European, as he'd asked. Now he had to use her courage as efficiently as possible and call her back before anything went wrong. He asked the most difficult question first, and the one he most needed an answer to.

"What is he, Carys?"

"I don't know," she said.

The tip of her tongue flickered out to spread a film of spit across her lips.

"So dark," she muttered.

It *was* dark in him: the same palpable darkness as in the room at Caliban Street. But, for the moment at least, the shadows were passive. The European didn't expect intruders here. He'd left no guardian terrors at the gates of his brain. She stepped deeper into his head. Darts of light burst at the corners of her thought's sight, like the colors that came after she'd rubbed her eyes, only more brilliant and more momentary. They came and went so quickly she was not certain if she saw anything in them or illuminated by them, but as she progressed and the bursts became more frequent, she began to see patterns there: commas, lattices, bars, dots, spirals.

Marty's voice interrupted the reverie, some foolish question that she had no patience with. She ignored it. Let him wait. The lights were becoming more intricate, their patterns cross-fertilizing, gaining depth and weight. Now she seemed to see tunnels and tumbling cubes; seas of rolling light; fissures opening and sealing; rains of white noise. She watched, entranced by the way they grew and multiplied, the world of his thought appearing in flickering Heavens above her; falling in showers on her and about her. Vast blocks of intersecting geometries thundered over, hovering inches above her skull, the weight of small moons.

Just as suddenly: gone. All of them. Darkness again, as relentless as ever, pressed on her from every side. For a moment she had the sensation of being smothered; she grabbed for breath, panicking.

"Carys?"

"I'm all right," she whispered to the distant inquirer. He was a world away, but he cared for her, or so she dimly remembered.

"Where are you?" he wanted to know.

She didn't have a clue, so she shook her head. Which way should she advance, if at all? She waited in the darkness, readying herself for whatever might happen next.

Suddenly the lights began again, at the horizon. This time—for their second performance—pattern had become form. Instead of spirals she saw rising columns of burning smoke. In place of seas of light, a landscape, with intermittent sunshine stabbing distant hillsides. Birds rose up on burning wings then turned into leaves of books, fluttering up from conflagrations that were even now flaring on every side.

"Where are you?" he asked her again. Her eyes roved maniacally behind her closed lids, taking in this burgeoning province. He could share none of it, except through her words, and she was dumb with admiration or terror, he couldn't tell which.

There was sound here too. Not much; the promontory she walked on had suffered too many ravages to shout. Its life was almost out. Bodies sprawled underfoot, so badly disfigured they might have been dropped out of the sky. Weapons; horses; wheels. She saw all of this as if by a show of lurid fireworks, with no sight glimpsed more than once. In the instant of darkness between one light-burst and the next the entire scene would change. One moment she was standing on an open road with a naked girl running toward her, bawling. The next, on a hillside looking down on a razed valley, snatched through a pall of smoke. Now a silver birch copse, now not. Now a ruin, with a headless man at her feet; again, not. But always the fires somewhere near; the smuts and the shrieks dirtying the air; the sense of relentless pursuit. She felt it could go on forever, these scenes changing before her—one moment a landscape, the next an atrocity—without her having time to correlate the disparate images.

Then, as abruptly as the first patterns had ceased, the fires did also, and the darkness was everywhere about her again.

"Where?"

Marty's voice found her. He was so agitated in his confusion, she answered him.

"I'm almost dead," she said, quite calmly.

"Carys?" He was terrified that naming her would alert Mamoulian, but he had to know if she spoke for herself, or for him.

"Not Carys," she replied. Her mouth seemed to lose its fullness; the lips thinning. It was Mamoulian's mouth, not hers.

She raised her hand a little way from her lap as if making to touch her face.

"Almost dead," she said again. "Lost the battle, you see. Lost the whole bloody war . . . "

"Which war?"

"Lost from the beginning. Not that it matters, eh? Find myself another war. There's always one around."

"Who are you?"

She frowned. "What's it to you?" she snapped at him. "None of your business."

"It doesn't matter," Marty returned. He feared pushing the interrogation too hard. As it was, his question was answered in the next breath.

"My name's Mamoulian. I'm a sergeant in the Third Fusiliers. Correction: *was* a sergeant."

"Not now?"

"No, not now. I'm nobody now. It's safer to be nobody these days, don't you think?"

The tone was eerily conversational, as though the European knew exactly what was happening, and had chosen to talk with Marty through Carys. Another game, perhaps?

"When I think of the things I've done," he said, "to stay out of trouble. I'm such a coward, you see? Always have been. *Loathe* the sight of blood." He began to laugh in her, a solid, unfeminine laugh.

"You're just a man?" Marty said. He could scarcely credit what he was being told. There was no Devil hiding in the European's cortex, just this half-mad sergeant, lost on some battlefield. "Just a man?" he said again.

"What did you want me to be?" the sergeant replied, quick as a flash, "I'm happy to oblige. Anything to get me out of this shit."

"Who do you think you're talking to?"

The sergeant frowned with Carys's face, puzzling this one out.

"I'm losing my mind," he said dolefully. "I've been talking to myself for days now on and off. There's no-one left, you see? The Third's been wiped out. And the Fourth. And the Fifth. All blown to Hell!" He stopped, and pulled a wry face. "Got no one to play cards with, damn it. Can't play with dead men, can I? They've got nothing I want . . ." The voice trailed away.

"What date is it?"

"Sometime in October, isn't it?" the sergeant came back. "I've lost track of time. Still, it's fucking cold at night, I tell you that much. Yes, must be October at least. There was snow in the wind yesterday. Or was it the day before?"

"What year is it?"

The sergeant laughed. "I'm not that far gone," he said. "It's 1811. That's right. I'm thirty-two on the ninth of November. And I don't look a day over forty."

If the sergeant was answering truthfully Mamoulian was two centuries old.

"Are you sure?" Marty asked. "The year is 1811; you're certain?"

"Shut your mouth!" the answer came.

"What?"

"Trouble."

Carys had drawn her arms up against her chest, as though constricted. She felt enclosed—but by what she wasn't certain. The open road she'd been standing on had abruptly disappeared, and now she sensed herself lying down, in darkness. It was warmer here than it had been on the road, but not a pleasant heat. It smelled putrid. She spat, not once but three or four times, to rid herself of a mouthful of muck. Where was she, for God's sake?

Close by she could hear the approach of horses. The sound was muffled, but it made her, or rather the man she occupied, panic. Off to her right, somebody moaned.

"Ssh . . ." she hissed. Didn't the moaner hear the horses too? They'd be discovered; and though she didn't know why, she was certain discovery would prove fatal.

"What's happening?" Marty asked.

She didn't dare to reply. The horsemen were too close to dare a word. She could hear them dismounting, and approaching her hiding place. She repeated a prayer, soundlessly. The riders were talking now; they were soldiers, she guessed. An argument had erupted among them as to who would tackle some distasteful duty. Maybe, she prayed, they'd give up their search before they started. But no. The debate was over, and they were grunting and complaining as several set about their labors. She heard them moving sacks, and flinging them down. A dozen; two dozen. Light seeped through to where she lay, scarcely breathing. More sacks were moved; more light fell on her. She opened her eyes, and finally recognized what refuge the sergeant had chosen.

"God Almighty," she said.

They weren't sacks she lay among, but bodies. He had hidden himself in a mound of corpses. It was the heat of putrefaction that made her sweat.

Now the hillock was being taken apart by the horsemen, who were pricking each of the bodies as they were hauled from the heap, in order to distinguish living from dead. The few who still breathed were pointed out to the officer. He dismissed them all as past the point of no return; they were swiftly dispatched. Before a bayonet could pierce his hide, the sergeant rolled over and showed himself.

"I surrender," he said. They jabbed him through the shoulder anyway. He yelled. Carys too.

Marty reached to touch her; her face was scrawled with pain. But he thought better of interfering at what was clearly a vital juncture: it might do more harm than good.

"Well, well," said the officer, high on the horse. "You don't look very dead to me."

"I was practicing," the sergeant replied. His wit earned him a second jab. To judge by the looks of the men who surrounded him, he'd be lucky to avoid a disemboweling. They were ready for some sport.

"You're not going to die," the officer said, patting his mount's gleaming neck. The presence of so much decay made the thoroughbred uneasy. "We need answers to some questions first. Then you can have your place in the pit."

Behind the officer's plumed head the sky had darkened. Even as he spoke the scene began to lose coherence, as though Mamoulian had forgotten how it went from here.

Under her lids Carys's eyes began to twitch back and forth again. Another welter of impressions had overtaken her, each moment delineated with absolute precision, but all coming too fast for her to make any sense of.

"Carys? Are you all right?"

"Yes, yes," she said breathlessly. "Just moments . . . living moments."

She saw a room, a chair. Felt a kiss, a slap. Pain; relief; pain again. Questions; laughter. She couldn't be certain, but she guessed that under pressure the sergeant was telling the enemy everything they wanted to know and more. Days passed in a heartbeat. She let them run through her fingers, sensing that the European's dreaming head was moving with mounting velocity toward some critical event. It was best to let him lead the way; he knew better than she the significance of this descent.

The journey finished with shocking suddenness.

A sky the color of cold iron opened above her head. Snow drifted from it, a lazy fall of goose down which instead of warming her made her bones ache. In the claustrophobic bed-sitting room, with Marty sitting bare-chested and sweating opposite her, Carys's teeth began to chatter.

The sergeant's captors were done with their interrogation, it seemed. They had led him and five other ragged prisoners out into a small quadrangle. He looked around. This was a monastery, or had been until its occupation. One or two monks stood in the shelter of the cloister walkway and watched events in the yard unfold with philosophical gaze.

The six prisoners waited in a line while the snow fell. They were not bound. There was nowhere in this square for them to run to. The sergeant, on the end of the line, chewed his nails and tried to keep his thoughts light. They were going to die here, that was an unavoidable fact. They were not the first to be executed this afternoon. Along one wall, arranged neatly for posthumous inspection, lay five dead men. Their lopped heads had been placed, the ultimate defamation, at their groins. Open-eyed, as if startled by the killing stroke, they stared at the snow as it descended, at the windows, at the one tree that was planted in a square of soil among the stones. In summer, it surely bore fruit; birds made idiot song in it. Now, it was leafless.

"They're going to kill us," she said matter-of-factly.

It was all very informal. The presiding officer, a fur coat pulled around his shoulders, was standing with his hands at a blazing brazier, his back to the prisoners. The executioner was with him, his bloody sword leaned jauntily on his shoulder. A fat, lumbering man, he laughed at some joke the officer made, and downed a cup of something warming before turning back to his business.

Carys smiled.

"What's happening now?"

She said nothing; her eyes were on the man who was going to kill them; she smiled on.

"Carys. What's happening?"

The soldiers had come along the line, and pushed them to the ground in the middle of the square. Carys had bowed her head, to expose the nape of her neck. "We're going to die," she whispered to her distant confidant.

At the far end of the line the executioner raised his sword and brought it down with one professional stroke. The prisoner's head seemed to leap from the neck, pushed forward by a geyser of blood. It was lurid against the gray walls, the white snow. The head fell face-forward, rolled a little way and stopped. The body curled to the ground. Out of the corner of his eye Mamoulian watched the proceedings, trying to stop his teeth from chattering. He wasn't afraid, and didn't want them to think he was. The next man in line had started to scream. Two soldiers stepped forward at the officer's barked command, and seized the man. Suddenly, after a calm in which you could hear the snow pat the ground, the line erupted with pleas and prayers; the man's terror had opened a floodgate. The sergeant said nothing. They were lucky to be dying in such style, he thought: the sword was for aristocrats and officers. But the tree was not yet tall enough to hang a man from. He watched the sword fall a second time, wondering if the tongue still wagged after death, sitting in the draining palate of the dead man's head.

"I'm not afraid," he said. "What's the use of fear? You can't buy it or sell it, you can't make love to it. You can't even wear it if they strip off your shirt and you're cold."

A third prisoner's head rolled in the snow; and a fourth. A soldier laughed. The blood steamed. Its meaty smell was appetizing to a man who hadn't been fed for a week.

"I'm not losing anything," he said in lieu of prayer. "I've had a useless life. If it ends here, so what?"

The prisoner at his left was young: no more than fifteen. A drummer boy, the sergeant guessed. He was quietly crying.

"Look over there," Mamoulian said. "Desertion if ever I saw it."

He nodded toward the sprawled bodies, which were already being vacated by their various parasites. Fleas and nits, aware that their host had ceased, crawled and leaped from head and hem, eager to find new residence before the cold caught them.

The boy looked and smiled. The spectacle diverted him in the moment it took for the executioner to position himself and deliver the killing stroke. The head sprang; heat escaped on to the sergeant's chest.

Idly, Mamoulian looked round at the executioner. He was slightly blood-spattered; otherwise his profession was not written upon him. It was a gorm-less face, with a shabby beard that needed trimming, and round, parboiled eyes. Shall I be murdered by this? the sergeant thought; well, I'm not ashamed. He spread his arms to either side of his body, the universal gesture of submission, and bowed his head. Somebody pulled at his shirt to expose his neck.

He waited. A noise like a shot sounded in his head. He opened his eyes, expecting to see the snow approaching as his head leaped from his neck; but no. In the middle of the square one of the soldiers was falling to his knees, his chest blown open by a shot from one of the upper cloister windows. Mamou-lian glanced behind him. Soldiers were swarming from every side of the quadrangle; shots sliced the snow. The presiding officer, wounded, fell clum-sily against the brazier, and his fur coat caught fire. Trapped beneath the tree, two soldiers were mown down, slumping together like lovers under the branches.

"Away." Carys whispered the imperative with his voice, "Quickly. Away."

He belly-crawled across the frozen stone as the factions fought above his head, scarcely able to believe that he'd been spared. Nobody gave him a sec-ond glance. Unarmed and skeletal-thin, he was no danger to anyone. Once out of the square, and into the backwaters of the monastery, he took a breath. Smoke had started to drift along the icy corridors. Inevitably, the place was being put to the torch by one side or the other: perhaps both. They were all imbeciles: he loved none of them. He began his way through the maze of the building, hoping to find his way out without encountering any stray fusiliers.

In a passageway far from the skirmishes he heard footsteps—sandaled, not booted—coming after him. He turned to face his pursuer. It was a monk, his scrawny features every inch the ascetic's. He arrested the sergeant by the tattered collar of his shirt.

"You're God-given," he said. He was breathless, but his grip was fierce.

"Let me alone. I want to get out."

"The fighting's spreading through the building; it's not safe anywhere."

"I'll take the risk," the sergeant grinned.

"You were chosen, soldier," the monk replied, still holding on. "Chance stepped in on your behalf. The innocent boy at your side died, but *you* sur-vived. Don't you see? Ask yourself why."

He tried to push the shaveling away; the mixture of incense and stale sweat was vile. But the man held fast, speaking hurriedly: "There are secret tunnels beneath the cells. We can slip away without being slaughtered."

"Yes?"

"Certainly. If you'll help me."

"How?"

"I've got writings to salvage; a life's work. I need your muscle, soldier. Don't fret yourself, you'll get something in return."

"What have you got that I'd want?" the sergeant said. What could this wild-eyed flagellant possibly possess?

"I need an acolyte," the monk said, "Someone to give my learning to."

"Spare me your spiritual guidance."

"I can teach you so much. How to live forever, if that's what you want." Mamoulian had started to laugh, but the monk went on with his dream-talk. "How to take life from other people, and have it for yourself. Or if you like, give it to the dead to resurrect them."

"Never."

"It's old wisdom," the monk said. "But I've found it again, written out in plain Greek. Secrets that were ancient when the hills were young. *Such* secrets."

"If you can do all that, why aren't you Tsar of All the Russias?" Mamoulian replied.

The monk let go of his shirt, and looked at the soldier with contempt freshly squeezed from his eyes. "What man," he said slowly, "what man with true ambition in his soul would want to be *merely* Tsar?"

The reply wiped the soldier's smile away. Strange words, whose significance—had he been asked—he would have had difficulty explaining. But there was a promise in them which his confusion couldn't rob them of. Well, he thought, maybe this is the way wisdom comes; and the sword didn't fall on me, did it?

"Show me the way," he said.

Carys smiled: a small but radiant smile. In the space of a wing beat winter melted away. Spring blossomed, the ground was green everywhere, especially over the burial pits.

"Where are you going?" Marty asked her. It was clear from her delighted expression that circumstances had changed. For several minutes she had spat out clues to the life she was sharing in the European's head. Marty had barely grasped the gist of what was going on. He hoped she would be able to furnish the details later. What country this was; what war.

Suddenly, she said: "I'm finished." Her voice was light; almost playful.

"Carys?"

"Who's Carys? Never heard of him. Probably dead. They're all dead but me."

"What have you finished?"

"Learning of course. All he can teach me. And it was true. Everything he promised: all true. Old wisdom."

"What have you learned?"

She raised her hand, the burned one, and spread it. "I can steal life," she said. "Easily. Just find the place, and drink. Easy to take; easy to give."

"Give?"

"For a while. As long as it suits me." She extended a finger: God to Adam. "Let there be life."

He began to laugh in her again.

"And the monk?"

"What about him?"

"Is he still with you?"

The sergeant shook Carys's head.

"I killed him, when he'd taught me everything he could." Her hands reached out and strangled the air. "I just throttled him one night, when he was sleeping. Of course he woke when he felt my grip around his throat. But he didn't struggle; he didn't make the slightest attempt to save himself." The sergeant was leering as he described the act. "He just let me murder him. I could scarcely believe my luck; I'd been planning the thing for weeks, terrified that he'd read my thoughts. When he went so easily, I was ecstatic—" The leer suddenly vanished. "Stupid," he murmured in her throat. "So, so *stupid*."

"Why?"

"I didn't see the trap he'd set. Didn't see how he'd planned it all along, nurtured me like a son *knowing* that I'd be his executioner when the time came. I never realized—not once—that I was just his tool. *He wanted to die.* He wanted to pass his wisdom"—the word was pronounced derisively—"along to me, and then have me put an end to him."

"Why did he want to die?"

"Don't you see how terrible it is to live when everything around you perishes? And the more the years pass the more the thought of death freezes your bowels, because the longer you avoid it the worse you imagine it must be? And you start to long—oh *how* you long—for someone to take pity on you, someone to embrace you and share your terrors. And, at the end, someone to go into the dark with you."

"And you chose Whitehead," Marty said, almost beneath his breath, "the way *you* were chosen; by chance."

"Everything is chance; and so nothing is," the sleeping man pronounced; then laughed again, at his own expense, bitterly. "Yes, I chose him, with a game of cards. And then I made a bargain with him."

"But he cheated you."

Carys nodded her head, very slowly, her hand inscribing a circle on the air.

"Round and round," she said. "Round and round."

"What will you do now?"

"Find the pilgrim. Wherever he is, find him! Take him with me. I swear I won't let him escape me. I'll take him, and show him."

"Show him what?"

No answer came. In its place, she sighed, stretching a little, and moving her head from left to right and back again. With a shock of recognition Marty realized that he was still watching her repeat Mamoulian's movements: that all the time the European had been asleep, and now, his energies repleted, he was preparing to wake. He snapped his previous question out again, determined to have an answer to his last, vital enquiry.

"Show him *what*?"

"*Hell*," Mamoulian said. "He cheated me! He squandered all my teachings, all my knowledge, threw it away for greed's sake, for power's sake, for the life of the body. *Appetite!* All gone for appetite. All my precious love, wasted!" Marty could hear, in this litany, the voice of the puritan—a monk's voice, perhaps?—the rage of a creature who wanted the world purer than it was and lived in torment because it saw only filth and flesh sweating to make more flesh, more filth. What hope of sanity in such a place? Except to find a soul to share the torment, a lover to hate the world with. Whitehead had been such a partner. And now Mamoulian was being true to his lover's soul: wanting, at the end, to go into death with the only other creature he had ever trusted. "We'll go to nothing . . . ," he breathed, and the breath was a promise. "All of us, go to nothing, Down! Down!"

He was waking. There was no time left for further questions, however curious Marty was.

"Carys."

"Down! Down!"

"Carys! Can you hear me? Come out of him! Quickly!"

Her head rolled on her neck.

"Carys!"

She grunted.

"*Quickly!*"

In Mamoulian's head the patterns had begun again, as enchanting as ever. Spurts of light which would become pictures in a while, she knew. What would they be this time? Birds, flowers, trees in blossom. What a wonderland it was.

"*Carys.*"

The voice of someone she had once known was calling her from some very distant place. But so were the lights. They were resolving themselves even now. She waited, expectantly, but this time they weren't memories that burst into view—

"*Carys! Quickly!*"

They were the real world, appearing as the European opened his lids. Her body tensed. Marty reached for her hand, and seized it. She exhaled, slowly, the breath coming out as a thin whine between her teeth, and suddenly she was awake to her imminent danger. She flung her thought out of the European's head and back across the miles to Kilburn. For an agonized instant she felt her will falter, and she was falling backwards, back into his waiting head. Terrified, she gasped like a stranded fish while her mind fought for propulsion.

Marty dragged her to a standing position, but her legs buckled. He held her up with his arms wrapped around her.

"Don't leave me," he whispered into her hair. "Gentle God, don't leave me."

Suddenly, her eyes flickered open.

"Marty," she mumbled. "Marty."

It was her: he knew her look too well for the European to deceive him.

"You came back," he said.

They didn't speak for several minutes, simply held on to each other. When they did talk, she had no taste for retelling what she'd experienced. Marty held his curiosity in check. It was enough to know they had no Devil on their backs.

Just old humanity, cheated of love, and ready to pull down the world on its head.

SIX

BESTIARY

Hieronymus Bosch, surely the greatest painter of invented creatures in Western art, is known best for an elaborate triptych which is now in the Prado in Madrid. On the left-hand panel Eden is depicted. On the right-hand panel is an extraordinary vision of Hell. And in the middle panel is a delirium that has tested the inventions of scholarly interpretation for centuries. The sheer profligacy of images in these pictures is breathtaking. Creatures abound, meticulously painted monsters that share the canvas with minutely observed renderings of real species.

I'd like my books and paintings to steal a little of that profligacy for themselves: to evoke for my audience a hallucinatory excess, forms proliferating, demanding new zoologies.

Some of these creatures can be repositories of strange wisdom. Lord Fox, for instance, from *Sacrament*, has a lot to say about the splendors of vulpine life; he's wise to his own condition. At the other end of that scale is the angel Uriel from *Weaveworld*, which has no knowledge of itself whatsoever. Indeed, it can only be bested if it can be brought to a state of self-comprehension.

And between these two extremes comes a parade of beasts. In *Cabal* these creatures have a city to themselves, from which, in the body of the story, they are exiled. And from the closing section of *Everville*, a passage which plays out as an almost self-contained story. Harry D'Amour, my Chandleresque private detective, finally confronts the entity Lazy Susan, which murdered his good friend Father Hess many years before. The creature has a problem, however; it doesn't really know what it is. Though it would like to think of itself as a good old-fashioned dreamer, the truth may be something stranger. Like the beasts who populate the middle panel of Bosch's triptych, Lazy Susan doesn't belong either in Heaven or Hell, but springs from the coils of the human imagination.

From *Sacrament*

J ust about everyone got high, except for Jack, who had become self-righteously sober the year before (after two decades of chemical excess) and Casper, who was forbidden to smoke the weed because Jack couldn't. Drew became democratically flirtatious under the influence, then, realizing where his best hopes of gratification lay, followed Will into the kitchen and offered up a graphic description of what he wanted to do when they got back to Sanchez Street.

As it turned out, by the time the party broke up, Drew was so much the worse for weed and beer he said he needed to go home and sleep it off. Will invited him back to the house, but he declined. He didn't want anyone, especially Will, watching him throw up in the toilet, he said: it was a private ritual. Will drove him home, made sure he got to his apartment safely, and then went home himself. Drew's verbal foreplay had left him feeling horny, however, and he contemplated a late-night cruise down to the Penitent to find some action. But the thought of getting geared up for the hunt at such a late hour dissuaded him. He needed sleep more than a stranger's hand. And Drew would be sober tomorrow.

Again, he seemed to wake, disturbed by sirens on Market, or a shout from the street. Seemed to wake, and seemed to sit up and study the shadowy room, just as he had two nights before. This time, however, he was wise to the trick his sleeping mind was playing. Resisting the urge to sleepwalk to the bathroom, he stayed in bed, waiting for the illusion of wakefulness to pass.

But after what seemed to be minutes, he grew bored. There was a ritual here, he realized, that his subconscious demanded he enact, and until he

221

played it out he wouldn't be allowed to dream something more restful. Resigned to the game, he got up and wandered out onto the landing. There was no shadow on the wall this time to coax him down the stairs, but he went anyway, following the same route as he had when he'd last come into the company of Lord Fox: along the hallway and into the file room. Tonight, however, there were no lights spilling from the photographs on the ground. Apparently the animal wanted to conduct the dream debate in darkness.

"Can we get this over with as quickly as possible?" Will said, stepping into the murk. "There's got to be a better dream than—"

He stopped. The air around him shifted, displaced by a motion in the room. Something was moving toward him, and it was a lot larger than a fox. He started to retreat; heard a hiss; saw a vast, gray bulk rise up in front of him, the slab of its head gaping, letting on to a darkness that made the murk seem bright—

A bear! Christ in Heaven! Nor was this just any bear. It was his wounder, coming at him with her own wounds gouting, her breath foul and hot on his face.

Instinctively, he did as he would have done in the wild: he dropped to his knees, lowered his head, and presented as small a target as possible. The boards beneath him reverberated with the weight and fury of the animal; his scars were suddenly burning in homage to their maker. It was all he could do not to cry out, even though he knew this was just some idiot dream; all he could do not to beg it to stop and let him alone. But he kept his silence, his palms against the boards, and waited. After a time, the reverberations ceased. Still he didn't move, but counted to ten, and only then dared to move his head an inch or two. There was no sign of the bear. But across the room, leaning against the window as nonchalantly as ever, was Lord Fox.

"There are probably a plethora of lessons here," the creature said, "but two in particular come to mind." Will gingerly got to his feet while the fox shared his wisdom. "That when you're dealing with animal spirits—and that's what you've got on your hands, Willy, whether you like it or not—it's best to remember that we're all one big happy family, and if I'm here then I've probably got company. That's the first lesson."

"And . . . what's the second?"

"*Show me some respect!*" the fox barked. Then, suddenly all reason: "You came in here saying you want to get it over with as quickly as possible. That's insulting, Willy."

"Don't call me Willy."

"Ask me politely."

"Oh for fuck's sake. *Please* don't call me Willy."

"Better."

"I need something to drink. My throat's completely dry."

"Go get yourself something," the fox said. "I'll come with you."

Will went into the kitchen, and the fox padded after him, instructing him not to turn on the light. "I much prefer the murk," the animal said. "It keeps my senses sharp."

Will opened the fridge and got out a carton of milk. "You want something?"

"I'm not thirsty," the fox said. "But thank you."

"Something to eat?"

"You know what I like to eat," the fox replied, and the image of Thomas Simeon lying dead in the grass entered Will's head with sickening clarity.

"Jesus," Will said, letting the fridge door slam closed.

"Come on," the fox said, "where's your sense of humor?" He stepped out of the deep shadows into a wash of gray light from the window. He looked, Will thought, more vicious than he had last time they'd met. "You know, I think you should ask yourself," he said, "in all seriousness, if perhaps you're not coming apart at the seams. And if you are, what the consequences are going to be for those around you. Particularly your new lover-boy. I mean, he's not the most *stable* of characters, is he?"

"Are you talking about Drew?"

"Right. Drew. For some reason, I was thinking his name was Brad. I think in all fairness you should let him go, or you'll end up dragging him down with you. He'll go nuts on you, or try to slit his wrists, one of the two. And you'll be responsible. You don't want that on your plate. Not with the rest of the shit you've got to deal with."

"Are you going to be more specific?"

"It's not his war, Will. It's yours and yours alone. You signed on for it the day you let Steep take you up the hill."

Will set down the carton of milk and put his head in his hands. "I wish I knew what the hell you wanted," he said.

"In the long view," the fox said, "I want what every animal—except maybe for the dogs—wants in its heart, I want your species gone. To the stars, if you can get there. To rot and ruin, more likely. We don't care. We just want you out of our fur."

"And then what?"

"Then nothing," the fox replied with a shrug. His voice went to a wistful murmur. "The planet keeps going round, and when it's bright it's day and when it's not it's night, and there's no end to the simple bliss of things."

"The simple bliss of things," Will said.

"It's a pretty phrase, isn't it? I think I got it from Steep."

"You'd miss all of that, if we were gone—"

"Words, you mean? I might, for a day or two. But it'd pass. In a week I'd have forgotten what good conversation was and I'd be a happy heart again. The way I was when Steep first clapped eyes on me."

"I know I'm just dreaming this, but while you're here . . . what do you know about Steep?"

"Nothing you don't," the fox said. "There's a good part of him in you, after all. You take a long look at yourself, one of these days." The fox approached the table now, lowering his voice to an insinuating whisper. "Do you really think you'd have wasted most of your natural span taking pictures of tormented wildlife if he hadn't put that knife in your hands? He *shaped* you, Will. He sowed the hopes and the disappointments, he sowed the guilt, and the yearning."

"And he sowed you at the same time?"

"For better or worse. You see, I'm nothing important. I'm just the innocent fox who ate Thomas Simeon's private parts. Steep saw me trotting away and he decided I was a villain. Which was very unfair of him, by the way. I was just doing what any fox with an empty belly would do, seeing a free meal. I didn't know I was eating anybody important."

"Was Simeon important?"

"Well, obviously he was to Steep. I mean Jacob really took this dick-eating business to heart. He came *after* me, like he was going to tear off my head. So I *ran*, I ran so far and so fast—" This wasn't Will's memory of the event, as he'd witnessed it through Steep's eyes, but Lord Fox was on a roll, and Will didn't dare interrupt. "And he kept coming after me. There was no escaping him. I was in his memory, you see? In his mind's eye. And let me tell you, he'd got a mind like a steel trap. Once he had me there was no tricking my way out. Even death couldn't spring me from his head." A raw sigh escaped the animal. "Let me tell you," he said, "it's not like being in your head. I mean, you've got a messed-up psyche, no doubt about it, but it's nothing compared with his. *Nothing.*"

Will knew bait when it was being trailed. But he couldn't help himself; he bit. "Tell me," he said.

"What's he like? Well . . . if *my* head's a hole in the ground and *yours* is a shack—no offense intended—then *his* is a fucking cathedral. I mean, it's all spires and choirs and flying buttresses. *Incredible.*"

"So much for the simple bliss of things."

"You're quick, aren't you?" the fox said appreciatively. "Soon as you see a little weakness in a fellow's argument, you're in."

"So he's got a mind like a cathedral?"

"That makes it sound too sublime. It isn't. It's decaying, year by year, day by day. It's getting darker and colder in there, and Steep doesn't know how to stay warm, except by killing things, and that doesn't work as well as it used to."

Will's fingers remembered the velvet of the moth's wings, and the heat of the fire that would soon consume them. Though he didn't speak the thought, the fox heard it anyway. "You've had experience of his methodologies, of course. I was forgetting that. You've seen his madness at firsthand. That should arm you against him, at least a little."

"And what happens if he dies?"

"I escape his head," the fox said. "And I'm free."

"Is that why you're haunting me?"

"I'm not *haunting* you. Haunting's for ghosts and I'm not a ghost. I'm a . . . what am I? I'm a memory Steep made into a little myth. The Animal That Devoured Men. That's who I am. I wasn't really interesting as a common or garden fox. So he gave me a voice. Stood me on my hind legs. Called me *Lord* Fox. He made me just as he made you." The admission was bitter. "We're both his children."

"And if he lets you go?"

"I told you: I'm away free."

"But in the real world you've been dead for centuries."

"So? I had children while I was alive. Three litters to my certain knowledge. And they had children, and their children had children. I'm still out there in some form or other. You should sow a few oats yourself, by the way, even if it does go against the grain. It's not as if you don't have the equipment." He glanced down at Will's groin. "I could feed a family of five on that."

"I think this conversation's at an end, don't you?"

"I certainly feel much better about things," the fox replied, as though they were two belligerent neighbors who'd just had a heart to heart.

Will got to his feet. "Does that mean I can stop dreaming now?" he said.

"You're not dreaming," the fox replied. "You've been wide awake for the last half-hour—"

"Not true," Will said, evenly.

"I'm afraid so," the fox replied. "You opened up a little hole in your head that night with Steep, and now the wind can get in. The same wind that blows through his head comes whistling through that shack of yours—"

Will had heard more than enough. "That's it!" he said, starting toward the door. "You're not going to start playing mind games with me."

Raising his paws in mock surrender, Lord Fox stood aside, and Will strode out into the hallway. The fox followed, his claws tap-tapping on the boards.

"Ah, Will," he whined, "we were doing so well—"

"I'm dreaming."

"No, you're not."

"I'm dreaming."

"No!"

At the bottom of the stairs, Will reeled around and yelled back, "Okay, I'm not! I'm crazy! I'm completely fucking ga-ga!"

"Good," the fox said calmly, "we're getting somewhere."

"You want me to go up against Steep in a straitjacket, is that it?"

"No. I just want you to let go of some of your saner suppositions."

"For instance?"

"I want you to accept the notion that you, William Rabjohns, and I, a semimythical fox, can and do coexist."

"If I accepted that I'd be certifiable."

"All right, try it this way: you recall the Russian dolls?"

"Don't start with them—"

"No, it's very simple. Everything fits inside everything else—"

"Oh, Christ . . . ," Will murmured to himself. The thought was now creeping upon him that if this was indeed a dream—and it was, it had to be—then maybe all that had gone before, back to his waking, was also a dream; that he *never woke*, but was still comatose in a bed in Winnipeg—

His body began to tremble.

"What's wrong?" the fox said.

"Just shut up!" he yelled, and started to stumble up the stairs.

The animal pursued him. "You've gone very pale. Are you sick? Get yourself some peppermint tea. It'll settle your stomach."

Did he tell the beast to shut up again? He wasn't sure. His senses were phasing in and out. One moment he was falling up the stairs, then he was practically crawling across the landing, then he was in the bathroom, puking, while the fox yattered on behind him about how he should take care, because he was in a very delicate frame of mind (as if he didn't know) and all manner of lunacies could creep up on him.

Then he was in the shower, his hand, ridiculously remote from him, struggling to grasp the handle. His fingers were as weak as an infant's; then the handle turned suddenly and he was struck by a deluge of icy water. At least his nerve-endings were fully operational, even if his wits weren't. In two heartbeats his body was solid goose flesh, his scalp throbbing with the cold.

Despite his panic, or perhaps because of it, his mind was uncannily agile, leaping instantly to the places where he'd felt such numbing cold before. In Balthazar, of course, as he lay wounded on the ice; and on the hill above Burnt Yarley, lost in the bitter rain. And on the banks of the River Neva, in the winter of the ice-palace—

Wait he thought. That isn't my memory.

—the birds dropping dead out of the sky—

That's a piece of Steep's life, not mine.

—the river like a rock, and Eropkin—poor, doomed Eropkin—building his masterwork out of ice and light—

He shook his head violently to dislodge these trespassers. But they wouldn't go. Frozen into immobility by the icy water, all he could do was stand there while Steep's unwanted memories came flooding into his head.

From *Cabal*
SUN AND SHADE

The sky was cloudless over Midian, the air effervescent. All the fretfulness she'd felt during her first visit here had disappeared. Though this was still the town where Boone had died, she could not hate it for that. Rather the reverse: she and it were allies, both marked by the man's passing.

It was not the town itself she'd come to visit, however; it was the graveyard, and it did not disappoint her. The sun gleamed on the mausoleums, the sharp shadows flattering their elaborate decor. Even the grass that sprouted between the tombs was a more brilliant green today. There was no wind from any quarter, no breath of the dream storms, bringing the dead. Within the high walls there was an extraordinary stillness, as if the outside world no longer existed. Here was a place sacred to the dead, who were *not* the living ceased, but almost another species, requiring rites and prayers that belonged uniquely to them. She was surrounded on every side by such signs: epitaphs in English, French, Polish, and Russian, images of veiled women and shattered urns, saints whose martyrdom she could only guess at, stone dogs sleeping upon their masters' tombs—all the symbolism that accompanied this other people. And the more she explored, the more she found herself asking the question she'd posed the day before: why was the cemetery so big? And why, as became apparent the more tombs she studied, were there so many nationalities laid here? She thought of her dream, of the wind that had come from all quarters of the earth. It was as if there'd been something prophetic in it. The thought didn't worry her. If that was the way the world worked—by omens and prophecies—then it was at least a *system*, and she had lived too long without one. Love had failed her; perhaps this would not.

It took her an hour, wandering down the hushed avenues, to reach the back wall of the cemetery, against which she found a row of animals' graves—cats interred beside birds, dogs beside cats, at peace with each other as common clay. It was an odd sight. Though she knew of other animal cemeteries, she'd never heard of pets being laid in the same consecrated ground as their owners. But then should she be surprised at anything here? The place was a law unto itself, built far from any who would care or condemn.

Turning from the back wall, she could see no sign of the front gate, nor could she remember which of the avenues led back there. It didn't matter. She felt secure in the emptiness of the place, and there was a good deal she wanted to see: sepulchers whose architecture, towering over their fellows, invited admiration. Choosing a route that would take in half a dozen of the most promising, she began an idling return journey. The sun was warmer by the minute now, as it climbed toward noon. Though her pace was slow she broke out into a sweat and her throat became steadily drier. It would be no short drive to find somewhere to quench her thirst. But parched throat or no, she didn't hurry. She knew she'd never come here again. She intended to leave with her memories well stocked.

Along the way were several tombs that had been virtually overtaken by saplings planted in front of them. Evergreens mostly, reminders of the life eternal, the trees flourished in the seclusion of the walls, fed well on rich soil. In some cases their spreading roots had cracked the very memorials they'd been planted to offer shade and protection. These scenes of verdancy and ruin she found particularly poignant. She was lingering at one when the perfect silence was broken.

Hidden in the foliage somebody, or some*thing*, was panting. She automatically stepped out of the tree's shadow and into the hot sun. Shock made her heart beat furiously, its thump deafening her to the sound that had excited it. She had to wait a few moments and listen hard to be sure she'd not imagined the sound. There was no error. Something was in hiding beneath the branches of the tree, which were so weighed by their burden of leaves they almost touched the ground. The sound, now that she listened more carefully, was not human; nor was it healthy. Its roughness and raggedness suggested a dying animal.

She stood in the heat of the sun for a minute or more, just staring into the mass of foliage and shadow, trying to catch some sight of the creature. Occasionally there was a movement: a body vainly trying to right itself, a desperate pawing at the ground as the creature tried to rise. Its helplessness touched her. If she failed to do what she could for it the animal would certainly perish, knowing—this was the thought that moved her to action—that someone had heard its agony and passed it by.

She stepped back into the shadow. For a moment the panting stopped completely. Perhaps the creature was fearful of her and, reading her approach as aggression, preparing some final act of defense. Readying herself to retreat before claws and teeth, she parted the outer twigs and peered through the mesh of branches. Her first impression was not one of sight or sound but of *smell*: a bittersweet scent that was not unpleasant, its source the pale-flanked creature she now made out in the murk, gazing at her wide-eyed. It was a young animal, she guessed, but of no species she could name. A wild cat of some kind, perhaps, but the skin resembled deer hide rather than fur. It watched her warily, its neck barely able to support the weight of its delicately marked head. Even as she returned its gaze it seemed to give up on life. Its eyes closed and its head sank to the ground.

The resilience of the branches defied any further approach. Rather than attempting to bend them aside, she began to break them in order to get to the failing creature. They were living wood, and fought back. Halfway through the thicket a particularly truculent branch snapped back in her face with such stinging force it brought a shout of pain from her. She put her hand to her cheek. The skin to the right of her mouth was broken. Dabbing the blood away she attacked the branch with fresh vigor, at last coming within reach of the animal. It was almost beyond responding to her touch, its eyes momentarily fluttering open as she stroked its flank, then closing again. There was no sign that she could see of a wound, but the body beneath her hand was feverish and full of tremors.

As she struggled to pick the animal up it began to urinate, wetting her hands and blouse, but she drew it to her nevertheless, a dead weight in her arms. Beyond the spasms that ran through its nervous system there was no power left in its muscles. Its limbs hung limply, its head the same. Only the smell she'd first encountered had any strength, intensifying as the creature's final moments approached.

Something like a sob reached her ears. She froze.

Again, the sound. Off to her left, some way, and barely suppressed. She stepped back, out of the shadow of the tree, bringing the dying animal with her. As the sunlight fell on the creature it responded with a violence that utterly belied its apparent frailty, its limbs jerking madly. She stepped back into the shade, instinct telling her the brightness was responsible. Only then did she look again in the direction from which the sob had come.

The door of one of the mausoleums farther down the avenue—a massive structure of cracked marble—stood ajar, and in the column of darkness beyond she could vaguely make out a human figure. Vaguely, because it was dressed in black and seemed to be veiled.

She could make no sense of this scenario. The dying animal tormented by light, the sobbing woman—surely a woman—in the doorway, dressed for mourning.

"Who are you?" she called out.

The mourner seemed to shrink back into the shadows as she was addressed, then regretted the move and approached the open door again, but so very tentatively the connection between animal and woman became clear.

She's afraid of the sun *too*, Lori thought. They belonged together, animal and mourner, the woman sobbing for the creature Lori had in her arms.

She looked at the pavement that lay between where she stood and the mausoleum. Could she get to the door of the tomb without having to step back into the sun, and so hasten the creature's demise? Perhaps, with care. Planning her route before she moved, she started to cross toward the mausoleum, using the shadows like stepping-stones. She didn't look up at the door—her attention was wholly focused on keeping the animal from the light—but she could feel the mourner's presence, willing her on. Once the woman gave voice, not with a word but with a soft sound, a cradle-side sound, addressed not to Lori but to the dying animal.

With the mausoleum door three or four yards from her, Lori dared to look up. The woman in the door could be patient no longer. She reached out from her refuge, her arms bared as the garment she wore rode back, her flesh exposed to the sunlight. The skin was white—as ice, as paper—but only for an instant. As the fingers stretched to relieve Lori of her burden, they darkened and swelled as though instantly bruised. The mourner made a cry of pain and almost fell back into the tomb as she withdrew her arms, but not before the skin broke and trails of dust—yellowish, like pollen—burst from her fingers and fell through the sunlight onto the patio.

Seconds later, Lori was at the door, then through it into the safety of the darkness beyond. The room was no more than an antechamber. Two doors led from it: one into a chapel of some sort, the other below ground. The woman in mourning was standing at this second door, which was open, as far from the wounding light as she could get. In her haste, her veil had fallen. The face beneath was fine-boned, and thin almost to the point of being wasted, lending additional force to her eyes, which caught, even in the darkest corner of the room, some trace of light from the open door, so that they seemed almost to glow.

Lori felt no trace of fear. It was the other woman who trembled as she nursed her sunstruck hands, her gaze moving from Lori's bewildered face to the animal.

"I'm afraid it's dead," Lori said, not knowing what disease afflicted this woman, but recognizing her grief from all too recent memory.

"No . . . ," the woman said with quiet conviction, "she can't die."

Her words were statement not entreaty, but the stillness in Lori's arms contradicted such certainty. If the creature wasn't yet dead it was surely beyond recall.

"Will you bring her to me?" the woman asked.

Lori hesitated. Though the weight of the body was making her arms ache, and she wanted the duty done, she didn't want to cross the chamber.

"Please," the woman said, reaching out with wounded hands.

Relenting, Lori left the comfort of the door and the sunlit patio beyond. She'd taken only two or three steps, however, when she heard the sound of whispering. There could only be one source: the stairs. There were people in the crypt. She stopped walking, childhood superstitions rising up in her. Fear of tombs, fear of stairs *descending*, fear of the Underworld.

"It's nobody," the woman said, her face pained. "Please, bring me Babette."

As if to further reassure Lori, she took a step away from the stairs, murmuring to the animal she'd called Babette. Either the words, or the woman's proximity, or perhaps the cool darkness of the chamber, won a response from the creature: a tremor ran down its spine like an electric charge, so strong Lori almost lost hold of it. The woman's murmurs grew louder, as if she were chiding the dying thing, her anxiety to claim it suddenly urgent. But there was an impasse. Lori was no more willing to approach the entrance to the crypt than the woman was to come another step toward the outer door, and in the seconds of stasis the animal found new life. One of its claws seized Lori's breast as it began to writhe in her embrace.

The chiding became a shout—

"*Babette!*"

But if the creature heard, it didn't care to listen. Its motion became more violent: a mingling of fit and sensuality. One moment it shuddered as though tortured, the next it moved like a snake sloughing off its skin.

"*Don't look, don't look!*" she heard the woman say, but Lori wasn't about to take her eyes off this horrendous dance. Nor could she give the creature over to the woman's charge; while the claw gripped her so tightly any attempt to separate them would draw blood.

But that *Don't look!* had purpose. Now it was Lori's turn to raise her voice in panic, as she realized that what was taking place in her arms defied all reason.

"*Jesus God!*"

The animal was changing before her eyes. In the luxury of slough and spasm it was losing its bestiality, not by reordering its anatomy but by liquefying its whole self—through to the bone—until what had been solid was a tumble of matter. Here was the origin of the bittersweet scent she'd met beneath the tree: the stuff of the beast's dissolution. In the moment it lost its coherence, the matter was ready to be out of her grasp, but somehow the essence of the thing—its will, perhaps, perhaps its *soul*—drew it back for the business of remaking. The last part of the beast to melt was the claw, its disintegration sending a throb of pleasure through Lori's body. It did not distract her from the fact that she was released. Horrified, she couldn't get what she held from her embrace fast enough, tipping it into the mourner's outstretched arms like so much excrement.

"Jesus," she said, backing away, "Jesus, Jesus."

There was no horror on the woman's face, however, only joy. Tears of welcome rolled down her pale cheeks, and fell into the melting pot she held. Lori looked away toward the sunlight. After the gloom of the interior it was blinding. She was momentarily disoriented, and closed her eyes to allow herself a reprieve from both tomb and light.

It was sobbing that made her open her eyes. Not the woman this time, but a child, a girl of four or five, lying naked where the muck of transformation had been.

"Babette," the woman said.

Impossible, reason replied. This thin white child could not be the animal she'd rescued from beneath the tree. It was sleight of hand, or some idiot delusion she'd foisted upon herself. Impossible, all impossible.

"She likes to play outside," the woman was saying, looking up from the child at Lori. "And I tell her: never, never in the sun. Never play in the sun. But she's a child. She doesn't understand."

Impossible, reason repeated. But somewhere in her gut Lori had already given up trying to deny. The animal had been real. The transformation had been real. Now here was a living child, weeping in her mother's arms. She too was real. Every moment she wasted saying No to what she *knew*, was a moment lost to comprehension. That her worldview couldn't contain such a mystery without shattering was its liability, and a problem for another day. For now she simply wanted to be away, into the sunlight where she knew these shape shifters feared to follow. Not daring to take her eyes off them until she was in the sun, she reached out to the wall to guide her tentative backward steps. But Babette's mother wanted to hold her awhile longer.

"I owe you something . . . ," she said.

"No," Lori replied, "I don't . . . want anything . . . from you."

She felt the urge to express her revulsion, but the scene of reunion before her—the child reaching up to touch her mother's chin, her sobs passing—were so tender. Disgust became bewilderment, fear, confusion.

"Let me help you," the woman said, "I know why you came here."

"I doubt it," Lori said.

"Don't waste your time here," the woman replied. "There's nothing for you here. Midian's a home for the Nightbreed. Only the Nightbreed."

Her voice had dropped in volume; it was barely above a whisper.

"The Nightbreed?" Lori said, more loudly.

The woman looked pained.

"Shh . . . ," she said. "I shouldn't be telling you this. But I owe you this much at least."

Lori had stopped her retreat to the door. Her instinct was telling her to wait.

"Do you know a man called Boone?" she said.

The woman opened her mouth to reply, her face a mass of contrary feelings. She wanted to answer, that much was clear, but fear prevented her from speaking. It didn't matter. Her hesitation was answer enough. She *did* know Boone, or had.

"Rachel."

A voice rose from the door that led down into the earth. A man's voice.

"Come away," it demanded, "you've nothing to tell."

The woman looked toward the stairs.

"Mr. Lylesburg," she said, her tone formal, "she saved Babette."

"We know," came the reply from the darkness, "we saw. Still, you must come away."

We, Lori thought. How many others were there below ground, how many more of the *Nightbreed?*

Taking confidence from the proximity of the open door, she challenged the voice that was attempting to silence her informant.

"I saved the child," she said. "I think I deserve something for that."

There was a silence from the darkness, then a point of heated ash brightened in its midst and Lori realized that Mr. Lylesburg was standing almost at the top of the stairs, where the light from outside should have illuminated him, albeit poorly, but that somehow the shadows were clotted about him, leaving him invisible but for his cigarette.

"The child has no life to save," he said to Lori, "but what she has is yours, if you want it." He paused. "Do you want it? If you do, take her. She belongs to you."

The notion of this exchange horrified her.

"What do you take me for?" she said.

"I don't know," Lylesburg replied. "You were the one who demanded recompense."

"I just want some questions answered," Lori protested. "I don't want the child. I'm not a savage."

"No," the voice said softly, "no, you're not. So go. You've no business here."

He drew on the cigarette and by its tiny light Lori glimpsed the speaker's features. She sensed that he willingly revealed himself in this moment, dropping the veil of shadow for a handful of instants to meet her gaze face-to-face. He, like Rachel, was wasted, his gauntness more acute because his bones were large and made for solid cladding. Now, with his eyes sunk into their sockets, and the muscles of his face all too plain beneath papery skin, it was the sweep of his brow that dominated, furrowed and sickly.

"This was never intended," he said. "You weren't meant to see."

"I know that," Lori replied.

"Then you also know that to speak of this will bring dire consequences."

"Don't threaten me."

"Not for you," Lylesburg said, "for *us*."

She felt a twinge of shame at her misunderstanding. She wasn't the vulnerable one, she who could walk in the sunlight.

"I won't say anything," she told him.

"I thank you," he said.

He drew on his cigarette again, and the dark smoke took his face from view.

"What's below," he said from behind the veil, "remains below."

Rachel sighed softly at this, gazing down at the child as she rocked it gently.

"Come away," Lylesburg told her, and the shadows that concealed him moved off down the stairs.

"I have to go," Rachel said, and turned to follow. "Forget you were ever here. There's nothing you can do. You heard Mr. Lylesburg. What's below—"

"Remains below. Yes, I heard."

"Midian's for the Breed. There's no one here who needs you—"

"Just tell me," Lori requested, "is Boone here?"

Rachel was already at the top of the stairs, and now began to descend.

"He is, isn't he?" Lori said, forsaking the safety of the open door and crossing the chamber toward Rachel. "You people stole the body!"

It made some terrible, macabre sense. These tomb dwellers, this Nightbreed, keeping Boone from being laid to rest.

"You *did! You stole him!*"

Rachel paused and looked back up at Lori, her face barely visible in the blackness of the stairs.

"We stole nothing," she said, her reply without rancor.

"*So where is he?*" Lori demanded.

Rachel turned away, and the shadows took her completely from view.

"*Tell me! Please God!*" Lori yelled down after her. Suddenly she was crying, in a turmoil of rage and fear and frustration. "*Tell me, please!*"

Desperation carried her down the stairs after Rachel, her shouts becoming appeals.

"Wait . . . talk to me . . ."

She took three steps, then a fourth. On the fifth she stopped, or rather her body stopped, the muscles of her legs becoming rigid without her instruction, refusing to carry her another step into the darkness of the crypt. Her skin was suddenly crawling with gooseflesh, her pulse thumping in her ears. No force of will could overrule the animal imperative forbidding her to descend; all she could do was stand rooted to the spot and stare into the depths. Even her tears had suddenly dried and the saliva gone from her mouth, so she could no more speak than walk. Not that she wanted to call down into the darkness now, for fear the forces there would answer her summons. Though she could see nothing of them her gut knew they were more terrible by far than Rachel and her beast-child. Shape-shifting was almost a natural act beside the skills these others had to hand. She felt their perversity as a quality of the air. She breathed it in and out. It scoured her lungs and hurried her heart.

If they had Boone's corpse as a plaything it was beyond reclamation. She would have to take comfort from the hope that his spirit was somewhere brighter.

Defeated, she took a step backward. The shadows seemed unwilling to relinquish her, however. She felt them weave themselves into her blouse and hook themselves on her eyelashes, a thousand tiny holds upon her, slowing her retreat.

"I won't tell anyone," she murmured. "Please let me go."

But the shadows held on, their power a promise of retribution if she defied them.

"I promise," she said. "What more can I do?"

And suddenly, they capitulated. She hadn't realized how strong their claim was until it was withdrawn. She stumbled backward, falling up the stairs into the light of the antechamber. Turning her back on the crypt, she fled for the door and out into the sun.

It was too bright. She covered her eyes, holding herself upright by gripping the stone portico so that she could accustom herself to its violence. It took several minutes, standing against the mausoleum, shaking and rigid by turns. Only when she felt able to see through half-closed eyes did she attempt to walk, her route back to the main gate a farrago of cul-de-sacs and missed turnings.

By the time she reached it, however, she'd more or less accustomed herself to the brutality of light and sky. Her body was still not back at her mind's disposal, however. Her legs refused to carry her more than a few paces up the hill to Midian without threatening to drop her to the ground. Her system, overdosed on adrenaline, was cavorting. But at least she was alive. For a short while there on the stairs it had been touch and go. The shadows that had held her by lash and thread could have taken her, she had no doubt of that. Claimed her for the Underworld and snuffed her out. Why had they released her? Perhaps because she'd saved the child, perhaps because she'd sworn silence and they'd trusted her. Neither, however, seemed the motives of monsters, and she had to believe that what lived beneath Midian's cemetery deserved that name. Who other than monsters made their nests among the dead? They might call themselves the Nightbreed, but neither words nor gestures of good faith could disguise their true nature.

She had escaped demons—things of rot and wickedness—and she would have offered up a prayer of thanks for her deliverance if the sky had not been so wide and bright, and so plainly devoid of deities to hear.

From *Weaveworld*
URIEL

Night came down like a dropped curtain. Jabir made a fire in the shelter of the wall, out of the remorseless assault of the wind, and there they ate bread and drank coffee. There was no conversation. Exhaustion had claimed their tongues. They simply sat hunched up, staring into the flames.

Though his bones ached, Shadwell couldn't sleep. As the fire burned low, and one by one the others succumbed to fatigue, he was left to keep watch. The wind dropped a little as the night deepened, its bellow becoming a moan. It soothed him like a lullaby, and at last, his eyelids dropped closed. Behind them, the busy patterns of his inner-eye. Then emptiness.

In sleep, he heard the boy Jabir's voice. It called him from darkness but he didn't want to answer. Rest was too sweet. It came again, however: a horrid shriek. This time he opened his lids.

The wind had died completely. Overhead the stars were bright in a perfect sky, trembling in their places. The fire had gone out, but their light was sufficient for him to see that both Ibn Talaq and Jabir were missing from their places. He got up, crossed to Hobart, and shook him awake.

As he did so, his eye caught sight of something on the ground a little way beyond Hobart's head. He stared—doubting what he saw.

There were *flowers* underfoot, or so he seemed to see. Clusters of blooms, set in abundant foliage. He looked up from the ground, and his parched throat unleashed a cry of astonishment.

The dunes had gone. In their place a jungle had risen up, a riot of trees that challenged the wall's height—vast, flower-laden species whose leaves were the size of a man. Beneath their canopy was a wilderness of vines and shrubs and grasses.

For a moment he doubted his sanity, until he heard Hobart say: "My God," at his side.

"You see it too?" said Shadwell.

"I see it . . . ," Hobart said, "a garden."

"Garden?"

At first sight the word scarcely described this chaos. But further scrutiny showed that there was order at work in what had initially seemed anarchy. Avenues had been laid under the vast, blossom-laden trees; there were lawns and terraces. This was indeed a garden of sorts, though there would be little pleasure to be had walking in it, for despite the surfeit of species—plants and bushes of every size and shape—there was not among them a single variety that had color. Neither bloom nor branch nor leaf nor fruit; all, down to the humblest blade, had been bled of pigment.

Shadwell was puzzling at this when a further cry issued from the depths. It was Ibn Talaq's voice this time; and it rose in a steep curve to a shriek. He followed it. The ground was soft beneath his feet, which slowed his progress, but the shriek went on, broken only by sobbing breaths. Shadwell ran, calling the man's name. There was no fear left in him; only an overwhelming hunger to see the Maker of this enigma face to face.

As he advanced down one of the shadowy boulevards, its pathway strewn with the same colorless plant-life, Ibn Talaq's cry stopped dead. Shadwell was momentarily disoriented. He halted, and scanned the foliage for some sign of movement. There was none. The breeze did not stir a single frond; nor—to further compound the mystery—was there a hint of perfume, however subtle, from the mass of blossoms.

Behind him, Hobart muttered a cautionary word. Shadwell turned, and was about to condemn the man's lack of curiosity when he caught sight of the trail his own footsteps had made. In the Gyre, his heels had brought forth life. Here, they'd destroyed it. Wherever he'd set foot the plants had simply crumbled away.

He stared at the blank ground where there'd previously been grasses and flowers, and the explanation for this extraordinary growth became apparent. Ignoring Hobart now, he walked toward the nearest of the bushes, the blooms of which hung like censers from their branches. Tentatively, he touched his fingers to one of the flowers. Upon this lightest of contacts the blossom fell apart, dropping from the branch in a shower of sand. He brushed its companion with his thumb: it too fell away, and with it the branch, and the exquisite leaves it bore; *all* returned to sand at a touch.

The dunes hadn't disappeared in the night, to make way for this garden. They had *become* the garden; risen up at some unthinkable command to create this sterile illusion. What had at first sight seemed a miracle of fecundity was a mockery. It was sand. Scentless, colorless, lifeless: a dead garden.

A sudden disgust gripped him. This trick was all too like the work of the Seerkind: some deceitful rapture. He flung himself into the midst of the shrubbery, flailing to right and left of him in his fury, destroying the bushes in stinging clouds. A tree, brushed by his hand, collapsed like an extinguished fountain. The most elaborate blossoms fell apart at his merest touch. But he wasn't satisfied. He flailed on until he'd cleared a small grove amid the press of foliage.

"*Raptures!*" he kept yelling, as the sand rained down on him. "*Raptures!*"

He might have gone on to more ambitious destruction, but that the Scourge's howl—the same he'd first heard days before, as he'd squatted in shit—began. That voice had brought him through desolation and emptiness; and to what? More desolation, more emptiness. His anger unassuaged by the damage he'd done, he turned to Hobart.

"Which way's it coming from?"

"I don't know," said Hobart, stumbling back a few steps. "*Everywhere.*"

"*Where are you?*" Shadwell demanded, yelling into the depths of the illusion. "Show yourself!"

"Don't—" said Hobart, his voice full of dread.

"This is your Dragon," Shadwell said. "We have to see it."

Hobart shook his head. The power that had made this place was not one he wanted sight of. Before he could retreat, however, Shadwell had hold of him.

"We meet it together," he said. "It's cheated us *both.*"

Hobart struggled to be free of Shadwell's grip, but his violence ceased as his panicked eyes caught sight of the form that now appeared at the far end of the avenue.

It was as tall as the canopy; twenty-five feet or more, its long, bone-white head brushing the branches, sand-petals spiraling down.

Though it still howled, it lacked a mouth, or indeed any feature on its face but eyes, which it had in terrifying numbers, twin rows of lidless, lashless slits which ran down each side of its head. There were perhaps a hundred eyes in all, but staring an age at it would not have revealed their true number, for the thing, despite its solidity, defied fixing. Were those wheels that moved at its heart, tied with lines of liquid fire to a hundred other geometries which informed the air it occupied? Did innumerable wings beat at its perimeters, and light burn in its bowels, as though it had swallowed stars?

Nothing was certain. In one breath it seemed to be enclosed in a matrix of darting light, like scaffolding struck by lightning; in the next the pattern became flame confetti, which swarmed at its extremities before it was snatched away. One moment, ether; the next, juggernaut.

And then, as suddenly as it had begun, the wail it was unleashing died away. The Scourge stopped moving.

Shadwell released Hobart, as the stench of shit rose from the man's trousers. Hobart fell to the ground, making small sobbing sounds. Shadwell left him where he lay, as the Scourge's head, mazed in geometries, located the creatures that had trespassed in its garden.

He didn't retreat. What use was retreat? In every direction from this place lay thousands of square miles of wasteland. There was nowhere to run to. All he could do was stand his ground and share with this terror the news he brought.

But before he could utter a word, the sand at his feet began to move. For an instant he thought the Scourge intended to bury him alive, as the ground liquefied. But instead the sand drew back like a sheet, and sprawled on the bed below—a few feet from where Shadwell stood—was the corpse of Ibn Talaq. The man was naked, and appalling torments had been visited upon him. Both his hands had been burned from his arms, leaving blackened stumps from which cracked bone protruded. His genitals had been similarly destroyed, and the eyes seared from his head. There was no use pretending the wounds had been delivered after death: his mouth still shaped his dying scream.

Shadwell was revolted, and averted his eyes, but the Scourge had more to show him. The sand moved again, to his right, and another body was uncovered. This time, Jabir, lying on his belly, his buttocks burned down to the bone, his neck broken and his head twisted round so that he stared up at the sky. His mouth was burned out.

"Why?" was the word on Shadwell's lips.

The Scourge's gaze made his bowels ache to empty themselves, but he still delivered the question.

"Why? We mean no harm here."

The Scourge made no sign that it had even heard the words. Had it perhaps lost the power of communication after an age here in the wilderness, its only response to the pain of being, that howl?

Then—somewhere amid the legion eyes—a skittering light, which was snatched by the burning wheels and spat toward Shadwell. In the breath before it struck him he had time to hope his death would be quick; then the light was on him. The agony of its touch was blinding; at its caress his body folded up beneath him. He struck the ground, his skull ready to split. But death didn't come. Instead the pain dropped away suddenly, and the burning wheel appeared in his mind's eye. The Scourge was in his head, its power circling in his skull.

Then the wheel went out, and in its place a vision, lent him by his possessor:

He was floating through the garden; high up in the trees. This is the Scourge's sight, he realized: he was sitting behind its eyes. Their shared gaze caught a motion on the ground below, and moved toward it.

There on the sand was Jabir—naked, and on all fours—with Ibn Talaq impaling him, grunting as he worked his flesh into the boy. To Shadwell's eyes the act looked uncomfortable, but harmless enough. He'd seen worse in his time; *done* worse, indeed. But it wasn't just sight he was sharing with the Scourge; its thoughts came too: and the creature saw a crime in this rutting, and judged it punishable by death.

Shadwell had seen the results of the Scourge's executions; he had no desire to watch them reenacted. But he had no choice. The Scourge owned his mind's eye; he was obliged to watch every terrible moment.

Brightness reached down and tore the pair from each other, then scoured out the offending parts—mouth, and eyes, and groin and buttocks—erasing them with fire. It was not quick. They had time to suffer—he heard again the shrieks that had brought him into the garden—and time to beg. But the fire was unforgiving. By the time it had done its work Shadwell was sobbing for it to stop. Finally it did, and a shroud of sand was drawn over the bodies. Only when that was done did the Scourge grant him his own sight back. The ground he lay on—stinking of his vomit—reappeared in front of him.

He lay where he'd fallen, trembling. Only when he was certain he wouldn't collapse did he raise his head and look up at the Scourge.

It had changed shape. No longer a giant, it sat on a hill of sand it had raised beneath itself, its many eyes turned up toward the stars. It had gone from judge and executioner to contemplative in a matter of moments.

Though the images that had filled his head had faded, Shadwell knew the creature still maintained its presence in his mind. He could feel the barbs of its thought. He was a human fish, and hooked.

It looked away from the sky, and down at him.

Shadwell . . .

He heard his name called, though in its new incarnation the Scourge still lacked a mouth. It needed none of course, when it could dabble in a man's head this way.

I see you, it said. Or rather, that was the thought it placed in Shadwell's head, to which he put words.

I see you. And I know your name.

"That's what I want," Shadwell said. "I want you to know me. Trust me. *Believe* me."

Sentiments like these had been part of his Salesman's spiel for more than half his life; he drew confidence from speaking them.

You're not the first to come here, the Scourge said. *Others have come. And gone.*

Shadwell knew all too well *where* they'd gone. He had a momentary glimpse—whether it was at the Scourge's behest or of his own making he couldn't be sure—of the bodies that were buried beneath the sand, their rot wasted on this dead garden. The thought should have made him afraid, but he'd felt all he was going to feel of fear, seeing the executions. Now, he would speak plainly, and hope the truth kept him from death.

"I came here for a reason," he said.

What reason?

This was the moment. The customer had asked a question and he had to reply to it. No use to try and prevaricate or prettify, in the hope of securing a better sale. The plain truth was all he had to bargain with. On that, the sale was either won or lost. Best to simply state it.

"The Seerkind," he said.

He felt the barbs in his brain twitch at the name, but there was no further response. The Scourge was silent. Even its wheels seemed to dim, as if at any moment the engine would flicker out.

Then, oh so quietly, it shaped the word in his head.

Seer. Kind.

And with the word came a spasm of energy, like lightning, that erupted in his skull. It was in the substance of the Scourge as well, this lightning. It flickered across the equation of its body. It ran back and forth in its eyes.

Seerkind.

"You know who they are?"

The sand hissed around Shadwell's feet.

I had forgotten.

"It's been a long time."

And you came here to tell me?

"To remind you."

Why?

The barbs twitched again. It could kill me at any moment, Shadwell thought. It's nervous, and that makes it dangerous. I must be careful; play it cunningly. Be a salesman.

"They hid from you," he said.

Indeed.

"All these years. Hid their heads so you'd never find them."

And now?

"Now they're awake again. In the human world."

I had forgotten. But I'm reminded now. Oh yes. Sweet Shadwell.

The barbs relaxed, and a wave of the purest pleasure broke over Shadwell, leaving him almost sick with the excess of it. It was a joy-bringer too, this Scourge. What power did not lie in its control?

"May I ask a question?" he said.

Ask.

"Who are you?"

The Scourge rose from its throne of sand, and in an instant it grew blindingly bright.

Shadwell covered his eyes, but the light shone through flesh and bone, and into his head, where the Scourge was pronouncing its eternal name.

I am called Uriel, it said. *Uriel, of the principalities.*

He knew the name, as he'd known by heart the rituals he'd heard at St. Philomena's: and from the same source. As a child he'd learned the names of all the angels and archangels by heart: and among the mighty Uriel was of the mightiest. The archangel of salvation; called by some the flame of God. The sight of the executions replayed in his head—the bodies withering beneath that merciless fire: an *Angel's* fire. What had he done, stepping into the presence of such power? This was Uriel, of the principalities . . .

Another of the Angel's attributes rose from memory now, and with it a sudden shock of comprehension. Uriel had been the angel left to stand guard at the gates of Eden.

Eden.

At the word, the creature blazed. Though the ages had driven it to grief and forgetfulness, it was still an Angel: its fires unquenchable. The wheels of its body rolled, the visible mathematics of its essence turning on itself and preparing for new terrors.

There were others here, the Seraph said, *that called this place Eden. But I never knew it by that name.*

"What, then?" Shadwell asked.

Paradise, said the Angel, and at the word a new picture appeared in Shadwell's mind. It was the garden, in another age. No trees of sand then, but a lush jungle that brought to mind the flora that had sprung to life in the Gyre: the same profligate fecundity, the same unnamable species that seemed on the verge of defying their condition. Blooms that might at any moment take breath, fruit about to fly. There was none of the urgency of the Gyre here, however; the atmosphere was one of inevitable rising up, things aspiring at their own pace to some higher state, which was surely *light*, for everywhere between the trees brightnesses floated like living spirits.

This was a place of making, the Angel said. *For ever and ever. Where things came to be.*

"To be?"

To find a form, and enter the world.

"And Adam, and Eve?"

I don't remember them, Uriel replied.

"The first parents of humanity."

Humanity was raised from dirt in a thousand places, but not here. Here were higher spirits.

"The Seerkind?" said Shadwell. "Higher spirits?"

The Angel made a sour sound. The image of the paradise garden convulsed, and Shadwell glimpsed furtive figures moving among the trees like thieves.

They began here, said the Angel; and in Shadwell's mind he saw the earth break open, and plants rise from it with human faces; and mist congeal . . . *But they were accidents. Droppings from greater stuff, that found life here. We did not know them, we spirits. We were about sublimer business.*

"And they grew?"

Grew. And grew curious.

Now Shadwell began to comprehend.

"They smelled the world," he prompted.

The Angel shuddered, and again Shadwell was bombarded with images. He saw the forefathers of the Seerkind, naked, every one, their bodies all colors and sizes—a crowd of freakish forms—tails, golden eyes and coxcombs, flesh on one with the sheen of a panther; another with vestigial wings—he saw them scaling the wall, eager to be out of the garden—

"They escaped."

Nobody escapes me, said Uriel. *When the spirits left, I remained here to keep watch until their return.*

That much, the Book of Genesis had been correct about: a guardian set at the gate. But little else, it seemed. The writers of that book had taken an image that mankind knew in its heart, and folded it into their narrative for their own moral purposes. What place God had here, if any, was perhaps as much a matter of definition as anything. Would the Vatican know this creature as an Angel, if it presented itself before the gates of that state? Shadwell doubted it.

"And the spirits?" he said. "The others who were here?"

I waited, said the Angel.

And waited, and waited, thought Shadwell, until loneliness drove it mad. Alone in the wilderness, with the garden withering and rotting, and the sand breaking through the walls . . .

"Will you come with me now?" said Shadwell. "I can lead you to the Seerkind."

The Angel turned its gaze on Shadwell afresh.

I hate the world, it said. *I was there before, once.*

"But if I take you to them," said Shadwell. "You can do your duty, and be finished with it."

Uriel's hatred of the Kingdom was like a physical thing; it chilled Shadwell's scalp. Yet the Angel didn't reject the offer, merely bided its time as it turned the possibility over. It wanted an end to its waiting, and soon. But its majesty was repulsed at the thought of contact with the human world. Like all pure things, it was vain, and easily spoiled.

Perhaps . . . it said.

Its gaze moved off Shadwell toward the wall. The Salesman followed its look, and there found Hobart. The man had taken the chance to creep away during the exchange with Uriel; but he'd not got far enough.

. . . *this time* . . . the Angel said, the light flickering in the concourse of its eyes, . . . *I will go* . . . The light was caught up by the wheels, and thrown out toward Hobart. . . . *in a different skin.*

With that, the entire engine flew apart, and not one but countless arrows of light fled toward Hobart. Uriel's gaze had bound him to the spot; he could not avoid the invasion. The arrows struck him from forehead to foot, their light entering him without breaking his skin.

In the space of a heartbeat all trace of the Angel had gone from the hill beside Shadwell; and with its disappearance into flesh came a new spectacle. A shudder ran through the ground from the wall where Hobart stood and through the garden. At its passage the sand forms began to decay, countless plants dropping into dust, avenues of trees shuddering and collapsing like arches in an earthquake. Watching the escalating destruction, Shadwell thought again of his first sight of the patterns in the dunes. Perhaps his assumptions then had been correct; perhaps this place *was* in some way a sign to the stars. Uriel's pitiful way of re-creating a lost glory, in the hope that some passing spirit would come calling, and remind it of itself.

Then the cataclysm grew too great, and he retreated before he was buried in a storm of sand.

Hobart was no longer on the garden's side of the breach, but had climbed the boulders, and stood looking out across the blank wastes of the desert.

There was no outward sign of Uriel's occupancy. To a casual eye this was the same Hobart. His gaunt features were as glacial as ever, and it was the same colorless voice that emerged when he spoke. But the question he posed told a different story.

"Am I the Dragon now?" he asked.

Shadwell looked at him. There was, he now saw, a brilliance in the hollows of Hobart's eyes that he'd not seen since he'd first seduced the man with promises of fire.

"Yes," he said. "You're the Dragon."

From *Everville*

September had been a month of recuperation for Harry. He'd made a project of tidying his tiny office on Forty-fifth Street; touched base with friends he hadn't seen all summer; even attempted to reignite a few amorous fuses around town. In this last he was completely unsuccessful: only one of the women for whom he left messages returned his call, and only to remind him that he'd borrowed fifty bucks.

He was not unhappy then, to find a girl in her late teens at his apartment door that Tuesday night in early October. She had a ring through her left nostril, a black dress too short for her health, and a package.

"Are you Harry?" she said.

"Yep."

"I'm Sabina. I got something for you." The parcel was cylindrical, four feet long, and wrapped in brown paper. "You want to take it from me?" she said.

"What is it?"

"I'm going to drop it—" the girl said, and let the thing go. Harry caught it before it hit the floor. "It's a present."

"Who from?"

"Could I maybe get a Coke or something?" the girl said, looking past Harry into the apartment.

The word *sure* was barely out of Harry's mouth and Sabina was pushing past him. What she lacked in manners she made up for in curves, he thought, watching her head on down the hall. He could live with that. "The kitchen's on your right," he told her, but she headed straight past it into the living room.

"Got anything stronger?" she said.

"There's probably some beers in the fridge," he replied, slamming the front door with his foot and following her into the living room.

"Beer gives me gas," she said.

Harry dropped the package in the middle of the floor. "I've got some rum, I think."

"Okay," she shrugged, as though Harry had been the one to suggest it and she really wasn't that interested.

He ducked into the kitchen to find the liquor, digging through the cupboard for an uncracked glass.

"You're not as weird as I thought you'd be," Sabina said to him meanwhile. "This place is nothing special."

"What were you expecting?"

"Something more crazy, you know. I heard you get into some pretty sick stuff."

"Who told you that?"

"Ted."

"You knew Ted?"

"I more than knew him," she said, appearing at the kitchen door. She was trying to look sultry, but her face, despite the kohl and the rouge and the blood-red lip gloss was too round and childlike to carry it off.

"When was this?" Harry asked her.

"Oh . . . three years ago. I was fourteen when I met him."

"That sounds like Ted."

"We never did anything I didn't want to do," she said, accepting the glass of rum from Harry. "He was always real nice to me, even when he was going through lousy times."

"He was one of the good guys," Harry said.

"We should drink to him," Sabina replied.

"Sure." They tapped glasses. "Here's to Ted."

"Wherever he is," Sabina added. "Now, are you going to open your present?"

It was a painting. Ted's great work, in fact, *D'Amour in Wyckoff Street*, taken from its frame, stripped off its support and somewhat ignominiously tied up with a piece of frayed string.

"He wanted you to have it," Sabina explained, as Harry pulled back the sofa to unroll the painting fully. The canvas was as powerful as Harry remembered. The seething color field in which the street was painted, the impasto from which his features had been carved, and of course that detail Ted had been so proud to point out to Harry in the gallery: the foot, the heel, the snake writhing as it was trodden lifeless. "I guess maybe if somebody had offered him ten grand for it," Sabina was saying, "he would have given you something else. But nobody bought it, so I thought I'd come and give it to you."

"And the gallery didn't mind?"

"They don't know it's gone," Sabina said. "They put it in storage with all the other pictures they couldn't sell. I guess they figured they'd find buyers sooner or later, but people don't want pictures like Ted's on their walls. They want stupid stuff." She had come to Harry's shoulder as she spoke. He could smell a light honey-scent off her. "If you like," she said, "I could come back and make a new support for the canvas. Then you could hang it over your bed—" she slid him a sly look, "or wherever."

Harry didn't want to offend the girl. No doubt she'd done as Ted would have wished, bringing the picture here, but the notion of waking to an image of Wyckoff Street every morning wasn't particularly comforting.

"I can see you want to think about it," Sabina said, and leaning across to Harry laid a quick kiss beside his mouth. "I'll stop by sometime next week, okay?" she said. "You can tell me then." She finished her rum and handed the empty glass to Harry. "It was really nice meeting you," she said, suddenly and sweetly formal. She was slowly retreating to the door as if waiting for a sign from Harry that she should stay.

He was tempted. But he knew he wouldn't think much of himself in the morning if he took advantage. She was seventeen, for God's sake. By Ted's standards that was practically senile, of course. But there was a part of Harry that still wanted seventeen year olds to be dreaming of love, not being plied with rum and coaxed into bed by men twice their age.

She seemed to realize that nothing was going to come of this, and gave him a slightly quizzical smile. "You really *aren't* the way I thought you'd be," she remarked, faintly disappointed.

"I guess Ted didn't know me as well as he thought he did."

"Oh it wasn't just Ted told me about you," she said.

"Who else?"

"Everyone and no one," she replied with a lazy shrug. She was at the door now. "See you, maybe," she said, and opening the door was away, leaving him wishing he'd kept her company a little longer.

Later, as he trailed to the john at three in the morning, he halted in front of the painting, and wondered if Mimi Lomax's house on Wyckoff Street was still standing. The question was still with him when he woke the following morning, and as he walked to his office, and as he sorted through his outstanding paperwork. It didn't matter either way, of course, except to the extent that the question kept coming between him and his business. He knew why: he was afraid. Though he'd seen terrors in Palomo Grove, and come face to face with the Iad itself in Everville, the specter of Wyckoff Street had never been properly exorcised. Perhaps it was time to do so now: to deal once and for all with that last corner of his psyche still haunted by the stale notion of an evil that coveted human souls.

He turned the notion over through the rest of the day, and through the day following that, knowing in his gut he would have to go sooner or later, or the subject would only gain authority over him.

On Friday morning, he got to his office to find that somebody had mailed him a mummified monkey's head, elaborately mounted on what looked suspiciously like a length of human bone. It was not the first time he'd had such items come his way—some of them warnings, some of them talismans from well-wishers, some of them simply ill-advised gifts—but today the presence of this object, its aroma stinging his sinuses, seemed to Harry a goad, to get him on his way. What are you afraid of? the gaping thing seemed to demand. Things die, and spoil, but look, I'm laughing.

He boxed the thing up, and was about to deposit it in the trash when some superstitious nerve in him twitched. Instead he left it where it lay in the middle of his desk and, telling it he'd be back soon, he headed off to Wyckoff Street.

———

It was a cold day. Not yet New York–bitter (that was probably a month, six weeks from now), but cold enough to know that there'd be no more shirt-sleeves days this side of winter. He didn't mind. The summer months had always brought him the most trouble—this summer had been no excep-tion—and he was relieved to feel things running down around him. So what if the trees shed, and the leaves rotted and the nights drew in? He needed the sleep.

He found that much of the neighborhood around Wyckoff Street had changed drastically since he'd last been here, and the closer he got the more he dared hope his destination would be so much rubble.

Not so. Wyckoff Street remained almost exactly as it had been ten years before, the houses as gray and grim as ever. Rock might melt in Oregon, and the sky crack like a dropped egg, but here earth was earth and sky was sky and whatever lived between was not going to be skipping anywhere soon.

He wandered along the littered sidewalk to Mimi Lomax's house, expecting to find it in a state of dilapidation. Again, not so. Its present owner was plainly attentive. The house had a new roof, a new chimney, new eaves. The door he knocked on had been recently painted.

There was no reply at first, though he heard the murmur of voices from inside. He knocked again, and this time, after a delay of a minute or so, the door was opened a sliver and a woman in late middle-age, her face taut and sickly, stared out at him with red-rimmed eyes.

"Are you him?" she said. Her voice was frail with exhaustion. "Are you De Amour?"

"I'm D'Amour, yes." Harry was already uneasy. He could smell the woman from where he stood; sour sweat and dirt. "How do you know who I am?" he asked her.

"She said—" the woman replied, opening the door a little wider.

"Who said?"

"She's got my Stevie upstairs. She's had him there for three days." Tears were pouring down the woman's cheeks as she spoke. She made no effort to wipe them away. "She said she wouldn't let him go till you got here." She stepped back from the door. "You gotta make her let him go. He's all I got."

Harry took a deep breath, and stepped into the house. At the far end of the hallway stood a woman in her early twenties. Long black hair, huge eyes shining in the gloom.

"This is Stevie's sister. Loretta."

The young woman clutched her rosary, and stared at Harry as though he was an accomplice of whatever was upstairs.

The older woman closed the front door and came to Harry's side. "How did it know you were coming here?" she murmured.

"I don't know," Harry replied.

"It said if we tried to leave—" Loretta said, her voice barely a whisper, "it'd kill Stevie."

"Why do you say *it?*"

"Because it's not human." She glanced up the flight, her face fearful. "It's from Hell," she breathed. "Can't you smell it?"

There was certainly a foul smell. This wasn't the fish-market stench of the Zyem Carasophia's chamber. This was shit and fire.

Heart cavorting, Harry went to the bottom of the stairs. "You stay down here," he told the two women, and started up the flight, stepping over the spot on the fifth stair where Father Hess's head had been resting when he expired. There was no noise from upstairs, and none now from below. He climbed in silence, knowing the creature awaiting him was listening for every creaking stair. Rather than let it think he was attempting to approach in silence and failing, he broke the hush himself.

"Coming, ready or not," he said.

The reply came immediately. And he knew within a syllable what thing this was.

"Harry—" said Lazy Susan. "Where have you been? No, don't tell me. You've been seeing the Boss Man, haven't you?"

While the demon talked, Harry reached the top of the stairs and crossed the landing to the door. The paint was blistered.

"You want a job, Harry?" Lazy Susan went on. "I don't blame you. Times are about to get *real bad.*"

The door was already open an inch. Harry pushed it, lightly, and it swung wide. The room beyond was almost completely dark, the drapes drawn, the lamp on the floor so encrusted with caked excrement it barely glimmered. The bed itself had been stripped down to the mattress, which in turn had been burned black. On it lay a youth, dressed in a filthy T-shirt and boxer shorts, face-down.

"Stevie?" Harry said.

The boy didn't move.

"He's asleep right now," said Lazy Susan's curdled voice from the darkness beyond the bed. "He's had a busy time."

"Why don't you just let the kid go? It's me you want."

"You overestimate your appeal, D'Amour. Why would I want a fucked-up soul like yours when I could have this pure little thing?"

"Then why did you bring me here?"

"I didn't. Sure, Sabina may have planted the thought in your head. But you came of your own accord."

"Sabina's a friend of yours?"

"She'd probably prefer mistress. Did you fuck her?"

"No."

"Ah, *D'Amour!*" the Nomad said, exasperated. "After all the trouble I went to getting her wet. You're not turning queer on me, are you? No. You're too straight for your own good. You're boring, D'Amour. Boring, boring—"

"Well maybe I should just piss off home," Harry said, turning back to the door.

There was a rush of motion behind him; he heard the bedsprings creak, and Stevie let out a little moan. "*Wait,*" the Nomad hissed. "*Don't you ever turn your back on me.*"

He glanced over his shoulder. The creature had shimmied up onto the bed and now had its bone and muck body poised over its victim. It was the color of the filth on the lamp, but wet, its too-naked anatomy full of peristaltic motions.

"Why's it always *shit?*" Harry said.

The Nomad cocked its head. Whatever features were upon it all resembled wounds. "Because shit's all we have, Harry, until we're returned to glory. It's all God allows us to play with. Maybe a little fire, once in a while, as long as He isn't looking. Speaking of fire, I saw Father Hess the other day, burning in his cell. I told him I might see you—"

Harry shook his head. "It doesn't work, Nomad," he said.

"What doesn't work?"

"The fallen angel routine. I don't believe it anymore." He started toward the bed. "You know why? I saw some of your relatives in Oregon. In fact, I almost got crucified by a couple of them. Brutish little fucks like you, except they didn't have any of your pretensions. They were just in it for the blood and the shit." He kept approaching the bed as he talked, far from certain what the creature would do. It had disemboweled Hess with a few short strokes and he had no reason to believe it had lost the knack. But, stripped of its phony autobiography, what was it? A thug with a few days' training in an abattoir.

"Stop right there," the creature said when Harry was a yard from the bed. It was shuddering from head to foot. "If you come any closer, I'll kill Little Stevie. And I'll throw him down the stairs, just like Hess."

Harry raised his hands in mock-surrender. "Okay," he said, "this is as close as I get. I just wanted to check the family resemblance. You know, it's uncanny."

The Nomad shook his head. "I was an angel, D'Amour," it said, its voice troubled. "I remember Heaven. I do. As though it were yesterday. Clouds and light and—"

"And the sea?"

"The sea?"

"Quiddity."

"*No!*" it yelled. "*I was in Heaven.* I remember God's heart, beating, beating, all the time—"

"Maybe you were born on a beach."

"I've warned you once," the creature said. "I'll kill the boy."

"And what will that *prove?* That you're a fallen angel? Or that you're the little bully I say you are?"

The Nomad raised its hands to its wretched face. "Ohh, you're clever, D'Amour," it sighed. "You're very clever. But so was Hess." The creature parted its fingers, exhaling its sewer breath. "And look what happened to him."

"Hess wasn't clever," Harry said softly. "I loved him and I respected him, but he was deluded. You're pretty much alike, now that I think about it." He leaned an inch or two closer to the entity. "*You* think you fell from Heaven. *He* thought he was serving it. You believed the same things, in the end. It was stupid to kill him, Nomad. It's not left you with very much."

"I've still got *you*," the creature replied. "I could fuck with your head until the Crack of Doom."

"Nah," Harry said, standing upright. "I'm not afraid of you any longer. I don't need prayers—"

"Oh don't you?" it growled.

"I don't need a crucifix. I just need the eyes in my head. And what I see—what I see is an anorexic little shit-eater."

At this, it launched itself at him, shrieking, all the wounds in its head wide. Harry retreated across the filthy floor, avoiding its whining talons by inches, until his back was flat against the wall. Then it closed on him, flinging its arms up at his head. He raised his hands to protect his eyes, but the creature didn't want them, at least not yet. Instead it dug its fingers into the flesh at the back of his neck, driving its spiked feet into the wall to either side of his body.

"Now *again*, D'Amour—" the creature said. Harry felt the blood pour down his spine. Heard his vertebrae crack. "Am I an angel?" Its face was inches from Harry's, its voice issuing from all the holes at once. "I want an answer, D'Amour. It's very important to me. I was in Heaven once, wasn't I? Admit it."

Very, very slowly, Harry shook his throbbing head.

The creature sighed. "Oh, D'Amour," it said, uprooting one of its hands from the back of Harry's neck and bringing it round to stroke his larynx. The growl had gone from its voice. It was no longer the Nomad; it was Lazy Susan. "I'll miss you," it said, its fingers breaking the skin of Harry's throat. "There hasn't been a night when I haven't thought of us"—its tone was sultry now—"here, in the dark together."

On the bed behind the creature, the boy moaned.

"*Hush . . . ,*" Lazy Susan said.

But Stevie was beyond being silenced. He wanted the comfort of a prayer. "Hail Mary, full of grace—" he began.

The creature glanced round at him, the Nomad surfacing again to shriek for the boy to shut the fuck up. As it did so, Harry caught hold of the hand at his neck, lacing his fingers with the talons. Then he threw his weight forward. The Nomad's feet were loosed from the wall and the two bodies, locked together, stumbled into the middle of the room.

Instantly, the creature drove its fingers deeper into Harry's nape. Blinded by pain, he swung around, determined that wherever they fell it wouldn't be on top of the boy. They reeled wildly, round and round, until Harry lost his balance and fell forward, carrying the Nomad ahead of him.

Its body struck the charred door, which splintered under the combined weight of their bodies. Through his tear-filled eyes Harry glimpsed the misbegotten face in front of him, its hands slack with shock. Then they were out onto the landing. It was bright after the murk of the bedroom. For the Nomad, painfully so. It convulsed in Harry's embrace, hot phlegm spurting from its maws. He seized the moment to wrest its talons from his neck, then their momentum carried them against the banisters, which cracked but did not break, and over they went.

It was a fall of perhaps ten feet, the Nomad under Harry, shrieking still. They hit the stairs, and rolled and rolled, finally coming to rest a few steps from the bottom.

The first thing Harry thought was: God, it's quiet. Then he opened his eyes. He was cheek to cheek with the creature, its sweat stinging his skin. Reaching out for the spattered banister he started to haul himself to his feet, his left arm, shoulder, ribs and neck all paining him, but none so badly he could not enjoy the spectacle at his feet.

The Nomad was in extremis, its body—which was even more pitiful and repulsive by the light of day than in the room above—a mass of degenerating tissue.

"Are . . . you . . . there?" the creature said.

It had lost its growl and its silkiness too, as though the selves it had pretended had flickered out along with its sight.

"I'm here," Harry replied.

It tried to raise one of its hands, but failed. "Are you . . . dying?" it wanted to know.

"Not today," Harry said softly.

"That's not right," the creature said. "We have to go together. *I . . . am . . . you . . .*"

"You haven't got much time," Harry told it. "Don't waste what you've got with that crap."

"But it's true," the thing went on. "*I am . . . I am you and . . . you are love . . .*"

Harry thought of Ted's painting; of the snake beneath his heel. Clinging to the banister, he raised his foot.

"Be quiet," he said.

The creature ignored him. "*You are love . . . ,*" it said again. "*And love is . . .*"

Harry laid his heel upon its head. "I'm warning you," he said.

"*Love is what . . .*"

He didn't warn it again, but ground his foot down into its suppurating face as hard as his weary body would allow. It was hard enough. He felt its muck cave in beneath his heel, layers of wafer-bone and ooze dividing under his weight. Small spasms ran out along the creature's limbs to its bloodied fingertips. Then, quite suddenly, it ceased, its schtick unfinished.

In the hallway below, Loretta was murmuring the prayer her brother had begun above.

"*Hail Mary, full of grace, the Lord is with thee, blessed art thou among women—*"

It sounded pretty to Harry's ears, after the shrieks and the threats.

"*And blessed be the fruit of thy womb, Jesus—*"

It would not turn death away, of course. It would not save the innocent from suffering. But prettiness was no insignificant quality, not in this troubled world.

While he listened he pulled his heel out of the Nomad's face. The creature's matter, stripped of the will that had shaped it, was already losing distinction and running off down the stairs.

Five steps to the bottom, Harry saw. Just like Hess.

The victory had taken its toll. In addition to his lacerated neck and punctured throat Harry had a broken collarbone, four cracked ribs, a fractured right arm, and mild concussion. As for Stevie, who had been the Nomad's hostage for three days, his traumas were more psychological than physical. They would take some time to heal, if they ever did, but the first step on that journey was made the day after the creature's death. The family moved out of the house on Wyckoff Street, leaving it to the mercy of gossip. This time there would be no attempt to redeem the house. Untenanted, it would fall into disrepair through the winter months, at what some thought an uncanny speed. Nobody would ever occupy it again.

One mystery remained unsolved. Why had the creature plotted to bring him back to Wyckoff Street in the first place? Had it begun to doubt its own mythology and arranged a rematch with an old enemy to confirm its sense of itself? Or had it simply been bored one September day and taken it into its head to play the old game of temptation and slaughter for the sheer hell of it?

The answer to those questions would, Harry assumed, join the long list of things he would never know.

As for Ted's magnum opus, after a few days of indecision Harry elected to hang it in the living room. Given that he was presently one-handed, this took him the better part of two hours to accomplish, but once it was up—

the canvas nailed directly to the wall—it looked better than it had in the gallery. Unbounded by a frame, Ted's vision seemed to bleed out across the wall.

Of the lovely Sabina, who had presumably been obeying the Nomad's instructions when she'd delivered the painting, there was no further sign. But Harry had two new dead bolts put on the front door anyway, just in case.

SEVEN

LOVE

Love is the engine of several of my novels. Certainly of *Galilee*, *Sacrament*, and *Imajica*; even, in a perverse way, of *The Damnation Game*. It also fires the narratives of some of my favorite stories: "Jacqueline Ess: Her Last Will and Testament," "The Life of Death," "The Forbidden." It isn't always a positive force. It sickens into obsession in several tales; it makes people crazy, even suicidal. But it is also, and often, the only source of illumination in an otherwise benighted landscape.

Some of the most interesting pieces here, I think, are those which deal with unconventional pairings. Jane Beck and the Devil, talking at cross-purposes with each other, testing each other's feelings, fearful of rejection. Marietta Barbarossa, chatting with her brother Maddox about their father's priapic excesses, while she combs Maddox's library to find a poem with which to seduce a woman she's met. Jacob Steep and Rosa McGee, the Macbeths of *Sacrament*, coupling in a fine old fury.

But this is also a chapter that contains its measure of unbridled romanticism. Witness Rachel and Galilee, on board his boat, the *Samarkand*, falling in love with each other; and more strange, but still I think, sweet, the blossoming romance between Gentle and the ambisexual Pie 'oh' pah from *Imajica*, which ends with one of the most bizarre nuptial scenes I've yet committed to paper.

As Edward Lear, the hero of *Subtle Bodies*, says, at his marriage to a gorilla: "Of course, it's all a complete mystery to me . . . What God can possibly mean, joining us in Roly-Poly Paddle Me"—he's a nonsense poet: he means to say "matrimony"—"But isn't that the sweetest thing; mystery?"

259

From *Galilee*

There was no trace of the day remaining when *The Samarkand* left the jetty; nor was there a moon. Only the stars, in brilliant array. Rachel sat on deck while the boat glided away from the island. The heavens got brighter the further they sailed, or such was her impression. She'd never seen so many stars, nor seen the Milky Way so clearly; a wide, irregular band of studded sky.

"What are you thinking about?" Galilee asked her.

"I used to work in a jewelry store in Boston," she said. "And we had this necklace that was called the Milky Way. It was supposed to look like *that*." She pointed to the sky. "I think it was eight hundred and fifty thousand dollars. You never saw so many diamonds."

"Did you want to steal it?" Galilee said.

"I'm not a thief."

"But did you?"

She grinned sheepishly. "I did try it on when nobody was looking. And it was *very* pretty. But the real thing's prettier."

"I would have stolen it for you," Galilee said. "No problem. All you needed to say was—*I want that*—and it would have been yours."

"Suppose you'd got caught?"

"I never get caught."

"So what have you stolen?"

"Oh my Lord . . . ," he said. "Where do I start?"

"Is that a joke?"

"No. I take theft very seriously."

"It *is* a joke."

"I stole this boat."

"You did not."

"How else was I going to get it?"

"Buy it?"

"You know how much vessels like this cost?" he said reasonably. She still wasn't sure whether he was joking or not. "I either stole the money to buy the boat, or stole the boat itself. It seemed simpler to steal the boat. That cut out the middle man." Rachel laughed. "Besides, the guy who had the boat didn't care about her. He left her tied up most of the time. I took her out, showed her the world."

"You make it sound like you married her."

"I'm not that crazy," Galilee replied. "I like sailing, but I like fucking better." An expression of surprise must have crossed her face, because he hurriedly said: "Sorry. That was crude. I mean—"

"No, if that's what you meant you should say it."

He looked sideways at her, his eyes gleaming by the light of the lamp. Despite his claim not to be crazy, that was exactly how he looked at that moment: sublimely, exquisitely crazy.

"You realize what you're inviting?" he said.

"No."

"Giving me permission to say what I mean? That's a dangerous invitation."

"I'll take the risk."

"All right," he said with a shrug. "But you remember . . . "

"I invited it."

He kept looking at her: that same gleaming gaze.

"I brought you on this boat because I want to make love to you."

"Make love is it now?"

"No, *fuck.* I want to fuck you."

"Is that your usual method?" she asked him. "Get the girl out to the sea where she hasn't got any choice?"

"You could swim," he said. He wasn't smiling.

"I suppose I could."

"But as they say on the islands: *Uliuli kai holo ka mano.*"

"Which means what?"

"*Where the sea is dark, sharks swim.*"

"Oh that's very reassuring," she said, glancing down at the waters slopping against the hull of *The Samarkand.* They were indeed dark.

"So that may not be the wisest option. You're safer here. With me. Getting what you want."

"I haven't said—"

"You don't need to tell me. You just need to be near me. I can smell what you want."

If Mitchell had ever said anything like that as a sexual overture it would have killed his chances stone dead. But she'd invited this man to say what was in his head. It was too late to play the Puritan. Besides, coming from him, right now, the idea was curiously beguiling. *He could smell her.* Her breath, her sweat; God knows what else. She was near him and he could smell her; she was wasting his time and hers protesting and denying . . .

So she said: "I thought we were going to fish?"

He grinned at her. "You want a lover who keeps his promises, huh?"

"Absolutely."

"I'll get a fish," he said, and standing up he stripped off his T-shirt, unbuckled his belt, and stepped out of his pants; all this so swiftly she didn't comprehend what he was intending to do until he threw himself overboard. It wasn't an elegant dive, it was a ragged plunge, and the splash soaked her. But that wasn't what got her up and shouting at him. It was what he'd said about sharks and dark water.

"Don't do this!" she yelled. She could barely see him. "Come out of there!"

"I'm not going to be long."

"*Galilee.* You said there were sharks."

"And the longer I talk to you the more likely they'll come and eat my ass, so can I please go fish?"

"I'm not hungry anymore."

"You will be," he said. She could hear the smile in his voice, then saw him throw his arms above his head and dive out of sight.

"You sonofabitch," she said to herself, her mind filling with unwelcome questions. How long could he hold his breath? When should she start to be concerned for his safety? And what if she saw a shark: what was she to do then? Lean over the side and beat on the hull of the boat to divert its attention? Not a very pleasant idea, with the water so concealing. The thing would be on her before she knew it; taking off her hand, her arm, dragging her overboard.

There was no doubt in her mind: when he got back on board she was going to tell him to take her straight back to the jetty; the sonofabitch, *the sonofabitch*, leaving her here staring down into the darkness with her heart in her mouth—

She heard a splashing sound on the other side of the boat.

"Is that you?" she called out. There was no reply. She crossed the deck, stumbling over something in the dark. "*Galilee, damn you! Answer me!*"

The splashing came again. She scanned the water, looking for some sign of life. Praying it was a man not a fin.

"Oh God, don't let anything happen to him," she found herself saying, "Please God, please, don't hurt him."

"You sound like a native."

She looked in the direction of the voice. There was something that looked like a black ball bobbing in the water. And around it, fish were leaping, their backs silvery in the starlight.

"Okay," she said, determined not to sound concerned for fear she encouraged his cavortings. "You got the fish? That's great."

"There was a shark god at Puhi, called Kaholia-Kane—"

"I don't want to hear it!" she yelled.

"But I heard you praying—"

"No—"

"*Please God*, you were saying."

"I wasn't praying to the fucking shark!" she yelled, her fury and fear getting the better of her.

"Well you should. They listen. At least this one did. The women used to call to him, whenever somebody was lost at sea—"

"Galilee?"

"Yes?"

"It's not funny anymore. I want you back on board."

"I'm coming," he said. "Let me just—" She saw his arm shoot out of the water and catch one of the leaping fish. "Gotcha! Okay. I'm on my way." He began to plow through the water toward the boat. She scanned the surface in every direction, superstitiously fearful that the fin would appear just as Galilee came in striking distance of the boat. But he made it to the side without incident.

"Here," he said, passing the fish up to her. It was large, and still very much intending to return to its native element, thrashing so violently that she had to use both hands to keep hold of it.

By the time she'd set the fish down where it couldn't dance its way back over the side, Galilee had hoisted himself up out of the water and was standing, dripping wet, just a step or two behind her.

"I'm sorry," he said, before she could start to tell him how angry she was. "I didn't realize I was upsetting you. I thought you knew it was all a joke."

"You mean there aren't any sharks?"

"Oh no. There are sharks out there. And the islanders do say *Uliuli kai holo ka mano*. But I don't think they're talking about real sharks when they say that."

"What are they talking about?"

"Men."

"Oh I see," Rachel said. "When it gets dark, the men come out—"

"Looking for something to eat." He nodded.

"But you could still have got attacked," she said, "if there *are* real sharks out there."

"They wouldn't have touched me."

"And why's that? Too tough?"

He reached out and took hold of her hand, escorting it back toward him, and laying her palm against the middle of his massive chest. His heart was thumping furiously. He felt as though there was just a single layer of skin between hand and heart; as though if she wanted to she could have reached into his chest and taken hold of it. And now it was she who could smell *him*. His skin like smoke and burned coffee; his breath salty.

"There's a lot of tales about sharks, men and gods," he said.

"More of your true stories?"

"Absolutely true," he replied. "I swear."

"Such as?"

"Well, they come in four varieties. Legends about men who are really shape-changing sharks; that's the first. These creatures walk the beaches at night, taking souls; sometimes taking children."

Rachel made a face. "Doesn't sound like a lot of fun."

"Then there are stories about men who decided to go into the sea and become sharks."

"Why would they do that?"

"For the same reason I got myself a boat and sailed away: they were fed up with pretending. They wanted to be in the water, always moving. Sharks die if they don't keep moving, did you know that?"

"No . . ."

"Well they do."

"So that's number two."

"Then there's the one you already know. Kaholia-Kane and his brothers and sisters."

"Shark gods."

"Protectors of sailors and ships. There's one in Pearl Harbor, watching over the dead. Her name's Ka'ahupahau. And the greatest of them is called Kuhaimuana. He's thirty fathoms long . . ."

Rachel shook her head. "Sorry. I don't like any of these stories," she said.

"That leaves us with just one category."

"Men who are gods?" Rachel said. Galilee nodded. "No, I'm not buying that either," she told him.

"Don't be so quick to judge," Galilee said. "Maybe you just haven't met the right man."

She laughed. "And maybe it's all just stories," she replied. "Look, I'm quite happy to talk about sharks and religion tomorrow. But tonight let's just be ordinary people."

"You make it sound easy," he said.

"It is," she told him. She moved closer to him, her hand still pressed against his chest. His heart seemed to beat more powerfully still. "I don't understand what's going on between us," she said, their faces so close she could feel the heat of his breath. "And to be honest I don't really care anymore." She kissed him. He was staring at her, unblinking, and continued to stare as he returned her kiss.

"What do you want to do?" he said, very quietly.

She slid her other hand down over the hard shallow dome of his stomach, to his sex. "Whatever you want," she said, unhooding him. He shuddered.

"There's so much I need to tell you," he said.

"Later."

"Things you have to know about me."

"Later."

"Don't say I didn't try," he said, staring at her with no little severity.

"I won't."

"Then let's go downstairs and be ordinary for a while."

She led the way. But before he followed her he walked back across the deck to where the fish lay, and going down on his haunches, picked it up. She watched his body by the lamplight; the muscles of his back and buttocks, the bunching of his thighs as he squatted down, the dark, laden sac hanging between his legs. He was glorious, she thought; perhaps the most glorious man she'd ever seen.

He stood up again—apparently unaware that she was watching him— and seemed to murmur a few words to the dead fish before tossing it overboard.

"What was that about?" she asked him.

"An offering," he explained. "To the shark god."

From *Galilee*

G lancing back over the last several chapters, I realize that I've left a thread of my story dangling (actually, I'm certain I've left a good many more than one, but the rest will be sewn into the design in due course). I'm speaking of my sister's adventures. You'll recall that the last time I saw her she was in flight from Cesaria, who was furious with her for some unspecified crime. If you'll allow me a moment here I'll tell you what all that was about. My fear is that if I don't tell you now, the urgency of what is about to happen in the lives of the Gearys will prevent me from breaking at a later point. In short, this may well be the last real breath I can take. After this, the deluge.

So; Marietta. She appeared in my chambers three or four days after my encounter with Cesaria, wearing a dreamy smile.

"What are you on?" I asked her.

"I've had a couple of mushrooms," she replied.

I was irritated with her, and I said so. She had too little sense of responsibility, I said: always in pursuit of some altered state or other.

"Oh, listen to you. So you didn't take the cocaine and Benedictine?"

I admitted that I had, but that I'd had a legitimate reason: it was helping me stay alert through the long hours of writing. It was quite a different situation, I said, to indulging day after day, the way she did.

"You're exaggerating," she said.

In my fine self-righteousness I made a list for her. There was nothing she wouldn't try. She smoked opium and chewed coca leaves; she ate pharmaceutical painkillers like candies and washed them down with tequila and rum; she liked heroin and cherries in brandy and hashish brownies.

"Lord, Maddox, you can be so tiresome sometimes. If I play music and the music's worth a damn, I'm altering my state. If I touch myself, and I give myself pleasure, I'm altering my state."

"They're not comparable."

"Why not?" I drew a breath before replying. "See? You don't have an answer."

"Wait, wait, wait—" I protested.

"Anyway," she went on, "I don't see that it's your business what I do with my head."

"It becomes my business if I have to deal with your mother."

Marietta rolled her eyes. "Oh Lord, I knew we'd get round to that eventually."

"I think I deserve an explanation."

"She found me going through some old clothes, that's all," Marietta replied.

"Old clothes?"

"Yes, . . . it was ridiculous. I mean, who cares after all this time?"

Despite her cavalier attitude she was plainly concealing something she felt guilty about. "Whose clothes were they?" I asked her.

"His," she said with a little shrug.

"Galilee's?"

"No . . . *his*." Another shrug. "Father's."

"You found clothes that belonged to our father—"

"Who art in Heaven . . . yes."

"And you were touching them?"

"Oh for God's sake, Maddox, don't you start. They were clothes. Old clothes. I don't think he'd even worn them. You know what a peacock he was."

"That's not what I remember."

"Well maybe he only did it for my benefit," she said with a sly smirk. "I had the pleasure of sitting in his dressing room with him many times—"

"I've heard enough, thank you," I told her. I didn't like the direction the conversation was taking; nor the gleam in Marietta's eye. But I was too late. The rebel in her was roused, and she wasn't about to be quelled.

"You started this," she said. "So you can damn well hear me out. It's all true; every word of it."

"I still—"

"*Listen to me*," she insisted. "You should know what he got up to when nobody else was looking. He was a priapic old bastard. Have you used that word yet by the way? *Priapic?*"

"No."

"Well now you can, quoting me."

"This isn't going in the book."

"Christ, you can be an old woman sometimes, Maddox. It's part of the story."

"It's got nothing to do with what I'm writing."

"The fact that the founding father of our family was so oversexed he used to parade around in front of his six-year-old daughter with a hard-on? Oh, I think that's got *everything* to do with what you're writing." She grinned at me, and I swear any God-fearing individual would have said the Devil was in that face. The beautiful exuberance of her features; the naked pleasure she took in shocking me.

"Of course I was fascinated. You know the origin of the word *fascinated*? It's Latin. *Fascinare* means to put under a spell. It was particularly attributed to serpents—"

"Why do you insist on doing this?"

"He had that power. No question. He waved his snake and I was . . . enchanted." She smiled at the memory. "I couldn't take my eyes off it. I would have followed it anywhere. Of course I wanted to touch it, but he told me no. When you're a little older, he said, then I'll show what it can do."

She stopped talking; stared out the window at the passing sky. "I was ashamed of my curiosity, but I couldn't help myself."

"And did he?" I said.

She kept staring. "No, he never did. He wanted to—I could see it in his eyes sometimes—but he didn't dare. You see I told Galilee all about it. That was my big mistake. I told him I'd seen Papa's snake and it was wonderful. I swore him to secrecy of course but I'm damn sure he told Cesaria, and she probably gave Papa hell. She was always jealous of me."

"That's ridiculous."

"She was. She still is. She threw a fit when she found me in the dressing room. After all these years she didn't want me near his belongings." She finally pulled her gaze from the clouds and looked back at me. "I love women more than life itself," she said. "I love everything about them. Their feel, their smell, the way they move when you stroke them . . . And I really can't bear men. Not in that way. They're so lumpen. But I'd have made an exception for Papa."

"You're grotesque, you know that?"

"Why?" I just made a pained face. "We don't have to live by the same rules as everybody else," she said. "Because we're not *like* everybody else."

"Maybe we'd all be a little happier if we were."

"Happy? I'm ecstatic. I'm in love. And I really mean it this time. I'm in love. With a farm girl no less."

"A farm girl."

"I know it doesn't sound very promising but she's extraordinary, Maddox. Her name's Alice Pennstrom, and I met her at a barn dance in Raleigh."

"They have lesbian barn dances these days?"

"It wasn't a dyke thing. It was men and women. You know me. I've always liked helping straight girls discover themselves. Anyway, Alice is wonderful. And I wanted to dress up in something special for our three-week anniversary."

"That's why you were looking through the clothes?"

"Yeah. I thought maybe I'd find something special. Something that would really get Alice going," Marietta said. "Which I did, by the way. So anyway thank you for taking the heat from Cesaria. I'll do the same for you one of these days."

"I'm going to hold you to that," I said.

"No problem," Marietta said. "If I make a promise, I'm good for it." She glanced at her watch. "Hey, I gotta go. I'm meeting Alice in half an hour. What I came in here for was a book of poems."

"Poems?"

"Something I can recite to her. Something sexy and romantic, to get her in the mood."

"You're welcome to look around," I said. "I presume, by the way, that all this means you think we've made peace?"

"Were we ever at war?" Marietta said, as though a little puzzled at my remark. "Where's the poetry section?"

"There isn't one. They're scattered all over."

"You need some organization in here."

"Thank you, but it suits me just the way it is."

"So point me to a poet."

"You want a lesbian poet? There's some Sappho up there, and a book of Marina Tsvetaeva."

"Is any of that going to make Alice moist?"

"Lord, you can be crude sometimes."

"Well is it or isn't it?"

"I don't know," I snapped. "Anyway, I thought you'd already seduced this woman."

"I have," Marietta said, scanning the shelves. "And it was amazing sex. So amazing that I've decided to propose to her."

"Is this a joke?"

"No. I want to marry my Alice. I want to set up house and adopt children. Dozens of children. But first I need a poem, to make her feel . . . you know what I mean . . . no, come to think of it, you probably don't . . . I want her to be so in love with me it hurts."

I pointed. "To your left—"

"What?"

"The little dark turquoise book. Try that." Marietta took it down.

"It's a book of poems by a nun."

"A nun?" Marietta went to put the book back.

"Wait," I said to her, "give it a chance. Here—" I went over to Marietta, and took the book—which she hadn't yet opened—from her hand. "Let me find something for you, then you can leave me alone." I flicked through the musty pages. It was years since I'd perused these lyrics, but I remembered one that had moved me.

"Who is she?" Marietta said.

"I told you: a nun. Her name was Mary-Elizabeth Bowen. She died in the forties, at the age of a hundred and one."

"A virgin?"

"Is that relevant?"

"Well it is if I'm trying to find something sexy."

"Try this," I said, and passed the book back to her.

"Which one?"

"I was a very narrow creature . . ."

Marietta read it aloud:

"*I was a very narrow creature at my heart,*
Until you came.
None got in and out of me with ease;
Yet when you spoke my name
I was unbounded, like the world—"

She looked up at me. "Oh I like this," she said. "Are you sure she was a nun?"

"Just read it . . ."

> "I was unbounded, like the world.
> I never felt such fear as then, being so limitless,
> When I'd known only walls and whisperings.
> I fled you foolishly;
> Looked in every quarter for a place to hide.
> Went into a bud, it blossomed.
> Went into a cloud, it rained.
> Went into a man, who died,
> And bore me out again,
> Into your arms."

"Oh my Lord," she said.

"You like that?"

"Who did she write it for?"

"Christ, I assume. But you needn't tell Alice that."

From *The History of the Devil*

THE DEVIL WANDERS TO CENTER STAGE, CARRYING A CROCODILE EGG.

THE DEVIL: I've seen men and women in the throes of bubonic plague, lying beside each other on diseased blankets under a dirty lamp, suddenly overcome with passion for each other's bodies, sores notwithstanding. I've seen them grind their last moments away, grunting out their lives, then collapsing onto each other, dead. When that's the way most of you touch Heaven, if at all, how can you believe that I, who didn't make you, am more malicious than the God who did?

ENTER JANE BECK. DURING THE OBLIQUE EXCHANGE THAT FOLLOWS, THE TWO FIGURES MOVE IN AND OUT OF MURKY PATCHES OF LIGHT. OFTEN THEY ARE BARELY VISIBLE.

THE DEVIL: You should go in: it's getting bitter. Did you enjoy the fireworks?

JANE BECK: Very pretty.

THE DEVIL: I noticed you today, looking at me.

JANE BECK: Returning your look.

THE DEVIL: Ah.

JANE BECK: You have a certain glamour. Evil does.

THE DEVIL: I don't feel evil.

JANE BECK: I don't feel like a woman, never having been a man.

THE DEVIL: I was an angel: I remember goodness. But here, everything explodes.

JANE BECK: Explodes?

THE DEVIL: Swells up, becomes overripe, bursts. Bang.

JANE BECK: I'm quite stable.

THE DEVIL: No, that bag of meat you occupy is getting tight and tender, getting too thin to hold your life.

JANE BECK: What do you suggest?

THE DEVIL: Burn it up. Heat is health.

JANE BECK: It just makes me sweat.

THE DEVIL: Passion's nothing to be ashamed of.

JANE BECK: (*Confounded*) Passion?

THE DEVIL: When we exchange looks.

JANE BECK: What are you telling me?

THE DEVIL: Have I been indelicate?

JANE BECK: (*She thinks she understands*) How could I be so slow? Growing tender—

THE DEVIL: It was unlooked for—

JANE BECK: I don't have any words.

THE DEVIL: Say nothing at all.

JANE BECK: I feel, I know it's absurd, honored—

THE DEVIL: Surely you've been in love.

JANE BECK: *I've* been in love?

THE DEVIL: Yes.

JANE BECK: Wait: you *are* telling me you're in love with me?

THE DEVIL: No, I thought you—

JANE BECK: Me?

THE DEVIL: Why would I?

JANE BECK: Well, why would I?

THE DEVIL: There seems to be a misunderstanding.

JANE BECK: Bang.

THE DEVIL: Will you smoke some hash?

JANE BECK: No thank you.

THE DEVIL: Already high enough?

THEY EXIT IN SEPARATE DIRECTIONS.

From *Imajica*

They were weighed down by what they'd seen, and the return journey took longer than the outward. By the time they made the safety of their niche in the rocks, to welcoming grunts from the surviving doeki, the sky was losing its golden sheen and dusk was on its way. They debated whether to proceed in darkness and decided against it. Though the air was calm at present, they knew from past experience that conditions on these heights were unpredictable. If they attempted to move by night, and a storm descended from the peaks, they'd be twice blinded and in danger of losing their way. With the High Pass so close, and the journey easier, they hoped, once they were through it, the risk was not worth taking.

Having used up the supply of wood they'd collected below the snow line, they were obliged to fuel the fire with the dead doeki's saddle and harness. It made for a smoky, pungent, and fitful blaze, but it was better than nothing. They cooked some of the fresh meat, Gentle observing as he chewed that he had less compunction about eating something he'd named than he thought, and brewed up a small serving of the herders' piss liquor. As they drank, Gentle returned the conversation to the women in the ice.

"Why would a God as powerful as Hapexamendios slaughter defenseless women?"

"Whoever said they were defenseless?" Pie replied. "I think they were probably very powerful. Their oracles must have sensed what was coming, so they had their armies ready—"

"Armies of women?"

"Certainly, warriors in their tens of thousands. There are places to the north of the Lenten Way where the earth used to move every fifty years or so and uncover one of their war graves."

"They were all slaughtered? The armies, the oracles—"

"Or driven so deep into hiding they forgot who they were after a few generations. Don't look so surprised. It happens."

"One God defeats how many Goddesses? Ten, twenty—"

"Innumerable."

"How?"

"He was One, and simple. They were many, and diverse."

"Singularity is strength—"

"At least in the short term. Who told you that?"

"I'm trying to remember. Somebody I didn't like much: Klein, maybe."

"Whoever said it, it's true. Hapexamendios came into the Dominions with a seductive idea: that wherever you went, whatever misfortune attended you, you needed only one name on your lips, one prayer, one altar, and you'd be in His care. And He brought a species to maintain that order once He'd established it. Yours."

"Those women back there looked human enough to me."

"So do I," Pie reminded him. "But I'm not."

"No . . . you're pretty diverse, aren't you?"

"I was once . . ."

"So that puts you on the side of the Goddesses, doesn't it?" Gentle whispered.

The mystif put its finger to his lips.

Gentle mouthed one word by way of response: "Heretic."

It was very dark now, and they both settled to studying the fire. It was steadily diminishing as the last of Chester's saddle was consumed.

"Maybe we should burn some fur," Gentle suggested.

"No," said Pie. "Let it dwindle. But keep looking."

"At what?"

"Anything."

"There's only you to look at."

"Then look at me."

He did so. The privations of the last many days had seemingly taken little toll on the mystif. It had no facial hair to disfigure the symmetry of its features, nor had their spartan diet pinched its cheeks or hollowed its eyes. Studying its face was like returning to a favorite painting in a museum. There it was: a thing of calm and beauty. But, unlike the painting, the face before him, which presently seemed so solid, had the capacity for infinite change. It was months since the night when he'd first seen that phenomenon. But now, as the fire burned itself out and the shadows deepened around them, he realized the same sweet miracle was imminent. The flicker of dying flame made the symmetry swim; the flesh before him seemed to lose its fixedness as he stared and stirred it.

"I want to watch," he murmured.

"Then watch."

"But the fire's going out . . ."

"We don't need light to see each other," the mystif whispered. "Hold on to the sight."

Gentle concentrated, studying the face before him. His eyes ached as he tried to hold on to it, but they were no competition for the swelling darkness.

"Stop looking," Pie said. in a voice that seemed to rise from the decay of the embers. "Stop looking, and *see*."

Gentle fought for the sense of this, but it was no more susceptible to analysis than the darkness in front of him. Two senses were failing him here—one physical, one linguistic—two ways to embrace the world slipping from him at the same moment. It was like a little death, and a panic seized him, like the fear he'd felt some midnights waking in his bed and body and knowing neither: his bones a cage, his blood a gruel, his dissolution the only certainty. At such times he'd turned on all the lights, for their comfort. But there were no lights here. Only bodies, growing colder as the fire died.

"Help me," he said. The mystif didn't speak. "Are you there, Pie? I'm afraid. Touch me, will you? *Pie?*"

The mystif didn't move. Gentle started to reach out in the darkness, remembering as he did so the sight of Taylor lying on a pillow from which they'd both known he'd never rise again, asking for Gentle to hold his hand. With that memory, the panic became sorrow: for Taylor, for Clem, for every soul sealed from its loved ones by senses born to failure, himself included. He wanted what the child wanted: knowledge of another presence, proved in touch. But he knew it was no real solution. He might find the mystif in the darkness, but he could no more hold on to its flesh forever than he could hold the senses he'd already lost. Nerves decayed, and fingers slipped from fingers at the last.

Knowing this little solace was as hopeless as any other, he withdrew his hand and instead said, "I love you."

Or did he simply think it? Perhaps it was thought, because it was the idea rather than the syllables that formed in front of him, the iridescence he remembered from Pie's transforming self shimmering in a darkness that was not, he vaguely understood, the darkness of the starless night but his mind's darkness; and this seeing not the business of eye and object but his exchange with a creature he loved, and who loved him back.

He let his feelings go to Pie, if there was indeed a going, which he doubted. Space, like time, belonged to the other tale—to the tragedy of separation they'd left behind. Stripped of his senses and their necessities, almost unborn again, he knew the mystif's comfort as it knew his, and that dissolution he'd woken in terror of so many times stood revealed as the beginning of bliss.

A gust of wind, blowing between the rocks, caught the embers at their side, and their glow became a momentary flame. It brightened the face in front of him, and the sight summoned him back from his unborn state. It was no great hardship to return. The place they'd found together was out of time and could not decay, and the face in front of him, for all its frailty (or perhaps because of it), was beautiful to look at. Pie smiled at him but said nothing.

"We should sleep," Gentle said. "We've got a long way to go tomorrow."

Another gust came along, and there were flecks of snow in it, stinging Gentle's face. He pulled the hood of his coat up over his head and got up to check on the welfare of the doeki. It had made a shallow bed for itself in the snow and was asleep. By the time he got back to the fire, which had found some combustible morsel and was devouring it brightly, the mystif was also asleep, its hood pulled up around its head. As he stared down at the visible crescent of Pie's face, a simple thought came: that though the wind was moaning at the rock, ready to bury them, and there was death in the valley behind and a city of atrocities ahead, he was happy. He lay down on the hard ground beside the mystif. His last thought as sleep came was of Taylor, lying on a pillow which was becoming a snowfield as he drew his final breaths, his face growing translucent and finally disappearing, so that when Gentle slipped from consciousness, it was not into darkness but into the whiteness of that deathbed, turned to untrodden snow.

The marriage of the Eurhetemec mystif and the fugitive John Furie Zacharias, called Gentle, took place that night in the depths of the asylum. Happily, their priest was passing through a period of lucidity and was willing to be addressed by his real name, Father Athanasius. He bore the evidence of his dementia, however: scars on his forehead, where the crowns of thorns he repeatedly fashioned and wore had dug deep, and scabs on his hands where he'd driven nails into his flesh. He was as fond of the frown as Scopique of the grin, though the look of a philosopher sat badly on a face better suited to a comedian: with its blob nose that perpetually ran, its teeth too widely spread, and eyebrows, like hairy caterpillars, that concertinaed when he furrowed his forehead. He was kept, along with twenty or so other prisoners judged exceptionally seditious, in the deepest part of the asylum, his windowless cell guarded more vigorously than those of the prisoners on higher floors. It had thus taken some fancy maneuvering on Scopique's part to get access to him, and the bribed guard, an Oethac, was only willing to turn a hooded eye for a few minutes. The ceremony was therefore short, conducted in an ad hoc mixture of Latin and English, with a few phrases pronounced in the language of Athanasius's Second Dominion order, the Dearthers, the music of which more than compensated for its unintelligibility. The oaths themselves were necessarily spare, given the constraints of time and the redundancy of most of the conventional vocabulary.

"This isn't done in the sight of Hapexamendios," Athanasius said, "nor in the sight of any God, or the agent of any God. We pray that the presence of our Lady may however touch this union with Her infinite compassion, and that you go together into the great union at some higher time. Until then, I can only be as a glass held up to your sacrament, which is performed in your sight for your sake."

The full significance of these words didn't strike Gentle until later, when, with the oaths made and the ceremony done, he lay down in his cell beside his partner.

"I always said I'd never marry," he whispered to the mystif.

"Regretting it already?"

"Not at all. But it's strange to be married and not have a wife."

"You can call me wife. You can call me whatever you want. Reinvent me. That's what I'm for."

"I didn't marry you to use you, Pie."

"That's part of it, though. We must be functions of each other. Mirrors, maybe." It touched Gentle's face. "I'll use *you*, believe me."

"For what?"

"For everything. Comfort, argument, pleasure."

"I do want to learn from you."

"About what?"

"How to fly out of my head again, the way I did this afternoon. How to travel by mind."

"By mote," Pie said, echoing the way Gentle had felt as he'd driven his thoughts through N'ashap's skull. "Meaning: a particle of thought, as seen in sunlight."

"It can only be done in sunlight?"

"No. It's just easier that way. Almost everything's easier in sunlight."

"Except this," Gentle said, kissing the mystif. "I've always preferred the night for this . . ."

He had come to their marriage bed determined that he would make love with the mystif as it truly was, allowing no fantasy to intrude between his senses and the vision he'd glimpsed in N'ashap's office. That oath made him as nervous as a virgin groom, demanding as it did a double unveiling. Just as he unbuttoned and discarded the clothes that concealed the mystif's essential sex, so he had to tear from his eyes the comfort of the illusions that lay between his sight and its object. What would he feel then? It was easy to be aroused by a creature so totally reconfigured by desire that it was indistinguishable from the thing desired. But what of the configurer itself, seen naked by naked eyes?

In the shadows its body was almost feminine, its planes serene, its surface smooth, but there was an austerity in its sinew he couldn't pretend was womanly; nor were its buttocks lush, or its chest ripe. It was not his wife, and though it was happy to be imagined that way, and his mind teetered over and over on the edge of giving in to such invention, he resisted, demanding his eyes hold to their focus and his fingers to the facts. He began to wish it were lighter in the cell, so as not to give ease to ambiguity. When he put his hand into the shadow between its legs and felt the heat and motion there, he said, "I want to see," and Pie dutifully stood up in the light from the window so that Gentle could have a plainer view. His heart was pumping furiously, but none of the blood was reaching his groin. It was filling his head, making his face burn. He was glad he sat in shadow, where his discomfort was less visible, though he knew that shadow concealed only the outward show, and the mystif was perfectly aware of the fear he felt. He took a deep breath and got up from the bed, crossing to within touching distance of this enigma.

"Why are you doing this to yourself?" Pie asked softly. "Why not let the dreams come?"

"Because I don't want to dream you," he said. "I came on this journey to understand. How can I understand anything if all I look at is illusions?"

"Maybe that's all there is."

"That isn't true," he said simply.

"Tomorrow, then," Pie said, temptingly. "Look plainly tomorrow. Just enjoy yourself tonight. I'm not the reason we're in the Imajica. I'm not the puzzle you came to solve."

"On the contrary," Gentle said, a smile creeping into his voice. "I think maybe you *are* the reason. And the puzzle. I think if we stayed here, locked up together, we could heal the Imajica from what's between us." The smile appeared on his face now. "I never realized that till now. That's why I want to see you clearly. Pie, so there're no lies between us." He put his hand against the mystif's sex. "You could fuck or be fucked with this, right?"

"Yes."

"And you could give birth?"

"I haven't. But it's been known."

"And fertilize?"

"Yes."

"That's wonderful. And is there something else you can do?"

"Like what?"

"It isn't all doer or done to, is it? I know it isn't. There's something else."

"Yes, there is."

"A third way."

"Yes."

"Do it with me, then."

"I can't. You're male, Gentle. You're a fixed sex. It's a physical fact." The mystif put its hand on Gentle's prick, still soft in his trousers. "I can't take this away. You wouldn't want me to." It frowned. "Would you?"

"I don't know. Maybe."

"You don't mean that."

"If it meant finding a way, maybe I do. I've used my dick every way I know how. Maybe it's redundant."

Now it was Pie's turn to smile, but such a fragile smile, as though the unease Gentle had felt now burdened the mystif instead. It narrowed its shining eyes.

"What are you thinking?" Gentle said.

"How you make me a little afraid."

"Of what?"

"Of the pain ahead. Of losing you."

"You're not going to lose me," Gentle said, putting his hand around the back of Pie's neck and stroking the nape with his thumb. "I told you, we could heal the Imajica from here. We're strong, Pie."

The anxiety didn't go from the mystif's face, so Gentle coaxed its face toward his and kissed it, first discreetly, then with an ardor it seemed reluctant to match. Only moments before, sitting on the bed, he'd been the tentative one. Now it was the other way around. He put his hand down to its groin, hoping to distract it from its sadness with caresses. The flesh came to meet his fingers, warm and fluted, trickling into the shallow cup of his palm a moisture his skin drank like liquor. He pressed deeper, feeling the elaboration grow at his touch. There was no hesitation here; no shame or sorrow in this flesh, to keep it from displaying its need, and need had never failed to arouse him. Seeing it on a woman's face was a sure aphrodisiac, and it was no less so now.

He reached up from this play to his belt, unbuckling it with one hand. But before he could take hold of his prick, which was becoming painfully hard, the mystif did so, guiding him inside it with an urgency its face still failed to betray. The bath of its sex soothed his ache, immersing him balls and all. He let out a long sigh of pleasure, his nerve endings—starved of this sensation for months—rioting. The mystif had closed its eyes, its mouth open. He put his tongue hard between its lips, and it responded with a passion he had never seen it manifest before. Its hands wrapped around his shoulders, and in possession of them both it fell back against the wall, so hard the breath went from it into Gentle's throat. He drew it down into his lungs, inciting a hunger for more, which the mystif understood without need of words, inhaling from the heated air between them and filling Gentle's chest as though he were a just-drowned man being pumped back to life. He answered its gift with thrusts, its fluids running freely down the inside of his thighs. It gave him another breath, and another. He drank them all, eating the pleasure off its face in the moments between, the breath received as his prick was given. In this exchange they were both entered and enterer: a hint, perhaps, of the third way Pie had spoken of, the coupling between unfixed forces that could not occur until his manhood had been taken from him. Now, as he worked his prick against the warmth of the mystif's sex, the thought of relinquishing it in pursuit of another sensation seemed ludicrous. There could be nothing better than this; only different.

He closed his eyes, no longer afraid that his imagination would put a memory, or some invented perfection, in Pie's place, only that if he looked at the mystif's bliss too much longer he'd lose all control. What his mind's eye pictured, however, was more potent still: the image of them locked together as they were, inside each other, breath and prick swelling inside each other's skins until they could swell no further. He wanted to warn the mystif that he could hold on no longer, but it seemed to have that news already. It grasped his hair, pulling him off its face, the sting of it just another spur now, and the sobs too, coming out of them both. He let his eyes open, wanting to see its face as he came, and in the time it took for his lashes to unknit, the beauty in front of him became a mirror. It was *his* face he was seeing, *his* body he was holding. The illusion didn't cool him. Quite the reverse. Before the mirror softened into flesh, its glass becoming the sweat on Pie's sweet face, he passed the point of no return, and it was with that image in his eye—his face mingled with the mystif's—that his body unleashed its little torrent. It was as ever exquisite and racking, a short delirium followed by a sense of loss he'd never made peace with.

The mystif began to laugh almost before he was finished, and when Gentle drew his first clear breath it was to ask, "What's so funny?"

"The silence," Pie said, suppressing the music so that Gentle could share the joke.

He'd lain here in this cell hour after hour, unable to make a moan, but he'd never heard a silence such as this. The whole asylum was listening, from the depths where Father Athanasius wove his piercing crowns to N'ashap's office, its carpet indelibly marked with the blood his nose had shed. There was not a waking soul who'd not heard their coupling.

"Such a silence," the mystif said.

As it spoke, the hush was broken by the sound of someone yelling in his cell, a rage of loss and loneliness that went on unchecked for the rest of the night, as if to cleanse the gray stone of the joy that had momentarily tainted it.

From *Sacrament*

He was standing in the crowded street in St. Petersburg; and if the cold had not already snatched his breath, the sight before him would have done so: Eropkin's palace, its walls raised forty feet high, and glittering in the light of the torches and bonfires that were blazing on every side. They were warm, those fires, but the palace did not shed a drop of water, for their heat could not compete with the frigid air.

He looked around at the throng who pressed at the barricades, daring the hussars who kept them in check with boots and threats. By Christ, how they stank tonight! Fetid clothes on fetid bodies.

"Rabble . . . ," he murmured.

To Steep's left, a beet-faced brat was shrieking on her father's shoulders, snot frozen at her nostrils. To his right a drunkard with a grease-clogged beard reeled about, with a woman in an even more incapacitated state clinging to his arm.

"I hate these people," said a voice close to his ear. "Let's come back later when it's quiet."

He looked around at the speaker, and there was Rosa, her exquisite face, pink from the cold, framed by her fur-lined hood. Oh but she was beautiful tonight, with the lantern flames flickering in her eyes.

"Please, Jacob," she said, tugging on his sleeve in that little-girl-lost fashion which she knew worked so well. "We could make a baby tonight, Jacob. Truly, I believe we could." She was pressing close to him now, and he caught the scent of her breath; a fragrance no Parisian perfumerie could ever hope to capture. Even here, in the heart of an iron winter, she had the smell of spring about her. "Put your hand on my belly, Jacob," she said, taking his hand in hers and placing it there. "Isn't that warm?" It was. "Don't you think we might make a life tonight?"

"Maybe," he said.

"So let's be away from these animals," she said. "Please, Jacob. *Please.*"

Oh, she could be persuasive when she was in this coquettish mood. And truth to tell he liked to play along.

"Animals, you say?"

"No better," she replied, with a growl of contempt in her voice.

"Would you have them dead?" he asked her.

"Every one of them."

"Every one?"

"But you and me. And from our love a new race of perfect people would come, to have the world the way God intended it."

Hearing this, he couldn't refrain from kissing her, though the streets of St. Petersburg were not like those of Paris or London, and any display of affection, especially one as passionate as theirs, would be bound to draw censure. He didn't care. She was his other, his complement, his completion. Without her, he was nothing. Taking her glorious face in his hands, he laid his lips on hers, her breath a fragrant phantom rising between their faces. The words that breath carried still astonished him, though he had heard them innumerable times.

"I love you," she told him. "And I will love you as long as I have life."

He kissed her again, harder, knowing there were envious eyes upon them, but caring not at all. Let the crowd stare and cluck and shake their heads. They would never feel in all their dreary lives what he and Rosa felt now: the supreme conjunction of soul and soul.

And then, in the midst of the kiss, the din of the crowd receded and completely disappeared. He opened his eyes. They were no longer standing on the street-side of the barricades, but were at the very threshold of the palace. The thoroughfare behind them was deserted. Half the night had passed in the time it took to draw breath. It was now long after midnight.

"Nobody's going to spy on us?" Rosa was asking him.

"I've paid all the guards to go and drink themselves stupid," he told her. "We've got four hours before the morning crowd starts to come and gawp. We can do what we like in here."

She slipped the hood back off her head, and combed her hair out with her fingers so that it lay abundantly about her shoulders. "Is there a bedroom?" she said.

He smiled. "Oh yes, there's a bedroom. And a big four-poster bed, all carved out of ice."

"Take me to it," she said, catching hold of his hand.

Into the palace they ventured, through the receiving room, which was handsomely appointed with mantelpiece and furniture; through the vast ballroom with its glittering stalactite chandelier; through the dressing room, where there was arranged a wardrobe of coats and hats and shoes, all perfectly carved out of ice.

"It's uncanny," Jacob said, glancing back toward the front door, "the way the light refracts." Though they had ventured deep into the heart of the structure, the glow from the torches set all around the palace was still bright, flickering through the translucent walls. To other eyes it would surely have aroused only wonder; but Jacob was discomfited. Something about the place awoke in him a memory he couldn't name.

"I've been somewhere like this before," he said to Rosa.

"Another ice palace?" she said.

"No. A place that's as bright inside as it is out."

She ruminated on this for a moment. "Yes. I've seen such a place," she said. She wandered from his side and ran her palm over the crystalline wall. "But it wasn't made of ice," she said. "I'm sure not . . ."

"What then?"

She frowned. "I don't know," she said. "Sometimes, when I try to remember things, I lose my way."

"So do I."

"Why is that?"

"Consorting with Rukenau maybe."

She spat on the floor at the sound of his name. "Don't talk about him," she said.

"But there's a connection, sweet," Steep said. "I swear there is."

"I won't hear you talk about him, Jacob," she said, and hurried away, her skirts hissing across the icy floor.

He followed her, telling her he'd say no more about Rukenau if it troubled her so much. She was angry now—her rages were always sudden, and sometimes brutal—but he was determined to placate her, as much for his own equilibrium as for hers. Once he had her on the bed, he'd kiss her rage away, easily; open her warm body to the cold air and lick her flesh till she sobbed. Her flesh could stand to be naked here. She complained of the cold, of course, and demanded he buy her furs to keep her from freezing, but it was all a sham. She'd heard other women demand such things from their husbands, and was playing the same petulant game. And just as it seemed to be her wifely duty to pout and stamp and flee him in some invented tantrum, so it was his to pursue and coerce, and end up taking her body—forcibly, if necessary—until she confessed that his only errors were errors of love, and she adored him for them. It was an absurd rigmarole, and they both knew it. But if they were to be husband and wife, then they were to play out the rituals as though they came naturally. And in truth, some portion of them did. This part, for instance; where he caught up to her and held her tight; told her not to be a ninny, or he'd have to fuck her all the harder. She squirmed in his arms, but made no attempt to escape him. Only told him to do his worst, his very worst.

"I'm not afraid of you, Jacob Steep," she said. "Nor your fucks."

"Well, that's good," he said, lifting her up and carrying her through to the bedroom. The bed itself was in every way a perfect replica of the real thing, even to the dent in the pillow, as though some frigid sleeper had a moment past risen from the spot. He gently laid her there, her hair spread upon the snowy linen, and began to unbutton her. She had forgiven his talk of Rukenau already, it seemed. Forgotten it, perhaps, in her hunger to have Steep's flesh in her, a desire as sudden as her rages, and sometimes just as brutal.

He had bared her breasts, and put his mouth to her nipple, sucking it into the heat of his mouth. She shuddered with pleasure, and pressed his head to the deed, reaching down to pull at his shirt. He was as hard as the bed on which they lay. Eschewing all tenderness, he hoisted up her skirt, found the place beneath where his prick ached to go, and slid his fingers there, whispering in her ear that she was the finest slut in all of Christendom, and deserved to be treated accordingly. She caught his face in her hands and told him to do his worst, at which invitation he removed his fingers and pressed his prick to service so suddenly her cry of complaint echoed through the glacial halls.

He took his time, as she demanded he did, laying his full weight upon her as he climbed to his discharge. And as he climbed, and her shouts of pleasure came back to him off the ceiling and walls, the feeling that had caught him in the passageway came again: that he had been in a place which this palace, for all its glories, could not approach in splendor.

"So bright—" he said, seeing its luminescence in his head.

"What's bright?" Rosa gasped.

"The deeper we go . . . ," he said, "the brighter it gets . . ."

"Look at me!" she demanded. "*Jacob! Look at me!*"

He thrust on mechanically, his arousal no longer in service of her pleasure, or even his own, but fueling the vision. The higher he climbed, the brighter it became; as though the spilling of his seed would bring him into the heart of this glory. The woman was writhing under his assault, but he paid her no mind; just pressed on, and on, as the brightness grew, and with it his hope that he would know this place by and by; name it, comprehend it.

The moment was almost upon him; the blaze of recognition certain. A few more seconds, a few more thrusts into her void, and he'd have his revelation.

Then she was pushing him away from her, pushing his body with all her strength. He held on, determined not to be denied his vision, but she was not going to indulge him. For all her squealing and sobbing, she only ever played at subjugation—the way she played at the lost girl, or the needy wife—and now, wanting him away from her, she had only to use her strength. Almost casually, she threw him out and off her, across the gelid bed. Instead of spilling his seed in the midst of revelation, he discharged meekly, in half-finished spurts, too distracted by her violence to catch the vision that had been upon him.

"You were thinking of Rukenau again!" she yelled, sliding off the bed and tucking her breasts from view. "I warned you, didn't I? I warned you I'd have no part of it!"

Jacob sealed his eyes, hoping to catch a glimpse of what had just escaped him. He'd been so close, so very close. But it had gone, like a firework dying in the heavens.

From *Sacrament*

The following day he went to visit Patrick, in his apartment up at the top of Castro. Though the pair had lived together on Sanchez Street for almost four of their six years together, Patrick had never given up the apartment, nor had Will ever pressured him to do so. The house, in its spare, functional way, was an expression of Will's undecorative nature. The apartment, by contrast, was so much a part of who Patrick was—warm, exuberant, enveloping—that to have given it up would have been tantamount to losing a limb. There at the top of the hill he had spent most of the money he earned in the city below (where he had been until recently an investment banker) creating a retreat from the city, where he and a few chosen lotus-eaters could watch the fog come and go. He was a big, broad handsome man, his Greek heritage as evident in his features as the Irish: heavy-lidded and laden eyes, a thug of a nose, a generous mouth beneath a fat black mustache. In a suit, he looked like somebody's bodyguard; in drag at Mardi Gras, like a fundamentalist's nightmare; in leather, sublime.

Today, when Rafael (who had apparently recanted and come home) escorted Will into the living room he found Patrick sitting at the window dressed in a baggy T-shirt and drawstring linen pants. He looked well. His hair was cropped to a graying crewcut, and he wasn't as beefy as he'd been, but his embrace was as powerful as ever.

"Lord, look at you," he said, standing back from Will to appreciate him. "You're finally starting to look like your photograph." (This was a backhanded compliment; and an ongoing joke, begun when Will had chosen an unflattering jacket photograph for his second book on the grounds that it made him look more authoritative.) "Come and sit down," he said, gesturing to the chair that had been put opposite his in the window. "Where the hell's Rafael gone? You want some tea?"

"No, I'm fine. Is he looking after you okay?"

"We're doing better," Patrick said, easing back into his own chair. Only now, in the tentativeness of this maneuver, did Will get a sense of his delicacy. "We argue, you know—"

"So I heard."

"From Adrianna?"

"Yeah, she said—"

"I just tell her the juicy bits," Patrick said. "She doesn't get to hear about what a sweetheart he is most of the time. Anyway, I have so many angels watching over me it's embarrassing."

Will looked back down the length of the room. "You've got some new things," he said.

"I inherited some heirlooms from dead queens," he said. "Though most of it doesn't mean much if you don't know the story that goes with it, which is kinda sad, because when I'm gone, nobody will know."

"Rafael isn't interested?"

Patrick shook his head. "It's old men's talk as far as he's concerned. That little table's got the strangest origins. It was made by Chris Powell. You remember Chris?"

"The Fix-it man with the beautiful butt."

"Yeah. He died last year, and when they went in his garage they found he'd been doing all this carpentry. Making chairs and tables and rocking-horses."

"Commissions?"

"Apparently not. He was just making them in his spare time, for his own satisfaction."

"And keeping them?"

"Yeah. Designing them, carving them, painting them, and leaving them all locked up in his garage."

"Did he have a lover?"

"A blue-collar honey like that, are ya kidding? He'd had hundreds." Before Will could protest. Patrick said: "I know what you're asking and no, he didn't have anyone permanent. It was his sister found all this beautiful work when she was cleaning out his house. Anyway, she asked me around to see if I wanted something to remember him by, and of course I said yes.

I really wanted a rocking-horse, but I didn't have the balls to ask. She was a rather prim little soul, from somewhere in Idaho. Obviously the last thing she wanted to be doing was going through her cute fag brother's belongings. God knows what she found under the bed. Can you imagine?" He gazed out toward the cityscape. "I've heard it happen so often now. Parents coming to see where their baby ran away to live, because now he's dying, and of course they find Queer City, the only surviving phallocracy." He mused a moment. "What must it be like for those people? I mean we do stuff in broad daylight here they haven't even invented in Idaho."

"You think so?"

"Well, you think back to Manchester, or, what was the place in Yorkshire?"

"Burnt Yarley?"

"Wonderful. Yeah. Burnt Yarley. You were the only queer in Burnt Yarley, right? And you left as soon as you could. We all leave. We leave so we can feel at home."

"Do you feel at home?"

"Right from the very first day. I walked along Folsom and I thought: this is where I want to be. Then I went into the Slot and got picked up by Jack Fisher."

"You did not," Will said. "You met Jack Fisher with me, at that art show in Berkeley."

"Shit! I cannot lie to you, can I?"

"No, you can lie," Will said magnanimously, "I just won't believe you. Which reminds me, Adrianna thought your father—"

"Was dead. Yeah. Yeah. She gave me hell. Thanks very much." He pursed his lips. "I'm beginning to have second thoughts about this party," he groused. "If you're going to go around telling the truth to everyone I'm going to have a shit time; and I know the party's for you, but if I'm not having fun then *nobody's* going to have fun—"

"Oh we can't have that. How about I promise not to contradict anything you've said to anybody as long as it's not a personal defamation?"

"Will. I could never defame you," Patrick said, with heavily feigned sincerity. "I might tell everyone you're a no-good egotistic sonofabitch who walked out on me. But defame you, the love of my life? Perish the thought." Performance over, he leaned forward and laid his hands on Will's knees. "We went through this phase, remember? Well at least I did—when we thought we were going to be the first queers in history never to get old? No, that's not true. Maybe we'd get old, but very, very slowly so that by the time we were sixty we could still pass for thirty-two in a good light? It's all in the bones; that's what Jack says. But black guys look good any age so he doesn't count."

"Do you have a point?" Will smiled.

"Yes. Us. Sitting here looking like two guys the world has not used kindly."

"I never—"

"I know what you're going to say: you never think about it. Well you wait till you go out cruising. You're going to find a lot of little muscle boys wanting to call you Daddy. I speak from experience. I think it must be a gay rite of passage. Straights feel old when they send their kids off to college. Queens feel old when one of those college kids comes up to them in a bar and tells them he wants to be spanked. Speaking of which—"

"Spanking or college boys?"

"Straights."

"Oh."

"Adrianna's going to bring Glenn on Saturday, and you mustn't laugh but he's had his ears pinned back surgically, and it makes him look weird. I never noticed before, but he's got a kind of pointy head. I think the protruding ears were a *distraction*. So, no laughing."

"I won't laugh," Will assured him, perfectly certain Patrick was only telling him for mischief's sake. "Is there anything you want me to do for Saturday?"

"Just turn up and be yourself."

"That I can do," he said. "Okay. I'm on my way." He leaned over and kissed Patrick lightly on the lips.

"You can see yourself out?"

"Blindfolded."

"Will you tell Rafael it's pill time? He'll be in his bedroom on the telephone."

Patrick had it right. Rafael was sprawled on his bed with the telephone glued to his ear, talking in Spanish. Seeing Will at the door he sat upright, blushing.

"Sorry—" Will said, "the door was open."

"Yeah, yeah, it was just a friend, you know?" Rafael said.

"Patrick said it's pill time."

"I know," Rafael replied. "I'm coming. I just got to finish with my friend."

"I'll leave you two alone," Will said. Before he'd even closed the door Will heard Rafael picking up the thread of his sex-talk while it was still warm. Will went back to the living room to tell Patrick the message had been delivered, but in the minute or so since his departure Patrick had fallen asleep, and was snoring softly in his chair. The wash of late afternoon light softened his features, but there was no erasing the toll of years and grief and sickness. If being called Daddy was a rite of passage, Will thought, so's this: looking in on a man I fell in love with in another life, and knowing that there was love there still, as plentiful as ever, but changed by time and circumstance into something more elusive.

He would gladly have watched Patrick a while longer, calmed by the familiarity of his face, but he didn't want to be hanging around when Rafael emerged, so he left the sleeper to his slumbers and headed off out of the apartment, down the stairs and into the street.

Why, he wondered, when there'd probably been more literary ink spilled on the subject of love than any other—including freedom, death, and God Almighty—could he not begin to grasp the complexities of what he felt for Patrick? There were many scars there, on both sides; cruel things said and done in anger and frustration. There were petty betrayals and desertions, again, on both sides. There were shared memories of wild sex and domestic high jinks and times of loving lucidity, when a glance or a touch or a certain song had been nirvana. And then there was now; feelings extricated from the past, but being woven into patterns neither of them had anticipated. Oh, they'd known they'd grow old, whatever Patrick remembered. They'd talked, half jokingly, about withering into happy alcoholics in Key West, or moving to Tuscany and owning an olive grove. What they'd never talked about because it had not seemed likely, was that they would be in here, in the middle of their lives, and talking like old men: remembering their dead peers and watching the clock until it was time for pills.

From *Subtle Bodies*

THE LIGHT IS FADING, TURNING A DUSKY PINK, AS IF BEFORE A MAJOR THUNDERSTORM.

MR. FOSS: Significance does seem to lie in insignificant places, doesn't it? In an arrangement of clouds, in the ink stain on my thumb.

ROB: In dreams.

MR. FOSS: Of course in dreams. There most of all.

TREADAWAY, WHO HAS TAKEN OVER AS PHOTOGRAPHER, COMES TO FETCH MR. FOSS AND ROB.

MR. TREADWAY: Please take your seats, or we'll never get to the Wedding Breakfast.

MR. FOSS: I hope everyone's in the mood for nuts and bananas.

MR. FOSS GOES TO STAND IN THE CENTER OF THE PICTURE, BESIDE HIS GORILLA. SOME OF THE GUESTS ARE SITTING, OTHERS STANDING. MRS. CORCORAN IS THERE, AS IS ULYSSES. SEAN, OF COURSE NOW ROB JOINS THE GROUP TOO.

MR. FOSS: Well, here we are. Finally.

MRS. CORCORAN: You have to say a few words.

MR. FOSS: Must I?

MRS. CORCORAN: It's traditional.

MR. FOSS: Well, I'm a great believer in tradition.

THE REST OF THE GUESTS APPLAUD. MR. FOSS QUIETENS THEM DOWN.

MR. FOSS: Of course, it's all a complete mystery to me. I freely admit it. Who proposed to who. What God can possibly mean, joining us in Roly-Poly Paddle Me. But isn't that the sweetest thing, mystery? To have that is, I think, to have everything. Everything.

TECHNICIAN: Poem!

MR. FOSS: No . . .

ALL: Yes! (*They chant*) Po! Em! Po! Em!

MR. FOSS: I have nothing prepared.

ROB: Make it up.

MR. FOSS: Then you'll have to help me.

ROB: I'll do my best.

MR. FOSS: So . . . *There once was a fellow called Lear* . . .

ROB: *Whose life was . . . exceedingly queer.*

MR. FOSS: *One day, for a jape. He married an ape . . .*

ROB: *And . . .*

> EVERYBODY WAITS, BREATHLESS, FOR THE NEXT LINE.

ROB: *And swung from a tree for a year.*

MR. FOSS: Yes! Yes! (*Applauds*)

> HE KISSES THE BRIDE.

MR. FOSS: Yes. Oh yes. Oh yes . . . *(Quietly, to Rob)* It's all nonsense of course. But it brings a tear to my eye nevertheless.

ROB: Ah, love!

MR. FOSS: Ah. *Love.*

> A FLASH. THE IMAGE FREEZES, AS HANDS ARE ABOUT TO CLAP AND TONGUES ABOUT TO MAKE WORDS. NOT THE DEAD SMILES OF PREVIOUS PHOTOGRAPHS. THIS IS AN INSTANT CAUGHT; FULL OF GENUINE PLEASURE.
>
> THUNDER RUMBLES.
>
> THE LIGHTS GO DOWN ON THE FROZEN MOMENT, THROUGH ROSE PINK TO DARKNESS.
>
> THE PLAY ENDS.

EIGHT

TERRORS

In search of a good scare, most people look to the cinema rather than to books, and for a very simple reason: films are more effective than ever at the business of making audiences jump. What they very often lack, of course, is an underbelly. They're all surface. And in a genre which gains much of its power from the meanings which lurk behind the scenes, that can be a fatal absence.

That said, it's undeniably fun simply to scare the fuck out of folks now and again. I've directed a few ghost-train rides of my own, and had a thoroughly good time doing it. In fact, two plays that are excerpted in this chapter—*Frankenstein in Love* and *The History of the Devil*—had more than a touch of the horror movie spirit in them when they were produced, and without having cut my teeth on their Grand Guignol excesses, I doubt I would have been confident enough to pursue the writing and directing of *Hellraiser*. A passage from the novella upon which that film is based also appears here, recording the first entrance of the demonic Cenobite who would eventually be dubbed "Pinhead." In fact, the image of a human head spiked with nails is a common symbol, the Jungians say, of *rage*. There is a tradition of African fetish heads that use that image. I'm sure I'd seen such heads in books, and they were the inspiration for Pinhead.

Also in this chapter, "In the Hills, the Cities," a short story which proved controversial before it was even published. My agent counseled against its publication; my editor at the time did the same. It was too surreal, and too blatantly homosexual. Fifteen years later, it still elicits responses from readers in practically every batch of mail. One of its inspirations is Goya's *Colossus*, which depicts a giant striding away from a valley packed with tiny panicking figures. Another is the eighteenth century's taste for rendering faces made from human figures (Archimboldo painted them, brilliantly, constructed from fish and vegetables). The third and final source is democracy itself: the notion that in exercising our democratic rights we make, as it were, a single will of our many wills.

Or so the idealists would have us believe. Since this story was written, the Soviet Union has dissolved, and what was once Yugoslavia has splintered into a number of warring factions. The atrocities from that region continue to make headlines. I claim no prophetic skills; but I think the story's portrait of collective insanity appears horribly accurate.

From *The Hellbound Heart*

S o intent was Frank upon solving the puzzle of Lemarchand's box that be
didn't hear the great bell begin to ring. The device had been constructed by a master craftsman, and the riddle was this—that though he'd
been told the box contained wonders, there simply seemed to be no way into
it, no clue on any of its six black lacquered faces as to the whereabouts of
the pressure points that would disengage one piece of this three-dimensional
jigsaw from another.

Frank had seen similar puzzles—mostly in Hong Kong, products of the
Chinese taste for making metaphysics of hard wood—but to the acuity
and technical genius of the Chinese the Frenchman had brought a perverse logic that was entirely his own. If there was a system to the puzzle,
Frank had failed to find it. Only after several hours of trial and error did a
chance juxtaposition of thumbs, middle, and last fingers bear fruit: an
almost imperceptible click, and then—victory!—a segment of the box slid
out from beside its neighbors.

There were two revelations.

The first, that the interior surfaces were brilliantly polished. Frank's
reflection—distorted, fragmented—skated across the lacquer. The second,
that Lemarchand, who had been in his time a maker of singing birds, had
constructed the box so that opening it tripped a musical mechanism,
which began to tinkle a short rondo of sublime banality.

Encouraged by his success, Frank proceeded to work on the box fever-
ishly, quickly finding fresh alignments of fluted slot and oiled peg which in
their turn revealed further intricacies. And with each solution—each new
half twist or pull—a further melodic element was brought into play—the

tune counterpointed and developed until the initial caprice was all but lost in ornamentation.

At some point in his labors, the bell had begun to ring—a steady somber tolling. He had not heard, at least not consciously. But when the puzzle was almost finished—the mirrored innards of the box unknotted—he became aware that his stomach churned so violently at the sound of the bell it might have been ringing half a lifetime.

He looked up from his work. For a few moments he supposed the noise to be coming from somewhere in the street outside—but he rapidly dismissed that notion. It had been almost midnight before he'd begun to work at the bird maker's box; several hours had gone by—hours he would not have remembered passing but for the evidence of his watch—since then. There was no church in the city—however desperate for adherents—that would ring a summoning bell at such an hour.

No. The sound was coming from somewhere much more distant, through the very door (as yet invisible) that Lemarchand's miraculous box had been constructed to open. Everything that Kircher, who had sold him the box, had promised of it was true! He was on the threshold of a new world, a province infinitely far from the room in which he sat.

Infinitely far; yet now, suddenly near.

The thought had made his breath quick. He had anticipated this moment so keenly, planned with every wit he possessed this rending of the veil. In moments they would be here—the ones Kircher had called the Cenobites, theologians of the Order of the Gash. Summoned from their experiments in the higher reaches of pleasure, to bring their ageless heads into a world of rain and failure.

He had worked ceaselessly in the preceding week to prepare the room for them. The bare boards had been meticulously scrubbed and strewn with petals. Upon the west wall he had set up a kind of altar to them, decorated with the kind of placatory offerings Kircher had assured him would nurture their good offices: bones, bonbons, needles. A jug of his urine—the product of seven days' collection—stood on the left of the altar, should they require some spontaneous gesture of self-defilement. On the right, a plate of doves' heads, which Kircher had also advised him to have on hand.

He had left no part of the invocation ritual unobserved. No cardinal, eager for the fisherman's shoes, could have been more diligent.

But now, as the sound of the bell became louder, drowning out the music box, he was afraid.

Too late, he murmured to himself, hoping to quell his rising fear. Lemarchand's device was undone; the final trick had been turned. There was no time left for prevarication or regret. Besides, hadn't he risked both life and sanity to make this unveiling possible? The doorway was even now opening to pleasures no more than a handful of humans had ever known existed, much less *tasted*—pleasures which would redefine the parameters of sensation, which would release him from the dull round of desire, seduction, and disappointment that had dogged him from late adolescence. He would be transformed by that knowledge, wouldn't he? No man could experience the profundity of such feeling and remain unchanged.

The bare bulb in the middle of the room dimmed and brightened. brightened and dimmed again. It had taken on the rhythm of the bell, burning its hottest on each chime. In the troughs between the chimes the darkness in the room became utter; it was as if the world he had occupied for twenty-nine years had ceased to exist. Then the bell would sound again, and the bulb burn so strongly it might never have faltered, and for a few precious seconds he was standing in a familiar place, with a door that led out and down and into the street, and a window through which—had he but the will (or strength) to tear the blinds back—he might glimpse a rumor of morning.

With each peal the bulb's light was becoming more revelatory. By it, he saw the east wall flayed; saw the brick momentarily lose solidity and blow away; saw, in that same instant, the place beyond the room from which the bell's din was issuing. A world of birds was it? Vast black birds caught in perpetual tempest? That was all the sense he could make of the province from which—even now—the hierophants were coming: that it was in confusion, and full of brittle, broken things that rose and fell and filled the dark air with their fright.

And then the wall was solid again, and the bell fell silent. The bulb flickered out. This time it went without a hope of rekindling.

He stood in the darkness, and said nothing. Even if he could remember the words of welcome he'd prepared, his tongue would not have spoken them. It was playing dead in his mouth.

And then, light.

It came from *them*: from the quartet of Cenobites who now, with the wall sealed behind them, occupied the room. A fitful phosphorescence, like the glow of deep-sea fishes: blue, cold, charmless. It struck Frank that he had never once wondered what they would look like. His imagination, though fertile when it came to trickery and theft, was impoverished in other regards. The skill to picture these eminences was beyond him, so he had not even tried.

Why then was he so distressed to set eyes upon them? Was it the scars that covered every inch of their bodies, the flesh cosmetically punctured and sliced and infibulated, then dusted down with ash? Was it the smell of vanilla they brought with them, the sweetness of which did little to disguise the stench beneath? Or was it that as the light grew, and he scanned them more closely, he saw nothing of joy, or even humanity, in their maimed faces: only desperation, and an appetite that made his bowels ache to be voided.

"What city is this?" one of the four inquired. Frank had difficulty guessing the speaker's gender with any certainty. Its clothes, some of which were sewn *to* and *through* its skin, hid its private parts, and there was nothing in the dregs of its voice, or in its willfully disfigured features that offered the least clue. When it spoke, the hooks that transfixed the flaps of its eyes and were wed, by an intricate system of chains passed through flesh and bone alike, to similar hooks through the lower lip, were teased by the motion, exposing the glistening meat beneath.

"I asked you a question," it said. Frank made no reply. The name of this city was the last thing on his mind.

"Do you understand?" the figure beside the first speaker demanded. Its voice, unlike that of its companion, was light and breathy—the voice of an excited girl. Every inch of its head had been tattooed with an intricate grid, and at every intersection of horizontal and vertical axes a jeweled pin driven through to the bone. Its tongue was similarly decorated. "Do you even know who we are?" it asked.

"Yes," Frank said at last. "I know."

Of course he knew; he and Kircher had spent long nights talking of hints gleaned from the diaries of Bolingbroke and Gilles de Rais. All that mankind knew of the Order of the Gash, he knew.

And yet . . . he had expected something different. Expected some sign of the numberless splendors they had access to. He had thought they would come with women, at least; oiled women, milked women; women shaved and muscled for the act of love: their lips perfumed, their thighs trembling to spread, their buttocks weighty, the way he liked them. He had expected sighs, and languid bodies spread on the floor underfoot like a living carpet; had expected virgin whores whose every crevice was his for the asking and whose skills would press him—*upward, upward*—to undreamed-of ecstasies. The world would be forgotten in their arms. He would be exalted by his lust, instead of despised for it.

But no. No women, no sighs. Only these sexless *things*, with their corrugated flesh.

Now the third spoke. Its features were so heavily scarified—the wounds nurtured until they ballooned—that its eyes were invisible and its words corrupted by the disfigurement of its mouth.

"What do you want?" it asked him.

He perused this questioner more confidently than he had the other two. His fear was draining away with every second that passed. Memories of the terrifying place beyond the wall were already receding. He was left with these decrepit decadents, with their stench, their queer deformity, their self-evident frailty. The only thing he had to fear was nausea.

"Kircher told me there would be five of you," Frank said.

"The Engineer will arrive should the moment merit," came the reply. "Now again, we ask you: *What do you want?*"

Why should he not answer them straight? "Pleasure," he replied. "Kircher said you know about pleasure."

"Oh we do," said the first of them. "Everything you ever wanted."

"Yes?"

"Of course. Of course." It stared at him with its all-too-naked eyes. "What have you dreamed?" it said.

The question, put so baldly, confounded him. How could he hope to articulate the nature of the phantasms his libido had created? He was still searching for words when one of them said:

"This world . . . it disappoints you?"

"Pretty much," he replied.

"You're not the first to tire of its trivialities," came the response. "There have been others."

"Not many," the gridded face put in.

"True. A handful at best. But a few have dared to use Lemarchand's Configuration. Men like yourself, hungry for new possibilities, who've heard that we have skills unknown in your region."

"I'd expected—" Frank began.

"We *know* what you expected," the Cenobite replied. "We understand to its breadth and depth the nature of your frenzy. It is utterly familiar to us."

Frank grunted. "So," he said, "you know what I've dreamed about. You can supply the pleasure."

The thing's face broke open, its lips curling back: a baboon's smile. "Not as you understand it," came the reply.

Frank made to interrupt, but the creature raised a silencing hand.

"There are conditions of the nerve endings," it said, "the like of which your imagination, however fevered, could not hope to evoke."

"Yes?"

"Oh yes. Oh most certainly. Your most treasured depravity is child's play beside the experiences we offer."

"Will you partake of them?" said the second Cenobite.

Frank looked at the scars and the hooks. Again, his tongue was deficient.

"*Will you?*"

Outside, somewhere near, the world would soon be waking. He had watched it wake from the window of this very room, day after day, stirring itself to another round of fruitless pursuits, and he'd known, *known*, that there was nothing left out there to excite him. No heat, only sweat. No passion, only sudden lust, and just as sudden indifference. He had turned his back on such dissatisfaction. If in doing so he had to interpret the signs these creatures brought him, then that was the price of ambition. He was ready to pay it.

"Show me," he said.

"There's no going back. You do understand that?"

"*Show me.*"

They needed no further invitation to raise the curtain. He heard the door creak as it was opened, and turned to see that the world beyond the threshold had disappeared, to be replaced by the same panic-filled darkness from which the members of the Order had stepped. He looked back toward the Cenobites, seeking some explanation for this. But they'd disappeared. Their passing had not gone unrecorded however. They'd taken the flowers with them, leaving only bare boards, and on the wall the offerings he had assembled were blackening, as if in the heat of some fierce but invisible flame. He smelled the bitterness of their consumption; it pricked his nostrils so acutely he was certain they would bleed.

But the smell of burning was only the beginning. No sooner had he registered it than half a dozen other scents filled his head. Perfumes he had scarcely noticed until now were suddenly overpoweringly strong. The lingering scent of filched blossoms; the smell of the paint on the ceiling and the sap in the wood beneath his feet—all filled his head. He could even smell the darkness outside the door, and in it, the ordure of a hundred thousand birds.

He put his hand to his mouth and nose, to stop the onslaught from overcoming him, but the stench of perspiration on his fingers made him giddy. He might have been driven to nausea had there not been fresh sensations flooding his system from each nerve ending and taste bud.

It seemed he could suddenly feel the collision of the dust motes with his skin. Every drawn breath chafed his lips; every blink, his eyes. Bile burned in the back of his throat, and a morsel of yesterday's beef that had lodged between his teeth sent spasms through his system as it exuded a droplet of gravy upon his tongue.

His ears were no less sensitive. His head was filled with a thousand dins, some of which he himself was father to. The air that broke against his eardrums was a hurricane; the flatulence in his bowels was thunder. But there were other sounds—innumerable sounds—which assailed him from somewhere beyond himself. Voices raised in anger, whispered professions of love, roars and rattlings, snatches of song, tears.

Was it the world he was hearing—morning breaking in a thousand homes? He had no chance to listen closely; the cacophony drove any power of analysis from his head.

But there was worse. The eyes! Oh god in heaven, he had never guessed that they could be such torment; he, who'd thought there was nothing on earth left to startle him. Now he reeled! Everywhere, *sight!*

The plain plaster of the ceiling was an awesome geography of brush-strokes. The weave of his plain shirt an unbearable elaboration of threads. In the corner he saw a mite move on a dead dove's head, and wink its eyes at him, seeing that he saw. Too much! *Too much!*

Appalled, he shut his eyes. But there was more *inside* than out; memories whose violence shook him to the verge of senselessness. He sucked his mother's milk, and choked; felt his sibling's arms around him (a fight, was it, or a brotherly embrace? Either way, it suffocated). And more; so much more. A short lifetime of sensations, all writ in a perfect hand upon his cortex, and breaking him with their insistence that they be remembered.

He felt close to exploding. Surely the world outside his head—the room, and the birds beyond the door—they, for all their shrieking excesses, could not be as overwhelming as his memories. Better that, he thought, and tried to open his eyes. But they wouldn't unglue. Tears or pus or needle and thread had sealed them up.

He thought of the faces of the Cenobites: the hooks, the chains. Had they worked some similar surgery upon him, locking him up behind his eyes with the parade of his history?

In fear for his sanity, he began to address them, though he was no longer certain that they were even within earshot.

"Why?" he asked. "Why are you doing this to me?"

The echo of his words roared in his ears, but he scarcely attended to it. More sense impressions were swimming up from the past to torment him. Childhood still lingered on his tongue (milk and frustration) but there were adult feelings joining it now. He was grown! He was mustached and mighty, hands heavy, gut large.

Youthful pleasures had possessed the appeal of newness, but as the years had crept on, and mild sensation lost its potency, stronger and stronger experiences had been called for. And here they came again, more pungent for being laid in the darkness at the back of his head.

He felt untold tastes upon his tongue: bitter, sweet, sour, salty, smelled spice and shit and his mother's hair; saw cities and skies; saw speed, saw deeps; broke bread with men now dead and was scalded by the heat of their spittle on his cheek.

And of course there were women.

Always, amid the flurry and confusion, memories of women appeared, assaulting him with their scents, their textures, their tastes.

The proximity of this harem aroused him, despite circumstances. He opened his trousers and caressed his cock, more eager to have the seed spilled and so be freed of these creatures than for the pleasure of it.

He was dimly aware, as he worked his inches, that he must make a pitiful sight: a blind man in an empty room, aroused for a dream's sake. But the wracking, joyless orgasm failed to even slow the relentless display. His knees buckled, and his body collapsed to the boards where his spunk had fallen. There was a spasm of pain as he hit the floor, but the response was washed away before another wave of memories.

He rolled onto his back, and screamed; screamed and begged for an end to it, but the sensations only rose higher still, whipped to fresh heights with every prayer for cessation he offered up.

The pleas became a single sound, words and sense eclipsed by panic. It seemed there was no end to this, but madness. No hope but to be lost to hope.

As he formulated this last, despairing thought, the torment stopped.

All at once; all of it. Gone. Sight, sound, touch, taste, smell. He was abruptly bereft of them all. There were seconds then when he doubted his very existence. Two heartbeats, three, four.

On the fifth beat, he opened his eyes. The room was empty, the doves and the piss pot gone. The door was closed.

Gingerly, he sat up. His limbs were tingling; his head, wrist and bladder ached.

And then—a movement at the other end of the room drew his attention.

Where, two moments before, there had been an empty space, there was now a figure. It was the fourth Cenobite, the one that had never spoken, nor shown its face. Not *it*, he now saw: but *she*. The hood it had worn had been discarded, as had the robes. The woman beneath was gray yet gleaming, her lips bloody, her legs parted so that the elaborate scarification of her pubis was displayed. She sat on a pile of rotting human heads, and smiled in welcome.

The collision of sensuality and death appalled him. Could he have any doubt that she had personally dispatched these victims? Their rot was beneath her nails, and their tongues—twenty or more—lay out in ranks on her oiled thighs, as if awaiting entrance. Nor did he doubt that the brains now seeping from their ears and nostrils had been driven to insanity before a blow or a kiss had stopped their hearts.

Kircher had lied to him—either that or he'd been horribly deceived. There was no pleasure in the air; or at least not as humankind understood it.

He had made a mistake opening Lemarchand's box. A very terrible mistake.

"Oh, so you've finished dreaming," said the Cenobite, perusing him as he lay panting on the bare boards. "Good."

She stood up. The tongues fell to the floor, like a rain of slugs.

"Now we can begin," she said.

From *The Great and Secret Show*

Tommy-Ray had been in the driver's seat of a car since his sixteenth birthday. Wheels had signaled freedom from Momma, the Pastor, the Grove, and all they stood for. Now he was heading back to the very place a few years ago he couldn't have escaped from fast enough, his foot on the accelerator every mile of the way. He wanted to walk the Grove again with the news his body carried, wanted to go back to his father, who'd taught him so much. Until the Jaff, the best life had offered was an offshore wind and a west swell at Topanga; him on a crest knowing the girls were all watching him from the beach. But he'd always known those high times couldn't last forever. New heroes came along, summer after summer. He'd been one of them, supplanting surfers no more than a couple of years older, who weren't quite as lithe. Boy-men like himself who'd been the cream of the swell the season before, suddenly old news. He wasn't stupid. He knew it was only a matter of time before he joined their ranks.

But now, he had a purpose in his belly and brain he'd never had before. He'd discovered ways to think and behave the airheads at Topanga never even guessed existed. Much of that he had to thank the Jaff for. But even his father, for all his wild advice, hadn't prepared him for what had happened at the Mission. He was a *myth* now. Death at the wheel of a Chevy, racing for home. He knew music that would have people dancing till they dropped. And when they dropped, and went to meat, he knew all about that too. He'd seen the spectacle at work on his own flesh. It gave him a boner remembering.

But the night's fun had only just started. Less than a hundred miles north of the Mission his route took him through a small village on the fringes of which lay a cemetery. The moon was still high. Its brightness gleamed on the tombs, washing the color from the flowers that were laid here and there. He stopped the car, to get a better look. After all, this was his territory from now on. It was home.

If he'd needed any further proof that what had happened at the Mission was not the invention of a crazy man, he got it when he pushed open the gate and wandered in. There was no wind to stir the grass, which grew to knee height in several places where tombs had been left untended. But there was movement there nevertheless. He advanced a few more paces, and saw human figures rising into view from a dozen places. They were dead. Had their appearance not testified to the fact the luminescence of their bodies—which were as bright as the bone shard he'd found beside the car—would have marked them as part of his clan.

They knew who had come to visit them. Their eyes, or in the case of the ancients among them, their *sockets*, were set on him as they moved to do him homage. None even glanced at the ground as they came, though it was uneven. They knew this turf too well, familiar with the spots where badly built tombs had toppled, or a casket been pushed back up to the surface by some motion in the earth. Their progress was, however, slow. He was in no hurry. He sat himself down on the grave which contained, the stone recorded, seven children and their mother, and watched the ghosts come his way. The closer they came the more of their condition he saw. It wasn't pretty. A wind blew out of them, twisting them out of true. Their faces were either too wide or too long, their eyes bulging, their mouths blown open, cheeks flopping. Their ugliness put Tommy-Ray in mind of a film he'd seen of pilots enduring G-force, the difference being that these were not volunteers. They suffered against their will.

He was not disturbed in the least by their distortions; nor by the holes in their wretched bodies, or their slashed and severed limbs. It was nothing he hadn't seen in comic books by the age of six; or on a ghost-train ride. The horrors were everywhere, if you wanted to look. On bubble-gum cards, and Saturday morning cartoons, or in the stores on T-shirts and album covers. He smiled to think of that. There were outposts of his empire everywhere. No place was untouched by the Death-Boy's finger.

The speediest of these, his first devotees, was a man who looked to have died young, and recently. He wore a pair of jeans two sizes too big for him, and a muscle shirt adorned with a hand presenting the fuck sign to the world. He also wore a hat, which he took off when he came within a few yards of Tommy-Ray. The head beneath had been practically shaved, exposing several long cuts to view. The fatal wounds, presumably. There was no blood out of them now; just a whine of the wind that blew through the man's gut.

A little distance from Tommy-Ray he stopped.

"Do you speak?" the Death-Boy asked him.

The man opened his mouth, which was already wide, a little wider, and proceeded to make a reply as best he could, by working it up from his throat. Watching him, Tommy-Ray remembered a performer he'd seen on a late show, who'd swallowed and then regurgitated live goldfish. Though it was several years ago the sight had struck a chord in Tommy-Ray's imagination. The spectacle of a man able to reverse his system by practice, vomiting up what he'd held in his throat—not in the stomach surely; no fish, however scaly, could survive in acid—had been worth the queasiness he'd felt while watching. Now the Fuck-You-Man was giving a similar performance, only with words instead of fishes. They came at last, but dry as his innards.

"Yes," he said, "I speak."

"Do you know who I am?" Tommy-Ray asked.

The man made a moan.

"Yes or no?"

"No."

"I'm the Death-Boy, and you're the Fuck-You-Man. How 'bout that? Don't we make a pair?"

"You're here for us," the dead man said.

"What do you mean?"

"We're not buried. Not blessed."

"Don't look at me for help," Tommy-Ray said. "I'm burying nobody. I came to look because this is my kind of place now. I'm going to be King of the Dead."

"Yes?"

"Depend on it."

Another of the lost souls—a wide-hipped woman—had approached, and puked up some words of her own.

"You . . ." she said, "are *shining*."

"Yeah?" said Tommy-Ray. "Doesn't surprise me. You're bright too. Real bright."

"We belong together," the woman said.

"All of us," said a third cadaver.

"Now you're getting the picture."

"Save us," said the woman.

"I already told the Fuck-You-Man," Tommy-Ray said, "I'm burying nobody."

"We'll follow you," the woman said.

"Follow?" Tommy-Ray replied, a shudder of excitement running down his spine at the idea of returning to the Grove with such a congregation in tow. Maybe there were other places he could visit along the way, and swell the numbers as he went.

"I like the idea," he said. "But how?"

"You lead. We'll follow," came the response.

Tommy-Ray stood up. "Why not?" he said, and started back toward the car. Even as he went he found himself thinking: this is going to be the end of me . . .

And thinking, didn't care.

Once at the wheel he looked back toward the cemetery. A wind had blown up from somewhere, and in it he saw the company that he'd chosen to keep seem to *dissolve*, their bodies coming undone as though they were made of sand, and being blown apart. Specks of their dust blew in his face. He squinted against it, unwilling to look away from the spectacle. Though their bodies were disappearing he could still hear their howls. They were like the wind, or *were* the wind, making their presence known. With their dissolution complete he turned from the blast, and put his foot on the accelerator. The car leaped forward, kicking up another spurt of dust to join the pursuing dervishes.

He had been right about there being more places along the route to gather ghosts. *I'll always be right from now on,* he thought. *Death's never wrong; never, ever wrong.* He found another cemetery within an hour's drive of the first, with a dust dervish of half-dissolved souls running back and forth along its front wall like a dog on a leash, impatiently awaiting the arrival of its master. Word of his coming had gone before him apparently. They were waiting, these souls, ready to join the throng. He didn't even have to slow the car. At his approach the dust storm came to meet him, momentarily smothering the vehicle before rising to join the souls behind. Tommy-Ray just drove straight on.

Toward dawn his unhappy band found yet more adherents. There had been a collision at a crossroads, earlier in the night. There was broken glass scattered across the road; blood; and one of the two cars—now barely recognizable as such—overturned at the side of the road. He slowed to look, not expecting there to be any haunters here, but even as he did so he heard the now familiar whining wind and saw two wretched forms, a man and a woman, appear from the darkness. They'd not yet got the trick of their condition. The wind that blew through them, or out of them, threatened with every faltering step they took to throw them over onto their broken heads. But newly dead as they were, they sensed their Lord in Tommy-Ray, and came obediently. He smiled to see them; their fresh wounds (glass in their faces, in their eyes) excited him.

There was no exchange of words. As they drew closer they seemed to take a signal from their comrades in death behind Tommy-Ray's car, allowing their bodies to erode completely, and join the wind.

His legion swelled, Tommy-Ray drove on.

There were other such meetings along the way; they seemed to multiply the further north he drove, as though word of his approach went through the earth, from buried thing to buried thing, graveyard whispers, so that there were dusty phantoms waiting all along the way. By no means all of them had come to join the party. Some had apparently come simply to stare at the passing parade. There was fear on their faces when they looked at Tommy-Ray. He'd become the Terror in the ghost-train now, and they were the chilled punters. There were hierarchies even among the dead it seemed, and he was too elevated a company for many of them to keep; his ambition too great, his appetite too depraved. They preferred quiet rot to such adventure.

It was early morning by the time he reached the nameless hick town in which he'd lost his wallet, but the daylight did not reveal the host in the dust storm that followed him. To any who chose to look—and few did, in such a blinding wind—a cloud of dirty air came in the car's wake; that was the sum of it.

He had other business here than the collecting of lost souls—though he didn't doubt for a moment that in such a wretched place life was quickly and violently over, and many bodies never laid to sanctified rest. No, his business here was revenge upon the pocket-picker. Or if not upon him, at least upon the den where it had happened. He found the place easily. The front door wasn't locked, as he'd expected at such an early hour. Nor, once he stepped inside, did he find the bar empty. Last night's drinkers were still scattered around the place, in various stages of collapse. One lay facedown on the floor, vomit spattered around him. Another two were sprawled at tables. Behind the bar itself was a man Tommy-Ray vaguely remembered as the doorman who'd taken his money for the backroom show. A lump of a man, with a face that looked to have been bruised so many times it'd never lose the stain.

"Looking for someone?" he demanded to know.

Tommy-Ray ignored him, crossing to the door that let on the arena where he'd seen the woman and the dog performing. It was open. The space beyond was empty, the players gone home to their beds and their kennels. The barman was a yard from him when he turned back into the bar.

"I asked a fucking question," he said.

Tommy-Ray was a little taken aback by the man's blindness. Did he not recognize the fact that he was speaking to a transformed creature? Had his perception been so dulled by years of drinking and dog shows he couldn't see the Death-Boy when he came visiting? More fool he.

"Get out of my way," Tommy-Ray said.

Instead, the man took hold of the front of Tommy-Ray's shirt. "You been here before," he said.

"Yeah."

"Left something behind, did you?"

He pulled Tommy-Ray closer, till they were practically nose to nose. He had a sick man's breath.

"I'd let go if I were you," Tommy-Ray warned.

The man looked amused at this. "You're looking to get your fucking balls ripped off," he said. "Or do you want to join the show?" His eyes widened at this notion. "Is that what you came looking for? An audition?"

"I told you . . . ," Tommy-Ray began.

"I don't give a fuck what you told me. I'm doing the talking now. Hear me?" He put one vast hand over Tommy-Ray's mouth. "So . . . do you want to show me something or not?"

The image of what he'd seen in the room behind him came back into Tommy-Ray's head as he stared up at his assaulter: the woman, glassy-eyed; the dog, glassy-eyed. He'd seen death here, in life. He opened his mouth against the man's palm, and pressed his tongue against the stale skin.

The man grinned.

"Yeah?" he said.

He dropped his hand from Tommy-Ray's face. "You got something to show?" he said again.

"*Here* . . . ," Tommy-Ray murmured.

"What?"

"*Come in . . . come in . . .*"

"What are you talking about?"

"Not talking to you. *Here. Come . . . in . . . here.*" His gaze went from the man's face to the door.

"Don't give me shit, kid," the man responded. "You're on your own."

"*Come in!*" Tommy-Ray yelled.

"Shut the fuck up!"

"*Come in!*"

His din maddened the man. He hit Tommy-Ray across the face, so hard the blow knocked the boy out of his grip to the floor. Tommy-Ray didn't get up. He simply stared at the door, and made his invitation one more time.

"*Please come in,*" he said, more quietly.

Was it because he *asked* this time instead of demanded, that the legion obeyed? Or simply that they'd been mustering themselves, and were only now ready to come to his aid? Either way, they began to rattle the closed doors. The barman grunted and turned. Even to his bleary eyes it must have been perfectly apparent that it was no natural wind that was pushing to come in. It pressed too rhythmically; it beat its fist too heavily. And its howls, oh its howls were nothing like the howls of any storm he'd heard before. He turned back to Tommy-Ray.

"What the fuck's out there?" he said.

Tommy-Ray just lay where he'd been thrown and smiled up at the man, that legendary smile, that forgive-me-my-trespasses smile, that would never be the same again now that he was the Death-Boy.

Die, that smile now said, *die while I watch you. Die slowly. Die quickly. I don't care. It's all the same to the Death-Boy.*

As the smile spread the doors opened, shards of the lock, and splinters of wood, thrown across the bar before the invading wind. Out in the sunlight the spirits in this storm had not been visible; but they made themselves so now, congealing their dust in front of the witnesses' eyes. One of the men slumped on the table roused himself in time to see three figures forming from the head down in front of him, their torsos trailing like innards of dust. He backed off against the wall, where they threw themselves upon him. Tommy-Ray heard his screech but didn't see what kind of death they gave him. His eyes were on the spirits that were coming at the bartender.

Their faces were all appetite, he saw; as though traveling together in that caravan had given them time to simplify themselves. They were no longer as distinct from each other as they'd been; perhaps their dust had mingled in the storm, and each had become a little like the other. Unparticularized, they were more terrible than they'd been at the cemetery wall. He shuddered at the sight, the remnants of the man he'd been in fear of them, the Death-Boy in bliss. These were soldiers in his army: eyes vast, mouths vaster, dust and want in one howling legion.

The bartender started to pray out loud, but he wasn't putting his faith in prayer alone. He reached down to his side and picked Tommy-Ray up one-handed, hauling him close. Then, with his hostage taken, he opened the door to the sex arena and backed through it. Tommy-Ray heard him repeating something as they went, the hook of the prayer perhaps? *Santo Dios! Santo Dios!* But neither words nor hostage slowed the advance of the wind and its dusty freight. They came after him, throwing the door wide.

Tommy-Ray saw their mouths grow huger still, and then the blur of faces was upon them both. He lost sight of what happened next. The dust filled his eyes before he had an opportunity to close them. But he felt the bartender's grip slide from him, and the next moment a rush of wet heat. The howling in the wind instantly rose in volume to a keening that he tried to stop his ears against, but it came anyway, boring into the bone of his head like a hundred drills.

When he opened his eyes he was red. Chest, arms, legs, hands: all red.

The bartender, the source of the color, had been dragged onto the stage where the night before Tommy had seen the woman and the dog. His head was in one corner, upended; his arms, hands locked in supplication, in another; the rest of him lay center stage, the neck still pumping.

Tommy-Ray tried not to be sickened (he was the Death-Boy, after all) but this was too much. And yet, he told himself, what had he expected when he'd invited them over the threshold? This was not a circus he had in tow. It was not sane; it was not civilized.

Shaking, sickened and chastened, he got to his feet and hauled himself back out into the bar. His legion's labors here were as cataclysmic as those he'd turned his back upon. All three of the bar's occupants had been brutally slaughtered. Giving the scene only the most casual perusal, he crossed through the destruction to the door.

Events inside the bar had inevitably attracted an audience outside, even at such an early hour. But the velocity of the wind—in which his ghost army was once more dissolved—kept all but the most adventurous, youths and children, from approaching the scene, and even they were cowed by the suspicion that the air howling around them was not entirely empty.

They watched the blond, blood-spattered boy emerge from the bar and cross to his car, but made no attempt to apprehend him. Their scrutiny made Tommy-Ray take note of his gait. Instead of slouching he walked more upright. When they remembered the Death-Boy, he thought, let them remember someone *terrible*.

From *Frankenstein in Love*

ENTER VERONIQUE, CARRYING A HEAVY BOX.

CARDINAL: Who are you?

VERONIQUE: The doctor's not here.

CARDINAL: Why not?

VERONIQUE: He's wounded.

CARDINAL: Badly?

VERONIQUE: He was shot trying to make his escape. He's dying.

CARDINAL: Animals! How did you get in here? The children at the doors are armed. They had instructions not to let anyone in but Frankenstein.

VERONIQUE: The boys have gone. There's nobody here.

CARDINAL: Oh yes, there's a whore— (*Can no longer see her*) somewhere. What is it smells?

VERONIQUE: Me. I came through the sewers. It's safer.

CARDINAL: Is there rioting?

VERONIQUE: Not now. They have entertainments, to keep the people happy. Fire-eating—

CARDINAL: Ha! When the Perez Junta took power they blindfolded the Democrats, gave them axes, and set them on each other. Now that's what I call entertainment. You know they've shot priests, these gentlemen fire-eaters? Godless bastards. In cold blood. At the altar. Wafer in hand. The body of Christ—

VERONIQUE: Dr. Frankenstein sends his love to you.

CARDINAL: And mine to him. The Holy Mother bless him and keep him.

VERONIQUE: And he sends you this. By way of farewell.

CARDINAL: A gift?

VERONIQUE: A gift.

CARDINAL: He's kind. He was the kindest man I ever knew. Too kind, with all his good works. What is this?

VERONIQUE: A keepsake.

CARDINAL: Is there a key?

VERONIQUE: In the lock.

THE CARDINAL TURNS THE KEY. A SMALL PANEL OPENS IN THE BOX.

CARDINAL: I can barely get my hands inside. Is this some sort of game? I can see Joseph's sense of humor in this. I know what it is. It's the ring, isn't it. It's the Auschwitz ring. I've always coveted it. He knew. Dear Joseph. (*Puts his hands in eagerly, the box makes a grinding noise*) It's empty. Ah! (*Screams*) Oh Christ in Heaven help me—my hands—ah! My hands!

(*Wrestles with the box*) Help me woman—help me, there's something skewering my hands. They're being cut to ribbons. Make it release me. Make it release me. Why has he done this to me? (*Screams and pulls his hands out*) I'm being crucified. (*His hands are transfixed by two blades, straight through the middle of the palms*) Why Joseph? Why, why, why?

VERONIQUE: This isn't his doing.

CARDINAL: Then who?

VERONIQUE: You won't remember me.

CARDINAL: Help me.

VERONIQUE: Veronique Flecker.

CARDINAL: It's excruciating.

VERONIQUE: I was in hell last time we met, naked under his needle, face-less. But I have friends you may remember.

> THE CARDINAL COLLAPSES TO THE FLOOR AS TWO EXTRAORDI-NARY MONSTERS ENTER: FOLLEZOU AND MATTOS. THEY ARE DRESSED IN A PATHETIC PARODY OF CIVILIZED CLOTHING. A SUIT, MAYBE A TIE EVEN, CAN BE GLIMPSED, SHITTY AND BLOODY, MIN-GLED WITH GANGRENED BANDAGES AND RAGS. PHYSICALLY, THEY FORM A CONTRAST. FOLLEZOU HAS THE FACE OF A CADAVER, WELL-PUTREFIED. HIS FLESH IS DARK GREEN, GRAY, AND BROWN, WITH LIVID SORES WHERE HIS WOUNDS FESTER. MATTOS RESEM-BLES A GROTESQUE FETUS, HIS CRANIUM UNNATURALLY LARGE, PALE PINK, AND ALMOST BALD. THEIR BODIES REFLECT THIS CON-TRAST. FOLLEZOU SKELETAL, MATTOS PULPY-FAT. MATTOS CAR-RIES A BUNDLE OF TOOLS.

VERONIQUE: Señor Edmundo Follezou. Eddie, the Cardinal.

FOLLEZOU: My pleasure.

VERONIQUE: And Salvador Mattos. Excuse me, Salvador doesn't hear well. (*Louder*) Salvador.

MATTOS: Huh?

VERONIQUE: The Cardinal.

MATTOS: At least he's not fat.

FOLLEZOU: You were present at Mattos's marriage, Cardinal, when good Dr. Frankenstein sewed his top half to his bottom half. Do you not remember?

CARDINAL: Help me.

MATTOS: He seems distracted.

CARDINAL: Somebody help me.

FOLLEZOU: The boys ran away.

MATTOS: They didn't like the looks of us.

FOLLEZOU: So we're your only hope.

CARDINAL: Hope? You?

FOLLEZOU: Oh yes.

MATTOS: Why not?

CARDINAL: Help me then. Staunch these wounds before I drain away.

MATTOS: No.

CARDINAL: Why not?

FOLLEZOU: You offend us, with that look of horror on your face.

MATTOS: Just because we've been tampered with, are we any less reasonable, any less sensitive?

FOLLEZOU: Close your eyes, listen to his voice — (*Mattos sings a fragment of "Ave Maria"*) Is that such a terrible sound? There's a sweet-natured soul in there. We're just men. I myself was a philosophy teacher before the purges. And a friend of Cicero. Remember Cicero?

MATTOS: I was a violinist at the Opera House. I'm going to play again.

CARDINAL: Won't you help me? Sensitive men.

FOLLEZOU: We are helping you.

CARDINAL: I'm dying.

MATTOS: There you are then.

CARDINAL: Veronique, is that your name? Veronique, a little mercy.

VERONIQUE: It was Follezou made the box. Fine handiwork, don't you think? His limbs don't have the strength to kill you personally, so he devised a trick.

CARDINAL: Why would anyone want to kill me?

VERONIQUE: You blessed the scalpels.

CARDINAL: A joke.

VERONIQUE: The slab was washed down with holy water.

CARDINAL: He made me do it.

VERONIQUE: You used to watch. Smiling. Why?

FOLLEZOU: Please explain. I want to understand how you could be so dispassionate. I'm a man you see, who can barely stand to crush a wood louse. To do what you did —

MATTOS: Was it morbid fascination?

CARDINAL: I hate you.

FOLLEZOU: Is it that simple?

CARDINAL: I hate every living thing, and I always have.

MATTOS: Women?

CARDINAL: Decay. Flatulence. Grease.

MATTOS: You must know some strange women.

CARDINAL: But Frankenstein, oh dear Joseph, he always loved humanity.

VERONIQUE: Never.

CARDINAL: Oh yes. He had a passion for its intricacies, its strength, its elasticity. So he wanted to stretch it, shape it, remake it by his own rules.

To make a law for the flesh, a physical morality he called it. I just saw a bloodletter, a tormentor. And it pleased me, watching him silence their complaints, sluice out their minds with agonies. I'd put my finger, sometimes, into their hot heads, buried in thought up to the knuckle, and see their lives go out a little further with each prod. That pleased me too. He worked out of love, I out of loathing.

MATTOS: Sounds like the perfect marriage.

FOLLEZOU: I understand. Thank you.

CARDINAL: He claimed he was sowing seeds that would one day change humanity. Drawing the sap out of vivisected fetuses and injecting it—

VERONIQUE: I don't want to hear.

MATTOS: I do. It makes me feel better hearing about people who are worse off.

CARDINAL: You for one.

VERONIQUE: I know.

CARDINAL: He tampered with you endlessly. You're just a jug, full of him.

VERONIQUE: No.

CARDINAL: He's changing you from inside.

MATTOS: She has pains.

VERONIQUE: Mattos.

MATTOS: Why not tell him? Her body—

VERONIQUE: You want to see the part of me that's sprouting wings? Or the fur? Or the feathers? You want to know what I crave these days, to eat, to drink, to sleep with?

MATTOS: I don't think he does.

FOLLEZOU: I think he's had enough. Lucky man.

CARDINAL: Will you let me go now?

FOLLEZOU: More or less.

CARDINAL: Help me before I'm bled white.

MATTOS: That's the idea.

CARDINAL: The idea?

MATTOS: To bleed you. We've no taste for blood. Lots of protein, but it makes me sick. It's the meat I want.

FOLLEZOU: We want.

CARDINAL: No.

VERONIQUE: They intend to eat you.

CARDINAL: No!

FOLLEZOU: I think it's time we took him away. His noise offends our lady.

CARDINAL: No! No! No!

FOLLEZOU: Maybe into the crypt.

CARDINAL: No! No! No!

MATTOS: For what we are about to receive may the Lord make us truly thankful.

FOLLEZOU AND MATTOS DRAG HIM AWAY.

From *The Damnation Game*

When were you born Marty?"

"Nineteen forty-eight. December."

"The war was over."

"Yes."

"You don't know what you missed."

It was an odd beginning for a confession.

"Such times."

"You had a good war?"

Whitehead reached for one of the less damaged chairs and righted it; then he sat down. For several seconds he didn't say anything.

"I was a thief, Marty," he said at last. "Well . . . black marketeer has a more impressive ring, I suppose, but it amounts to the same thing. I was able to speak three or four languages adequately, and I was always quick-witted. Things fell my way very easily."

"You were lucky."

"Luck had no bearing on it. Luck's out for people with no *control*. I *had* control; though I didn't know it at the time. I made my own luck, if you like." He paused. "You must understand, war isn't like you see in the cinema; or at least my war wasn't. Europe was falling apart. Everything was in flux. Borders were changing, people were being shipped into oblivion: the world was up for grabs." He shook his head. "You can't conceive of it. You've always lived in a period of relative stability. But war changes the rules you live by. Suddenly it's *good* to hate, it's *good* to applaud destruction. People are allowed to show their true selves—"

Marty wondered where this introduction was taking them, but Whitehead was just getting into the rhythm of his telling. This was no time to divert him.

"And when there's so much uncertainty all around, the man who can shape his own destiny can be king of the world. Forgive the hyperbole, but it's how I felt. King of the World. I was clever, you see. Not *educated*, that came later, but clever. Streetwise, you'd call it now. And I was determined to make the most of this wonderful war God had sent me. I spent two or three months in Paris, just before the Occupation, then got out while the going was good. Later on, I went south. Enjoyed Italy; the Mediterranean. I wanted for nothing. The worse the war became, the better it was for me. Other people's desperation made me into a rich man.

"Of course I frittered the money away. Never really held on to my earnings for more than a few months. When I think of the paintings that went through my hands, the objets d'art, the sheer *loot*. Not that I knew that when I pissed in the bucket I splashed a Raphael. I bought and sold these things by the Jeep load.

"Toward the end of the European war I took off north, into Poland. The Germans were in a bad way: they knew the game was coming to an end, and I thought I could strike a few deals. Eventually—it was an error really—I wound up in Warsaw. There was practically nothing left by the time I got there. What the Russians hadn't flattened, the Nazis had. It was one wasteland from end to end." He sighed, and pulled a face, making an effort to find the words. "You can't imagine it," he said. "This had been a great city. But now? How can I make you understand? You have to see through my eyes, or none of this makes sense."

"I'm trying," Marty said.

"You live in *yourself*," Whitehead went on. "As I live in *myself*. We have very strong ideas of what we are. That's why we value ourselves; by what's unique in us. Do you follow what I'm saying?"

Marty was too involved to lie. He shook his head.

"No; not really."

"The *isness* of things: that's my point. The fact that everything of any value in the world is very specifically *itself*. We celebrate the individuality of appearance, of being, and I suppose we assume that some part of that individuality goes on forever, if only in the memory of the people who experienced it. That's why I valued Evangeline's collection, because I delight in the *special* thing. The vase that's unlike any other, the carpet woven with special artistry."

Then suddenly, they were back in Warsaw—

"There'd been such glories there, you know. Fine houses; beautiful churches; great collections of paintings. So much. But by the time I arrived it was all gone, pounded to dust.

"Everywhere you walked it was the same. Underfoot there was muck. Gray muck. It caked your boots, its dust hung in the air, it coated the back of your throat. When you sneezed, your snot was gray; your shit the same. And if you looked closely at this filth you could see it wasn't just dirt, it was flesh, it was rubble, it was porcelain fragments, newspapers. All of Warsaw was in that mud. Its houses, its citizens, its art, its history: all ground down to something that you scraped off your boots."

Whitehead was hunched up. He looked his seventy years; an old man lost in remembering. His face was knotted up, his hands were fists. He was older than Marty's father would have been had he survived his lousy heart: except that his father would never have been able to speak this way. He'd lacked the power of articulation, and, Marty thought, the depth of pain. Whitehead was in agonies. The memory of muck. More than that: the *anticipation* of it.

Thinking of his father, of the past, Marty alighted upon a memory that made some sense of Whitehead's reminiscences. He'd been a boy of five or six when a woman who'd lived three doors down the terrace died. She'd had no relatives apparently, or none that cared sufficiently to remove what few possessions she'd had from the house. The council had reclaimed the property and summarily emptied it, carting off her furniture to be auctioned. The day after, Marty and his playmates had found some of the dead woman's belongings dumped in the alley behind the row of houses. The council workmen, pressed for time, had simply emptied all the drawers of worthless personal effects into a pile, and left them there. Bundles of ancient letters roughly tied up with faded ribbon; a photograph album (she was there repeatedly: as a girl; as a bride; as a middle-aged harridan, diminishing in size as she dried up); much valueless bric-a-brac; sealing wax, inkless pens, a letter opener. The boys had fallen on these leavings like hyenas in search of something nourishing. Finding nothing, they scattered the torn-up letters down the alley; they dismembered the album, and laughed themselves silly at the photographs, although some superstition in them prevented them tearing those. They had no need to do so. The elements soon vandalized them more efficiently than their best efforts could have done. In a week of rain and night frost the faces on the photographs had been spoiled, dirtied, and finally eroded entirely. Perhaps the last existing portraits of people now dead went to mush in that alley, and Marty, passing down it daily, had watched the gradual extinction; seen the ink on the scattered letters rained off until the old woman's memorial was gone away utterly, just as her body had gone. If you'd up-ended the tray that held her ashes on to the trampled remains of her belongings they would have been virtually indistinguishable: both gray dirt, their significance irretrievably lost. Muck held the whip hand.

All this Marty recalled mistily. It wasn't quite that he saw the letters, the rain, the boys—as much as retouching the feelings the events had aroused: the buried sense that what had happened in that alley was unbearably poignant. Now his memory meshed with Whitehead's. All the old man had said about muck, about the isness of things, made some sense.

"I see," he murmured.

Whitehead looked up at Marty.

"Perhaps," he said.

"I was a gambling man in those days; far more than I am now. War brings it out in you, I think. You hear stories all the time, about how some lucky man escaped death because he sneezed, or died for the same reason. Tales of benign providence, or fatal bad fortune. And after a while you get to look at the world a little differently: you begin to see chance at work everywhere. You become alive to its mysteries. And of course to its flipside; to determinism. Because take it from me there are men who make their own luck. Men who can *mold* chance like putty. You talked yourself of feeling a tingle in your hands. As though today, whatever you did, you couldn't lose."

"Yes . . ." That conversation seemed an age away; ancient history.

"Well, while I was in Warsaw, I heard about a man who never once lost a game. A card-player."

"Never lost?" Marty was incredulous.

"Yes, I was as cynical as you. I treated the stories I heard as fable, at least for a while. But wherever I went, people told me about him. I got to be curious. In fact I decided to stay in the city, though God knows there was precious little to keep me there, and find this miracle worker for myself."

"Who did he play against?"

"All comers, apparently. Some said he'd been there in the last days before the Russian advance, playing against Nazis, and then when the Red Army entered the city he stayed on."

"Why play in the middle of nowhere? There can't have been much money around."

"Practically none. The Russians were betting their rations, their boots."

"So again: why?"

"That's what fascinated me. I couldn't understand it either. Nor did I believe he won every game, however good a player he was."

"I don't see how he kept finding people to play him."

"Because there's always somebody who thinks they can bring the champion down. I was one. I went searching for him to prove the stories wrong. They offended my sense of reality, if you like. I spent every waking hour of every day searching the city for him. Eventually I found a soldier who'd played against him, and, of course lost. Lieutenant Konstantin Vasiliev."

"And the card player . . . what was his name?"

"I think you know . . . ," Whitehead said.

"Yes," Marty replied, after a moment. "Yes, you know I saw him. At Bill's club?"

"When was this?"

"When I went to buy my suit. You told me to gamble what was left of the money."

"Mamoulian was at the academy? And did he play?"

"No. Apparently he never does."

"I tried to get him to play, when he came here last, but he wouldn't."

"But in Warsaw? You played him there?"

"Oh yes. That's what he'd been waiting for. I see that now. All these years I pretended I was in charge, you know? That I'd gone to him, that I'd won by my own skills—"

"You won?" Marty exclaimed.

"Certainly I won. But he let me. It was his way of seducing me, and it worked. He made it look difficult of course, to give some weight to the illusion, but I was so full of myself I never once contemplated the possibility that he'd lost the game deliberately. I mean, there was no reason for him to do that, was there? Not that I could see. Not at the time."

"Why did he let you win?"

"I told you: seduction."

"What, do you mean he wanted you in bed?"

Whitehead made the gentlest of shrugs. "It's possible, yes." The thought seemed to amuse him; vanity bloomed on his face. "Yes, I think I probably was a temptation." Then the smile faded. "But sex is nothing, is it? I mean, as possessions go, to fuck somebody is trite stuff. What he wanted me for went far deeper and was far more permanent than any physical act."

"Did you always win when you played him?"

"I never played against him again, that was the first and only time. I know it sounds unlikely. He was a gambler and so was I. But as I told you, he wasn't interested in cards for the betting."

"It was a test."

"Yes. To see if I was worthy of him. Fit to build an empire. After the war, when they started rebuilding Europe, he used to say there were no *real* Europeans left—they'd all been wiped out by one holocaust or another—and he was the last of the line. I believed him. All the talk of empires and traditions. I was flattered to be lionized by him. He was more cultured, more persuasive, more penetrating than any man I had met or have met since." Whitehead was lost in this reverie, hypnotized by the memory. "All that's left now is a husk of course. You can't really appreciate what an impression he made. There was nothing he couldn't have been or done if he'd put his mind to it. But when I said to him: why do you bother with the likes of me, why don't you go into politics, some sphere where you can wield power directly, he'd give me this look, and say: it's all been done. At first I thought he meant those lives were predictable. But I think he meant something else. I think he was telling me that he'd *been* these people, *done* those things."

"How's that possible? One man."

"I don't know. It's all conjecture. It was from the beginning. And here I am forty years later, still juggling rumors."

He stood up. By the look on his face it was obvious that his sitting position had caused some stiffness in the joints. Once he was upright, he leaned against the wall, and put his head back, staring up at the blank ceiling.

"He had one great love. One all-consuming passion. Chance. It obsessed him. 'All life is chance' he used to say, 'the trick is learning how to use it.'"

"And all this made sense to you?"

"It took time; but I came to share his fascination over a period of years, yes. Not out of intellectual interest. I've never had much of that. But because I knew it could bring power. If you can make Providence work for you—" he glanced down at Marty, "work out its *system* if you like—the world succumbs to you." The voice soured, "I mean, look at me. See how well I've done for myself . . . ," he let out a short, bitter laugh, "he cheated," he said, returning to the beginning of their conversation. "He didn't obey the rules."

"This was to be the Last Supper," Marty said. "Am I right? You were going to escape before he came for you."

"In a way."

"How?"

Whitehead didn't reply. Instead he began the story again, where he'd left off.

"He taught me so much. After the war we traveled around for a while, picking up a small fortune. Me with my skills, him with his. Then we came to England, and I went into chemicals."

"And got rich."

"Beyond the dreams of Croesus. It took a few years, but the money came, the power came."

"With his help."

Whitehead frowned at this unwelcome observation. "I applied his principles, yes," he replied. "But *he* prospered every bit as much as I did. He shared my houses, my friends. Even my wife."

Marty made to speak, but Whitehead cut him off.

"Did I tell you about the lieutenant?" he said.

"You mentioned him. Vasiliev."

"He died, did I tell you *that*?"

"No."

"He didn't pay his debts. His body was dragged out of the sewers of Warsaw."

"Mamoulian killed him?"

"Not personally. But yes I think—" Whitehead stopped in midflow, almost cocked his head, listening. "Did you hear something?"

"What?"

"No. It's all right. In my head. What was I saying?"

"The lieutenant."

"Oh yes. This piece of the story . . . I don't know if it'll mean too much to you . . . but I have to explain, because without it the rest doesn't quite make sense. You see, the night I found Mamoulian was an incredible evening. Useless to try and describe it really, but you know the way the sun can catch the tops of clouds; they were blush-colored, love-colored. And I was so full of myself, so *certain* that nothing could ever harm me." He stopped and licked his lips before going on. "I was an imbecile," self-contempt stung the words from him, "I walked through the ruins—smell of putrefaction everywhere, muck under my feet—and I *didn't care*, because it wasn't *my* ruin, *my* putrefaction. I thought I was above all that: especially that night. I felt like the victor, because *I* was alive and the dead were dead." The words stopped pressing forward for a moment. When he spoke again, it was so quietly it hurt the ears to catch the words. "What did I know? Nothing at all." He covered his face with his shaking hand, and said, "Oh Jesus," quietly into it.

In the silence that followed, Marty thought he heard something outside the door: a movement in the hallway. But the sound was too soft for him to be certain, and the atmosphere in the room demanded his absolute fixedness. To move now, to speak, would ruin the confessional, and Marty, like a child hooked by a master storyteller, wanted to hear the end of this narrative. At that moment it seemed to him more important than anything else.

Whitehead's face was concealed behind his hand as he attempted to stem tears. After a moment he took up the tail of the story again—carefully, as if it might strike him dead.

"I've never told anyone this. I thought if I kept my silence—if I let it become another rumor—sooner or later it would disappear."

There was another noise in the hall, a whine like wind through a tiny aperture. And then, a scratching at the door. Whitehead didn't hear it. He was in Warsaw again, in a house with a bonfire and a flight of steps and a room with a table and a guttering flame. Almost like the room they were in now, in fact, but smelling of old fire rather than souring wine.

"I remember," he said, "when the game was over Mamoulian stood up and shook hands with me. Cold hands. Icy hands. Then the door opened behind me. I half-turned to see. It was Vasiliev."

"The lieutenant?"

"Horribly burned."

"He'd survived," Marty breathed.

"No," came the reply. "He was quite dead."

Marty thought maybe he'd missed something in the story that would justify this preposterous statement. But no; the insanity was presented as plain truth. "Mamoulian was responsible," Whitehead went on. He was trembling, but the tears had stopped, boiled away by the glare of the memory. "He'd raised the lieutenant from the dead, you see. Like Lazarus. He needed functionaries I suppose."

As the words faltered the scratching began again at the door, an unmistakable appeal for entry. This time Whitehead heard it. His moment of weakness had passed apparently. His head jerked up. "Don't answer it," he commanded.

"Why not?"

"It's him," he said, eyes wild.

"No. The European's gone. I saw him leave."

"Not the European," Whitehead replied. "It's the lieutenant. *Vasiliev*."

Marty looked incredulous. "No," he said.

"You don't know what Mamoulian can do."

"You're being ridiculous!"

Marty stood up, and picked his way through the glass. Behind him, he heard Whitehead say "no" again, "please, Jesus, no," but he turned the handle and opened the door. Meager candlelight found the would-be entrant.

It was Bella, the Madonna of the kennels. She stood uncertainly on the threshold, her eyes, what was left of them, turned balefully up to look at Marty, her tongue a rag of maggoty muscle which hung from her mouth as if she lacked the strength to withdraw it. From somewhere in the pit of her body, she exhaled a thin whistle of air, the whine of a dog seeking human comfort.

Marty took two or three stumbling steps back from the door.

"It isn't him," Whitehead said, smiling.

"Jesus Christ."

"It's all right, Martin. It isn't him."

"Close the door!" Marty said, unable to move and do it himself. Her eyes, her stench, kept him at bay.

"She doesn't mean any harm. She used to come up here sometimes, for tidbits. She was the only one of them I trusted. Vile species."

Whitehead pushed himself away from the wall and walked across to the door, kicking broken bottles ahead of him as he went. Bella shifted her head to look at him, and her tail began to wag. Marty turned away, revolted, his reason thrashing around to find some sane explanation, but there was none to be had. The dog had been dead: he'd parceled her up himself. There was no question of premature burial.

Whitehead was staring at Bella across the threshold.

"No, you can't come in," he told her, as if she were a living thing.

"Send it away," Marty groaned.

"She's lonely," the old man replied, chiding him for his lack of compassion. It crossed Marty's mind that Whitehead had lost his wits. "I don't believe this is happening," he said.

"Dogs are nothing to him, believe me."

Marty remembered watching Mamoulian standing in the woods, staring down at the earth. He had seen no gravedigger because there'd been none. They'd exhumed themselves; squirming out of their plastic shrouds and pawing their way to the air.

"It's easy with dogs," Whitehead said. "Isn't it Bella? You're trained to obey."

She was sniffing at herself, content now that she'd seen Whitehead. Her God was still in His Heaven, and all was well with the world. The old man left the door ajar, and turned back to Marty.

"There's nothing to be afraid of," he said. "She's not going to do us any harm."

"He brought them to the house?"

"Yes; to break up my party. Pure spite. It was his way of reminding me what he's capable of."

Marty stooped and righted another chair. He was shaking so violently, he feared if he didn't sit down he'd fall down.

"The lieutenant was worse," the old man said, "because he didn't obey like Bella. He knew what had been done to him was an abomination. That made him angry."

Bella had woken with an appetite. That was why she'd made her way up to the room she remembered most fondly; a place where a man who knew the best spot to scratch behind her ear would coo soft words to her, and feed her morsels off his plate. But tonight she'd come up to find things changed. The man was odd with her, his voice jangling, and there was someone else in the room, one she vaguely knew the scent of, but couldn't place. She was *still* hungry, such deep hunger, and there was an appetizing smell very close to her. Of meat left in the earth, the way she liked it, still on the bone and half gone to putrescence. She sniffed, almost blind, looking for the source of the smell, and having found it, began to eat.

"Not a pretty sight."

She was devouring her own body, taking gray, greasy bites from the decayed muscle of her haunch. Whitehead watched as she pulled at herself. His passivity in the face of this new horror broke Marty.

"Don't let her!" he pushed the old man aside.

"But she's hungry," he responded, as though this horror were the most natural sight in the world.

Marty picked up the chair he'd been sitting on and slammed it against the wall. It was heavy, but his muscles were brimming, and the violence was a welcome release. The chair broke.

The dog looked up from her meal; the meat she was swallowing fell from her cut throat.

"Too much," Marty said, picking up a leg of the chair and crossing the room to the door before Bella could register what he intended. At the last moment she seemed to understand that he meant her harm, and tried to get to her feet. One of her back legs, the haunch almost chewed through, would no longer support her, and she staggered, teeth bared, as Marty swung his makeshift weapon down on her. The force of his blow shattered her skull. The snarling stopped. The body backed off, dragging the ruined head on a rope of a neck, the tail tucked between its back legs in fear. Two or three trembling steps of retreat and it could go no further.

Marty waited, hoping to God he wouldn't have to strike a second time. As he watched the body seemed to deflate. The swell of its chest, the remnants of its head, the organs hanging in the vault of its torso all collapsed into an abstraction, one part indistinguishable from the next. He closed the door on it, and dropped the blooded weapon at his side.

Whitehead had taken refuge across the room. His face was as gray as Bella's body.

"How did he do this?" Marty said. "*How* is it possible?"

"He has power," Whitehead stated. It was as simple as that apparently. "He can steal life, and he can give it."

Marty dug in his pocket for the linen handkerchief he'd bought specially for this night of dining and conversation. Shaking it out, its edges pristine, he wiped his face. The handkerchief came away dirtied with specks of rot. He felt as empty as the sac in the hall outside.

"You asked me once if I believed in Hell," he said. "Do you remember?"

"Yes."

"Is that what you think Mamoulian is? Something—" he wanted to laugh, "something from Hell?"

"I've considered the possibility. But I'm not by nature a supernaturalist. Heaven and Hell. All that paraphernalia. My system revolts at it."

"If not devils: what?"

"Is it so important?"

Marty wiped his sweaty palms on his trousers. He felt contaminated by this obscenity. It would take a long time to wash the horror out, if he ever could. He'd made the error of digging too deep, and the story he'd heard— that and the dog at the door—were the consequence.

"You look sick," Whitehead said.

"I never thought . . ."

"What? That the dead can get up and walk? Oh Marty, I took you for a Christian, despite your protestations."

"I'm getting out," Marty said. "Both of us."

"*Both?*"

"Carys and me. We'll go away. From him. From you."

"Poor Marty. You're more bovine than I thought you were. You won't see her again."

"Why not?"

"She's with *him*, damn you! Didn't it occur to you? *She went with him!*" So that had been the unthinkable solution to her abrupt vanishing trick. "Willingly, of course."

"No."

"Oh yes, Marty. He had a claim on her from the beginning. He rocked her in his arms when she was barely born. Who knows what kind of influence he has. I won her back of course, for a while." He sighed. "I made her love me."

"She wanted to be away from you."

"Never. She's *my* daughter, Strauss. She's as manipulative as I am. Anything between you and she was purely a marriage of her convenience."

"You're a fucking bastard."

"That's a given, Marty. I'm a monster; I concede the point." He threw up his hands, palms out, innocent of everything but guilt.

"I thought you said she loved you. Still she went."

"I told you: she's my daughter. She thinks the way I do. She went with him to learn how to use her powers. I did the same, remember?"

This line of argument, even from vermin like Whitehead, made a kind of sense. Beneath her strange conversation hadn't there always lurked a contempt for Marty and the old man alike, contempt earned by their inability to sum her up? Given the opportunity, wouldn't Carys go dance with the Devil if she felt she'd understand more of herself by doing so?

"Don't concern yourself with her," Whitehead said. "Forget her; she's gone."

Marty tried to hold on to the image of her face, but it was deteriorating. He was suddenly very tired, exhausted to his bones.

"Get some rest, Marty. Tomorrow we can bury the whore together."

"I'm not getting involved in this."

"I told you once, didn't I, if you stayed with me, there was nowhere I couldn't take you. It's more true now than ever. You know Toy's dead."

"When? How?"

"I didn't ask the details. The point is, he's gone. There's only you and I now."

"You made a fool out of me."

Whitehead's face was a portrait of persuasion. "An error of taste," he said. "Forgive me."

"Too late."

"I don't want you to leave me, Marty. *I won't let you leave me!* You hear?" his finger jabbed the air. "You came here to help me! What have you done? Nothing! *Nothing!*"

Blandishment had turned into accusations of betrayal in mere seconds. One moment tears, the next curses, and behind it all, the same terror of being left alone. Marty watched the old man's trembling hands fist and unfist.

"Please . . . ," he appealed, "don't leave me."

"I want you to finish the story."

"*Good* boy."

"Everything, you understand me. Everything."

"What more is there to tell?" Whitehead said. "I became rich. I had entered one of the fastest growing postwar markets: pharmaceuticals. Within half a decade I was up there with the world leaders." He smiled to himself. "What's more, there was very little illegality in the way I made my fortune. Unlike many, I played by the rules."

"And Mamoulian? Did he help you?"

"He taught me not to agonize over the moral issues."

"And what did he want in return?"

Whitehead narrowed his eyes. "You're not so stupid, are you?" he said appreciatively. "You manage to get right to the hurt when it suits you."

"It's an obvious question. You'd made a deal with him."

"No!" Whitehead interrupted, face set. "I made no deal, not in the way you mean it anyway. There was, perhaps, a gentleman's agreement, but that's long past. He's had all he's getting from me."

"Which was?"

"To live through me," Whitehead replied.

"Explain," Marty said, "I don't understand."

"He *wanted* life, like any other man. He had *appetites*. And he satisfied them through me. Don't ask me how. I don't understand myself. But sometimes I could feel him at the back of my eyes . . ."

"And you let him?"

"At first I didn't even know what he was doing: I had other calls on my attention. I was getting richer by the hour, it seemed. I had houses, land, art, women. It was easy to forget that he was always there, watching; living by proxy.

"Then in 1959 I married Evangeline. We had a wedding that would have shamed royalty: it was written up in newspapers from here to Hong Kong. Wealth and Influence marries Intelligence and Beauty: it was the ideal match. It crowned my happiness, it really did."

"You were in love."

"It was impossible not to love Evangeline. I think—" he sounded surprised as he spoke, "I think she even loved me."

"What did she make of Mamoulian?"

"Ah, there's the rub," he said. "She loathed him from the start. She said he was too puritanical; that his presence made her feel perpetually guilty. And she was right. He loathed the body; its functions disgusted him. But he couldn't be free of it, or its appetites. That was a torment to him. And as time went by that streak of self-hatred worsened."

"Because of her?"

"I don't know. Perhaps. Now I think back, he probably *wanted* her, the way he'd wanted beauties in the past. And of course she despised him, right from the beginning. Once she was mistress of the house this war of nerves just escalated. Eventually she told me to get rid of him. This was just after Carys was born. She said she didn't like him handling the baby— which he seemed to like to do. She just didn't want him in the house. I'd known him two decades by now—he'd lived in my house, he'd shared my life—and I realized I knew *nothing* about him. He was still the mythical card player I'd met in Warsaw."

"Did you ever ask him?"

"Ask him what?"

"Who he was? Where he came from? How he got his skills?"

"Oh yes, I asked him. On each occasion the answer was a little different from the time before."

"So he was lying to you?"

"Quite blatantly. It was a sort of joke, I think: his idea of a party piece, never to be the same person twice. As if he didn't quite exist. As if this man called *Mamoulian* was a construction, covering something else altogether."

"What?"

Whitehead shrugged. "I don't know. Evangeline used to say: he's empty. That was what she found foul about him. It wasn't his presence in the house that distressed her, it was his *absence*, the nullity of him. And I began to think maybe I'd be better getting rid of him, for Evangeline's sake. All the lessons he had to teach me I'd learned. I didn't need him anymore.

"Besides, he'd become a social embarrassment. God, when I think back

I wonder—I really wonder—how we let him rule us for so long. He'd sit at the dinner table and you could feel the spell of depression he'd cast on the guests. And the older he got the more his talk was all futility.

"Not that he visibly aged; he didn't. He doesn't look a year older now than when I first met him."

"No change at all?"

"Not physically. There's something altered maybe. He's got an air of defeat about him now."

"He didn't seem defeated to me."

"You should have seen him in his prime. He was terrifying then, believe me. People would fall silent when he stepped through the door: he seemed to soak up the joy in anyone; kill it on the spot. It got to the point where Evangeline couldn't bear to be in the same room with him. She got paranoid about him plotting to kill her and the child. She had somebody sit with Carys every night, to make certain that he didn't touch her. Come to think of it, it was Evangeline who first coaxed me into buying the dogs. She knew he had an abhorrence of them."

"But you didn't do as she asked? I mean, you didn't throw him out."

"Oh I knew I'd have to act sooner or later; I just lacked the balls to do it. Then he started petty power games, just to prove I still needed him. It was a tactical error. The novelty value of an inhouse puritan had worn very thin. I told him so. Told him he'd have to change his whole demeanor or go. He refused, of course. I knew he would. All I wanted was an excuse to break our association off, and he gave it to me on a plate. Looking back, of course, he knew damn well what I was doing. Anyway, the upshot was—I threw him out. Well, not me personally. Toy did the deed."

"Toy worked for you personally?"

"Oh yes. Again, it was Evangeline's idea: she was always so protective of me. She suggested I hire a bodyguard. I chose Toy. He'd been a boxer, and he was as honest as the day's long. He was always unimpressed by Mamoulian. Never had the least qualm about speaking his mind. So when I told him to get rid of the man, he did just that. I came home one day and the card player had gone.

"I breathed easy that day. It was as though I'd been wearing a stone around my neck and not known it. Suddenly it was gone: I was light-headed.

"Any fears I'd had about the consequences proved utterly groundless. My fortune didn't evaporate. I was as successful as ever without him. More so perhaps. I found new confidence."

"And you didn't see him again?"

"Oh no, I saw him. He came back to the house twice, each time unannounced. Things hadn't gone well for him, it seemed. I don't know what it was, but he'd lost the magic touch somehow. The first time he came back he was so decrepit I scarcely recognized him. He looked ill, he smelled foul. If you'd seen him in the street you'd have crossed over the road to avoid him. I could scarcely credit the transformation. He didn't want even to step into the house—not that I would have let him—all he wanted was money, which I gave him, and then he went away."

"And it was genuine?"

"What do you mean, *genuine?*"

"The beggar performance: it was real, was it? I mean, it wasn't another story . . . ?"

Whitehead raised his eyebrows. "All these years . . . I never thought of that. Always assumed . . . ," he stopped, and began again on a different tack. "You know, I'm not a sophisticated man, despite appearances to the contrary. I'm a thief. My father was a thief, and probably his father too. All this culture I surround myself with, it's a façade. Things I've picked up from other people. Received good taste, if you like.

"But after a few years you begin to believe your own publicity; you begin to think you actually *are* a sophisticate, a man of the world. You start to be ashamed of the instincts that got you where you are, because they're part of an embarrassing history. That's what happened to me. I lost any sense of what I was.

"Well, I think it's time the thief had his say again: time I started to use *his* eyes, *his* instinct. You taught me that, though Christ knows you weren't aware of it."

"Me?"

"We're the same. Don't you see? Both thieves. Both victims."

The self-pity in Whitehead's pronouncement was too much. "You can't tell me you're a victim," Marty said, "the way you've lived."

"What do you know about my feelings?" Whitehead snapped back. "Don't *presume,* you hear me? Don't think you understand because you don't! He took everything away from me; *everything!* First Evangeline, then Toy, now Carys. Don't tell me whether I've suffered or not!"

"What do you mean, he *took* Evangeline? I thought she died in an accident?"

Whitehead shook his head. "There's a limit to what I can tell you," he said.

"Some things I can't express. Never will." The voice was ashen. Marty let the point go, and moved on.

"You said he came back twice."

"That's right. He came again, a year or two after his first visit. Evangeline wasn't at home that night. It was November. Toy answered the door, I remember, and though I hadn't heard Mamoulian's voice I *knew* it was him. I went into the hallway. He was standing on the step, in the porch light. It was drizzling. I can see him now, the way his eyes found me. 'Am I welcome?' he said. Just stood there and said 'Am I welcome?'

"I don't know why, but I let him in. He didn't look in bad shape. Maybe I thought he'd come to apologize, I can't remember. Even then I would have been friends with him, if he'd offered. Not on the old basis. As business acquaintances, perhaps. I let my defenses down. We started talking about the past together—" Whitehead chewed the memory over, trying to get a better taste of it, "and then he started to tell me how lonely he was, how he needed my companionship. I told him Warsaw was a long time gone. I was a married man, a pillar of the community, and I had no intention of changing my ways. He started to get abusive: accused me of ingratitude. Said I'd cheated him. Broken the covenant between us. I told him there'd never been a covenant, I'd just won a game of cards once, in a distant city, and as a result, he'd chosen to help me, for his own reasons. I said I felt I'd acceded to his demands sufficiently to feel that any debt to him had been paid. He'd shared my house, my friends, my *life* for a decade: everything that I had, had been his to share. 'It's not enough,' he said, and he began again: the same pleas as before, the same demands that I give up this pretense to respectability and go off somewhere with him, be a wanderer, be his pupil, learn new, terrible lessons about the way of the world. And I have to say he made it sound almost attractive. There were times when I tired of the masquerade; when I smelled war, dirt; when I saw the clouds over Warsaw, and I was homesick for the thief I used to be. But I wasn't going to throw everything away for nostalgia's sake. I told him so. I think he must have known I was immovable, because he became desperate. He started to ramble, started to tell me he was frightened without me, lost. I was the one he'd given years of his life and his energies to, and how could I be so callous and unloving? He laid hands on me, wept, tried to paw my face. I was horrified by the whole thing. He disgusted me with his melodrama; I wanted no part of it, or him. But he wouldn't leave. His demands turned into threats, and I suppose I lost my temper. No suppose about it. I've never been so angry. I wanted an end to him and all he stood for:

my grubby past. I hit him. Not hard at first, but when he wouldn't stop staring at me I lost control. He didn't make any attempt to defend himself, and his passivity only inflamed me more. I hit him and hit him, and he just took it. Kept offering up his face to be beaten—" He took a trembling breath. "God knows I've done worse things. But nothing I feel so ashamed of. I didn't stop 'til my knuckles began to split. Then I gave him to Toy, who really worked him over. And all the time not a peep out of him. I go cold to think about it. I can still see him against the wall, with Bill at his throat and his eyes not looking at where the next blow was coming from but at me. Just at me.

"I remember he said: 'Do you know what you've done?' Just like that. Very quietly, blood coming out with the words.

"Then something happened. The air got thick. The blood on his face started to crawl around like it was alive. Toy let him go. He slid down the wall; left a smear down it. I thought we'd killed him. It was the worst moment of my life, standing here with Toy, both of us staring down at this bag of bones we'd beaten up. That was our mistake of course. We should never have backed down. We should have finished it then and there, and killed him."

"Jesus."

"Yes! Stupid, not to have finished it. Bill was loyal: there would have been no comeback. But we didn't have the courage. *I* didn't have the courage. I just made Toy clean Mamoulian up, then drive him to the middle of the city and dump him."

"You wouldn't have killed him," Marty said.

"Still you insist on reading my mind," Whitehead replied, wearily. "Don't you see that's what he wanted. *What he'd come for?* He would have let me be his executioner then, if I'd only had the nerve to follow through. He was sick of life. I could have put him out of his misery, and that would have been the end of it."

"You think he's mortal?"

"Everything has its season. His is past. He knows it."

"So all you need do is wait, right? He'll die, given time." Marty was suddenly sick of the story now; of thieves, of chance. The whole sorry tale, true or untrue, repulsed him. "You don't need me anymore," he said. He stood, and crossed to the door. The sound of his feet in the glass was too loud in the small room.

"Where are you going?" the old man wanted to know.

"Away. As far as I can get."

"You promised to stay."

"I promised to listen. I *have* listened. And I don't want any of this bloody place."

Marty began to open the door. Whitehead addressed his back.

"You think the European'll let you be? You've seen him in the flesh, you've seen what he can do. He'll have to silence you sooner or later. Have you thought of that?"

"I'll take the risk."

"You're safe here."

"Safe?" Marty repeated incredulously. "You can't be serious. *Safe?* You really are pathetic, you know that?"

"If you go—" Whitehead warned.

"What?" Marty turned on him, spitting contempt. "What will you do, *old man?*"

"I'll have them after you in two minutes flat; you're skipping parole."

"And if they find me, I'll tell them everything. About the heroin, about her out there in the hall. Every dirty thing I can dig up to tell them. I don't give a monkey's toss for your fucking threats, you hear?"

Whitehead nodded. "So. Stalemate."

"Looks like it," Marty replied, and stepped out into the corridor without looking back.

There was a morbid surprise awaiting him: the pups had found Bella. They had not been spared Mamoulian's resurrecting hand, though they could not have served any practical purpose. Too small, too blind. They lay in the shadow of her empty belly, their mouths seeking teats that had long since gone. One of them was missing, he noted. Had it been the sixth child he'd seen move in the grave, either buried too deeply, or too profoundly degenerated, to follow where the rest went?

Bella raised her neck as he sidled past. What was left of her head swung in his general direction. Marty looked away, disgusted; but a rhythmical thumping made him glance back.

She had forgiven him his previous violence apparently. Content now, with her adoring litter in her lap, she stared, eyeless, at him, while her wretched tail beat gently on the carpet.

In the room where Marty had left him Whitehead sat slumped with exhaustion.

Though it had been difficult to tell the story at first, it had become easier with the telling, and he was glad to have been unburdened of it. So many times he'd wanted to tell Evangeline. But she had signaled, in her elegant, subtle way, that if there were indeed secrets he had from her, she didn't want to know them. All those years, living with Mamoulian in their home, she had never directly asked Whitehead *why*, as though she'd known the answer would be no answer at all, merely another question.

Thinking about her brought so many sorrows to his throat; they brimmed in him. The European had killed her, he had no doubt of that. He or his agents had been on the road with her; her death had not been chance. Had it been chance he would have known. His unfailing instinct would have sensed its rightness, however terrible his grief. But there had been no such sense, only the recognition of his oblique complicity in her death. She had been killed as revenge upon him. One of many such acts, but easily the worst.

And had the European taken her, after death? Had he slipped into the mausoleum and touched her into life, the way he had the dogs? The thought was repugnant, but Whitehead entertained it nevertheless, determined to think the worst for fear that if he didn't Mamoulian might still find terrors to shake him with.

"*You won't,*" he said aloud to the room of glass. Won't: *frighten me, intimidate me, destroy me.* There were ways and means. He could escape still, and hide at the ends of the earth. Find a place where he could forget the story of his life.

There *was* something he hadn't told; a fraction of the tale, scarcely pivotal but of more than passing interest, that he'd withheld from Strauss as he would withhold it from any interrogator. Perhaps it was unspeakable. Or perhaps it touched so centrally, so profoundly, upon the ambiguities that had pursued him through the wastelands of his life that to speak it was to reveal the color of his soul.

He pondered this last secret now, and in a strange way the thought of it warmed him:

He had left the game, that first and only game with the European, and scrambled through the half-choked door into Muranowski Square. No stars were burning; only the bonfire at his back.

As he'd stood in the gloom, reorienting himself, the chill creeping up through the soles of his boots, the lipless woman had appeared in front of him. She'd beckoned. He assumed she intended to lead him back the way he'd come, and so followed. She'd had other intentions however. She'd led him away from the Square to a house with barricaded windows, and—ever curious—he'd pursued her into it, certain that tonight of all nights no harm could possibly come to him.

In the entrails of the house was a tiny room whose walls were draped with pirated swaths of cloth, some rags, others dusty lengths of velvet that had once framed majestic windows. Here, in this makeshift boudoir, there was one piece of furniture only. A bed, upon which the dead Lieutenant Vasiliev—whom he had so recently seen in Mamoulian's gaming room—was making love. And as the thief stepped through the door, and the lipless woman stood aside, Konstantin had looked up from his labors, his body continuing to press into the woman who lay beneath him on a mattress strewn with Russian and German and Polish flags.

The thief stood, disbelieving, wanting to tell Vasiliev that he was performing the act incorrectly, that he'd mistaken one hole for another, and it was no natural orifice he was using so brutally, but a wound.

The lieutenant wouldn't have listened of course. He grinned as he worked, the red pole rooting and dislodging, rooting and dislodging. The corpse he was pleasuring rocked beneath him, unimpressed by her paramour's attentions.

How long had the thief watched? The act showed no sign of consummation. At last the lipless woman had murmured *"Enough?"* in his ear, and he had turned a little way to her while she had put her hand on the front of his trousers. She seemed not at all surprised that he was aroused, though in all the years since he had never understood how such a thing was possible. He had long ago accepted that the dead could be woken. But that he had felt heat in their presence—that was another crime altogether, more terrible to him than the first.

There is no Hell, the old man thought, putting the boudoir and its charred Casanova out of his mind. Or else Hell is a room and a bed and appetite everlasting, and I've been there and seen its rapture and, if the worst comes to the worst, I will endure it.

From *The History of the Devil*

A JOYLESS LIGHT FALLS THROUGH LEAVES. ENTER GEORG KEIPENHAUER, A YOUNG SOLDIER, WITH A BABY WRAPPED IN A BLOOD- AND DIRT-STAINED CLOTH, AND—FROM THE MURK BETWEEN THE TREES—THE DEVIL, WITH A BOOK AND PEN. GUNS CAN BE HEARD, NOT FAR OFF.

KEIPENHAUER: Are you Russian? There's a curfew—

THE DEVIL: I'm sorry?

KEIPENHAUER: Get back to your house. You want your head blown off?

THE DEVIL: I'm not a local man.

KEIPENHAUER: This is forbidden territory.

THE DEVIL: I'm a historian.

KEIPENHAUER: Just keep out of this forest.

THE DEVIL: What's your name?

KEIPENHAUER: Why?

THE DEVIL: Answer me.

KEIPENHAUER: *(Almost mesmerized)* Georg Keipenhauer.

THE DEVIL: I need some assistance from you.

KEIPENHAUER: I've no time. This child—

THE DEVIL: Dead?

KEIPENHAUER: Not quite. I found her among—why am I telling you this?

THE DEVIL: Could you just direct me to the mass graves? That is where you brought her from?

KEIPENHAUER: *(Nods)* They pile them up. Some of them are still breathing.

THE DEVIL: There have been atrocities, then? I thought I'd finished: but there's no rest for the wicked.

KEIPENHAUER: Finished?

THE DEVIL: I've taken it upon myself these last three years to chronicle the names of the casualties in Europe, especially the Jews. I've just come up from Dachau, thinking the work was done, and what do I find?

KEIPENHAUER: Why?

THE DEVIL: Why what?

KEIPENHAUER: Why chronicle the dead?

THE DEVIL: We've committed genocide, you and I, Germany: the least we can do is make an account. So I've been asking the dead their names before they go to dirt.

KEIPENHAUER: All the names?

THE DEVIL: As many as I can find.

KEIPENHAUER: You write them down?

THE DEVIL: Here.

KEIPENHAUER: Such a small book.

THE DEVIL: I have a neat hand. Germany, why do you look so unhappy? All the engineers of Hell couldn't conceive of this. I'm humbled. The teacher, taught. You've set the standard for a coming generation.

KEIPENHAUER: It wasn't me—

THE DEVIL: It never is, Germany, that's the trick of it. How shall we ever stop it, when we can't find the culprit? Owning up to evil takes the courage of an innocent: an unresolvable state of affairs. Do you want to give me the child?

KEIPENHAUER: What for?

THE DEVIL: Aren't you withdrawing? I heard artillery close. You don't want to be weighed down—

KEIPENHAUER: No, I'll take her.

THE DEVIL: What's her name?

KEIPENHAUER: I don't know.

THE DEVIL: For the records.

KEIPENHAUER: She isn't dead.

THE DEVIL: (Reaching) Give her to me.

KEIPENHAUER: (Refusing) She's not dead.

THE DEVIL: A little gestural, isn't it, looking after a single baby when somebody's laid her whole country to waste? Give her to me. You must save your spotless skin, Georg. No doubt you have a family of your own. Children, grandchildren. Give me the child and no bullet will touch you.

KEIPENHAUER: She's so small.

THE DEVIL: Dispossessed, Georg. She doesn't want life. She'll only resent you for it. Oh, everything's confusion isn't it? You don't know which way to turn. But between us we are architects of the solution. The world's ending, Georg. This is wise. There's no light to go by. There's only the engine demanding ceaselessly, ceaselessly demanding to continue. Relinquish the mite. No harm. Let her go. (He takes the baby) There. There. Which way are the graves?

KEIPENHAUER: Back along the path, to your left. Two hundred yards.

THE DEVIL: Thank you. You have my deepest respect and admiration. I'll always remember you. Please excuse me; I must take her into history. EXIT THE DEVIL.

KEIPENHAUER: I let her go: to my shame I let him take the living child and bury her. Criminals I've known, always apparent; brutal men. I've showered with them. They were flesh enough. But this bland evil, so reasonable, so understanding. I never knew it. But it's The Devil himself.

From *The Books of Blood, Vol. I*
"In the Hills, the Cities"

It wasn't until the first week of the Yugoslavian trip that Mick discovered what a political bigot he'd chosen as a lover. Certainly, he'd been warned. One of the queens at the Baths had told him Judd was to the right of Attila the Hun, but the man had been one of Judd's ex-affairs, and Mick had presumed there was more spite than perception in the character assassination.

If only he'd listened. Then he wouldn't be driving along an interminable road in a Volkswagen that suddenly seemed the size of a coffin, listening to Judd's views on Soviet expansionism. Jesus, he was so boring. He didn't converse, he lectured, and endlessly. In Italy the sermon had been on the way the Communists had exploited the peasant vote. Now, in Yugoslavia, Judd had really warmed to this theme, and Mick was just about ready to take a hammer to his self-opinionated head.

It wasn't that he disagreed with everything Judd said. Some of the arguments (the ones Mick understood) seemed quite sensible. But then, what did he know? He was a dance teacher. Judd was a journalist, a professional pundit. He felt, like most journalists Mick had encountered, that he was obliged to have an opinion on everything under the sun. Especially politics; that was the best trough to wallow in. You could get your snout, eyes, head, and front hooves in that mess of muck and have a fine old time splashing around. It was an inexhaustible subject to devour, a swill with a little of everything in it, because everything, according to Judd, was political. The arts were political. Sex was political. Religion, commerce, gardening, eating, drinking, and farting—all political.

Jesus, it was mind-blowingly boring; killingly, love-deadeningly boring.

Worse still, Judd didn't seem to notice how bored Mick had become, or if he noticed, he didn't care. He just rambled on, his arguments getting windier and windier, his sentences lengthening with every mile they drove.

Judd, Mick had decided, was a selfish bastard, and as soon as their honeymoon was over he'd part with the guy.

It was not until their trip, that endless, motiveless caravan through the graveyards of mid-European culture, that Judd realized what a political lightweight he had in Mick. The guy showed precious little interest in the economics or the politics of the countries they passed through. He registered indifference to the full facts behind the Italian situation, and yawned, yes, yawned when he tried (and failed) to debate the Russian threat to world peace. He had to face the bitter truth: Mick was a queen; there was no other word for him; all right, perhaps he didn't mince or wear jewelry to excess, but he was a queen nevertheless, happy to wallow in a dreamworld of early Renaissance frescoes and Yugoslavian icons. The complexities, the contradictions, even the agonies that made those cultures blossom and wither were just tiresome to him. His mind was no deeper than his looks; he was a well-groomed nobody.

Some honeymoon.

The road south from Belgrade to Novi Pazar was, by Yugoslavian standards, a good one. There were fewer potholes than on many of the roads they'd traveled, and it was relatively straight. The town of Novi Pazar lay in the valley of the River Raska, south of the city named after the river. It wasn't an area particularly popular with the tourists. Despite the good road it was still inaccessible, and lacked sophisticated amenities; but Mick was determined to see the monastery at Sopocani, to the west of the town, and after some bitter argument, he'd won.

The journey had proved uninspiring. On either side of the road the cultivated fields looked parched and dusty. The summer had been unusually hot, and droughts were affecting many of the villages. Crops had failed, and livestock had been prematurely slaughtered to prevent them dying of malnutrition. There was a defeated look about the few faces they glimpsed at the roadside. Even the children had dour expressions; brows as heavy as the stale heat that hung over the valley.

Now, with the cards on the table after a row at Belgrade, they drove in silence most of the time; but the straight road, like most straight roads, invited dispute. When the driving was easy, the mind rooted for something to keep it engaged. What better than a fight?

"Why the hell do you want to see this damn monastery?" Judd demanded.

It was an unmistakable invitation.

"We've come all this way . . . ," Mick tried to keep the tone conversational. He wasn't in the mood for an argument.

"More fucking Virgins, is it?"

Keeping his voice as even as he could, Mick picked up the Guide and read aloud from it: "there, some of the greatest works of Serbian painting can still be seen and enjoyed, including what many commentators agree to be the enduring masterpiece of the Raska school: *The Dormition of the Virgin.*"

Silence.

Then Judd: "I'm up to here with churches."

"It's a masterpiece."

"They're all masterpieces according to that bloody book."

Mick felt his control slipping.

"Two and a half hours at most—"

"I told you, I don't want to see another church; the smell of the places makes me sick. Stale incense, old sweat, and lies . . ."

"It's a short detour; then we can get back on to the road and you can give me another lecture on farming subsidies in the Sandzak."

"I'm just trying to get some decent conversation going instead of this endless tripe about Serbian fucking masterpieces—"

"Stop the car!"

"What?"

"Stop the car!"

Judd pulled the Volkswagen onto the side of the road. Mick got out.

The road was hot, but there was a slight breeze. He took a deep breath, and wandered into the middle of the road. Empty of traffic and of pedestrians in both directions. In every direction, empty. The hills shimmered in the heat off the fields. There were wild poppies growing in the ditches. Mick crossed the road, squatted on his haunches, and picked one.

Behind him he heard the VW's door slam.

"What did you stop us for?" Judd said. His voice was edgy, still hoping for that argument, begging for it.

Mick stood up, playing with the poppy. It was close to seeding, late in the season. The petals fell from the receptacle as soon as he touched them, little splashes of red fluttering down on to the gray tarmac.

"I asked you a question," Judd said again.

Mick looked around. Judd was standing the far side of the car, his brows a knitted line of burgeoning anger. But handsome; oh yes; a face that made women weep with frustration that he was gay. A heavy black mustache (perfectly trimmed) and eyes you could watch forever, and never see the same light in them twice. Why in God's name, thought Mick, does a man as fine as that have to be such an insensitive little shit?

Judd returned the look of contemptuous appraisal, staring at the pouting pretty boy across the road. It made him want to puke, seeing the little act Mick was performing for his benefit. It might just have been plausible in a sixteen-year-old virgin. In a twenty-five-year-old, it lacked credibility.

Mick dropped the flower, and untucked his T-shirt from his jeans. A tight stomach, then a slim, smooth chest were revealed as he pulled it off. His hair was ruffled when his head reappeared, and his face wore a broad grin. Judd looked at the torso. Neat, not too muscular. An appendix scar peering over his faded jeans. A gold chain, small but catching the sun, dipped in the hollow of his throat. Without meaning to, he returned Mick's grin, and a kind of peace was made between them.

Mick was unbuckling his belt.

"Want to fuck?" he said, the grin not faltering.

"It's no use," came an answer, though not to that question.

"What isn't?"

"We're not compatible."

"Want to bet?"

Now he was unzipped, and turning away toward the wheat field that bordered the road.

Judd watched as Mick cut a swathe through the swaying sea, his back the color of the grain, so that he was almost camouflaged by it. It was a dangerous game, screwing in the open air—this wasn't San Francisco, or even Hampstead Heath. Nervously, Judd glanced along the road. Still empty in both directions. And Mick was turning, deep in the field, turning and smiling and waving like a swimmer buoyed up in a golden surf. What the hell . . . there was nobody to see, nobody to know. Just the hills, liquid in the heat haze, their forested backs bent to the business of the earth, and a lost dog, sitting at the edge of the road, waiting for some lost master.

Judd followed Mick's path through the wheat, unbuttoning his shirt as he walked. Field mice ran ahead of him, scurrying through the stalks as the giant came their way, his feet like thunder. Judd saw their panic, and smiled. He meant no harm to them, but then how were they to know that? Maybe he'd put out a hundred lives, mice, beetles, worms, before he reached the spot where Mick was lying, stark bollock naked, on a bed of trampled grain, still grinning.

It was good love they made, good, strong love, equal in pleasure for both; there was a precision to their passion, sensing the moment when effortless delight became urgent, when desire became necessity. They locked together, limb around limb, tongue around tongue, in a knot only orgasm could untie, their backs alternately scorched and scratched as they rolled around exchanging blows and kisses. In the thick of it, creaming together, they heard the *phut-phut-phut* of a tractor passing by; but they were past caring.

They made their way back to the Volkswagen with body-threshed wheat in their hair and their ears, in their socks and between their toes. Their grins had been replaced with easy smiles: the truce, if not permanent, would last a few hours at least.

The car was baking hot, and they had to open all the windows and doors to let the breeze cool it before they started toward Novi Pazar. It was four o'clock, and there was still an hour's driving ahead.

As they got into the car Mick said, "We'll forget the monastery, eh?"

Judd gaped.

"I thought—"

"I couldn't bear another fucking Virgin—"

They laughed lightly together, then kissed, tasting each other and themselves, a mingling of saliva, and the aftertaste of salt semen.

The following day was bright, but not particularly warm. No blue skies: just an even layer of white cloud. The morning air was sharp in the lining of the nostrils, like ether, or peppermint.

Vaslav Jelovsek watched the pigeons in the main square of Popolac courting death as they skipped and fluttered ahead of the vehicles that were buzzing around. Some about military business, some civilian. An air of sober intention barely suppressed the excitement he felt on this day, an excitement he knew was shared by every man, woman, and child in Popolac. Shared by the pigeons too for all he knew. Maybe that was why they played under the wheels with such dexterity, knowing that on this day of days no harm could come to them.

He scanned the sky again, that same white sky he'd been peering at since dawn. The cloud layer was low; not ideal for the celebrations. A phrase passed through his mind, an English phrase he'd heard from a friend, "to have your head in the clouds." It meant, he gathered, to be lost in a reverie, in a white, sightless dream. That, he thought wryly, was all the West knew about clouds, that they stood for dreams. It took a vision they lacked to make a truth out of that casual turn of phrase. Here, in these secret hills, wouldn't they create a spectacular reality from those idle words? A living proverb.

A head in the clouds.

Already the first contingent was assembling in the square. There were one or two absentees owing to illness, but the auxiliaries were ready and waiting to take their places. Such eagerness! Such wide smiles when an auxiliary heard his or her name and number called and was taken out of line to join the limb that was already taking shape. On every side, miracles of organization. Everyone with a job to do and a place to go. There was no shouting or pushing: indeed, voices were scarcely raised above an eager whisper. He watched in admiration as the work of positioning and buckling and roping went on.

It was going to be a long and arduous day. Vaslav had been in the square since an hour before dawn, drinking coffee from imported plastic cups, discussing the half-hourly meteorological reports coming in from Pristina and Mitrovica, and watching the starless sky as the gray light of morning crept across it. Now he was drinking his sixth coffee of the day, and it was still barely seven o'clock. Across the square Metzinger looked as tired and as anxious as Vaslav felt.

They'd watched the dawn seep out of the east together. Metzinger and he. But now they had separated, forgetting previous companionship, and would not speak until the contest was over. After all, Metzinger was from Podujevo. He had his own city to support in the coming battle. Tomorrow they'd exchange tales of their adventures, but for today they must behave as if they didn't know each other, not even to exchange a smile. For today they had to be utterly partisan, caring only for the victory of their own city over the opposition.

Now the first leg of Popolac was erected, to the mutual satisfaction of Metzinger and Vaslav. All the safety checks had been meticulously made, and the leg left the square, its shadow falling hugely across the face of the Town Hall.

Vaslav sipped his sweet, sweet coffee and allowed himself a little grunt of satisfaction. Such days, such days. Days filled with glory, with snapping flags and high, stomach-turning sights, enough to last a man a lifetime. It was a golden foretaste of Heaven.

Let America have its simple pleasures, its cartoon mice, its candy-coated castles, its cults, and its technologies, he wanted none of it. The greatest wonder of the world was here, hidden in the hills.

Ah, such days.

In the main square of Podujevo the scene was no less animated, and no less inspiring. Perhaps there was a muted sense of sadness underlying this year's celebration, but that was understandable. Nita Obrenovic, Podujevo's loved and respected organizer, was no longer living. The previous winter had claimed her at the age of ninety-four, leaving the city bereft of her fierce opin-

ions and her fiercer proportions. For sixty years Nita had worked with the citizens of Podujevo, always planning for the next contest and improving on the
designs, her energies spent on making the next creation more ambitious and
more lifelike than the last.

Now she was dead, and sorely missed. There was no disorganization in
the streets without her, the people were far too disciplined for that, but
they were already falling behind schedule, and it was almost 7:25. Nita's
daughter had taken over in her mother's stead, but she lacked Nita's power
to galvanize the people into action. She was, in a word, too gentle for the
job at hand. It required a leader who was part prophet and part ringmaster,
to coax and bully and inspire the citizens into their places. Maybe, after
two or three decades, and with a few more contests under her belt, Nita
Obrenovic's daughter would make the grade. But for today Podujevo was
behindhand; safety checks were being overlooked; nervous looks replaced
the confidence of earlier years.

Nevertheless, at six minutes before eight the first limb of Podujevo
made its way out of the city to the assembly point, to wait for its fellow.

By that time the flanks were already lashed together in Popolac, and
armed contingents were awaiting orders in the Town Square.

Mick woke promptly at seven, though there was no alarm clock in their
simply furnished room at the Hotel Beograd. He lay in his bed and listened to Judd's regular breathing from the twin bed across the room. A
dull morning light whimpered through the thin curtains, not encouraging
an early departure. After a few minutes' staring at the cracked paintwork
on the ceiling, and a while longer at the crudely carved crucifix on the
opposite wall, Mick got up and went to the window. It was a dull day, as he
had guessed. The sky was overcast, and the roofs of Novi Pazar were gray
and featureless in the flat morning light. But beyond the roofs, to the east,
he could see the hills. There was sun there. He could see shafts of light
catching the blue-green of the forest, inviting a visit to their slopes.

Today maybe they would go south to Kosovska Mitrovica. There was a
market there, wasn't there, and a museum? And they could drive down the
valley of the Ibar, following the road beside the river, where the hills rose
wild and shining on either side. The hills, yes; today he decided they
would see the hills.

It was 8:15.

By nine the main bodies of Popolac and Podujevo were substantially assembled. In their allotted districts the limbs of both cities were ready and waiting to join their expectant torsos.

Vaslav Jelovsek capped his gloved hands over his eyes and surveyed the sky. The cloud base had risen in the last hour, no doubt of it, and there were breaks in the clouds to the west; even, on occasion, a few glimpses of the sun. It wouldn't be a perfect day for the contest perhaps, but certainly adequate.

Mick and Judd breakfasted late on *hemendeks*—roughly translated as ham and eggs—and several cups of good black coffee. It was brightening up, even in Novi Pazar, and their ambitions were set high. Kosovska Mitrovica by lunchtime, and maybe a visit to the hill-castle of Zvecan in the afternoon.

About nine-thirty they motored out of Novi Pazar and took the Srbovac road south to the Ibar valley. Not a good road, but the bumps and potholes couldn't spoil the new day.

The road was empty, except for the occasional pedestrian; and in place of the maize and cornfields they'd passed on the previous day the road was flanked by undulating hills, whose sides were thickly and darkly forested. Apart from a few birds, they saw no wildlife. Even their infrequent traveling companions petered out altogether after a few miles, and the occasional farmhouse they drove by appeared locked and shuttered up. Black pigs ran unattended in the yard, with no child to feed them. Washing snapped and billowed on a sagging line, with no washerwoman in sight.

At first this solitary journey through the hills was refreshing in its lack of human contact, but as the morning drew on, an uneasiness grew on them.

"Shouldn't we have seen a signpost to Mitrovica, Mick?"

He peered at the map.

"Maybe . . ."

"We've taken the wrong road."

"If there'd been a sign, I'd have seen it. I think we should try and get off this road, bear south a bit more—meet the valley closer to Mitrovica than we'd planned."

"How do we get off this bloody road?"

"There've been a couple of turns . . ."

"Dirt tracks."

"Well, it's either that or going on the way we are."

Judd pursed his lips.

"Cigarette?" he asked.

"Finished them miles back."

In front of them, the hills formed an impenetrable line. There was no sign of life ahead; no frail wisp of chimney smoke, no sound of voice or vehicle.

"All right," said Judd, "we take the next turn. Anything's better than this."

They drove on. The road was deteriorating rapidly, the potholes becoming craters, the hummocks feeling like bodies beneath the wheels.

Then:

"There!"

A turn: a palpable turn. Not a major road, certainly. In fact barely the dirt track Judd had described the other roads as being, but it was an escape from the endless perspective of the road they were trapped on.

"This is becoming a bloody safari," said Judd as the VW began to bump and grind its way along the doleful little track.

"Where's your sense of adventure?"

"I forgot to pack it."

They were beginning to climb now, as the track wound its way up into the hills. The forest closed over them, blotting out the sky, so a shifting patchwork of light and shadow scooted over the hood as they drove. There was birdsong suddenly, vacuous and optimistic, and a smell of new pine and undug earth. A fox crossed the track, up ahead, and watched a long moment as the car grumbled up toward it. Then, with the leisurely stride of a fearless prince, it sauntered away into the trees.

Wherever they were going, Mick thought, this was better than the road they'd left. Soon maybe they'd stop, and walk a while, to find a promontory from which they could see the valley, even Novi Pazar, nestled behind them.

The two men were still an hour's drive from Popolac when the head of the contingent at last marched out of the Town Square and took up its position with the main body.

This last exit left the city completely deserted. Not even the sick or the old were neglected on this day; no one was to be denied the spectacle and the triumph of the contest. Every single citizen, however young or infirm, the blind, the crippled, babes in arms, pregnant women—all made their way up from their proud city to the stamping ground. It was the law that they should attend: but it needed no enforcing. No citizen of either city would have missed the chance to see that sight—to experience the thrill of that contest.

The confrontation had to be total, city against city. This was the way it had always been.

So the cities went up into the hills. By noon they were gathered, the citizens of Popolac and Podujevo, in the secret well of the hills, hidden from civilized eyes, to do ancient and ceremonial battle.

Tens of thousands of hearts beat faster. Tens of thousands of bodies stretched and strained and sweated as the twin cities took their positions. The shadows of the bodies darkened tracts of land the size of small towns; the weight of their feet trampled the grass to a green milk; their movement killed animals, crushed bushes, and threw down trees. The earth literally reverberated with their passage, the hills echoing with the booming din of their steps.

In the towering body of Podujevo, a few technical hitches were becoming apparent. A slight flaw in the knitting of the left flank had resulted in a weakness there: and there were consequent problems in the swiveling mechanism of the hips. It was stiffer than it should be, and the movements were not smooth. As a result there was considerable strain being put upon that region of the city. It was being dealt with bravely; after all, the contest was intended to press the contestants to their limits. But breaking point was closer than anyone would have dared to admit. The citizens were not as resilient as they had been in previous contests. A bad decade for crops had produced bodies less well-nourished, spines less supple, wills less resolute. The badly knitted flank might not have caused an accident in itself, but further weakened by the frailty of the competitors it set a scene for death on an unprecedented scale.

They stopped the car.

"Hear that?"

Mick shook his head. His hearing hadn't been good since he was an adolescent. Too many rock shows had blown his eardrums to hell.

Judd got out of the car.

The birds were quieter now. The noise he'd heard as they drove came again. It wasn't simply a noise: it was almost a motion in the earth, a roar that seemed seated in the substance of the hills.

Thunder, was it?

No, too rhythmical. It came again, through the soles of the feet—

Boom.

Mick heard it this time. He leaned out of the car window.

"It's up ahead somewhere. I hear it now."

Judd nodded.

Boom.

The earth-thunder sounded again.

"What the hell is it?" said Mick.

"Whatever it is, I want to see it—"

Judd got back into the Volkswagen, smiling.

"Sounds almost like guns," he said, starting the car. "Big guns."

Through his Russian-made binoculars Vaslav Jelovsek watched the start-ing-official raise his pistol. He saw the feather of white smoke rise from the barrel, and a second later heard the sound of the shot across the valley.

The contest had begun.

He looked up at twin towers of Popolac and Podujevo. Heads in the clouds—well almost. They practically stretched to touch the sky. It was an awesome sight, a breath-stopping, sleep-stabbing sight. Two cities swaying and writhing and preparing to take their first steps toward each other in this ritual battle.

Of the two, Podujevo seemed the less stable. There was a slight hesitation as the city raised its left leg to begin its march. Nothing serious, just a little dif-ficulty in coordinating hip and thigh muscles. A couple of steps and the city would find its rhythm; a couple more and its inhabitants would be moving as one creature, one perfect giant set to match its grace and power against its mirror-image.

The gunshot had sent flurries of birds up from the trees that banked the hidden valley. They rose up in celebration of the great contest, chattering their excitement as they swooped over the stamping-ground.

"Did you hear a shot?" asked Judd.

Mick nodded.

"Military exercises . . . ?" Judd's smile had broadened. He could see the headlines already—exclusive reports of secret maneuvers in the depths of the Yugoslavian countryside. Russian tanks perhaps, tactical exercises being held out of the West's prying sight. With luck, he would be the car-rier of this news.

Boom.

Boom.

There were birds in the air. The thunder was louder now.

It did sound like guns.

"It's over the next ridge . . . ," said Judd.

"I don't think we should go any farther."

"I have to see."

"I don't. We're not supposed to be here."

"I don't see any signs."

"They'll cart us away; deport us—I don't know—I just think—"

Boom.

"I've got to see."

The words were scarcely out of his mouth when the screaming started.

Podujevo was screaming: a death cry. Someone buried in the weak flank had died of the strain, and had begun a chain of decay in the system. One man loosed his neighbor and that neighbor loosed his, spreading a cancer of chaos through the body of the city. The coherence of the towering structure deteriorated with terrifying rapidity as the failure of one part of the anatomy put unendurable pressure on the other.

The masterpiece that the good citizens of Podujevo had constructed of their own flesh and blood tottered and then—a dynamited skyscraper, it began to fall.

The broken flank spewed citizens like a slashed artery spitting blood. Then, with a graceful sloth that made the agonies of the citizens all the more horrible, it bowed toward the earth, all its limbs dissembling as it fell.

The huge head, that had brushed the clouds so recently, was flung back on its thick neck. Ten thousand mouths spoke a single scream for its vast mouth, a wordless, infinitely pitiable appeal to the sky. A howl of loss, a howl of anticipation, a howl of puzzlement. How, that scream demanded, could the day of days end like this, in a welter of falling bodies?

"Did you hear that?"

It was unmistakably human, though almost deafeningly loud. Judd's stomach convulsed. He looked across at Mick, who was as white as a sheet.

Judd stopped the car.

"No," said Mick.

"Listen—for Christ's sake—"

The din of dying moans, appeals, and imprecations flooded the air. It was very close.

"We've got to go on now," Mick implored.

Judd shook his head. He was prepared for some military spectacle—all the Russian army massed over the next hill—but that noise in his ears was the noise of human flesh—too human for words. It reminded him of his childhood imaginings of Hell; the endless, unspeakable torments his mother had threatened him with if he failed to embrace Christ. It was a terror he'd forgotten for twenty years. But suddenly, here it was again, fresh-faced. Maybe the pit itself gaped just over the next horizon, with his mother standing at its lip, inviting him to taste its punishments.

"If you won't drive, I will."

Mick got out of the car and crossed in front of it, glancing up the track as he did so. There was a moment's hesitation, no more than a moment's, when his eyes flickered with disbelief, before he turned toward the windscreen, his face even paler than it had been previously and said: "Jesus Christ . . ." in a voice that was thick with suppressed nausea.

His lover was still sitting behind the wheel, his head in his hands, trying to blot out memories.

"Judd . . ."

Judd looked up, slowly. Mick was staring at him like a wild man, his face shining with a sudden, icy sweat. Judd looked past him. A few meters ahead the track had mysteriously darkened, as a tide edged toward the car, a thick, deep tide of blood. Judd's reason twisted and turned to make any other sense of the sight than that inevitable conclusion. But there was no saner explanation. It was blood, in unendurable abundance, blood without end—

And now, in the breeze, there was the flavor of freshly opened carcasses: the smell out of the depths of the human body, part sweet, part savory.

Mick stumbled back to the passenger's side of the VW and fumbled weakly at the handle. The door opened suddenly and he lurched inside, his eyes glazed.

"Back up," he said.

Judd reached for the ignition. The tide of blood was already sloshing against the front wheels. Ahead, the world had been painted red.

"Drive, for fuck's sake, drive!"

Judd was making no attempt to start the car.

"We must look," he said, without conviction, "we have to."

"We don't have to do anything," said Mick, "but get the hell out of here. It's not our business . . ."

"Plane crash—"

"There's no smoke."

"Those are human voices."

Mick's instinct was to leave well enough alone. He could read about the tragedy in a newspaper—he could see the pictures tomorrow when they were gray and grainy. Today it was too fresh, too unpredictable—

Anything could be at the end of that track, bleeding—

"We must—"

Judd started the car, while beside him Mick began to moan quietly. The VW began to edge forward, nosing through the river of blood, its wheels spinning in the queasy, foaming tide.

"No," said Mick, very quietly. "Please, no . . ."

"We must," was Judd's reply. "We must. We must."

Only a few yards away the surviving city of Popolac was recovering from its first convulsions. It stared, with a thousand eyes, at the ruins of its ritual enemy, now spread in a tangle of rope and bodies over the impacted ground, shattered forever. Popolac staggered back from the sight, its vast legs flattening the forest that bounded the stamping-ground, its arms flailing the air. But it kept its balance, even as a common insanity, woken by the horror at its feet, surged through its sinews and curdled its brain. The order went out: the body thrashed and twisted and turned from the grisly carpet of Podujevo, and fled into the hills.

As it headed into oblivion, its towering form passed between the car and the sun, throwing its cold shadow over the bloody road. Mick saw nothing through his tears, and Judd, his eyes narrowed against the sight he feared seeing around the next bend, only dimly registered that something had blotted the light for a minute. A cloud, perhaps. A flock of birds.

Had he looked up at that moment, just stolen a glance out toward the northeast, he would have seen Popolac's head, the vast, swarming head of a maddened city, disappearing below his line of vision, as it marched into the hills. He would have known that this territory was beyond his comprehension; and that there was no healing to be done in this corner of Hell. But he didn't see the city, and he and Mick's last turn had passed. From now on, like Popolac and its dead twin, they were lost to sanity, and to all hope of life.

They rounded the bend, and the ruins of Podujevo came into sight.

Their domesticated imaginations had never conceived of a sight so unspeakably brutal.

Perhaps in the battlefields of Europe as many corpses had been heaped together: but had so many of them been women and children, locked together with the corpses of men? There had been piles of dead as high, but ever so many so recently abundant with life? There had been cities laid waste as quickly, but ever an entire city lost to the simple dictate of gravity?

It was a sight beyond sickness. In the face of it the mind slowed to a snail's pace, the forces of reason picked over the evidence with meticulous hands, searching for a flaw in it, a place where it could say:

This is not happening. This is a dream of death, not death itself.

But reason could find no weakness in the wall. This was true. It was death indeed.

Podujevo had fallen.

Thirty-eight thousand, seven hundred and sixty-five citizens were spread on the ground, or rather flung in ungainly, seeping piles. Those who had not died of the fall, or of suffocation, were dying. There would be no survivors from that city except that bundle of onlookers that had traipsed out of their homes to watch the contest. Those few Podujevians, the crippled, the sick, the ancient few, were now staring, like Mick and Judd, at the carnage, trying not to believe.

Judd was first out of the car. The ground beneath his suedes was sticky with coagulating gore. He surveyed the carnage. There was no wreckage: no sign of a plane crash, no fire, no smell of fuel. Just tens of thousands of fresh bodies, all either naked or dressed in an identical gray serge, men, women, and children alike. Some of them, he could see, wore leather harnesses, tightly buckled around their upper chests, and snaking out from these contraptions were lengths of rope, miles and miles of it. The closer he looked, the more he saw of the extraordinary system of knots and lashings that still held the bodies together. For some reason these people had been tied together, side by side. Some were yoked on their neighbors' shoulders, straddling them like boys playing at horseback riding. Others were locked arm in arm, knitted together with threads of rope in a wall of muscle and bone. Yet others were trussed in a ball, with their heads tucked between their knees. All were in some way connected up with their fellows, tied together as though in some insane collective bondage game.

Another shot.

Mick looked up.

Across the field a solitary man, dressed in a drab overcoat, was walking among the bodies with a revolver, dispatching the dying. It was a pitifully inadequate act of mercy, but he went on nevertheless, choosing the suffering children first. Emptying the revolver, filling it again, emptying it, filling it, emptying it—

Mick let go.

He yelled at the top of his voice over the moans of the injured.

"What is this?"

The man looked up from his appalling duty, his face as dead gray as his coat.

"Uh?" he grunted, frowning at the two interlopers through his thick spectacles.

"What's happened here?" Mick shouted across at him. It felt good to shout, it felt good to sound angry at the man. Maybe he was to blame. It would be a fine thing, just to have someone to blame.

"Tell us—" Mick said. He could hear the tears throbbing in his voice. "Tell us, for God's sake. Explain."

Gray-coat shook his head. He didn't understand a word this young idiot was saying. It was English he spoke, but that's all he knew. Mick began to walk toward him, feeling all the time the eyes of the dead on him. Eyes like black, shining gems set in broken faces: eyes looking at him upside down, on heads severed from their seating. Eyes in heads that had solid howls for voices. Eyes in heads beyond howls, beyond breath.

Thousands of eyes.

He reached Gray-coat, whose gun was almost empty. He had taken off his spectacles and thrown them aside. He too was weeping, little jerks ran through his big, ungainly body.

At Mick's feet, somebody was reaching for him. He didn't want to look, but the hand touched his shoe and he had no choice but to see its owner. A young man, lying like a flesh swastika, every joint smashed. A child lay under him, her bloody legs poking out like two pink sticks.

He wanted the man's revolver, to stop the hand from touching him. Better still he wanted a machine-gun, a flame-thrower, anything to wipe the agony away.

As he looked up from the broken body, Mick saw Gray-coat raise the revolver.

"Judd—" he said, but as the word left his lips the muzzle of the revolver was slipped into Gray-coat's mouth and the trigger was pulled.

Gray-coat had saved the last bullet for himself. The back of his head opened like a dropped egg, the shell of his skull flying off. His body went limp and sank to the ground, the revolver still between his lips.

"We must—" began Mick, saying the words to nobody. "We must . . ."

What was the imperative? In this situation, what *must* they do?

"We must—"

Judd was behind him.

"Help—" he said to Mick.

"Yes. We must get help. We must—"

"Go."

Go! That was what they must do. On any pretext, for any fragile, cowardly reason, they must go. Get out of the battlefield, get out of the reach of a dying hand with a wound in place of a body.

"We have to tell the authorities. Find a town. Get help—"

"Priests," said Mick. "They need priests."

It was absurd, to think of giving the Last Rites to so many people. It would take an army of priests, a water cannon filled with holy water, a loudspeaker to pronounce the benedictions.

They turned away, together, from the horror, and wrapped their arms around each other, then picked their way through the carnage to the car.

It was occupied.

Vaslav Jelovsek was sitting behind the wheel, and trying to start the Volkswagen. He turned the ignition key once. Twice. Third time the engine caught and the wheels spun in the crimson mud as he put her into reverse and backed down the track. Vaslav saw the Englishmen running toward the car, cursing him. There was no help for it—he didn't want to steal the vehicle, but he had work to do. He had been a referee, he had been responsible for the contest, and the safety of the contestants. One of the heroic cities had already fallen. He must do everything in his power to prevent Popolac from following its twin. He must chase Popolac, and reason with it. Talk it down out of its terrors with quiet words and promises. If he failed there would be another disaster the equal of the one in front of him, and his conscience was already broken enough.

Mick was still chasing the VW, shouting at Jelovsek. The thief took no notice, concentrating on maneuvering the car back down the narrow, slippery track. Mick was losing the chase rapidly. The car had begun to pick up speed. Furious, but without the breath to speak his fury, Mick stood in the road, hands on his knees, heaving and sobbing.

"Bastard!" said Judd.

Mick looked down the track. Their car had already disappeared.

"Fucker couldn't even drive properly."

"We have . . . we have . . . to catch . . . up . . . ," said Mick through gulps of breath.

"How?"

"On foot . . ."

"We haven't even got a map . . . it's in the car."

"Jesus . . . Christ . . . Almighty."

They walked down the track together, away from the field.

After a few meters the tide of blood began to peter out. Just a few congealing rivulets dribbled on toward the main road. Mick and Judd followed the bloody tide marks to the junction.

The Srbovac road was empty in both directions. The tide marks showed a left turn. "He's gone deeper into the hills," said Judd, staring along the lovely road toward the blue-green distance. "He's out of his mind!"

"Do we go back the way we came?"

"It'll take us all night on foot."

"We'll hop a lift."

Judd shook his head: his face was slack and his look lost. "Don't you see, Mick, they all knew this was happening. The people in the farms—they got the hell out while those people went crazy up there. There'll be no cars along this road, I'll lay you anything—except maybe a couple of shit-dumb tourists like us—and no tourist would stop for the likes of us."

He was right. They looked like butchers—splattered with blood. Their faces were shining with grease, their eyes maddened.

"We'll have to walk," said Judd, "the way he went."

He pointed along the road. The hills were darker now; the sun had suddenly gone out on their slopes.

Mick shrugged. Either way he could see they had a night on the road ahead of them. But he wanted to walk somewhere—anywhere—as long as he put distance between him and the dead.

In Popolac a kind of peace reigned. Instead of a frenzy of panic, there was a numbness, a sheeplike acceptance of the world as it was. Locked in their positions, strapped, roped, and harnessed to each other in a living system that allowed for no single voice to be louder than any other, nor any back to labor less than its neighbor's, they let an insane consensus replace the tranquil voice of reason. They were convulsed into one mind, one thought, one ambition. They became, in the space of a few moments, the single-minded giant whose image they had so brilliantly re-created. The illusion of petty individuality was swept away in an irresistible tide of collective feeling—not a mob's passion, but a telepathic surge that dissolved the voices of thousands into one irresistible command.

And the voice said: go!

The voice said: take this horrible sight away, where I need never see it again.

Popolac turned away into the hills, its legs taking strides half a mile long. Each man, woman, and child in that seething tower was sightless. They saw only through the eyes of the city. They were thoughtless, but to think the city's thoughts. And they believed themselves deathless, in their lumbering, relentless strength. Vast and mad and deathless.

Two miles along the road Mick and Judd smelled petrol in the air, and a little farther along they came upon the VW. It had overturned in the reed-clogged drainage ditch at the side of the road. It had not caught fire.

The driver's door was open, and the body of Vaslav Jelovsek had tumbled out. His face was calm in unconsciousness. There seemed to be no sign of injury, except for a small cut or two on his sober face. They gently pulled the thief out of the wreckage and up out of the filth of the ditch onto the road. He moaned a little as they fussed about him, rolling Mick's sweater up to pillow his head and removing his jacket and tie.

Quite suddenly, he opened his eyes.

He stared at them both.

"Are you all right?" Mick asked.

The man said nothing for a moment. He seemed not to understand.

Then:

"English?" he said. His accent was thick, but the question was quite clear.

"Yes."

"I heard your voices. English."

He frowned and winced.

"Are you in pain?" said Judd.

The man seemed to find this amusing.

"Am I in pain?" he repeated, his face screwed up in a mixture of agony and delight.

"I shall die," he said, through gritted teeth.

"No," said Mick. "You're all right—"

The man shook his head, his authority absolute.

"I shall die," he said again, the voice full of determination. "I want to die."

Judd crouched closer to him. His voice was weaker by the moment.

"Tell us what to do," he said. The man had closed his eyes. Judd shook him awake, roughly.

"Tell us," he said again, his show of compassion rapidly disappearing. "Tell us what this is all about."

"About?" said the man, his eyes still closed. "It was a fall, that's all. Just a fall . . ."

"What fell?"

"The city. Podujevo. My city."

"What did it fall from?"

"Itself, of course."

The man was explaining nothing; just answering one riddle with another.

"Where were you going?" Mick inquired, trying to sound as unaggressive as possible.

"After Popolac," said the man.

"Popolac?" said Judd.

Mick began to see some sense in the story.

"Popolac is another city. Like Podujevo. Twin cities. They're on the map—"

"Where's the city now?" said Judd.

Vaslav Jelovsek seemed to choose to tell the truth. There was a moment when he hovered between dying with a riddle on his lips, and living long enough to unburden his story. What did it matter if the tale was told now? There could never be another contest: all that was over.

"They came to fight," he said, his voice now very soft, "Popolac and Podujevo. They come every ten years—"

"Fight?" said Judd. "You mean all those people were slaughtered?"

Vaslav shook his head.

"No, no. They fell. I told you."

"Well, how do they fight?" Mick said.

"Go into the hills," was the only reply.

Vaslav opened his eyes a little. The faces that loomed over him were exhausted and sick. They had suffered, these innocents. They deserved some explanation.

"As giants," he said. "They fought as giants. They made a body out of their bodies, do you understand? The frame, the muscles, the bone, the eyes, nose, teeth all made of men and women."

"He's delirious," said Judd.

"You go into the hills," the man repeated. "See for yourselves how true it is."

"Even supposing—" Mick began.

Vaslav interrupted him, eager to be finished. "They were good at the game of giants. It took many centuries of practice: every ten years making the figure larger and larger. One always ambitious to be larger than the other. Ropes to tie them all together, flawlessly. Sinews . . . ligaments . . . There was food in its belly . . . there were pipes from the loins, to take away the waste. The best-sighted sat in the eye sockets, the best voiced in the mouth and throat. You wouldn't believe the engineering of it."

"I don't," said Judd, and stood up.

"It is the body of the state," said Vaslav, so softly his voice was barely above a whisper, "it is the shape of our lives."

There was a silence. Small clouds passed over the road, soundlessly shedding their mass to the air.

"It was a miracle," he said. It was as if he realized the true enormity of the fact for the first time. "It was a miracle."

It was enough. Yes. It was quite enough.

His mouth closed, the words said, and he died.

Mick felt this death more acutely than the thousands they had fled from; or rather this death was the key to unlock the anguish he felt for them all.

Whether the man had chosen to tell a fantastic lie as he died, or whether this story was in some way true, Mick felt useless in the face of it. His imagination was too narrow to encompass the idea. His brain ached with the thought of it, and his compassion cracked under the weight of misery he felt.

They stood on the road, while the clouds scudded by, their vague, gray shadows passing over them toward the enigmatic hills.

It was twilight.

Popolac could stride no further. It felt exhaustion in every muscle. Here and there in its huge anatomy deaths had occurred; but there was no grieving in the city for its deceased cells. If the dead were in the interior, the corpses were allowed to hang from their harnesses. If they formed the skin of the city they were unbuckled from their positions and released, to plunge into the forest below.

The giant was not capable of pity. It had no ambition but to continue until it ceased.

As the sun slunk out of sight Popolac rested, sitting on a small hillock, nursing its huge head in its huge hands.

The stars were coming out, with their familiar caution. Night was approaching, mercifully bandaging up the wounds of the day, blinding eyes that had seen too much.

Popolac rose to its feet again, and began to move, step by booming step. It would not be long surely, before fatigue overcame it: before it could lie down in the tomb of some lost valley and die.

But for a space yet it must walk on, each step more agonizingly slow than the last, while the night bloomed black around its head.

Mick wanted to bury the car thief, somewhere on the edge of the forest. Judd, however, pointed out that burying a body might seem, in tomorrow's saner light, a little suspicious. And besides, wasn't it absurd to concern themselves with one corpse when there were literally thousands of them lying a few miles from where they stood?

The body was left to lie, therefore, and the car to sink deeper into the ditch.

They began to walk again.

It was cold, and colder by the moment, and they were hungry. But the few houses they passed were all deserted, locked and shuttered, every one.

"What did he mean?" said Mick, as they stood looking at another locked door.

"He was talking metaphor—"

"All that stuff about giants?"

"It was some Trotskyist tripe—" Judd insisted.

"I don't think so."

"I know so. It was his deathbed speech, he'd probably been preparing for years."

"I don't think so," Mick said again, and began walking back toward the road.

"Oh, how's that?" Judd was at his back.

"He wasn't towing some party line."

"Are you saying you think there's some giant around here someplace? For God's sake!"

Mick turned to Judd. His face was difficult to see in the twilight. But his voice was sober with belief.

"Yes. I think he was telling the truth."

"That's absurd. That's ridiculous. No."

Judd hated Mick that moment. Hated his naïveté, his passion to believe any half-witted story if it had a whiff of romance about it. And this? This was the worst, the most preposterous . . .

"No," he said again, "No. No. No."

The sky was porcelain smooth, and the outline of the hills black as pitch.

"I'm fucking freezing," said Mick out of the ink, "Are you staying here or walking with me?"

Judd shouted: "We're not going to find anything this way."

"Well, it's a long way back."

"We're just going deeper into the hills."

"Do what you like—I'm walking."

His footsteps receded: the dark encased him.

After a minute, Judd followed.

The night was cloudless and bitter. They walked on, their collars up against the chill, their feet swollen in their shoes. Above them the whole sky had become a parade of stars. A triumph of spilled light, from which the eye could make as many patterns as it had patience for. After a while, they slung their tired arms around each other, for comfort and warmth.

About eleven o'clock, they saw the glow of a window in the distance.

The woman at the door of the stone cottage didn't smile, but she understood their condition, and let them in. There seemed to be no purpose in trying to explain to either the woman or her crippled husband what they had seen. The cottage had no telephone, and there was no sign of a vehicle, so even had they found some way to express themselves, nothing could be done.

With mimes and face-pullings they explained that they were hungry and exhausted. They tried further to explain that they were lost, cursing themselves for leaving their phrasebook in the VW. She didn't seem to understand very much of what they said, but sat them down beside a blazing fire and put a pan of food on the stove to heat.

They ate thick unsalted pea soup and eggs, and occasionally smiled their thanks at the woman. Her husband sat beside the fire, making no attempt to talk, or even look at the visitors.

The food was good. It buoyed their spirits.

They would sleep until morning and then begin the long trek back. By dawn the bodies in the field would be being quantified, identified, parceled up and dispatched to their families. The air would be full of reassuring noises, canceling out the moans that still rang in their ears. There would be helicopters, lorry loads of men organizing the clearing-up operations. All the rites and paraphernalia of a civilized disaster.

And in a while, it would be palatable. It would become part of their history: a tragedy, of course, but one they could explain, classify, and learn to live with. All would be well, yes, all would be well. Come morning.

The sleep of sheer fatigue came on them suddenly. They lay where they had fallen, still sitting at the table, their heads on their crossed arms. A litter of empty bowls and bread crusts surrounded them.

They knew nothing. Dreamed nothing. Felt nothing.

Then the thunder began.

In the earth, in the deep earth, a rhythmical tread, as of a titan, that came, by degrees, closer and closer.

The woman woke her husband. She blew out the lamp and went to the door. The night sky was luminous with stars: the hills black on every side.

The thunder still sounded: a full half-minute between every boom, but louder now. And louder with every new step.

They stood at the door together, husband and wife, and listened to the night hills echo back and forth with the sound. There was no lightning to accompany the thunder.

Just the boom—

Boom—

Boom—

It made the ground shake: it threw dust down from the door lintel, and rattled the window latches.

Boom—

Boom—

They didn't know what approached, but whatever shape it took, and whatever it intended, there seemed no sense in running from it. Where they stood, in the pitiful shelter of their cottage, was as safe as any nook of the forest. How could they choose, out of a hundred thousand trees, which would be standing when the thunder had passed? Better to wait: and watch.

The wife's eyes were not good, and she doubted what she saw when the blackness of the hill changed shape and reared up to block the stars. But her husband had seen it too: the unimaginably huge head, vaster in the deceiving darkness, looming up and up, dwarfing the hills themselves with ambition.

He fell to his knees, babbling a prayer, his arthritic legs twisted beneath him.

His wife screamed: no words she knew could keep this monster at bay—no prayer, no plea, had power over it.

In the cottage, Mick woke and his outstretched arm, twitching with a sudden cramp, wiped the plate and the lamp off the table.

They smashed.

Judd woke.

The screaming outside had stopped. The woman had disappeared from the doorway into the forest. Any tree, any tree at all, was better than this sight. Her husband still let a string of prayers dribble from his slack mouth, as the great leg of the giant rose to take another step—

Boom—

The cottage shook. Plates danced and smashed off the dresser. A clay pipe rolled from the mantelpiece and shattered in the ashes of the hearth.

The lovers knew the noise that sounded in their substance: that earth-thunder.

Mick reached for Judd, and took him by the shoulder.

"You see," he said, his teeth blue-gray in the darkness of the cottage. "See? See?"

There was a kind of hysteria bubbling behind his words. He ran to the door, stumbling over a chair in the dark. Cursing and bruised he staggered out into the night—

Boom—

The thunder was deafening. This time it broke all the windows in the cottage. In the bedroom one of the roof-joists cracked and flung debris downstairs.

Judd joined his lover at the door. The old man was now face down on the ground, his sick and swollen fingers curled, his begging lips pressed to the damp soil.

Mick was looking up, towards the sky. Judd followed his gaze.

There was a place that showed no stars. It was a darkness in the shape of a man, a vast, broad human frame, a colossus that soared up to meet heaven. It was not quite a perfect giant. Its outline was not tidy; it seethed and swarmed.

He seemed broader too, this giant, than any real man. His legs were abnormally thick and stumpy, and his arms were not long. The hands, as they clenched and unclenched, seemed oddly-jointed and over-delicate for its torso.

Then it raised one huge, flat foot and placed it on the earth, taking a stride towards them.

Boom—

The step brought the roof collapsing in on the cottage. Everything that the car-thief had said was true. Popolac was a city and a giant; and it had gone into the hills. . .

Now their eyes were becoming accustomed to the night light. They could see in ever more horrible detail the way this monster was constructed. It was a masterpiece of human engineering: a man made entirely of men. Or rather, a sexless giant, made of men and women and children. All the citizens of Popolac writhed and strained in the body of this flesh-knitted giant, their muscles stretched to breaking point, their bones close to snapping.

They could see how the architects of Popolac had subtly altered the proportions of the human body; how the thing had been made squatter to lower its center of gravity; how its legs had been made elephantine to bear the weight of the torso; how the head was sunk low on the wide shoulders, so that the problems of a weak neck had been minimized.

Despite these malformations, it was horribly lifelike. The bodies that were bound together to make its surface were naked but for their harnesses, so that its surface glistened in the starlight, like one vast human torso. Even the muscles were well copied, though simplified. They could see the way the roped bodies pushed and pulled against each other in solid cords of flesh and bone. They could see the intertwined people that made up the body: the backs like turtles packed together to offer the sweep of the pectorals; the lashed and knotted acrobats at the joints of the arms and the legs alike; rolling and unwinding to articulate the city.

But surely the most amazing sight of all was the face.

Cheeks of bodies; cavernous eye sockets in which heads stared, five bound together for each eyeball; a broad, flat nose and a mouth that opened and closed, as the muscles of the jaw bunched and hollowed rhythmically. And from that mouth, lined with teeth of bald children, the voice of the giant, now only a weak copy of its former powers, spoke a single note of idiot music.

Popolac walked and Popolac sang.

Was there ever a sight in Europe the equal of it?

They watched, Mick and Judd, as it took another step toward them.

The old man had wet his pants. Blubbering and begging, he dragged himself away from the ruined cottage into the surrounding trees, dragging his dead legs after him.

The Englishmen remained where they stood, watching the spectacle as it approached. Neither dread nor horror touched them now, just an awe that rooted them to the spot. They knew this was a sight they could never hope to see again; this was the apex—after this there was only common experience. Better to stay then, though every step brought death nearer, better to stay and see the sight while it was still there to be seen. And if it killed them, this monster, then at least they would have glimpsed a miracle, known this terrible majesty for a brief moment. It seemed a fair exchange.

Popolac was within two steps of the cottage. They could see the complexities of its structure quite clearly. The faces of the citizens were becoming detailed: white, sweat-wet, and content in their weariness. Some hung dead from their harnesses, their legs swinging back and forth like the hanged. Others, children particularly, had ceased to obey their training, and had relaxed their positions, so that the form of the body was degenerating, beginning to seethe with the boils of rebellious cells.

Yet it still walked, each step an incalculable effort of coordination and strength.

Boom—

The step that trod the cottage came sooner than they thought.

Mick saw the leg raised; saw the faces of the people in the shin and ankle and foot—they were as big as he was now—all huge men chosen to take the full weight of this great creation. Many were dead. The bottom of the foot, he could see, was a jigsaw of crushed and bloody bodies, pressed to death under the weight of their fellow citizens.

The foot descended with a roar.

In a matter of seconds the cottage was reduced to splinters and dust.

Popolac blotted the sky utterly. It was, for a moment, the whole world, heaven and earth, its presence filled the senses to overflowing. At this proximity one look could not encompass it, the eye had to range backward and forward over its mass to take it all in, and even then the mind refused to accept the whole truth.

A whirling fragment of stone, flung off from the cottage as it collapsed, struck Judd full in the face. In his head he heard the killing stroke like a ball hitting a wall: a play-yard death. No pain: no remorse. Out like a light, a tiny, insignificant light; his death cry lost in the pandemonium, his body hidden in the smoke and darkness. Mick neither saw nor heard Judd die.

He was too busy staring at the foot as it settled for a moment in the ruins of the cottage, while the other leg mustered the will to move.

Mick took his chance. Howling like a banshee, he ran toward the leg, longing to embrace the monster. He stumbled in the wreckage, and stood again, bloodied, to reach for the foot before it was lifted and he was left behind. There was a clamor of agonized breath as the message came to the foot that it must move; Mick saw the muscles of the shin bunch and marry as the leg began to lift. He made one last lunge at the limb as it began to leave the ground, snatching a harness or a rope, or human hair, or flesh itself—anything to catch this passing miracle and be part of it. Better to go with it wherever it was going, serve it in its purpose, whatever that might be; better to die with it than live without it.

He caught the foot, and found a safe purchase on its ankle. Screaming his sheer ecstasy at his success he felt the great leg raised, and glanced down through the swirling dust to the spot where he had stood, already receding as the limb climbed.

The earth was gone from beneath him. He was a hitchhiker with a god: the mere life he had left was nothing to him now, or ever. He would live with this thing, yes, he would live with it—seeing it and seeing it and eating it with his eyes until he died of sheer gluttony.

He screamed and howled and swung on the ropes, drinking up his triumph. Below, far below, he glimpsed Judd's body, curled up pale on the dark ground, irretrievable. Love and life and sanity were gone, gone like the memory of his name, or his sex, or his ambition.

It all meant nothing. Nothing at all.

Boom—

Boom—

Popolac walked, the noise of its steps receding to the east. Popolac walked, the hum of its voice lost in the night.

After a day, birds came, foxes came, flies, butterflies, wasps came. Judd moved, Judd shifted, Judd gave birth. In his belly maggots warmed themselves, in a vixen's den the good flesh of his thigh was fought over. After that, it was quick. The bones yellowing, the bones crumbling: soon, an empty space which he had once filled with breath and opinions.

Darkness, light, darkness, light. He interrupted neither with his name.

NINE

THE BODY

If the genre we conventionally call "fantasy" has been largely defined by its concern with landscapes (we think of the "world" of these books before we think of the people who populate that world) then the genre we dub "horror" has been about the most intimate landscape of all: the body. The mutability of the flesh has often been the wellspring from which horror fiction has taken its power.

I've tried to reappraise these conventions in my stories. Here are four examples of that reappraisal. One, "Jacqueline Ess: Her Last Will and Testament," is probably a horror story, in that it elicits, at times, a sense of revulsion. But it turns into something altogether stranger by the end, a kind of brutal romance, in which the site of coitus is not simply the genitals, but the entire body. I put beside it a passage from *Imajica* which visits the same territory, but within the context of what is essentially a religious quest novel. Here, the marriage of flesh is more surreal than in "Jacqueline Ess," but there is a similarity of intention. The lovers want to go beyond the limits of the physical: to transgress in pursuit of the ultimate union.

The other two pieces in this chapter are both from *Sacrament*, which is neither a horror novel nor a fantasy novel. It has no invented worlds, and its imagery is seldom horrific. But it does have a character—its hero, Will Rabjohns—whose flesh is protean.

In these scenes we see him first discover the vision that flickers inside him, then he goes out on the town, wearing its skin. Or does he? Is Will a were-fox, or simply a man who turns into an animal when he gets a hard-on (which might be said for many of us)? The book provides no simple answers. It allows the readers plenty of room to inform the text with their own knowledge of what the body is capable of being and becoming.

From *Sacrament*

That night, around eleven or so, he decided to forgo a sleeping pill and go out for a drink. It was Friday, so the streets were alive and kicking, and on the five-minute walk up Sanchez to 16th he met the appreciative eyes of enough guys to be certain he could get lucky tonight if the urge took him. Some of that cockiness was knocked out of him, however, when he stepped into the Gestalt, a bar which according to Jack (whom he'd called for the inside scoop) had opened two months before and was the hot place for the summer. It was filled to near capacity, some of the customers locals here for a casual beer with friends, but many more geared up and wired for the weekend. In the old days there had been certain tribal divisions in the Castro: leather men had their watering-holes, drug aficionados, theirs; the preppie boys had gathered in a different spot than the hustlers; the queens, especially the older guys, would never have been seen in a black bar, or vice versa. Here, however, there were representatives of every one of those clans, and more. Was that a man in a rubber suit, leaning against the bar sipping his bourbon? Yes it was. And the guy waiting his turn at the pool table, his nose pierced and his hair carved in concentric circles, was he the lover of the Latino man in the well-cut suit who was making a beeline for him? To judge by their smiles and kisses, yes. There was even a good proportion of women in the throng; a few, Will thought, straight girls come to ogle the queers with their boyfriends (this was a risky business; any boyfriend who agreed to the trip was probably half-hoping to be gang-banged on the pool table), the rest lesbians (again, of every variation, from the kittenish to the mustached). Though he was a little intimidated at the sheer exuberance of the scene, he was too much of a voyeur to leave. He eased his way through the crowd to the bar, and

371

found a niche at the far end where he had a wide-angle view of the room. Two beers in, and he started to feel a little more mellow. Excepting a few glances cast his way nobody took much notice of him, which was fine, he told himself, just fine. And then, as he was ordering a third beer (his last for the night, he'd decided) somebody stepped up to the bar beside him and said: "I'll have the same. No I won't. I'll have a tequila straight up. And he's paying."

"I am?" said Will, looking around at a man maybe five years his junior, whose present hapless expression he vaguely knew. Narrowed brown eyes watched him under upturned brows, a smile, with dimples, waited in readiness for when Will said—

"Drew?"

"Shit! I shoulda taken the bet. I was with this guy—" He glanced back down the bar at a husky fellow in a leather jacket; the guy waved, obviously chomping at the bit for an invitation to join them. Drew looked back at Will, "He said you wouldn't recognize me after all this time. I said betcha. And you did."

"It took a moment."

"Yeah. Well . . . the hairline's not what it used to be," Drew said. A decade and a half before, when they'd had their fling, Drew had sported a curly clump of golden brown hair that hung over his forehead, its most ambitious curls tickling the bridge of his nose. Now it was gone. "You don't mind?" he said. "The tequila, I mean? I wasn't even sure it was you at first. I mean I heard . . . well, you know what you hear. I don't know half the time what to believe and what not to believe."

"You heard I was dead?"

"Yeah."

"Well," said Will, clinking his beer can against Drew's brimming glass of tequila. "I'm not."

"Good," Drew said, clinking back. "Are you still living in the city?"

"I just returned."

"You bought a house on Sanchez, right?" Their affair had preceded the purchase, and upon its cooling they'd not remained friends. "Still got it?"

"Still got it."

"I dated somebody on Sanchez, and he pointed it out to me. 'That's where the famous photographer lives.'" Drew's eyes widened at the quoted description. "Of course, I didn't know who. Then he told me and I said—"

"Oh, *him*."

"No, I was really proud," Drew said, with sweet sincerity. "I don't keep up with art stuff, you know, so I hadn't really put two and two together. I mean, I knew you took pictures, but I just remembered seals."

Will roared with laughter. "Christ, the seals!"

"You remember? We went to Pier 39 together? I thought we were going to get buzzed and watch the ocean, but you got obsessed with the seals. I was so pissed off." He emptied half his tequila glass in one. "Funny, the things that stick in your head."

"Your buddy's waving at you, by the way," Will said.

"Oh, Lord. It's a sad case. I had one date with him and now every time I come in here he's all over me."

"Do you need to get back to him?"

"Absolutely not. Unless you want to be on your own? I mean, you've got the pick of the crowd here."

"I wish."

"You're still in great shape," Drew said. "I'm kinda running to seed here." He looked down at a belly that was no longer the washboard it had been. "It took me an hour to put these jeans on, and it'll take me twice as long to get 'em off." He glanced up at Will. "Without help, that is," he said. He patted his stomach. "You took some pictures of me, do you remember?"

Will remembered: a sticky afternoon of beefcake and baby oil. Drew had been quite the muscle-boy back then, competition standards, and proud of it. A little too proud perhaps. They'd broken up on Halloween Night, when he'd found Drew stark naked and painted gold from head to foot, standing in the backyard of a house on Hancock like an ithyphallic idol surrounded by devotees.

"Have you still got those pictures?" Drew asked.

"Oh, I'm sure. Somewhere."

"I'd love to see 'em . . . sometime." He shrugged, as though when was of no consequence, though both of them had known two minutes before, when he'd mentioned his jeans, that Will would be helping him out of them tonight.

As they made their way back to the house Will wondered if perhaps he'd made a mistake. Drew kept up a virtually unbroken monologue, none of it particularly enlightening, about his job selling advertising space at the *Chronicle*, about the unwanted attentions of Al, and the adventures of his ineptly neutered cat. A few yards from the door, however, he stopped in midflow and said: "I'm running off at the mouth, aren't I? Sorry. I'm just nervous I guess."

"If it's any comfort," Will said, "so am I."

"Really?" Drew sounded doubtful.

"I haven't had sex with anyone in eight or nine months."

"Jeez," Drew said, plainly relieved. "Well we can just take it real slowly."

They were at the front door. "That's good," Will said, letting them in, "slowly's good."

In the old days sex with Drew had been quite a show; a lot of posing and boasting and wrestling around. Tonight it was mellow. Nothing acrobatic; nothing risky. Little, in fact, beyond the simple pleasure of lying naked together in Will's big bed with the pallid light from the street washing over their bodies, holding and being held. The greed for sensuality Will would once have felt in this situation, the need to exhaustively explore every sensation, seemed very remote. Yes, it was still there; another night, perhaps, another body—one he didn't remember in its finest hour—and perhaps he'd be just as possessed as he'd been in the past. But for tonight, gentle pleasures and modest satisfactions. There was just one moment, as they were undressing, and Drew first saw the scars on Will's body, when the liaison threatened to become something a little headier.

"Oh my, oh my," Drew said, his voice breathy with admiration. "Can I touch them?"

"If you really want to."

Drew did so; not with his fingers but with his lips, tracing the shiny path the bear's claws had left on Will's chest and belly. He went down on his knees in the process, and pressing his face against Will's lower abdomen, said: "I could stay down here all night." He'd slipped his hands behind his back; plainly he was quite ready to have them tied there if it took Will's fancy. Will ran his fingers through the man's hair, half-tempted to play the game. Bind him up; have him kissing scars and calling him sir. But he decided against it.

"Another night," he said, and pulling Drew up and into his arms, escorted him to bed.

He woke to the sound of rain, pattering on the skylight overhead. It was still dark. He glanced at his watch—it was 4:15—then over to Drew, who was lying on his back, snoring slightly. Will wasn't sure what had woken him, but now that he was conscious he decided to get up and empty his bladder. But as he eased out of bed he caught, or thought he caught, a motion in the shadows across the room. He froze. Had somebody broken into the house? Was that what had woken him? He studied the darkness, looking and listening for further signs of an intruder; but now there was nothing. The shadows were empty. He looked back at his bedmate. Drew was wearing a tiny smile in his sleep, and was rubbing his bare belly gently, back and forth. Will watched him for a moment, curiously enraptured. Of all the unlikely people to have broken his sexual fast with, he thought; Drew the muscle-boy, softened by time.

The rain got suddenly heavier, beating a tattoo on the roof. It stirred him to get up and go to the bathroom, a route he could have covered in his sleep. Out through the bedroom door, then first left onto the cold tile; three paces forward, turn to the right and he could piss in certain knowledge his aim was true. He drained his bladder contentedly, then headed back to the bedroom, thinking as he went how good it would feel to slip his arms around Drew.

Then, two paces from the door, he again glimpsed a motion from the corner of his eye. This time he was quick enough to catch sight of the intruder's shadow, as the man made his escape down the stairs.

"*Hey—*" he said, and followed, thinking as he did so that there was something suspiciously playful about what was happening. For some reason he didn't feel in the least threatened by the presence of this trespasser; it was as though he knew already there was no harm here. As he reached the bottom of the stairs, and pursued the shadow back down the hallway toward the file room he realized why: he was dreaming. And what more certain proof of that than the sight awaiting him when he entered the room? There, casually leaning on the windowsill twenty feet from him and silhouetted against the raining glass, was Lord Fox.

"You're naked," the creature remarked.

"So are you," Will observed.

"It's different for animals. We're more comfortable in our skins." He cocked his head. "The scars suit you."

"So I've been told."

"By the fellow in your bed?"

"Yep."

"You can't have him hanging around, you realize that? Not the way things are going. You'll have to get rid of him."

"This is a ridiculous conversation," Will said, turning to go. "I'm heading back to bed." He was already there, of course, and asleep, but even in dream form he didn't want to linger down here chatting with the fox. The animal belonged to another part of his psyche; a part he'd begun to put at a healthier distance tonight, with Drew's compliance.

"Wait a moment," said the fox. "Just take a look at this."

There was a crisp enthusiasm in the animal's words that made Will glance back. There was more light in the room than there'd been moments before, its source not shed from street lamps outside, but from the photographs, his poor consumptives, which were still scattered on the floor where he'd tossed them. Leaving his place at the window Lord Fox stepped between the pictures, coming into the middle of the room. By the strange luminescence the photographs were giving off, Will could see a voluptuous smile upon the animal's face.

"These are worth a moment's study, don't you think?" the fox said.

Will looked. The light that emanated from the photographs was uncertain, and for good reason. The bright, blurred forms in the pictures were *moving*: fluttering, flickering, as though they were being consumed by a slow fire. And in their throes, Will recognized them. A skinned lion, hanging from a tree. A pitiful tent of elephant hide, hanging in rotted scraps over one of the poles of its bones. A tribe of lunatic baboons beating each other's children to death with rocks. Pictures of the corrupted world, no longer fixed and remote, but thrashing and twitching and blazing out into his room.

"Don't you wish they looked like this when people saw them?" the fox said. "Wouldn't it change the world if they could see the horror this way?"

Will glanced up at the fox. "No," he said, "it wouldn't change a thing."

"Even this," the animal said, staring down at a picture that lay between them. It was darker than the others, and at first he couldn't make out the subject.

"What is it?"

"You tell me," the fox said.

Will went down on his haunches and looked at the picture more closely. There was motion in this one too: a deluge of flickering light falling on a form sitting at the center of the picture.

"Patrick?" he murmured.

"Could be," the fox replied. It was Patrick for sure. He was slumped in his chair beside his window, except that somehow the roof had been

stripped off his house and the rain was pouring in, running down over his
head and body, glistening on his forehead and his nose and his lips, which
were drawn back a little, so that his teeth showed. He was dead, Will knew.
Dead in the rain. And the more the deluge beat upon him the more his
flesh bruised and swelled. Will wanted to look away. This wasn't an ape,
this wasn't a lion, it was Patrick, his beloved Patrick. But he'd trained his
eyes too well. They kept looking, like the good witnesses they were, while
Patrick's face smeared beneath the assault of the rain, all trace of who or
even what he'd been steadily erased.

"Oh God . . . ," Will murmured.

"He feels nothing, if that's any comfort," the fox said.

"I don't believe you."

"So look away."

"I can't. It's in my head now." He advanced on the animal, suddenly
enraged. "What the fuck have I done to deserve this?"

"That's the mother of all questions, isn't it?" he said, unperturbed by
Will's rage.

"And?"

The animal shrugged. "God wants you to see. Don't ask me why. That's
between you and God. I'm just the go-between." Flummoxed by this, Will
glanced back down at the picture of Patrick. The body had disappeared,
dissolved in the rain. "Sometimes it's too much for people," the fox went
on, in its matter-of-fact fashion. "God says: *take a look at this*, and people
just lose their sanity. I hope it doesn't happen to you, but there are no
guarantees."

"I don't want to lose him . . . ," Will murmured.

"I can't help you there," the animal replied. "I'm just the messenger."

"Well you tell God from me—" Will started to say.

"*Will?*"

There was another voice behind him. He glanced over his shoulder,
and there was Drew standing in the doorway, with a sheet wrapped around
his middle.

"Who are you talking to?" he said.

Will looked back into the room, and for a moment—though he was
now awake—he thought he glimpsed the animal's silhouette against the
glass. Then the vision was gone, and he was standing naked in the cold,
with Drew coming to drape the sheet over his shoulders.

"You're clammy," Drew said.

He was: running with a sickly sweat. Drew put his arms around Will's chest, locking his hands against his breastbone and laying his head against Will's neck. "Do you often go walkabout in your sleep?"

"Once in a while," Will replied, staring at the littered floor, still half-thinking he might catch a glittering light in one of the pictures. But there was nothing.

"Shall we go back to bed then?" Drew said.

"No, actually I'd prefer to stay up for a while," Will said. He'd had enough dreams for one night. "You go back up. I'm going to make myself some tea."

"I can stay with you, if you want."

"I'm okay," Will told him. "I'll be up in a while."

Drew bequeathed the sheet to Will and headed on upstairs, leaving Will to go brew himself a pot of Earl Grey. He didn't particularly want to revisit the images that had just come to find him, but as he sat sipping his tea he couldn't help but picture the uncanny life his littered photographs had taken on as he dreamed them. It was as though they contained some freight of meaning he'd neglected to see or understand, and had chosen to communicate it to him in his sleep. But what? That death was terrible? He knew that better than most. That Patrick was going to die, and there was nothing Will could do about it? He knew that too. He chewed it over and over, but he couldn't make much sense of the experience. Perhaps he was looking for significance where there was none. How much credence should he be giving a dream that showcased a talking fox claiming to be God's messenger? Probably very little.

And yet, hadn't there been a hairbreadth moment at the end, after Drew had called his name, and he'd woken, when the fox had lingered, as though it were testing the limits of its jurisdiction, ready to trespass where it had no business being?

He returned to bed at last. The rainstorm had passed over the city and the only sound in the room was Drew's peaceful breath. Will slipped between the sheets as delicately as possible so as not to wake him, but somewhere in his slumber, Drew knew his bedmate had come back, because he turned to face Will, his eyes still closed, his breathing even, and found a place against Will's body where they fitted together comfortably. Will was certain he wouldn't sleep, but he did; and deeply. There were no further visits. God and his messenger left him undisturbed for the rest of the night, and when he woke it was to sunlight and kisses.

From *Sacrament*

There was a club on Folsom called the Penitent. At the height of its notoriety in the mid-seventies, it had been called the Serpent's Tooth, and had been to San Francisco what the Mineshaft had been to New York: a club where nothing was *verboten* if it got you hard. On the wild nights, moving down the streets of the Castro, the serious leather crowd had counted off their pleasuredomes on the knuckles of one well-greased fist, and the Tooth had always been one of the five. Chuck and Jean-Pierre, the owners of the club, had long since gone, dying within three weeks of one another in the early years of the plague, and for a time the site had remained untaken, as though in deference to the men who'd played there and passed away. But in 1987 the Sons of Priapus, a group of onanists who'd restored masturbation to the status of a respectable handicraft, had occupied the building for their Monday night circle jerks. The ghosts of the building had smiled on them, it seemed, because word of the atmosphere there soon swelled the number of the Sons. They organized a second weekly gathering, on Thursdays, and then when that become overcrowded, a third. Almost overnight the building had become a paean to the democracy of the palm. An element of the fetishistic gradually crept into the Thursday and Friday assemblies (Monday remained vanilla) and before long the leaders of the Sons had turned into businessmen, leased the building, and were running the most successful sex club in San Francisco. Chuck and Jean-Pierre would have been proud. The Penitent had been born.

The club wasn't particularly busy. Tuesdays were usually slow, and tonight was no exception. But for the thirty or so individuals who were wandering the Penitent's bare-brick halls, or chatting around the juice bar (unlike the back room, this was an alcohol-free party), or idling in the television lounge, watching porno of strictly historical interest, there would be reason to remember tonight.

Just before eleven-thirty, a man appeared in the hallway, whose identity would be described variously by people who later talked about the evening's events. Good-looking, certainly, in a man-who's-seen-the-world kind of way. Hair slicked back or receding, depending on who was telling you the story. Eyes dark and deep set, or invisible behind sunglasses, depending, again, on who was recounting the tale. Nobody really remembered what he was wearing in any detail. (He wasn't naked, as a few of the more exhibitionist patrons were; that was agreed.) Nor was he dressed for casting in any specific scenario. He wasn't a biker or a cowboy, or a hardhat or a cop. He didn't carry a paddle or a whip. Hearing this, a certain kind of listener would inevitably ask: "Well what the hell was he *into?*" to which the storytellers universally replied: *sex.* Well, not universally. The more pretentious may have said *the pleasures of the flesh,* and the cruder said *meat,* but it amounted to the same thing: this man—who within the space of an hour and a half had created a stir so potent it would become local myth inside a day—was an embodiment of the spirit of the Penitent: a creature of pure sensation, ready to take on any partner heated enough to match the fierceness of his desires. In this brave brotherhood, there were only three or four members equal to the challenge, and—not coincidentally—they were the only celebrants that night who said nothing about the experience afterward. They kept their silence and their fantasies intact, leaving the rest to chatter on what they'd seen and heard. In truth, no more than half a dozen people remained purely witnesses. As had happened often in the long ago, but infrequently now, the presence of one unfettered imagination in the crowd had been the signal for general license. Men who had only ever come to the Penitent to watch dared a touch, and more, tonight. Two love affairs began there, and both prospered; four people caught crabs, and one traced his gonorrhea to his loss of control on the stained sofa of the television lounge.

As for the man who'd initiated this orgy, he came several times, and went, leaving the couplings to continue until closing time. Several people claimed he spoke to them, though he said nothing. One claimed they knew him to be a sometime porn star who'd retired from the business and moved to Oregon. He'd returned to his old hunting grounds, this account went, for sentimental reasons, only to vanish again into the wilderness that always claims the sexual professional.

One part of this was certainly true. The man vanished and did not return, though every one of the thirty patrons that night came back, crabs and gonorrhea notwithstanding, within the next few days (most of them the next night) in the hope of seeing him again. When he did not appear, a few then made it their private mission to discover him in some other watering hole, but a man seen by the yellowing light of a dim lamp in a secret place is not easily identified elsewhere. The more they thought about him and talked about him, the less clear the memory of him became, so that a week after the event, no two witnesses could have readily agreed on any of his personal details.

And as for the man himself, he could not remember the events of the night clearly, and thanked God for the fact.

From *Imajica*

As soon as they got back to the flat Jude threw open the windows to let the breeze, which was still balmy though the night had long since fallen, come and go. News from the streets outside came with it, of course, but nothing momentous: the inevitable sirens; chatter from the pavement; jazz from the club down the block. With the windows wide, she sat down on the bed beside Gentle. It was time for them to speak without any other agenda but the truth.

"I didn't think we'd end up this way," she said. "Here, together."

"Are you glad we have?"

"Yes, I'm glad," she said, after a pause. "It feels right."

"Good," he replied. "It feels perfectly natural to me too."

He slid around the back of her and, threading his hands through her hair, began to work his fingers against her scalp. She sighed.

"You like that?" he asked.

"I like that."

"Do you want to tell me how you feel?"

"About what?"

"About me. About us."

"I told you, it feels right."

"That's all?"

"No."

"What else?"

She closed her eyes, the persuasive fingers almost easing the words out of her. "I'm glad you're here because I think we can learn from one another. Maybe even love each other again. How does that sound?"

"Fine by me," he said softly.

"And what about you? What's in your head?"

"That I'd forgotten how strange this Dominion is. That I need your help to make me strong. That I'm afraid I may act strangely sometimes, make mistakes, and I want you to love me enough to forgive me if I do. Will you?"

"You know I will," she said.

"I want you to share my visions, Judith. I want you to see what's shining in me and not be afraid of it."

"I'm not afraid."

"That's good to hear," he said. "That's so very good." He leaned toward her, putting his mouth close to her ear. "We make the rules from now on," he whispered. "And the world follows. Yes? There's no law but us. What we want. What we feel. We'll let that consume us, and the fire'll spread. You'll see."

He kissed the ear into which he'd poured these seductions, then her cheek, and finally her mouth. She started to kiss him back, fervently, putting her hands around his head as he had hers, kneading the flesh from which his hair sprang and feeling its motion against his skull. He had his hands on the neck of her blouse, but he didn't bother to unbutton it. Instead he tore it open, not in a frenzy but rhythmically, rent after rent, like a ritual of uncovering. As soon as her breasts were bare his mouth was on them. Her skin was hot, but his tongue was hotter, painting her with spiral tracks of spittle, then closing his mouth around her nipples until they were harder than the tongue that teased them. His hands were reducing her skirt to tatters in the same efficient way he'd torn open her blouse. She let herself drop back onto the bed, with the rags of blouse and skirt beneath her. He looked down at her, laying his palm at her crotch, which was still protected from his touch by the thin fabric of her underwear.

"How many men have had this?" he asked her, the question murmured without inflection. His head was silhouetted against the pale billows at the window, and she could not read his expression. "How many?" he said, moving the ball of his hand in a circular motion. From any other source but this the question would have offended or even enraged her. But she liked his curiosity.

"A few."

He ran his fingers down into the space between her legs and worked his middle fingers under the fabric to touch her other hole. "And this?" he said, pushing at the place.

She was less comfortable with this inquiry, verbal or digital, but he insisted. "Tell me," he said. "Who's been in here?"

"Just one," she said.

"Godolphin?" he replied.

"Yes."

He removed his finger and rose from the bed. "A family enthusiasm," he remarked.

"Where are you going?"

"Just closing the curtains," he said. "The dark's better for what we're going to do." He drew the drapes without closing the window. "Are you wearing any jewelry?" he asked her.

"Just my earrings."

"Take them off," he said.

"Can't we have a little light?"

"It's too bright as it is," he replied, though she could barely see him. He was watching her as she undressed, that much she knew. He saw her slide her earrings from the holes in her lobes and then take off her underwear. By the time she was completely naked so was he.

"I don't want a little part of you," he said, approaching the bottom of the bed. "I want all of you, every last piece. And I want you to want all of me."

"I do," she said.

"I hope you mean that."

"How can I prove it?"

His gray form seemed to darken as she spoke, receding into the shadows of the room. He'd said he'd be invisible, and now he was. Though she felt his hand graze her ankle, and looked down the bed to find him, he was beyond the grasp of her eye. But pleasure flowed from his touch nevertheless.

"I want this," he said as he caressed her foot. "And this." Now her shin and thigh. "And this"—her sex—"as much as the rest, but no more. And this, and these." Belly, breasts. His touch was on them all, so he had to be very close to her now, but still invisible. "And this sweet throat, and this wonderful head." Now the hands slid away again, down her arms. "And these," he said, "to the ends of your fingers."

The touch was back at her foot again, but everywhere his hands had been—which was to say her entire body—trembled with anticipation at the touch coming again. She raised her head from the pillow a second time in the hope of glimpsing her lover.

"Lie back," he told her.

"I want to see you."

"I'm here," he said, his eyes stealing a gleam from somewhere as he spoke: two bright dots in a space that, had she not known it was bounded, could have been limitless. After his words, there was only his breath. She couldn't help but let the rhythm of her own inhalations and exhalations fall in with his, a lulling regularity which steadily slowed.

After a time, he raised her foot to his mouth and licked the sole from heel to toe in one motion. Then his breath again, cooling the fluid he'd bathed her with, and slowing still further as it came and went, until her system seemed to teeter on termination at the end of each breath, only to be coaxed back into life again as she inhaled. This was the substance of every moment, she realized: the body—never certain if the next lungful would be its last— hovering for a tiny time between cessation and continuance. And in that space out of time, between a breath expelled and another drawn, the mirac-ulous was easy, because neither flesh nor reason had laid their edicts there. She felt his mouth open wide enough to encompass her toes and then, impossible as it was, slide her foot into his throat.

He's going to swallow me, she thought, and the notion conjured once again the book she'd found in Estabrook's study, with its sequence of lovers enclosed in a circle of consumption: a devouring so prodigious it had ended with mutual eclipse. She felt no unease at the prospect. This wasn't the busi-ness of the visible world, where fear got fat because there was so much to win and lose. This was a place for lovers, where there was only ever gain.

She felt him draw her other leg up to his head and immerse it in the same heat; then felt him take hold of her hips and use them as purchase to impale himself upon her, inch by inch. Perhaps he'd become vast: his maw mon-strous, his throat a tunnel; or perhaps she was pliant as silk, and he was draw-ing her into him like a magician threading fake flowers into a wand. She reached up toward him in the darkness, to feel the miracle, but her fingers couldn't interpret what buzzed beneath them. Was this *her* flesh or *his*? Ankle or cheek? There was no way of knowing. Nor, in truth, any need to know. All she wanted now was to do as the lovers in the book had done and match his devouring with her own.

She reached for the edge of the bed and turned herself half over, bringing him down beside her. Now, though her eyes were besotted by darkness, she saw the outline of his body, folded into the shadows of her own. There was nothing changed about his anatomy. Though he was consuming her, his body was in no way distorted. He lay beside her like a sleeper. She reached out to touch him a second time, not expecting to make sense of his body now but finding she could. This was his thigh; this his shin; this his ankle and foot. As she ran her palm across his flesh a delicate wave of change came with it, and his substance seemed to soften beneath her touch. The scent of his sweat was appetizing. It quickened the juices in her throat and belly. She drew her head toward his feet and touched her lips to the substance of him. Then she was feeding; spreading her hunger around him like a mouth and closing her mind on his glistening skin. He shuddered as she took him in, and she felt the thrill of his pleasure as her own. He had already consumed her to the hips, but she quickly matched his appetite, taking his legs down into her, swallowing both his prick and the belly it lay hard against. She loved the excess of this, and its absurdity, their bodies defying physics and physique, or else making fresh proofs of both as the configuration closed upon itself. Was anything ever so easy, and yet so impossible, besides love? And what was this, if not that paradox laid on a sheet? He had slowed his swallows to allow her to catch up, and now, in tandem, they closed the loop of their consumption, until their bodies were figments, and they were mouth to mouth.

Something from outside—a shout in the street, a sour saxophone chord— threw her back into the plausible world again, and she saw the root from which their invention had flowered. It was a commonplace conjunction: her legs crossed around his hips, his erection high inside her. She couldn't see his face, but she knew he wasn't here in this fugitive place with her. He was still dreaming their devouring. She panicked, wanted to regain the vision but not knowing how. She tightened her grip on his body and, in so doing, inspired his hips to motion. He began to move in her, breathing oh so slowly against her face. She forgot her panic and let her rhythm once again slow until it matched his. The solid world dissolved as she did so, and she returned to the place from which she'd been called to find that the loop was tightening by the moment, his mind enveloping her head as she enveloped his, like layers of an impossible onion, each one smaller than the layer it concealed: an enigma that could only exist where substance collapsed into the very mind which begged its being.

This bliss could not be sustained indefinitely, however. Before long it began once more to lose its purity, tainted by further sounds from the outside world, and this time she sensed that he was also relinquishing his hold on the delirium. Perhaps, as they learned to be lovers again, they'd find a way to sustain the state for longer: spend nights and days, perhaps, lost in the precious space between a breath expelled and another drawn. But for now she would have to be content with the ecstasy they'd had. Reluctantly, she let the tropic night in which they'd devoured each other be subsumed into a simpler darkness, and, without quite knowing where consciousness began and ended, she fell asleep.

When she awoke she was alone in the bed. That disappointment apart, she felt both lively and light. What they'd shared was a commodity more marketable than a cure for the common cold: a high without a hangover. She sat up, reaching for a sheet to drape around her, but before she could stand she heard his voice in the predawn gloom. He was standing by the window, with a fold of curtain clipped between middle and forefinger, his eye to the chink he'd opened.

"It's time for me to get working," he said softly.

"It's still early," she said.

"The sun's almost up," he replied. "I can't waste time."

He let the curtain drop and crossed to the bed. She sat up and put her arms around his torso. She wanted to spend time with him, luxuriating in the calm she felt, but his instinct was healthier. They both had work to do.

"I'd rather stay here than return to the studio," he said. "Would you mind?"

"Not at all," she replied. "In fact, I'd like you to stay."

"I'll be coming and going at odd hours."

"As long as you find your way back into bed once in a while," she said.

"I'll be with you," he said, running his hand down from her neck to rub her belly. "From now on, I'll be with you night and day."

From *The Books of Blood, Vol. II*
"Jacqueline Ess: Her Will and Testament"

My God, she thought, this can't be living. Day in, day out: the boredom, the drudgery, the frustration.

My Christ, she prayed, let me out, set me free, crucify me if you must, but put me out of my misery.

In lieu of his euthanasian benediction, she took a blade from Ben's razor, one dull day in late March, locked herself in the bathroom, and slit her wrists.

Through the throbbing in her ears, she faintly heard Ben outside the bathroom door.

"Are you in there, darling?"

"Go away," she thought she said.

"I'm back early, sweetheart. The traffic was light."

"Please go away."

The effort of trying to speak slid her off the toilet seat and on to the white-tiled floor, where pools of her blood were already cooling.

"Darling?"

"Go."

"Darling."

"Away."

"Are you all right?"

Now he was rattling at the door, the rat. Didn't he realize she couldn't open it, wouldn't open it?

"Answer me, Jackie."

She groaned. She couldn't stop herself. The pain wasn't as terrible as she'd expected, but there was an ugly feeling, as though she'd been kicked in the head. Still, he couldn't catch her in time, not now. Not even if he broke the door down.

He broke the door down.

She looked up at him through an air grown so thick with death you could have sliced it.

Too late, she thought she said.

But it wasn't.

My God, she thought, this can't be suicide. I haven't died.

The doctor Ben had hired for her was too perfectly benign. Only the best, he'd promised, only the very best for my Jackie.

"It's nothing," the doctor reassured her, "that we can't put right with a little tinkering."

Why doesn't he just come out with it? she thought. He doesn't give a damn. He doesn't know what it's like.

"I deal with a lot of these women's problems," he confided, fairly oozing a practiced compassion. "It's got to epidemic proportions among a certain age bracket."

She was barely thirty. What was he telling her? That she was prematurely menopausal?

"Depression, partial or total withdrawal, neuroses of every shape and size. You're not alone, believe me."

Oh yes I am, she thought. I'm here in my head, on my own, and you can't know what it's like.

"We'll have you right in two shakes of a lamb's tail."

I'm a lamb, am I? Does he think I'm a lamb?

Musing, he glanced up at his framed qualifications, then at his manicured nails, then at the pens on his desk and notepad. But he didn't look at Jacqueline. Anywhere but at Jacqueline.

"I know," he was saying now, "what you've been through, and it's been traumatic. Women have certain needs. If they go unanswered—"

What would he know about women's needs?

You're not a woman, she thought she thought.

"What?" he said.

Had she spoken? She shook her head: denying speech. He went on; finding his rhythm once more: "I'm not going to put you through interminable therapy sessions. You don't want that, do you? You want a little reassurance, and you want something to help you sleep at nights."

He was irritating her badly now. His condescension was so profound it had no bottom. All-knowing, all-seeing Father; that was his performance. As if he were blessed with some miraculous insight into the nature of a woman's soul.

"Of course, I've tried therapy courses with patients in the past. But between you and me—"

He lightly patted her hand. Father's palm on the back of her hand. She was supposed to be flattered, reassured, maybe even seduced.

"Between you and me it's so much talk. Endless talk. Frankly, what good does it do? We've all got problems. You can't talk them away, can you?"

You're not a woman. You don't look like a woman, you don't feel like a woman—

"Did you say something?"

She shook her head.

"I thought you said something. Please feel free to be honest with me."

She didn't reply, and he seemed to tire of pretending intimacy. He stood up and went to the window.

"I think the best thing for you—"

He stood against the light: darkening the room, obscuring the view of the cherry trees on the lawn through the window. She stared at his wide shoulders, at his narrow hips. A fine figure of a man, as Ben would have called him. No childbearer he. Made to remake the world, a body like that. If not the world, remaking minds would have to do.

"I think the best thing for you—"

What did he know, with his hips, with his shoulders? He was too much a man to understand anything of her.

"I think the best thing for you would be a course of sedatives—"

Now her eyes were on his waist.

"And a holiday."

Her mind had focused now on the body beneath the veneer of his clothes. The muscle, bone and blood beneath the elastic skin. She pictured it from all sides, sizing it up, judging its powers of resistance, then closing on it. She thought:

Be a woman.

Simply, as she thought that preposterous idea, it began to take shape. Not a fairy-tale transformation, unfortunately, his flesh resisted such magic. She willed his manly chest into making breasts of itself and it began to swell most fetchingly, until the skin burst and his sternum flew apart. His pelvis, teased to breaking point, fractured at its center; unbalanced, he toppled over onto his desk and from there stared up at her, his face yellow with shock. He licked his lips, over and over again, to find some wetness to talk with. His mouth was dry: his words were stillborn. It was from between his legs that all the noise was coming; the splashing of his blood; the thud of his bowel on the carpet.

She screamed at the absurd monstrosity she had made, and withdrew to the far corner of the room, where she was sick in the pot of the rubber plant.

My God, she thought, this can't be murder. I didn't so much as touch him.

What Jacqueline had done that afternoon, she kept to herself. No sense in giving people sleepless nights, thinking about such peculiar talent.

The police were very kind. They produced any number of explanations for the sudden departure of Dr. Blandish, though none quite described how his chest had erupted in that extraordinary fashion, making two handsome (if hairy) domes of his pectorals.

It was assumed that some unknown psychotic, strong in his insanity, had broken in, done the deed with hands, hammers and saws, and exited, locking the innocent Jacqueline Ess in an appalled silence no interrogation could hope to penetrate.

Person or persons unknown had clearly dispatched the doctor to where neither sedatives nor therapy could help him.

She almost forgot for a while. But as the months passed it came back to her by degrees, like a memory of a secret adultery. It teased her with its forbidden delights. She forgot the nausea, and remembered the power. She forgot sordidity, and remembered strength. She forgot the guilt that had seized her afterward and longed, longed to do it again.

Only better.

"Jacqueline."

Is this my husband, she thought, actually calling me by my name? Usually it was Jackie, or Jack, or nothing at all.

"Jacqueline."

He was looking at her with those big baby blues of his, like the college boy she'd loved at first sight. But his mouth was harder now, and his kisses tasted like stale bread.

"Jacqueline."

"Yes."

"I've got something I want to speak to you about."

A conversation? she thought. It must be a public holiday.

"I don't know how to tell you this."

"Try me," she suggested.

She knew that she could think his tongue into speaking if it pleased her. Make him tell her what she wanted to hear. Words of love, maybe, if she could remember what they sounded like. But what was the use of that? Better the truth.

"Darling, I've gone off the rails a bit."

"What do you mean?" she said.

Have you, you bastard, she thought.

"It was while you weren't quite yourself. You know, when things had more or less stopped between us. Separate rooms . . . you wanted separate rooms . . . and I just went bananas with frustration. I didn't want to upset you, so I didn't say anything. But it's no use me trying to live two lives."

"You can have an affair if you want to, Ben."

"It's not an affair, Jackie. I love her—"

He was preparing one of his speeches, she could see it gathering momentum behind his teeth. The justifications that became accusations, those excuses that always turned into assaults on her character. Once he got into full flow there'd be no stopping him. She didn't want to hear.

"She's not like you at all, Jackie. She's frivolous in her way. I suppose you'd call her shallow."

It might be worth interrupting here, she thought, before he ties himself in his usual knots.

"She's not moody like you. You know, she's just a normal woman. I don't mean to say you're not normal: you can't help having depressions. But she's not so sensitive."

"There's no need, Ben—"

"No, damn it, I want it all off my chest."

Onto mine, she thought.

"You've never let me explain," he was saying. "You've always given me one of those damn looks of yours, as if you wished I'd—"

Die.

"Wished I'd shut up."

Shut up.

"You don't care how I feel!" He was shouting now. "Always in your own little world."

Shut up, she thought.

His mouth was open. She seemed to wish it closed, and with the thought his jaws snapped together, severing the very tip of his pink tongue. It fell from between his lips and lodged in a fold of his shirt.

Shut up, she thought again.

The two perfect regiments of his teeth ground down into each other, cracking and splitting, nerve, calcium, and spit making a pinkish foam on his chin as his mouth collapsed inward.

Shut up, she was still thinking as his startled baby blues sank back into his skull and his nose wormed its way into his brain.

He was not Ben any longer, he was a man with a red lizard's head, flattening, battening down upon itself, and, thank God, he was past speechmaking once and for all.

Now she had the knack of it, she began to take pleasure in the changes she was willing upon him.

She flipped him head over heels onto the floor and began to compress his arms and legs, telescoping flesh and resistant bone into a smaller and yet smaller space. His clothes were folded inward, and the tissue of his stomach was plucked from his neatly packaged entrails and stretched around his body to wrap him up. His fingers were poking from his shoulder blades now, and his feet, still thrashing with fury, were tipped up in his gut. She turned him over one final time to pressure his spine into a foot-long column of muck, and that was about the end of it.

As she came out of her ecstasy she saw Ben sitting on the floor, shut up into a space about the size of one of his fine leather suitcases, while blood, bile, and lymphatic fluid pulsed weakly from his hushed body.

My God, she thought, this can't be my husband. He's never been as tidy as that.

This time she didn't wait for help. This time she knew what she'd done (guessed, even, how she'd done it) and she accepted her crime for the too-rough justice it was. She packed her bags and left the home.

I'm alive, she thought. For the first time in my whole, wretched life, I'm alive.

Vassi's Testimony: Part One

To you who dream of sweet, strong women I leave this story. It is a promise, as surely as it is a confession, as surely as it's the last words of a lost man who wanted nothing but to love and be loved. I sit here trembling, waiting for the night, waiting for that whining pimp Koos to come to my door again, and take everything I own from me in exchange for the key to her room.

I am not a courageous man, and I never have been: so I'm afraid of what may happen to me tonight. But I cannot go through life dreaming all the time, existing through the darkness on only a glimpse of heaven. Sooner or later, one has to gird one's loins (that's appropriate) and get up and find it. Even if it means giving away the world in exchange.

I probably make no sense. You're thinking, you who chanced on this testimony, you're thinking, who was he, this imbecile?

My name was Oliver Vassi. I am now thirty-eight years old. I was a lawyer, until a year or more ago, when I began the search that ends tonight with that pimp and that key and that holy of holies.

But the story begins more than a year ago. It is many years since Jacqueline Ess first came to me.

She arrived out of the blue at my offices, claiming to be the widow of a friend of mine from law school, one Benjamin Ess, and when I thought back, I remembered the face. A mutual friend who'd been at the wedding had shown me a photograph of Ben and his blushing bride. And here she was, every bit as elusive a beauty as her photograph promised.

I remember being acutely embarrassed at that first interview. She'd arrived at a busy time, and I was up to my neck in work. But I was so enthralled by her, I let all the day's interviews fall by the wayside, and when my secretary came in she gave me one of her steely glances as if to throw a bucket of cold water over me. I suppose I was enamored from the start, and she sensed the electric atmosphere in my office. Me, I pretended I was merely being polite to the widow of an old friend. I didn't like to think about passion: it wasn't a part of my nature, or so I thought. How little we know—I mean *really* know—about our capabilities.

Jacqueline told me lies at that first meeting. About how Ben had died of cancer, of how often he had spoken of me, and how fondly. I suppose she could have told me the truth then and there, and I would have lapped it up—I believe I was utterly devoted from the beginning.

But it's difficult to remember quite how and when interest in another human being flares into something more committed, more passionate. It may be that I am inventing the impact she had on me at that first meeting, simply reinventing history to justify my later excesses. I'm not sure. Anyway, wherever and whenever it happened, however quickly or slowly, I succumbed to her, and the affair began.

I'm not a particularly inquisitive man where my friends, or my bed partners, are concerned. As a lawyer one spends one's time going through the dirt of other people's lives, and frankly, eight hours a day of that is quite enough for me. When I'm out of the office my pleasure is in letting people be. I don't pry. I don't dig, I just take them at face value.

Jacqueline was no exception to this rule. She was a woman I was glad to have in my life whatever the truth of her past. She possessed a marvelous sangfroid, she was witty, bawdy, oblique. I had never met a more enchanting woman. It was none of my business how she'd lived with Ben, what the marriage had been like, etc., etc. That was her history. I was happy to live in the present, and let the past die its own death. I think I even flattered myself that whatever pain she had experienced, I could help her forget it.

Certainly her stories had holes in them. As a lawyer, I was trained to be eagle-eyed where fabrications were concerned, and however much I tried to put my perceptions aside I sensed that she wasn't quite coming clean with me. But everyone has secrets: I knew that. Let her have hers, I thought.

Only once did I challenge her on a detail of her pretended life story. In talking about Ben's death, she let slip that he had got what he deserved. I asked her what she meant. She smiled, that Gioconda smile of hers, and told me that she felt there was a balance to be redressed between men and women. I let the observation pass. After all, I was obsessed by that time, past all hope of salvation; whatever argument she was putting, I was happy to concede it.

She was so beautiful, you see. Not in any two-dimensional sense: she wasn't young, she wasn't innocent, she didn't have that pristine symmetry so favored by ad men and photographers. Her face was plainly that of a woman in her early forties: it had been used to laugh and cry, and usage leaves its marks. But she had a power to transform herself, in the subtlest way, making that face as various as the sky. Early on, I thought it was a makeup trick. But as we slept together more and more, and I watched her in the mornings, sleep in her eyes, and in the evenings, heavy with fatigue, I soon realized she wore nothing on her skull but flesh and blood. What transformed her was internal: it was a trick of the will.

And, you know, that made me love her all the more.

Then one night I woke with her sleeping beside me. We slept often on the floor, which she preferred to the bed. Beds, she said, reminded her of marriage. Anyway, that night she was lying under a quilt on the carpet of my room, and I, simply out of adoration, was watching her face in sleep.

If one has given oneself utterly, watching the beloved sleep can be a vile experience. Perhaps some of you have known that paralysis, staring down at features closed to your inquiry, locked away from you where you can never, ever go, into the other's mind. As I say, for us who have given ourselves, that is a horror. One knows, in those moments, that one does not exist, except in relation to that face, that personality. Therefore, when that face is closed down, that personality is lost in its own unknowable world, one feels completely without purpose. A planet without a sun, revolving in darkness.

That's how I felt that night, looking down at her extraordinary features, and as I chewed on my soullessness, her face began to alter. She was clearly dreaming; but what dreams must she have been having. Her very fabric was on the move, her muscle, her hair, the down on her cheek moving to the dictates of some internal tide. Her lips bloomed from her bone, boiling up into a slavering tower of skin: her hair swirled around her head as though she were lying in water; the substance of her cheeks formed furrows and ridges like the ritual scars on a warrior; inflamed and throbbing patterns of tissue, swelling up and changing again even as a pattern formed. This fluxion was a terror to me, and I must have made some noise. She didn't wake, but came a little closer to the surface of sleep, leaving the deeper waters where these powers were sourced. The patterns sank away in an instant, and her face was again that of a gently sleeping woman.

That was, you can understand, a pivotal experience, even though I spent the next few days trying to convince myself that I hadn't seen it.

The effort was useless. I knew there was something wrong with her; and at that time I was certain she knew nothing about it. I was convinced that something in her system was awry, and that it was best to investigate her history before I told her what I had seen.

On reflection, of course, that seems laughably naïve. To think she wouldn't have known that she contained such a power. But it was easier for me to picture her as prey to such skill, than as mistress of it. That's a man speaking of a woman; not just me, Oliver Vassi, of her, Jacqueline Ess. We cannot believe, we men, that power will ever reside happily in the body of a woman, unless that power is a male child. Not true power. The power must be in male hands, God-given. That's what our fathers tell us, idiots that they are.

Anyway, I investigated Jacqueline, as surreptitiously as I could. I had a contact in York, where she had lived with Ben, and it wasn't difficult to get some inquiries moving. It took a week for my contact to get back to me, because he'd had to cut through a good deal of shit from the police to get a hint of the truth, but the news came, and it was bad.

Ben was dead, that much was true. But there was no way he had died of cancer. My contact had only got the vaguest clues as to the condition of Ben's corpse, but he gathered it had been spectacularly mutilated. And the prime suspect? My beloved Jacqueline Ess. The same innocent woman who was occupying my flat, sleeping by my side every night.

So I put it to her that she was hiding something from me. I don't know what I was expecting in return. What I got was a demonstration of her power. She gave it freely, without malice, but I would have been a fool not to have read a warning into it. She told me first how she had discovered her unique control over the sum and substance of human beings. In her despair, she said, when she was on the verge of killing herself, she had found, in the very deep-water trenches of her nature, faculties she had never known existed. Powers which came up out of those regions as she recovered, like fish to the light.

Then she showed me the smallest measure of these powers, plucking hairs from my head, one by one. Only a dozen; just to demonstrate her formidable skills. I felt them going. She just said: one from behind your ear, and I'd feel my skin creep and then jump as fingers of her volition snatched a hair out. Then another, and another. It was an incredible display; she had this power down to a fine art, locating and withdrawing single hairs from my scalp with the precision of tweezers.

Frankly, I was sitting there rigid with fear, knowing that she was just toying with me. Sooner or later, I was certain the time would be right for her to silence me permanently.

But she had doubts about herself. She told me how the skill, though she had honed it, scared her. She needed, she said, someone to teach her how to use it best. And I was not that somebody. I was just a man who loved her, who had loved her before this revelation, and would love her still, in spite of it.

In fact, after that display I quickly came to accommodate a new vision of Jacqueline. Instead of fearing her, I became more devoted to this woman who tolerated my possession of her body.

My work became an irritation, a distraction that came between me and thinking of my beloved. What reputation I had began to deteriorate; I lost briefs, I lost credibility. In the space of two or three months my professional life dwindled away to almost nothing. Friends despaired of me, colleagues avoided me.

It wasn't that she was feeding on me. I want to be clear about that. She was no lamia, no succubus. What happened to me, my fall from grace with ordinary life if you like, was of my own making. She didn't bewitch me; that's a romantic lie to excuse rape. She was a sea: and I had to swim in her. Does that make any sense? I'd lived my life on the shore, in the solid world of law, and I was tired of it. She was liquid; a boundless sea in a single body, a deluge in a small room, and I will gladly drown in her, if she grants me the chance. But that was my decision. Understand that. This has always been my decision. I have decided to go to the room tonight, and be with her one final time. That is of my own free will.

And what man would not? She was (is) sublime.

For a month after that demonstration of power I lived in a permanent ecstasy of her. When I was with her she showed me ways to love beyond the limits of any other creature on God's earth. I say beyond the limits: with her there were no limits. And when I was away from her the reverie continued: because she seemed to have changed my world.

Then she left me.

I knew why: she'd gone to find someone to teach her how to use her strength. But understanding her reasons made it no easier.

I broke down: lost my job, lost my identity, lost the few friends I had left in the world. I scarcely noticed. They were minor losses, beside the loss of Jacqueline. . . .

"Jacqueline."

My God, she thought, can this really be the most influential man in the country? He looked so unprepossessing, so very unspectacular. His chin wasn't even strong.

But Titus Pettifer was power.

He ran more monopolies than he could count; his word in the financial world could break companies like sticks, destroying the ambitions of hundreds, the careers of thousands. Fortunes were made overnight in his shadow, entire corporations fell when he blew on them, casualties of his whim. This man knew power if any man knew it. He had to be learned from.

"You wouldn't mind if I called you J., would you?"

"No."

"Have you been waiting long?"

"Long enough."

"I don't normally leave beautiful women waiting."

"Yes you do."

She knew him already: two minutes in his presence was enough to find his measure. He would come quickest to her if she was quietly insolent.

"Do you always call women you've never met before by their initials?"

"It's convenient for filing; do you mind?"

"It depends."

"On what?"

"What I get in return for giving you the privilege."

"It's a privilege, is it, to know your name?"

"Yes."

"Well . . . I'm flattered. Unless of course you grant that privilege widely?"

She shook her head. No, he could see she wasn't profligate with her affections.

"Why have you waited so long to see me?" he said. "Why have I had reports of your wearing my secretaries down with your constant demands to meet with me? Do you want money? Because if you do you'll go away empty-handed. I became rich by being mean, and the richer I get, the meaner I become."

The remark was truth; he spoke it plainly.

"I don't want money," she said, equally plainly.

"That's refreshing."

"There's richer than you."

He raised his eyebrows in surprise. She could bite, this beauty.

"True," he said. There were at least half a dozen richer men in the hemisphere.

"I'm not an adoring little nobody. I haven't come here to screw a name. I've come here because we can be together. We have a great deal to offer each other."

"Such as?" he said.

"I have my body."

He smiled. It was the straightest offer he'd heard in years.

"And what do I offer you in return for such largesse?"

"I want to learn—"

"Learn?"

"How to use power."

She was stranger and stranger, this one.

"What do you mean?" he replied, playing for time. He hadn't got the measure of her; she vexed him, confounded him.

"Shall I recite it for you again, in bourgeois?" she said, playing insolence with such a smile he almost felt attractive again.

"No need. You want to learn to use power. I suppose I could teach you—"

"I know you can."

"You realize I'm a married man. Virginia and I have been together eighteen years."

"You have three sons, four houses, a maid-servant called Mirabelle. You loathe New York, and you love Bangkok; your shirt collar is $16^1/_2$, your favorite color green."

"Turquoise."

"You're getting subtler in your old age."

"I'm not old."

"Eighteen years a married man. It ages you prematurely."

"Not me."

"Prove it."

"How?"

"Take me."

"What?"

"Take me."

"Here?"

"Draw the blinds, lock the door, turn off the computer terminus, and take me. I dare you."

"Dare?"

How long was it since anyone had *dared* him to do anything?

"Dare?"

He was excited. He hadn't been so excited in a dozen years. He drew the blinds, locked the door, turned off the video display of his fortunes.

My God, she thought, I've got him.

It wasn't an easy passion, not like that with Vassi. For one thing, Pettifer was a clumsy, uncultured lover. For another, he was too nervous of his wife to be a wholly successful adulterer. He thought he saw Virginia everywhere: in the lobbies of the hotels they took a room in for the afternoon, in cabs cruising the street outside their rendezvous, once even (he swore the likeness was exact) dressed as a waitress, and swabbing down a table in a restaurant. All fictional fears, but they dampened the spontaneity of the romance somewhat.

Still, she was learning from him. He was as brilliant a potentate as he was inept a lover. She learned how to be powerful without exercising power, how to keep one's self uncontaminated by the foulness all charisma stirs up in the uncharismatic; how to make the plain decisions plainly; how to be merciless. Not that she needed much education in that particular quarter. Perhaps it was more truthful to say he taught her never to regret her lack of instinctive compassion, but to judge with her intellect alone who deserved extinction and who might be numbered among the righteous.

Not once did she show herself to him, though she used her skills in the most secret of ways to tease pleasure out of his stale nerves.

In the fourth week of their affair they were lying side by side in a lilac room, while the midafternoon traffic growled in the street below. It had been a bad bout of sex; he was nervous, and no tricks would coax him out of himself. It was over quickly, almost without heat.

He was going to tell her something. She knew it: it was waiting, this revelation, somewhere at the back of his throat. Turning to him she massaged his temples with her mind, and soothed him into speech.

He was about to spoil the day.

He was about to spoil his career.

He was about, God help him, to spoil his life.

"I have to stop seeing you," he said.

He wouldn't dare, she thought.

"I'm not sure what I know about you, or rather, what I *think* I know about you, but it makes me . . . cautious of you, J. Do you understand?"

"No."

"I'm afraid I suspect you of . . . crimes."

"Crimes?"

"You have a history."

"Who's been rooting?" she asked. "Surely not Virginia?"

"No, not Virginia, she's beyond curiosity."

"Who then?"

"It's not your business."

"Who?"

She pressed lightly on his temples. It hurt him and he winced.

"What's wrong?" she asked.

"My head's aching."

"Tension, that's all, just tension. I can take it away, Titus." She touched her finger to his forehead, relaxing her hold on him. He sighed as relief came.

"Is that better?"

"Yes."

"Who's been snooping, Titus?"

"I have a personal secretary. Lyndon. You've heard me speak of him. He knew about our relationship from the beginning. Indeed, he books the hotels, arranges my cover stories for Virginia."

There was a sort of boyishness in this speech that was rather touching. As though he was embarrassed to leave her, rather than heartbroken. "Lyndon's quite a miracle worker. He's maneuvered a lot of things to make it easier between us. So he's got nothing against you. It's just that he happened to see one of the photographs I took of you. I gave them to him to shred."

"Why?"

"I shouldn't have taken them; it was a mistake. Virginia might have. . . ."

He paused, began again. "Anyhow, he recognized you, although he couldn't remember where he'd seen you before."

"But he remembered eventually."

"He used to work for one of my newspapers, as a gossip columnist. That's how he came to be my personal assistant. He remembered you from your previous incarnation, as it were. Jacqueline Ess, the wife of Benjamin Ess, deceased."

"Deceased."

"He brought me some other photographs, not as pretty as the ones of you."

"Photographs of what?"

"Your home. And the body of your husband. They said it was a body, though in God's name there was precious little human being left in it."

"There was precious little to start with," she said simply, thinking of Ben's cold eyes, and colder hands. Fit only to be shut up, and forgotten.

"What happened?"

"To Ben? He was killed."

"How?" Did his voice waver a little?

"Very easily." She had risen from the bed, and was standing by the window. Strong summer light carved its way through the slates of the blind, ridges of shadow and sunlight charting the contours of her face.

"You did it."

"Yes." He had taught her to be plain. "Yes, I did it."

He had taught her an economy of threat too. "Leave me, and I'll do the same again."

He shook his head. "Never. You wouldn't dare."

He was standing in front of her now.

"We must understand each other, J. I am powerful and I am pure. Do you see? My public face isn't even touched by a glimmer of scandal. I could afford a mistress, a dozen mistresses, to be revealed. But a murderess? No, that would spoil my life."

"Is he blackmailing you? This Lyndon?"

He stared at the day through the blinds, with a crippled look on his face. There was a twitch in the nerves of his cheek, under his left eye.

"Yes, if you must know," he said in a dead voice. "The bastard has me for all I'm worth."

"I see."

"And if he can guess, so can others. You understand?"

"I'm strong: you're strong. We can twist them around our little fingers."

"No."

"Yes! I have skills, Titus."

"I don't want to know."

"You *will* know," she said.

She looked at him, taking hold of his hands without touching him. He watched, all astonished eyes, as his unwilling hands were raised to touch her face, to stroke her hair with the fondest of gestures. She made him run his trembling fingers across her breasts, taking them with more ardor than he could summon on his own initiative.

"You are always too tentative, Titus," she said, making him paw her almost to the point of bruising. "This is how I like it." Now his hands were lower, fetching out a different look from her face. Tides were moving over it, she was all alive —

"Deeper —"

His finger intruded, his thumb stroked.

"I like that, Titus. Why can't you do that to me without me demanding?"

He blushed. He didn't like to talk about what they did together. She coaxed him deeper, whispering.

"I won't break, you know. Virginia may be Dresden china, I'm not. I want feeling; I want something that I can remember you by when I'm not with you. Nothing is everlasting, is it? But I want something to keep me warm through the night."

He was sinking to his knees, his hands kept, by her design, on her and in her, still roving like two lustful crabs. His body was awash with sweat. It was, she thought, the first time she'd ever seen him sweat.

"Don't kill me," he whimpered.

"I could wipe you out." Wipe, she thought, then put the image out of her mind before she did him some harm.

"I know. I know," he said. "You can kill me easily."

He was crying. My God, she thought, the great man is at my feet, sobbing like a baby. What can I learn of power from this puerile performance? She plucked the tears off his cheeks, using rather more strength than the task required. His skin reddened under her gaze.

"Let me be, J. I can't help you. I'm useless to you."

It was true. He was absolutely useless. Contemptuously, she let his hands go. They fell limply by his sides.

"Don't ever try and find me, Titus. You understand? Don't ever send your minions after me to preserve your reputation, because I will be more merciless than you've ever been."

He said nothing; just knelt there, facing the window, while she washed her face, drank the coffee they'd ordered, and left.

Lyndon was surprised to find the door of his office ajar. It was only 7:36. None of the secretaries would be in for another hour. Clearly one of the cleaners had been remiss, leaving the door unlocked. He'd find out who: sack her.

He pushed the door open.

Jacqueline was sitting with her back to the door. He recognized the back of her head, that fall of auburn hair. A sluttish display; too teased, too wild. His office, an annex to Mr. Pettifer's, was kept meticulously ordered. He glanced over it: everything seemed to be in place.

"What are you doing here?"

She took a little breath, preparing herself.

This was the first time she had planned to do it. Before it had been a spur-of-the-moment decision.

He was approaching the desk, and putting down his briefcase and his neatly folded copy of the *Financial Times*.

"You have no right to come in here without my permission," he said.

She turned on the lazy swivel of his chair; the way he did when he had people in to discipline.

"Lyndon," she said.

"Nothing you can say or do will change the facts, Mrs. Ess," he said, saving her the trouble of introducing the subject, "you are a cold-blooded killer. It was my bounden duty to inform Mr. Pettifer of the situation."

"You did it for the good of Titus?"

"Of course."

"And the blackmail, that was also for the good of Titus, was it?"

"Get out of my office—"

"Was it, Lyndon?"

"You're a whore! Whores know nothing: they are ignorant, diseased animals," he spat. "Oh, you're cunning, I grant you that—but then so's any slut with a living to make."

She stood up. He expected a riposte. He got none; at least not verbally. But he felt a tautness across his face: as though someone was pressing on it.

"What . . . are . . . you . . . doing?" he asked.

"Doing?"

His eyes were being forced into slits like a child imitating a monstrous Oriental, his mouth was hauled wide and tight, his smile brilliant. The words were difficult to say—

"Stop . . . it . . . "

She shook her head.

"Whore . . . ," he said again, still defying her.

She just stared at him. His face was beginning to jerk and twitch under the pressure, the muscles going into spasm.

"The police . . . ," he tried to say, "if you lay a finger on me . . ."

"I won't," she said, and pressed home her advantage.

Beneath his clothes he felt the same tension all over his body, pulling his skin, drawing him tighter and tighter. Something was going to give; he knew it. Some part of him would be weak, and tear under this relentless assault. And if he once began to break open, nothing would prevent her ripping him apart. He worked all this out quite coolly, while his body twitched and he swore at her through his enforced grin.

"Cunt," he said. "Syphilitic cunt."

He didn't seem to be afraid, she thought.

In extremis he just unleashed so much hatred of her, the fear was entirely eclipsed. Now he was calling her a whore again; though his face was distorted almost beyond recognition.

And then he began to split.

The tear began at the bridge of his nose and ran up, across his brow, and down, bisecting his lips and his chin, then his neck and chest. In a matter of seconds his shirt was dyed red, his dark suit darkening further, his cuffs and trouser legs pouring blood. The skin flew off his hands like gloves off a surgeon, and two rings of scarlet tissue lolled down to either side of his flayed face like the ears of an elephant.

His name-calling had stopped.

He had been dead of shock now for ten seconds, though she was still working him over vengefully, tugging his skin off his body and flinging the scraps around the room, until at last he stood, steaming, in his red suit, and his red shirt, and his shiny red shoes, and looked, to her eyes, a little more like a sensitive man. Content with the effect, she released him. He lay down quietly in a blood puddle and slept.

My God, she thought, as she calmly took the stairs out the back way, that was murder in the first degree.

She saw no reports of the death in any of the papers, and nothing on the news bulletins. Lyndon had apparently died as he had lived, hidden from public view.

But she knew wheels, so big their hubs could not be seen by insignificant individuals like herself, would be moving. What they would do, how they would change her life, she could only guess at. But the murder of Lyndon had not simply been spite, though that had been a part of it. No, she'd also wanted to stir them up, her enemies in the world, and bring them after her. Let them show their hands: let them show their contempt, their terror. She'd gone through her life, it seemed, looking for a sign of herself, only able to define her nature by the look in others' eyes. Now she wanted an end to that. It was time to deal with her pursuers.

Surely now everyone who had seen her, Pettifer first, then Vassi, would come after her, and she would close their eyes permanently: make them forgetful of her. Only then, the witnesses destroyed, would she be free.

Pettifer didn't come, of course, not in person. It was easy for him to find agents, men without scruple or compassion, but with a nose for pursuit that would shame a bloodhound.

A trap was being laid for her, though she couldn't yet see its jaws. There were signs of it everywhere. An eruption of birds from behind a wall, a peculiar light from a distant window, footsteps, whistles, dark-suited men reading the news at the limit of her vision. As the weeks passed they didn't come any closer to her, but then neither did they go away. They waited, like cats in a tree, their tails twitching, their eyes lazy.

But the pursuit had Pettifer's mark. She'd learned enough from him to recognize his circumspection and his guile. They would come for her eventually, not in her time, but in theirs. Perhaps not even in theirs: in his. And though she never saw his face, it was as though Titus was on her heels personally.

My God, she thought, I'm in danger of my life and I don't care.

It was useless, this power over flesh, if it had no direction behind it. She had used it for her own petty reasons, for the gratification of nervous pleasure and sheer anger. But these displays hadn't brought her any closer to other people: they just made her a freak in their eyes.

Sometimes she thought of Vassi, and wondered where he was, what he was doing. He hadn't been a strong man, but he'd had a little passion in his soul. More than Ben, more than Pettifer, certainly more than Lyndon. And, she remembered, fondly, he was the only man she'd ever known who called her Jacqueline. All the rest had manufactured unendearing corruptions of her name: Jackie, or J., or, in Ben's more irritating moods, Ju-ju. Only Vassi had called her Jacqueline, plain and simple, accepting, in his formal way, the completeness of her, the totality of her. And when she thought of him, tried to picture how he might return to her, she feared for him.

Vassi's Testimony: Part Two

Of course I searched for her. It's only when you've lost someone, you realize the nonsense of that phrase "it's a small world." It isn't. It's a vast, devouring world, especially if you're alone.

When I was a lawyer, locked in that incestuous coterie, I used to see the same faces day after day. Some I'd exchange words with, some smiles, some nods. We belonged, even if we were enemies at the bar, to the same complacent circle. We ate at the same tables, we drank elbow to elbow. We even shared mistresses, though we didn't always know it at the time. In such circumstances, it's easy to believe the world means you no harm. Certainly you grow older, but then so does everyone else. You even believe, in your self-satisfied way, that the passage of years makes you a little wiser. Life is bearable; even the 3 A.M. sweats come more infrequently as the bank balance swells.

But to think that the world is harmless is to lie to yourself, to believe in so-called certainties that are, in fact, simply shared delusions.

When she left, all the delusions fell away, and all the lies I had assiduously lived by became strikingly apparent.

It's not a small world, when there's only one face in it you can bear to look upon, and that face is lost somewhere in a maelstrom. It's not a small world when the few, vital memories of your object of affection are in danger of being trampled out by the thousands of moments that assail you every day, like children tugging at you, demanding your sole attention.

I was a broken man.

I would find myself (there's an apt phrase) sleeping in tiny bedrooms in forlorn hotels, drinking more often than eating, and writing her name, like a classic obsessive, over and over again. On the walls, on the pillow, on the palm of my hand. I broke the skin of my palm with my pen, and the ink infected it. The mark's still there, I'm looking at it now. Jacqueline it says. Jacqueline.

Then one day, entirely by chance, I saw her. It sounds melodramatic, but I thought I was going to die at that moment. I'd imagined her for so long, keyed myself up for seeing her again, that when it happened I felt my limbs weaken, and I was sick in the middle of the street. Not a classic reunion. The lover, on seeing his beloved, throws up down his shirt. But then, nothing that happened between Jacqueline and myself was ever quite normal. Or natural.

I followed her, which was difficult. There were crowds, and she was walking fast. I didn't know whether to call out her name or not. I decided not. What would she have done anyway, seeing this unshaven lunatic shambling toward her, calling her name? She would have run probably. Or worse, she would have reached into my chest, seizing my heart in her will, and put me out of my misery before I could reveal her to the world.

So I was silent, and simply followed her, doggedly, to what I assumed was her apartment. And I stayed there, or in the vicinity, for the next two and a half days, not quite knowing what to do. It was a ridiculous dilemma. After all this time of watching for her, now that she was within speaking distance, touching distance, I didn't dare approach.

Maybe I feared death. But then, here I am, in this stinking room in Amsterdam, setting my testimony down and waiting for Koos to bring me her key, and I don't fear death now. Probably it was my vanity that prevented me from approaching her. I didn't want her to see me cracked and desolate; I wanted to come to her clean, her dream lover.

While I waited, they came for her.

I don't know who they were. Two men, plainly dressed. I don't think policemen: too smooth. Cultured even. And she didn't resist. She went smilingly, as if to the opera.

At the first opportunity I returned to the building a little better dressed, located her apartment from the porter, and broke in. She had been living plainly. In one corner of the room she had set up a table, and had been writing her memoirs. I sat down and read, and eventually took the pages away with me. She had got no further than the first seven years of her life. I wondered, again in my vanity, if I would have been chronicled in the book. Probably not.

I took some of her clothes too; only items she had worn when I had known her. And nothing intimate: I'm not a fetishist. I wasn't going to go home and bury my face in the smell of her underwear. But I wanted something to remember her by; to picture her in. Though on reflection I never met a human being more fitted to dress purely in her skin.

So I lost her a second time, more the fault of my own cowardice than circumstance.

Pettifer didn't come near the house they were keeping Mrs. Ess in for four weeks. She was given more or less everything she asked for, except her freedom, and she only asked for that in the most abstracted fashion. She wasn't interested in escape: though it would have been easy to achieve. Once or twice she wondered if Titus had told the two men and the woman who were keeping her a prisoner in the house exactly what she was capable of: she guessed not. They treated her as though she were simply a woman Titus had set eyes on and desired. They had procured her for his bed, simple as that.

With a room to herself, and an endless supply of paper, she began to write her memoirs again, from the beginning.

It was late summer, and the nights were getting chilly. Sometimes, to warm herself, she would lie on the floor (she'd asked them to remove the bed) and will her body to ripple like the surface of a lake. Her body, without sex, became a mystery to her again; and she realized for the first time that physical love had been an exploration of that most intimate, and yet most unknown region of her being: her flesh. She had understood herself best embracing someone else: seen her own substance clearly only when another's lips were laid on it, adoring and gentle. She thought of Vassi again; and the lake, at the thought of him, was roused as if by a tempest. Her breasts shook into curling mountains, her belly ran with extraordinary tides, currents crossed and recrossed her flickering face, lapping at her mouth and leaving their mark like waves on sand. As she was fluid in his memory, so as she remembered him, she liquefied.

She thought of the few times she had been at peace in her life; and physical love, discharging ambition and vanity, had always preceded those fragile moments. There were other ways presumably; but her experience had been limited. Her mother had always said that women, being more at peace with themselves than men, needed fewer distractions from their hurts. But she'd not found it like that at all. She'd found her life full of hurts, but almost empty of ways to salve them.

She left off writing her memoirs when she reached her ninth year. She despaired of telling her story from that point on, with the first realization of oncoming puberty. She burned the papers on a bonfire she lit in the middle of her room the day that Pettifer arrived.

My God, she thought, this can't be power.

Pettifer looked sick; as physically changed as a friend she'd lost to cancer. One month seemingly healthy, the next sucked up from the inside, self-devoured. He looked like a husk of a man: his skin gray and mottled. Only his eyes glittered, and those like the eyes of a mad dog.

He was dressed immaculately, as though for a wedding.

"J."

"Titus."

He looked her up and down.

"Are you well?"

"Thank you, yes."

"They give you everything you ask for?"

"Perfect hosts."

"You haven't resisted."

"Resisted?"

"Being here. Locked up. I was prepared, after Lyndon, for another slaughter of the innocents."

"Lyndon was not innocent, Titus. These people are. You didn't tell them."

"I didn't deem it necessary. May I close the door?"

He was her captor: but he came like an emissary to the camp of a greater power. She liked the way he was with her, cowed but elated. He closed the door, and locked it.

"I love you, J. And I fear you. In fact, I think I love you because I fear you. Is that a sickness?"

"I would have thought so."

"Yes, so would I."

"Why did you take such a time to come?"

"I had to put my affairs in order. Otherwise there would have been chaos. When I was gone."

"You're leaving?"

He looked into her, the muscles of his face ruffled by anticipation.

"I hope so."

"Where to?"

Still she didn't guess what had brought him to the house, his affairs neatened, his wife unknowingly asked forgiveness of as she slept, all channels of escape closed, all contradictions laid to rest.

Still she didn't guess he'd come to die.

"I'm reduced by you, J. Reduced to nothing. And there is nowhere for me to go. Do you follow?"

"No."

"I cannot live without you," he said. The cliché was unpardonable. Could he not have found a better way to say it? She almost laughed, it was so trite.

But he hadn't finished.

"And I certainly can't live *with* you." Abruptly, the tone changed. "Because you revolt me, woman, your whole being disgusts me."

"So?" she asked, softly.

"So . . ." He was tender again and she began to understand. "Kill me.'

It was grotesque. The glittering eyes were steady on her.

"It's what I want," he said. "Believe me, it's all I want in the world. Kill me, however you please. I'll go without resistance, without complaint."

She remembered the old joke. Masochist to Sadist: Hurt me! For God's sake, hurt me! Sadist to Masochist: No.

"And if I refuse?" she said.

"You can't refuse. I'm loathsome."

"But I don't hate you, Titus."

"You should. I'm weak. I'm useless to you. I taught you nothing."

"You taught me a great deal. I can control myself now."

"Lyndon's death was controlled, was it?"

"Certainly."

"It looked a little excessive to me."

"He got everything he deserved."

"Give me what I deserve, then, in my turn. I've locked you up. I've rejected you when you needed me. Punish me for it."

"I survived."

"J!"

Even in this extremity he couldn't call her by her full name.

"Please to God. Please to God. I need only this one thing from you. Do it out of whatever motive you have in you. Compassion, or contempt, or love. But do it, please do it."

"No," she said.

He crossed the room suddenly, and slapped her, very hard.

"Lyndon said you were a whore. He was right; you are. Gutterslut, nothing better."

He walked away, turned, walked back, hit her again, faster, harder, and again, six or seven times, backward and forward.

Then he stopped, panting.

"You want money?" Bargains now. Blows, then bargains.

She was seeing him twisted through tears of shock, which she was unable to prevent.

"Do you want money?" he said again.

"What do you think?"

He didn't hear her sarcasm, and began to scatter notes around her feet, dozens and dozens of them, like offerings around the Statue of the Virgin.

"Anything you want," he said, "*Jacqueline.*"

In her belly she felt something close to pain as the urge to kill him found birth, but she resisted it. It was playing into his hands, becoming the instrument of his will: powerless. Usage again; that's all she ever got. She had been bred like a cow, to give a certain supply. Of care to husbands, of milk to babies, of death to old men. And, like a cow, she was expected to be compliant with every demand made of her, whenever the call came. Well, not this time.

She went to the door.

"Where are you going?"

She reached for the key.

"Your death is your own business, not mine," she said.

He ran at her before she could unlock the door, and the blow—in its force, in its malice—was totally unexpected.

"Bitch!" he shrieked, a hail of blows coming fast upon the first.

In her stomach, the thing that wanted to kill grew a little larger.

He had his fingers tangled in her hair, and pulled her back into the room, shouting obscenities at her, an endless stream of them, as though he'd opened a dam full of sewer water on her. This was just another way for him to get what he wanted, she told herself, if you succumb to this you've lost: he's just manipulating you. Still the words came: the same dirty words that had been thrown at generations of unsubmissive women. Whore; heretic; cunt; bitch; monster.

Yes, she was that.

Yes, she thought: monster I am.

The thought made it easy. She turned. He knew what she intended even before she looked at him. He dropped his hands from her head. Her anger was already in her throat, coming out of her—crossing the air between them.

Monster he calls me: monster I am.

I do this for myself, not for him. Never for him. For myself!

He gasped as her will touched him, and the glittering eyes stopped glittering for a moment, the will to die became the will to survive, all too late of course, and he roared. She heard answering shouts, steps, threats on the stairs. They would be in the room in a matter of moments.

"You are an animal," she said.

"No," he said, certain even now that his place was in command.

"You don't exist," she said, advancing on him. "They'll never find the part that was Titus. Titus is gone. The rest is just—"

The pain was terrible. It stopped even a voice coming out from him. Or was that her again, changing his throat, his palate, his very head? She was unlocking the plates of his skull, and reorganizing him.

No, he wanted to say, this isn't the subtle ritual I had planned. I wanted to die folded into you, I wanted to go with my mouth clamped to yours, cooling in you as I died. This is not the way I want it.

No. No. No.

They were at the door, the men who'd kept her here, beating on it. She had no fear of them, of course, except that they might spoil her handiwork before the final touches were added to it.

Someone was hurling himself at the door now. Wood splintered: the door was flung open. The two men were both armed. They pointed their weapons at her, steady-handed.

"Mr. Pettifer?" said the younger man. In the corner of the room, under the table, Pettifer's eyes shone.

"Mr. Pettifer?" he said again, forgetting the woman.

Pettifer shook his snouted head. Don't come any closer, please, he thought.

The man crouched down and stared under the table at the disgusting beast that was squatting there; bloody from its transformation, but alive. She had killed his nerves: he felt no pain. He just survived, his hands knotted into paws, his legs scooped up around his back, knees broken so he had the look of a four-legged crab, his brain exposed, his eyes lidless, lower jaw broken and swept up over his top jaw like a bulldog, ears torn off, spine snapped, humanity bewitched into another state.

"You are an animal," she'd said. It wasn't a bad facsimile of beasthood.

The man with the gun gagged as he recognized fragments of his master. He stood up, greasy-chinned, and glanced around at the woman.

Jacqueline shrugged.

"You did this?" Awe mingled with the revulsion.

She nodded.

"Come, Titus," she said, clicking her fingers.

The beast shook its head, sobbing.

"Come, Titus," she said more forcefully, and Titus Pettifer waddled out of his hiding place, leaving a trail like a punctured meat sack.

The man fired at Pettifer's remains out of sheer instinct. Anything, anything at all to prevent this disgusting creature from approaching him.

Titus stumbled two steps back on his bloody paws, shook himself as if to dislodge the death in him, and failing, died.

"Content?" she asked.

The gunman looked up from the execution. Was the power talking to him? No; Jacqueline was staring at Pettifer's corpse, asking the question of him.

Content?

The gunman dropped his weapon. The other man did the same.

"How did this happen?" asked the man at the door. A simple question: a child's question.

"He asked," said Jacqueline. "It was all I could give him."

The gunman nodded, and fell to his knees.

Vassi's Testimony: Final Part

Chance has played a worryingly large part in my romance with Jacqueline Ess. Sometimes it's seemed I've been subject to every tide that passes through the world, spun around by the merest flick of accident's wrist. Other times I've had the suspicion that she was masterminding my life, as she was the lives of a hundred others, a thousand others, arranging every fluke meeting, choreographing my victories and my defeats, escorting me, blindly, toward this last encounter.

I found her without knowing I'd found her, that was the irony of it. I'd traced her first to a house in Surrey, a house that had a year previous seen the murder of one Titus Pettifer, a billionaire shot by one of his own bodyguards. In the upstairs room, where the murder had taken place, all was serenity. If she had been there, they had removed any sign. But the house, now in virtual ruin, was prey to all manner of graffiti; and on the stained plaster wall of that room someone had scrawled a woman. She was obscenely overendowed, her gaping sex blazing with what looked like lightning. And at her feet there was a creature of indeterminate species. Perhaps a crab, perhaps a dog, perhaps even a man. Whatever it was it had no power over itself. It sat in the light of her agonizing presence and counted itself among the fortunate. Looking at that wizened creature, with its eyes turned up to gaze on the burning Madonna, I knew the picture was a portrait of Jacqueline.

I don't know how long I stood looking at the graffiti, but I was interrupted by a man who looked to be in a worse condition than me. A beard that had never been trimmed or washed, a frame so wasted I wondered how he managed to stand upright, and a smell that would not have shamed a skunk.

I never knew his name: but he was, he told me, the maker of the picture on the wall. It was easy to believe that. His desperation, his hunger, his confusion were all marks of a man who had seen Jacqueline.

If I was rough in my interrogation of him I'm sure he forgave me. It was an unburdening for him, to tell everything he'd seen the day that Pettifer had been killed, and know that I believed it all. He told me his fellow bodyguard, the man who had fired the shots that had killed Pettifer, had committed suicide in prison.

His life, he said, was meaningless. She had destroyed it. I gave him what reassurances I could; that she meant no harm, and that he needn't fear that she would come for him. When I told him that, he cried, more, I think, out of loss than relief.

Finally I asked him if he knew where Jacqueline was now. I'd left that question to the end, though it had been the most pressing inquiry, because I suppose I didn't dare hope he'd know. But my God, he did. She had not left the house immediately after the shooting of Pettifer. She had sat down with this man, and talked to him quietly about his children, his tailor, his car. She'd asked him what his mother had been like, and he'd told her his mother had been a prostitute. Had she been happy? Jacqueline had asked. He'd said he didn't know. Did she ever cry? she'd asked. He'd said he never saw her laugh or cry in his life. And she'd nodded, and thanked him.

Later, before his suicide, the other gunman had told him Jacqueline had gone to Amsterdam. This he knew for a fact, from a man called Koos. And so the circle begins to close, yes?

I was in Amsterdam seven weeks, without finding a single clue to her whereabouts, until yesterday evening. Seven weeks of celibacy, which is unusual for me. Listless with frustration I went down to the red-light district, to find a woman. They sit there you know, in the windows, like mannequins, beside pink-fringed lamps. Some have miniature dogs on their laps; some read. Most just stare out at the street, as if mesmerized.

There were no faces there that interested me. They all seemed joyless, lightless, too much unlike her. Yet I couldn't leave. I was like a fat boy in a sweet shop, too nauseous to buy, too gluttonous to go.

Toward the middle of the night, I was spoken to out of the crowd by a young man who, on closer inspection, was not young at all, but heavily made up. He had no eyebrows, just pencil marks drawn on to his shiny skin. A cluster of gold earrings in his left ear, a half-eaten peach in his white-gloved hand, open sandals, lacquered toenails. He took hold of my sleeve, proprietorially.

I must have sneered at his sickening appearance, but he didn't seem at all upset by my contempt. You look like a man of discernment, he said. I looked nothing of the kind: you must be mistaken, I said. No, he replied, I am not mistaken. You are Oliver Vassi.

My first thought, absurdly, was that he intended to kill me. I tried to pull away; his grip on my cuff was relentless.

You want a woman, he said. Did I hesitate enough for him to know I meant yes, though I said no? I have a woman like no other, he went on, she's a miracle. I know you'll want to meet her in the flesh.

What made me know it was Jacqueline he was talking about? Perhaps the fact that he had known me from out of the crowd, as though she was up at a window somewhere, ordering her admirers to be brought to her like a diner ordering lobster from a tank. Perhaps too the way his eyes shone at me, meeting mine without fear because fear, like rapture, he felt only in the presence of one creature on God's cruel earth. Could I not also see myself reflected in his perilous look? He knew Jacqueline, I had no doubt of it.

He knew I was hooked, because once I hesitated he turned away from me with a mincing shrug, as if to say: you missed your chance. Where is she? I said, seizing his twig-thin arm. He cocked his head down the street and I followed him, suddenly as witless as an idiot, out of the throng. The road emptied as we walked; the red lights gave way to gloom, and then to darkness. If I asked him where we were going once I asked him a dozen times; he chose not to answer, until we reached a narrow door in a narrow house down some razor-thin street. We're here, he announced, as though the hovel were the Palace of Versailles.

Up two flights in the otherwise empty house there was a room with a black door. He pressed me to it. It was locked.

"See," he invited, "she's inside."

"It's locked," I replied. My heart was fit to burst: she was near, for certain, I knew she was near.

"See," he said again, and pointed to a tiny hole in the panel of the door. I devoured the light through it, pushing my eye toward her through the tiny hole.

The squalid interior was empty, except for a mattress and Jacqueline. She lay spread-eagled, her wrists and ankles bound to rough posts set in the bare floor at the four corners of the mattress.

"Who did this?" I demanded, not taking my eye from her nakedness.

"She asks," he replied. "It is her desire. She asks."

She had heard my voice; she cranked up her head with some difficulty and stared directly at the door. When she looked at me all the hairs rose on my head, I swear it, in welcome, and swayed at her command.

"Oliver," she said.

"Jacqueline." I pressed the word to the wood with a kiss.

Her body was seething, her shaved sex opening and closing like some exquisite plant, purple and lilac and rose.

"Let me in," I said to Koos.

"You will not survive one night with her."

"Let me in."

"She is expensive," he warned.

"How much do you want?"

"Everything you have. The shirt off your back, your money, your jewelry; then she is yours."

I wanted to beat the door down, or break his nicotine-stained fingers one by one until he gave me the key. He knew what I was thinking.

"The key is hidden," he said, "and the door is strong. You must pay, Mr. Vassi. You want to pay."

It was true. I wanted to pay.

"You want to give me all you have ever owned, all you have ever been. You want to go to her with nothing to claim you back. I know this. It's how they all go to her."

"All? Are there many?"

"She is insatiable," he said, without relish. It wasn't a pimp's boast: it was his pain, I saw that clearly. "I am always finding more for her, and burying them."

Burying them.

That, I suppose, is Koos's function; he disposes of the dead. And he will get his lacquered hands on me after tonight; he will fetch me off her when I am dry and useless to her, and find some pit, some canal, some furnace to lose me in. The thought isn't particularly attractive.

Yet here I am with all the money I could raise from selling my few remaining possessions on the table in front of me, my dignity gone, my life hanging on a thread, waiting for a pimp and a key.

It's well dark now, and he's late. But I think he is obliged to come. Not for the money, he probably has few requirements beyond his heroin and his mascara. He will come to do business with me because she demands it and he is in thrall to her, every bit as much as I am. Oh, he will come. Of course he will come.

Well, I think that is sufficient.

This is my testimony. I have no time to reread it now. His footsteps are on the stairs (he limps) and I must go with him. This I leave to whoever finds it, to use as they think fit. By morning I shall be dead, and happy. Believe it.

My God, she thought, *Koos has cheated me*.

Vassi had been outside the door, she'd felt his flesh with her mind and she'd embraced it. But Koos hadn't let him in, despite her explicit orders. Of all men, Vassi was to be allowed free access, Koos knew that. But he'd cheated her, the way they'd all cheated her except Vassi. With him (perhaps) it had been love.

She lay on the bed through the night, never sleeping. She seldom slept now for more than a few minutes: and only then with Koos watching her. She'd done herself harm in her sleep, mutilating herself without knowing it, waking up bleeding and screaming with every limb sprouting needles she'd made out of her own skin and muscle, like a flesh cactus.

It was dark again, she guessed, but it was difficult to be sure. In this heavily curtained, bare-bulb-lit room, it was perpetual day to the senses, perpetual night to the soul. She would lie, bedsores on her back, on her buttocks, listening to the far sounds of the street, sometimes dozing for a while, sometimes eating from Koos's hand, being washed, being toileted, being used.

A key turned in the lock. She strained from the mattress to see who it was. The door was opening . . . opening . . . opened.

Vassi. Oh God, it was Vassi at last, she could see him crossing the room toward her.

Let this not be another memory, she prayed, please let it be him this time: true and real.

"Jacqueline."

He said the name of her flesh, the whole name.

"Jacqueline." It *was* him.

Behind him, Koos stared between her legs, fascinated by the dance of her labia.

"Koo . . . ," she said, trying to smile.

"I brought him," he grinned at her, not looking away from her sex.

"A day," she whispered. "I waited a day, Koos. You made me wait—"

"What's a day to you?" he said, still grinning.

She didn't need the pimp any longer, not that he knew that. In his innocence he thought Vassi was just another man she'd seduced along the way; to be drained and discarded like the others. Koos believed he would be needed tomorrow; that's why he played this fatal game so artlessly.

"Lock the door," she suggested to him. "Stay if you like."

"Stay?" he said, leering. "You mean, and watch?"

He watched anyway. She knew he watched through that hole he had bored in the door; she could hear him pant sometimes. But this time, let him stay forever.

Carefully, he took the key from the outside of the door, closed it, slipped the key into the inside, and locked it. Even as the lock clicked she killed him, before he could even turn round and look at her again. Nothing spectacular in the execution; she just reached into his pigeon chest and crushed his lungs. He slumped against the door and slid down, smearing his face across the wood.

Vassi didn't even turn round to see him die; she was all he ever wanted to look at again.

He approached the mattress, crouched, and began to untie her ankles. The skin was chafed, the rope scabby with old blood. He worked at the knots systematically, finding a calm he thought he'd lost, a simple contentment in being here at the end, unable to go back, and knowing that the path ahead was deep in her.

When her ankles were free, he began on her wrists, interrupting her view of the ceiling as he bent over her. His voice was soft.

"Why did you let him do this to you?"

"I was afraid."

"Of what?"

"To move; even to live. Every day, agony."

"Yes."

He understood so well that total incapacity to exist.

She felt him at her side, undressing, then laying a kiss on the sallow skin of the stomach of the body she occupied. It was marked with her workings; the skin had been stretched beyond its tolerance and was permanently criss-crossed.

He lay down beside her, and the feel of his body against hers was not unpleasant.

She touched his head. Her joints were stiff, the movements painful, but she wanted to draw his face up to hers. He came, smiling, into her sight, and they exchanged kisses.

My God, she thought, we are together.

And thinking they were together, her will was made flesh. Under his lips her features dissolved, becoming the red sea he'd dreamed of, and washing up over his face, that was itself dissolving: common waters made of thought and bone.

Her keen breasts pricked him like arrows; his erection, sharpened by her thought, killed her in return with his only thrust. Tangled in a wash of love they thought themselves extinguished, and were.

Outside, the hard world mourned on, the chatter of buyers and sellers continuing through the night. Eventually indifference and fatigue claimed even the eagerest merchant. Inside and out there was a healing silence: an end to losses and to gains.

TEN

WORLDS

Sometimes a list can be almost enough. Thus, in this chapter you'll find: some observations on the Western Isles; on Yzordderrex; an incident in a shanty town on the outskirts of Patashoqua; some descriptions of the Patashoquan Highway; of Mai-ké, Iahmandhas, and L'Himby; the glories of Gamut Street; the star-crossed lovers Howie and Jo-Beth, swept to the Ephemeris; Joe and Noah on the shores of Quiddity; and later, a theory advanced by Carasophia concerning the distance between Sapas Humana and the dream-sea; b'Kether Sabbat, a city in defiance of gravity; Cal Mooney in the Weaveworld, encountering Boaz and Ganza; and a performance of poems in the orchard of Lemuel Lo.

Many of the names contained in these passages are of course invented. But I learned many years ago, from Blake and from Lord Dunsany (a now scarcely published writer of fantastic fragments), that there is something marvelous about inventing words. If they have the right music they can do more to enchant a reader in the space of a few syllables than paragraphs of poetic prose.

From *Sacrament*

There were among the Western Isles places of great historical and mythological significance; where battles had been fought and princes hid, and stories made that haunted listeners still. Tiree was not among them. The island had not passed an entirely uneventful life; but it had been at best a footnote to events that flowered in their full splendor in other places.

There was no more obvious example of this than the exploits of St. Columba, who had in his time carried the Gospel throughout the Hebrides, founding seats of devotion and learning on a number of islands. Tiree was not thus blessed, however. The good man had lingered on the island only long enough to curse a rock in Gott Bay for the sin of letting his boat's mooring rope slip. It would be henceforth barren, he declared. The rock was dubbed *Mallachdaig*, or Little Cursed One, and no seaweed had grown on it since. Columba's associate, St. Brendan, had been in a more benign mood during his fleeting visit, and had blessed a hill, but if the blessing had conferred some inspirational power on the place nobody had noticed: there had been no revelations or spontaneous healings on the spot. The third of these visiting mystics, St. Kenneth, had caused a chapel to be built in the dunes near the township of Kilkenneth, which had been so named in the hope of persuading him to linger. The ruse had failed. Kenneth had gone on to greater things, and the dunes—more persuaded by wind than metaphysics—had subsequently buried the chapel.

There were a handful of stories through which St. Columba and his gang did not wander, all of which remained part of the anecdotal landscape, but most of them were dispiritingly domestic in scale. A well on the side of Beinn Hough, for instance, called *Tobar nan naoi beo*, the Well of

423

the Nine Living, because it had miraculously supplied a widow and her eight homeless children with a lifetime's supply of shellfish. A pool close to the shore at Vaul where the ghost of a girl who had drowned in its depths could be seen on moonless nights, singing a lonely lullaby to lure living souls into the water with her. In short, nothing out of the ordinary; islands half the size of Tiree boasted legends far more ambitious.

But there was a numinosity here none of the rest of the Isles possessed, and at its heart a phenomenon which would have turned St. Columba from a gentle meditative into a wild-eyed prophet had he witnessed it. In fact, this wonderment had not yet come to pass when the saint had hop-scotched through the islands, but even if it had he would most likely have been denied sight of it, for those few islanders who had glimpsed the mira-cle (and presently living they numbered eight) never mentioned the sub-ject, not even to those they loved. This was the great secret of their lives, a thing unseen, yet more certain than the sun, and they were not about to dilute its enchantment by speaking of it. In fact, many of them limited their own contemplation of what they'd sensed, for fear of exhausting its power to enrapture them. Some, it was true, returned to the place where they'd been touched in the hope of a second revelation, and though none of them saw anything on their return visits, many were granted a certainty that kept them content for the rest of their lives: they left the place with the conviction that what they had failed to see had *seen them*. They were no longer frail mortals, who would live their lives and pass away. The power on the hill at Kenavara had witnessed them, and in that witnessing had drawn them into an immortal dance.

For it lived in the island's very being, this power; it moved in sand and pasture and sea and wind, and the souls it saw became part of these eter-nals, imperishable. Once witnessed, what did a man or woman have to fear? Nothing, except perhaps the discomforts that attended death. Once their corporeal selves were shed, however, they moved where the power moved, and witnessed as it witnessed, glory on glory. When on summer nights the Borealis drooped its color on the stratosphere, they would be there. When the whales came to breach in exaltation, they would rise, too. They would be with the kittiwakes and the hares and with every star that trembled on Loch an Eilein. It was in all things, this power. In the sandy pastures adjoining the dunes (or the *machair* as it was called in Gaelic); and in the richer, damper fields of the island's midst, where the grass was lush and the cattle grazed themselves creamy.

It did not much concern itself with the griefs and travails of those men and women who never saw it, but it kept a tally of their comings and goings. It knew who was buried in the churchyards at Kirkapol and Vaul; it knew how many babies were born each year. It even watched the visitors, in a casual fashion, not because they were as interesting as whales or kitti-wakes, they weren't, but because there might be among them some soul who would do it harm. This was not beyond the bounds of possibility. It had been witnessing long enough to have seen stars disappear from the heavens. It was not more permanent than they.

From *Imajica*

Until the rise of Yzordderrex, a rise engineered by the Autarch for reasons more political than geographical, the city of Patashoqua, which lay on the edge of the Fourth Dominion, close to where the In Ovo marked the perimeter of the Reconciled worlds, had just claim to be the preeminent city of the Dominions. Its proud inhabitants called it *casje au casje*, simply meaning the hive of hives, a place of intense and fruitful labor. Its proximity to the Fifth made it particularly prone to influences from that source, and even after Yzordderrex had become the center of power across the Dominions it was to Patashoqua that those at the cutting edge of style and invention looked for the coming thing. Patashoqua had a variation on the motor vehicle in its streets long before Yzordderrex. It had rock and roll in its clubs long before Yzordderrex. It had hamburgers, cin-emas, blue jeans, and countless other proofs of modernity long before the great city of the Second. Nor was it simply the trivialities of fashion that Patashoqua reinvented from Fifth Dominion models. It was philosophies and belief systems. Indeed, it was said in Patashoqua that you knew a native of Yzordderrex because he looked like you did yesterday and believed what you'd believed the day before.

As with most cities in love with the modern, however, Patashoqua had deeply conservative roots. Whereas Yzordderrex was a sinful city, notorious for the excesses of its darker Kesparates, the streets of Patashoqua were quiet after nightfall, its occupants in their own beds with their own spouses, plotting vogues. This mingling of chic and conservatism was nowhere more apparent than in architecture. Built as it was in a temperate

region, unlike the semitropical Yzordderrex, the buildings did not have to
be designed with any climatic extreme in mind. They were either ele-
gantly classical, and built to remain standing until Doomsday, or else
functions of some current craze, and likely to be demolished within a
week.

But it was on the borders of the city where the most extraordinary sights
were to be seen, because it was here that a second, parasitical city had
been created, peopled by inhabitants of the Four Dominions who had fled
persecution and had looked to Patashoqua as a place where liberty of
thought and action were still possible. How much longer this would
remain the case was a debate that dominated every social gathering in the
city. The Autarch had moved against other towns, cities, and states which
he and his councils judged hotbeds of revolutionary thought. Some of
those cities had been razed; others had come under Yzordderrexian edict
and all sign of independent thought had been crushed. The university city
of Hezoir, for instance, had been reduced to rubble, the brains of its students literally scooped out of their skulls and heaped up in the streets. In
the Azzimulto the inhabitants of an entire province had been decimated,
so rumor went, by a disease introduced into that region by the Autarch's
representatives. There were tales of atrocities from so many sources that
people became almost blasé about the newest horror, until, of course,
somebody asked how long it would be until the Autarch turned his unforgiving eyes on the hive of hives. Then their faces drained of color, and
people talked in whispers of how they planned to escape or defend themselves if that day ever came; and they looked around at their exquisite city,
built to stand until Doomsday, and wondered just how near that day was.

Walking through the narrow spaces between the shanties was like passing
through a country in which the very air had evolutionary ambition, and to
breathe was to change. A hundred kinds of eye gazed out at them from
doorways and windows, while a hundred forms of limb got about the business of the day—cooking, nursing, crafting, conniving, making fires and
deals and love—and all glimpsed so briefly that after a few paces Gentle
was obliged to look away, to study the muddy gutter they were walking in,
lest his mind be overwhelmed by the sheer profusion of sights. Smells, too:
aromatic, sickly, sour and sweet; and sounds that made his skull shake and
his gut quiver.

There had been nothing in his life to date, either waking or sleeping, to prepare him for this. He'd studied the masterworks of great imaginers—he'd painted a passable Goya, once, and sold an Ensor for a little fortune—but the difference between paint and reality was vast, a gap whose scale he could not by definition have known until now, when he had around him the other half of the equation. This wasn't an invented place, its inhabitants variations on experienced phenomena. It was independent of his terms of reference: a place unto and of itself.

When he looked up again, daring the assault of the strange, he was grateful that he and Pie were now in a quarter occupied by more human entities, though even here there were surprises. What seemed to be a three-legged child skipped across their path only to look back with a face wizened as a desert corpse, its third leg a tail. A woman sitting in a doorway, her hair being combed by her consort, drew her robes around her as Gentle looked her way, but not fast enough to conceal the fact that a second consort, with the skin of a herring and an eye that ran all the way around its skull, was kneeling in front of her, inscribing hieroglyphics on her belly with the sharpened heel of its hand. He heard a range of tongues being spoken, but English seemed to be the commonest parlance, albeit heavily accented or corrupted by the labial anatomy of the speaker. Some seemed to sing their speech; some almost to vomit it up.

But the voice that called to them from one of the crowded alleyways off to their right might have been heard on any street in London: a lisping, pompous holler demanding they halt in their tracks. They looked in its direction. The throng had divided to allow the speaker and his party of three easy passage.

"Play dumb," Pie muttered to Gentle as the lisper, an overfed gargoyle, bald but for an absurd wreath of oiled kiss curls, approached.

He was finely dressed, his high black boots polished and his canary yellow jacket densely embroidered after what Gentle would come to know as the present Patashoquan fashion. A man much less showily garbed followed, an eye covered by a patch that trailed the tail feathers of a scarlet bird as if echoing the moment of his mutilation. On his shoulders he carried a woman in black, with silvery scales for skin and a cane in her tiny hands with which she tapped her mount's head to speed him on his way. Still farther behind came the oddest of the four.

"A Nullianac," Gentle heard Pie murmur.

He didn't need to ask if this was good news or bad. The creature was its own best advertisement, and it was selling harm. Its head resembled nothing so much as praying hands, the thumbs leading and tipped with lobster's eyes, the gap between the palms wide enough for the sky to be seen through it, but flickering, as arcs of energy passed from side to side. It was without question the ugliest living thing Gentle had ever seen. If Pie had not suggested they obey the edict and halt, Gentle would have taken to his heels there and then, rather than let the Nullianac get one stride closer to them.

The lisper had halted and now addressed them afresh. "What business have you in Vanaeph?" he wanted to know.

"We're just passing through," Pie said, a reply somewhat lacking in invention, Gentle thought.

"Who are you?" the man demanded.

"Who are *you*?" Gentle returned.

The patch-eyed mount guffawed and got his head slapped for his troubles.

"Loitus Hammeryock," the lisper replied.

"My name's Zacharias," Gentle said, "and this is—"

"Casanova," Pie said, which earned him a quizzical glance from Gentle.

"Zooical!" the woman said. "D'yee speakat te gloss?"

"Sure," said Gentle. "I speakat te gloss."

"Be careful," Pie whispered at his side.

"Bone! Bone!" the woman went on, and proceeded to tell them, in a language which was two parts English, or a variant thereof, one part Latin, and one part some Fourth Dominion dialect that consisted of tongue clicks and teeth tappings, that all strangers to this town, Neo Vanaeph, had to register their origins and intentions before they were allowed access: or, indeed, the right to depart. For all its ramshackle appearance, Vanaeph was no lawless stew, it appeared, but a tightly policed township, and this woman—who introduced herself in this flurry of lexicons as Pontiff Farrow—was a significant authority here.

When she'd finished, Gentle cast a confounded look in Pie's direction. This was proving more difficult terrain by the moment. Unconcealed in the Pontiff's speech was threat of summary execution if they failed to answer their inquiries satisfactorily. The executioner among this party was not hard to spot: he of the prayerful head—the Nullianac—waiting in the rear for his instructions.

"So," said Hammeryock. "We need some identification."

"I don't have any," Gentle said.

"And you?" he asked the mystif, which also shook its head.

"Spies," the Pontiff hissed.

"No, we're just . . . tourists," Gentle said.

"Tourists?" said Hammeryock.

"We've come to see the sights of Patashoqua." He turned to Pie for support. "Whatever they are."

"The tombs of the Vehement Loki Lobb," Pie said, clearly scratching around for the glories Patashoqua had to offer, "and the Merrow Ti' Ti'."

That sounded pretty to Gentle's ears. He faked a broad smile of enthusiasm. "The Merrow Ti' Ti'!" he said. "Absolutely! I wouldn't miss the Merrow Ti' Ti' for all the tea in China."

"*China?*" said Hammeryock.

"Did I say China?"

"You did."

"Fifth Dominion," the Pontiff muttered. "Spiatits from the Fifth Dominion."

"I object strongly to that accusation," said Pie 'oh' pah.

"And so," said a voice behind the accused, "do I."

Both Pie and Gentle turned to take in the sight of a scabrous, bearded individual, dressed in what might generously have been described as motley and less generously as rags, standing on one leg and scraping shit off the heel of his other foot with a stick.

"It's the hypocrisy that turns my stomach. Hammeryock," he said, his expression a maze of wiles. "You two pontificate," he went on, eyeing his pun's target as he spoke, "about keeping the streets free from undesirables, but you do nothing about the dog shite!"

"This isn't your business, Tick Raw," Hammeryock said.

"Oh, but it is. These are my friends, and you've insulted them with your slurs and your suspicions."

"Friends, sayat?" the Pontiff murmured.

"Yes, ma'am. Friends. Some of us still know the difference between conversation and diatribe. I have friends, with whom I talk and exchange ideas. Remember *ideas*? They're what make life worth living."

Hammeryock could not disguise his unease, hearing his mistress thus addressed, but whoever Tick Raw was he wielded sufficient authority to silence any further objection.

"My dearlings," he said to Gentle and Pie, "shall we repair to my home?"

As a parting gesture he lobbed the stick in Hammeryock's direction. It landed in the mud between the man's legs.

"Clean up, Loitus," Tick Raw said. "We don't want the Autarch's heel sliding in shite, now, do we?"

The two parties then went their separate ways, Tick Raw leading Pie and Gentle off through the labyrinth.

"We want to thank you," Gentle said.

"What for?" Tick Raw asked him, aiming a kick at a goat that wandered across his path.

"Talking us out of trouble," Gentle replied. "We'll be on our way now."

"But you've got to come back with me," Tick Raw said.

"There's no need."

"Need? There's *every* need! Have I got this right?" he said to Pie. "Is there need or isn't there?"

"We'd certainly like the benefit of your insights," Pie said. "We're strangers here. Both of us." The mystif spoke in an oddly stilted fashion, as if it wanted to say more, but couldn't. "We need reeducating," it said.

"Oh?" said Tick Raw. "Really?"

"Who is this Autarch?" Gentle asked.

"He rules the Reconciled Dominions, from Yzordderrex. He's the greatest power in the Imajica."

"And he's coming here?"

"That's the rumor. He's losing his grip in the Fourth, and he knows it. So he's decided to put in a personal appearance. Officially, he's visiting Patashoqua, but this is where the trouble's brewing."

"Do you think he'll definitely come?" Pie asked.

"If he doesn't, the whole of the Imajica's going to know he's afraid to show his face. Of course that's always been a part of his fascination, hasn't it? All these years he's ruled the Dominions without anybody really knowing what he looks like. But the glamour's worn off. If he wants to avoid revolution he's going to have to prove he's a charismatic."

"Are you going to get blamed for telling Hammeryock we were your friends?" Gentle asked.

"Probably, but I've been accused of worse. Besides, it's almost true. Any stranger here's a friend of mine." He cast a glance at Pie. "Even a mystif," he said. "The people in this dung heap have no poetry in them. I know I should be more sympathetic. They're refugees, most of them. They've lost their lands, their houses, their tribes. But they're so concerned with their itsy-bitsy little sorrows they don't see the broader picture."

"And what *is* the broader picture?" Gentle asked.

"I think that's better discussed behind closed doors," Tick Raw said, and would not be drawn any further on the subject until they were secure in his hut.

Gentle and Pie were six days on the Patashoquan Highway, days measured not by the watch on Pie's wrist but by the brightening and darkening of the peacock sky. On the fifth day the watch gave up the ghost anyway, maddened, Pie supposed, by the magnetic field surrounding a city of pyramids they passed. Thereafter, even though Gentle wanted to preserve some sense of how time was proceeding in the Dominion they'd left, it was virtually impossible. Within a few days their bodies were accommodating the rhythm of their new world, and he let his curiosity feast on more pertinent matters: chiefly, the landscape through which they were traveling.

It was diverse. In that first week they passed out of the plain into a region of lagoons—the Cosacosa—which took two days to cross, and thence into tracts of ancient conifers so tall that clouds hung in their topmost branches like the nests of ethereal birds. On the other side of this stupendous forest, the mountains Gentle had glimpsed days before came plainly into view. The range was called the Jokalaylau, Pie informed him, and legend had it that after the Mount of Lipper Bayak these heights had been Hapexamendios's next resting place as He'd crossed through the Dominions. It was no accident, it seemed, that the landscapes they passed through recalled those of the Fifth: they had been chosen for that similarity. The Unbeheld had strode the Imajica dropping seeds of humanity as He went—even to the very edge of His sanctum—in order to give the species He favored new challenges, and like any good gardener He'd dispersed them where they had the best hope of prospering. Where the native crop could be conquered or accommodated; where the living was hard enough to make sure only the most resilient survived, but the land fertile enough to feed their children; where rain came; where light came; where all the vicissitudes that strengthened a species by occasional calamity— tempest, earthquake, flood—were to hand.

But while there was much that any terrestrial traveler would have recognized, nothing, not the smallest pebble underfoot, was quite like its counterpart in the Fifth. Some of these disparities were too vast to be missed: the green-gold of the heavens, for instance, or the elephantine snails that grazed beneath the cloud-nested trees. Others were smaller but equally bizarre, like the wild dogs that ran along the highway now and then, hairless and shiny as patent leather; or grotesque, like the horned kites that swooped on any animal dead or near-dead on the road and only rose from their meals, purple wings opening like cloaks, when the vehicle was almost upon them; or absurd, like the bone-white lizards that congregated in their thousands along the edge of the lagoons, the urge to turn somersaults passing through their colonies in waves.

Twenty-two days after emerging from the icy wastes of the Jokalaylau into the balmier climes of the Third Dominion—days which had seen Pie and Gentle's fortunes rise dramatically as they journeyed through the Third's diverse territories—the wanderers were standing on a station platform outside the tiny town of Mai-ké, waiting for the train that once a week came through on its way from the city of Iahmandhas, in the northeast, to L'Himby, half a day's journey to the south.

They were eager to be departing. Of all the towns and villages they'd visited in the past three weeks, Mai-ké had been the least welcoming. It had its reasons. It was a community under siege from the Dominion's two suns, the rains which brought the region its crops having failed to materialize for six consecutive years. Terraces and fields that should have been bright with shoots were virtually dust bowls, stocks hoarded against this eventuality critically depleted. Famine was imminent, and the village was in no mood to entertain strangers. The previous night the entire populace had been out in the drab streets praying aloud, these imprecations led by their spiritual leaders, who had about them the air of men whose invention was nearing its end. The noise, so unmusical Gentle had observed that it would irritate the most sympathetic of deities, had gone on until first light, making sleep impossible. As a consequence, exchanges between Pie and Gentle were somewhat tense this morning.

They were not the only travelers waiting for the train. A farmer from Mai-ké had brought a herd of sheep onto the platform, some of them so emaciated it was a wonder they could stand, and the flock had brought with them clouds of the local pest: an insect called a zarzi, that had the wingspan of a dragonfly and a body as fat and furred as a bee. It fed on sheep ticks, unless it could find something more tempting. Gentle's blood fell into this latter category, and the lazy whine of the zarzi was never far from his ears as he waited in the midday heat. Their one informant in Mai-ké, a woman called Hairstone Banty, had predicted that the train would be on time, but it was already well overdue, which didn't augur well for the hundred other pieces of advice she'd offered them the night before.

Swatting zarzi to left and right, Gentle emerged from the shade of the platform building to peer down the track. It ran without crook or bend to its vanishing point, empty every mile of the way. On the rails a few yards from where he stood, rats—a gangrenous variety called graveolents—to-ed and fro-ed, gathering dead grasses for the nests they were constructing between the rails and the gravel the rails were set upon. Their industry only served to irritate Gentle further.

"We're stuck here forever," he said to Pie, who was squatting on the platform making marks on the stone with a sharp pebble. "This is Hairstone's revenge on a couple of hoopreo."

He'd heard this term whispered in their presence countless times. It meant anything from exotic stranger to repugnant leper, depending on the facial expression of the speaker. The people of Mai-ké were keen facepullers, and when they'd used the word in Gentle's company there was little doubt which end of the scale of affections they had in mind.

"It'll come," said Pie. "We're not the only ones waiting."

Two more groups of travelers had appeared on the platform in the last few minutes: a family of Mai-kéacs, three generations represented, who had lugged everything they owned down to the station; and three women in voluminous robes, their heads shaved and plastered with white mud, nuns of the Goetic Kicaranki, an order as despised in Mai-ké as any well-fed hoopreo. Gentle took some comfort from the appearance of these fellow travelers, but the track was still empty, the graveolents, who would surely be the first to sense any disturbance in the rails, going about their nest building unperturbed. He wearied of watching them very quickly and turned his attention to Pie's scrawlings.

"What are you doing?"

"I'm trying to work out how long we've been here."

"Two days in Mai-ké, a day and a half on the road from Attaboy—"

"No, no," said the mystif, "I'm trying to work it out in Earth days. Right from first arriving in the Dominions."

"We tried that in the mountains, and we didn't get anywhere."

"That's because our brains were frozen stiff."

"So have you done it?"

"Give me a little time."

"Time, we've got," Gentle said, returning his gaze to the antics of grave-olents. "These little buggers'll have grandchildren by the time the damn train arrives."

The mystif went on with its calculations, leaving Gentle to wander back into the comparative comfort of the waiting room, which, to judge by the sheep droppings on the floor, had been used to pen entire flocks in the recent past. The zarzi followed him, buzzing around his brow. He pulled from his ill-fitting jacket (bought with money he and Pie had won gambling in Attaboy) a dog-eared copy of *Fanny Hill*—the only volume in English, besides *Pilgrim's Progress*, which he'd been able to purchase—and used it to flail at the insects, then gave up. They'd tire of him eventually, or else he'd become immune to their attacks. Whichever; he didn't care.

He leaned against the graffiti-covered wall and yawned. He was bored. Of all things, bored! If, when they'd first arrived in Vanaeph, Pie had suggested that a few weeks later the wonders of the Reconciled Dominions would have become tedious, Gentle would have laughed the thought off as nonsense. With a gold-green sky above and the spires of Patashoqua gleaming in the distance, the scope for adventure had seemed endless. But by the time he'd reached Beatrix—the fond memories of which had not been entirely erased by images of its ruin—he was traveling like any man in a foreign land, prepared for occasional revelations but persuaded that the nature of conscious, curious bipeds was a constant under any heaven. They'd seen a great deal in the last few days, to be sure, but nothing he might not have imagined had he not stayed at home and got seriously drunk.

Yes, there had been glorious sights. But there had also been hours of discomfort, boredom, and banality. On their way to Mai-ké, for instance, they'd been exhorted to stay in some nameless hamlet to witness the community's festival: the annual donkey drowning. The origins of this ritual were, they were told, shrouded in fabulous mystery. They declined, Gentle remarking that this surely marked the nadir of their journey, and traveled on in the back of a wagon whose driver informed them that the vehicle had served his family for six generations as a dung carrier. He then proceeded to explain at great length the life cycle of his family's ancient foe, the pensanu, or shit rooster, a beast that with one turd could render an entire wagonload of dung inedible. They didn't press the man as to who in the region dined thusly, but they peered closely at their plates for many days following.

As he sat rolling the hard pellets of sheep dung under his heel. Gentle turned his thoughts to the one high point in their journey across the Third. That was the town of Effatoi, which Gentle had rechristened Attaboy. It wasn't that large—the size of Amsterdam, perhaps, and with that city's charm—but it was a gambler's paradise, drawing souls addicted to chance from across the Dominion. Here every game in the Imajica could be played. If your credit wasn't good in the casinos or the cock pits, you could always find a desperate man somewhere who'd bet on the color of your next piss if it was the only game on offer. Working together with what was surely telepathic efficiency. Gentle and the mystif had made a small fortune in the city—in eight currencies, no less—enough to keep them in clothes, food, and train tickets until they reached Yzordderrex. It wasn't profit that had almost seduced Gentle into setting up house there, however. It was a local delicacy: a cake of strudel pastry and the honey-softened seeds of a marriage between peach and pomegranate, which he ate before they gambled to give him vim, then while they gambled to calm his nerves, and then again in celebration when they'd won. It was only when Pie assured him that the confection would be available elsewhere (and if it wasn't they now had sufficient funds to hire their own pastry chef to make it) that Gentle was persuaded to depart.

If the divine engineers who had raised the Jokalaylau had one night set their most ambitious peak between a desert and an ocean, and returned the next night and for a century of nights thereafter to carve its steeps and sheers from foothills to clouded heights with lowly habitations and magnificent plazas, with streets, bastions, and pavilions—and if, having carved, they had set in the core of that mountain a fire that smoldered but never burned—then their handiwork, when filled to overflowing with every manner of life, might have deserved comparison with Yzordderrex. But given that no such masterwork had ever been devised, the city stood without parallel throughout the Imajica.

The travelers first sight of it came as they crossed the causeway that skipped like a well-aimed stone across the delta of the River Noy, rushing in twelve white torrents to meet the sea. It was early morning when they arrived, the fog off the river conspiring with the uneasy light of dawn to keep the city from sight until they were so close to it that when the fog was snatched the sky was barely visible, the desert and the sea no more than marginal, and all the world was suddenly Yzordderrex.

As they'd walked the Lenten Way, passing from the Third Dominion into the Second, Huzzah had recited all she'd read about the city from her father's books. One of the writers had described Yzordderrex as a god, she reported, a notion Gentle had thought ludicrous until he set eyes upon it. Then he understood what the urban theologian had been about, deifying this termite hill. Yzordderrex was worthy of worship; and millions were daily performing the ultimate act of veneration, living on or within the body of their Lord. Their dwellings clung like a million panicked climbers to the cliffs above the harbor and teetered on the plateaus that rose, tier on tier, toward the summit, many so crammed with houses that those closest to the edge had to be buttressed from below, the buttresses in turn encrusted with nests of life, winged, perhaps, or else suicidal. Everywhere, the mountain teemed, its streets of steps, lethally precipitous, leading the eye from one brimming shelf to another: from leafless boulevards lined with fine mansions to gates that let onto shadowy arcades, then up to the city's six summits, on the highest of which stood the palace of the Autarch of the Imajica. There was an abundance of a different order here, for the palace had more domes and towers than Rome, their obsessive elaboration visible even at this distance. Rising above them all was the Pivot Tower, as plain as its fellows were baroque. And high above that again, hanging in the white sky above the city, the comet that brought the Dominion's long days and languid dusks: Yzordderrex's star, called Giess, the Witherer.

They stood for only a minute or so to admire the sight. The daily traffic of workers who, having found no place of residence on the back or in the bowels of the city, commuted in and out daily, had begun, and by the time the newcomers reached the other end of the causeway they were lost in a dusty throng of vehicles, bicycles, rickshaws, and pedestrians all making their way into Yzordderrex. Three among tens of thousands: a scrawny young girl wearing a wide smile; a white man, perhaps once handsome but sickly now, his pale face half lost behind a ragged brown beard; and a Eurhetemec mystif, its eyes, like so many of its breed, barely concealing a private grief. The crowd bore them forward, and they went unresisting where countless multitudes had gone before: into the belly of the city-god Yzordderrex.

From *The Great and Secret Show*

*E*phemeris.

  The name had echoed in Howie's head since he'd first heard it spoken, by Fletcher.

What's on Ephemeris? he'd asked, imagining some paradise island. His father's reply hadn't been particularly illuminating. *The Great and Secret Show*, he'd said, an answer which begged a dozen more questions. Now, as the island came into view ahead of him, he wished he'd pursued his questions with more persistence. Even from a distance it was quite clear his picturing of the place had been spectacularly short of the mark. Just as Quiddity wasn't in any conventional sense a sea, so Ephemeris demanded a redefinition of the word *island*. For one, it was not a single land mass but many, perhaps hundreds, joined by arches of rock, the whole archipelago resembling a vast, floating cathedral, the bridges like buttresses, the islands towers which mounted in scale as they approached the central island, from which solid pillars of smoke rose to meet the sky. The similarity was too strong to be coincidence. This image was surely the subconscious inspiration of architects the world over. Cathedral builders, tower raisers, even—who knew?—children playing with building blocks, had this dream place somewhere at the back of their minds, and paid homage as best they could. But their masterworks could only be approximations, compromises with gravity and the limitations of their medium. Nor could they ever aspire to a work so massive. The Ephemeris was many miles across, Howie guessed, and there was no portion of it that had not been touched by genius. If it was a natural phenomenon (and who knew what *natural* was, in a place of mind?) then it was nature in a frenzy of invention. It made solid matter play games only cloud or light would be capable of in the world he'd left behind. Made towers as fine as reeds on which globes the size of houses balanced; made sheer cliff faces fluted like shells and canyon walls that seemed to billow like curtains at a window; made spiral hills; made boulders like breasts, and dogs, and the sweepings from some vast table. So many likenesses, but none he could be certain were intended. A fragment in which he'd seen a face was part of another likeness the glance after, each interpretation subject to change at a moment's notice. Perhaps they were all true, all intended. Perhaps none were, and this game of resemblances was, like the creation of the pier when he'd first approached Quiddity, his mind's way of taming the immensity. If so, there was one sight it failed to master: the island at the center of the archipelago, which rose straight out of Quiddity, sheer, the smoke that gouted from countless fissures on its walls rising with the same verticality. Its pinnacle was completely concealed by the smoke, but whatever mystery lay behind it was nectar to the spirit-lights, who rose to it unburdened by flesh and blood, not entering the smoke but grazing its blossom. He wondered if it was fear that kept them from moving into the smoke, or if it was a more solid barrier than it seemed. Perhaps when he got closer, he'd discover the answer. Eager to be there as quickly as possible, he aided the tide with strokes of his own, so that within ten or fifteen minutes of first seeing the Ephemeris he was hauling himself up onto its beach. It was dark, though not as dark as Quiddity, and harsh beneath his palms, not sand but encrustations, like coral. Was it possible, he suddenly wondered, that the archipelago had been created the way the island he'd seen floating among the flotsam from the Vance house had been created, formed around the presence of human beings in Quiddity? If so, how long ago must they have come into the dream-sea, to have grown so massive?

From *Everville*

T here's something wrong with the sea."
        Joe sat up, and looked down the shore toward the booming surf. The waters were almost velvety, the waves large enough to tempt a surfer, but curling and breaking more slowly than those on any terrestrial shore. Flecks of iridescence rose in their lavish curl, and glittered on their crests.

"It's beautiful," he said.

Noah grunted. "Look out there," he said, and pointed out beyond the breakers, to the place where the horizon should have been. Black and gray and green pillars of clouds were apparently rising from the sea as though some titanic heat was turning the waters to steam. The heavens, meanwhile, were falling in floods and fires. It was a spectacle the scale of which Joe had never conceived before, like a scene from the making of the world, or its unmaking.

"What's causing all that?"

"I don't want to speak the words until I'm certain," Noah said. "But I begin to think we should be careful, even here."

"Careful about what?"

"About waiting for the likes of that to come our way," he said, and pointed along the shore.

Three or four miles from where they stood he could see the roofs and spires of a city. Liverpool, he presumed. In between, perhaps a quarter of that distance away, was an approaching procession.

"That's a Blessedm'n," Noah said, "I think we're better away, Joe."

"Why?" Joe wanted to know. "What's a Blessedm'n?"

"One who conjures," Noah said. "Perhaps the one who opened this door."

"Don't you want to wait and *thank* him?" Joe said, still studying the procession. There were perhaps thirty in the line, some of them on horseback; one, it seemed, on a camel.

"The door wasn't opened for me," Noah replied.

"Who was it opened *for*?" There was no answer. Joe looked round to see that Noah was once again staring out toward the apocalyptic storm that blocked the horizon. "Something out there?" he said.

"Maybe," Noah replied.

Half a dozen questions appeared in Joe's head at the same time. If what was out *there* was coming *here*, what would happen to the shore? And to the city? And if it passed over the threshold, would the storm it brought go with it? Down the mountain, to Everville? To Phoebe?

Oh my God, to Phoebe?

"I have to go back," he said.

"You can't."

"I can and I will," Joe said, turning and starting back toward the crack. It was not hidden here, as it was on the mountain. It crackled like a rod of black lightning against the shifting sky. Was it his imagination, or was it wider and taller than it had been?

"I promised you power, Joe," Noah called after him. "And I still have it to give."

Joe turned on his heel. "So give it to me and let me go," he said.

Noah stared at the ground. "It's not as easy as that, my friend."

"What do you mean?"

"I can't grant you power here."

"On the other side, you said."

"Yes, I did. I know I did. But that wasn't quite the truth." He looked up at

Joe now, his oversized head seeming to teeter on his frail neck. "I'd hoped that once you got here and saw the glories of the dream-sea, you'd want to travel with me a little way. I can give you power. Truly I can. But only in my own country."

"How far?" Joe said.

There was no answer forthcoming. Infuriated, Joe went back to Noah, moving at such speed the creature raised its arms to ward off a blow. "I'm not going to hit you," Joe said. Noah lowered his guard six inches. "I just want an honest answer."

Noah sighed. "My country is the Ephemeris," he said.

"And where's the Ephemeris?" Joe wanted to know.

Noah looked at him for perhaps ten seconds, and then pointed out to sea.

"No shit," Joe said, deadpan. "You really put one over on me."

"Put one over?" Noah said.

"Tricked me, asshole." He pushed his face at Noah, until they were almost nose to nose. "You tricked me."

"I believed you'd been sent to take me home," Noah said.

"Don't be pathetic."

"It's true, I did. I still do." He looked up at Joe. "You think that's ridiculous, that our lives could be intertwined that way?"

"Yes," said Joe.

Noah nodded. "So you must go back," he said. "And I'll stay. I feel stronger here, under my own sky. No doubt you'll feel stronger under yours."

Joe didn't miss the irony. "You know damn well what I'll be when I get back there."

"Yes," said Noah, getting to his feet. "Powerless." With that he started to hobble away down the beach. "Good-bye, Joe," he called after him.

"Asshole," Joe said, staring back up the shore at the sliver of night sky visible in the crack. What use would he be to himself or to Phoebe if he returned home now? He was a wounded fugitive. And just as Noah had pointed out, he was utterly powerless.

He turned again to scan the strange world into which he'd stepped. The distant city, the approaching procession, the storm raging over Quiddity's tumultuous waters: none of it looked particularly promising. But perhaps—just perhaps—there was hope for him here. A means to get power of some kind, *any* kind, that would make him a man to be reckoned with when he got back to his own world. Perhaps he'd have to sweat for it, but he'd sweated in the Cosm, hadn't he, and what had he got for his efforts? Broken balls.

"All right," he said, going down the shore after Noah. "I'll stay. But I'm not carrying you, understand?"

Noah smiled back at him. "May I . . . put my arm around your shoulder, until I get some nourishment in me, and my legs are stronger?"

"I guess," said Joe.

Noah hooked his arm around Joe's neck. "There's a beached boat down there," he said, "we'll take refuge until the procession's gone."

"What's so bad about these Blessedm'n?" Joe asked him as they made their hobbling way down to the vessel.

"No one ever knows what's in a Blessedm'n's heart. They have secret reasons and purposes for everything. Perhaps this one is benign, but we've no way of knowing."

They walked on in silence, until they reached the vessel. It was two-masted, perhaps twenty-five feet long, its boards and wheelhouse painted scarlet and blue, though its voyages had taken their toll on both paintwork and boards. Its name, *The Fanacapan*, had been neatly lettered on its bow.

Hunger was beginning to gnaw at Joe, so he left Noah squatting in the lee of the vessel, and clambered on board to look for some sustenance. The narcotic effect of the painkillers was finally wearing off, and as he went about the boat, looking above and below for a loaf of bread or a bottle of beer, he felt a mingling of negative feelings creep upon him. One of them was unease, another trepidation, a third, disappointment. He had found his way into another world, only to discover that things here weren't so very different. Perhaps Quiddity was indeed a dream-sea as Noah had claimed, but this boat, which had apparently crossed it, showed no sign of having been built or occupied by creatures of vision. Its two cabins were squalid, its galley unspeakable, the woodwork of its wheelhouse crudely etched with drawings of the obscenest kind.

As for nourishment, there was none to be found. There were a few scraps of food left in the galley, but nothing remotely edible, and though Joe searched through the strewn clothes and filthy blankets in the cabins in the hope of finding a bar of chocolate or a piece of fruit, he came up empty-handed. Frustrated, and hungrier than ever after his exertions, he clambered back down onto the shore to find that Noah was sitting cross-legged on the ground, staring up the shore with tears on his face.

"What's wrong?"

"It just reminds me . . . ," Noah said, nodding toward the procession. Its destination was the crack, no doubt of that. Five or six celebrants, who looked to be children, and nearly naked, had broken from the front of the procession and were strewing a path of leaves or petals between their lord and the threshold.

"Reminds you of what?"

"Of my wedding day," Noah said. "And of my beloved. We had a procession three, four times that one. You never saw such finery. You never heard such music. It was to be the end of an age of war, and the beginning . . ." He faltered, shuddering. "I want to see my country again, Joe," he said after a time. "If it's only to be buried there."

"You haven't waited all this time just to die."

"It won't be so bad," Noah murmured. "I've had the love of my life. There could never be another like her, nor do I want there to be. I couldn't bear to even think such a thought until now, but it's the truth, Joe. So it won't be so bad, if I die in my own country, and I'm laid in the dirt from which I came. You understand that, don't you?" Joe didn't reply. Noah looked round at him. "No?"

"No," he said, "I don't have a country, Noah. I hate America."

"Africa then."

"I was never there. I don't think I'd much like that either." He drew a long, slow breath. "So I don't give a fuck where I'm buried." There was another long silence. Then he said: "I'm hungry. There's nothing on the boat. I'm going to have to eat soon or I'm going to start falling down."

"Then you must catch yourself something," Noah said, and getting to his feet, led Joe down to the water's edge. The waves were not breaking as violently as they had been, Joe thought. "See the fish?" Noah said, pointing into curling waves.

The streaks of iridescence Joe had seen from the threshold were in fact living things: fishes and eels, bright as lightning, leaping in the water in their thousands.

"I see them."

"Take your fill."

"You mean, just catch them in my hands?"

"And swallow them down," Noah said. He smiled, seeing the disgusted look on Joe's face. "They're best alive," he said. "Trust me."

The ache in Joe's stomach was now competing with that in his balls. This was, he knew, no time to be persnickety about his options. He shrugged and strode out into the water. It was balmy warm, which came as a pleasant surprise, and if he hadn't known better he'd have said it was eager to have him in its midst, the way it curled around his shins, and leaped up toward his groin. The fish were *everywhere*, he saw; and they came in a number of shapes and sizes, some as large as salmon, which surprised him given the shallowness of the waters, others tiny as hummingbirds and almost as defiant of gravity, leaping around him in their glittering thousands. He had to exert almost no effort at all to catch hold of one. He simply closed his hand in their midst, and opening it again found he'd caught not one but three—two a reddish silver, the third blue—all flapping wildly in his palm. They didn't look remotely appetizing, with their black, black eyes and their gasping flanks. But as long as he and Noah were trapped here he had little choice. He either ate the fish, or went hungry.

He plucked one of the reddish variety off the plate of his palm, and without giving himself time to regret what he was doing, threw back his head and dropped it into his mouth. There was a moment of disgust when he thought he'd vomit, then the fish was gone down his gullet. He'd tasted nothing, but what the hell. This wasn't a gourmet meal; it was eating at its most primal. He took one more look at his palm, then he popped both the remaining fish into his mouth at the same time, throwing back his head so as to knock them back. One slipped down his throat as efficiently as the first, but the other flapped against his tonsils, and found its way back onto his tongue. He spat it out.

"Bad taste?" Noah said, wading into the surf beside Joe.

"It just didn't want to get eaten," Joe replied.

"You can't blame it," Noah replied, and strode on until he was hip deep in the waters.

"You're feeling stronger," Joe yelled to him over the crash of surf.

"All the time," Noah replied. "The air nourishes me." He plunged his hands into the water and came up not with a fish, but something that resembled a squid, its huge eyes a vivid gold.

"Don't tell me to eat *that*," Joe said.

"No. No, never," Noah replied. "This is a Zehrapushu; a spirit-pilot. See how it looks at you?"

Joe saw. There was an eerie curiosity in the creature's unblinking gaze, as though it were studying him.

"It's not used to seeing your species in flesh and blood," Noah said. "If you could speak its language it would surely tell you to go home. Perhaps you want to touch it?"

"Not much."

"It would please the Zehrapushu," Noah said, proffering the creature. "And if you please one you please many."

Joe waded out toward Noah, watching the animal watch him.

"You mean this thing's connected to other . . . what'd you call them . . . Zehra-what?"

"People call them 'shu, it's easier." He pressed the creature into Joe's arms. "It's not going to bite," he said.

Joe took hold of it, gingerly. It lay quite passively in his hands, its gaze turned up toward Joe's face.

"The oldest temples on the twelve continents were raised to the 'shu," Noah went on, "and it's still worshiped in some places."

"But not by your people?"

Noah shook his head. "My wife was a Catholic," he said. "And I'm . . . I'm a nonbeliever. You'd better put it back before it perishes. I think it'd happily die just watching you."

Joe stooped and set the 'shu back in the water. It lingered between his palms several seconds, the gleam of its eye still bright, then with one twitch of its boneless body it was away, out into deeper waters. Watching it go, Joe could not help but wonder if even now it was telling tales of the black man to its fellows.

"There are some people," Noah said, "who believe that the 'shu are all parts of the Creator, who split into a billion pieces so as to pilot human souls in Quiddity, and has forgotten how to put the pieces back together again."

"So I just had a piece of God in my hands?"

"Yes." Noah reached down into the water again, and this time brought up a foot-long fish. "Too big?" he said.

"Too big!"

"The little ones slip down more easily, is that it?"

"Much easier," Joe said, and reaching into the waters plucked out two handfuls of the tiny fish. His encounter with the 'shu had taken the edge off his pickiness. Plainly these blank-eyed minnows were of a much lower order of being than the creature that had studied him so carefully. He could swallow them without concerning himself about the niceties of it. He downed two handfuls in as many seconds and then found himself something a little larger, which he bit into as though it were a sandwich. The meat of it was bright orange, and sweetly tender, and he chewed on it careless of how the thing thrashed in his grip, tossing it back only when one of its bones caught between his teeth.

"I'm done for now," he announced to Noah, working to ease the bone out.

"You won't drink?" Noah said.

"It's salty," Joe said, "isn't it?"

"Not to my palate," Noah said, lifting a cupped handful of Quiddity's waters to his lips and sucking it up noisily. "I think it's good."

Joe did the same and was not disappointed. The water had a pleasant pungency about it. He swallowed several mouthfuls and then waded back to the shore, feeling more replete than he'd imagined possible given the fare.

In the time he and Noah had been discussing fish and God, the entire procession had arrived at the crack—which was indeed growing larger: it was half as tall again as it had been when he'd stepped through it—the members of the procession now gathered at the threshold.

"Are they going through?" he said.

"It looks that way," Noah replied. He glanced up at the sky, which though it had no sun in it was darker than it had been. "If some of them remain," he said, "we may find our crew among them."

"For what ship?"

"What other ship do we have but *this*?" Noah said, slamming his palm against *The Fanacapan*.

"There are others in the harbor," Joe said, pointing along the shore toward the city. "Big ships. This thing doesn't even look seaworthy. And even if it is, how the hell are we going to persuade anyone to come with us?"

"That's my problem," Noah said. "Why don't you rest a while? Sleep if you can. We've a busy night ahead of us."

"Sleep?" Joe said. "You've gotta be kidding."

He thought about getting a blanket and a pillow out of one of the cabins, but decided it wasn't worth being lice-ridden for the little snugness they'd afford, and instead made himself as comfortable as he could on the bare stones. It was undoubtedly the most uncomfortable bed he'd ever attempted to lie upon, but the serenity of the sky made a powerful soporific, and though he never fell into a deep enough sleep to dream, he drifted for a while.

From *Everville*

The distance between the shores of Mem-é b'Kether Sabbat and the mountainside where Tesla and Phoebe were climbing was not readily measured. Though generations of thinkers in both the Cosm and the Metacosm had attempted to evolve a theory of distance between the two worlds, there was little consensus on the subject. The only thing the various factions agreed upon was that this distance could not be measured with a rule and an abacus. After all, it was not simply the distance between two points: it was the distance between two *states*. Some said it was best viewed as an entirely symbolic space, like that between worshiper and deity, and proposed an entirely new system of measurement applicable to such cases. Others argued that a soul moving from the Helter Incendo into Quiddity underwent such a radical altering that the best way to describe and analyze the distance, if the word *distance* were still applicable (which they doubted), was to derive it from the vocabulary of spiritual reformation. The notion proved untenable, however, one man's reformation being another's heresy.

Finally, there were those who argued that the relationships between Sapas Humana and the dream-sea were all in the mind, and any attempt to measure distance was doomed to failure. Surely, they opined, the space between one thought and another was beyond the wit of any man to measure. They were accused of defeatism by some of their enemies; of shoddy metaphysics by others. Men and women only entered the dream-sea three times, they were reminded. For the rest of their lives Quiddity was a lot further than a thought away. Not so, the leader of this faction—a mystic from Joom called Carasophia—argued. The wall between the Cosm and the Metacosm was getting steadily thinner, and would—he predicted—soon disappear altogether, at which point the minds of Sapas Humana, which seemed so pathetically literal, would be revealed to be purveyors of the miraculous, even in their present, primal state.

Carasophia had died for his theories, assassinated in a field of sunflowers outside Eliphas, but he would have found comforting evidence for his beliefs had he wandered through the minds of the people gathered along the parade route in Everville. People were dreaming today, even though their eyes were wide open.

Parents dreaming of being free as their children; children dreaming of having their parents' power.

Lovers seeing the coming night in each other's eyes; old folks, staring at their hands, or at the sky, seeing the same.

Dreams of sex, dreams of oblivion; dreams of circus and bacchanalia.

And further down the parade route, sitting by the window from which he'd so recently fallen, a man dreaming of how it would be when he had the Art for himself, and time and distance disappeared forever.

Though the trees that bounded the shore of Ephemeris grew so close together their exposed roots knotted like the fingers of praying hands, and the canopy overhead was so dense the sky was blotted out altogether, there was not a leaf, twig, or patch of moss that didn't exude light, which eased Joe's progress considerably. Once in the midst of the forest, he had to rely upon his sense of direction to bring him out the other side, which indeed it did. After perhaps half an hour the trees began to thin, and he stumbled into the open air.

There, a scene lay before him of such scale he could have stood and studied it for a week and not taken in every detail. Stretching in front of his feet for perhaps twenty miles was a landscape of bright fields and water-meadows, the former blazing green and yellow and scarlet, the latter sheets of silver and gold. Rising overhead, like a vast wave that had climbed to titanic height and now threatened to break over the perfection below, was a wall of darkness, which surely concealed the lad. It was not black, but a thousand shades of gray, tinged here and there with red and purple. It was impossible to judge the matter of which it was made. It had the texture of smoke in some places, in others it glistened like skinned muscle; in others still it divided in convulsions, and divided again, as though it were reproducing itself. Of the legion, or nation, that lurked behind it, there was no sign. The wave teetered, and teetered, and did not fall.

But there was another sight that was in its way more extraordinary still, and that was the city that stood in the shadow of this toppling sky: b'Kether Sabbat. The glory of the Ephemeris, Noah had called it and, had Joe's journey taken him not one step closer to the city's limits, he would have believed the boast.

It was shaped, this city, like an inverted pyramid, balanced on its tip. There was no sign of any structure supporting it in this position. Though there were myriad means of ascent from the ground to its underbelly, which was encrusted with what he assumed to be dwellings (though their occupants would have to have the attributes of bats to live there), the sum of these ladders and stairways was nowhere near sufficient to bear the city's weight. He had no way to judge its true scale, but he was certain Manhattan would have fitted upon the upper surface with room to spare, which meant that the dozen or so towers that rose there, each resembling a vast swathe of fabric, plucked up by one corner and falling in countless folds, were many hundreds of stories high.

Despite the lights that blazed from their countless windows, Joe doubted the towers were occupied. B'Kether Sabbat's citizens were choking the roads that led from the city, or rising from its streets and towers in wheeling flocks.

Such was the sheer immensity of this spectacle he was almost tempted to find himself a comfortable spot among the roots, and watch it until the wave broke, and it was obliterated. But the same curiosity that had brought him from the shore now pressed him on, down the slope and across a swampy field, where a crop of crystalline flowers sprouted, to the nearest of the roads. Despite the vast diversity of faces and forms in the throng upon that road, there was a certain desperation in their faces and in their forms a common dread. They shuddered and sweated as they went, their eyes—white, golden, blue, and black—cast over their shoulders now and again toward the city they'd deserted, and the teetering darkness that shadowed it.

Few showed any interest in Joe. And those few that did looked at him pityingly, judging him crazy, he supposed, for being the only traveler on this highway who was not fleeing b'Kether Sabbat, but heading back toward it.

From *Weaveworld*
CAL, AMONG MIRACLES

True joy is a profound remembering; and true grief the same.

Thus it was, when the dust storm that had snatched Cal up finally died, and he opened his eyes to see the Fugue spread before him, he felt as though the few fragile moments of epiphany he'd tasted in his twenty-six years—tasted but always lost—were here redeemed and wed. He'd grasped fragments of this delight before. Heard rumor of it in the womb-dream and the dream of love; known it in lullabies. But never, until now, the whole, the thing entire.

It would be, he idly thought, a fine time to die.

And a finer time still to live, with so much laid out before him.

He was on a hill. Not high, but high enough to offer a vantage point. He got to his feet and surveyed this newfound land.

The unknotting of the carpet had by no means finished; the raptures of the Loom were far too complex to be so readily reversed. But the ground-work was laid: hills, fields, forest, and much else besides.

Last time he'd set eyes on this place it had been from a bird's-eye view, and the landscape had seemed various enough. But from the human per-spective its profusion verged on the riotous. It was as if a vast suitcase, packed in great haste, had been upturned, its contents scattered in hope-less disarray. There appeared to be no system to the geography, just a ran-dom assembling of spots the Seerkind had loved enough to snatch from destruction. Butterfly copses and placid water meadows; lairs and walled sanctuaries; keeps, rivers, and standing stones.

Few of these locations were complete: most were slivers and snatches, fragments of the Kingdom ceded to the Fugue behind humanity's back. The haunted corners of familiar rooms that would neither be missed nor mourned, where children had perhaps seen ghosts or saints; where the fugitive might be comforted and not know why, and the suicide find rea-son for another breath.

Amid this disorder, the most curious juxtapositions abounded. Here a bridge, parted from the chasm it had crossed, sat in a field, spanning pop-pies; there an obelisk stood in the middle of a pool, gazing at its reflection.

One sight in particular caught Cal's eye.

It was a hill, which rose almost straight-sided to a tree-crowned summit. Lights moved over its face, and danced among the branches. Having no sense of direction here, he decided to make his way down toward it.

There was music playing somewhere in the night. It came to him by fits and starts, at the behest of the breeze. Drums and violins; a mingling of Strauss and Sioux. And occasionally, evidence of people too. Whispers in the trees; shadowed figures beneath a canopy which stood in the middle of a waist-high field of grain. But the creatures were fugitive; they came and went too quickly for him to gain more than a fleeting impression. Whether this was because they knew him for the Cuckoo he was, or simply out of shyness, only time would tell. Certainly he felt no threat here, despite the fact that he was, in a sense, trespassing. On the contrary, he felt utterly at peace with the world and himself. So much so that his concern for the others here— Suzanna, Apolline, Jerichau, Nimrod—was quite remote. When his thoughts did touch upon them it was only to imagine them wandering as he was wandering, lost among miracles. No harm could come to them; not here. Here was an end to harm, and malice, and envy too. Having this living rapture wrapping him round, what was left to envy or desire?

He was within a hundred yards of the hill and stood before it in amazement. The lights he'd seen from a distance were in fact human fireflies; wingless, but describing effortless arabesques around the hill. There was no communication between them that he could hear, yet they had the precision of daredevils, their maneuvers repeatedly bringing them within a hairbreadth of each other.

"You must be Mooney."

The speaker's voice was soft, but it broke the hold the lights had on him. Cal looked off to his right. Two figures were standing in the shade of an archway, their faces still immersed in darkness. All he could see were the two blue-gray ovals of their faces, hanging beneath the arch like lanterns.

"Yes. I'm Mooney," he said. *Show yourselves*, he thought. "How do you know my name?"

"News travels fast here," came the reply. The voice seemed slightly softer and more fluting than the first, but he couldn't be certain it wasn't the same speaker. "It's the air," said his informant. "It gossips."

Now one of the pair stepped into the night light. The soft illumination from the hill moved on his face, lending it strangeness, but even had Cal seen it by daylight this was a face to be haunted by. He was young, yet completely bald, his features powdered to remove any modulation in skin tone, his mouth and eyes almost too wet, too vulnerable, in the mask of his features.

"I'm Boaz," he said. "You're welcome, Mooney."

He took Cal's hand, and shook it, and as he did so his companion broke her covenant with shadow.

"You can see the Amadou?" she said.

It took Cal several seconds to conclude that the second speaker was indeed a woman, the processes of his doubt in turn throwing doubt on the sex of Boaz, for the two were very close to being identical twins.

"I'm Ganza," said the second speaker. She was dressed in the same plain black trousers and loose tunic as her brother, or lover, or whatever he was; and she too was bald. That, and their powdered faces, seemed to confuse all the clichés of gender. Their faces were vulnerable, yet implacable; delicate, yet severe.

Boaz looked toward the hill, where the fireflies were still cavorting.

"This is the Rock of the First Fatality," he told Cal. "The Amadou always gather here. This is where the first victims of the Scourge died."

Cal looked back toward the Rock, but only for a moment. Boaz and Ganza fascinated him more; their ambiguities multiplied the more he watched them.

"Where are you going tonight?" said Ganza.

Cal shrugged. "No idea," he said. "I don't know a yard of this place."

"Yes, you do," she said. "You know it very well."

While she spoke she was idly locking and unlocking her fingers, or so it seemed, until Cal's eyes lingered on the exercise for two or three seconds. Then it became apparent that she was passing her fingers *through* the palms of the other hand, left through right, right through left, defying their solidity. The motion was so casual, the illusion—if illusion it was—so quick, that Cal was by no means certain he was interpreting it correctly.

"How do they look to you?" she inquired.

He looked back at her face. Was the finger-trick some kind of test of his perception? It wasn't her hands she was talking about, however.

"The Amadou," she said. "How do they appear?"

He glanced toward the Rock again.

"Like human beings," he replied.

She gave him a tiny smile.

"Why do you ask?" he wanted to know. But she didn't have time to reply before Boaz spoke.

"There's a Council been called," he said. "At Capra's House. I think they're going to reweave."

"That can't be right," said Cal. "They're going to put the Fugue back?"

"That's what I hear," said Boaz.

It seemed to be fresh news to him; had he just lifted it off the gossiping air? "The times are too dangerous, they're saying," he told Cal. "Is that true?"

"I don't know any other," Cal said. "So I've got nothing to compare them with."

"Do we have the night?" Ganza asked.

"Some of it," said Boaz.

"Then we'll go to see Lo; yes?"

"It's as good a place as any," Boaz replied. "Will you come?" he asked the Cuckoo.

Cal looked back toward the Amadou. The thought of staying and watching their performance a while longer was tempting, but he might not find another guide to show him the sights, and if time here was short then he'd best make the most of it.

"Yes. I'll come."

The woman had stopped lacing her fingers.

"You'll like Lo," she said, turning away, and starting off into the night.

He followed, already full to brimming with questions, but knowing that if indeed he only had hours to taste Wonderland he should not waste time and breath asking.

From *Weaveworld*
THE ORCHARD OF LEMUEL LO

Neither Boaz nor Ganza were voluble guides. They led the way through the Fugue in almost complete silence, only breaking that silence to warn Cal that a stretch of ground was treacherous, or to keep close to them as they moved down a colonnade in which he heard dogs panting. In a sense he was glad of their quietness. He didn't want a guided tour of the terrain, at least not tonight. He'd known, when he'd first looked down at the Fugue from the wall in Mimi's yard, that it couldn't be mapped, nor its contents listed and committed to memory like his beloved timetables. He would have to understand the Weaveworld in a different fashion: not as hard fact but as feeling. The schism between his mind and the world it was attempting to grasp was dissolving. In its place was a relationship of echo and counter echo. They were thoughts inside each other's heads, he and this world; and that knowledge, which he could never have found the words to articulate, turned the journey into a tour of his own history. He'd known from Mad Mooney that poetry was heard differently from ear to ear. Poetry was like that. The same, he began to see, was also true of geography.

They climbed a long slope. He thought maybe a tide of crickets leaped before their feet; the earth seemed alive.

At the top of the slope they looked across a field. At the far side of the field was an orchard.

"Almost there," said Ganza, and they began toward it.

The orchard was the biggest single feature he'd seen in the Fugue so far; a plot of maybe thirty or forty trees, planted in rows and carefully pruned so that their branches almost touched. Beneath this canopy were passages of neatly clipped grass, dappled by velvet light.

"This is the orchard of Lemuel Lo," Boaz said, as they stood on the perimeter. His gentle voice was softer than ever. "Even among the fabled, it's fabled."

Ganza led the way beneath the trees. The air was still and warm and sweet. The branches were laden with a fruit that Cal did not recognize.

"They're Jude pears," Boaz told him. "One of the species we've never shared with the Cuckoos."

"Why not?"

"There are reasons," said Boaz. He looked around for Ganza, but she'd disappeared down one of the avenues. "Help yourself to the fruit," he said, moving away from Cal in search of his companion. "Lem won't mind."

Though Cal thought he could see all the way down the corridor of trees his eyes deceived him. Boaz took three steps from him, and was gone.

Cal reached toward one of the low-slung branches and put his hand on one of the fruits. As he did so there was a great commotion in the tree and something ran down the branch toward him.

"Not that one!"

The voice was bass profundo. The speaker was a monkey.

"They're sweeter upstairs," the beast said, throwing its brown eyes skyward. Then it ran back the way it had come, its passage bringing leaves down around Cal. He tried to follow its progress, but the animal moved too fast. It was back in half a dozen seconds, with not one but two fruits. Perched in the branches, it threw them down to Cal.

"Peel them," it said. "One each."

Despite their name, they didn't resemble pears. They were the size of a plum, but with a leathery skin. It was tough, but it couldn't disguise the fragrance of the meat inside.

"What are you waiting for?" the monkey demanded to know. "They're tasty, these Giddys. Peel it and see."

The fact of the talking monkey—which might have stopped Cal dead in his tracks a week before—was just part of the local color now.

"You call them Giddys?" he said.

"Jude pears; Giddy Fruit. It's all the same meat."

The monkey's eyes were on Cal's hands, willing him to peel the fruit. He proceeded to do just that. They were more difficult to skin than any fruit he'd encountered; hence the monkey's bargain with him, presumably. Viscous juice ran from the broken skin and over his hands; the smell was ever more appetizing. Before he'd quite finished peeling the first of them, the monkey snatched it from his grasp and wolfed it down.

"Good—" it said, between mouthfuls.

Its pleasure was echoed from beneath the tree. Somebody made a sound of appreciation, and Cal glanced away from his labors to see that there was a man squatting against the trunk, rolling a cigarette. He looked back up to the monkey, then down at the man, and the voice from the beast made new sense.

"Good trick," he said.

The man looked up at Cal. His features were distressingly close to mongoloid; the smile he offered huge, and seemingly uncomprehending.

"What is?" said the voice from the branches.

Confounded as he was by the face below him, Cal pursued his assumption, and addressed his reply not to the puppet but the puppeteer.

"Throwing your voice like that."

The man still grinned, but showed no sign that he'd understood. The monkey, however, laughed loudly.

"Eat the fruit," it said.

Cal's fingers had worked at the peeling without his direction. The Giddy was skinned. But some lingering superstition about stolen fruit kept him from putting it to his lips.

"Try it," said the monkey. "They're not poisonous—"

The smell was too tantalizing to resist. He bit.

"At least not to us," the monkey added, laughing again.

The fruit tasted even better than its scent had promised. The meat was succulent, the juice strong as a liqueur. He licked it off his fingers, and the palms of his hand.

"Like it?"

"Superb."

"Food and drink all in one." The monkey looked at the man beneath the tree. "Want one, Smith?" it asked.

The man put a flame to his cigarette and drew on it.

"D'you hear me?"

Getting no response, the monkey scampered back up into the higher reaches of the tree.

Cal, still eating the pear, had found the pips at its center. He chewed them up. Their slight bitterness only complemented the sweetness of the rest.

There was music playing somewhere between the trees, he now noticed. One moment lilting, the next manic.

"Another?" said the monkey, reappearing with not two but several fruit.

Cal swallowed the last of his first.

"Same deal," the monkey said.

Suddenly greedy, Cal took three, and started to peel.

"There's other people here," he said to the puppeteer.

"Of course," said the monkey. "This has always been a gathering place."

"Why do you speak through the animal?" Cal asked, as the monkey's fingers claimed a peeled fruit from his hands.

"The name's Novello," said the monkey. "And who says he's speaking at all?"

Cal laughed, as much at himself as at the performance.

"Fact is," said the monkey, "neither of us is quite sure who does what any longer. But then love's like that, don't you find?"

It threw back its head and squeezed the fruit in its hand, so that the liquor ran down its throat.

The music had found a fresh intoxication. Cal was intrigued to find out what instruments it was being played upon. Violins certainly, and whistles and drums. But there were sounds among these that he couldn't place.

"Any excuse for a party," said Novello.

"Must be the biggest breakfast in history."

"I daresay. Want to go see?"

"Yes."

The monkey ran along the branch, and scurried down the trunk to where Smith was sitting. Cal, chewing the seeds of his second Giddy, reached up and claimed a further handful of fruit from among the foliage, pocketing half a dozen against future hunger, and skinning another to be consumed on the spot.

The sound of monkey chatter drew his gaze down to Novello and Smith. The beast was perched on the man's chest, and they were talking to each other, a babble of words and grunts. Cal looked from man to beast and back to man again. He could not tell who was saying what to whom.

The debate ended abruptly, and Smith stood up, the monkey now sitting on his shoulder. Without inviting Cal to follow, they threaded their way between the trees. Cal pursued, peeling and eating as he went.

Some of the visitors here were doing as he'd done, standing beneath the trees, consuming Jude pears. One or two had even climbed up and were draped among the branches, bathing in the perfumed air. Others, either indifferent to the fruit or sated upon it, lay sprawled in the grass and talked together in low voices. The atmosphere was all tranquillity.

Heaven is an orchard, Cal thought as he walked; and God is plenty.

"That's the fruit talking," said Novello. Cal wasn't even aware that he'd spoken aloud. He looked round at the monkey, feeling slightly disoriented.

"You should watch yourself," the animal said, "an excess of Judes isn't good for you."

"I've got a strong stomach," Cal replied.

"Who said anything about your stomach?" the monkey replied. "They're not called Giddy Fruit for nothing."

Cal ignored him. The animal's condescending tone irritated him. He picked up his pace, overtaking man and beast.

"Have it your way," said the monkey.

Somebody darted between the trees a little way ahead of Cal, trailing laughter. To Cal's eyes the sound was momentarily *visible*; he saw the rise and fall of notes as splashes of light, which flew apart like dandelion heads in a high wind. Enchantment upon enchantment. Plucking and peeling yet another of Lo's remarkable fruits as he went, he hurried on toward the music.

And ahead of him, the scene came clear. A blue and ocher rug had been laid on the ground between the trees, with wicks in oil flickering along its borders; and at its edge the musicians he'd heard. There were five of them: three women and two men, dressed formally in suits and dresses, in the dark threads of which brilliant designs were somehow concealed, so that the subtlest motion of the folds in the flame light revealed a glamour that brought to Cal's mind the iridescence of tropical butterflies. More startling, however, was the fact that this quintet had not a single instrument between them. They were *singing* these violins, pipes, and drums, and offering in addition sounds no instrument could hope to produce. Here was a music which did not imitate natural sound—it was not bird or whale song, nor tree nor stream—but instead expressed experiences which lay between words: the off-beat of the heart, where intellect could not go.

Hearing it, shudders of pleasure ran down Cal's spine.

The show had drawn an audience of perhaps thirty Seerkind, and Cal joined them. His presence was noted by a few, who threw mildly curious glances in his direction.

Surveying the crowd, he attempted to allot these people to one or other of the four Families, but it was near enough impossible. The choral orchestra were presumably Aia; hadn't Apolline said that it was Aia blood that had given her a good singing voice? But among the rest, who was who? Which of these people were of Jerichau's Family, for instance: the Babu? Which of the Ye-me, or the Lo? There were Negro and Caucasian faces, and one or two with an Oriental cast; there were some who boasted traits not quite human— one with Nimrod's golden eyes (and tail too, presumably); another pair whose features carried symmetrical marking that crept down from the scalp; yet others who bore—either at the dictates of fashion or theology—elaborate tattoos and hairstyles. There was the same startling variety in the clothes they wore, the formal designs of their late-nineteenth-century garb refashioned to suit the wearer. And in the fabrics of skirts, suits, and waistcoats, the same barely concealed iridescence: threads of carnival brilliance in wait behind the monochrome.

Cal's admiring gaze went from one face to another, and he felt he wanted each of these people as a friend, wanted to know them and walk with them and share his pittance of secrets with them. He was vaguely aware that this was probably the fruit talking. But if so, then it was wise fruit.

Though his hunger was assuaged, he took another of the pears from his pocket and was about to peel it when the music came to an end. There was applause and whistling. The quintet took their bows. As they did so a bearded man with a face as lined as a walnut, who had been sitting on a stool close to the edge of the rug, stood up. He looked directly at Cal and said:

"My friends . . . my friends . . . we have a stranger among us . . ."

The applause was dying down. Faces turned in Cal's direction; he could feel himself blush.

"Come out, Mr. Mooney! Mr. *Calhoun Mooney!*"

Ganza told the truth: the air *did* gossip.

The man was beckoning. Cal made a murmur of protest.

"Come on. Entertain us a while!" came the reply.

At this Cal's heart started to thump furiously. "I can't," he said.

"Of course you can," the man grinned. "Of course you can!"

There was more applause. The shining faces smiled around him. Somebody touched his shoulder. He glanced round. It was Novello.

"That's Mr. Lo," said the monkey. "You mustn't refuse him."

"But I can't *do* anything—"

"Everybody can do *something*," said the monkey. "If it's only fart."

"Come on, come on," Lemuel Lo was saying. "Don't be shy."

Much against his will, Cal edged through the crowd toward the rectangle of wicks.

"Really . . . ," he said to Lo. "I don't think . . ."

"You've eaten freely of my fruit," said Lo, without rancor. "The least you can do is entertain us."

Cal looked about him for some support, but all he saw were expectant faces.

"I can't sing, and I've two left feet," he pointed out, still hoping self-depreciation might earn him an escape route.

"Your great-grandfather was a poet, wasn't he?" said Lemuel, his tone almost rebuking Cal for not making mention of the fact.

"He was," said Cal.

"And can you not quote your own great-grandfather?" said Lemuel.

Cal thought about this for a moment. It was clear he was not going to be released from this circle without at least making some stab at recompense for his greed, and Lemuel's suggestion was not a bad one. Many years ago Brendan had taught Cal one or two fragments of Mad Mooney's verse. They'd meant little enough to Cal at the time—he'd been about six years old—but their rhymes had been intriguing.

"The rug is yours," said Lemuel, and stood aside to let Cal have access to the performing area. Before he'd had an opportunity to run any of the lines through his head—it was two decades since he'd learned them; how much would he remember?—he was standing on the rug, staring across the flickering footlights at his audience.

"What Mr. Lo says is true . . . ," he said, all hesitation, "my great-grandfather . . ."

"Speak up," somebody said.

"My great-grandfather was a poet. I'll try and recite one of his verses. I don't know if I can remember them, but I'll do my best."

There was scattered applause at this, which made Cal more uneasy than ever.

"What's it called, this poem?" said Lemuel.

Cal wracked his brain. The title had meant even less than the lines when he'd first been taught it, but he'd learned it anyway, parrot-fashion.

"It's called *Six Commonplaces*," he said, his tongue quicker to shape the words than his brain was to dust them off.

"Tell it, my friend," said the orchard-keeper.

The audience stood with bated breath; the only movement now was that of the flames around the rug.

Cal began.

"*One part of love . . .*"

For a terrible instant his mind went totally blank. If somebody had asked him his name at that juncture he would not have been able to reply. Four words, and he was suddenly speechless.

In that moment of panic he realized that he wanted more than anything in the world to please this gracious gathering; to show them how glad he was to be among them. But his damn tongue—

At the back of his head, the poet said:

"Go on, boy. Tell them what you know. Don't try and remember. Just speak."

He began again, not falteringly this time, but strongly, as though he knew these lines perfectly well. And damn it, he did. They flowed from him easily, and he heard himself speaking them in a voice he'd never have thought himself capable of. A bard's voice, declaiming.

> One part of love is innocence,
> One part of love is guilt,
> One part the milk, that in a sense
> Is soured as soon as spilt.
> One part of love is sentiment,
> One part of love is lust,
> One part is the presentiment
> Of our return to dust."

Eight lines, and it was all over; over, and he was standing, the lines buzzing in his head, both pleased that he'd got through the verse without fumbling, and wishing it could have gone on a while longer. He looked at the audience. They were not smiling any longer, but staring at him with an odd puzzlement in their eyes. For an instant he thought maybe he'd offended them. Then came the applause, hands raised above their heads. There were shouts and whistles.

"It's a fine poem!" Lo said, applauding heartily as he spoke. "And finely delivered!"

So saying, he stepped out of the audience again and embraced Cal with fervor.

"Do you hear?" Cal said to the poet in his skull. "They like you."

And back came another fragment, as if fresh from Mad Mooney's lips. He didn't speak it this time: but he heard it clearly.

> *Forgive my Art. On bended knees,*
> *I do confess: I seek to please.*

And it was a fine thing, this pleasing business. He returned Lemuel's hug.

"Help yourself, Mr. Mooney," the orchard-keeper said, "to all the fruit you can eat."

"Thank you," said Cal.

"Did you ever know the poet?" he asked.

"No," said Cal. "He was dead before I was born."

"Who can call a man dead whose words still hush us and whose sentiments move?" Mr. Lo replied.

"That's true," said Cal.

"Of course it's true. Would I tell a lie on a night like this?"

Having spoken, Lemuel called somebody else out of the crowd: another performer brought to the rug. Cal felt a pang of envy as he stepped over the footlights. He wanted that breathless moment again: wanted to feel the audience held by his words, moved and marked by them. He made a mental note to learn some more of Mad Mooney's verses if and when he saw his father's house again, so that next time he was here he had new lines to enchant with.

His hand was shaken and his face kissed half a dozen times as he made his way back through the crowd. When he turned round to face the rug once more, he was surprised to find that the next performers were Boaz and Ganza. Doubly surprised: they were both naked. There was nothing overtly sexual in their nakedness: indeed it was as formal in its way as the clothes they'd shrugged off. Nor was there any trace of discomfort among the audience: they watched the pair with the same grave and expectant looks as they'd watched him.

Boaz and Ganza had gone to opposite sides of the carpet, halted there a beat, then turned and begun to walk toward each other. They advanced slowly, until they were nose to nose, lip to lip. It crossed Cal's mind that maybe some erotic display *was* in the offing, and in a way that confounded his every definition of erotic, that was true, for they continued to walk toward each other, or so his eyes testified, pressing into each other, their faces disappearing, their torsos congealing, their limbs too, until they were one body, the head an almost featureless ball.

The illusion was absolute. But there was more to come; for the partners were still moving forward, their faces appearing now to press through the back of each other's craniums, as though the bone was soft as marshmallow. And *still* they advanced, until they were like Siamese twins born back to back, their single skull now teased out, and boasting two faces.

As if this weren't enough, there was a further twist to the trick, for somehow in the flux they'd exchanged genders, to stand finally—quite separate once more—in their partner's place.

Love's like that, the monkey had said. Here was the point proved, in flesh and blood.

As the performers bowed, and fresh applause broke out, Cal detached himself from the crowd and began to wander back through the trees. Several vague thoughts were in his head. One, that he couldn't linger here all night, and should soon go in search of Suzanna. Another that it might be wise to seek a guide. The monkey, perhaps?

But first, the laden branches drew his eye again. He reached, took another handful of fruit, and began to peel. Lo's ad hoc vaudeville was still going on behind him. He heard laughter, then more applause, and the music began again.

He felt his limbs growing heavier; his fingers were barely the equal of the peeling; his eyelids drooped. Deciding he'd better sit down before he fell down, he settled beneath one of the trees.

Drowsiness was claiming him, and he had no power to resist it. There was no harm in dozing for a while. He was safe here, in the wash of starlight and applause. His eyes flickered closed. It seemed he could see his dreams approaching—their light growing brighter, their voices louder. He smiled to greet them.

It was his old life he dreamed.

He stood in the shuttered room that lay between his ears and let the lost days appear on the wall like a lantern show; moments retrieved from some stockpile he hadn't even known he'd owned. But the scenes that were paraded before him now—these passages from the unfinished book of his life—no longer seemed quite real. It was fiction, that book; or at best momentarily real, when some part of him had leaped from that stale story, and glimpsed the Fugue in waiting.

The sound of applause called him to the surface of sleep, and his eyes flickered open. The stars were still set among the branches of the Giddy trees; there was still laughter and flame light near at hand; all was well with his newfound land.

I wasn't born 'til now, he thought, as the lantern show returned. I wasn't even born.

Content with that thought, his mind's eye peeled another of Lo's sweet fruits, and put it to his lips.

Somewhere, somebody was applauding him. Hearing it, he took a bow. But this time he did not wake.

ELEVEN

MAKING AND UNMAKING

In non-Western cosmologies the beginning and the end are not the defining moments of a story made to frighten us into righteousness, but two parts of a loop of possibilities. Deities both make and unmake, often in the same instant. It's as though the Madonna were re-created with the Holy Child nestled in the crook of one arm, and an arsenal of assassins' knives in the other.

Art can show us this process at work: make an entertainment of it, even. And sometimes the tension between a Western, or more correctly a Judeo-Christian, view and that of a cyclic cosmology becomes part of the drama. In *Galilee,* for instance, the narrator, Maddox Barbarossa, is motivated to set down all that he knows about the world before it ends, only to find—as the story unfolds—that it contains evidence of its own continuation. In *Weaveworld* a scene of apocalyptic destruction houses the seeds of its own strange renewal. Even in *The Thief of Always,* a book written primarily for children, a metaphysical system is at work. As Harvey Swick unmakes his enemy, Mr. Hood, the dying villain gives up the souls he's stolen and his victims are resurrected. In the same moment Hood's oldest servant happily goes to her death, released from the burden of living. It becomes impossible to judge where the making ends and the unmaking begins. It's all one.

From *Galilee*

W *hat must I do, in the time remaining? Only everything.*
I don't yet know how much I know; but it's a great deal. There are vast tracts of my nature I never knew existed until now. I lived, I suppose, in a cell of my own creation, while outside its walls lay a landscape of unparalleled richness. But I could not bear to venture there. In my self-delusion I thought I was a minor king, and I didn't want to step beyond the bounds of what I knew for fear I lost my dominion. I daresay most of us live in such pitiful realms. It takes something profound to transform us; to open our eyes to our own glorious *diversity*.

Now my eyes were open, and I had no doubt that with my sight came great responsibility. I had to write about what I saw; I had to put it into the words that appear on the very pages you are reading.

But I could bear the weight of that responsibility. Gladly. For now I had the answer to the question: what lay at the center of all the threads of my story? It was myself. I wasn't an abstracted recanter of these lives and loves. I was—*I am*—the story itself; its source, its voice, its music. Perhaps to you that doesn't seem like much of a revelation. But for me, it changes everything. It makes me see, with brutal clarity, the person I once was. It makes me understand for the first time who I am now. And it makes me shake with anticipation of what I must become.

I must tell you not only how the living human world fared, but also how it went among the animals, and among those who had passed from life, yet still wandered the earth. I must tell you about those creatures God made, but also of those who made *themselves* by force of will or appetite. In other words, there must inevitably be unholy business here, just as there will be sacred, but I cannot guarantee to tell you—or even sometimes to know—which is which.

And in my heart I realize I want most to *romance* you; to share with you a vision of the world that puts order where there has been discordance and chaos. Nothing happens carelessly. We're not brought into the world without reason, even though we may never understand that reason. An infant that lives an hour, that dies before it can lay eyes on those who made it, even that soul did not live without purpose: this is my sudden certainty. And it is my duty to sweat until I convince you of the same. Sometimes the stories will recount epic events—wars and insurrection; the fall of dynasties. Sometimes they'll seem, by contrast, inconsequential, and you'll wonder what business they have in these pages. Bear with me. Think of these fragments as the shavings off a carpenter's floor, swept together after some great work has been made. The masterpiece has been taken from the workshop, but what might we learn from a study of some particular curl of wood about the moment of creation? How here the carpenter hesitated, or there moved to complete a form with unerring certainty? Are these shavings then, that seem at first glance redundant, not also part of the great work, being that which has been removed to reveal it?

I won't be staying here at L'Enfant, searching for these shavings. We have great cities to visit: New York and Washington, Paris and London; and further east, and older than any of these, the legendary city of Samarkand, whose crumbling palaces and mosques still welcome travelers on the Silk Road. Weary of cities? Then we'll take to the wilds. To the islands of Hawaii and the mountains of Japan, to forests where the Civil War dead still lie, and stretches of sea no mariner ever crossed. They all have their poetry: the glittering cities and the ruined, the watery wastes and the dusty; I want to show you them all. I want to show you everything.

Only everything: prophets, poets, soldiers, dogs, birds, fishes, lovers, potentates, beggars, ghosts. Nothing is beyond my ambition right now, and nothing is beneath my notice. I will attempt to conjure common divinities, and show you the loveliness of filth.

Wait! What am I saying? There's a kind of madness in my pen; promising all this. It's suicidal. I'm bound to fail. But it's what I want to do. Even if I make a wretched fool of myself in the process, it's what I want to do.

I want to show you bliss; my own, among others. And I will most certainly show you despair. That I promise you without the least hesitation. Despair so deep it will lighten your heart to discover that others suffer so much more than you do.

And how will it all end? This showing, this failing. Honestly? I don't have the slightest idea.

Sitting here, looking out across the lawn, I wonder how far from the borders of our strange little domain the invading world is. Weeks away? Months away? A year? I don't believe any of us here know the answer to that question. Even Cesaria, with all her powers of prophecy, couldn't tell me how fast the enemy will be upon us. All I know is that they will come. *Must* come, indeed, for everybody's sake. I no longer cling to the idea of this house as a blessed refuge for enchantment. Perhaps it was once that. But it has fallen into decadence; its fine ambitions rotted. Better it be taken apart, hopefully with some measure of dignity; but if not, not.

All I want now is the time to enchant you. After that, I suppose I'm history, just as this house is history. I wouldn't be surprised if we didn't both end up at the bottom of the swamp together. And truth to tell, that prospect doesn't entirely distress me, as long as I've done all I need to do before I go.

Which is only everything.

From *Weaveworld*

Always, worlds within worlds.

In the Kingdom of the Cuckoo, the Weave; in the Weave, the Fugue; in the Fugue, the world of Mimi's book, and now this: the Gyre.

But nothing that she'd seen in the pages or places she'd visited could have prepared Suzanna for what she found waiting behind the Mantle.

For one thing, though it had seemed as she stepped through the cloud-curtain that there'd been only night awaiting her on the other side, that darkness had been an illusion.

The landscape of the Gyre was lit with an amber phosphorescence that rose from the very earth beneath her feet. The reversal upset her equilibrium completely. It was almost as if the world had turned over, and she was treading the sky. And the true heavens? They were another wonder. The clouds pressed low, their innards in perpetual turmoil, as if at the least provocation they'd rain lightning on her defenseless head.

When she'd advanced a few yards she glanced behind her, just to be certain that she knew the route back. But the door, and the battlefield of the Narrow Bright beyond, had already disappeared; the cloud was no longer a curtain but a wall. A spasm of panic clutched her belly. She soothed it with the thought that she wasn't alone here. Somewhere up ahead was Cal.

But where? Though the light from the ground was bright enough for her to walk by, it—and the fact that the landscape was so barren—conspired to make a nonsense of distance. She couldn't be certain whether she was seeing twenty yards ahead of her, or two hundred. Whichever, there was no sign of human presence within range of her eyesight. All she could do was follow her nose, and hope to God she was heading in the right direction.

And then, a fresh wonder. At her feet, a trail had appeared; or rather two trails, intermingled. Though the earth was impacted and dry—so much so that neither Shadwell nor Cal's footfalls had left an indentation, where the invaders had trodden the ground seemed to be vibrating. That was her first impression, at least. But as she followed their route the truth became apparent: the soil along the path pursuer and pursued had taken was *sprouting*.

She stopped walking and went down on her haunches to confirm the phenomenon. Her eyes weren't misleading her. The earth was cracking, and yellow-green tendrils, their strength out of all proportion to their size, were corkscrewing up out of the cracks, their growth so fast she could watch it happening. Was this some elaborate defense mechanism on the Gyre's part? Or had those ahead of her carried seeds into this sterile world, which the raptures here had urged into immediate life? She looked back. Her own route was similarly marked, the shoots only just appearing, while those in Cal and Shadwell's path—with a minute or more's headway—were already six inches high. One was uncurling like a fern; another had pods; a third was spiny. At this rate of growth they'd be trees within an hour.

Extraordinary as the spectacle was, she had no time to study it. Following this trail of proliferating life, she pressed on.

Though she'd picked up her pace to a trot, there was still no sign of those she was following. The flowering path was the only proof of their passing.

She was soon obliged to run well off the trail, for the plants, growing at exponential rate, were spreading laterally as well as vertically. As they swelled it became clear how little they had in common with the Kingdom's flora. If they had sprung from seeds brought in on human heels, the enchantments here had wrought profound changes in them.

Indeed the resemblance was less to a jungle than to some undersea reef, not least because the plants' prodigious growth made them sway as if moved by a tide. Their colors and their forms were utterly various; not one was like its neighbor. All they had in common was their enthusiasm for growth, for fruitfulness. Clouds of scented pollen were being expelled like breaths; pulsing blossoms were turning their heads to the clouds, as if the lightning was a kind of sustenance; roots were spreading underfoot with such violence the earth trembled.

Yet there was nothing threatening in this surge of life. The eagerness here was simply the eagerness of the new born. They grew for the pleasure of growing.

Then, from off to her right, she heard a cry; or something like a cry. Was it Cal? No; there was no sign of the trail dividing. It came again, somewhere between a sob and a sigh. It was impossible to ignore, despite her mission. Promising herself only the briefest of detours, she followed the sound.

Distance was so deceptive here. She'd advanced perhaps two dozen yards from the trail when the air unveiled the source of the sound.

It was a plant, the first living thing she'd seen here beyond the limits of the trail, with which it shared the same multiplicity of forms and brilliance of color. It was the size of a small tree, its heart a knot of boughs so complex she suspected it must be several plants growing together in one spot. She heard rustling in the blossom-laden thicket, and among the serpentine roots, but she couldn't see the creature whose call had brought her here.

Something did become apparent, however: that the knot at the center of the tree, all but lost among the foliage, was a human corpse. If she needed further confirmation it was in plain sight. Fragments of a fine suit, hanging from the boughs like the sloughed skins of executive snakes; a shoe, parceled up in tendrils. The clothes had been shredded so that the dead flesh could be claimed by flora; green life springing up where red had failed. The corpse's legs had grown woody, and sprouted knotted roots; shoots were exploding from its innards.

There was no time to linger and look; she had work to do. She made one circuit of the tree, and was about to return to the path when she saw a pair of living eyes staring out at her from the leaves. She yelped. They blinked. Tentatively, she reached forward, and parted the twigs.

The head of the man she'd taken for dead was on almost back to front, and his skull had been cracked wide open. But everywhere the wounds had bred sumptuous life. A beard, lush as new grass, grew around a mossy mouth which ran with sap; floret-laden twigs broke from the cheeks.

The eyes watched her intently, and she felt moist tendrils reaching up to investigate her face and hair.

Then, its blossoms shaking as it drew breath, the hybrid spoke. One long, soft word.

"Amialive."

Was it naming itself? When she'd overcome her surprise, she told it she didn't understand.

It seemed to frown. There was a fall of petals from its crown of flowers. The throat pulsed, and then regurgitated the syllables, this time better punctuated.

"Am ia live?"

"Are you alive?" she said, comprehending now. "Of course. Of course you're alive."

"I thought I was dreaming," it said, its eyes wandering from its perusal of her a while, then returning. "Dead, or dreaming. Or both. One moment . . . bricks in the air, breaking my head . . ."

"Shearman's house?" she said.

"Ah. You were there?"

"The Auction. You were at the Auction."

It laughed to itself, and its humor tingled against her cheek.

"I always wanted . . . to be inside . . . ," he said, "inside . . ."

And now she understood the how and why of this. Though it was odd to think—odd? it was *incredible*—that this creature had been one of Shadwell's party, that was what she construed. Injured, or perhaps killed in the destruction of the house, he'd somehow been caught up in the Gyre, which had turned his broken body to this flowering purpose.

Her face must have registered her distress at his state, for the tendrils empathized, and grew jittery.

"So I'm not dreaming then," the hybrid said.

"No."

"Strange," came the reply. "I thought I was. It's so like paradise."

She wasn't sure she'd heard correctly.

"Paradise?" she said.

"I never dared hope . . . life would be such pleasure."

She smiled. The tendrils were soothed.

"This is Wonderland," the hybrid said.

"Really?"

"Oh yes. We're near to where the Weave began; near to the Temple of the Loom. Here everything transforms, everything *becomes*. Me? I was lost. Look at me now. How I am!"

Hearing his boast her mind went back to the adventures she'd had in the book; how, in that no-man's-land between words and the world, everything had been transforming and becoming, and her mind, married in hatred with Hobart's, had been the energy of that condition. She the warp to his weft. Thoughts from different skulls, crossing, and making a material place from their conflict.

It was all part of the same procedure.

The knowledge was slippery; she wanted an equation in which she could fix the lesson, in case she could put it to use. But there were more pressing issues now than the higher mathematics of the imagination.

"I must go," she said.

"Of course you must."

"There are others here."

"I saw," said the hybrid. "Passing overhead."

"Overhead?"

"Toward the Loom."

Toward the Loom.

She retraced her steps to the trail with fresh enthusiasm. The fact of the buyer's existence in the Gyre, apparently accepted by the forces here— even welcomed—gave her some hope that the mere presence of a trespasser was not sufficient to make the Gyre turn itself inside out. Its sensitivity had apparently been overestimated. It was strong enough to deal with an invading force in its own inimitable fashion.

Her skin had begun to itch, and there was a restlessness in her gut. She tried not to think too hard of what this signified, but the irritation increased as she again followed the trail. The atmosphere was thickening now; the world around her darkening. It wasn't night's darkness, coaxing sleep. The murk buzzed with life. She could taste it, sweet and sour. She could see it, busy behind her eyes.

She'd gone only a little way when something ran across her feet. She looked down to see an animal—an unlikely cross between squirrel and centipede, eyes bright, legs innumerable, cavorting between the roots. Nor, she now realized, was the creature alone. The forest was inhabited.

Animals, as numerous and as remarkable as the plant life, were spilling out from the undergrowth, changing even as they hopped and squirmed, more ambitious by the breath.

Their origins?: the plants. The flora had parented its own fauna; its buds flowering into insects, its fruits growing fur and scales. A plant opened, and butterflies rose in a flickering cloud; in a thorn thicket birds were fluttering into life; from a tree trunk, white snakes poured like sentient sap.

The air was so thick now she could have sliced it, new creatures crossing her path with every yard she advanced, only to be eclipsed by the murk. Something that was a distant relation of the armadillo waddled in front of her; three variations on the theme of ape came and went; a golden dog cavorted among the flowers. And so on. And so forth.

She had no doubt now why her skin itched. It longed to join this game of changes, to throw itself back into the melting pot and find a new design. Her mind, too, was half seduced by the notion. Among such joyous invention it seemed churlish to cleave to a single anatomy.

Indeed she might have succumbed in time to these temptations of the flesh, but that ahead of her a building now emerged from the fog: a plain brick building which she caught sight of for an instant before the air enclosed it again. Plain as it was, this could only be the Temple of the Loom.

A huge parrot swooped in front of her, speaking in tongues, then flitted away. She began to run. The golden dog had elected to keep pace with her; it panted at her heels.

Then, the shock wave. It came from the direction of the building, a force that convulsed the living membrane of the air, and rocked the earth. She was thrown off her feet amid sprawling roots, which instantly attempted to incorporate her into their design. She disengaged them from around about her, and pulled herself to her feet. Either the contact with the earth, or the wave of energy from the Temple, had sent her into paroxysms. Though she was standing quite still her whole body seemed to be *dancing*. There was no other word for it. Every part of her, from eyelash to marrow, had caught the rhythm of power here; its percussion ordered her heart to a different beat; her blood sped then slowed; her mind soared and plummeted by turns.

But that was only flesh. Her other anatomy—the subtle body which the menstruum had quickened—was beyond the control of the forces here; or else was already in such accord with them it was left to its own work.

She occupied it now—telling it to keep her feet from rooting, and her head from sprouting wings and flying off. It soothed her. She'd been a dragon, and emerged again, hadn't she? This was no different.

Yes it is, said her fears. This is flesh and bone business; the dragon was all in my mind.

Haven't you learned yet? came the reply, there *is* no difference.

As the answer rang in her head, the second shock wave struck; and this time it was no petit mal, but the full fit. The ground beneath her began to roar. She started to run toward the Temple once more, as the noise mounted, but she'd got five yards at best when the roar became the hard din of breaking stone, and a zigzag crack appeared to the right of her; and to the left another; and another.

The Gyre was tearing itself apart.

Outside the Temple, the quake tremors were worsening. Inside, however, an uneasy peace reigned. Suzanna started to advance down the darkened corridors, the itching in her body subdued now that she was out of the turbulence, in this, the eye of the hurricane.

There was light ahead. She turned a corner, and another, and finding a door in the wall, slipped through into a second passageway, as spartan as the one she'd left. The light was still tantalizingly out of reach. Around the next corner, it promised; just a little further, a little further.

The menstruum was quiet inside her, as though it feared to show itself. Was that the natural respect one miracle paid to a greater? If so, the raptures here were hiding their faces with no little skill; there was nothing about these corridors suggestive of revelation or power: just bare brick. Except for the light. That coaxed her still, through another door and along further passageways. The building, she now realized, was built on the principle of a Russian doll, one within another. *Worlds within worlds.* They couldn't diminish infinitely, she told herself. Or could they?

Around the very next corner she had her answer, or at least part of it, as a shadow was thrown up against the wall and she heard somebody shouting:

"*What in God's name?*"

For the first time since setting foot here, she felt the ground vibrate. There was a fall of brick dust from the ceiling.

"Shadwell," she said.

As she spoke it seemed she could see the two syllables—*Shad Well*— carried along the corridor toward the next door. A fleeting memory came too: of Jerichau speaking his love to her; word as reality.

The shadow on the wall shifted, and suddenly the Salesman was standing in front of her. All trace of the Prophet had gone. The face revealed beneath was bloated and pale; the face of a beached fish.

"Gone," he said.

He was shaking from head to foot. Sweat droplets decorated his face like pearls.

"It's all gone."

Any fear she might once have had of this man had disappeared. He was here unmasked as ludicrous. But his words made her wonder. *What* had gone? She began to walk toward the door he'd stepped through.

"It was *you* —" he said, his shakes worsening. "*You* did this."

"I did nothing."

"Oh yes —"

As she came within a yard of him he reached for her, his clammy hands suddenly about her neck.

"*There's nothing there!*" he shrieked, pulling her close.

His grip intended harm, but the menstruum didn't rise to her aid. She was left with only muscle power to disengage him, and it was not enough.

"You want to see?" he screamed into her face. "You want to see how I've been cheated? *I'll show you!*"

He dragged her toward the door, and pitched her through into the room at the heart of the Temple: the inner sanctum in which the miracles of the Gyre had been generated; the powerhouse which had held the many worlds of the Fugue together for so long.

It was a room some fifteen feet square, built of the same naked brick as the rest of the Temple, and high. She looked up to see that the roof had a skylight of sorts, open to the heavens. The clouds that swirled around the Temple roof shed a milky brightness down, as if the lightning from the Gyre was being kindled in the womb of troubled air above. The clouds were not the only movement overhead, however. As she gazed up she caught sight of a form in the corner of the roof. Before her gaze could focus on it, Shadwell was approaching her.

"Where is it?" he demanded. "Where's the Loom?"

She looked around the sanctum, and discovered now that it was not entirely bare. In each of the four corners a figure was sitting, gazing toward the center of the room. Her spine twitched. Though they sat bolt upright on their high-backed chairs, the quartet were long dead, their flesh like stained paper on their bones, their clothes hanging in rotted rags.

Had these guardians been murdered where they sat, so that thieves could remove the Loom unchallenged? So it seemed. Yet there was nothing in their posture that suggested a violent death; nor could she believe that this charmed place would have sanctioned bloodshed. No; something else had happened here—*was happening still, perhaps*—some essential point both she and Shadwell could not yet grasp.

He was still muttering to himself, his voice a decaying spiral of complaint. She was only half-listening; she was far more interested in the object she now saw lying in the middle of the floor. There it lay, the kitchen knife Cal had brought into the Auction Room all those months ago; the commonplace domestic tool which the look between them had somehow drawn into the Weave, to this very spot, the absolute center of the Fugue.

Seeing it, pieces of the riddle began to slot together in her head. Here, where the glances of the sentinels intersected, lay the knife that *another* glance—between herself and Cal—had empowered. It had entered this chamber and somehow cut the last knot the Loom had created; and the Weave had released its secrets. All of which was well and good, except that the sentinels were dead, and the Loom, as Shadwell kept repeating, was gone.

"You were the one," he growled. "You knew all along."

She ignored his accusations, a new thought forming. If the magic *had* gone, she reasoned, why did the menstruum hide itself?

As she shaped the question Shadwell's fury drove him to attack.

"*I'll kill you!*" he yelled.

His assault caught her unawares, and she was flung back against the wall. The breath went out of her in a rush, and before she could defend herself his thumbs were at her throat, his bulk trapping her.

"Thieving bitch," he said. "You cheated me!"

She raised her hands to beat him off, but she was already growing weak. She struggled to draw breath, desperate for a mouthful of air even if it was the flatulent breath he was expelling, but his grip on her throat prevented so much as a mouthful reaching her. I'm going to die, she thought; I'm going to die looking into this curdled face.

And then her upturned eyes caught a glimpse of movement in the roof, and a voice said:

"The Loom is here."

Shadwell's grip on Suzanna relaxed. He turned, and looked up at the speaker.

Immacolata, her arms spread out like a parachutist in free-fall, was hovering above them.

"Do you remember me?" she asked Shadwell.

"Jesus Christ."

"I missed you, Shadwell. Though you were unkind."

"Where's the Loom?" he said. "Tell me."

"There is no Loom," she replied.

"But you just said—"

"The Loom is here."

"Where then? *Where?*"

"There is no Loom."

"You're out of your mind," he yelled up at her. "Either there *is* or there *isn't!*"

The Incantatrix had a skull's smile as she gazed down on the man below.

"*You're* the fool," she said mildly. "You don't understand, do you?"

Shadwell put on a gentler tone. "Why don't you come down?" he said. "My neck aches."

She shook her head. It cost her effort to hang in the air that way, Suzanna could see; she was defying the sanctity of the Temple by working her raptures here. But she flew in the face of such edicts, determined to remind Shadwell of how earthbound he was.

"Afraid, are you?" said Shadwell.

Immacolata's smile did not falter. "I'm not afraid," she said, and began to float down toward him.

Keep out of his way, Suzanna willed her. Though the Incantatrix had done terrible harm, Suzanna had no desire to see her felled by Shadwell's mischief. But the Salesman stood face to face with the woman and made no move. He simply said:

"You reached here before me."

"I almost forgot you," Immacolata replied. Her voice had lost any trace of stridency. It was full of sighs. "But *she* reminded me," she glanced at Suzanna. "It was a fine service you did me, sister," she said. "To remind me of my enemy."

Her eyes went back to Shadwell.

"You drove me mad," she said. "And I forgot you. But I remember now."

Suddenly the smile and the sighs had gone entirely. There was only ruin, and rage.

"I remember very well."

"Where's the Loom?" Shadwell demanded.

"You were always so *literal*," Immacolata replied, contemptuously. "Did you really expect to find a *thing*? Another object to be possessed? Is that your Godhood, Shadwell? Possession?"

"*Where the fuck is it?*"

She laughed then, though the sound from her throat had nothing to do with pleasure.

Her ridicule pressed Shadwell to breaking point; he flung himself at her. But she was not about to let herself be touched by his hands. As he snatched hold of her it seemed to Suzanna that her whole ruined face cracked open, spilling a force that might once have been the menstruum—that cool, bright river Suzanna had first plunged into at Immacolata's behest—but was now a damned and polluted stream, breaking from the wounds like pus. It had force nevertheless. Shadwell was thrown to the ground.

Overhead, the clouds threw lightning across the roof, freezing the scene below by its scalpel light. The killing blow could only be a glance away, surely.

But it didn't come. The Incantatrix hesitated, the broken face leaking tainted power, and in that instant Shadwell's hand closed on the kitchen knife at his side.

Suzanna cried a warning, but Immacolata either failed to hear or chose not to. Then Shadwell was on his feet, his ungainly rise offering his victim a moment to strike him down, which was missed—and drove the blade up into her abdomen, a butcher's stroke which opened a traumatic wound.

At last she seemed to know he meant her death, and responded. Her face began to blaze afresh, but before the spark could become fire Shadwell's blade was dividing her to the breasts. Her innards slid from the wound. She screamed, and threw back her head, the unleashed force wasted against the sanctum walls.

On the instant, the room was filled with a roaring that seemed to come from both the bricks and the innards of Immacolata. Shadwell dropped the blood-slicked knife, and made to retreat from his crime, but his victim reached out and pulled him close.

The fire had entirely gone from Immacolata's face. She was dying, and quickly. But even in her failing moments her grip was strong. As the roaring grew louder she granted Shadwell the embrace she'd always denied him, her wound besmirching his jacket. He made a cry of repugnance, but she wouldn't let him go. He struggled, and finally succeeded in breaking her hold, throwing her off and staggering from her, his chest and belly plastered with blood. He cast one more look in her direction then started toward the door, making small moans of horror. As he reached the exit he looked up at Suzanna.

"I didn't . . . ," he began, his hands raised, blood trickling between his fingers. "It wasn't me . . ."

The words were as much appeal as denial.

"*It was magic!*" he said, tears starting to his eyes. Not of sorrow, she knew, but of a sudden righteous rage.

"*Filthy magic!*" he shrieked. The ground rocked to hear its glory denied.

He didn't wait to have the roof fall on his head, but fled from the chamber as the roars rose in intensity.

Suzanna looked back at Immacolata.

Despite the grievous wounding she'd sustained she was not yet dead. She was standing against one of the walls, clinging to the brick with one hand and keeping her innards from falling with the other.

"Blood's been spilled," she said, as another tremor, more fierce than any that had preceded it, unknitted the foundations of the building. "Blood's been spilled in the Temple of the Loom."

She smiled that terrible, twisted smile.

"The Fugue's undone, sister—" she said.

"What do you mean?"

"I came here intending to spill his blood and bring the Gyre down. Seems it's me who's done the bleeding. It's no matter." Her voice grew weaker. Suzanna stepped close, to hear her better. "It's all the same in the end. *The Fugue is finished.* It'll be dust. All dust . . ."

She pushed herself off the wall. Suzanna reached and kept her from falling. The contact made her palm tingle.

"They're exiles forever," Immacolata said, and frail as it was, there was triumph in her voice. "The Fugue ends here. Wiped away as if it had never been."

At this, her legs buckled beneath her. Pushing Suzanna away, she stumbled back against the wall. Her hand slipped from her belly; her guts unspooled.

"I used to dream . . . ," she said, "terrible emptiness . . ."

She stopped speaking, as she slid down the wall, strands of her hair catching on the brick.

"Sand and nothingness," she said. "That's what I dreamed. Sand and nothingness. And here it is."

As if to bear out her remark the din grew cataclysmic.

Satisfied with her labors, Immacolata sank to the ground.

Suzanna looked toward her escape route, as the bricks of the Temple began to grind upon each other with fresh ferocity. What more could she do here? The mysteries of the Loom had defeated her. If she stayed she'd be buried in the ruins. There was nothing left to do but get out while she still could.

As she moved to the door, two pencil beams of light sliced through the grimy air, and struck her arm. Their brightness shocked her. More shocking still, their source. They were coming from the eye sockets of one of the sentinels. She stepped out of the path of the light, and as the beams struck the corpse opposite lights flared there too; then in the third sentinel's head, and the fourth.

These events weren't lost on Immacolata.

"The Loom . . . ," she whispered, her breath failing.

The intersecting beams were brightening, and the fraught air was soothed by the sound of voices, softly murmuring words so unfixable they were almost music.

"You're too late," said the Incantatrix, her comment made not to Suzanna but to the dead quartet. "You can't save it now."

Her head began to slip forward.

"Too late . . . ," she said again.

Then a shudder went through her. The body, vacated by spirit, keeled over. She lay dead in her blood.

Despite her dying words, the power here was still building. Suzanna backed toward the door, to clear the beams' route completely. With nothing to bar their way they immediately redoubled their brilliance, and from the point of collision threw up new beams at every angle. The whispering that filled the chamber suddenly found a fresh rhythm; the words, though still alien to her, ran like a melodious poem. Somehow, they and the light were part of one system; the raptures of the four Families—Aia, Lo, Ye-me, and Babu—working together: word music accompanying a woven dance of light.

This was the Loom; of course. *This was the Loom.*

No wonder Immacolata had poured scorn on Shadwell's literalism. Magic might be bestowed upon the physical, but it didn't *reside* there. It resided in the word, which was mind spoken, and in motion, which was mind made manifest; in the system of the Weave and the evocations of the melody: all *mind*.

Yet damn it, this recognition was not enough. Finally she was still only a Cuckoo, and all the puzzle-solving in the world wouldn't help her mellow the rage of this desecrated place. All she could do was watch the Loom's wrath shake the Fugue and all it contained apart.

In her frustration her thoughts went to Mimi, who had brought her into this adventure, but had died too soon to entirely prepare her for it. Surely even she would not have predicted this: the Fugue's failing, and Suzanna at its heart, unable to keep it beating.

The lights were still colliding and multiplying, the beams growing so solid now she might have walked upon them. Their performances transfixed her. She felt she could watch them forever, and never tire of their complexities. And still they grew more elaborate, more solid, until she was certain they would not be bound within the walls of the sanctum, but would burst out—

Into the Fugue, where she had to go. Out to where Cal was lying, to comfort him as best she could in the imminent maelstrom.

With this thought came another. That perhaps Mimi *had* known, or feared, that in the end it would simply be Suzanna and the magic—and that maybe the old woman had after all left a signpost.

She reached into her pocket, and brought out the book. *Secrets of the Hidden Peoples*. She didn't need to open the book to remember the epigraph on the dedication page:

"What can be imagined need never be lost."

She'd tussled with its meaning repeatedly, but her intellect had failed to make much sense of it. Now she forsook her analytical thinking and let subtler sensibilities take over.

The light of the Loom was so bright it hurt her eyes, and as she stepped out of the sanctum she discovered that the beams were exploiting chinks in the brick—either that or eating at the wall—and breaking through. Needle-thin lines of light stratified the passageway.

Her thoughts as much on the book in her hand as on her safety, she made her way back via the route she'd come: door and passageway, door and passageway. Even the outer layers of corridor were not immune to the Loom's glamour. The beams had broken through three solid walls and were growing wider with every moment. As she walked through them, she felt the menstruum stir in her for the first time since she'd entered the Gyre. It rose not to her face, however, but through her arms and into her hands, which clasped the book, as though charging it.

What can be imagined—

The chanting rose; the light beams multiplied.

—*need never be lost.*

The book grew heavier; warmer; like a living thing in her arms. And yet, so full of dreams. A thing of ink and paper in which another world awaited release. Not one world perhaps, but many; for as she and Hobart's time in the pages had proved, each adventurer reimagined the stories for themselves. There were as many Wild Woods as there were readers to wander there.

She was out into the third corridor now, and the whole Temple had become a hive of light and sound. There was so much energy here, waiting to be channeled. If she could only be the catalyst that turned its strength to better ends than destruction.

Her head was full of images, or fragments thereof:

She and Hobart in the forest of their story, exchanging skins and fictions;

She and Cal in the Auction Room, their glance the engine that turned the knife above the Weave.

And finally, the sentinels sitting in the Loom chamber. Eight eyes that had, even in death, the power to unmake the Weave. And . . . *make* it again?

Suddenly, she wasn't walking any longer. She was running, not for fear that the roof would come down on her head but because the final pieces of the puzzle were coming clear, and she had so little time.

Redeeming the Fugue could not be done alone. Of course not. No rapture could be performed alone. Their essence was in exchange. That was why the Families sang and danced and wove: their magic blossomed *between people*: between performer and spectator, maker and admirer.

And wasn't there rapture at work between her mind and the mind in the book she held? her eyes scanning the page and soaking up another soul's dreams? It was like love. Or rather love was its highest form: mind shaping mind, visions pirouetting on the threads between lovers.

"*Cal!*"

She was at the last door, and flinging herself into the turmoil beyond.

The light in the earth had turned to the color of bruises, blue-black and purple. The sky above writhed, ripe to discharge its innards. From the music and the exquisite geometry of light inside the Temple, she was suddenly in bedlam.

Cal was propped against the wall of the Temple. His face was white, but he was alive.

She went to him and knelt by his side.

"What's happening?" he said, his voice lazy with exhaustion.

"I've no time to explain," she said, her hand stroking his face. The menstruum played against his cheek. "You have to trust me."

"Yes," he said.

"Good. You have to think for me, Cal. Think of everything you remember."

"Remember . . . ?"

As he puzzled at her a crack, fully a foot wide, opened in the earth, running from the threshold of the Temple like a messenger. The news it carried was all grim. Seeing it, doubts filled Suzanna. How could anything be claimed from this chaos? The sky shed thunder; dust and dirt were flung up from the crevasses that gaped on every side.

She endeavored to hold on to the comprehension she'd found in the corridors behind her. Tried to keep the images of the Loom in her head. The beams intersecting. Thought over and under thought. Minds filling the void with *shared* memories and *shared* dreams.

"Think of everything you remember about the Fugue," she said.

"Everything?"

"Everything. All the places you've seen."

"Why?"

"Trust me!" she said. "Please God, Cal, trust me. What do you remember?"

"Just bits and pieces."

"Whatever you can find. Every little piece."

She pressed her palm to his face. He was feverish, but the book in her other hand was hotter.

In recent times she'd shared intimacies with her greatest enemy, Hobart. Surely she could share knowledge with this man, whose sweetness she'd come to love.

"Please . . . ," she said.

"For you . . . ," he replied, seeming to know at last all she felt for him, "anything."

And the thoughts came. She felt them flow into her, and through her; she was a conduit, the menstruum the stream on which his memories were carried. Her mind's eye saw glimpses only of what he'd seen and felt here in the Fugue, but they were things fine and beautiful.

An orchard; firelight; fruit; people dancing; singing. A road; a field; de

Bono and the rope-dancers. The Firmament (rooms full of miracles); a rickshaw; a house, with a man standing on the step. A mountain, and planets. Most of it came too fast for her to focus upon, but *her* comprehension of what he'd seen wasn't the point. She was just part of a cycle—as she'd been in the Auction Room.

Behind her, she felt the beams breaking through the last wall, as though the Loom was coming to meet her, its genius for transfiguration momentarily at her disposal. They hadn't got long. If she missed this wave there'd be no other.

"Go on," she said to Cal.

He had his eyes closed now, and the images were still pouring out of him. He'd remembered more than she'd dared hope. And she in her turn was adding sights and sounds to the flow—

The lake; Capra's House; the forest; the streets of Nonesuch—

They came back, razor sharp, and she felt the beams pick them up and speed them on their way.

She'd feared the Loom would reject her interference, but not at all; it married its power to that of the menstruum, transforming all that she and Cal were remembering.

She had no control over these processes. They were beyond her grasp. All she could do was be a part of the exchange between meaning and magic, and trust that the forces at work here comprehended her intentions better than she did.

But the power behind her was growing too strong for her; she could not channel its energies much longer. The book was getting too hot to hold, and Cal was shuddering beneath her hand.

"Enough!" she said.

Cal's eyes flew open.

"I haven't finished."

"*Enough I said.*"

As she spoke, the structure of the Temple began to shudder.

Cal said: "Oh God."

"Time to go," said Suzanna. "Can you walk?"

"Of course I can walk."

She helped him to his feet. There were roars from within, as one after another the walls capitulated to the rage of the Loom.

They didn't wait to watch the final cataclysm, but started away from the Temple, brick-shards whining past their heads.

Cal was as good as his word: he could indeed walk, albeit slowly. But running would have been impossible in the wasteland they were now obliged to cross. As Creation had been the touchstone of the outward journey, wholesale Destruction marked their return. The flora and fauna that had sprung into being in the footsteps of the trespassers were now suffering a swift dissolution. Flowers and trees were withering, the stench of their rot carried on the hooligan winds that scoured the Gyre.

With the earth-light dimmed, the scene was murky, the gloom further thickened by dust and airborne matter. From the darkness animal cries rose as the earth opened and consumed the very creatures it had produced mere minutes before. Those not devoured by the bed from which they'd sprung were subject to a fate still more terrible, as the powers that had made them unknitted their children. Pale, skeletal things that had once been bright and alive now littered the landscape, breathing their last. Some turned their eyes up to Cal and Suzanna, looking for hope or help, but they had none to offer.

It was as much as they could do to keep the cracks in the earth from claiming them too. They stumbled on, arms about each other, heads bowed beneath a barrage of hailstones which the Mantle, as though to perfect their misery, had unleashed.

"How far?" Cal said.

They halted and Suzanna stared ahead; she could not be certain they were not simply walking in circles. The light at their feet was now all but extinguished. Here and there it flared up, but only to illuminate another pitiable scene: the last wracking moments of the glory that their presence here had engendered.

Then:

"*There!*" she said, pointing through the curtain of hail and dust. "*I see a light.*"

They set off again, as fast as the suppurating earth would allow. With every step, their feet sank deeper into a swamp of decaying matter, in which the remnants of life still moved; the inheritors of this Eden: worms and cockroaches.

But there was a distinct light at the end of the tunnel; she glimpsed it again through the thick air.

"Look up, Cal," she said.

He did just that, though only with effort.

"Not far now. A few more steps."

He was becoming heavier by the moment; but the tear in the Mantle was sufficient to spur them on over the last few yards of treacherous earth.

And finally they stepped out into the light, almost spat from the entrails of the Gyre as it went into its final convulsions.

They stumbled away from the Mantle, but not far before Cal said:

"I can't . . . ," and fell to the ground.

She knelt beside him, cradling his head, then looked around for help. Only then did she see the consequences of events in the Gyre.

Wonderland had gone.

The glories of the Fugue had been shredded and torn, their tatters evaporating even as she watched. Water, wood, and stone; living animal tissue and dead Seerkind: all gone, as though it had never been. A few remnants lingered, but not for long. As the Gyre thundered and shook, these last signs of the Fugue's terrain became smoke and threads, then empty air. It was horribly quick.

Suzanna looked behind her. The Mantle was receding too, now that it had nothing left to conceal, its retreat uncovering a wasteland of dirt and fractured rock. Even its thunder was diminishing.

"Suzanna!"

She looked back to see de Bono coming toward her.

"What happened in there?"

"Later," she said. "First, we have to get help for Cal. He's been shot."

"I'll fetch a car."

Cal's eyes flickered open.

"Is it gone?" he murmured.

"Don't think about it now," she said.

"I want to know," he demanded, with surprising vehemence, and struggled to sit up. Knowing he wouldn't be placated, Suzanna helped him.

He moaned, seeing the desolation before them.

Groups of Seerkind, with a few of Hobart's people scattered among them, stood in the valley and up the slopes of the surrounding hills, neither speaking nor moving. They were all that remained.

"What about Shadwell?" said Cal.

Suzanna shrugged. "I don't know," she said. "He escaped the Temple before me."

The din of a revved car-engine canceled further conversation, as de Bono drove one of the invaders' vehicles across the dead grass, bringing it to a halt a few feet from where Cal lay.

"I'll drive," said Suzanna, once Cal had been laid on the backseat.

"What do we tell the doctors?" Cal said, his voice getting fainter. "I've got a bullet in me."

"We'll cross that bridge when we come to it," said Suzanna. As she got into the driver's seat, which de Bono had only reluctantly vacated, somebody called her name. Nimrod was running toward the car.

"Where are you going?" he said to her.

She directed his attention to the passenger.

"My friend," he said, seeing Cal, "you look the worse for wear." He tried a smile of welcome, but tears came instead.

"It's over," he said, sobbing. "Destroyed. Our sweet land . . ." He wiped his eyes and nose with the back of his hand. "What do we do now?" he said to Suzanna.

"We get out of harm's way," she told him. "As quickly as we can. We still have enemies—"

"It doesn't matter anymore," he said. "The Fugue's gone. Everything we ever possessed, *lost*."

"We're alive, aren't we?" she said. "As long as we're alive . . ."

"Where will we go?"

"We'll find a place."

"You have to lead us now," said Nimrod. "There's only you."

"Later. First, we have to help Cal—"

"Yes," he said. "Of course." He'd taken hold of her arm, and was loath to let her go. "You *will* come back?"

"Of course," she said.

"I'll take the rest of them North," he told her. "Two valleys from here. We'll wait for you there."

"Then *move*," she said. "Time's wasting."

"You will remember?" he said.

She would have laughed his doubts off, but that remembering was all. Instead she touched his wet face, letting him feel the menstruum in her fingers.

It was only as she drove away that she realized she'd probably blessed him.

From *The Thief of Always*

Hood didn't waste any time. He'd no sooner made his final offer to Harvey than the balmy wind grew gusty, carrying off the lamb's wool clouds that had been drifting through the summer sky. In their place came a juggernaut: a thunderhead the size of a mountain, which loomed over the House like a shadow thrown against Heaven.

It had more than lightning at its dark heart. It had the light rains that came at early morning to coax forth the seeds of another spring; it had the drooping fogs of autumn, and the spiraling snows that had brought so many midnight Christmases to the House. Now all three fell at once— rains, snows, and fogs—as a chilly sleet that all but covered the sun. It would have killed the flowers on the slope with cold, had the wind not reached them first, tearing through the blossoms with such vehemence that every petal and leaf was snatched up into the air.

Standing between this fragrant tide and the plummeting curtain of ice and cloud, Harvey was barely able to stay upright. But he planted his feet wide apart, and resisted every blast and buffet, determined not to take shelter. This spectacle might be the last he set eyes upon as a free spirit; indeed as a *living* spirit. He intended to enjoy it.

It was a sight to behold; a battle the likes of which the planet had never seen.

To his left, shafts of sunlight pierced the storm clouds in the name of Summer, only to be smothered by Autumn's fogs, while to his right Spring coaxed its legions out of bough and earth, then saw its buds murdered by Winter's frosts before they could show their colors.

Attack after attack was mounted and repulsed, reveille and retreat sounded a hundred times, but no one season was able to carry the day. It was soon impossible to distinguish defeats from victories. The rallies and the feints, the diversions and encirclements all became one confusion. Snows melted into rains as they fell; rains were boiled into vapor, and sweated new shoots out through the rot of their brothers.

And somewhere in the midst of this chaos, the power that had brought it about raised its voice in a rage, demanding that it cease.

"*Enough!*" the Hood-House yelled. "*Enough!*"

But its voice—which had once carried such terrible authority—had grown weak. Its orders went unnoticed; or if noticed, then disobeyed.

The seasons raged on, throwing themselves against each other with rare abandon, and in passing tearing at the House which stood in the midst of their battlefield.

The walls, which had begun to teeter as Hood's power diminished, were thrown over by the raging wind. The chimneys were wracked by thunder, and toppled; the lightning rods struck so many times they melted, and fell through the slateless roof in a burning rain, setting fire to every floorboard, banister, and stick of furniture they touched. The porch, pummeled by hail, was reduced to matchwood. The staircase, rocked to its foundations by the growth in the dirt around it, collapsed like a tower of cards.

Squinting against the face of the storm, Harvey witnessed all of this, and rejoiced. He'd come to the House hoping to steal back the years that Hood had tricked from him, but he'd never dared believe he could bring the whole edifice down. Yet here it was, falling as he watched. Loud though the dins of wind and thunder were, they couldn't drown out the sound of the House as it perished and went to dust. Every nail and sill and brick seemed to shriek at once, a cry of pain that only oblivion could comfort.

Harvey was denied a glimpse of Hood's last moments. A cloud of dirt rose like a veil to cover the sight. But he knew the moment his battle with the Vampire King was over, because the warring seasons suddenly turned to peace. The thunderhead softened its furies, and dispersed; the wind dropped to an idling breeze; the fierce sun grew watery, and veiled itself in mist.

There was debris in the air, of course: petals and leaves, dust and ash. They fell like a dream rain, though their fall marked the end of a dream.

"Oh, child . . . ," said Mrs. Griffin.

Harvey turned to her. She was standing just a few yards from him, gazing up at the sky. There was a little patch of blue above their heads; the first glimpse of real sky these few acres of ground had seen since Hood had founded his empire of illusions. But it was not the patch she was watching, it was a congregation of floating lights—the same that Harvey had seen Hood feeding upon in the attic—which had been freed by the collapse of the House. They were now moving in a steady stream toward the lake.

"The children's souls," she said, her voice growing thinner as she spoke the word. "Beautiful."

Her body was no longer solid, Harvey saw; she was fading away in front of him.

"Oh no," he murmured.

She took her eyes off the sky and stared down at her arms, and the cat she was carrying in them. It too was growing insubstantial.

"Look at us," Mrs. Griffin said, with a smile upon her weary face. "It feels so wonderful."

"But you're disappearing."

"I've lingered here far too long, sweet boy," she said. There were tears glistening on her face, but they were tears of joy, not of sadness. "It's time to go . . ." She kept stroking Stew-Cat as they both faded from sight. "You *are* the brightest soul I ever met, Harvey Swick," she said. "Keep shining, won't you?"

Harvey wished he had some words to persuade her to stay a little while longer. But even if he'd had such words, he knew it would have been selfish to speak them. Mrs. Griffin had another life to go to, where every soul shone.

"Good-bye, child," she said. "Wherever I go, I will speak of you with love."

Then her ghostly form flickered out, leaving Harvey alone in the ruins.

From *Sacrament*

Halfway along the track that led from the crossroads to the Courthouse, Will heard the squeaking of ill-oiled wheels behind him. He glanced over his shoulder to see not one but two bicycle headlamps a little distance behind him. Breathing an inventive little curse, he stood and waited until Frannie and Sherwood caught up with him.

"Go home," were his first words to them.

"No," said Frannie breathlessly. "We decided to come with you."

"I don't want you to come," Will said.

"It's a free country," Sherwood replied. "We can go wherever we want. Can't we, Frannie?"

"Shut up," Frannie said. Then to Will: "I only wanted to make sure you were okay."

"So why'd you bring him?" Will said.

"Because . . . he asked me . . . ," Frannie said. "He won't be a bother."

Will shook his head. "I don't want you coming inside," he said.

"It's a free—" Sherwood began again, but Frannie shushed him.

"All right, we won't," she said. "We'll just wait."

Knowing this was the best deal he was going to be able to make, Will headed for the Courthouse, with Frannie and Sherwood trailing behind. He made no further recognition of their presence, until he got to the hedgerow adjacent to the Courthouse. Only then did he turn and tell them in a whisper that if they made a sound they'd spoil everything and he would never ever speak to them again. With the warning given, he dug through the hawthorn and started up the gently sloping meadow toward the building. It loomed larger by night than it had by day, like a vast mausoleum, but he could see a light flickering within; there was nothing but exhilaration in his heart as he made his way down the passage toward it.

Jacob was sitting in the judge's chair, with a small fire burning on the table in front of him. He looked up when he heard the door creak, and by the flames' light Will had sight of the face he had conjured so many ways. In every detail, he had fallen short of its power. He had not made a brow wide or clear enough, nor eyes deep enough, nor imagined that Steep's hair, which he had seen in silhouette falling in curly abundance, would be cropped back to a shadow on the top of his skull. He had not imagined the gloss of his beard and mustache, or the delicacy of his lips, which he licked, and licked again, before saying:

"Welcome, Will. You come at a strange time."

"Does that mean you want me to go?"

"No. Far from it." He added a few pieces of tinder to the fire before him. It crackled and spat. "It is, I know, the custom to paint a smile over sorrow; to pretend there is joy in you when there is not. But I hate wiles and pretenses. The truth is I'm melancholy tonight."

"What's . . . melancholy?" Will said.

"There's honest," Jacob replied appreciatively. "Melancholy is sad, but more than sad. It's what we feel when we think about the world and how little we understand; when we think of what we must come to."

"You mean dying and stuff?"

"Dying will do," Jacob said. "Though that's not what concerns me tonight." He beckoned to Will. "Come closer," he said, "it's warmer by the fire."

The few flames on the table offered, Will thought, little prospect of heat, but he gladly approached. "So why are you sad?" Will said.

Jacob sat back in the ancient chair, and contemplated the fire. "It's business between a man and a woman," he replied. "You need not concern yourself with it for a little time yet and you should be grateful. Hold it off as long as you can." As he spoke he reached into his pocket and pulled out more fuel for his tiny bonfire. This time, Will was close enough to see that this tinder was moving. Fascinated, and faintly sickened, Will approached the table, and saw that Steep's captive was a moth, the wings of which he had caught between thumb and forefinger. Its legs and antennae flailed as it was dropped into the flames, and for an instant it seemed the draught of heat would waft it to safety, but before it could gain sufficient height its wings ignited and down it went. "Living and dying we feed the fire," Steep said softly. "That is the melancholy truth of things."

"Except that you just did the feeding," Will said, surprised by his own eloquence.

"So we must," Jacob replied. "Or there'd be darkness in here. And how would we see each other then? I daresay you'd be more comfortable with fuel that didn't squirm as you fed it to the flame."

"Yes . . . ," Will said, "I would."

"Do you eat sausages, Will?"

"Yes."

"You like them, I'm sure. A nicely browned pork sausage? Or a good steak and kidney pie?"

"Yes. I like steak and kidney pie."

"But do you think of the beast, shitting itself in terror as it is shunted to its execution? Hanging by one leg, still kicking, while the blood spurts from its neck? Do you?"

Will had heard his father debate often enough to know that there was a trap here. "It's not the same," he protested.

"Oh, but it is."

"No, it's not. I need food to stay alive."

"So eat turnips."

"But I like sausages."

"You like light too, Will."

"There are candles," Will said, "right there."

"And the living earth gave up wax and wick in their making," Steep said. "Everything is *consumed*, Will, sooner or later. Living and dying we feed the fire." He smiled, just a little. "Sit," he said softly. "Go on. We're equals here. Both a little melancholy."

Will sat. "I'm not melancholy," he said, liking the gift of the word. "I'm happy."

"Are you really? Well that's good to hear. And why are you so happy?"

Will was embarrassed to admit the truth, but Jacob had been honest, he thought; so should he. "Because I found you here," he said.

"That pleases you?"

"Yes."

"But in an hour you'll be bored with me —"

"No, I won't."

"And the sadness will still be there, waiting for you." As he spoke, the fire began to dwindle. "Do you want to feed the fire, Will?" Steep said.

His words carried an uncanny power. It was as though this dwindling meant more than the extinguishing of a few flames. This fire was suddenly the only light in a cold, sunless world, and if somebody didn't feed it soon the consequences would be grim.

"Well, Will?" Jacob said, digging in his pocket and taking out another moth. "Here," he said, proffering it.

Will hesitated. He could hear the soft flapping of the moth's panic. He looked past the creature to its captor. Jacob's face was utterly without expression.

"Well?" Jacob said.

The fire had almost gone out. Another few seconds and it would be too late. The room would be given over to darkness, and the face in front of Will, its symmetry and its scrutiny, would be gone.

That thought was suddenly too much to bear. Will looked back at the moth: at its wheeling legs and its flapping antennae. Then, in a kind of wonderful terror, he took it from Jacob's fingers.

From *Sacrament*

I t had always been Steep's preference, when he was about the business of slaughtering mating couples, to kill the male first. If he was dealing with the last of a species, of course—which was his great and glorious labor—the dispatch of both genders was academic. All he needed to do was kill one to ensure that the line was ended. But he liked to be able to kill both, for neatness' sake, starting with the male. He had a number of practical reasons for this. In most species the male was the more aggressive of the sexes, and for his own protection it made sense to incapacitate the husband before the wife. He'd also observed that females were more likely to demonstrate grief at the demise of their mates, in the throes of which they could be readily killed. The male, by contrast, became vengeful. All but two of the serious injuries he'd sustained over the years had come from males that he had unwisely left to kill after the female and that had thrown themselves upon him with suicidal abandon. A century and a half since the extinction of the great auk on the cliffs of St. Kilda, and he still bore the scar on his forearm where the male had opened him up. And in cold weather there was still an ache in his thigh where a blaubok had kicked him, seeing its lady bleeding to death before its eyes.

Both were painful lessons. But more painful than either the scars or the ill-knit bones was the memory of those males who had, through some failing of his, outmaneuvered him and escaped. It had happened seldom, but when it had he had mounted heroic searches for the escapee, driving Rosa to distraction with his doggedness. Let the brute go, she'd tell him, ever the pragmatist; just let him die of loneliness.

Oh, but that was what haunted him. The thought of a rogue animal out in the wild, circling its territory, looking for something that was its like, and coming back at last to the place where its mate had perished, seeking a vestige of her being—a scent, a feather, a shard of bone—was almost unbearable. He had caught fugitives several times under such circumstances; waiting for them to return to that fatal place, and murdering them on the spot where they mourned. But there were some animals that escaped him completely, whose final hours were not his to have dominion over, and these were a source of great distress to him. He dreamed and imagined them for months after. Saw them wandering in his mind's eye; growing ragged, growing rogue. And then, when a season or two had passed, and they had not encountered any of their own species, losing the will to live; flea-bitten and bony-shanked, becoming phantoms of veldt or forest or ice floe, until they finally gave up all hope, and died.

He would always know when this finally happened; or such was his conviction. He would feel the animal's passing in his gut, as though a physical procedure as real as digestion had come to its inevitable end. Another dinning thing had gone into memory (and into his journal) never to be known again.

This will not come again. Nor this. Nor this . . .

TWELVE

MEMORY

I probably have more life to remember than I do to live. That calculation would once have made me clammy; now there's something almost comforting in it. Plenty still to do, plenty still to experience; but plenty, too, accumulated. Plenty stored where circumstance cannot spoil it.

In some measure my books are a repository of memories: of friends, places, insights, feelings. And several of the novels use the theme of memory, and forgetfulness, as a narrative element. The Nilotic, in *Sacrament*, has forgotten its own identity. Cal Mooney, in *Weaveworld*, is induced into a dreamy forgetfulness of miracles by the world in which he lives. In *Imajica*, the memory loss is self-induced, the consequence of a character having felt too much grief and failure.

The memories which that character, a man called Gentle, is repressing, come back to him in a sequence I've chosen for this chapter. His confrontation isn't just a reclamation of who he was, but of who he is. The man who is remembering must take the responsibility for what he remembers.

From *Sacrament*

A s the afternoon light began to fail, the wind veered, and came out of the northeast across Hudson Bay, rattling the door and windows of Guthrie's shack, like something lonely and invisible, wanting comfort at the table. The old man sat in his old leather armchair and savored the gale's din like a connoisseur. He had long ago given up on the charms of the human voice. It was more often than not a courier of lies and confusions, or so he had come to believe; if he never heard another syllable uttered in his life he would not think himself the poorer. All he needed by way of communication was the sound he was listening to now. The wind's mourn and whine was wiser than any psalm, prayer or profession of love he'd ever heard.

But tonight the sound failed to soothe him as it usually did. He knew why. The responsibility lay with the visitor who'd come knocking on his door the night before. He'd disturbed Guthrie's equilibrium, raising the phantoms of faces he'd tried so hard to put from his mind. Jacob Steep, with his soot-and-gold eyes, and black beard, and pale poet's hands; and Rosa, glorious Rosa, who had the gold of Steep's eyes in her hair, and the black of his beard in her gaze, but was as fleshy and passionate as he was sweatless and unmoved. Guthrie had known them for such a short time, and many years ago, but he had them in his mind's eye so clearly he might have met them that morning.

He had Rabjohns there too: with his green milk eyes, too gentle by half, and his hair in unruly abundance, curling at his nape, and the wide ease of his face, nicked with scars on his cheek and brow. He hadn't been scarred half enough, Guthrie thought; there was still some measure of hope in him.

Why else had he come asking questions, except in the belief that they could be answered? He'd learn, if he lived long enough. There were no answers. None that made sense anyhow.

The wind gusted hard against the window, and loosened one of the boards Guthrie had taped over a cracked pane. He raised himself out of the pit of his chair and, picking up the roll of tape he'd used to secure the board, crossed to the window to fix it. Before he stuck it back in place, blocking out the world, he stared through the grimy glass. The day was close to departure, the thickening waters of the Bay the color of slate, the rocks black. He kept staring, distracted from his task not by the sight but by the memories which came to him still, unbidden, unwanted, but impossible to put from his head.

Words first. No more than a murmur. But that was all he needed.

These will not come again—

Steep was speaking, his voice majestic.

—nor this. Nor this—

And as he spoke the pages appeared in front of Guthrie's grieving eyes; the pages of Steep's terrible book. There, a perfect rendering of a bird's wing, exquisitely colored—

—nor this—

And here, on the following page, a beetle, copied in death; every part documented for posterity: mandible, wing-case, and segmented limb.

—nor this—

"Jesus," he sobbed, the roll of tape dropping from his trembling fingers. Why couldn't Rabjohns have left him alone? Was there no corner of the world where a man might listen to the wail of the wind, without being discovered and reminded of his crimes?

The answer, it seemed, was no; at least for a soul as unredeemed as his. He could never hope to forget, not until God struck life and memory from him, which prospect seemed at this moment far less dreadful than living on, day and night, in fear of another Will coming to his door and naming names.

Nor this . . .

Shut up, he murmured to memories. But the pages kept flipping in his head. Picture after picture, like some morbid bestiary. What fish was that, that would never again silver the sea? What bird, that would never tune its song to the sky?

On and on the pages flew, while he watched, knowing that at last

Steep's fingers would come to a page where he himself had made a mark. Not with a brush or a pen, but with a bright little knife.

And then the tears would begin to come in torrents, and it wouldn't matter how hard the northeasterly blew, it could not carry the past away.

From *Sacrament*

O n Easter Sunday, he did something he'd been putting off since the mellowing of the weather. He retraced the journey he'd taken with Jacob, from the Courthouse to the copse where he'd killed the birds. The Courthouse itself had the previous year inspired much morbid interest among sightseers, and had as a consequence been fenced off, the wire hung with signs warning trespassers that they would be liable to prosecution. Will was tempted to scramble under the fence and take a look at the place, but the day was too fine to waste indoors, so he began to climb. There was a warm gusty wind blowing, herding white clouds, all innocent of rain, down the valley. On the slopes, the sheep were stupid with spring, and watched him unalarmed, only darting off if he yelled at them. The climb itself was hard (he missed Jacob's hand at his neck) but every time he paused to look around, the vista widened, the fells rolling away in every direction.

He had remembered the wood with uncanny accuracy, as though—despite his sickness and fatigue—that night his sight had been preternaturally sharp. The trees were budding now, of course, every twig an arrow aiming high. And underfoot, blades of brilliant green where there'd been a frosted carpet.

He went straight to the place where he'd killed the birds. There was no trace of them. Not so much as a bone. But simply standing on the same spot, such a wave of yearning and sorrow passed through him that it made him gasp for breath. He'd been so proud of what he'd done here. (*Wasn't that quick? Wasn't that beautiful?*) But now he felt a bit more ambiguous about it. Burning moths to keep the darkness at bay was one thing, but killing birds just because it felt good to do so? That didn't feel so brave; not today, when the trees were budding and the sky was wide. Today it felt like a dirty memory, and he swore to himself there and then that he'd told the story for the last time. Once Faraday and Parsons had filed away their notes and forgotten them, it would be as though it had never happened.

He went down on his haunches, to check one final time for evidence of the victims, but even as he did so he knew he'd invited trouble. He felt a tiny tremor in the air as a breath was drawn, and looked up to see that the wood itself had not changed in any detail but one. There was a fox a short distance from him, watching him intently. He stood on all fours like any other fox, but there was something about the way he stared that made Will suspicious. He'd seen this defiant gaze before, from the dubious safety of his bed.

"Go *away!*" he shouted. The fox just looked at him, unblinking and unmoved. "*D'you hear me?*" Will yelled at the top of his voice. "*Shoo!*" But what had worked like a charm on sheep didn't work on foxes. Or at least not this fox.

"Look," Will said. "Coming to bother me in dreams is one thing, but you don't *belong* here. This is the real world."

The fox shook its head, preserving the illusion of its artlessness. To any gaze but Will's, it seemed to be dislodging a flea from its ear. But Will knew better: it was contradicting him.

"Are you telling me I'm dreaming *this* as well?" he said.

The animal didn't bother to nod. It simply perused Will, amiably enough, while he worked the problem out for himself. And now, as he puzzled over this curious turn of events, he vaguely recalled something Lord Fox had mentioned in his rambling. What had he said? There'd been some talk of Russian dolls, but that wasn't it. An anecdote about a debate with a dog; no, that wasn't it either. There'd been something else his visitor had mentioned. Some message that had to be passed along. But *what? What?*

The fox was plainly close to giving up on him. It was no longer staring in his direction, but sniffing the air in search of its next meal.

"Wait a moment," Will said. A minute ago, he'd been wanting to drive it away. Now he was afraid it would do as he'd wished, and go about its business before he'd solved the puzzle of its presence.

"Don't leave yet," he said to it. "I'll *remember*. Just give me a chance—"

Too late. He'd lost the animal's attention. Off it trotted, its brush flicking back and forth.

"Oh, *come on*—" Will said, rising to follow it. "I'm trying my best."

The trees were close together, and in his pursuit of the fox their bark gouged him and their branches raked his face. He didn't care. The faster he ran, the harder his heart pumped and the harder his heart pumped the clearer his memory became—

"I'll get it!" he yelled after the fox. "Wait for me, will you?"

The message was there, on the tip of his tongue, but the fox was outpacing him, weaving between the trees with astonishing agility. And all at once, twin revelations. One, that this was *not* Lord Fox he was following, just a passing animal that was fleeing for its flea-bitten life. And two, that the message was to wake, wake from dreams of foxes, Lords or no, *into the world*—

He was running so fast now, the trees were a blur around him. And up ahead, where they thinned out, was not the hill but a growing brightness; not the past, but something more painful. He didn't want to go there, but it was too late to slow his flight, much less halt it. The trees were a blur because they were no longer trees, they'd become the wall of a tunnel, down which he was hurtling, out of memory, out of childhood.

Somebody was speaking at the far end of the tunnel. He couldn't catch hold of precisely what was being said, but there were words of encouragement, he thought, as though he were a runner on a marathon, being coaxed to the finishing line.

Before he reached it, however—before he was back in that place of wakefulness—he was determined to take one last look at the past. Ungluing his eyes from the brightness ahead, he glanced back over his shoulder, and for a few precious seconds glimpsed the world he was leaving. There was the wood, sparkling in the spring light—every bud a promise of green to come. And the fox! Lord, there it was, darting away about the business of the morning. He pressed his sight to look harder, knowing he had only moments left, and it went where he willed, back the way he'd come, to look down the hillside to the village. One last heroic glance, fixing the sight in all its myriad details. The river, sparkling; the Courthouse, moldering; the roofs of the village, rising in slated tiers; the bridge, the post office, the telephone box from which he'd called Frannie that night long ago, telling her he was running away.

So he was. Running back into his life, where he would never see this sight again, so finely, so perfectly—

They were calling him again, from the present. "Welcome back, Will . . ." somebody was saying to him softly.

Wait, he wanted to tell them. Don't welcome me yet. Give me just another second to dream this dream. The bells are ringing for the end of the Sunday service. I want to see the people. I want to see their faces, as they come out into the sun. I want to see—

The voice again, a little more insistent. "Will. *Open your eyes.*"

There was no time left. He'd reached the finishing line. The past was consumed by brightness. River, bridge, church, houses, hill, trees, and fox, gone, all gone, and the eyes that had witnessed them, weaker for the passage of years, but no less hungry, opened to see what he'd become.

From *Imajica*

Gentle's thoughts had not often turned to Taylor as he and Pie journeyed, but when, in the streets outside the palace, Nikaetomaas had asked him why he'd come to the Imajica, it had been Taylor's death he'd spoken of first, and only then of Judith and the attempt upon her life. Now, as he and Nikaetomaas passed through the balmy, benighted courtyards and up into the palace itself, he thought of the man again, lying on his final pillow, talking about floating and charging Gentle to solve mysteries that he'd not had time to solve himself.

"I had a friend in the Fifth who would have loved this place," Gentle said. "He loved desolation."

It was here, in every courtyard. Gardens had been planted in many of them and left to riot. But riot took energy, and nature was weary here, the plants throttling themselves after a few spurts and withering back into earth the color of ash. The scene was not so different once they got inside, wandering mapless down galleries where the dust was as thick as the soil in the dead gardens, into forsaken annexes and chambers laid out for guests who had breathed their last decades before. Most of the walls, whether of chambers or galleries, were decorated: some with tapestries, many others with immense frescoes, and while there were scenes Gentle recognized from his travels—Patashoqua under a green-gold sky, with a flight of air balloons rising from the plain outside its walls; a festival at the L'Himby temples—the suspicion grew on him that the finest of these images were of earth; or, more particularly, of England. Doubtless the pastoral was a universal mode, and shepherds wooed nymphs in the Reconciled Dominions just as sonnets described them doing in the Fifth, but there were details of these scenes that were indisputably English: swallows swooping in mild summer skies; cattle drinking in water meadows while their herders slept; the Salisbury spire rising from a bank of oaks; the distant towers and domes of London, glimpsed from a slope on which maids and swains made dalliance: even Stonehenge, relocated for drama's sake to a hill and set against thunderheads.

"England," Gentle said as they went. "Somebody here remembers England."

He waited until the first stars appeared in a sky of elegiac blue before he raised the blinds. The street outside was quiet, but given that he lacked the cash for a cab he knew he'd have to brush shoulders with a lot of people before he reached Clerkenwell. On a fine evening like this, the Edgware Road would be busy, and there'd be crowds on the Underground. His best hope of reaching his destination unscrutinized was to dress as blandly as possible, and he took some time hunting through his depleted wardrobe for those clothes that would render him most invisible. Once dressed, he walked down to Marble Arch and boarded the Underground. It was only five stations to Chancery Lane, which would put him on the borders of Clerkenwell, but after two he had to get off, gasping and sweating like a claustrophobic. Cursing this new weakness in himself, he sat in the station for half an hour while more trains passed through, unable to bring himself to board. What an irony! Here he was, a sometime wanderer in the wilds of the Imajica, incapable of traveling a couple of miles by tube without panicking. He waited until his shaking subsided and a less crowded train came along. Then he reboarded, sitting close to the door with his head in his hands until the journey was over.

By the time he emerged at Chancery Lane the sky had darkened, and he stood for several minutes on High Holborn, his head thrown back, soaking up the sky. Only when the tremors had left his legs did he head up Gray's Inn Road toward the environs of Gamut Street. Almost all the property on the main thoroughfares had long since been turned to commercial use, but there was a network of streets and squares behind the barricade of darkened office buildings which, protected perhaps by the patronage of notoriety, had been left untouched by the developers. Many of these streets were narrow and mazy, their lamps unlit, their signs missing, as though blind eyes had been turned to them over the generations. But he didn't need signs and lamps; his feet had trodden these ways countless times. Here was Shiverick Square, with its little park all overgrown, and Flaxen Street, and Almoth, and Sterne. And in their midst, cocooned by anonymity, his destination.

He saw the corner of Gamut Street twenty yards ahead and slowed his pace to take pleasure in the moment of reunion. There were innumerable

memories awaiting him there, the mystif among them. But not all would
be so sweet, or so welcome. He would have to ingest them carefully, like a
diner with a delicate stomach coming to a lavish table. Moderation was
the way. As soon as he felt a surfeit, he'd retreat and return to the studio to
digest what he'd learned, let it strengthen him. Only then would he return
for a second helping. The process would take time, he knew, and time was
of the essence. But so was his sanity. What use would he be as a Reconciler
if he choked on the past?

With his heart thumping hard, he came to the corner and, turning it,
finally laid his eyes upon the sacred street. Perhaps, during his years of forgetfulness, he'd wandered through these backwaters all unknowing and
seen the sight before him now. But he doubted it. More likely, his eyes
were seeing Gamut Street for the first time in two centuries. It had
changed scarcely at all, preserved from the city planners and their hammer-
wielding hordes by the feits whose makers were still rumored here. The
trees planted along the pavement were weighed down with unkempt
foliage, but their sap's tang was sharp, the air protected from the fumes of
Holborn and Gray's Inn Road by the warren of thoroughfares between.
Was it just his fancy, or was the tree outside number 28 particularly lush,
fed perhaps by a seepage of magics from the step of the Maestro's house?

He began toward them, tree and step, the memories already returning
in force. He heard the children singing behind him, the song that had so
tormented him when the Autarch had told him who he was. *Sartori*, he'd
said, and this charmless ditty, sung by piping voices, had come in pursuit
of the name. He'd loathed it then. Its melody was banal; its words were
nonsense. But now he remembered how he'd first heard it, walking along
this very pavement with the children in procession on the opposite shore,
and how flattered he'd been that he was famous enough to have reached
the lips of children who would never read or write or, most probably,
reach the age of puberty. All of London knew who he was, and he liked his
fame. He was talked about at court, Roxborough said, and should soon
expect an invitation. People who'd not so much as touched his sleeve were
claiming intimate association.

But there were still those, thank God, who kept an exquisite distance, and
one such soul had lived, he remembered, in the house opposite: a nymph
called Allegra who liked to sit at her dressing table near the window with her
bodice half unlaced, knowing she had an admirer in the Maestro across the
street. She'd had a little curly haired dog, and sometimes in the evening he'd

hear her piping voice summon the lucky hound onto her lap, where she'd let it snuggle. One afternoon, a few paces from where he stood now, he'd met the girl out walking with her mother and had made much of the dog, suffering its little tongue on his mouth for the smell of her sex in its fur. What had become of that child? Had she died a virgin or grown old and fat, wondering about the man who'd been her most ardent admirer?

He glanced up at the window where Allegra had sat. No light burned in it now. The house, like almost all these buildings, was dark. Sighing, he turned his gaze toward number 28 and, crossing the street, went to the door. It was locked, of course, but one of the lower windows had been broken at some point and never repaired. He reached through the smashed pane and unlocked it, then slid the window up and himself inside. Slowly, he reminded himself: go slowly. Keep the flow under control.

It was dark, but he'd come prepared for that eventuality, with candle and matches. The flame guttered at first, and the room rocked at its indecision, but by degrees it strengthened, and he felt a sensation he'd not expected swelling like the light: pride. In its time, this, his house, had been a place of great souls and great ambition, where all commonplace debate had been banned. If you wanted to talk politics or tittle-tattle you went to the coffeehouse; if you wanted commerce, to the Exchange. Here, only miracles. Here, only the rising of the spirit. And, yes, love, if it was pertinent (which it was, so often); and sometimes bloodletting. But never the prosaic, never the trivial. Here the man who brought the strangest tale was the most welcome. Here every excess was celebrated if it brought visions, and every vision analyzed for the hints it held to the nature of the Everlasting.

He lifted the candle and, holding it high, began to walk through the house. The rooms—there were many—were badly dilapidated, the boards creaking under his feet, weakened by rot and worms, the walls mapping continents of damp. But the present didn't insist upon him for long. By the time he reached the bottom of the stairs, memory was lighting candles everywhere, their luminescence spilling through the dining-room door and from the rooms above. It was a generous light, clothing naked walls, putting lush carpets underfoot, and setting fine furniture on their pile. Though the debaters here might have aspired to pure spirit, they were not averse to comforting the flesh while still cursed with it. Who would have guessed, seeing the modest façade of the house from the street, that the interior would be so finely furnished and ornamented? And seeing these glories appear, he heard the voices of those who'd wallowed in that luxury.

Laughter first; then vociferous argument from somebody at the top of the stairs. He couldn't see the debaters yet—perhaps his mind, which he'd instructed in caution, was holding the flood back—but he could put names to both of them, sight unseen. One was Horace Tyrwhitt, the other Isaac Abelove. And the laughter? That was Joshua Godolphin, of course. He had a laugh like the Devil's laugh, full and throaty.

"Come on, then," Gentle said aloud to the memories. "I'm ready to see your faces."

And as he spoke, they came: Tyrwhitt on the stairs, overdressed and overpowdered, as ever, keeping his distance from Abelove in case the magpie his pursuer was nursing flew free.

"It's bad luck," Tyrwhitt was protesting. "Birds in the house are bad luck!"

"Luck's for fishermen and gamblers," Abelove replied.

"One of these days you'll turn a phrase worth remembering," Tyrwhitt replied. "Just get the thing out before I wring its neck." He turned toward Gentle. "Tell him, Sartori."

Gentle was shocked to see the memory's eyes fix so acutely upon him. "It does no harm," he found himself replying. "It's one of God's creatures."

At which point the bird rose flapping from Abelove's grasp, emptying its bowels as it did so on the man's wig and face, which brought a hoot of laughter from Tyrwhitt.

"Now don't wipe it off," he told Abelove as the magpie fluttered away. "It's good luck."

The sound of his laughter brought Joshua Godolphin, imperious as ever, out of the dining room. "What's the row?"

Abelove was already clattering after the bird, his calls merely alarming it more. It fluttered around the hallway in panic, cawing as it went.

"Open the damned door!" Godolphin said. "Let the bloody thing out!"

"And spoil the sport?" Tyrwhitt said.

"If everyone would but calm their voices," Abelove said, "it would settle."

"Why did you bring it in?" Joshua wanted to know.

"It was sitting on the step," Abelove replied. "I thought it was injured."

"It looks quite well to me," Godolphin said, and turned his face, ruddied with brandy, toward Gentle. "Maestro," he said, inclining his head a little. "I'm afraid we began dinner without you. Come in. Leave these bird brains to play."

Gentle was crossing to the dining room when there was a thud behind him, and he turned to see the bird dropping to the floor beneath one of the windows, where it had struck the glass. Abelove let out a little moan, and Tyrwhitt's laughter ceased.

"There now!" he said. "You killed the thing!"

"Not me!" Abelove said.

"You want to resurrect it?" Joshua murmured to Gentle, his tone conspiratorial.

"With a broken neck and wings?" Gentle mourned. "That wouldn't be very kind."

"But amusing," Godolphin replied with mischief in his puffy eyes.

"I think not," Gentle said, and saw his distaste wipe the humor off Joshua's face. He's a little afraid of me, Gentle thought; the power in me makes him nervous.

Joshua headed into the dining room, and Gentle was about to step through the door after him when a young man—eighteen at most, with a plain, long face and chorister's curls—came to his side.

"Maestro?'" he said.

Unlike Joshua and the others, these features seemed more familiar to Gentle. Perhaps there was a certain modernity in the languid, lidded gaze and the small, almost effeminate, mouth. He didn't look that intelligent, in truth, but his words, when they came, were well turned, despite the boy's nervousness. He barely dared look at Sartori, but with those lids downcast begged the Maestro's indulgence.

"I wondered, sir, if you had perhaps considered the matter of which we spoke?"

Gentle was about to ask, What matter?, when his tongue replied, his intellect seizing the memory as the words spilled out. "I know how eager you are, Lucius."

Lucius Cobbitt was the boy's name. At seventeen he already had the great works by heart, or at least their theses. Ambitious and apt at politics, he'd taken Tyrwhitt as a patron (for what services only his bed knew, but it was surely a hanging offense) and had secured himself a place in the house as a menial. But he wanted more than that, and scarcely an evening went by without his politely plying the Maestro with coy glances and pleas.

"I'm more than eager, sir," he said. "I've studied all the rituals. I've mapped the In Ovo, from what I've read in Flute's *Visions*. They're just beginnings, I know, but I've also copied all the known glyphs, and I have them by heart."

He had a little skill as an artist, too: something else they shared, besides ambition and dubious morals.

"I can help you, Maestro," he was saying. "You're going to need somebody beside you on the night."

"I commend you on your discipline, Lucius, but the Reconciliation's a dangerous business. I can't take the responsibility—"

"I'll take that, sir."

"Besides, I have my assistant."

The boy's face fell. "You do?" he said.

"Certainly. Pie 'oh' pah."

"You'd trust your life to a familiar?"

"Why shouldn't I?"

"Well, because . . . because it's not even human."

"That's why I trust it. Lucius," Gentle said. "I'm sorry to disappoint you—"

"Could I at least *watch*, sir? I'll keep my distance, I swear, I swear. Everybody else is going to be there."

This was true enough. As the night of the Reconciliation approached, the size of the audience swelled. His patrons, who'd at first taken their oaths of secrecy very seriously, now sensed triumph and had become indiscreet. In hushed and often embarrassed tones they'd admit to having invited a friend or a relation to witness the rites, and who was he, the performer, to forbid his paymasters their moment of reflected glory? Though he never gave them an easy time when they made these confessions, he didn't much mind. Admiration charged the blood. And when the Reconciliation had been achieved, the more tongues there were to say they'd seen it done, and sanctify the doer, the better.

"I beg you, sir," Lucius was saying. "I'll be in your debt forever."

Gentle nodded, ruffling the youth's ginger hair. "You may watch," he said.

Tears started to the boy's eyes, and he snatched up Gentle's hand, laying his lips to it. "I am the luckiest man in England," he said. "Thank you, sir, thank you."

Quieting the boy's profusions, Gentle left him at the door and stepped through into the dining room. As he did so he wondered if all these events and conversations had actually dovetailed in this fashion, or whether his memory was collecting fragments from different nights and days, knitting them together so that they appeared seamless. If the latter was the case—

and he guessed it was—then there were probably clues in these scenes to mysteries yet to be unveiled, and he should try to remember their every detail. But it was difficult. He was both Gentle and Sartori here, both witness and actor. It was hard to live the moments when he was also observing them, and harder still to dig for the seam of their significance when their surface gleamed so fetchingly, and when he was the brightest jewel that shone there. How they had idolized him! He'd been like a divinity among them, his every belch and fart attended to like a sermon, his cosmological pronouncements—of which he was too fond—greeted with reverence and gratitude, even by the mightiest.

Three of those mighty awaited him in the dining room, gathered at one end of a table, set for four but laden with sufficient food to sate the street for a week. Joshua was one of the trio, of course. Roxborough and his longtime foil Oliver McGann were the others, the latter well in his cups, the former, as ever, keeping his counsel, his ascetic features, dominated by the long hook of his nose, always half masked by his hands. He despised his mouth, Gentle thought, because it betrayed his nature, which despite his incalculable wealth and his pretensions to metaphysics was peevish, penurious, and sullen.

"Religion's for the faithful," McGann was loudly opining. "They say their prayers, their prayers aren't answered, and their faith increases. Whereas magic—" He stopped, laying his inebriated gaze on the Maestro at the door. "Ah! The very man! The *very* man! Tell him, Sartori! Tell him what magic is."

Roxborough had made a pyramid of his fingers, the apex at the bridge of his nose. "Yes, Maestro," he said. "Do tell."

"My pleasure," Gentle replied, taking the glass of wine McGann poured for him and wetting his throat before he provided tonight's profundities. "Magic is the first and last religion of the world," he said. "It has the power to make us whole. To open our eyes to the Dominions and return us to ourselves."

"That sounds very fine," Roxborough said flatly. "But what does it mean?"

"It's obvious what it means," McGann protested.

"Not to me it isn't."

"It means we're born divided, Roxborough," the Maestro replied. "But we long for union."

"Oh, we do, do we?"

"I believe so."

"And why should we seek union with ourselves?" Roxborough said. "Tell me that. I would have thought we're the only company we're certain we have."

There was a riling smugness to the man's tone, but the Maestro had heard these niceties before and had his answers well honed.

"Everything that isn't us is also ourselves," he said. He came to the table and set down his glass, peering through the smoky candle flames at Roxborough's black eyes. "We're joined to everything that was, is, and will be," he said. "From one end of the Imajica to another. From the tiniest mote dancing over this flame to the Godhead Itself."

He took breath, leaving room for a retort from Roxborough. But none came.

"We'll not be subsumed at our deaths," he went on. "We'll be increased: to the size of Creation."

"Yes . . . ," McGann said, the word coming long and loud from between teeth clenched in a tigerish smile.

"Magic's our means to that Revelation," the Maestro said, "while we're still in our flesh."

"And is it your opinion that we are *given* that Revelation?" Roxborough replied. "Or are we stealing it?"

"We were born to know as much as we *can* know."

"We were born to suffer in our flesh," Roxborough said.

"You may suffer; I don't."

The reply won a guffaw from McGann.

"The flesh isn't punishment," the Maestro said, "it's there for joy. But it also marks the place where we end and the rest of Creation begins. Or so we believe. It's an illusion, of course."

"Good," said Godolphin. "I like that."

"So are we about God's business or not?" Roxborough wanted to know.

"Are you having second thoughts?"

"Third and fourth, more like," McGann said.

Roxborough gave the man at his side a sour glance. "Did we swear an oath not to doubt?" he said. "I don't think so. Why should I be castigated because I ask a simple question?"

"I apologize," McGann said. "Tell the man. Maestro. We're doing God's work, aren't we?"

"Does God want us to be more than we are?" Gentle said. "Of course. Does God want us to love, which is the desire to be joined and made whole? Of course. Does It want us in Its glory, forever and ever? Yes. It does."

"You always say It," McGann observed. "Why's that?"

"Creation and its maker are one and the same. True or false?"

"True."

"And Creation's as full of women as it is of men. True or false?"

"Oh, true, true."

"Indeed, I give thanks for the fact night and day," Gentle said, glancing at Godolphin as he spoke. "Beside my bed and in it."

Joshua laughed his Devil's laugh.

"So the Godhead is both male and female. For convenience, an It."

"Bravely said!" Joshua announced. "I never tire of hearing you speak, Sartori. My thoughts get muddy, but after I've listened to you awhile they're like spring water, straight from the rock!"

"Not too clean, I hope," the Maestro said. "We don't want any Puritan souls spoiling the Reconciliation."

"You know me better than that," Joshua said, catching Gentle's eye.

Even as he did so, Gentle had proof of his suspicion that these encounters, though remembered in one continuous stream, had not occurred sequentially but were fragments his mind was knitting together as the rooms he was walking through evoked them. McGann and Roxborough faded from the table, as did most of the candlelight and the litter of carafes, glasses, and food it had illuminated. Now there was only Joshua and himself, and the house was still above and below. Everyone asleep, but for these conspirators.

"I want to be with you when you perform the working," Joshua was saying. There was no hint of laughter now. He looked harassed and nervous. "She's very precious to me, Sartori. If anything were to happen to her I'd lose my mind."

"She'll be perfectly safe," the Maestro said, sitting down at the table.

There was a map of the Imajica laid out in front of him, with the names of the Maestros and their assistants in each Dominion marked beside their places of conjuration. He scanned them and found he knew one or two. Tick Raw was there, as the deputy to Uter Musky; Scopique was there too, marked as an assistant to an assistant to Heratae Hammeryock, the latter a distant relation, perhaps, of the Hammeryock whom Gentle and Pie had encountered in Vanaeph. Names from two pasts, intersecting here on the map.

"Are you listening to me?" Joshua said.

"I told you she'd be perfectly safe," came the Maestro's reply. "The workings are delicate, but they're not dangerous."

"Then let me be there," Godolphin said, wringing his hands. "I'll be your assistant instead of that wretched mystif."

"I haven't even told Pie 'oh' pah what we're up to. This is our business and only ours. You just bring Judith here tomorrow evening, and I'll see to the rest."

"She's so vulnerable."

"She seems very self-possessed to me," the Maestro observed. "Very heated."

Godolphin's fretful expression soured into ice. "Don't parade it, Sartori," he said. "It's not enough that I've got Roxborough at my ear all yesterday, telling me he doesn't trust you; I have to bear you parading your arrogance."

"Roxborough understands nothing."

"He says you're obsessed with women, so he understands that, at least. You watch some girl across the street, he says—"

"What if I do?"

"How can you give yourself to the Reconciliation if you're so distracted?"

"Are you trying to talk me out of wanting Judith?"

"I thought magic was a religion to you."

"So's she."

"A discipline, a sacred mystery."

"Again, so's she." He laughed. "When I first saw her, it was like my first glimpse of another world. I knew I'd risk my life to be inside her skin. When I'm with her, I feel like an adept again, creeping toward a miracle, step by step. Tentative, excited—"

"Enough!"

"Really? You don't want to know why I need to be inside her so badly?"

Godolphin eyed him ruefully. "Not really," he said. "But if you don't tell me, I'll only wonder."

"Because for a little time, I'll forget who I am. Everything petty and particular will go out of me. My ambition. My history. Everything. I'll be unmade. And that's when I'm closest to divinity."

"Somehow you always manage to bring everything back to that. Even your lust."

"It's all One."

"I don't like your talk of the One," Godolphin said. "You sound like Roxborough with his dictums! *Simplicity is strength* and all the rest."

"That's not what I mean and you know it. It's just that women are where everything begins, and I like—how shall I put it?—to touch the source as often as possible."

"You think you're perfect, don't you?" Godolphin said.

"Why so sour? A week ago you were doting on my every word."

"I don't like what we're doing," Godolphin replied. "I want Judith for myself."

"You'll have her. And so will I. That's the glory of this."

"There'll be no difference between them?"

"None. They'll be identical. To the pucker. To the lash."

"So why must I have the copy?"

"You know the answer to that. Because the original loves me, not you."

"I should never have let you set eyes on her."

"You couldn't have kept us apart. Don't look so forlorn. I'm going to make you a Judith that'll dote on you and your sons, and your son's sons, until the name Godolphin disappears off the face of the earth. Now where's the harm in that?"

As he asked the question all the candles but the one he held went out, and the past was extinguished with them. He was suddenly back in the empty house, a police siren whooping nearby. He stepped back into the hallway as the car sped down Gamut Street, its blue light pulsing through the windows. Seconds later, another came howling after. Though the din of the sirens faded and finally disappeared, the flashes did not. They brightened from blue to white, however, and lost their regularity. By their brilliance he saw the house once more restored to glory. It was no longer a place of debate and laughter however. There was sobbing above and below, and the animal smells of fear in every corner. Thunder rattled the roof, but there was no rain to soothe its choler.

I don't want to be here, he thought. The other memories had entertained him. He'd liked his role in the proceedings. But this darkness was another matter entirely. It was full of death, and he wanted to run from it.

The lightning came again, horribly livid. By it, he saw Lucius Cobbitt standing halfway up the stairs, clutching the banister as though he'd fall if he didn't. He'd bitten his tongue or lip, or both, and blood dribbled from his mouth and chin, made stringy by the spit with which it was mingled. When Gentle climbed the stairs he smelled excrement. The boy had loosed his bowels in his breeches. Seeing Gentle, he raised his eyes.

"How did it fail, Maestro?" he sobbed. "*How?*"

Gentle shuddered as the question brought images flooding into his head, more horrendous than all the scenes he'd witnessed at the Erasure. The failure of the Reconciliation had been sudden, and calamitous, and had caught the Maestros representing the five Dominions at such a delicate time in the working that they'd been ill-equipped to prevent it. The spirits of all five had already risen from their circles across Imajica and, carrying the analogues of their worlds, had converged on the Ana, the zone of inviolability that appeared every two centuries in the heart of the In Ovo. There, for a tender time, miracles could be worked, as the Maestros, safe from the In Ovo's inhabitants but freed and empowered by their immaterial state, unburdened themselves of their similitudes and allowed the genius of the Ana to complete the fusing of the Dominions. It was a precarious time, but they'd been reaching its conclusion when the circle in which the Maestro Sartori's physical body sat, its stones protecting the outside world from the flux which let on to the In Ovo, broke. Of all the potential places for failure in the ceremonies, this was the unlikeliest: tantamount to transubstantiation failing for want of salt in the bread. But fail it did, and once the breach was opened, there was no way to seal it until the Maestros had returned to their bodies and mustered their feits. In that time the hungry tenants of the In Ovo had free access to the Fifth. Not only to the Fifth, but to the exulted flesh of the Maestros themselves, who vacated the Ana in confusion, leading the hounds of the In Ovo back to their flesh.

Sartori's life would certainly have been forfeited along with all the others had Pie 'oh' pah not intervened. When the circle broke, Pie was being forcibly removed from the Retreat on Godolphin's order, for voicing a prophetic murmur of alarm and disturbing the audience. The duty of removal had fallen to Abelove and Lucius Cobbitt, but neither had possessed the strength to hold the mystif. It had broken free, racing across the Retreat and plunging into the circle, where its master was visible to the assembly only as a blaze of light. The mystif had learned well at Sartori's feet. It had defenses against the flux of power that roared in the circle and had pulled the Maestro from under the noses of the approaching Oviates.

The rest of the assembly, however, caught between the mystif's yells of warning and Roxborough's attempts to maintain the status quo, were still standing around in confusion when the Oviates appeared.

The entities were swift. One moment the Retreat was a bridge to the transcendental; the next, it was an abattoir. Dazed by his sudden fall from grace, the Maestro had seen only snatches of the massacre, but they were burned on his eyes, and Gentle remembered them now in all their wretched detail: Abelove, scrabbling at the ground in terror as an Oviate the size of a felled bull, but resembling something barely born, opened its toothless maw and drew him between its jaws with tongues the length of whips; McGann, losing his arm to a sleek dark animal that rippled as it ran but hauling himself away, his blood a scarlet fountain, while the thing was distracted by fresher meat; and Flores—poor Flores, who'd come to Gamut Street the day before, carrying a letter of introduction from Casanova—caught by two beasts whose skulls were as flat as spades and whose translucent skin had given Sartori a terrible glimpse of their victim's agony as his head was taken down the throat of one while his legs were devoured by the other.

But it was the death of Roxborough's sister that Gentle remembered with profoundest horror, not least because the man had been at such pains to keep her from coming and had even abased himself to the Maestro, begging him to talk to the woman and persuade her to stay away. He'd had the talk, but he'd knowingly made his caution a seduction—almost literally, in fact—and she'd come to see the Reconciliation as much to meet the eyes of the man who'd wooed her with his warnings as for the ceremony itself. She'd paid the most terrible price. She'd been fought over like a bone among hungry wolves, shrieking a prayer for deliverance as a trio of Oviates drew out her entrails and dabbled in her open skull. By the time the Maestro, with Pie 'oh' pah's help, had raised sufficient feits to drive the entities back into the circle, she was dying in her own coils, thrashing like a fish half filleted by a hook.

Only later did the Maestro hear of the atrocities visited on the other circles. It was the same story there as in the Fifth: the Oviates appearing in the midst of innocents; carnage ensuing, which was only brought to a halt when one of the Maestro's assistants drove them back. With the exception of Sartori, the Maestros themselves had all perished.

"It would be better if I'd died like the others," he said to Lucius.

The boy tried to persuade him otherwise, but tears overwhelmed him. There was another voice, however, rising from the bottom of the stairs, raw with grief but strong.

"Sartori! Sartori!"

He turned. Joshua was there in the hallway, his fine powder-blue coat covered with blood. As were his hands. As was his face.

"What's going to happen?" he yelled. "This storm! It's going to tear the world apart!"

"No, Joshua."

"Don't lie to me! There's never been a storm like this! Ever!"

"Control yourself—"

"Jesus Christ our Lord, forgive us our trespasses."

"That's not going to help, Joshua."

Godolphin had a crucifix in his hand and put it to his lips.

"You Godless trash! Are you a demon? Is that it? Were you sent to have our souls?" Tears were pouring down his crazed face. "What Hell did you come out of?"

"The same as you. The human hell."

"I should have listened to Roxborough. He knew! He said over and over you had some plan, and I didn't believe him, wouldn't believe him, because Judith loved you, and how could anything so pure love anything unholy? But you hid yourself from her too, didn't you? Poor, sweet Judith! How did you make her love you? How did you do it?"

"Is that all you can think of?"

"Tell me! *How?*"

Barely coherent in his fury, Godolphin started up the stairs toward the seducer.

Gentle felt his hand go to his mouth. Godolphin halted. He knew this power.

"Haven't we shed enough blood tonight?" the Maestro said.

"*You,* not me," Godolphin replied. He jabbed a finger in Gentle's direction, the crucifix hanging from his fist. "You'll have no peace after this," he said. "Roxborough's already talking about a purge, and I'm going to give him every guinea he needs to break your back. You and all your works are damned!"

"Even Judith?"

"I never want to see that creature again."

"But she's yours, Joshua," the Maestro said flatly, descending the stairs as he spoke. "She's yours forever and ever. She won't age. She won't die. She belongs to the family Godolphin until the sun goes out."

"Then I'll kill her."

"And have her innocent soul on your blotted conscience?"

"She's got no soul!"

"I promised you Judith to the last, and that's what she is. A religion. A discipline. A sacred mystery. Remember?"

Godolphin buried his face in his hands.

"She's the one truly innocent soul left among us, Joshua. Preserve her. Love her as you've never loved any living thing, because she's our only victory." He took hold of Godolphin's hands and unmasked him. "Don't be ashamed of our ambition," he said. "And don't believe anyone who tells you it was the Devil's doing. We did what we did out of love."

"Which?" Godolphin said. "Making her, or the Reconciliation?"

"It's all One," he replied. "Believe that, at least."

Godolphin claimed his hands from the Maestro's grip. "I'll never believe anything again," he said and, turning his back, began his weary descent.

Standing on the stairs, watching the memory disappear, Gentle said a second farewell. He had never seen Godolphin again after that night. A few weeks later the man had retreated to his estate and sealed himself up there, living in silent self-mortification until despair had burst his tender heart.

"It was my fault," said the boy on the stairs behind him.

Gentle had forgotten Lucius was still there, watching and listening. He turned back to the child.

"No," he said. "You're not to blame."

Lucius had wiped the blood from his chin, but he couldn't control his trembling. His teeth chattered between his stumbling words. "I did everything you told me to do," he said. "I swear. I swear. But I must have missed some words from the rites or . . . I don't know . . . maybe mixed up the stones."

"What are you talking about?"

"The stones you gave me, to replace the flawed ones."

"I gave you no stones, Lucius."

"But Maestro, you did. Two stones, to go in the circle. You told me to bury the ones I took, at the step. Don't you remember?"

Listening to the boy, Gentle finally understood how the Reconciliation had come to grief. His other—born in the upper room of this very house—had used Lucius as his agent, sending him to replace a part of the circle with stones that resembled the originals (forging ran in the blood), knowing they would not preserve the circle's integrity when the ceremony reached its height.

But while the man who was remembering these scenes understood how all this had come about, to Maestro Sartori, still ignorant of the other self he'd created in the womb of the doubling circle, this remained an unfathomable mystery.

"I gave you no such instruction," he said to Lucius.

"I understand," the youth replied. "You have to lay the blame at my feet. That's why Maestros need adepts. I begged you for the responsibility, and I'm glad to have had it even if I failed." He reached into his pocket as he spoke. "Forgive me, Maestro," he said and, drawing out a knife, had it at his heart in the space of a thunderclap. As the tip drew blood the Maestro caught hold of the youth's hand and, wrenching the blade from his fingers, threw it down the stairs.

"Who gave you permission to do that?" he said to Lucius. "I thought you wanted to be an adept?"

"I did," the boy said.

"And now you're out of love with it. You see humiliation and you want no more of the business."

"No!" Lucius protested. "I still want wisdom. But I failed tonight."

"We *all* failed tonight!" the Maestro said. He took hold of the trembling boy and spoke to him softly. "I don't know how this tragedy came about," he said. "But I sniff more than your shite in the air. Some plot was here, laid against our high ambition, and perhaps if I hadn't been blinded by my own glory I'd have seen it. The fault isn't yours, Lucius. And stopping your own life won't bring Abelove, or Esther, or any of the others back. Listen to me."

"I'm listening."

"Do you still want to be my adept?"

"Of course."

"Will you obey my instructions now, to the letter?"

"Anything. Just tell me what you need from me."

"Take my books, all that you can carry, and go as far from here as you're able to go. To the other end of the Imajica, if you can learn the trick of it. Somewhere Roxborough and his hounds won't ever find you. There's a hard winter coming for men like us. It'll kill all but the cleverest. But you can be clever, can't you?"

"Yes."

"I knew it." The Maestro smiled. "You must teach yourself in secret, Lucius, and you must learn to live outside time. That way, the years won't wither you, and when Roxborough's dead you'll be able to try again."

"Where will you be, Maestro?"

"Forgotten, if I'm lucky. But never forgiven, I think. That would be too much to hope for. Don't look so dejected, Lucius. I have to know there's some hope, and I'm charging you to carry it for me."

"It's my honor, Maestro."

As he replied, Gentle was once again grazed by the déjà vu he'd first felt when he'd encountered Lucius outside the dining-room door. But the touch was light, and passed before he could make sense of it.

"Remember. Lucius, that everything you learn is already part of you, even to the Godhead Itself. Study nothing except in the knowledge that you already knew it. Worship nothing except in adoration of your true self. And fear nothing—" There the Maestro stopped and shuddered, as though he had a presentiment. "Fear nothing except in the certainty that you are your enemy's begetter and its only hope of healing. For everything that does evil is in pain. Will you remember those things?"

The boy looked uncertain. "As best I can," he said.

"That will have to suffice," the Maestro said. "Now . . . get out of here before the purgers come."

He let go of the boy's shoulders, and Cobbitt retreated down the stairs, backward, like a commoner from the king, only turning and heading away when he was at the bottom.

The storm was overhead now, and with the boy gone, taking his sewer stench with him, the smell of electricity was strong. The candle Gentle held flickered, and for an instant he thought it was going to be extinguished, signaling the end of these recollections, at least for tonight. But there was more to come.

"That was kind," he heard Pie 'oh' pah say, and turned to see the mystif standing at the top of the stairs. It had discarded its soiled clothes with its customary fastidiousness, but the plain shirt and trousers it wore were all the finery it needed to appear in perfection. There was no face in the Imajica more beautiful than this, Gentle thought, nor form more graceful, and the scenes of terror and recrimination the storm had brought were of little consequence while he bathed in the sight of it. But the Maestro he had been had not yet made the error of losing this miracle and, seeing the mystif, was more concerned that his deceits had been discovered.

"Were you here when Godolphin came?" he asked.

"Yes."

"Then you know about Judith?"

"I can guess."

"I kept it from you because I knew you wouldn't approve."

"It's not my place to approve or otherwise. I'm not your wife, that you should fear my censure."

"Still, I do. And I thought, well, when the Reconciliation was done this would seem like a little indulgence, and you'd say I deserved it because of what I'd achieved. Now it seems like a crime, and I wish it could be undone."

"Do you? Truly?" the mystif said.

The Maestro looked up. "No, I don't," he said, his tone that of a man surprised by a revelation. He started to climb the stairs. "I suppose I must believe what I told Godolphin, about her being our . . ."

"Victory," Pie prompted, stepping aside to let the summoner step into the Meditation Room. It was, as ever, bare. "Shall I leave you alone?" Pie asked.

"No," the Maestro said hurriedly. Then, more quietly: "Please. No."

He went to the window from which he had stood those many evenings watching the nymph Allegra at her toilet. The branches of the tree he'd spied her through thrashed themselves to splinter and pulp against the panes.

"Can you make me forget, Pie 'oh' pah? There are such feits, aren't there?"

"Of course. But is that what you want?"

"No, what I really want is death, but I'm too afraid of that at the moment. So . . . it will have to be forgetfulness."

"The true Maestro folds pain into his experience."

"Then I'm not a true Maestro," he returned. "I don't have the courage for that. Make me forget, mystif. Divide me from what I've done and what I am forever. Make a feit that'll be a river between me and this moment, so that I'm never tempted to cross it."

"How will you live?"

The Maestro puzzled over this for a few moments. "In increments," he finally replied. "Each part ignorant of the part before. Well. You can do this for me?"

"Certainly."

"It's what I did for the woman I made for Godolphin. Every ten years she'll start to undo her life and disappear. Then she'll invent another one and live it, never knowing what she left behind."

Listening to himself plot the life he'd lived, Gentle heard a perverse satisfaction in his voice. He had condemned himself to two hundred years of waste, but he'd known what he was doing. He'd made the same arrangements precisely for the second Judith and had contemplated every consequence on her behalf. It wasn't just cowardice that made him shun these memories. It was a kind of revenge upon himself for failing, to banish his future to the same limbo he'd made for his creature.

"I'll have pleasure, Pie," he said. "I'll wander the world and enjoy the moments. I just won't have the sum of them."

"And what about me?"

"After this, you're free to go," he said.

"And do what? Be what?"

"Whore or assassin, I don't care," the Maestro said.

The remark had been thrown off casually, surely not intended as an order to the mystif. But was it a slave's duty to distinguish between a command made for the humor of it and one to be followed absolutely? No, it was a slave's duty to obey, especially if the dictate came, as did this, from a beloved mouth. Here, with a throwaway remark, the master had circumscribed his servant's life for two centuries, driving it to deeds it had doubtless abhorred.

Gentle saw the tears shining in the mystif's eyes and felt its suffering like a hammer pounding at his heart. He hated himself then, for his arrogance and his carelessness, for not seeing the harm he was doing a creature that only wanted to love him and be near him. And he longed more than ever to be reunited with Pie, so that he could beg forgiveness for this cruelty.

"Make me forget," he said again. "I want an end to this."

The mystif was speaking, Gentle saw, though whatever incantations its lips shaped were spoken in a voice he couldn't hear. The breath that bore them made the flame he'd set on the floor flicker, however, and as the mystif instructed its master in forgetfulness the memories went out with the flame.

Gentle rummaged for the box of matches and struck one, using its light to find the smoking wick, then reigniting it. But the night of storm had passed back into history, and Pie 'oh' pah, beautiful, obedient, loving Pie 'oh' pah, had gone with it. He sat down in front of the candle and waited, wondering if there was some coda to come. But the house was dead from cellar to eaves.

"So," he said to himself. "What now, Maestro?"

He had his answer from his stomach, which made a little thunder of its own.

"You want food?" he asked it, and it gurgled its reply. "Me too," he said.

He got up and started down the stairs, preparing himself for a return to modernity. As he reached the bottom, however, he heard something scraping across the bare boards. He raised the candle, and his voice.

"Who's there?"

Neither the light nor his demand brought an answer. But the sound went on, and others joined it, none of them pleasant: a low, agonized moan; a wet, dragging sound; a whistling inhalation. What melodrama was his memory preparing to stage for him, he wondered, that had need of these hoary devices? They might have inspired fear in him once upon a time, but not now. He'd seen too many horrors face to face to be chilled by imitations.

"What's this about?" he asked the shadows, and was somewhat surprised to have his question answered.

"We've waited for you a long time," a wheezing voice told him.

"Sometimes we thought you'd never come home," another said. There was a fluting femininity in its tone.

Gentle took a step in the direction of the woman, and the rim of the candle's reach touched what looked to be the hem of a scarlet skirt, which was hastily twitched out of sight. Where it had lain, the bare boards shone with fresh blood. He didn't advance any further, but listened for another pronouncement from the shadows. It came soon enough. Not the woman this time, but the wheezer.

"The fault was yours," he said. "But the pain's been ours. All these years, waiting for you."

Though corrupted by anguish, the voice was familiar. He'd heard its lilt in this very house.

"Is that Abelove?" he said.

"Do you remember the maggot-pie?" the man said, confirming his identity. "The number of times I've thought: that was my error, bringing the bird into the house. Tyrwhitt would have no part of it, and he survived, didn't he? He died in his dotage. And Roxborough, and Godolphin, and you. All of you lived and died intact. But me, I just suffered here, flying against the glass but never hard enough to cease." He moaned, and though his rebuke was as absurd as it had been when first uttered, this time Gentle shuddered. "I'm not alone, of course," Abelove said. "Esther's here. And Flores. And Byam-Shaw. And Bloxham's brother-in-law; do you remember him? So there'll be plenty of company for you."

"I'm not staying," Gentle said.

"Oh, but you are," said Esther. "It's the least you can do."

"Blow out the candle," Abelove said. "Save yourself the distress of seeing us. We'll put out your eyes, and you can live with us blind."

"I'll do no such thing," Gentle said, raising the light so that it cast its net wider.

They appeared at its farthest edge, their viscera catching the gleam. What he'd taken to be Esther's skirt was a train of tissue, half flayed from her hip and thigh. She clutched it still, pulling it up around her, seeking to conceal her groin from him. Her decorum was absurd, but then perhaps his reputation as a womanizer had so swelled over the passage of the years that she believed he might be aroused by her, even in this appalling state. There was worse, however. Byam-Shaw was barely recognizable as a human being, and Bloxham's brother-in-law looked to have been chewed by tigers. But whatever their condition they were ready for revenge, no doubt of that. At Abelove's command they began to close upon him.

"You've already been hurt enough," Gentle said. "I don't want to hurt you again. I advise you to let me pass."

"Let you pass to do what?" Abelove replied, his terrible wounding clearer with every step he took. His scalp had gone, and one of his eyes lolled on his cheek. When he lifted his arm to point his next accusation at Gentle, it was with the littlest finger, which was the only one remaining on that hand. "You want to try again, don't you? Don't deny it! You've got the old ambition in your head!"

"You died for the Reconciliation," Gentle said. "Don't you want to see it achieved?"

"It's an abomination!" Abelove replied. "It was never meant to be! We died proving that. You render our sacrifice worthless if you try, then fail again."

"I won't fail," Gentle said.

"No, you won't," Esther replied, dropping her skirt to uncoil a garrote of her gut. "Because you won't get the chance."

He looked from one wretched face to the next and realized that he didn't have a hope of dissuading them from their intentions. They hadn't waited out the years to be diverted by argument. They'd waited for revenge. He had no choice but to stop them with a pneuma, regrettable as it was to add to their sum of suffering. He passed the candle from his right hand to his left, but as he did so somebody reached around him from behind and pinned his arms to his torso. The candle went from his fingers and rolled across the floor in the direction of his accusers. Before it could drown in its own wax, Abelove picked it up in his fingered hand.

"Good work, Flores," Abelove said.

The man clutching Gentle grunted his acknowledgment, shaking his prey to prove he had it securely caught. His arms were flayed, but they held Gentle like steel bands.

Abelove made something like a smile, though on a face with flaps for cheeks and blisters for lips it was a misbegotten thing.

"You don't struggle," he said, approaching Gentle with the candle held high. "Why's that? Are you already resigned to joining us, or do you think we'll be moved by your martyrdom and let you go?" He was very close to Gentle now. "It is pretty," he said. He cocked his eye a little, sighing. "How your face was loved!" he went on. "And this chest. How women fought to lay their heads upon it!" He slid his stump of a hand into Gentle's shirt and tore it open. "Very pale! And hairless! It's not Italian flesh, is it?"

"Does it matter?" said Esther. "As long as it bleeds, what do you care?"

"He never deigned to tell us anything about himself. We had to take him on trust because he had power in his fingers and his wits. He's like a little God, Tyrwhitt used to say. But even little Gods have fathers and mothers." Abelove leaned closer, allowing the candle flame within singeing distance of Gentle's lashes. "Who are you *really?*" Abelove said. "You're not an Italian. Are you Dutch? You could be Dutch. Or a Swiss. Chilly and precise. Huh? Is that you?" He paused. Then: "Or are you the Devil's child?"

"Abelove," Esther protested.

"I want to know!" Abelove yelped. "I want to hear him admit he's Lucifer's son." He peered at Gentle more closely. "Go on," he said. "Confess it."

"I'm not," Gentle said.

"There was no Maestro in Christendom could match you for feits. That kind of power has to come from somebody. *Who,* Sartori?"

Gentle would have gladly told, if he'd had an answer. But he had none. "Whoever I am," he said, "and whatever hurt I've done—"

"'Whatever,' he says!" Esther spat. "Listen to him! *Whatever! Whatever!*"

She pushed Abelove aside and tossed a loop of her gut over Gentle's head. Abelove protested, but he'd prevaricated long enough. He was howled down from all sides, Esther's howls the loudest. Tightening the noose around Gentle's neck, she tugged on it, preparing to topple him. He felt rather than saw the devourers awaiting him when he fell. Something was gnawing at his leg, something else punching his testicles. It hurt like hell, and he started to struggle and kick. There were too many holds upon him, however—gut, arms, and teeth—and he earned himself not an inch of latitude with his thrashings.

Past the red blur of Esther's fury, he caught sight of Abelove, crossing himself with his one-fingered hand, then raising the candle to his mouth.

"*Don't!*" Gentle yelled. Even a little light was better than none. Hearing him shout, Abelove looked up and shrugged. Then he blew out the flame. Gentle felt the wet flesh around him rise like a tide to claw him down. The fist gave up beating at his testicles and seized them instead. He screamed with pain, his clamor rising an octave as someone began to chew on his hamstrings.

"Down!" he heard Esther screech. "Down!"

Her noose had cut off all but the last squeak of breath. Choked, crushed, and devoured, he toppled, his head thrown back as he did so. They'd take his eyes, he knew, as soon as they could, and that would be the end of him. Even if he was saved by some miracle, it would be worthless if they'd taken his eyes. Unmanned, he could go on living; but not blind. His knees struck the boards, and fingers clawed for access to his face. Knowing he had mere seconds of sight left to him, he opened his eyes as wide as he could and stared up into the darkness overhead, hoping to find some last lovely thing to spend them on: a beam of dusty moonlight; a spider's web, trembling at the din he raised. But the darkness was too deep. His eyes would be thumbed out before he could use them again.

And then, a motion in that darkness. Something unfurling, like smoke from a conch, taking figmental shape overhead. His pain's invention, no doubt, but it sweetened his terror a little to see a face, like that of a beatific child, pour his gaze upon him.

"Open yourself to me," he heard it say. "Give up the struggle and let me be in you."

Another cliché, he thought. A dream of intercession to set against the nightmare that was about to geld and blind him. But one was real—his pain was testament to that—so why not the other?

"Let me into your head and heart," the infant's lips said.

"I don't know how," he yelled, his cry taken up in parody by Abelove and the rest.

"How? How? How?" they chanted.

The child had its reply. "Give up the fight," he said.

That wasn't so hard, Gentle thought. He'd lost it anyway. What was there left to lose? With his eyes fixed on the child, Gentle let every muscle in his body relax. His hands gave up their fists; his heels, their kicks. His head tipped back, mouth open.

"Open your heart and head," he heard the infant say.

"Yes," he replied.

Even as he uttered his invitation, a moth's-wing doubt fluttered in his ear. At the beginning hadn't this smacked of melodrama? And didn't it still? A soul snatched from Purgatory by cherubim; opened, at the last, to simple salvation. But his heart was wide, and the saving child swooped upon it before doubt could seal it again. He tasted another mind in his throat and felt its chill in his veins. The invader was as good as its word. He felt his tormentors melt from around him, their holds and howls fading like mists.

He fell to the floor. It was dry beneath his cheek, though seconds before Esther's skirts had been seeping on it. Nor was there any trace of the creatures' stench in the air. He rolled over and cautiously reached to touch his hamstrings. They were intact. And his testicles, which he'd presumed nearly pulped, didn't even ache. He laughed with relief to find himself whole and, while he laughed, scrabbled for the candle he'd dropped. Delusion! It had all been delusion! Some final rite of passage conducted by his mind so that he might supersede his guilt and face his future as a Reconciler unburdened. Well, the phantoms had done their duty. Now he was free.

His fingers had found the candle. He picked it up, fumbled for the matches, struck one, and put the flame to the wick. The stage he'd filled with ghouls and cherubim was empty from boards to gallery. He got to his feet. Though the hurts he'd felt had been imagined, the fight he'd put up against them had been real enough, and his body—which was far from healed after the brutalities of Yzordderrex—was the worse for his resistance.

As he hobbled toward the door, he heard the cherub speak again. "Alone at last," it said.

He turned on his heel. The voice had come from behind him, but the staircase was empty. So was the landing and the passageways that led off the hall. The voice came again, however.

"Amazing, isn't it?" the putto said. "To hear and not to see. It's enough to drive a man mad."

Again Gentle wheeled, the candle flame fluttering at his speed.

"I'm still here," the cherub said. "We'll be together for quite a time, just you and I, so we'd better get to like each other. What do you enjoy chatting about? Politics? Food? I'm good for anything but religion."

This time, as he turned, Gentle caught a glimpse of his tormentor. It had put off the cherubic illusion. What he saw resembled a small ape, its face either anemic or powdered, its eyes black beads, its mouth enormous.

Rather than waste his energies pursuing something so nimble (it had hung from the ceiling minutes before), Gentle stood still and waited. The tormentor was a chatterbox. It would speak again and eventually show itself entirely. He didn't have to wait long.

"Those demons of yours must have been appalling," it said. "The way you kicked and cursed."

"You didn't see them?"

"No. Nor do I want to."

"But you've got your fingers in my head, haven't you?"

"Yes. But I don't delve. It's not my business."

"What *is* your business?"

"How do you live in this brain? It's so small and sweaty."

"Your business?"

"To keep you company."

"I'm leaving soon."

"I don't think so. Of course, that's just my opinion . . ."

"Who are you?"

"Call me Little Ease."

"That's a name?"

"My father was a jailer. Little Ease was his favorite cell. I used to say, Thank God he didn't circumcise for a living, or I'd be—"

"Don't."

"Just trying to keep the conversation light. You seem very agitated. There's no need. You're not going to come to any harm, unless you defy my Maestro."

"Sartori."

"The very man. He knew you'd come here, you see. He said you'd pine and you'd preen, and how very right he was. But then I'm sure he'd have done the same thing. There's nothing in your head that isn't in his. Except for me, that is. I must thank you for being so prompt, by the way. He said I'd have to be patient, but here you are, after less than two days. You must have wanted these memories badly."

The creature went on in similar vein, burbling at the back of Gentle's head, but he was barely aware of it. He was concentrating on what to do now. This creature, whatever it was, had tricked its way into him—*Open your head and heart*, it had said, and he'd done just that, fool that he was: opened himself up to its possession—and now he had to find some way to be rid of it.

"There's more where those came from, you know," it was saying.

He'd temporarily lost track of its monologue and didn't know what it was prattling about.

"More of what?" he said.

"More memories," it replied. "You wanted the past, but you've only had a tiny part of a tiny part. The best's still to come."

"I don't want it," he said.

"Why not? It's *you*, Maestro, in all your many skins. You should have what's yours. Or are you afraid you'll drown in what you've been?"

He didn't answer. It knew damn well how much damage the past could do if it came over him too suddenly; he'd laid plans for that very eventuality as he'd come to the house.

Little Ease must have heard his pulse quicken, because it said, "I can see why it'd frighten you. There's so much to be guilty for, isn't there? Always, so much."

He had to be out and away, he thought. Staying here, where the past was all too present, invited disaster.

"Where are you going?" Little Ease said as Gentle started toward the door.

"I'd like to get some sleep," he said. An innocent enough request.

"You can sleep here," his possessor replied.

"There's no bed."

"Then lie down on the floor. I'll sing a lullaby."

"And there's nothing to eat or drink."

"You don't need sustenance right now," came the reply.

"I'm hungry."

"So fast for a while."

Why was it so eager to keep him here? he wondered. Did it simply want to wear him down with sleeplessness and thirst before he even stepped outside? Or did its sphere of influence cease at the threshold? That hope leaped in him, but he tried not to let it show. He sensed that the creature, though it had spoken of entering his head and heart, did not have access to every thought in his cranium. If it did, it'd have no need of threats in order to keep him here. It would simply direct his limbs to be leaden and drop him to the ground. His intentions were still his own, even if the entity had his memories at its behest, and it followed therefore that he might get to the door, if he was quick, and be beyond its grasp before it opened the floodgates. In order to placate it until he was ready to make his move, he turned his back on the door.

"Then I suppose I stay," he said.

"At least we've got each other for company," Little Ease said. "Though let me make it clear, I draw the line at any carnal relations, however desperate you get. Please don't take it personally. It's just that I know your reputation, and I want to state here and now I have no interest in sex."

"Will you never have children?"

"Oh, yes, but that's different. I lay them in the heads of my enemies."

"Is that a warning?" he asked.

"Not at all," it replied. "I'm sure you could accommodate a family of us. It's all One, after all. Isn't that right?" It left off its voice for a moment and imitated him perfectly. "*We'll not be subsumed at our deaths, Roxborough, we'll be increased to the size of Creation.* Think of me as a little sign of that increase, and we'll get along fine."

"Until you murder me."

"Why would I do that?"

"Because Sartori wants me dead."

"You do him an injustice," Little Ease said. "I've no brief as an assassin. All he wants me to do is keep you from your work until after midsummer. He doesn't want you playing the Reconciler and letting his enemies into the Fifth. Who can blame him? He intends to build a New Yzordderrex here, to rule over the Fifth from pole to pole. Did you know that?"

"He did mention it."

"And when that's done. I'm sure he'll embrace you as a brother."

"But until then—"

"I have his permission to do whatever I must to keep you from being a Reconciler. And if that means driving you insane with memories—"

"Then you will."

"Must, Maestro, *must*. I'm a dutiful creature."

Keep talking, Gentle thought, as it waxed poetic describing its powers of subservience. He wouldn't make for the door, he'd decided. It was probably double- or treble-locked. Better that he went for the window by which he'd entered. He'd fling himself through if need be. If he broke a few bones in the process, it'd be a small price to pay for escape.

He glanced around casually, as if deciding where he was going to lay his head, never once allowing his eyes to stray to the front door. The room with the open window lay ten paces at most from where he stood. Once inside, there'd be another ten to reach the window. Little Ease, meanwhile, was lost in loops of its own humility. Now was as good a time as any.

He took a pace toward the bottom of the stairs as a feint, then changed direction and darted for the door. He'd made three paces before it even realized what he was up to.

"Don't be so stupid!" it snapped.

He'd been conservative in his calculation, he realized. He'd be through the door in eight paces, not ten, and across the room in another six.

"I'm warning you," it shrieked, then, realizing its appeals would gain it nothing, acted.

Within a pace of the door, Gentle felt something open in his head. The crack through which he allowed the past to trickle suddenly gaped. In a pace the rivulet was a stream; in two, white waters: in three, a flood. He saw the window across the room, and the street outside, but his will to reach it was washed away in the deluge of the past.

He'd lived nineteen lives between his years as Sartori and his time as John Furie Zacharias, his unconscious programmed by Pie to ease him out of one life and into another in a fog of self-ignorance that only lifted when the deed was done, and he awoke in a strange city, with a name filched from a telephone book or a conversation. He'd left pain behind him, of course, wherever he'd gone. Though he'd always been careful to detach himself from his circle, and cover his tracks when he departed, his sudden disappearances had undoubtedly caused great grief to everyone who'd held him in their affections. The only one who'd escaped unscathed had been himself. Until now. Now all these lives were upon him at once, and the hurts he'd scrupulously avoided caught up with him. His head filled with fragments of his past, pieces of the nineteen unfinished stories that he'd left behind, all lived with the same infantile greed for sensation that had marked his existence as John Furie Zacharias. In every one of these lives he'd had the comfort of adoration. He'd been loved and lionized: for his charm, for his profile, for his mystery. But that fact didn't sweeten the flood of memories. Nor did it save him from the panic he felt as the little self he knew and understood was overwhelmed by the sheer profusion of details that arose from the other histories.

For two centuries he'd never had to ask the questions that vexed every other soul at some midnight or other: 'Who am I? What was I made for, and what will I be when I die?'

Now he had too many answers, and that was more distressing than too few. He had a small tribe of selves, put on and off like masks. He had trivial purposes aplenty. But there had never been enough years held in his memory at one time to make him plumb the depths of regret or remorse, and he was the poorer for that. Nor, of course, had there been the imminence of death or the hard wisdom of mourning. Forgetfulness had always been on hand to smooth his frowns away, and it had left his spirit unproved.

Just as he'd feared, the assault of sights and scenes was too much to bear, and though he fought to hold on to some sense of the man he'd been when he'd entered the house, it was rapidly subsumed. Halfway between the door and the window his desire to escape, which had been rooted in the need to protect himself, went out of him. The determination fell from his face, as though it were just another mask. Nothing replaced it. He stood in the middle of the room like a stoic sentinel, with no flicker of his inner turmoil rising to disturb the placid symmetry of his face.

The night hours crawled on, marked by a bell in a distant steeple, but if he heard it he showed no sign. It wasn't until the first light of day crept over Gamut Street, slipping through the window he'd been so desperate to reach, that the world outside his confounded head drew any response from him. He wept. Not for himself, but rather for the delicacy of this amber light falling in soft pools on the hard floor. Seeing it, he conceived the vague notion of stepping out into the street and looking for the source of this miracle, but there was somebody in his head, its voice stronger than the muck of confusion that swilled there, who wanted him to answer a question before it would allow him out to play. It was a simple enough inquiry.

"Who are you?" it wanted to know.

The answer was difficult. He had a lot of names in his head, and pieces of lives to go with them, but which one of them was his? He'd have to sort through many fragments to get a sense of himself, and that was too wretched a task on a day like this, when there were sunbeams at the window, inviting him out to spy their father in Heaven.

"Who are you?" the voice asked him again, and he was obliged to tell the simple truth.

"I don't know."

The questioner seemed content with this. "You may as well go, then," it said. "But I'd like you to come back once in a while, just to see me. Will you do that?"

He said that of course he would, and the voice replied that he was free to go. His legs were stiff, and when he tried to walk he fell instead, and had to crawl to where the sun was brightening the boards. He played there for a time and then, feeling stronger, climbed out of the window into the street.

Had he possessed a cogent memory of the previous night's pursuits he'd have realized, as he jumped down onto the pavement, that his guess concerning Sartori's agent had been correct, and its jurisdiction did indeed halt at the limits of the house. But he comprehended not at all the fact of his escape. He'd entered number 28 the previous night as a man of purpose, the Reconciler of the Imajica come to confront the past and be strengthened by self-knowledge. He left it undone by that same knowledge and stood in the street like a bedlamite, staring up at the sun in ignorance of the fact that its arc marked the year's progression to midsummer, and thus to the hour when the man of purpose he'd been had to act—or fail forever.

If coming to the moment of Reconciliation had been for Gentle a series of rememberings, leading him back to himself, then the greatest of those rememberings, and the one he was least prepared for, was the Reconciliation itself.

Though he'd performed the working before, the circumstances had been radically different. For one, there'd been all the hoopla of a grand event. He'd gone into the circle like a prizefighter, with an air of congratulation hanging around his head before he'd even worked up a sweat, his patrons and admirers a cheering throng at the sidelines. This time he was alone. For another, he'd had his eyes on what the world would shower on him when the work was done: what women would fall to him, what wealth and glory would come. This time, the prize in sight was a different thing entirely, and wouldn't be counted in stained sheets and coinage. He was the instrument of a higher and wiser power.

That fact took the fear away. When he opened his mind to the process, he felt a calm come upon him, subduing the unease he'd felt climbing the stairs. He'd told Jude and Clem that forces would run through the house the likes of which its bricks had never known, and it was true. He felt them fuel his weakening mind, ushering his thoughts out of his head to gather the Dominion to the circle.

That gleaning began with the place he was sitting in. His mind spread to all compass points, and up and down, to have the sum of the room. It was an easy space to grasp. Generations of prison poets had made the analogies for him, and he borrowed them freely. The walls were his body's limits, the door his mouth, the windows his eyes: commonplace similitudes, taxing his power of comparison not a jot. He dissolved the boards, the plaster, the glass, and all the thousand tiny details in the same lyric of confinement and, having made them part of him, broke their bounds to stray farther afield.

As his imagination headed down the stairs and up onto the roof, he felt the beginnings of momentum. His intellect, dogged by literalism, was already lagging behind a sensibility more mercurial, which was delivering back to him similitudes for the whole house before his logical faculties had even reached the hallway.

Once again, his body was the measure of all things: the cellar, his bowels; the roof, his scalp; the stairs, his spine. Their proofs delivered, his thoughts flew out of the house, rising up over the slates and spreading through the streets. He gave passing consideration to Sartori as he went, knowing his other was out here in the night somewhere, skulking. But his mind was quicksilver, and too exhilarated by its speed and capacity to go searching in the shadows for an enemy already defeated.

With speed came ease. The streets were no more difficult to claim than the house he'd already devoured. His body had its conduits and its intersections, had its places of excrement and its fine, dandified façades; had its rivers, moving from a springing place, and its parliament, and its holy seat.

The whole city, he began to see, could be analogized to his flesh, bone, and blood. And why should that be so surprising? When an architect turned his mind to the building of a city, where would he look for inspiration? To the flesh where he'd lived since birth. It was the first model for any creator. It was a school and an eating house and an abattoir and a church; it could be a prison and a brothel and bedlam. There wasn't an edifice in any street in London that hadn't begun somewhere in the private city of an architect's anatomy, and all Gentle had to do was open his mind to that fact and the districts were his, running back to swell the assembly in his head.

He flew north, through Highbury and Finsbury Park, to Palmer's Green and Cockfosters. He went east with the river, past Greenwich, where the clock that marked the coming of midnight stood, and on toward Tilbury. West took him through Marylebone and Hammersmith, south through Lambeth and Streatham, where he'd first met Pie 'oh' pah, long ago.

But the names soon became irrelevant. Like the ground seen from a rising plane, the particulars of a street or a district became part of another pattern, even more appetizing to his ambitious spirit. He saw the Wash glittering to the east, and the Channel to the south, becalmed on this humid night. Here was a fine new challenge. Was his body, which had proved the equal of a city, also the measure of this vaster geography? Why not? Water flowed by the same laws everywhere, whether the conduit was a groove in his brow or a rift between the continents. And were his hands not like two countries, laid side by side in his lap, their peninsulas almost touching, their landscapes scarred and grooved?

There was nothing outside his substance that was not mirrored within: no sea, no city, no street, no roof, no room. He was in the Fifth, and the Fifth in him, gathering to be carried into the Ana as a proof and a map and a poem, written in praise of all things being One.

From *Weaveworld*

The third week of September brought rain. Not the torrents of August, which had poured from operatic skies, but drizzles and piddlings. The days grew grayer; and so, it seemed, did Brendan. Though Cal made daily attempts to persuade his father downstairs, he would no longer come. Cal also made two or three valiant efforts to talk about what had happened a month before, but the old man was simply not interested. His eyes became glazed as soon as he sensed the drift of the conversation, and if Cal persisted he grew irritable.

The professionals judged that Brendan was suffering from senile dementia, an irreversible process which would finally make him impossible for Cal to nurse. It might be best for all concerned, they advised, if a place were found in a nursing home, where Brendan could be cared for twenty-four hours a day.

Cal rejected the suggestion. He was certain that Brendan's cleaving to a room he knew—one he'd shared with Eileen for so many years—was all that was keeping him from total breakdown.

He was not alone in his attempts to nurse his father. Two days after he'd failed to set the pigeons flying, Geraldine had appeared at the house. There was ten minutes of hesitant apologies and explanations, then Brendan's condition entered the exchange and Geraldine's good sense came triumphantly to the fore. Forget our differences, she said, I want to help. Cal was not about to refuse the offer. Brendan responded to Geraldine's presence as a child to a

long-lost teat. He was cosseted and indulged, and with Geraldine in the
house in Eileen's place, Cal found himself falling back into the old domestic routines. The affection he felt for Geraldine was painless, which was
surely the most certain sign of how slight it was. When she was there he was
happy to be with her. But he seldom, if ever, missed her.

As to the Fugue, he did his best to keep his memories of it sharp, but it
was by no means easy. The Kingdom had ways to induce forgetfulness so
subtle and so numerous he was scarcely aware of how they dulled him.

It was only when, in the middle of a dreary day, something reminded
him—a scent, a shout—that he had once been in another place, and
breathed its air and met its creatures, it was only then that he realized how
tentative his recall was. And the more he went in pursuit of what he was
forgetting the more it eluded him.

The glories of the Fugue were becoming mere words, the reality of
which he could no longer conjure. When he thought of an orchard it was
less and less that extraordinary place he'd slept in (slept, and dreamed that
this life he was now living was the dream) and more a commonplace stand
of apple trees.

The miracles were drifting from him, and he seemed to be unable to
hold on to them.

Surely dying was like this, he thought; losing things dear and unable to
prevent their passing.

Yes; this was a kind of dying.

Brendan, for his part, continued to continue. As the weeks passed, Geraldine managed to talk him into joining them downstairs, but he was interested in little but tea and television, and his conversation was now scarcely
more than grunts. Sometimes Cal would watch Brendan's face as he sat
slumped in front of the television—his expression unchanging whether
the screen offered pundits or comedians—and wondered what had happened to the man he'd known. Was the old Brendan still in hiding somewhere, behind those addled eyes, or had he been an illusion all along, a
son's dream of his father's permanence which, like the letter from Eileen,
had simply evaporated? Perhaps it was for the best, he thought, that Brendan was shielded from his pain, then drew himself up short at such a
thought. Wasn't that what they said as the coffin was marched past: it was
all for the best? Brendan wasn't dead yet.

As time went by, Geraldine's presence began to prove as comforting to

Cal as to the old man. Her smiles were the brightest thing those dismal months could boast. She came and went, more indispensable by the day, until, in the first week of December, she suggested it might be more convenient all round if she slept at the house. It was a perfectly natural progression.

"I don't want to marry you," she told him quite plainly. The sorry spectacle of Theresa's marriage—five months old and already rocky—had confirmed her worst suspicions of matrimony. "I did want to marry you once," she said. "But now I'm happy just to be with you."

She proved easy company; down-to-earth, unsentimental: as much companion as lover. She it was who made certain the bills were paid on time, and saw that there was tea in the caddy. She it was too who suggested that Cal sell the pigeons.

"Your father doesn't show any interest in them any longer," she said on more than one occasion. "He wouldn't even notice if they were gone."

That was certainly true. But Cal refused to contemplate the sale. Come spring and the fine weather his father might well show fresh interest in the birds.

"You know that's not true," she'd tell him when he put this point. "Why do you want to keep them so much? They're just a burden." Then she'd let the subject drop for a few days, only to raise it again when a cue was presented.

History was repeating itself. Often in the course of these exchanges, which gradually became more heated, Cal could hear echoes of his mother and father: the same routes were being trodden afresh. And, like his father, Cal—though malleable on almost every other issue—was immovable on this. He would not sell the birds.

The real reason for his bullishness was not, of course, hope of Brendan's rehabilitation, but the fact that the birds were his last concrete link with the events of the previous summer.

In the weeks after Suzanna's disappearance he'd bought a dozen newspapers a day, scanning each page for some report of her, or the carpet, or Shadwell. But there was nothing, and eventually—unable to bear the daily disappointment—he'd stopped looking. Nor was there any further visit from Hobart or his men—which was in its way bad news. He, Cal, had become an irrelevancy. The story, if it was still being written, was running on without him.

He became so frightened he'd forget the Fugue that he took the risk of writing down all that he could remember of the night there, which, when he set himself to the task, was depressingly little. He wrote the names down too: Lemuel Lo; Apolline Dubois; Frederick Cammell . . . ; set them all down at the back of his diary, in the section reserved for telephone numbers, except that there were no numbers for these people; nor addresses either. Just uncommon names to which he was less and less able to attach faces.

On some nights he had dreams, from which he would wake with tears on his face.

Geraldine consoled him as best she could, given that he claimed not to recall these dreams when he woke. That was in a sense true. He brought nothing into consciousness that words could encapsulate: only an aching sadness. She would lie beside him then, and stroke his hair, and tell him that though these were difficult times things could be much worse. She was right, of course. And by and by the dreams dwindled, until they finally ceased altogether.

In the last week of January, with Christmas bills still outstanding and too little money to pay them with, he sold the pigeons, with the exception of 33 and his mate. This pair he kept, though the reason why was harder and harder to remember; and by the end of the following month had been forgotten entirely.

THIRTEEN

ART

The sentence that opens the final excerpt of this chapter, *Nothing ever begins*, was at one point going to be the opening of the book itself. But it seemed better placed here, a happy admission that all that's gone before has been rooted in something else: a legend, a rumor, a memory.

Two of the excerpts here are concerned with the making of images. In the excerpt from *Everville*, Harry D'Amour visits an exhibition and finds that one of the paintings is a portrait of himself, battling the Devil. The passage was written at a time when I was regularly exhibiting my paintings in New York, and had the scars to prove it. The second piece is from *Imajica*, and conjures, I hope, a little of the power painting can have in an unlikely setting. There was a period in the seventies when it was quite the thing in London to paint the walls of derelict buildings with elaborate and often hallucinatory murals. The vogue has largely passed, regrettably. Now if a wall is covered with an image, it's likely to be selling us something.

The selection from *Weaveworld* which opens this section tells a self-contained tale: one in which storytelling becomes a means of revelation. Two characters, the heroine Suzanne and a villain called Hobart, enter—by force of their animosity—the pages of a book of fairy tales. There they discover the true nature of their relationship with each other, which powerfully impacts the Weaveworld itself.

Stories within stories, worlds within worlds.

From *Weaveworld*

The Law had come to Nonesuch.

It had come to root out dissension: it had found none. It had come with truncheons, riot shields, and bullets, prepared for armed rebellion: it had found no whisper of that either. All it had found was a warren of shadowy streets, most of them deserted, and a few pedestrians who bowed their heads at the first sign of a uniform.

Hobart had immediately ordered a house-to-house search. It had been greeted with a few sour looks, but little more than that. He was disappointed; it would have been gratifying to have found something to sharpen his authority upon. All too easy, he knew, to be lulled into a false sense of security, especially when an anticipated confrontation had failed to materialize. Vigilance was the key word now; unending vigilance.

That was why he'd occupied a house with a good view of the township from its upper stories, where he could take up residence for the night. Tomorrow would bring the big push on the Gyre, which could surely not go unopposed. And yet, who could be certain with these people? They were so docile; like animals, rolling over at the first sign of a greater power.

The house he'd commandeered had little to recommend it, beyond its view. A maze of rooms; a collection of faded murals, which he didn't care to study too closely; spare and creaking furniture. The discomfort of the place didn't bother him: he liked spartan living. But the atmosphere did; the sense he had that the ousted tenants were still here, just out of sight. If he'd been a man who believed in ghosts, he'd have said the house was haunted. He wasn't, so he kept his fears to himself, where they multiplied.

Evening had fallen, and the streets below were dark. He could see little from his high window now, but he could hear laughter drifting up from below. He'd given his men the evening to enjoy themselves, warning them never to forget that the township was enemy territory. The laughter grew more riotous, then faded down the street. Let them indulge themselves, he thought. Tomorrow the crusade would take them onto ground the people here thought of as sacred: if they were going to show any resistance, it would be then. He'd seen the same happen in the world outside: a man who wouldn't lift a finger if his house were burned down throwing a fit if someone touched a trinket he called *holy*. Tomorrow promised to be a busy day, and a bloody one too.

Richardson had declined the opportunity to take the night off, preferring to stay in the house, and make a report of the day's events for his personal records. He kept a ledger of his every move, set down in a tiny, meticulous hand. He worked on it now, as Hobart listened to the laughter disappearing below.

Finally, he put down his pen.

"Sir?"

"What is it?"

"These people, sir. It seems to me—" Richardson halted, unsure of how best to voice a question that had been vexing him since they'd arrived, "it seems to me they don't look quite *human*."

Hobart studied the man. His hair was immaculately cut, his cheeks immaculately shaved, his uniform immaculately pressed.

"You may be right," he said.

A flicker of distress crossed Richardson's face.

"I don't understand . . . sir."

"While you're here, you should believe nothing you see."

"*Nothing*, sir?"

"Nothing at all," Hobart said. He put his fingers to the glass. It was cold; his body heat lent the tips misty haloes. "The whole place is a mass of illusions. Tricks and traps. None of it's to be trusted."

"It's not real?" Richardson said.

Hobart stared across the roofs of this little nowhere, and turned the question over. *Real* was a word he'd once had no problem using. Real was what made the world go round, what was solid and true. And its flip side, *unreal*, that was what some lunatic in a cell shouted at four in the morning; unreal was dreams of power without the flesh to give them weight.

But his view of these matters had subtly changed since his first encounter with Suzanna. He had wanted her capture as he'd wanted no other, and his pursuit of her had led from one strangeness to another, until he was so fatigued he scarcely knew right from left. Real? What *was* real? Perhaps (this thought would have been unthinkable before Suzanna) real was merely what he *said* was real. He was the general, and the soldier needed an answer, for his sanity's sake. A plain answer, that would let him sleep soundly.

He gave it:

"Only the Law's real here," he said. "We have to hang on to that. All of us. Do you understand?"

Richardson nodded. "Yes, sir."

There was a long pause, during which somebody outside began whooping like a drunken Cherokee. Richardson closed his ledger, and went to the second window.

"I wonder . . . ," he said.

"Yes?"

"Perhaps I *should* go out. Just for a while. To see these illusions face to face."

"Maybe."

"Now that I know it's all a lie—" he said, "I'm safe, aren't I?"

"As safe as you're ever going to be," said Hobart.

"Then, if you don't mind . . ."

"Go on. See for yourself."

Richardson was away in seconds, and down the stairs. A few moments later Hobart caught sight of his shadowy form moving away down the street.

The Inspector stretched. He was tired to the marrow. There was a mattress in the next room, but he was determined not to avail himself of it. Laying his head on a pillow would offer the rumors of occupancy here an easy victim.

Instead he sat down in one of the plain chairs and took the book of fairy tales from his pocket. It had not left his presence since its confiscation; he'd lost count of the times he'd scanned its pages. Now he did the same again. But the lines of prose grew steadily hazier in front of him, and though he tried to check himself, his lids became heavier and heavier.

Long before Richardson had found himself an illusion to call his own, the Law that had come to Nonesuch had fallen asleep.

Suzanna didn't find it so difficult to avoid Hobart's men when she stepped back into the township. Though they swarmed through the alleyways the shadows had become unnaturally dense there, and she was always able to stay a few steps ahead of the enemy. Getting access to Hobart was another matter, however. Though she wanted to be finished with her work here as quickly as possible there was no use in risking arrest. She'd escaped custody twice; three times might be pressing her luck. Though impatience gnawed at her, she decided to wait until the light faded. The days were still short this early in the year; it would only be a few hours.

She found herself an empty house—availing herself of some plain food that the owners had left there—and wandered around the echoing rooms until the light outside began to dwindle. Her thoughts turned back, and back again, to Jerichau, and the circumstances of his death. She tried to remember the way he looked, and had some success with his eyes and hands, but couldn't create anything like a complete portrait. Her failure depressed her. He was so soon gone.

She had just about decided that it was dark enough to risk venturing out when she heard voices. She went to the bottom of the stairs, and peered through to the front of the house. There were two silhouetted figures on the threshold.

"Not here . . . ," she heard a girl's voice whisper.

"Why not?" said her male companion, his words slurred. One of Hobart's company, no doubt. "Why not? It's as good as any."

"There's somebody here already," said the girl, staring into the mystery of the house.

The man laughed. "Dirty fuckers!" he called. Then he took the woman roughly by the arm. "Let's find somewhere else," he said. They moved away, into the street.

Suzanna wondered if Hobart had sanctioned such fraternization. She couldn't believe he had.

It was time she put an end to stalking him in her imagination; time to find him and get her business with him done. She slipped through the house, scanned the street, then stepped out into the night.

The air was balmy, and with so few lights burning in the houses, and those that did burn mere candle flames, the sky was bright above, the stars like dewdrops on velvet. She walked a little way with her face turned skyward, entranced by the sight. But not so entranced she didn't sense Hobart's proximity. He was somewhere near. But where? She could still waste precious hours going from house to house, trying to find him.

When in doubt, ask a policeman. It had been one of her mother's favorite saws, and never more apt. A few yards from where she stood one of

Hobart's horde was pissing against a wall, singing a ragged rendition of "Land of Hope and Glory" to accompany the flood.

Trusting that his inebriation would keep him from recognizing her, she asked Hobart's whereabouts.

"You don't need *him*," the man said. "Come on in. We've got a party going."

"Maybe later. I've got to see the Inspector."

"If you must," the man said. "He's in the big house with the white walls." He pointed back the way she'd come, splashing his feet as he did so. "Somewhere off to the right," he said.

The instructions, despite the provider's condition, were good. Off to the right was a street of silent dwellings, and at the corner of the next intersection a sizable house, its walls pale in the starlight. There was nobody standing sentry at the door; the guards had presumably succumbed to whatever pleasures Nonesuch could offer. She pushed the door open and stepped inside unchallenged.

There were riot-shields propped against the wall of the room she'd entered, but she needed no confirmation that this was indeed the house. Her gut already knew that Hobart was in one of the upper rooms.

She started up the stairs, not certain what she would do when she confronted him. His pursuit of her had made her life a nightmare, and she wanted to make him regret it. But she couldn't kill him. Dispatching the Magdalene had been terrible enough; killing a human being was more than her conscience would allow. Best just to claim her book, and go.

At the top of the stairs was a corridor, at the end of which a door stood ajar. She went to it, and pushed it open. He was there, her enemy; alone, slumped in a chair, his eyes closed. In his lap lay the book of fairy tales. The very sight of it made her nerves flutter. She didn't hesitate in the doorway, but crossed the bare boards to where he slumbered.

In his sleep, Hobart was floating in a misty place. Moths flew around his head, and beat their dusty wings against his eyes, but he couldn't raise his arms to brush them away. Somewhere near he sensed danger, but from which direction would it come?

The mist moved to his left, then to his right.

"Who. . . ?" he murmured.

The word he spoke froze Suzanna in her tracks. She was a yard from the chair, no more. He muttered something else; words she couldn't comprehend. But he didn't wake.

Behind his eyelids Hobart glimpsed an unfixable form in the mist. He struggled to be free of the lethargy that weighed him down; fought to waken, and defend himself.

Suzanna took another step toward the sleeper.

He moaned again.

She reached for the book, her fingers trembling. As they closed around it, his eyes sprang wide open. Before she could snatch the book away from him, his grip on it tightened. He stood up.

"No!" he shouted.

The shock of his waking almost made her lose her hold, but she wasn't going to give her prize up now: the book was *her* property. There was a moment of struggle between them, as they fought for possession of the volume.

Then—without warning—a veil of darkness rose from their hands, or more correctly from the book they held between them.

She looked up into Hobart's eyes. He was sharing her shock at the power that was suddenly released from between their woven fingers. The darkness rose between them like smoke, and blossomed against the ceiling, immediately tumbling down again, enclosing them both in a night within a night.

She heard Hobart loose a yell of fear. The next moment words seemed to rise from the book, white forms against the smoke, and as they rose they became what they meant. Either that or she and Hobart were falling, and becoming symbols as the book opened to receive them. Whichever; or both; it was all one in the end.

Rising or falling, as language or life, they were delivered into storyland.

. . .

It was dark in the state they'd entered; dark, and full of rumor. Suzanna could see nothing in front of her, not even her fingertips, but she could hear soft whispers, carried to her on a warm, pine-scented wind. Both touched her face, whispers and wind; both excited her. They knew she was here, the people that inhabited the stories in Mimi's book: for it was there, *in the book*, that she and Hobart now existed.

Somehow, in the act of struggling, they'd been transformed—or at least their thoughts had. They'd entered the common life of words.

Standing in the darkness, and listening to the whispers all around her, she didn't find the notion so difficult to comprehend. After all hadn't the author of this book turned his thoughts into words, in the act of writing it, knowing his readers would decode them as they read, making thoughts of them again? More: making an imagined life. So here was she now, living that life. Lost in *Geschichten der Geheimen Orte*; or found there.

There were hints of light moving to either side of her she now realized; or was it *she* that was moving: running perhaps, or flying? Anything was possible here: this was fairy land. She concentrated, to get a better grasp of what these flashes of light and darkness meant, and realized all at once that she was traveling at speed through avenues of trees, vast primeval trees, and the light between them was growing brighter.

Somewhere up ahead, Hobart was waiting for her, or for the thing she'd become as she flew through the pages.

For she was not Suzanna here; or rather, not *simply* Suzanna. She could not simply be herself here, any more than he could be simply Hobart. They were grown mythical in this absolute forest. They had drawn to themselves the dreams that this state celebrated: the desires and faiths that filled the nursery stories, and so shaped all subsequent desires and faiths.

There were countless characters to choose from, wandering in the Wild Woods; sooner or later every story had a scene played here. This was the place orphaned children were left to find either their deaths or their destinies: where virgins went in fear of wolves, and lovers in fear of their hearts. Here birds talked, and frogs aspired to the throne, and every grove had its pool and well, and every tree a door to the Netherworld.

What, among these, was *she*? The Maiden, of course. Since childhood she'd been the Maiden. She felt the Wild Woods grow more luminous at this thought, as though she'd ignited the air with it.

I'm the Maiden . . .

she murmured,

. . . and he's the Dragon.

Oh yes. That was it; of course that was it.

The speed of her flight increased; the pages flipped over and over. And now ahead she saw a metallic brightness between the trees, and there the Great Worm was, its gleaming coils wrapped around the roots of a Noahic tree, its vast, flat-snouted head laid on a bed of blood-red poppies as it bided its terrible time.

Yet, perfect as it was, in every scaly detail, she saw Hobart there too. He was woven with the pattern of light and shade, and so—most oddly—was the word *Dragon*. All three occupied the same space in her head: a living text of man, word, and monster.

The Great Worm Hobart opened its one good eye. A broken arrow protruded from its twin, the work of some hero or other no doubt, who'd gone his tasseled and shining way in the belief that he'd dispatched the beast. It was not so easily destroyed. It lived still, its coils no less tremendous for the scars they bore, its glamour untarnished. And the living eye? It held enough malice for a tribe of dragons.

It saw her, and raised its head a little. Molten stone seethed between its lips, and murdered the poppies.

Her flight toward it faltered. She felt its glance pierce her. Her body began to tremble in response. She tumbled toward the dark earth like a swatted moth. The ground beneath her was strewn with words; or were they bones? Whichever, she fell among them, shards of nonsense thrown up in all directions by her flailing arms.

She got to her feet, and looked about her. The colonnades were empty in every direction: there was no hero to call upon, nor mother to take comfort with. She was alone with the Worm.

It raised its head a few feet higher, this minor motion causing a slow avalanche of coils.

It was a beautiful worm, there was no denying that, its iridescent scales glittering, the elegance of its malice enchanting. She felt, looking at it, that same combination of yearning and anxiety which she remembered so well from childhood. Its presence *aroused* her, there was no other word for it. As if in response to that confession, the Dragon roared. The sound it made was hot and low, seeming to begin in its bowels and winding down its length to break from between the countless needles of its teeth, a promise of greater heat to come.

All light had gone from between the trees. No birds sang or spoke, no animal, if any lived so close to the Dragon, dared move a whisker in the undergrowth. Even the bone-words and the poppies had disappeared, leaving these two elements, Maiden and Monster, to play out their legend.

"*It finishes here,*" Hobart said, with the Dragon's laval tongue. Each syllable he shaped was a little fire, which cremated the specks of dust around her head. She was not afraid of all this; rather, exhilarated. She had only ever been an observer of these rites; at last she was a performer.

"Have you nothing more *to tell me?*" the Dragon demanded, spitting the words from between its serried teeth. "*No blessings? No explanations?*"

"Nothing," she said defiantly. What was the purpose of talk, when they were so perfectly transparent to each other? They knew who they were, didn't they; knew what they meant to one another? In the final confrontation of any great tale dialogue was redundant. With nothing left to say, only action remained: a murder or a marriage.

"Very well," said the Dragon, and it moved toward her, drawing its length over the wasteland between them with vestigial forelegs.

He means to kill me, she thought; *I have to act quickly.* What did the Maiden do to protect herself in such circumstances as this? Did she flee, or try to sing the beast to sleep?

The Dragon was towering over her now. But it didn't attack. Instead it threw back its head, exposing the pale, tender flesh of its throat.

"Please be quick," it growled.

She was bewildered by this.

"Be quick?" she said.

"Kill me and be done," it instructed her.

Though her mind didn't fully comprehend this volte-face, the body she occupied did. She felt it changing in response to the invitation; felt a new ripeness in it. She'd thought to live in this world as an innocent; but that she couldn't be. She was a grown woman; a woman who'd changed in the last several months, sloughed off years of dead assumptions; found magic inside herself; suffered loss. The role of Maiden—all milk and soft sighs—didn't fit.

Hobart knew that better than she. He hadn't come into these pages as a child, but as the man he was, and he'd found a role here that suited his most secret and forbidden dreams. This was no place for pretense. She was not the virgin, he was not the devouring worm. He, in his private imaginings, was power besieged, and seduced, and finally—painfully—*martyred*. That was why the Dragon before her raised its milky throat.

Kill me and be done, he said, lowering his head a little to look at her. In his surviving eye she saw for the first time how wounded he was by his obsession with her; how he'd come to be in thrall to her, sniffing after her like a lost dog, hating her more with every day that passed for the power she had over him.

In the other reality—in the room from which they'd stepped, which was in turn hidden in a larger Kingdom (worlds within worlds)—he would be brutal with her. Given the chance he'd kill her for fear of the truth he could only admit in the sacred grove of his dreams. But here there was no story to tell except the true one. That was why he raised his palpitating throat, and fluttered his heavily lidded eye. He was the virgin, frightened and alone, ready to die rather than sacrifice his tattered virtue.

And what did that make her? The beast, of course. She was the beast. *No sooner thought than felt.*

She sensed her body growing larger, and larger, and larger still. Her bloodstream ran colder than a shark's. A furnace flared up in her belly.

In front of her Hobart was shrinking. The dragon-skin fell away from him in silky folds, and he was revealed, naked and white: a human male, covered in wounds. A chaste knight at the end of a weary road, bereft of strength or certitude.

She had claimed the skin he'd lost; she felt it solidify around her, its armor glittering. The size of her body was a joy to her. She exulted in the way it felt to be so dangerous and so impossible. This was how she *truly* dreamed of herself; this was the real Suzanna. She was a Dragon.

With that lesson learned, what was she to do? Finish the story as the man before her wished? Burn him? Swallow him?

Looking down at his insipidity from her rearing height, smelling the dirt off him, the sweat off him—she could easily find it in her heart to do her Dragon's duty, and *devour*. It would be easy.

She moved toward him, her shadow engulfing him. He was weeping, and smiling up at her with gratitude. She opened her vast jaws. Her breath singed his hair. She would cook him and swallow him in one swift motion. But she was not quick enough. As she was about to devour him she was distracted by a voice nearby. Was there somebody else in the grove? The sounds certainly belonged in these pages. They were far from human, though there were words attempting to surface through the barking and grunting. Pig; dog; man: a combination of all three, and all panicking.

The Knight Hobart opened his eyes, and there was something new in them, something besides tears and fatigue. He too had heard the voices; and hearing them, he was reminded of the place that lay beyond these Wild Woods.

The Dragon's moment of triumph was already sliding away. She roared her frustration, but there was nothing to be done. She felt herself shedding her scales, dwindling from the mythical to the particular, while Hobart's scarred body fluttered like a flame in a breeze, and went out.

Her instant of questioning would surely cost her dearly. In failing to finish the story, to satisfy her victim's desire for death, she'd given him fresh motive for hatred. What change might it have wrought in Hobart to have dreamed himself devoured; to have made a second womb in the Worm's belly until he was born back into the world?

Too late, damn it; far too late. The pages could contain them no longer. Leaving their confrontation unfinished they broke from the words in a burst of punctuation. They didn't leave the din of the animals behind them: it grew louder as the darkness of the Wild Woods lifted.

Her only thought was for the book. She felt it in her hands once more, and took fiercer hold of it. But Hobart had the same idea. As the room appeared around them in all its solidity she found his fingers clawing at hers, tearing at her skin in his eagerness to claim the prize back.

"You should have killed me," she heard him murmur.

She glanced up at his face. He looked even sicklier than the knight he'd been, sweat running down his sallow cheeks, gaze desperate. Then he seemed to realize himself, and the eyes grew arctic.

Somebody was beating on the other side of the door, from which the pained cacophony of animals still came.

"Wait!" Hobart yelled to his visitors, whoever they were. As he shouted he took one hand from the book and drew a gun from the inside of his jacket, digging the muzzle into Suzanna's abdomen.

"Let the book go, or I'll kill you."

She had no choice but to comply. The menstruum would not be swift enough to incapacitate him before he pulled the trigger.

As her hands slipped from the volume, however, the door was thrown open, and all thought of books was eclipsed by what stood on the threshold.

Once, this quartet had been among the pride of Hobart's Squad: the smartest, the hardest. But their night of drinking and seduction had unbuttoned more than their trousers. It had undone their minds as well. It was as if the splendors Suzanna had first seen on Lord Street, the haloes that sainted Human and Seerkind alike, had somehow been drawn *inside* them, for the skin of their limbs and faces was swollen and raw, bubbles of darkness scurrying around their anatomies like rats under sheets.

In their panic at this disease, they'd clawed their clothes to tatters; their torsos shone with sweat and blood. And from their throats came the cacophony that had called the Dragon and the Knight out of the book; a bestiality that was echoed in a dozen horrid details. The way this one's face had swollen to lend him a snout; the way another's hands were fat as paws.

This, she presumed, was how the Seerkind had opposed the occupation of their homeland. They'd feigned passivity to seduce the invading army into their raptures, and this nightmare menagerie was the result. Apt as it was, she was appalled.

One of the pack now staggered into the room, his lips and forehead swollen to the brink of bursting. He was clearly trying to address Hobart, but all his spellbound palate could produce was the complaint of a cat having its neck wrung.

Hobart had no intention of deciphering the mewls, but instead leveled his gun at the wreckage shambling toward him.

"Come no closer," he warned.

The man, spittle running from his open mouth, made a incoherent appeal.

"Get out!" was Hobart's response. He took a step toward the quartet.

The leader retreated, as did those in the doorway. Not for the gun's sake, Suzanna thought, but because Hobart was their master. These new anatomies only confirmed what their training had long ago taught them: that they were unthinking animals, in thrall to the Law.

"Out!" said Hobart again.

They were backing off along the corridor now, their din subdued by their fear of Hobart.

In a matter of moments his attention would no longer be diverted, Suzanna knew. He'd turn on her again, and the slim advantage gained by this interruption would have been squandered.

She had to let her instinct lead; she might have no other opportunity.

Seizing the moment, she ran at Hobart and snatched the book from his hand. He shouted out, and glanced her way, his gun still keeping the howling quartet at bay. With his eye off them, the creatures set up their racket afresh.

"There's no way out—" Hobart said to her, "except by this door. Maybe you'd like to go that way. . . ?"

The creatures clearly sensed that something was in the air, and redoubled their din. It was like feeding time at the zoo. She'd not get two steps down the passage before they were upon her. Hobart had her trapped.

At that realization, she felt the menstruum rise in her, coming with breath-snatching suddenness.

Hobart knew instantly she was gathering strength. He crossed quickly to the door, and slammed it on the howling breed outside, then turned on her again.

"We saw some things, didn't we?" he said. "But it's a story you won't live to tell."

He aimed the gun at her face.

It wasn't possible to analyze what happened next. Perhaps he fired and the shot miraculously went wide, shattering the window behind her. Whatever, she felt the night air invade the room, and the next moment the menstruum was bathing her from head to foot, turning her on her heel, and she was running toward the window with no time to consider the sense of this escape route until she was up on the sill and hurling herself out.

The window was three stories up. But it was too late for such practicalities. She was committed to the leap, or fall, or—*flight!*

The menstruum scooped her up, throwing its strength against the wall of the house opposite, and letting her slide from window to roof on its cool back. It wasn't true flight, but it felt like the real thing.

The street reeled beneath her as she tumbled on solid air to meet the eaves of the other house, only to be scooped up a second time and carried over the roof, Hobart's shouts diminishing behind her.

She could not be held aloft for long, of course; but it was an exhilarating ride while it lasted. She slid helter skelter down another roof, catching sight in that moment of a streak of dawn light between the hills, then over gables and chimney stacks and down, swooping, into a square where the birds were already tuning up for the day.

As she flew down they scattered, startled by the twist evolution had taken to produce such a bird as this. Her landing must have reassured them that there was much design work still to do. She skidded across the paving stones, the menstruum cushioning the worst of the impact, and came to a halt inches from a mosaic-covered wall.

Shaking, and faintly nauseous, she stood up. The entire flight had probably lasted no more than twenty seconds, but already she heard voices raising the alarm in an adjacent street.

Clutching Mimi's gift, she slipped from the square and out of the township by a route that took her once in a circle and twice almost threw her into the arms of her pursuers. Every step of the way she discovered a new bruise, but she was at least alive, and wiser for the night's adventures.

Life and wisdom. What more could anybody ask?

From *Everville*

"T hat," said the man with the salmon-pink tie, gesturing toward the canvas on the gallery wall, "is an abomination. What the hell's it called?" He peered at his price sheet.

"*Bronx Apocalypse*," the man at his side said.

"*Bronx Apocalypse*," the critic snorted. "Jesus!"

He eyed the man who'd supplied the title. "You're not him, are you?" he said. "You're not this fellow Dusseldorf?"

The other man—a well-made fellow in his late thirties, with three days' growth of beard and the eyes of an insomniac—shook his head. "No. I'm not."

"You *are* in one of the paintings though, aren't you?" said the Asian woman at Salmon Tie's side.

"Am I?"

She took the sheet from her companion's hand and scanned the twenty or so titles upon it. "There," she said. "*D'Amour in Wyckoff Street*. It's the big painting next door," she said to Salmon Tie, "with that bilious sky."

"Loathsome," the man remarked. "Dusseldorf should go back to pushing heroin or whatever the hell he was doing. He's got no business foisting this crap on people."

"Ted didn't push," D'Amour said. He spoke softly, but there was no doubting the warning in his voice.

"I was simply stating my opinion," the man said, somewhat defensively.

"Just don't spread lies," D'Amour said. "You'll put the Devil out of work."

It was July 8, a Friday, and the Devil was much on Harry's mind tonight. New York was a stew as ever, and, as ever, Harry wished he could be out of the pot and away, but there was nowhere to go; nowhere he wouldn't be followed and found. And here, at least, in the sweet-and-sour streets he knew so well, he had niches and hiding places; he had people who owed him, people who feared him. He even had a couple of friends.

One of whom was Ted Dusseldorf, reformed heroin addict, sometime performance artist, and now, remarkably, a painter of metropolitan apocalypses.

There he was, holding court in front of one of his rowdier pieces, all five foot nothing of him, dressed in a baggy plaid suit, and chewing on a contender for the largest damn cigar in Manhattan.

"Harry! Harry!" he said, laying eyes on D'Amour. "Thanks for coming." He deserted his little audience and hooked his arm over Harry's shoulder. "I know you hate crowds, but I wanted you to see I got myself some admirers."

"Any sales?"

"Yeah, would you believe it? Nice Jewish lady, big collector, lives on the park, fancy address, buys that—" he jabbed his cigar in the direction of *Slaughtered Lambs on the Brooklyn Bridge*, "for her dining room. I guess maybe she's a vegetarian," he added, with a catarrhal laugh. "Sold a couple of drawings too. I mean, I ain't gonna get rich, you know, but I proved something, right?"

"That you did."

"I want you to see the masterwork," Ted said, leading Harry through the throng, which was divided into three distinct camps. The inevitable fashion victims, here to be seen and noted in columns. A smattering of well-heeled collectors, slumming. And Ted's friends, several of whom had tattoos as colorful as anything on the walls.

"I had this guy come up to me," Ted said, "fancy shoes, designer haircut, he says: Fantasy's so *passé*. I said: What fantasy? He looks at me like I farted. He says: These works of yours. I said: This isn't fantasy. This is my life. He shakes his head, walks away." Ted leaned closer to Harry. "I think sometimes there's two different kinds of people in the world. The people who understand and the people who don't. And if they don't, it's no use trying to explain, 'cause it's just beyond them, and it always will be."

There was an eight-by-six foot canvas on the wall ahead, its colors more livid and its focus more strident than anything else in the exhibition.

"You know, it keeps me sane, doin' this shit. If I hadn't started lettin' all this out onto canvas, man, I'd have lost my fuckin' mind. I don't know how you keep your head straight, Harry. I really don't. I mean, knowing what you know, seeing what you see . . ."

The knot of people standing in front of the picture parted, seeing the artist and his model approach, giving them plain view of the masterpiece. Like most of the other works it too depicted a commonplace street. Only this was a street Harry could name. This was Wyckoff Street, in Brooklyn, where one sunny Easter Sunday almost a decade before Harry had first been brushed by infernal wings.

Ted had painted the street pretty much as it looked—drab and uncomfortable—and had placed the figure of D'Amour in the middle of the thoroughfare, regarding the viewer with a curious gaze, as if to say: do you see what I see? At first glance it seemed there was nothing untoward about the scene, but further study gave the lie to that. Rather than simply accruing a host of disturbing details on the canvas, Ted had worked a subtler effect. He'd laid down a field of mushy scarlets and ochers, like the guts of an overripe pomegranate, and then stroked the details of Wyckoff Street over this seething backcloth, the grays and sepias of brick and iron and asphalt never completely concealing the rotted hues beneath, so that for all the carefully rendered detail, Wyckoff Street looked like a veil drawn over a more insistent and powerful reality.

"Good likeness, huh?" Ted said.

Harry assumed it was, given that he'd been recognized from it, but hell, it was less than comforting. He had good bones—Norma had told him so the first time she'd touched his face—but did they have to *protrude* quite so much? The way Ted had laid the paint down on Harry's face he'd practically *carved* the features: long nose, strong jaw, wide brow, and all. As for the marks of age, he hadn't stinted. The gray hairs and the frown lines were much in evidence. It wasn't a bad face to be wearing into his forties, Harry supposed. Sure, there was none of the serenity that was rumored to be compensation for losing the bloom and ease of youth—his stare was troubled, the smile on his lips tentative to say the least—but it was a picture of a sane man with all his limbs and faculties intact, and of the people who'd wrestled with the beasts of the abyss, that pretty much put Harry in a league of one.

"Do you see it?" Ted said.

"See what?"

Ted brought Harry a couple of steps closer to the canvas and pointed to the lower half.

"There." Harry looked. First at the sidewalk, then at the gutter. "Under your foot," Ted prompted.

There, squirming under Harry's right heel, was a thin black snake, with burning coals for eyes.

"The Devil Himself," Ted said.

"Got him where I want him, have I?" Harry said.

Ted grinned. "Hey, it's art. I'm allowed to lie a little."

From *Sacrament*

C lem's duties were done for the night. He'd been out since seven the previous evening, about the same business that took him out every night: the shepherding of those among the city's homeless too frail or too young to survive long on its streets with only concrete and cardboard for a bed. Midsummer Night was only two days away, and the hours of darkness were short and relatively balmy, but there were other stalkers besides the cold that preyed on the weak—all human—and the work of denying them their quarry took him through the empty hours after midnight and left him, as now, exhausted, but too full of feeling to lay down his head and sleep. He'd seen more human misery in the three months he'd been working with the homeless than in the four decades preceding that. People living in the extremes of deprivation within spitting distance of the city's most conspicuous symbols of justice, faith, and democracy: without money, without hope, and many (these the saddest) without much left of their sanity. When he returned home after these nightly treks, the hole left in him by Taylor's passing not filled but at least forgotten for a while, it was with expressions of such despair in his head that his own, met in the mirror, seemed almost blithe.

Tonight, however, he lingered in the dark city longer than usual. Once the sun was up he knew he'd have little or no chance of sleeping, but sleep was of little consequence to him at the moment. It was two days since he'd had the visitation that had sent him to Judy's doorstep with tales of angels, and since then there'd been no further hint of Taylor's presence. But there were other hints, not in the house but out here in the streets, that powers were abroad which his dear Taylor was just one sweet part of.

He'd had evidence of this only a short time ago. Just after midnight a man called Tolland, apparently much feared among the fragile communities that gathered to sleep under the bridges and in the stations of Westminster, had gone on a rampage in Soho. He'd wounded two alcoholics in a back street, their sole offense to be in his path when his temper flowed. Clem had witnessed none of this, but had arrived after Tolland's arrest to see if he could coax from the gutter some of those whose beds and belongings had been demolished. None would go with him, however, and in the course of his vain persuasions one of the number, a woman he'd never seen without tears on her face until now, had smiled at him and said he should stay out in the open with them tonight rather than hiding in his bed, because the Lord was coming, and it would be the people on the streets who saw Him first. Had it not been for Taylor's fleeting reappearance in his life, Clem would have dismissed the woman's blissful talk, but there were too many imponderables in the air for him to ignore the vaguest signpost to the miraculous. He'd asked the woman what Lord this was that was coming, and she'd replied, quite sensibly, that it didn't matter. Why should she care what Lord it was, she said, as long as He came?

Now it was an hour before dawn, and he was trudging across Waterloo Bridge because he'd heard the psychopathic Tolland had usually kept to the South Bank and something odd must have happened to drive him across the river. A faint clue, to be sure, but enough to keep Clem walking, though hearth and pillow lay in the opposite direction.

The concrete bunkers of the South Bank complex had been a favorite *bête grise* of Taylor's, their ugliness railed against whenever the subject of contemporary architecture came up in conversation. The darkness presently concealed their drab, stained façades, but it also turned the maze of underpasses and walkways around them into terrain no bourgeois would tread for fear of his life or his wallet. Recent experience had taught Clem to ignore such anxieties. Warrens such as this usually contained individuals more aggressed against than aggressive, souls whose shouts were a defense against imagined enemies and whose tirades, however terrifying they might seem emerging from shadow, usually dwindled into tears.

In fact, he'd not heard a whisper from the murk as he descended from the bridge. The cardboard city was visible where its suburbs spilled out into the meager lamplight, but the bulk of it lay under cover of the walkways, out of sight and utterly quiet. He began to suspect that the lunatic Tolland was not the only tenant who'd left his plot to travel north and, stooping to peer into the boxes on the outskirts, had that suspicion confirmed. He headed into shadow, fishing his pencil torch from his pocket to light the way. There was the usual detritus on the ground: spoiled scraps of food, broken bottles, vomit stains. But the boxes, and the beds of newspaper and filthy blankets they contained, were empty. More curious than ever, he wandered on through the rubbish, hoping to find a soul here too weak or too crazy to leave, who could explain this migration. But he passed through the city without finding a single occupant, emerging into what the planners of this concrete hell had designed as a children's playground. All that remained of their good intentions were the grimy bones of a slide and a jungle gym. The paving beyond them, however, was covered in fresh color, and advancing to the spot Clem found himself in the middle of a kitsch exhibition: crude chalk copies of movie-star portraits and glamour girls everywhere underfoot.

He ran the beam over the ground, following the trail of images. It led him to a wall, which was also decorated, but by a very different hand. Here was no mere copyist's work. This image was on such a grand scale Clem had to play his torch beam back and forth across it to grasp its splendor. A group of philanthropic muralists had apparently taken it upon themselves to enliven this underworld, and the result was a dream landscape, its sky green, with streaks of brilliant yellow, the plain beneath orange and red. Set on the sands, a walled city, with fantastical spires.

The torch beam caught a glint off the paint, and Clem approached the wall to discover that the muralists had only recently left off their labors. Patches of the paint were still tacky. Seen at close quarters, the rendering was extremely casual, almost slapdash. Barely more than half a dozen marks had been used to indicate the city and its towers, and only a single snaking stroke to show the highway running from the gates. Moving his beam off the picture to illuminate the way ahead, Clem realized why the muralists had been so haphazard. They had been at work on every available wall, creating a parade of brightly colored images, many of which were far stranger than the landscape with the green sky. To Clem's left was a man with two cupped hands for a head, lightning jumping between the palms; to his right a family of freaks, with fur on their faces. Farther on was an alpine scene, fantasticated by the addition of several naked women, hovering above the snows; beyond it a skull-strewn veldt, with a distant train belching smoke against a dazzling sky; and beyond that again, an island set in the middle of a sea disturbed by a single wave, in the foam of which a face could be discovered. All were painted with the same passionate haste as the first, which fact lent them the urgency of sketches and added to their power. Perhaps it was his exhaustion, or simply the bizarre setting for this exhibition, but Clem found himself oddly moved by the images. There was nothing ingratiating or sentimental about them. They were glimpses into the minds of strangers, and he was exhilarated to find such wonders there.

From *Weaveworld*

N othing ever begins.
      There is no first moment; no single word or place from which this or any other story springs.

The threads can always be traced back to some earlier tale, and to the tales that preceded that; though as the narrator's voice recedes the connections will seem to grow more tenuous, for each age will want the tale told as if it were of its own making.

Thus the pagan will be sanctified, the tragic become laughable; great lovers will stoop to sentiment, and demons dwindle to clockwork toys.

Nothing is fixed. In and out the shuttle goes, fact and fiction, mind and matter, woven into patterns that may have only this in common: that hidden among them is a filigree which will with time become a world.

APPENDIX

THE BOOKS OF BLOOD
First published in 1984 and 1985

Written originally for the entertainment of his friends, *The Books of Blood* were published in six volumes over a period of two years. Their powerful and provocative content earned a word of mouth reputation that made Clive Barker a household name. *The Books of Blood* won the 1985 World Fantasy Award for Best Anthology/Collection.

Volume I: "The Book of Blood"; "The Midnight Meat Train"; "The Yattering and Jack"; "Pig Blood Blues"; "Sex, Death and Starshine"; "In the Hills, the Cities."

Volume II: "Dread"; "Hell's Event"; "Jacqueline Ess: Her Will and Testament"; "The Skins of the Fathers"; "New Murders in the Rue Morgue."

Volume III: "Son of Celluloid"; "Rawhead Rex"; "Confession of a (Pornographer's) Shroud"; "Scapegoats"; "Human Remains."

Volume IV: "The Body Politic"; "The Inhuman Condition"; "Revelations"; "Down, Satan!"; "The Age of Desire."

Volume V: "The Forbidden"; "The Madonna"; "Babel's Children"; "In the Flesh."

Volume VI: "The Life of Death"; "How Spoilers Bleed"; "Twilight at the Towers"; "The Last Illusion"; "The Book of Blood (a postscript): On Jerusalem Street."

"Clive Barker completes a sextet of imaginative forays into the grandest of guignol." —*Time Out*

THE DAMNATION GAME
First published in 1985

Barker's debut novel, published between *Volumes III* and *IV* of *The Books of Blood*, is a modern reworking of the Faustian myth. A London criminal, Marty Strauss, is sprung from prison to act as bodyguard to Joseph White-head, a millionaire industrialist and former gambler who owes his empire to Mamoulian, who sacrificed his soul in return for terrifying powers. As Marty learns the disturbing truth about just who he is protecting his employer from, the narrative takes the reader through a variety of striking landscapes: from the blasted streets of postwar Warsaw to the gaming clubs and back alleys of modern-day London; from vast country estates and impenetrable fortresses to a nightworld filled with ghostly assassins.

"Wonderful, moving and apocalyptic. Death and damnation hang at the end of every chapter." —*Seattle Post*

WEAVEWORLD
First published in 1987

Cal Mooney is drawn into a world of mystery and revelation when he first sees an old carpet in the back yard of Mimi Laschenski's house. When Mimi dies her grand-daughter, Suzanna, becomes the custodian of the carpet; but she and Cal soon find themselves hunted by the witch Imma-colata and her accomplice, the salesman Shadwell. The carpet contains the last refuge of the Seerkind, a magical tribe cast out of Eden, and the Immacolata and Shadwell are ready to sell the exotic refugees into slavery. Only Cal and Suzanna stand in their way. *Weaveworld* redefined the para-meters of genre fiction, creating a vast epic narrative played out against the dual backdrops of a bleak, industrialized Liverpool and the strange, fantas-tic landscape of the Fugue, a magical world hidden within the ancient carpet.

"His most ambitious and imaginative work . . . strands of Joyce, Poe, Tolkien . . . an irresistible yarn."   —*Time*

"An epic tale of a magic carpet and the wondrous world within its weave [that] towers above his earlier work . . . the most ambitious and visionary horror novel of the decade . . . a raging flood of image and situation so rich as to overflow. Barker has unleashed literary genius."   —*Kirkus*

THE HELLBOUND HEART
First published in 1987

Frank becomes obsessed with trying to open a Chinese puzzle-box, but the eventual solution opens a doorway into Hell, and through it come the Cenobites, demons who have dedicated an eternity to the pursuit of pleasure–and pain. This is the novella which inspired the groundbreaking horror film classic, *Hellraiser*.

"A real marrow-melter."   —*The Scotsman*

CABAL
First published in 1989

Aaron Boone, a psychiatric patient suffering from disturbing dreams of a place called Midian, finds himself accused of a series of mass murders. On the run, he learns from a fellow patient that Midian does indeed exist. Boone is killed trying to get there but returns from the dead, knowing that his journey is not yet over. Expanded from a novella which first appeared in the U.S. edition of *The Books of Blood, Volume VI, Cabal* was made into the film, *Nightbreed*, and directed by Barker himself.

"A complete but open-ended system of multi-layered dark magic. On the one hand it's a simple macabre tale; on the other it shows a deep and dreadful understanding of society and its outcasts . . . a rare, powerful fantasy."   —*Fear*

THE GREAT AND SECRET SHOW
First published in 1989

The First Book of The Art. Two men's obsession with gaining access to Quiddity, the dream sea that separates us from the nightmare world of the Iad Uroboros, leads screenwriter Tesla Bombeck into a conflict which leaves her transformed into a powerful shaman. This obsession also sets in motion a chain of events which lead to a destructive battle in Palomo Grove, as both men gather armies from the souls of the quiet Californian town. And as a schism is opened into Quiddity, the terrifying Iad Uroboros approach the opening, intent on invading our world.

> "Clive Barker's career has been building up to *The Great and Secret Show.* It is nothing so much as a cross between *Gravity's Rainbow* and *The Lord of the Rings;* allusive and mythic, complex and entertaining ... extravagantly metaphorical, wildly symbolic, skillful and funny."   —*New York Times Book Review*

IMAJICA
First published in 1991

The Imajica – five Dominions, four reconciled. The fifth, Earth, is cut off from the others, its people living in ignorance of the surrounding wonder. But a time of Reconciliation is approaching, and this represents both opportunity and threat to all the peoples of the Imajica. Three very different people bound by one secret – Gentle, a master forger; Judith, a beautiful independent woman; and Pie'oh' Pah, an assassin – all seeking a deeper understanding to their lives, are brought together in a deadly quest for Reconciliation as they journey through the fantastic, exotic worlds of the Imajica.

> "Tears and blood and nightmare imagery are passionate and ingenious. *Imajica* is a ride with remarkable views."
>
> —*Times Literary Supplement*

> "Rich in plot twists, Byzantine intrigues, and hidden secrets, *Imajica* is a Chinese puzzle book constructed on a universal scale ... Barker has an unparalleled talent for envisioning other worlds."   —*Washington Post*

THE THIEF OF ALWAYS
First published in 1992

Mr. Hood's Holiday House has stood for a thousand years, a place of miracles offering everything a child could wish for. But when young Harvey Swick discovers its darker secrets he finds himself trapped inside, and must battle the sinister Mr. Hood in a bid for freedom. This fable for all ages, richly illustrated in black and white by the author, represented a change of style which was critically acclaimed the world over.

> "A dashingly produced fantasy with powerful drawings by the author." —*Daily Telegraph*

> "Barker's book puts the grim back into fairy tales and continues a noble tradition of scaring kids witless. Neatly nasty drawings too." —*Time Out*

EVERVILLE
First published in 1994

The Second Book of the Art. A door stands open on a mountain high above the city of Everville, revealing the shores of the dream sea, Quiddity. This extraordinary event draws together three exceptional people: Phoebe Cobb, searching for her lover who stepped through the door; Tesla Bombeck, who must learn Everville's secrets to prevent the horrors of the Iad Uroboros from crossing the threshold; and Harry D'Amour, who has tracked evil across America and finds it invading the streets of Everville. But the mysterious and ageless Buddenbaum is intent on stopping them, and draws upon the power of his deadly patrons to ensure that the door stands open.

> "*Everville* confirms the author's position as one of modern fiction's premier metaphysicians . . . a spectacular sequel to his masterpiece of dark fantasy, *The Great and Secret Show*." —*Publishers Weekly*

INCARNATIONS
First published in 1995

Before Clive Barker wrote novels he wrote plays for the theater, which continue to be performed all over the world. Collected here are three of them: *Colossus*, a powerful study of the painter, Goya; *Frankenstein in Love*, a bizarre and horrifying wedding in the Grand Guignol style; and *The History of the Devil*, in which Lucifer himself is brought to trial, revealing a truly unique personality.

"Excellent mystical work."   —*Liverpool Echo*

FORMS OF HEAVEN
First published in 1996

The second volume of collected plays. Contained here are: *Crazyface*, following the life of a great clown cast adrift in the Dark Ages; *Paradise Street*, in which the gray streets of Liverpool are transformed by an extraordinary band of time travelers; and *Subtle Bodies*, in which the power of desire and rage transforms an ordinary hotel into a ship which sails on a dream-sea, until misfortune overtakes it–an idea which was later expanded in *The Great and Secret Show* and *Everville*.

"A great collection."   —*SFX*

SACRAMENT
First published in 1996

A near-fatal encounter with a polar bear leaves Will Rabjohns, a world-famous wildlife photographer, in a coma. While unconscious he revisits his childhood, and a traumatic event which shaped his life. Upon waking he realizes that he must journey from the familiar streets of San Francisco to wildernesses of England, and once again face the mysterious couple who nurtured and tormented him as a boy, and who will finally reveal the secret that links his destiny to that of every soul on the planet.

"A gripping book that weaves a compulsive spell almost to the final page. . . . Vintage Barker."   —*The Times* (of London)

GALILEE
First published in 1998

Shop assistant Rachel Pallenburg never dreamed of meeting Mitchell Geary, heir to the Geary fortune, let alone marrying him. But life as part of the richest family in America has turned sour, and Rachel finds herself trapped in the most destructive of relationships. Then she meets Galilee, prodigal prince of the mythical Barbarossa clan; and they fall passionately in love, a love which will ignite an age-old feud between the two families. As secrets are laid bare, the pent-up loathing between the two dynasties will erupt into a mutually destructive frenzy.

> "*Galilee* leaps through time and space to reveal an impressively majestic vision told in beautiful prose. A fantastic, engrossing war of the worlds." —*People*

PERMISSIONS